"YOU KNOW WHAT WE'RE DOING IS WRONG, DON'T YOU?" PAUL ASKED.

But even as he spoke, Paul Larrabee's eyes were feasting on Gigi, her body illuminated in the moonlight. He had never seen anything so exquisite before in his life. Her waist was small, her hips well rounded, her breasts full and sensitive. As he touched them, the nipples surged up hard and firm in answer, and she moaned, her hands moving up to caress his neck.

"Yes!" she said. "But I don't care. I can't go on like this, Paul. It's driving me crazy. I have to know, Paul. I have to know what it's like. I have to stop the ache inside."

"And so you shall," he whispered against her mouth. "I'll make you forget everything, my darling, everything but this."

For Gigi Rouvier and Paul Larrabee, there would be no forgetting what was about to happen—and no escaping the price they would have to pay. . . .

Hold Back The Sun

![Signet logo]

Fabulous Fiction from SIGNET

Hold Back
the Sun

June Lund Shiplett

A SIGNET BOOK
NEW AMERICAN LIBRARY
TIMES MIRROR

PUBLISHER'S NOTE

This novel is a work of fiction. Names, characters, places, and incidents are either the product of the author's imagination or are used fictitiously, and any resemblance to actual persons, living or dead, events, or locales is entirely coincidental.

SIGNET TRADEMARK REG. U.S. PAT. OFF. AND FOREIGN COUNTRIES
REGISTERED TRADEMARK—MARCA REGISTRADA
HECHO EN CHICAGO, U.S.A.

SIGNET, SIGNET CLASSICS, MENTOR, PLUME, MERIDIAN AND NAL BOOKS are published by The New American Library, Inc., 1633 Broadway, New York, New York 10019

First Printing, September, 1981

3   4   5   6   7   8   9

PRINTED IN THE UNITED STATES OF AMERICA

This book is dedicated to all of my wonderful fans across the country and especially to Dorothy Sheppard in Sierra Vista, Arizona, whose husband Jack was such a great help when I needed research about the Texas and Mexican territory. God bless all of you.

1

Sitting up cross-legged in the four-poster, she tucked the brightly colored patchwork quilt about her waist, then held out the hand mirror, scrutinizing her face. Long tapered fingers ran slowly along the high arch of her dark brows and down the smooth contours of her cheek. The skin was petal-soft and creamy, with just a faint dusky hue. Large, long-lashed blue-green eyes watched as her fingers moved over onto the end of her small nose, then traced the outline of her full rosy lips. It was a young face, perhaps not yet twenty, and it was her face. But whose face? Who was she really? She bit her lip, staring hard into the depths of the blue-green eyes. My God, she thought frantically, what name goes with this face? But the eyes couldn't answer, and only gazed back at her with the same empty stare she'd seen the first time she'd looked into the mirror.

She lowered the mirror hesitantly, toying with it as she contemplated her predicament. She was angry and frustrated. It wasn't only her name she couldn't remember, it was everything that had happened to her before yesterday morning when she'd come to and found herself lying in this big bed.

Mrs. Thornapple, whose house she was in, told her she'd been pulled from the wreckage of a burning train the night before and brought here because the hospital was already overflowing with injured passengers.

She exhaled angrily. Why couldn't she remember? She could talk and think and walk, even with a bruised, burned leg. She glanced about apprehensively. There was nothing familiar about Mrs. Thornapple's guest room, yet a strange sensation swept over her as she looked at everything. She knew that was a chair over in the corner, with a fancy needlepoint cushion, a vanity against the far wall, and a Per-

sian rug on the floor. She held the mirror in front of her face
again.

"And you're a person!" she whispered stubbornly. "But
who?"

Even looking in the mirror didn't help. She knew so much,
yet the most important details were gone. She set the mirror
back on the marble-topped stand beside the bed and picked
up a pink silk handbag that Mrs. Thornapple told her she'd
been clutching when they found her battered and bruised
body sprawled about ten feet from one of the burning
coaches. Apparently, when the bridge collapsed, the coach
she was in smashed on impact and she was thrown through
the resulting hole onto the soft sand on the riverbank. The
lanterns had shattered, spilling their contents, setting the
coach on fire, and everyone in it had perished. The rest of
the line of cars had either landed in the river or smashed
onto the opposite bank, and she shuddered to think how horrible it must have been.

A piece of the wreckage had fallen across her own legs as
she lay stunned, bruising them and burning one leg badly
where the fire had charred through the skirt of her dress before they'd had a chance to pull her clear. She remembered
none of it, and had no idea whatsoever as to why she'd been
on the train or where she'd been going.

She stared uneasily at the handbag, then reached in, pulling out a letter, turning it over in her hands, inspecting it
carefully, reading the return address. It had been mailed in
New York City on February 20, 1893, and was from a Mr.
Jason Larrabee. She turned the envelope back over to the
front. It was addressed to a Miss Gigi Rouvier in care of a
convent in Texas. She and Mrs. Thornapple had read the letter the day before, and whoever Mr. Larrabee was, he'd
expressed his delight that Miss Rouvier had decided to honor
his request and pay him a visit, and he'd be anxiously waiting
her arrival.

"So you see," Mrs. Thornapple told her yesterday as she'd
handed the letter back to her, "you do have somewhere to go,
and you do have a name."

Now, as she sat cross-legged staring at the name, she
frowned. Gigi Rouvier. It was a pretty name, but who was
Gigi Rouvier? What kind of a person was she? And more-
over, who was Jason Larrabee and why had he invited her to
his home?

She reached in the handbag again, rummaging against its satiny lining, then pulled her hand back out, her fingers holding tightly to a beautiful brooch encrusted with diamonds. In the center, delicately alive and glittering, were small rubies spelling the name Gigi, and on the back of the brooch were engraved the words "Love, Jason."

Was the man she was on her way to see the man she was to marry? They said the brooch had been fastened on the front of her shawl, holding it together. If she'd been wearing it, then she must be Gigi Rouvier. She clutched the brooch tightly, her fingers hurting against the brilliant gems. If her name was really Gigi, why couldn't she remember, and why did it sound so alien to her when Mrs. Thornapple called her Gigi? If only she could remember. It was terrifying.

She was restless, and shifted her position, wincing as she hit her sore leg against the mattress. The doctor said there were no bones broken, but the burn was deep and hurt terribly, and she was sure it'd scar. She shouldn't complain, though, because she was fortunate to be alive, if you could call someone fortunate who had no memory. She moved her leg into a better position, then put the brooch and letter back into the handbag as Mrs. Thornapple came in to light the lamps.

It was almost dark outside, and deep shadows were beginning to fill the corners of the room. She watched Mrs. Thornapple studiously. She was a motherly woman, softly rounded, with gray hair and a pert smile, always fussing, worried that things wouldn't be right.

She saw the hand mirror on the nightstand when she started lighting the lamp, and glanced over briefly at the young woman almost lost in the huge four-poster.

"You're going to wear it out looking at yourself, dear," she said affectionately, striking the match, holding it against the damp wick.

"And it doesn't help," said Gigi, watching the flames from the match begin to catch hold, forming a circle.

"The doctor said you'd remember eventually," Mrs. Thornapple went on. "But it'll take time. You have to be patient." She put the globe chimney back over the flame and walked to the dresser to light another lamp. "At least you know your name."

"Gigi Rouvier?"

"That's who the letter was addressed to."

She sat up straighter. "But I don't know any Gigi Rouvier!"

Mrs. Thornapple finished lighting the other lamp, then stood for a moment listening as she stared at the young woman in the bed. And she was a woman, not a young girl, there was no doubt of that. Her full breasts and sensuous figure attested to it, even though her eyes held a vibrantly youthful innocence.

"I hear a carriage out front," the older woman finally said, handing her a bed-jacket from the foot of the bed. "Here, slip this on, we're to have visitors."

Gigi's eyes widened, catching yellow flecks of light from the flickering lamps. "Who?"

"I sent word to New York City. To the man whose name was on the letter. That should be him."

"But I don't know him!"

Mrs. Thornapple frowned. "Maybe it'll jog your memory," she said, ignoring her protest. "I'm sorry, I had to. You can't stay here indefinitely, you know," and she left the room hurriedly, giving the young woman no chance to argue.

Gigi watched indignantly as Mrs. Thornapple shut the door firmly behind her; then she reluctantly slipped into the soft, lacy pink bed-jacket, smoothing the covers about her, stretching her legs out, leaning back against the propped-up pillows, wondering.

A good five minutes went by before Mrs. Thornapple returned, but when she did, she was accompanied by a tall dark-haired man who looked to be in his late twenties. His appearance took the young woman in the bed completely by surprise, for he was wearing a full set of evening clothes, including flowing white-silk-lined cape, white gloves, pearl-handled walking stick, and carrying a high silk opera hat. His smoky gray eyes caught hers and held as he followed Mrs. Thornapple into the room, and he stood rigidly erect, staring at her, his face grim.

"This is Mr. Paul Larrabee," Mrs. Thornapple said, introducing them as she walked over to her bedside, and the young woman felt herself flush uncomfortably beneath the man's intense gaze.

She eyed him warily. "Paul Larrabee?" she questioned. "The name on the letter is Jason Larrabee."

"My father," he volunteered, still scowling, and his eyes

sifted over her as if he were looking for some fault. "And you're Gigi Rouvier."

"I am?"

His scowl deepened. "What makes you say it like that?"

She tilted her head flippantly, making the lustrous curls of her long black hair twist about her shoulders. "I just don't feel like a Gigi Rouvier, that's all," she replied.

His eyes changed slowly, hinting at a smile, yet his mouth stayed firm. "But you are."

"You know me?"

"I've never seen you before in my life."

She sneered, then asked saucily, "Then how can you be sure? Who is Gigi Rouvier anyway, and what does she have to do with you?"

He hesitated, still staring at her, remembering the description his father had given him of Gigi Rouvier's mother. Looking at this enticingly lovely young woman with her provocative face and brilliant turquoise eyes was like seeing in the flesh what his father had described. Was it any wonder his father had loved her mother? A woman like this could arouse the desires of any man, yet she was barely out of her teens and probably unaware of the powers her beauty possessed. There was something vaguely naive about her, like the appealing innocence of a child, and he wondered if she'd understand what he was going to have to tell her.

He glanced quickly at Mrs. Thornapple. "Do you mind if I speak to the young lady alone, ma'am?" he asked abruptly, and saw her flush.

"Oh, to be sure, sir," she said, her face reddening even more. "I didn't mean to be listening." She glanced at the young woman, then to Mr. Larrabee and back again to Gigi. "I'll just be in the next room," she assured her. "In case you need me," and she left, shutting the door hesitantly.

Paul Larrabee watched the door close, then turned his gaze once more toward the young woman propped up in the bed, trying not to notice the way the soft pink bed-jacket draped across her full breasts, but failing miserably, and cursing himself silently for it.

She straightened, not realizing she was making the bed-jacket pull even tighter, then addressed him again more forcefully, asking him once more who Gigi Rouvier was and at the same time appreciating the fact that in spite of the apparent bad mood he was in, he was extremely attractive. His eyes held a hint of warmth and repressed desire that was fascinating, belying his outward irritability.

"Well, I'll ask again," she said stubbornly. "Who is Gigi Rouvier?"

This time Paul Larrabee's eyes hardened and he fidgeted nervously with his walking stick. "Gigi Rouvier's my half-sister," he said curtly, and watched the expression on her face change as his words sank in.

"Your . . . ? But how?"

He pulled a chair up to the side of the bed and sat down. "I'm afraid I have a bit of explaining to do," he said, and she agreed, so he set his gloves, hat, and walking stick on the nightstand, then threw the cape back from his broad shoulders and began. "You see, my father, unfortunately, wasn't the most faithful husband," he explained somewhat bitterly. "Some twenty years ago he fell in love with an actress named Gigi Rouvier. My mother learned of the affair the day after Miss Rouvier told my father she was expecting a child, his child."

He caught the shocked look in her eyes, yet went on.

"As you can probably guess, my mother's demands brought an end to the affair, and Miss Rouvier left town. Father never heard from her until the child was born, when she wrote saying she'd had a girl and named her after herself. Again she dropped from sight, and nothing more was heard from her until the end of January this year, when Father received a letter telling him that she was dying and the girl would be left alone without anyone to care for her." He paused momentarily, staring at her, then reluctantly continued. "My father's made up his mind that since Mother's dead and there's no reason for silence anymore, he's going to acknowledge you, Gigi Rouvier, as his daughter. And since my father's now an invalid in a wheelchair, I've come to take you to him."

She sat motionless, staring at him, her eyes troubled, stunned by his confession. "Are . . . are you telling me I'm a bastard?" she gasped incredulously, and his eyebrows raised in wonder.

"Miss Rouvier!" he blurted abruptly, yet his eyes were amused as his voice deepened huskily. "Nice ladies don't use such language," he admonished softly.

She glowered at him belligerently, her eyes snapping. "And

nice men don't go around telling stories that aren't true, either," she replied.

"I assure you, Miss Rouvier," he said, "the story I just told is true, although I wish it weren't." His gray eyes grew turbulent, like the sky before a storm. "I'll warn you, though, that my father's the only one looking forward to your arrival. I have a brother and sister at home who're anything but happy about the whole affair."

"And you?" she asked.

He let his eyes sift over her again at some length, aware of the delicate yet sensuous blue-green eyes that were staring back at him, blatantly hostile.

"I haven't made up my mind yet," he said slowly, and her eyes narrowed cautiously.

"And yet you expect me to go with you?"

"You're Gigi Rouvier, aren't you?" he said with conviction.

She laughed skeptically. "You say I am, and that's the name on the letter, but how do I really know? Didn't Mrs. Thornapple tell you I can't remember?"

"She did." He leaned toward her, his eyes softening as they searched her face. "But please believe me, you couldn't be anyone else. Father described your mother to me, and it's more as if he described you. How can you deny it? And the brooch?" he questioned. "You have the brooch?"

He saw her eyes dart toward the handbag, and they both reached for it at the same time, his hand covering hers, and suddenly, as their flesh touched, a shock ran through them both, although neither was immediately aware of the other's plight. Then, without warning, their eyes met, clashing violently, and something strange and compelling passed between them.

Gigi stared at him, alarmed, unable to cope with the weird sensations sweeping over her, and Paul stared back, shocked by the sudden effect she was having on him. He swallowed hard, fighting it, then retreated into a façade of cold reserve, his eyes hardening.

She inhaled sharply, battling her discomfiture, and wrenched the handbag away, holding it in front of her, her breasts heaving as she tried to calm her nerves. There was something electric about this man. Something vibrantly masculine that she somehow knew she'd never experienced before, and it scared her. She pushed back farther against the pillows, as if trying to get away from him, but his eyes were still there, devouring her.

"It's no use fighting the facts," he finally said, finding his voice again, deliberately forcing himself to look at her, hoping to conquer the tingling sensations that were making his heart beat erratically. This was insane! He clenched his jaw stubbornly and went on. "You're Gigi Rouvier, my half-sister, and you might as well accept it," he said flatly, trying to convince himself as well as her that what he knew they'd both experienced when their hands touched was nothing to be concerned about.

She was close to tears. "Maybe I am, and maybe I'm not," she said defensively, trying unsuccessfully to compose herself. "But that doesn't mean I have to go with you and be humiliated."

"Humiliated?" He frowned. "Who's going to humiliate you?"

"Your brother and sister. You said they don't want me there."

"Father does, and that's what counts," he said, at last managing to force his mind and body back to why he was here. "Father's a wealthy man, Gigi," he went on more confidently, "and you'll never want for anything, and no one would dare humiliate you. He'd never let them."

"It's enough humiliation just to know you've been born out of wedlock, Mr. Larrabee," she said softly, "without flaunting it before the world. How will he explain me to his friends?"

He flushed. "He'll introduce you as his daughter. As I said, he's influential. Everyone'll have to accept you."

"You mean, he'll simply tell them I'm his daughter?"

Paul sighed. "That's what he has in mind."

"But . . . people don't do that, do they?"

"Jason Larrabee does what he damn well pleases," he blurted roughly; then his voice softened. "And right now it'll please him if you'll come home with me."

She hesitated. "Then you . . . you're convinced I'm Gigi Rouvier, your half-sister?"

"May I see the brooch?"

She took it from the handbag and gave it to him, then watched as he examined it. His dark hair waved above hauntingly gray eyes that could be warm one minute and like cold steel the next, and his firm, broad chin ended what was a long, ruggedly tanned face, as if he spent a good deal of time outdoors. He was truly the handsomest man she'd ever seen. At least she thought he must be. Funny, she knew he was a man, and a handsome one at that, but yet, except for the doctor, she couldn't name one single man she could compare him to, and she swallowed hard, cursing her brain for being so fuzzy.

Her hand reached to her temple, rubbing it lightly. Not only did she not know who she was, but she didn't know who anyone was. Even if she met people she knew, she'd never remember them. Why did she remember some things, but not others? Why couldn't she say for sure, yes, I'm Gigi Rouvier? Why did she have to rely on other people telling her who she was? She frowned unhappily. It was so complicated.

He glanced at her, handing the brooch back, his eyes somber. "You're Gigi Rouvier," he said with conviction, and she could swear he looked disappointed.

"Then I guess that's that," she said, sighing wistfully, then added more spiritedly, "but I still don't like it. I don't like being your father's illegitimate daughter, and I never will, so don't expect me to be glad about it!"

He laughed lightly and smiled, a deep smile that was both cynical and unnerving. "I think you'll change your mind once we get to New York City," he said sardonically. "Now, we have a long way to travel, so I suggest we have Mrs. Thornapple bring your clothes so we can get started."

She gasped, startled. "We're leaving now?"

He stood up. "Miss Rouvier, I was at a party after the opera last night when my father sent word that I was to leave immediately to come here." He picked up his gloves and things from the stand. "I haven't slept since leaving, unless you call the short naps I had while jogging in the carriage sleep. If you don't mind, the sooner we leave, the better."

He summoned Mrs. Thornapple and told her to bring Gigi's clothes, then stared at the woman dismayed when she told him they'd been ruined and she threw them out.

"But surely you've got something she could wear," he protested vigorously.

She flushed, flustered. "She's so small, sir . . . my cothes would be far too big."

Gigi looked down at the frilly bed-jacket and cotton nightgown and blushed, embarrassed. She had nothing. Except for the pink handbag with the letter, the brooch, her shoes, and underclothes, she was destitute.

Paul grew impatient, his mind sobering to the fact that he had to find something to put on her. He certainly couldn't take her home in a nightgown. Then he remembered the sign out front that stated Mrs. Thornapple was a dressmaker, and he also remembered the mannequin he'd walked past in the parlour when he'd arrived. And if he remembered right, the mannequin had on a dress that looked like it was made for Gigi, but he wasn't prepared for Mrs. Thornapple's protest.

"Oh, mercy, sir," she cried when he suggested it, and her hand covered her mouth in consternation. "I can't let you take that dress! That's Miss Warren's wedding dress. I've just finished it."

He stared at her, his eyes narrowing shrewdly. "When is Miss Warren getting married?" he asked, and she swallowed nervously.

"Next Saturday."

"Could you make another just like it before then?" he asked.

She fluttered anxiously. "Why . . ." She shrugged. "Yes . . . I guess I could." she said, distressed. "But the material was sent for special from New York City. There's none like it in town."

His jaw tightened stubbornly. "Then I'll send you more from New York," he assured her, and reached in his pocket, pulling out some bills. holding them toward her. "Here, take this, it'll compensate some, and I'll see you have everything you need to make a new one." He shoved the bills in her hand, then headed for the door, nodding toward Gigi. "Now, see that she gets dressed. and I'll wait outside," he said quickly. "And don't take half the night," and he left the room with an arrogant stride.

Mrs. Thornapple stared at the money in her hand, then gazed at the young woman in the bed. "Well," she said, astonished. "Did you ever . . . he does seem sure of himself, doesn't he?"

Gigi nodded, staring at the open doorway through which Paul Larrabee had disappeared. "Well, I'll say one thing for him," she said, frowning. "He doesn't let anything stand in his way. does he?" and while she waited for Mrs. Thornapple to go bring the dress, she wasn't quite sure she liked the idea of having to go with him.

Gigi sat opposite Paul in the plush carriage, staring out into the darkness, watching the shadows of the bare trees. It was early April and the leaves were just beginning to open on them, and she watched them go by. She'd managed, rather awkwardly with her injured leg, to get into the white satin dress, and insisted on walking from the small bungalow to the carriage unaided. Each step had been agonizing, but she was stubborn.

The night air was chilly, and Paul Larrabee had taken the cape from his shoulders, placing it about her as she stepped from the house. It was so large she could wrap it about herself twice, and the white silk lining felt sensuous against her bare throat when she pulled it closer, trying to cover the exposed flesh above her breasts.

Before leaving the bedroom, she'd come to the conclusion that the dress Paul confiscated for her was actually becoming. It was an off shade of white slipper satin with low tucked bodice, huge bouffant sleeves, and tiny seed pearls scattered over the flounced skirt. The hipline was bolstered with tucked folds of more slipper satin. She wondered if Miss Warren, whoever she was, would be angry because they'd taken it. Now, as she sat in the carriage, she smoothed the soft, shiny, cream-colored skirt across her lap and wrapped the cloak tighter about her.

"How long will it take us to reach New York City?" she asked as the carriage rolled along.

"We won't arrive until daybreak."

"You mean I have to try sleeping with this awful jogging?"

"Now you know what I've been through," he said, and she made a face at him, only he wasn't able to see it in the darkness.

She was curious. Here she was on a journey to who knows where, with a man she knew nothing about, except that he claimed to be her brother. Well, her half-brother anyway.

"Tell me," she asked, making sure to be heard above the creak of the carriage and rhythmic beating of the horse's hooves, "do you go to the opera often?"

"The opera?"

"You said you'd been at a party after the opera . . ."

He laughed lightly, and she liked the sound of his laugh. "I'd forgotten," he said slowly, his voice deep and resonant. "I usually see about three a season, if that can be considered often. Have you ever been to the opera?"

She stared toward him silently in the darkness, then made an attempt to answer. "I . . . I . . ." she stammered, and he cut in quickly, realizing his mistake.

"I'm sorry," he apologized, feeling ridiculous about the blunder. "How stupid of me. I keep forgetting you can't remember."

She gazed harder into the darkness toward where he was sitting, and wondered. Had he really forgotten, or was he testing her? Maybe he thought she was pretending, although she couldn't think of any logical reason why he'd think that. He was the one who'd convinced her she was his sister. There were dozens of other people she'd probably much rather be, so it couldn't be that. She shrugged, turning toward the window again, looking out, watching the night go by. Oh, well, maybe he had forgotten.

She sighed. If only he knew the empty feeling that overwhelmed her every time she tried to remember. "You can't imagine how horrible it is not to be able to remember anything," she murmured, and her voice broke as she fought back tears of frustration. She felt so lost and alone in the darkened, unfriendly confines of the carriage.

Either he sensed her unease or heard the tremor in her voice, for without hesitating, he left his seat, moving over beside her, handing her his handkerchief.

"Here, blow hard," he ordered, and she wiped her eyes, then did as she was told.

"I'll be all right," she sniffed after a few minutes, embarrassed to be caught crying. "Only, I wish I knew . . ." She closed her eyes and leaned her head back, holding his handkerchief clenched in her lap.

"Why don't you get some sleep?" he suggested. "It's a long ride."

She sighed, trying to relax, realizing that she still knew very little about him except he offered crying women his handkerchief, went to the opera, and bothered her in a way she couldn't quite fathom. He also has a soft shoulder, she thought as her head lolled against it, and since he made no protest, she settled back on it comfortably, cuddling close, closed her eyes, and fell asleep while the carriage continued to make its way through the countryside toward New York City.

The sun was barely peeping up over the horizon as the carriage made its way up the winding circular drive toward the

front of a magnificent stone mansion nestled on the riverbank, with the back of the huge house overlooking the Hudson River, only a few miles from the heart of the city. The
house was long and high, like a castle, with stone columns
supporting a portico across the second story in the front.
Leaded French windows with small panes were used throughout, and its elegance was enhanced by white birch trees just
beginning to burst forth with the first leaves of spring, and
they lined the drive and graced the edge of the soon to be
flowering gardens at the back and side of the house. The
house itself sat on a green slope, and as the sun's rays struck
it, it took on a glow as if it were on fire, and Gigi held her
breath in awe as Paul pointed it out to her.

"It's so big!" she exclaimed.

"Are you frightened?"

She looked back over her shoulder, directly into his eyes,
and a strange warm feeling spread through her, making her
tingle all over. "I'm scared to death," she said softly, then realized how fast her heart was pounding. "I wish I'd never
come with you," she whispered. "I wish I could go back to
Mrs. Thornapple's and start all over again. I wish . . ."

"What do you really wish?" he suddenly asked, watching
the distressed look in her startlingly brilliant eyes.

She inhaled sharply. "I wish I weren't Gigi Rouvier," she
whispered breathlessly; then she suddenly trembled, embarrassed, and looked away toward the door of the mansion as
the carriage pulled up to it and stopped.

Paul made her stay seated while he climbed down; then he
reached up to help her. She tried to stand on her leg, but the
long ride and inactivity of just sitting had left it sore and stiff,
and it hurt so badly it wouldn't hold her when she tried to
step down. She fell, and Paul moved quickly, letting her fall
against him as she let out a soft cry, and his arms enfolded
her, swinging her into them, cradling her against him.

"You're light as a feather," he said, smiling that provocatively unnerving smile of his, and she started struggling to get
down.

"I can walk," she said stubbornly, but he disagreed.

"Your leg's too sore."

"Don't be silly. I can walk!"

"I'll carry you," he insisted obstinately, and started for the
house. She began to squirm. "Stop struggling!" he ordered.

"It won't do you a bit of good," and he held her even tighter so she could barely move.

She was lost in his cape, twisting awkwardly as she struggled in his arms; then, as he reached the door, she stopped.

"Good," he said, pleased, and reached out, pulling the leather bell cord hanging beside the door.

Seconds later the door swung open and Paul stepped in, carrying her across the threshold into the foyer.

Gigi was dumbfounded as she gazed about. The foyer was extremely large and looked more like a museum, with portraits and statues lining the dark paneled walls. Two huge crystal chandeliers hung from the ceiling, and the back wall was a series of French doors. She looked through them out onto a flagstone terrace where wrought-iron furniture was set up in front of a magnificent fountain.

Her eyes adjusted slowly to the light in the foyer, and she glanced inquisitively about her, taking in the details. It was bare of furniture except for an occasional straight-backed chair or small stand, and deep blue plush carpeting covered the full length of the floor, making it appear even more spacious. As it was, the foyer traversed the full width of the house, from front to back.

"You look impressed," said Paul as she lay motionless in his arms, her eyes roaming the room, and she gasped.

"This is where you live?" she asked breathlessly, and her eyes moved back to look at his face.

He nodded, their eyes meeting again, and suddenly she was very much aware of his arms about her, holding her close, and the same strange warm feeling flooded through her that she'd felt before, making her uncomfortable and disconcerted.

"Please," she whispered self-consciously. "I can walk now. Please put me down."

"Yes," said a woman's voice from behind them, and Paul whirled about, still holding her in his arms. "Do put her down, Paul," the woman continued coldly, "so we can get a better look."

Paul moved deftly, gently setting Gigi on her feet so she faced the young woman, who was standing in front of a sullen man who'd obviously opened the door for them.

"Rose and Bruce," said Paul, introducing them, "this is Gigi Rouvier." He looked down at Gigi, so small beside him.

"Gigi, your half-sister and half-brother, Rose and Bruce Larrabee."

Gigi stared at them shyly. He'd been right. They didn't look any too pleased. "How do you do," she murmured softly.

"Well," said Rose, tilting her head back, looking down her nose at Gigi. "You certainly don't look like a Larrabee, I'll say that much for you," and Gigi's eyebrows raised in surprise; then she realized Rose was right. They looked nothing alike.

Rose's nose was long and aquiline, but for some reason, with her heart-shaped face and large brown eyes, it was an asset rather than a liability. She was about Gigi's age, attractive, but not beautiful. In fact, in less gracious surroundings, with less expensive clothes and coiffure, she'd probably be considered ordinary-looking.

"Maybe she's glad she doesn't look like a Larrabee," commented Bruce dryly as he pushed a lock of dark brown hair back from his forehead. She could see his slight resemblance to Paul, only Bruce was far less commanding in appearance. Shorter than Paul and lighter in stature, he had a weak chin and a voice with a slight nasal twang, unpleasant to the ear. He looked to be younger than Paul, mid-twenties perhaps.

It was obvious they were all set to dislike her long before she arrived. Gigi glowered at them, her defenses roused, head high. "Not only do I dislike the thought of looking like a Larrabee," she said bitterly, staring at them, "but I don't even like the idea that I might be one!"

Rose and Bruce looked startled.

"There's been a train wreck," explained Paul quickly. "And Gigi's had a lapse of memory. She didn't even know who she was or where she was going."

"Then how can you be sure, Paul?" Rose asked skeptically. "Maybe she isn't Gigi Rouvier."

"My dear Rose," he said, annoyed. "I assure you I wouldn't have brought her here if I wasn't sure. She had the letter, the brooch, and besides, she fits the description Father gave me."

"Then let's let Father be the judge," said Bruce.

Paul's eyes narrowed. "Then why don't you wake him," he suggested angrily. "Since you don't trust my judgment."

Bruce sneered insolently. "Don't have to," he replied flippantly. "He hasn't been to bed yet. He's been up all night, dozing off and on in his chair. Why do you think we're dressed so early? He wouldn't let us go to bed either. Insisted we wait." He sighed wearily, looking at Gigi in disgust. "I'm so tired I'll probably sleep all day," he said lazily.

Gigi flushed. Was it any wonder they resented her. It was bad enough to discover your father committed adultery, but to be forced to lose sleep waiting for the results of his folly was asking too much, and she began to wonder just what sort of man Jason Larrabee was.

"Is he in the drawing room or his quarters?" Paul asked gruffly.

Rose answered, "The drawing room, where he had a full view of the drive. We saw you coming."

Gigi felt weak, and the pain in her leg was getting worse. She looked up at Paul anxiously. "Do I have to meet him now?" she asked, trembling.

"There's no use prolonging it," he said softly. "It'll only make it worse." His eyes met hers and held, softening. "Do you think you can walk on your leg?"

She bit her lip and nodded, watching the concern that filled his eyes.

He glanced at Rose and Bruce, realizing they were staring at her curiously. "She was hurt in the wreck," he explained briefly, then looked down once more at Gigi. "Here, let me help," he said, and reached down, supporting her about the waist, letting her lean against him so her full weight wasn't on her leg.

They moved cautiously to the center of the foyer as he half-carried her, then entered a long hallway on the right. The plush carpeting helped cushion her steps, but she was thankful for Paul's help, although being so close to him was unsettling.

At the far end of the hall, a wide archway opened on the right, revealing the drawing room. It was huge, decorated with brocades, satins, and velvets in shades of white, gold, and green, with dashes of red and pink here and there to lend color, and as they moved under the arch, stopping just inside, Gigi stared intently across the room. A man moved out from the shadows of the green brocade and satin drapes near the front window, maneuvering his wheelchair into the light from the crystal chandelier overhead so he could get a better look, and his face paled as his eyes fell on her face.

Gigi could only stand, staring back, unable to move. He

was an older version of Paul. Not quite as handsome, but the resemblance was uncanny. He had on a scarlet robe with white ascot at the throat, and his legs were covered with an embroidered lap robe of red velvet. Dark hair spattered with gray waved to just below his ears, and his steely gray eyes, moist with tears, were set in a strong masculine face. Now she knew where Paul had inherited his striking personality and looks. Evidently Rose and Bruce resembled their mother more than their father.

Jason Larrabee held his hand out, motioning for her to come forward.

"She hurt her leg, Father," said Paul, still holding her about the waist, letting her body rest against him, unaware that his nearness was causing her a good deal of trepidation.

"Then let her sit down, Paul," he said quickly. "Help her to the sofa," and Paul helped her walk farther into the room, where she sat on the white brocade sofa that graced the inside wall, her dress of slipper satin blending with it luxuriously.

Jason wheeled his chair close, unable to take his eyes from her, watching the light from the chandelier play through her dark lustrous hair, bringing her startlingly blue-green eyes to life.

Gigi was uneasy. "Please," she finally said. "Is something wrong?" She glanced up at Paul. "I knew I shouldn't have come," she said softly, but Jason shook his head.

"On the contrary," he protested, still watching her closely, and she looked back at him. "Everything is fine . . . fine . . ." he said. "It's just that . . . you look so much like your mother, and it's brought back so many memories."

"I do?" she gasped, her hand moving to her throat.

Jason wheeled his chair even closer, reaching out, taking her other hand in his. "My dear, it's as if I've been taken back twenty years," he said, his voice deepening passionately. "You look just like her, and she was the most beautiful, vivacious woman I've ever known."

"Really, Father!" exclaimed Rose disgustedly, and her eyes blazed. "It's bad enough you brought her here. Do we have to stand here and listen to you extolling her mother's charms too?"

Jason's eyes snapped. "Hold your tongue, Rose," he ordered tartly. "You may not like the idea, but Gigi's your sister, whether you want to accept it or not, and I won't have her feelings hurt by you or anyone else in this house. Is that understood?"

Rose paled, making her brown eyes look even larger in her small face, and gave Gigi a dark, hateful look Jason missed because he too was busy again gazing at Gigi; then Rose walked over angrily and plunked down in one of the over-stuffed chairs, where she sat fuming, her mouth held rigidly to control her wayward tongue.

"One thing," Jason said, motioning toward a corner of the room, and Gigi was startled to see a man silently slip from the shadows where he'd been standing motionless. He was as tall as Paul and wore an ordinary dark suit, but a bright red turban adorned his head, accentuating the slight slant to his eyes and high cheekbones set in a lean, swarthy face. "This is my manservant, Ahmed," Jason explained, introducing her. "He's invaluable to a man in my circumstances," and his hands touched the arms of his wheelchair. "He can hear, but can't speak, due to an unfortunate incident when he was young," he went on. "He moves about rather silently, and I don't want you to be frightened of him." He looked understandingly at Ahmed. "My daughter Gigi, Ahmed," he said, and the man bowed low, his ebony eyes steady on her as she greeted him.

She felt strange and uneasy as she looked into his eyes. They were so dark they looked black, yet were unusually alert, not missing a detail as they looked her over from head to toe.

"Now," said Jason, as Gigi hesitantly drew her eyes from the forceful personality of this strange man. "If you'll all leave, there's so much I want to ask Gigi about her mother, and so many questions that have to be answered."

Gigi looked at Paul desperately.

"I'm afraid it'll have to wait, Father," Paul interrupted hurriedly. "Gigi has amnesia and can't remember anything. It was the train wreck. The fact is, I had to convince her she was Gigi Rouvier."

Jason glanced at her, startled, then shook his head. "Oh, no, my dear, don't worry about that," he assured her affectionately, then chuckled to himself. "There's no doubt, believe me," he said. "None at all. You're Gigi Rouvier. You couldn't be anyone else." He reached out, tilting her face toward his, his fingers beneath her chin. "I have no doubts, my dear, you're definitely my daughter, and you're the image of your mother."

"You're sure?" she asked. "Absolutely sure?"

"I'm positive." Suddenly realizing that she must be tired, he dropped his hand abruptly, wheeling his chair about, fighting the memories she aroused in him, yet reveling in the joy they brought him. "Now, then, Paul," he said briskly, "take her to her room and see she's made comfortable. Since we've been up all night, and since she's unable to remember, we'll talk later. And send for the doctor to look at her leg," he instructed him, "then have her get some rest so she can dine with us tonight. Oh, and don't let her walk on her leg, carry her upstairs."

He took one last look at her, reaching out, squeezing her hand, then wheeled his chair over where he could look out the window, and Paul could tell he was pleased with himself. There was a smile on his face and a gleam in his eyes that hadn't been there for a long time. Paul sighed.

A beautiful, carpeted winding staircase was on the outside wall of the room, and Gigi never said a word as Paul reached down, picked her up, then walked over, slowly mounting them. When he reached the top, he paused momentarily, looking back. Rose and Bruce were already disappearing into the hallway, while his father still sat quietly staring out the front window.

"Are you convinced now who you really are?" he asked, once more looking into the eyes of the young woman he held in his arms.

She nodded, glancing below, then back to him. "Yes," she said, her voice hushed.

He hefted her closer in his arms, continuing on, turning into the upstairs hall, walking down it, stopping in front of one of the many doors.

"Yours is the third on the left," he said, and bent down, still holding her, awkwardly opening it.

For the second time that morning as he held her against him, she was suddenly aware again of the strength in his arms and how tall and ruggedly good-looking he was. It made her uneasy. There was a magnetism about him that seemed to draw her to him, making her feel unsteady and trembly inside, especially when he looked into her eyes. She was sure you weren't supposed to feel like this toward a relative, especially a brother, and she shivered slightly, trying to ignore the sensations, but it was so hard, especially when they entered the room and he laid her on the bed, asking if she were cold. He'd felt her tremble, and frowned.

"No, I'm all right," she assured him, but his eyes narrowed.

He stood looking down at her, and there was a strange expression on his face. Her heart began to pound erratically, and she felt herself getting warm all over.

His eyes unconsciously sifted over her, enjoying the curvaceous display she made as she stretched on the bed.

"I almost forgot," she suddenly said. "I'm still wearing your cape," and she started to arch her body upward, to pull it out from beneath her, but he stopped her.

"No," he said, reaching out, and his hand on her arm seemed to burn the flesh when he touched her.

She stared at him uneasily, afraid of the strong emotions that were overwhelming her, not knowing what to do with them, yet afraid to let go, because they felt so good.

"It's all right," he said huskily, drawing his hand away as if he too had been burned. "I'll get the cloak later," and he stood, looking down at her, trying to grasp what was happening, because for the first time in his life, without having to even touch a woman to become aroused, he felt a quickening inside that took his breath away.

No wonder his father loved her mother. God, Gigi was provocative beyond belief, and he realized angrily that ever since he'd first laid eyes on her, he'd been comparing her to Lenore. But then, there was no comparison, really, was there? And he knew it. Lenore was from partly Scandinavian stock. Tall, blond, fair-skinned, reserved, gracious, always in control of her emotions, never a hair out of place. Calm, cool Lenore.

He remembered last night when he'd told her he had to leave the party to run an errand for his father, and the matter-of-fact way she'd kissed him good-bye. He'd thought nothing of it at the time, but now, gazing down at Gigi's hauntingly alive eyes, he suddenly remembered, and it bothered him.

Gigi lay staring back at him. She was bewildered, and her mouth parted slowly, invitingly, and he watched it curve at the corners. She'd never kiss a man like that, he thought, watching its sensuous movement. She'd put her heart and soul in every fiery kiss. She was warm, vibrant. He suddenly pulled himself back to reality. Hell! What was he thinking of?

He pulled his thoughts together as best he could, trying to force himself to forget what he'd just been thinking, and he straightened guiltily. What did it matter anyway what he thought? He was her brother; besides, the fact that she was so attractive was only going to complicate things. She'd have every young swain in New York at her feet. His face became cold, remote.

"I'll send for the doctor right away," he said, irritated with himself as he wrenched his eyes from her and turned toward the door. "Oh, yes, and I'll send Biddy up to take your measurements."

"Who's Biddy?"

He stopped, turning back to face her. "Rose's personal maid," he said. "I don't think she'll mind sharing her."

"Sharing her? You're crazy. Your sister hates me. She'll never share her maid."

"She's your sister too," he said.

She sighed, exasperated. "Don't remind me!"

He headed for the door again, and she raised up on her elbows as he reached it, grabbing the doorknob.

"What does Biddy need my measurements for?" she asked curiously, and he hesitated, turning again, his eyes sifting over her once more.

"You'll need something to wear tonight at dinner," he answered coldly. "I don't think Miss Warren's wedding dress is appropriate, do you?"

She glanced down at the beautiful satin dress billowing about her on the bed, feeling quite glamorous in it. "What's wrong with it?" she asked softly. "I thought it was rather becoming."

His eyes hardened. He didn't dare tell her how he really felt, how becoming it really was, and he was certain she had no idea how provocative she looked.

"You're not getting married, that's what's wrong with it," he said sullenly, and swung the door open. "I'm sure Biddy'll find something more appropriate," and he left abruptly, closing the door firmly behind him.

Gigi stared at the closed door, then sighed, frowning. What a strange man this brother of hers was. And what extraordinary feelings he provoked in her. She lay back on the pillow, closing her eyes, and wondered if maybe she'd made a mistake by coming to New York after all.

2

It was some twenty minutes later when Biddy walked into the bedroom. She was an extremely short woman, under five feet, and in her forties, quite thin, with fiery red hair swirling haphazardly about a sallow, sullen face. Her hands and feet were exceptionally tiny, and she was so short, a few inches taken from her height would have turned her into a dwarf.

She walked over, pulling the cords, opening the pink damask draperies, letting in the morning light, and Gigi realized she hadn't even given the room any thought until now. It was done up luxuriously in pink and white, with light gray carpeting. The deep pink damask draperies had hidden French doors that opened onto the portico at the front of the house, and everything in the room was soft and feminine, the headboard of the bed tufted and covered with pale pink satin.

For some reason, Gigi felt out of place. Although she couldn't remember, it was as if she knew she'd never seen elegance like this before.

"If you'll just sit up, miss," the little maid said, bringing her back to reality, "I can take your measurements without you having to stand. They told me you hurt your leg."

Gigi smoothed the satin bedspread beneath her fingers, then sat up on the edge of the bed, letting Biddy wield the tape measure in her deft hands.

"Surely you can't make a dress in just one day," said Gigi as Biddy frowned, writing the measurements down on a piece of paper as she took them.

"No, miss," she answered coolly, her brown eyes hostile. "But we can send to one of the shops in town and have something sent out. Do you have any color preference?"

Gigi shook her head. "No," she said. "Anything you think appropriate."

Biddy was very efficient. Too efficient. She did her work briskly, hurriedly. There was no warmth or delight in being of service, and Gigi knew the woman resented the task given her.

"How long have you been Rose's personal maid?" Gigi asked, trying to be friendly, hoping the woman wouldn't resent her too much.

Biddy slipped the piece of paper with the measurements on it into her apron pocket, and her head straightened proudly. "I tended the late Mrs. Larrabee for many years before she passed away," she said haughtily. "And I took over with Miss Rose when she made her debut into society."

Gigi's eyebrows raised. "Then you've been with the Larrabees a long time."

"I certainly have, miss," she said bitterly, then went on. "Long enough to know that you've made a terrible mistake by coming here." She laced the measuring tape in and out of her fingers nervously, then straightened as tall as she could, her eyes flashing. "I was eighteen when I came here, miss, and I've seen what goes on in this family and I've kept my mouth shut, but what Mr. Larrabee has done to his children by bringing you here is unforgivable," she said. "It's disgraceful, and for your sake and for the good of all concerned, I think you should go back to where you came from." She looked relieved. "There, I've said it," she finished forcefully.

Gigi was dumbfounded. "Really, Biddy!" she exclaimed, amazed at the woman's audacity.

"Well, it's true," she said angrily. "I was here then, and I knew what was happening. I knew he was seeing that wicked woman." She sighed, shaking her head. "Poor Mrs. Larrabee, bless her soul, was never the same after that." Her eyes suddenly darkened, the hatred in them intense. "Your mother brought tragedy to this family, young woman, and you'll do the same," she said viciously. "You mark my words!" She turned and headed for the door. "And I think you'd better inform Mr. Paul that you'll need your own personal maid from now on," she said defiantly. "I have too many duties serving Miss Rose to be of any more help to you," and she left the room, leaving Gigi staring after her flabbergasted.

Now, just who on earth did the woman think she was, thought Gigi. Of all the gall! Being devoted to one's employer was one thing, but being brazen and arrogant was another. It was bad enough to be cast into the part she had to play in this house without having to put up with something like this.

She stirred, moving back farther onto the bed, sitting in the middle of the fancy bedspread. She hadn't wanted to come in the first place. Maybe she should take the maid's advice and go—but where? She exhaled disgustedly, knowing she had no place to go and no one else to help her. She had no other choice but to stay. Well, as long as she had to, she'd try to make the most of the situation. She lay back on the bed again, trying to rest, while she waited for the doctor.

It was close to dinnertime already. Her leg was feeling better now that the doctor had cleaned and tended it, and she was managing to get about quite well, although she was limping badly. She glanced at herself in the full-length mirror covering the closet door.

The dress they'd sent up for her was lovely. It was pale gold with a draped bodice covering her full breasts, baring her neck and throat, and billowing sleeves edged with gold lace just above the elbow. The deep girdle at her small waist was covered with the same lace, and it met at the back, forming a train of lace that trailed to the floor in layers. The effect was enchanting, and she had to admit that it was more appropriate than Miss Warren's wedding dress.

Gigi kept twirling from side to side, watching in the mirror as the train swished behind her. She'd piled her hair atop her head herself, securing it with hairpins she'd confiscated from the dressing table, declining Biddy's reluctant last-minute offer of assistance, and the results were pleasing. She studied herself in the mirror.

There was a knock on the door.

"Come in," she called over her shoulder, and closed the closet door, limping toward the center of the room. She stopped abruptly halfway to the bed, and inhaled breathlessly as Paul came in.

He hesitated just inside the door, staring, and she could swear it looked like his face paled when his eyes struck her.

"Is this dress appropriate enough?" she asked timidly, holding her arms out, showing it off demurely. She was self-conscious under his searing gaze.

He nodded. "It's fine," he said abruptly, and looked away hurriedly, then closed the door behind him. "I wanted to talk to you before we go downstairs," he said, avoiding her eyes, walking toward the open French doors. "There's been a slight complication."

"Oh?"

He thrust his hands into the pockets of his blue dinner jacket and walked out onto the portico, standing motionless for a few minutes; then he turned toward her reluctantly. "Father's invited guests for dinner," he said suddenly, and watched the expression on her face.

"Guests? Who?"

"My fiancée and her parents," he said. "And he intends to introduce you to them as his daughter. I thought you should be forewarned."

She frowned. "You mean without any explanation to try to ease the shock? Just, this is my daughter?" she asked.

"Oh, he'll explain," said Paul. "That's not what's bothering me. What worries me is how they're going to take it. Especially when they see you."

She stared at him curiously. "What is that supposed to mean? What's wrong with me?"

Paul blushed, embarrassed. "Nothing, that's just the trouble."

Her frown deepened. "I . . . I don't understand."

"Don't you see?" he said, walking over to look down into her eyes. "If you were a quiet little nobody, a timid little soul, shy, homely, and conservative, they could merely ignore you if they wished, or second best, tolerate you." The depths of his eyes darkened to a slate gray. "But you're not the sort of person one can ignore or push to the background," he said, unsmiling. "I can see it in your eyes now. You'll make people notice, whether they want to or not."

"And you don't think they'll want to?"

"I have my doubts."

She stared at him, wishing she knew what he was thinking. "You said it was your fiancée and her parents?"

"Yes."

She turned from him and limped ungracefully toward the vanity. "What's she like?" she asked as she glanced into the mirror for one last look.

"Lenore?" He watched her put a curl back into place, his eyes studying her delicately tapered fingers. "She's tall, blond. I've known Lenore for a long time," he said. "You might say we grew up together. She's spent a good deal of time in Europe, though, the past few years, up until about two years ago."

Gigi turned and eyed him curiously. "How old are you, Paul?" she suddenly asked.

He was taken by surprise, and straightened, his shoulders looking even broader beneath his formal dinner jacket. "Now, what makes you ask that?"

She left the vanity and slowly limped to the French doors, then went outside onto the portico and stood looking at the evening shadows descending on the trees and lawn, then turned to face him again where he stood just inside the room.

"I bet you're every bit of twenty-eight, aren't you?" she finally said. "It seems strange you've waited all these years to marry someone you've known for so long, don't you think?"

He didn't answer, but stood staring at her, his eyes unwavering.

"Well, don't you think I'm right?" she urged again, and this time she saw a spark of anger ignite behind those gray eyes.

"I told you," he explained, "she's been in Europe. Besides"—his voice had an edge to it—"what business is it of yours whom I marry?"

"None," she said, shrugging as she came back in the room. "I was just curious."

His eyes narrowed. "Well, don't go prying into my life," he said angrily. For some reason her question had irritated him.

"Why not? You've pried into mine!"

"Pried? I've tried to help you. I could have easily told Father you weren't Gigi Rouvier. That Gigi Rouvier was dead. Where would you be then? Out on the streets somewhere trying to beg, borrow, steal, or sell yourself trying to survive, that's where you'd be." His eyes blazed. "And now, I only came up here to do you a favor. I thought it only fair to tell you what's going on, what to expect, but if that's the way you want it!" He started to leave.

She moved quickly, grabbing his arm. "Wait, Paul . . . please!"

He stopped, staring at her, his face like granite.

"I'm sorry," she apologized. "I didn't mean to make you mad." She flushed. "Here we are fighting like brother and sister already, and for nothing," she said, trying to coax him. "It's your business when and whom you marry. I know that. I don't have any right to say anything," and she tried to smile at him. "I'll be only too glad to meet your fiancée, even if she isn't glad to meet me, only don't leave me," she pleaded, and the smile faded forlornly. "Don't let me walk down there alone, Paul, please," she begged.

He gazed deep into her eyes, and felt a warm sensation run through him, wild and abandoned, making him feel good all over, and for a second he wished . . .

"Oh, hell," he said, angry with himself and everything about the whole sordid affair. "Grab hold," and he held his arm out for her to take as they heard a carriage pulling up out front.

Her smile appeared once more and deepened as she slipped her arm through his, tucking it in the warmth of his elbow. "Thanks," she murmured softly, and they left the room.

Jason had parked his wheelchair at the foot of the stairs, and now he leaned back comfortably, waiting. Paul had said he'd escort Gigi down for dinner, and Jason wanted to make sure he hadn't forgotten. When he'd received the letter from Texas, at first he'd been apprehensive. So many years had passed. He wasn't sure whether he wanted to bring out the past or just let it rest, but then his conscience had gotten the better of him, as did his curiosity, and he decided to meet this young woman he'd fathered. Now, having seen her face to face, he couldn't deny it. She was a daughter to be proud of, and the image of her mother.

He thought of his marriage. A marriage that had been more of a merger of wealth rather than love. He hadn't minded at first, because he'd never really known what love was; then he'd met Gigi Rouvier, only it was too late. At least for him. Now, seeing her daughter, having her in the house, a part of him, of them both, was like a tonic to him.

He smiled as Gigi and Paul appeared at the top of the stairs, and his eyes followed her as they descended slowly, Paul letting her favor her sore leg.

"You look lovely tonight, my dear," he said as they reached the bottom, his voice reflecting his feelings.

She squeezed Paul's arm tighter. "Thank you, sir," she said.

Jason moved away from the bottom of the stairs, then turned his wheelchair about so he was facing them. "Well," he said confidently, "I assume Paul's told you about our dinner guests."

She nodded.

"Good." He glanced at Paul. "Then shall we join them?" and he led the way from the room, heading toward the other wing of the house.

Later that evening, when all the excitement was over, Gigi sat in her bedroom on the edge of the bed, wearing only her underthings, staring vacantly at her dress flung across the chaise longue. She'd felt like a princess in it. Maybe that's why the evening had affected her the way it did.

She stood up slowly, beginning to take off the rest of her things, tossing them down beside the dress, going over in her mind everything that happened. Before going to dinner they'd gone to the music room directly across from the dining room, where she'd met Jason's closest friends, Nels and Katrin Van Der Linden and their daughter, Lenore, who was Paul's fiancée.

Nels was extremely tall, a giant of a man, massively built, with a flushed, fair complexion and graying blond hair, and his wife complemented him well. She too was tall for a woman, and stately, her blond hair a shade lighter than his.

Jason had greeted them warmly as Paul and Gigi followed him into the room; then he turned toward a young blond woman who was walking toward him from the piano where she'd been standing listening to Rose play.

Lenore Van Der Linden's hair was coiled toward the nape of her neck into a plump chignon, without a hair out of place, and the sea-green dress she wore gave an aquatic cast to her pale blue eyes set below finely arched brows that wore a faint hint of artificial color to make them stand out, for beneath the color, they were as fair as the meticulously groomed hair on her head. She greeted Jason affectionately, then stopped abruptly, staring at the beautiful young woman being escorted into the room behind him by her fiancé.

"Ah, yes," said Jason, smiling as he wheeled his chair about to face Gigi and Paul. "Now for the reason I asked you all to come."

He held out his hand. "Come here, my dear," he ordered Gigi, and she left the security of Paul's arm, joining her father, trying not to limp. "I want you all to meet Miss Gigi Rouvier," he said enthusiastically. "Gigi, this is Nels and Katrin Van Der Linden, two of my dearest friends," he said, "and their daughter, Lenore, who, in case he hasn't mentioned it, is engaged to Paul."

Gigi greeted them as calmly as she could, in spite of the cold, hateful look that was accompanying Lenore's greeting.

Jason sensed what Lenore was thinking, and he suddenly laughed, gazing at her reproachfully. "Lenore, my dear, don't look so disturbed," he said, calming her affectionately. "You've no reason to be jealous, I assure you." He looked up at her, his face beaming. "Let me explain," he said softly, "and you'll see." He took a deep breath, then let it explode. "She's my daughter!" he announced, and for a moment the silence was frightening.

Nels's face turned white, as did Katrin's, and they just stood staring at him.

"Well . . . haven't you anything to say?" asked Jason, looking from one to the other.

Nels swallowed hard, shaking his head. "You're . . . you're joking, surely, Jason," he said in disbelief.

Jason sighed. "I assure you, it's no joke," he said. "Let me explain." He maneuvered his wheelchair to a more command-ing position, then began. "I'm afraid I haven't always been the faithful husband I intended to be," he confessed, trying to tell it the best he knew how. "Once, and only once, I strayed. I fell in love with an actress. The result of that affair is here before you, and I'm proud now to be able to claim her as my own," and he motioned toward Gigi, whose face was crim-son.

"Jason, you're out of your mind!" blurted Katrin, her face livid beneath her graying blond hair. "Do you realize what you're saying? And in front of Lenore?"

Jason moaned. "Good God, Katrin," he said heatedly. "Lenore's all of twenty-three, and if she doesn't know the facts of life and love by now," he said, "then I suggest you call her engagement off until you teach her a few things."

Katrin's face fell. "Jason! Really! Your daughter!" and she sat back down, her knees too weak to support her.

"This is madness," agreed Nels. "You can't go about an-nouncing to the world that . . . well, you just can't, Jason!"

"Why not?" he asked, his jaw tightening arrogantly. "Why can't I? What's past is done and over with," he said. "Why should Gigi suffer ostracism for my mistakes? Besides, I could name you a dozen men in this city who've fathered more than one child out of wedlock, only they're too ashamed to own up to it."

Nels ran his hand through his hair and shook his head, while Lenore turned to Paul.

"You agree with your father?" she asked, somewhat bewildered.

It was the first time Paul had ever seen her visibly shaken, and he could see the disturbance in her blue eyes. "You heard him," he said.

"But . . . but . . ." she stammered. "What will people say?"

"As Father has already said," he said quietly, "they'll gossip and talk, and . . . really, now, what does it matter? If Father's happy and it's what he wants . . . and it's the truth, he's not trying to hide her away like most men have done . . . well, anyway, why not?" He looked at Gigi, seeing the pained confusion in her eyes. He had to do something to make her feel less hurt. "Besides," he said defiantly, "she makes a rather pretty sister at that," and as Gigi's eyes raised to his again, he half-smiled, trying to let her know it was all right. He didn't know why he was suddenly agreeing with his father. Maybe because they were so much alike.

"What do Rose and Bruce think about it?" Lenore asked, studying the look that Paul was giving this newly found sister of his, and Paul drew his eyes from Gigi's to look at Lenore.

"Why don't you ask them?" he queried, and motioned toward his brother and sister.

There was a staircase in the music room identical to the one in the drawing room, and Bruce was standing near the bottom, leaning on the banister, taking in the conversation, one hand resting in the pocket of his burgundy dinner jacket.

Lenore turned to him. "Well, Bruce?" she asked.

He waited until all eyes were on him, then descended one more step, emphasizing the sharp creases in his buff-colored trousers. "Since I wasn't consulted when this whole thing started," he said flippantly, "I suppose I have no right to condone or condemn." His eyes hardened. "But in respect for our mother's memory," he suddenly said angrily, "Rose and I both feel that the situation could have been handled more delicately by providing for Miss Rouvier financially without disrupting our lives and jeopardizing the family name!"

Jason snorted. "What family name?" he yelled, staring at his son. "Larrabee? Son, before I decided to clean it up, the name Larrabee was tagged on rum-runners, slave traders, and horse thieves, and since I pulled it out of the gutter, then I guess I've got a right to jeopardize it, isn't that right?"

He turned to Lenore. "If this has any bearing on the status of your engagement, my dear, I'm sorry," he said, suddenly realizing by the look on her face that she was anything but pleased. "I never expected you to be narrow-minded. All I want is for my friends to recognize that a man can make a mistake and own up to it without the world falling apart. Tomorrow I intend to have some reporters come out so I can tell the world what I've told you here tonight, and I want my daughter treated with the respect due her." He looked at Nels and Katrin, his closest friends. "Well?" he asked.

Nels pleaded with Katrin. "Friends are friends, Katrin," he said slowly.

She glanced at Jason. "It's hard to believe," she said. "I've known you for years, Jason, and I never dreamed . . ."

"Is it wrong, Katrin, for a man to fall in love . . . truly in love?" he asked. "You and Nels have been fortunate that your lives haven't been complicated by passion."

"Oh, Jason . . . I don't know what to say, and Lenore . . . this puts her in an awkward position."

"It needn't," blustered Jason. "Paul is no less the man he's always been, and this should have no effect whatsoever on their engagement."

Nels turned to his daughter. "This is your affair as well as ours, Lenore, dear," he said, running a hand through his gray hair. "Will you be able to handle it? There'll be a lot of gossip and talk."

Lenore looked at Paul. She'd made up her mind when they were children that someday she'd be Mrs. Paul Larrabee. She couldn't lose him now, she'd be a laughingstock. What his father was about to do was unheard-of in the best of circles, but if anyone could pull it off, Jason Larrabee could.

She stared at her father, her decision made, and stepped next to Paul, deliberately taking his arm. "If Paul's willing to accept her as his sister, then it wouldn't be ethical for me to tell him no," she said graciously, trying to sound convincing. "I'm afraid what you and Mother decide will have to be your own affair."

Nels rubbed his sideburns, as if thinking, then turned to his wife. "Katrin?"

"I know, Nels, I know," she said reluctantly, then looked at Jason. "All right, Jason," she conceded.

Now, as Gigi raised her arms, pulling on the silk night-gown that had been left for her on the bed, she remembered it all as if in a dream. The whole thing seemed so unreal.

When she woke up in Mrs. Thornapple's huge four-poster and realized she had no memories to cling to, no identity to base her life on, she'd been terrified. Now, in just a short time she felt as if she'd been handed the world on a silver platter. Jason Larrabee had really accepted her as his daughter.

She reached up, taking the pins from her hair, letting it fall about her shoulders, then pulled the covers back and climbed into bed, nestling down into the warm covers, closing her eyes. It wasn't going to be all sweetness and light, she knew. There were Rose and Bruce to contend with, and a lot of people were going to despise her for no other reason except that she was who she was. They wouldn't care that she had feelings. All they'd care about was that her parents had never married. And there'd probably be other things, too. Things she had no way of even imagining now.

But it was better than having nothing. She was starting to have a past again. It encompassed only two days, but they were two days filled with so many surprises, so many twists and turns. As she lay now, with her eyes shut, glorying in the ability to remember even this much of her life, she knew there was one thing she was never going to forget. One person who would always be a part of her memories, even though he had no right to be, and she drifted off to sleep, dreaming of Paul.

3

Gigi had been prepared to dislike Jason Larrabee. She didn't really know why. Maybe because he had so much money, or perhaps because at first meeting he seemed so arrogantly sure of himself. But she couldn't dislike him, it was impossible. He treated her with such warmth and kindness that her heart ached inside. If only she could remember her mother and her past. Her mother must have spoken to her of him often. She had to. One didn't forget a man like this.

The morning after the dinner with the Van Der Lindens, Jason fulfilled his vows of the night before. By ten o'clock, all the newspapers in New York had dispatched reporters to the Larrabee mansion for a news conference with none other than Jason Larrabee himself. This in itself was something new. Before this, no reporter had ever set foot inside the Larrabee home. Jason was a reclusive, private man who didn't accept publicity gracefully, and shunned reporters. But that evening when the story broke, every newsboy in the city was hawking his own version of the headlines given to the reporters by the old tycoon himself.

"Extra! Extra! Read all about it!" they yelled from every street corner. "Millionaire Confesses!—Jason Larrabee Shocks Society—Scandal Hits Wall Street Financier—Jason Larrabee Fathers Illegitimate Child!"

There were dozens of versions, each one as explosive as the other, and Jason just sat back waiting to see what would happen.

That afternoon, after the reporters left, it was hectic for Gigi. A dressmaker was sent for, and she was kept busy choosing the latest styles from Paris. Creations of Worth, Doucet, and Virot. Feather- and lace-trimmed gowns, beaded, pleated, and draped, for dress and every day, with parasols, gloves, capes, and fancy hats. Paul, who she learned was Jason's right-hand man in his business dealings, supervised her himself, at his father's request. It seemed Jason would be tied up all afternoon in his quarters with business associates.

The right wing of the house, opposite the drawing room, had been made into a separate apartment for Jason's use, with everything he needed close at hand. It consisted of his bedroom and an all-purpose room where he could while away his time and where some of his meals were served. No one entered Jason's quarters unless invited. Most of his business was conducted there, and this afternoon, after the arrival of several men with briefcases and worried looks, the door to Jason's quarters remained locked.

Paul smiled faintly when the dressmaker finally left, and Gigi plunked herself down on the window seat in the sewing room, breathing a sigh of relief.

"Now, don't tell me you haven't enjoyed being able to order whatever you want," he said, watching her with interest. "All women enjoy buying clothes."

"Not this one," she said emphatically. "I thought she'd never leave. I still feel like I've got pins in me. And why do I need so many things?" she asked, leaning toward him, her violet dressing gown pulling tightly across her breasts. "And those riding clothes . . . what if I don't know how to ride?"

"Then I'll teach you."

She eyed him skeptically. "You don't hate me, do you, Paul?" she asked.

"No."

"Why not? Rose and Bruce do."

He hesitated, not knowing quite how to explain.

"Or is it that your father hasn't given you much choice? After all, he did order you to look after me."

He shook his head. "Don't be silly," he said, smiling. "You know I don't hate you. This afternoon's been enjoyable, watching you trying to decide what fabrics to choose, and the enthusiasm you give to everything you do. Besides, it took me away from a lot of boring paperwork. Now, how can I hate you for that?"

"But the embarrassment I'm going to cause you and Lenore."

"If it's anybody's fault, it's Father's, not yours," he said.

"Yet you don't hate him either." She was puzzled.

Paul had been sitting in an armchair in the corner, and now he stood up, walking over to stand in front of her, staring out the window behind her toward the drive, watching the white birch trees swaying in the breeze.

"Maybe Rose and Bruce don't understand Father the way I do," he tried to explain, his hands in the pockets of his gray sport pants. "Maybe because I'm more like him than they are. They're wishy-washy and selfish, and if I must admit it, quite snobbish. Mother was like that, I'm afraid. She was a cold person who lived by the blue book. You did things because you were supposed to do them, not because it brought you pleasure. Father's not like that, and I guess maybe I'm more like he is. Perhaps I can understand why he did what he did."

"He must have loved my mother very much," she said softly, and her eyes took on a dreamy, faraway look. "I wonder what she was like."

"She was just like you," he said passionately, and gazed down into her face, their eyes meeting, and for a few moments he forgot who she was. He was aware only of her beauty and the soft warmth in her eyes. Now he knew how his father must have felt looking into the depths of her mother's eyes. Suddenly he inhaled sharply, remembering who she was, and who he was, and he flushed with embarrassment.

"Shall we go have some tea?" he suggested awkwardly, as he tried to put his emotions back into their proper perspective, and she stared at him bewildered, then quickly recovered.

"One thing first," she said, and he hesitated. "I'm afraid Biddy won't do, Paul," she informed him. "She told me she was far too busy looking after Rose to be bothered with me. Do I really need a personal maid?" she asked abruptly. "Can't I just take care of myself?"

He shook his head. "Father'd never allow it." He gazed at her thoughtfully. "I'll see what I can do," he finally said. "There's a servant girl in the kitchen, rather young, but she seems pleasant. Maybe she'd enjoy getting away from Mrs. Sharp's eagle eye."

"Mrs. Sharp?"

"The cook," he explained. "I'll see to it myself right now. You go to the terrace, and I'll have tea brought out and let

you know. The girl's name is Bridget." He opened the door
for them to leave.

"Thank you," she said, and he watched as she moved down
the hall toward the foyer, the sweep of her violet dressing
gown following her rhythmically; then he went to his left
toward the kitchen.

After getting a promise from Mrs. Sharp that she'd send
Bridget to help Gigi, Paul went down the hall, across the
foyer, and was about to step outside onto the terrace, when
he realized Gigi wasn't alone. Bruce and Rose were with her.
He stopped, unconsciously eavesdropping.

"You can't imagine." Gigi was talking. "Everything's so
strange. I know what the things are, like I know this is a
dressing gown I'm wearing, and that's a fountain." She
pointed to the beautiful marble fountain in the center of the
terrace, with water cascading into the pool below. "But I
don't ever remember seeing them before. When I opened my
eyes in that bedroom, I knew I was in a bed, but I didn't
know how I knew. My mind's a blank, yet it isn't. It's hard to
explain. Sometimes I see something and I feel it's right, that
it should be, but I don't know why. There's no yesterday, and
nothing to compare today or tomorrow with. If only I could
remember . . ." Her voice rose desperately. "You don't think
I like not remembering, do you?" she asked, and Bruce
cleared his throat, watching her closely.

"Rose thinks you're pretending," he said, and saw her look
of disbelief.

"Pretending? Why on earth should I pretend?"

Rose fingered the pages of the *Harper's Bazaar* that lay in
her lap, and smirked. "It'd be a convenient way of not having
to reveal your past," she said.

Gigi's eyes flashed. "Not having to reveal my past? What
are you talking about?"

"Well . . ." Rose sneered. "If you can't remember, then
you won't have to tell about the sordid life you and your
mother led while you were growing up, will you?"

Gigi pursed her lips indignantly. "Sordid? How dare you!"
She glared at them. "Who gave you the right to judge my
mother and say what she was or wasn't?" she asked heatedly.

"She seduced my father, didn't she?" said Rose. "I wonder
how many other men she went after!"

Paul exhaled furiously, stepping onto the terrace. "I think
you owe Gigi an apology, Rose," he demanded, interrupting

them, and Rose whirled about, almost dropping her magazine on the floor.

She hadn't seen him until he spoke, but quickly composed herself. "Why should I apologize for telling the truth?" she said.

"Because I said so. And if you don't stop harassing her, I'll—"

"What will you do, big brother?" cut in Bruce. "Why are you sticking up for Father, anyway?"

Rose glanced at Bruce, then back to Paul. "Don't you see, Bruce, dear," she said sarcastically, her gold-flecked brown eyes sparking as they studied Paul. "He's preparing people. Everybody says he's so much like father. Tell me, Paul, are you planning to treat Lenore as shabbily as Father treated Mother? Are you?" She let out a vicious half-laugh. "How many women will you sleep with after you're married?"

Paul's lips quivered and his face went white, then red, and his jaw set hard. "If you weren't my sister, Rose, I'd lay you out cold!" he said venomously.

Rose gave Gigi a nasty look, then turned to Bruce. "I do believe Paul's angry with us, Bruce," she said flippantly, then turned once more to Paul. "Don't think you're going to tell Father, either, Paul," she admonished, pleased with herself. "Because if you do, I'll tell Father you're lying and Bruce'll back me up. Just make sure you take good care of your sweet little charge here, only don't be surprised if all your old friends suddenly decide they've been seeing too much of you. Father may be able to influence the older generation, but he doesn't have any hold over our set." She turned back to Bruce. "Let's go, Bruce," she said nastily. "I promised Natalie we'd be at her party tonight, and I've so many things to get ready." She sauntered off triumphantly toward the foyer, her blue taffeta afternoon dress swishing as she moved, followed by brother Bruce in his white pants and blue Prince Albert frock coat.

Gigi was heartsick as she watched them go. She stood up and turned to face Paul. "Biddy was right," she said self-consciously. "I should never have come here with you!"

Paul's eyes hardened. "You mean Biddy's been working on you too?" he asked.

Gigi nodded. "Yesterday when she came to take my measurements. I wasn't going to tell you."

His eyes turned a deep, violent gray, like storm clouds on a summer day. "What else did she tell you?" he asked softly.

"That I'd cause nothing but trouble and heartache. . . . Maybe she's right, Paul. Maybe I should go somewhere else," she said. "Bruce was right last night. I don't have to live here."

Paul reached out and held her by the shoulders, holding her so she faced him. "Don't ever say that, Gigi," he said, and felt her tremble. "Besides," he added softly, "it's too late to leave now. The newspapers are on the streets by now, and the whole city'll know who you are. There's no backing out. You're staying! Do you hear?"

She started to cry. "Oh, Paul! If I could only remember!" Huge tears rolled down her cheeks.

His arms went about her, and he pulled her to him, holding her close, trying to comfort her. She was so fragile, and she felt so small and soft against him. Suddenly he felt a shock run through him, with a warm quickening response deep in his loins as her body pressed close. He'd been aroused before, but never this easily, not even with Lenore, and he tried to fight it. He kept telling himself over and over again that she was his sister, but it didn't seem to be doing any good.

He felt himself hardening. This was madness! This soft, warm, fragrant bundle in his arms was his sister. Oh, God! His head was reeling. He had to let go . . . he had to pull himself together so he wouldn't give himself away.

Reluctantly he loosened his arms, but just couldn't seem to drop them from around her. "Gigi," he said hoarsely, reaching down, tilting her face to his. "Don't worry, please, Gigi," he whispered huskily. "Everything'll be all right. Please. Rose and Bruce'll change. They'll accept you eventually."

She sniffed in, wrinkling her nose, and her full lips looked so voluptuous he had a hard time keeping his mind on what she was saying. "You're just saying that," she said, "to be nice."

He shook his head. "No . . . really." There was a softness in his face she hadn't seen before, and it was doing peculiar things to her. "And even if they don't," he went on, "the important thing is that you've made Father happy. Please, Gigi, don't ever leave him!"

"What if my memory comes back?"

"I hope it does," he whispered. "Maybe it'd help."

She looked up at him, into his eyes, and suddenly realized what he meant. His arms were still holding her, and her body, molded close to his, was throbbing with a desire she'd never known before, and she knew he felt it too. She could see it in his eyes. Her heart sank to her stomach, where it tightened into a knot that nearly tore her in two.

"Would it help, Paul?" she asked abruptly, and her blue-green eyes stared into his passionately. "Would it really solve anything for us, or would it only make things worse?"

He stared back and saw her tremble.

She felt all warm and weak inside when he held her like this. It was the same feeling she'd had yesterday when he'd laid her on the bed in her room and stood looking down at her. A tingling in her loins and an awareness that puzzled her. There was something about the atmosphere whenever they were together, and she knew now that she wasn't the only one who felt it.

His arms dropped quickly from about her, and he walked away, standing by the fountain, gazing off toward the river. She watched him for a long time, not saying anything, and he finally turned to face her again.

"I guess you're right, Gigi," he said slowly, his face flushed. "Nothing's going to solve our problem, is it?" and just then one of the girls from the kitchen came out with their tea.

They were silent as the girl poured for them, their eyes on each other, the words unspoken. Then Paul tried to be casual as he told her Mrs. Sharp had agreed to spare Bridget from the kitchen. As Paul talked, he glanced toward the foyer and saw his father saying good-bye to the men he'd been in conference with, and a few minutes later Jason joined them on the terrace.

"Well, well," he said, glancing at Gigi. "Just the two people I wanted to see," and his eyes filled with admiration. "Did you get everything ordered, young lady?" he asked enthusiastically.

"Yes, sir," she answered.

He smiled. "Fine, because you'll need all those fancy clothes." He turned to Paul. "Did you tell the dressmaker to get a daytime dress ready for tomorrow afternoon like I told you, Paul?" he asked.

"It'll be ready."

"Good." His face beamed. "Sousa's band is playing in Central Park tomorrow afternoon, and we're all going," he announced proudly, and Paul looked startled.

"All of us?" he asked.

His father seldom went out since his crippling accident. In fact, for Jason Larrabee to appear in public at anything other than an important social event was unheard-of. He had business representatives who reported to him regularly, and if an invitation came from someone he felt obligated to acknowledge, he'd usually send Paul in his place. Consequently, few people had ever come face to face with him. For Jason Larrabee to attend a band concert in the park was truly an innovation.

"All of us, Paul," he said, smiling broadly. He breathed in deeply, his eyes dancing. "I feel like a new man, Paul," he said, enjoying the clean, fresh river air and forsythia that was blooming along its banks. "A new man."

"How did Redding, Fitzsimmons, and the others take your news?" asked Paul, trying to turn his thoughts back to business.

Jason snorted. "Like I thought they would," he said. "They stormed and fumed and yelled and cursed, then asked to see her. Cy Redding's making arrangements for a dinner party at Delmonico's for tomorrow evening, and I told them they could meet her then."

Paul stared at his father curiously. "You know, I think you're actually enjoying yourself," he said, watching the animated look on the older man's face.

Jason lit up. "I am, Paul," he said boisterously, the hint of a smile in his eyes. "I am! Now, tell me, where are Rose and Bruce? I have to tell them about tomorrow's plans."

Paul glanced quickly at Gigi, then back to his father. "Rose mentioned getting ready for a party at Natalie's, and I'm sure Bruce tagged along."

Jason scowled. "I wish they felt differently about your coming, Gigi," he said sadly, shaking his head; then his tone changed abruptly to a gayer mood. "But I'm sure with a little time we can change things." He wheeled his chair toward the fountain. "It's a lovely day, isn't it?" he said, smiling, pleased with himself as he gazed up at the blue sky, then on out toward the river. "Yes, a lovely day."

Gigi and Paul's eyes met above Jason's head, and Gigi remembered Paul's words: "Don't leave him." Now she knew why he'd said them, because right now, at this moment, Jason Larrabee looked like he could be just about the happiest man on the face of the earth.

The next day, Gigi's new personal maid, Bridget, handed her the newspaper. She was reclining on the tufted gray velvet chaise, and carefully looked over the front page, reading it again while Bridget put a fresh bandage on her leg. She wasn't limping anymore, thank God, and the leg was healing beautifully, although she'd been right, there would be a scar.

Gigi held the paper up and stared at the picture on the front page. It was a picture her father had had the newspapermen take the day before, and surprisingly, it was a good likeness. Well, all of New York knew now, she thought. Some of the papers had written favorably, and others . . . well, the general impression was one of shock.

"I bet you can tell by the headlines how many newspapers Mr. Larrabee has stock in, can't you?" she said to Bridget, putting the paper down as Bridget tied off the bandage, looking at her mistress sheepishly, knowing Gigi was right.

Bridget was about sixteen, with large brown eyes and honey-blond hair, and her flair for fashion was surprising. She loved doing Gigi's hair and taking care of her things, and seemed to thoroughly enjoy her new job. She sighed. "I suppose," she said, then walked over and picked up the dress Gigi was to wear to the band concert. It had arrived barely an hour ago, and much to their surprise, it was a perfect fit.

The pink skirt was pleated all around, with a pink satin sash at the waist, and satin and lace trim around the bottom. Layers of lace hung on the sleeves, with satin bows at the elbows and more satin collaring the high neckline, while pink lace covered the top of the bodice, and there was a parasol to match.

Gigi rose from the chaise, joining her, and Bridget held the dress out for her to slip into.

"I think there's some people who'll understand, Miss Gigi," said Bridget as she slid the dress down over Gigi's head, then fastened it up the back.

"Do you understand, Bridget?" Gigi asked.

Bridget's eyes darkened. "Miss Gigi, I never knew who my father or mother was," she said softly, and Gigi craned her neck sharply to look at the girl as she fastened the last hook; then Gigi turned all the way around to face her.

"You didn't know either of them?" she asked.

Bridget nodded. "They told me at the orphanage she was a nice lady who made a mistake and couldn't face up to it. You know, it's terrible not knowing. But then again, sometimes you're glad you don't know, because you might not like what you find. You're lucky, though, Miss Gigi," she reassured her, "you at least know who your parents are."

Gigi stared at her for a minute, then understood. "Does Paul Larrabee know you were born out of wedlock, Bridget?" she asked.

Bridget nodded. "Yes, ma'am. He found me crying about it one day, and before I realized it, I'd told him the whole story. I wish Miss Rose and Mr. Bruce were more like Mr. Paul," she said. "This house would be a pleasure to work in. Oh, I know, he seems stern and aloof at times, and when he's angry he can be frightening, but he's fair and treats us decent, and that's what counts. And at least now, taking care of you, I won't have Miss Rose bawling me out all the time for being clumsy with the tea and making mistakes at the dinner table."

Gigi liked the girl. She was wholesome and truthful and pleasant to be around, and she smiled as she realized why Paul had probably chosen this particular girl. She silently thanked him, then remembered Bridget's words.

Paul frightening? Never, she thought. Not Paul, and she smiled to herself. She sat down, and Bridget began doing her hair, humming a sprightly tune, and suddenly Gigi felt a strange twinge in her breast as she continued to think of Paul. She was so mixed up. From the moment he'd stepped into her room at Mrs. Thornapple's, there'd been something about him. She was drawn to him somehow, some way, and it was frightening. Could it be the fact that they were related? Was it a form of bond between them? She wondered. It was strange and alien to think of him as a brother. When he looked at her, she always felt a piercing tingle spread all the way around her, deep down, all the way to her loins. Oh, God! It wasn't right. She had to think of something else. She had to stop thinking of him like this—it wasn't healthy. She pursed her lips stubbornly. He was her brother, she told herself angrily, her brother, and nothing could change the fact.

Besides, he was engaged to Lenore, and she should be happy for them.

She sighed, trying hard to think of him only as a brother.

Bridget put her pink hat in place and stood back surveying her handiwork. "You look lovely," she told Gigi, and Gigi glanced at her, startled, realizing she hadn't been watching what the girl was doing.

"Oh, yes, it does, doesn't it?" she said abruptly, pulled forcefully from her thoughts.

"You'll enchant everyone," assured Bridget. "You look beautiful."

Gigi thanked her, then stood up, picking up her parasol. "They'll be delivering another dress for me to wear this evening," she said as she took one last look in the mirror. "Make sure it's hung up, will you, please?" she said. "Then for the rest of the afternoon, just do as you'd like. I don't have any idea when we'll return."

"Don't worry," said Bridget. "I'll be here when you need me."

"Thank you," said Gigi, and looked down to make sure she had her gloves and fan. Pink was becoming on her, she thought, smoothing the skirt of her dress, and she hoped everyone else would think so too.

She left the room and went downstairs, where everyone was waiting in the foyer for the carriage to be brought around front.

"I didn't mean to be late," she said, greeting them hurriedly. "I'm sorry."

But Jason didn't mind. "You're not late, my dear, you're just on time," he said, smiling robustly. "We're merely waiting for the carriage, that's all," and she took a deep breath, stopping to stand quietly beside his wheelchair.

She glanced at all of them. Jason and Bruce were both wearing black suits with black-velvet-trimmed frock coats, but Paul's suit was a soft blue-gray and he looked more handsome than ever.

"It's pulling up out front now," said Rose as she walked over and pulled the curtain back from one of the front windows.

Rose looked exceptionally nice this afternoon. Her dress was pale green layers of organza with a velvet sash at the waist, and huge puff sleeves that tapered tightly from the elbows down. The neckline was rounded just below the hollow in her throat, scalloped with velvet trim, and she wore a single strand of pearls about her neck, with earrings to match. Her hat was of pale green straw. She didn't look too happy, however, and Gigi guessed she was being forced to go along.

The front door opened, and Ahmed stepped in. He stood motioning for them to leave, then helped Jason out the doorway and down the steps to the carriage.

Gigi was surprised when, after seating Jason in the carriage, Ahmed stowed the wheelchair in a specially made compartment at the rear of the carriage. She'd been wondering what they were going to do with it, and how Jason was going to manage.

Ahmed helped her in and seated her beside Jason, then helped Rose in and put her on the opposite side of the huge carriage to face them; then he sat down on the other side of Jason. Bruce climbed in beside Rose, and Paul got in, sitting directly opposite Ahmed.

"Nels, Katrin, and Lenore will meet us at the park," said Jason as the carriage pulled away from the house and started down the drive.

"Then they've accepted the invitation?" asked Paul.

"I forgot to tell you, son," he said. "I received a telephone call a short time ago. We're to meet them by the bandstand."

"Really, Father," said Rose disgustedly. "This is ridiculous. You know you haven't been out for ages. And Central Park, of all places! Why do we suddenly have to go slumming?" She hated going out among the common people. "Why couldn't we have waited?" she went on haughtily. "I'm sure Mr. Sousa's band would have played someplace more appropriate to our social standing."

Jason eyed his daughter and shook his head. Poor Rose. "When are you going to learn, Rose," he said defensively, "that you're no better than anyone else? Just because you're fortunate enough to have a father with a knack for making money . . ." He sighed. "Besides, what's wrong with the park? It's a wonderful place to spend a Saturday afternoon. Now, stop grumbling and at least look happy, even if you're not."

She pouted, and turned away, looking out the window of the closed carriage.

When they arrived at the park, a crowd had already

gathered. People and carriages were lined up everywhere, and the seats were filling quickly.

At first, when they emerged from the carriage and started to make their way to the bandstand, no one paid any particular attention to them, until someone spotted Ahmed's red turban and Jason in his wheelchair. Then, as they recognized Gigi from her pictures in the paper the day before, the whispering started, and by the time they reached the front of the bandstand where the Van Der Lindens waited, all eyes were on them.

Gigi swallowed hard and held her head high as she fastened her arm through Paul's and they walked beside Jason. She could tell as she studied Lenore's face while they were approaching that Lenore was uncomfortable in this new role. She was wearing a frothy blue dress that was striking with her ash-blond hair, yet it seemed to emphasize her coolness toward those around her, reminding Gigi of a large, cold chunk of ice.

"You're creating quite a sensation," said Nels as he greeted his longtime friend, shaking hands all around and smiling.

"Surprising, isn't it," said Jason as he glanced surreptitiously at the crowd, "how one man's sins can be of interest to so many people."

"You knew it would be like this," said Katrin. "So why on earth did you come?"

"I find it interesting," said Paul as he too surveyed the crowd. "I imagine all these good, pious people staring at us have broken at least one or more of the commandments at one time or another in their lives, yet, because Father's sin is the kind you can't hide away, they're all so quick to cast stones."

Lenore glanced at Paul. "Do you have to talk about it so freely here in public, Paul?" she said furtively. "Good Lord, it's bad enough everyone's staring at us!"

"Don't get squeamish now, Lenore," said Paul. "The fun's just starting," and Gigi, who was still hanging on to Paul's arm, felt his hand squeeze hers through her lace glove.

Lenore looked at him coldly. "I'm glad you consider it fun, because I don't," she said. "I'm going along with it because it's what you want, Paul, but believe me, I don't think it's fun! Not one bit."

Gigi was surprised to see the dark look in Paul's eyes as he stared at Lenore, and she wondered what he was thinking. He looked anything but pleased.

Members of the band started making their way toward the platform, and someone suggested they sit down, so Paul escorted her congenially to one of the seats. Ordinarily a band concert such as this never held reserved seats, but Jason had used his money and influence, and they were ushered to eight empty seats in the front row, with "Reserved" signs on them. This also caused a tittering among the crowd, and more than one disgruntled catcall.

In spite of the whisperings and disgusted looks, however, Gigi lost herself in the music, enjoying herself immensely, as did Paul and Jason, who'd remained in his wheelchair. But the rest of Jason's party remained nervous, and never seemed to lose their awareness of the crowd and the stares.

They arrived back home just in time to change clothes and leave for Delmonico's. Bridget had Gigi's dress ready and waiting.

"Why, Bridget," said Gigi as she slipped into the dress after a warm, soothing bath. "They couldn't possibly have made this dress since yesterday." She felt the material, running her hand slowly across the bodice. "A dress like this takes hours to do, and I don't remember picking out this material or design," she said.

The dress was perfect for her. It was of deep turquoise-blue satin, the exact color of her eyes, with a low, heart-shaped neckline and huge puffed sleeves that ended at her elbows with lace ruffles of the same color. The girdle was beaded with minute seed pearls, and seed pearls were scattered here and there about the skirt, with rows of lace ruffles adorning the hemline.

"I think perhaps it's a dress Madame Benoit had made up already and knew would be perfect for you," offered Bridget as she fastened it up the back, and Gigi was entranced.

"There's a cape to match, Miss Gigi," said Bridget. "And I swear, I've never seen anything so beautiful."

"I feel guilty," said Gigi, running her hand across the seed pearls that encrusted the bodice. "Mr. Larrabee's been so kind to me, yet I just can't seem to make myself call him Father, and I don't know why."

"Don't worry," Bridget assured her. "As soon as your memory comes back, you'll feel differently."

"I hope you're right, Bridget," she said. "I certainly hope

you're right, but somehow I feel that this is all a ⟨
soon I'll wake up. Did you ever have that feeling?"

Bridget shook her head as she made Gigi sit down o⟨
vanity seat and she began working on her hair. "No, M⟨ ⟩
Gigi, I can't say I have," she said, holding the hairpins between her teeth as she talked. "But I'm sure it's only because
of the amnesia."

"I don't know," said Gigi. She watched Bridget twist a lustrous curl about her finger and tuck it high to the back of
her head. "I just feel so out of place . . ."

Delmonico's was crowded when they arrived, and the
people there turned in unison to stare as they saw the red-turbaned Ahmed pushing Jason's wheelchair into the dining
room, with Paul beside him, resplendent in white tie and
tails, escorting Gigi, one of the most beautiful women they'd
ever seen.

Cy Redding was Jason's top lawyer and business manager,
a slightly built man sporting a small mustache and sideburns.
His wife, seated beside him, was twice his size, with two
chins, and was loaded with oversized jewelry. They were already at the table when the Larrabees arrived, and with them
were the presidents and representatives of the many companies in which Jason was either leading stockholder or sole
owner. The men's wives accompanied them and were an assortment of the usual ladies of wealthy New York society.

It was an exceptionally large dinner party. However, from
the looks on the faces of the women around the table, Gigi
knew they were there only at the insistence of their husbands,
and she could sense their aloofness and reserve.

"You all know my son Paul," said Jason as the men stood,
acknowledging their arrival. "Now I'd like you to meet my
daughter Miss Gigi Rouvier."

Admiration showed in the men's eyes, but the women's
eyes were conveniently masked. They were used to disguising
their feelings. Anything to help their husbands' business
careers. So Gigi wasn't really sure of her reception.

Jason hadn't made Rose and Bruce come this evening, and
Gigi was relieved. It wouldn't do to let these people see their
hostility toward her. As it was, she felt uneasy all evening listening to the conversation around her, and was quick at
catching the underlying sarcasm in some of the remarks the
women made. Only Jason seemed oblivious of the sly innuen-

dos accompanied by supposedly friendly smiles, but it was obvious to Gigi that these people were anything but pleased with her presence.

When they finally left Delmonico's, Gigi breathed a sigh. She had made her second public appearance today, and to her the results were shattering. Everyone was merely tolerating her for Jason's sake and because there was nothing else to do if they wished to stay in his good graces. Now more than ever she wished she'd never come to New York.

4

The next few weeks were filled with more engagements. They all attended the opera, the theater, took a tour through the museum and aquarium at Old Castle Garden, then watched the horse shows, boat races, and polo games, with lawn parties sandwiched in between. Their pictures appeared on the society pages over and over again as their comings and goings became news.

Jason was exposing her to what Rose and Bruce had grown up with, New York society, and Gigi's life was in a constant turmoil.

New Yorkers became more and more accustomed to seeing the man in the wheelchair with the red-turbaned servant and beautiful dark-haired girl at his side. Paul couldn't always accompany them because of Lenore, and it was on these occasions that Gigi felt most out-of-place. Paul always made her feel comfortable and wanted, and although Jason tried to, she could never really feel secure with him, even though she was becoming more and more fond of him. But Jason was a hard, ruthless man in spite of his warmth toward her, and there were times she wished she'd never heard of him. He was stubborn and bullheaded, used to having things his way.

Rose and Bruce begged off constantly, so Jason made fewer and fewer attempts to force their attendance at social functions. The few lawn parties they did attend with her, however, were disastrous as far as Gigi was concerned, and she was glad Jason decided to leave them on their own. They let the world know, without Jason being aware of it, their true feelings for her too often. They were never going to accept her, and she knew it.

It was a few days before the annual charity masquerade ball being held in the main ballroom of the Waldorf Hotel.

Everyone was going to be there, including the Larrabees. Paul was going as a swashbuckling pirate and Lenore as a Casket Girl.

"It was strictly her idea," said Paul as he and Gigi discussed it early one morning while they sat on the terrace finishing breakfast and trying to decide what Gigi should wear.

"Then I think I'll go as your colored cabin boy," Gigi said, and Paul looked at her skeptically.

"With your face all blacked up?" He laughed, his deep resonant voice making her gooseflesh rise and her insides turn upside down, as always. "Who'd recognize you like that?" he said.

"That's the general idea, isn't it?" she asked. "Not to be recognized?"

"Well, yes, but . . ."

"Besides"—she tossed her head stubbornly—"then maybe I wouldn't have to unmask, and no one would know I was even there."

He gazed at her long and hard. "You're not happy, are you, Gigi?" he said thoughtfully, and she turned away.

They were sitting near the fountain, and he stood up, walking over, pulling her from her chair, taking her by the shoulders, turning her around so she had to face him. "You didn't answer me," he said.

"It isn't right, Paul," she whispered, her eyes misty. "Your father's done so much for me, but wherever I go, I can see people whispering, and I know the ones who do speak to me are doing it out of a morbid curiosity, or else because they're forced to tolerate me. I don't like being stared at and pointed out wherever I go!" Huge tears rimmed her eyes. "It just isn't working," she said dejectedly.

He frowned, his voice low. "I know just what you need," he said, gazing deep into her eyes. "You need a day to yourself. I'm going to take you somewhere where no one will know you. Someplace where you can be yourself without worrying about what people will say or do."

She looked surprised. "But when? How? Your father has every evening planned."

He smiled. "Now, right now." His gray eyes lit up. "Go upstairs and get your hat," he ordered her. "I'll tell Father we're going to spend the day in the city and meet you out front." He looked down at her dress. She looked magnificent in yellow, like an exotic tropical flower. "And don't change the dress," he said wistfully. "You look lovely just as you are."

"But where can we go this hour of the morning?" she asked, puzzled.

He only smiled that long luxurious smile of his that always transformed his face and made him look like a naughty little boy. "Let me worry about that," he said enthusiastically, and pulled her into the foyer. "Now, go get your things," and he headed her toward the drawing room and stairs, giving her a hurried push.

Less than ten minutes later Paul drove a small one-horse buggy down the drive, while Gigi looked back toward the house curiously.

"I feel like we're doing something illegal," she said as she watched the beautiful stone mansion disappear in the distance. But he didn't seem perturbed.

"Maybe we are at that," he said, laughing. It felt good to get away in the warm sunshine, with no demands being made on him for a change. Today would be good for him too. He set the horse into an easy trot.

A little over three hours later they arrived at Jewell's Wharf. Gigi hadn't minded the long ride at all. It was a gorgeous day and she was with Paul, that's all that mattered. He found a livery where he could leave the horse and buggy, and they had just enough time to catch the steamboat for the trip across to the island. Gigi was fascinated by the boat ride. There was music, people eating and playing cards, others dancing, and she watched the paddlewheels hypnotically as they seemed to keep time to the music the string orchestra near the railing was playing.

By one o'clock in the afternoon they finally stepped off the steamboat at Coney Island, and somehow Gigi knew she'd never seen anything like it before. Most of Paul's friends spent their time on the island at St. Thomas' Hotel. But that wasn't for Paul. Not today. He wanted Gigi to just be a part of the crowd, to enjoy herself and relax, so he stayed clear of the hotel.

They spent the next couple of hours wearing themselves out like children on a holiday, and no one gave them a second look. Few people here on the midway read the society pages, and to them they were merely another couple out for an afternoon of fun. Gigi never saw Paul so relaxed and lighthearted. He tried his prowess with the sledgehammer while she held her hand over her mouth to keep from smirking, and to her surprise he won her a fancy souvenir plate. Then he proceeded to win fancy dolls, stuffed animals, and pennants by knocking over plates with little white balls and pitching hoops over the ends of wooden pegs.

Gigi's arms were full as she perched atop a horse on the carousel and hummed along with the music as they whirled round and round. Her dark hair was flying loose, cascading to her shoulders, and more than once she had to brush the curling tangles from her face.

"Don't look outside, watch me," called Paul, who was sitting on the horse next to her toward the center of the carousel. "If you watch the things going by, you'll get dizzy, and I don't want a sick woman on my hands."

She leaned toward him, laughing, and her eyes shone. "You're too late, I've already made that discovery," she said, and sighed. "Why do you think I've been staring a hole through you?"

He grinned, patting his mount on its wooden head, and she saw his eyes linger on her curvaceous torso before settling on her face.

She blushed, and glanced back sheepishly toward an elderly couple sitting in the chariot a few rows behind them, aware that they were watching the two of them intently, probably thinking they were lovers, and the blush on her face deepened.

A few minutes later, at an old Gypsy fortune-teller's along the boardwalk, the same mistake was made.

"You'll find much happiness together," said the withered old crone as she studied the lines in Gigi's palm, referring to Paul as the love of her life, and they were both too embarrassed right away to tell her any differently. "But before this happens," she went on, "there'll be much danger for you." She studied Gigi's hand, engrossed, her eyes piercingly direct. "You will go on a long, dangerous trip," she said after a few moments. "A trip to a hot, dry land where the moon runs red with the blood of innocent people."

She peered at Paul, standing behind Gigi, her eyes narrowing. "Remember what I say, sir," she said, moving a thick tongue across crooked teeth. "Be wary, very wary." She waved a finger at him dramatically, and reached her clawlike hand out so he could cross her palm with more silver, but he declined, his face suddenly impassive and unsmiling.

"I think my sister has been frightened enough by all this nonsense," he told the old woman, taking Gigi's arm, helping her from the chair.

But the old woman protested. "Oh, no, sir! Please," she begged. "You must listen. Please, sir. Madame Zaleda is never wrong." Her eyes crinkled until they were barely slits under her painted brows. "This lady, I do not see her as your sister! Oh, no, sir!" she protested.

"Perhaps because we didn't have the same mother," explained Paul, irritated.

"No . . . no, it is more than that," she cried hurriedly, trying to keep them from leaving. "There is no tie, no blood tie, only a tie of love," she said, but Paul brushed her aside.

"Enough!" he said angrily. "You don't know what you're talking about, old woman. I've heard enough!" and he escorted Gigi to the door, angry at the old woman's stubbornness and his own foolishness for bringing Gigi here. Her arms were laden with his winnings, and she almost dropped one of the fancy dolls as he hurried her away.

The old woman stood for a long time watching after them, shaking her head and muttering to herself, until they were long out of sight.

The encounter had shaken Gigi, and Paul could see she was upset, but there was nothing he could do about it now. He cursed himself for his stupidity, but then, how could he have known what the woman would say and do? They headed for the edge of the boardwalk, not saying much, both very aware of the old woman's mistake.

"I'll never forget today," said Gigi after a while as she cuddled one of the fuzzy little stuffed animals to her breast and kicked the sand aside with her shoe. They were off the boardwalk now, at the edge of the sand, walking along, watching the waves come up onto the beach. She hadn't felt so carefree for days, and even the old Gypsy woman's ravings were beginning to fade from her thoughts. "It was wonderful just to be one of the crowd," she said.

The day was hot, but because it was a weekday, there weren't too many people on the beach. "If we had time, I'd take you for a dip in the ocean," Paul said, and glanced toward the edge of the water, where men and women were in their swimsuits playing in the surf.

Gigi's hand flew to her breast, and her eyes widened as she watched the women cavorting in the cumbersome swimsuits that exposed their legs beneath billowing bloomers. The wet suits clung to them, revealing their curves. "Oh, dear, I've never worn one of those," she said, shocked. "They're too revealing. I . . ." She stopped suddenly and looked at Paul, frowning. "Did you hear what I just said, Paul?" she asked.

He nodded, the smile leaving his face. "You said you'd never worn a bathing suit," he said slowly.

"But how do I know?" Her brows furrowed. "Somehow I know I've never worn one," she said. "Or even seen one before today. Do you think my memory's coming back?"

He searched her eyes, and it made Gigi quiver inside. "I don't know, Gigi," he said, frowning. "Maybe it is."

She stared up at him for a long time, then sighed, and they headed back toward the pier where the steamboat would soon be docking to pick up passengers. They felt like truants, guilty and a little disturbed yet, but happy.

It was almost seven in the evening when they arrived home, giving them just enough time to dress for dinner. But Rose and Bruce were eating out, and Jason wasn't feeling well and stayed in his private quarters, so the only one who discovered where they'd been was Bridget. She saw the stuffed animals Gigi smuggled into her room, and knew immediately, and as she helped Gigi dress for dinner, she was pleased to see her looking so radiantly happy for a change.

It was Bridget's suggestion and insistence that Gigi go to the masquerade ball as a Spanish señorita.

"With your dark hair and beautiful eyes, you'll look exotic," she'd said.

So Gigi let her fit her into a dress of red satin, with gold-trimmed ruffles cascading down the skirt, and a long black lace mantilla held atop her head with a gold comb. The bodice of the dress was covered with shiny glass beads, and was low in the front, hugging her small but voluptuous figure. Now she stood at the side of the ballroom, her face hidden behind a red satin mask, watching Lenore and Paul dancing together.

The full sleeves of Paul's costume billowed gracefully above the tight-fitting black pants he wore tucked into buckled boots, and a jeweled sword graced the sheath in his belt. He'd even tucked a gold earring onto one ear. Gigi loved it; Lenore didn't. Paul insisted it stay there, however, so it glinted now under the ballroom lights.

Gigi's eyes settled on Lenore, watching her sway in Paul's

arms. He definitely looked like a pirate, but she resembled very little one of the Casket Girls who'd come to this country years before to find husbands. Not a hair on her head was out of place, as usual, and the clothes she wore, that were supposed to belong to a peasant, were satins and silk. Only the small white hat covering her blond hair looked anywhere near real. She'd never win a prize for authenticity, thought Gigi, and she looked away quickly.

Tonight was one of the few evenings Jason hadn't accompanied them. Bruce, dressed as Ben Franklin, had brought Natalie Worthington, and Rose, trying her best to look like Cleopatra, was with Cy Redding's son Harvey.

The first thing Lenore said when she realized Paul was escorting both herself and Gigi was, "What's the matter, darling, couldn't you find anyone good enough to escort your sister tonight?" to which he'd replied without the slightest show of anger, "How did you guess?" Lenore's face had turned crimson.

As Gigi watched them now, she smiled, remembering. She really should try to like Lenore, but there was something about her that left Gigi cold. Maybe the way she always looked down her nose at her, or the way she tried to dominate Paul without trying to be too obvious. Gigi could see right through her.

Gigi was suddenly brought out of her daydreaming by a man's voice at her side, low and husky. "My dear, señorita, can it be true? I'm in luck, you're standing here alone?"

She turned quickly to look.

The voice came from a Spanish cavalier standing solidly at her elbow. A neat black mustache was visible just below his mask, and a set of beautiful white teeth shone below the well-trimmed mustache as he smiled broadly. He swept the ostrich-plumed cavalier's hat from his head, waving it in front of himself as he bowed low, the feather touching the floor.

"I'm André, at your service, my lovely one," he said. "And you are . . .?"

She frowned at his brashness. "I'm nobody," she answered politely.

"Oh, but no, señorita." He waved a finger in front of her face, his accent heavy. "You're wrong. You're somebody. Sí. You're the most beautiful woman in the room, and to be

standing here alone . . ." He gestured helplessly. *"Por favor,*
take pity on a stranger," he said.

This was ridiculous. He was looking at her so strangely.
His mouth was saying one thing, but his eyes another. His
words were flirtatious and devil-may-care, but his eyes studied
her with an intensity that made her uneasy.

"If you knew who I was, you'd want to stay a stranger,"
she said seriously, but he shook his head.

"Madre de Dios!" He laughed lightheartedly. "That I'd
never do," he replied. "Besides, I'm only jesting." His smiling
mouth grew a little more serious as he gazed into her eyes. "I
know who you are. You're Miss Gigi Rouvier, the daughter
of Jason Larrabee."

She blushed beneath the mask. "You knew?"

"Why do you think I came tonight?" he asked suddenly,
his smile fading completely. "I've seen you before many times
these past few days, señorita, but alas, I wasn't able to meet
you. Your brother keeps too tight a rein on you, I'm afraid."

His accent was heavy, and she began to wonder if perhaps
he really was Spanish, and it seemed weird to hear him referring to Paul as her brother.

"May I have this dance?" he asked suddenly as the music
started up again, and she frowned, uncertain of what to say.
After all, they hadn't been properly introduced. "Please?" he
coaxed. *"Por favor?"*

She shrugged. "I'd be delighted," she finally said, and
moved into his arms, then out onto the dance floor.

As he and Lenore danced, Paul had been watching the exchange of conversation between Gigi and the Spanish cavalier
who'd suddenly come up and started talking to her. In fact,
he'd kept an eye on her all evening as the different men escorted her about the ballroom floor. Even when the music
stopped, he continued to watch them, and now, as the music
started up again and the cavalier put his arms around Gigi,
starting to dance, Lenore glanced at Paul irritably.

"Is he suitable enough for her, Paul?" she asked abruptly.
"Or are you going to demand he unhand her?"

He paused, then looked at her unexpectedly. "Huh? Oh
. . . yes . . . what did you say?" he asked absentmindedly.

"I said, I think we'd better talk, Paul," she said, bristling
angrily. "Shall we go outside?"

He glanced at her quickly, scowling, then elbowed his way
to the portico at the end of the ballroom, ushering her ahead

of him. Fortunately, no one else was on the small balcony as they stepped outside.

"What's the matter?" he asked, his thoughts fully on her now as she walked over and leaned against the stone railing, looking out at the city.

She turned. "The matter? With me?" She shook her head. "There's nothing the matter with me, Paul," she said, facing him. "But there certainly seems to be with you. You seem so preoccupied lately. I talk to you, and you don't even hear me."

"I hadn't noticed."

"I know. That's just it," she lamented. "You don't notice anything anymore. I rarely see you, and when I do, your sister's always with us. I never get to see you alone anymore." She moved toward him, putting her hand up, toying with the collar on the fancy buccaneer's shirt he was wearing. "I feel like an intruder."

He laughed lightly, trying to be casual. "Why, you're jealous of Gigi, aren't you?" he said.

She bit her lip, and Paul could tell she was trying to control her emotions. He didn't want to hurt her. He put his arms around her and drew her close.

"Gigi's my sister, Lenore," he assured her. "You're being ridiculous. There's no reason for you to be jealous."

"Isn't there? You spend all your time with her. I hardly even get to see you anymore."

His arms tightened around her. "Have I really been neglecting you that much?" he said softly. "I didn't realize . . . but Father gave me the responsibility of seeing to it that everything goes well. I can't let him down."

"And your fiancée doesn't count? Is that it?"

"You know that's not true."

"Do I?" she asked bitterly. Her hand moved to his shirt, where it was open low in front, and she began to caress his broad chest, running her fingers through the soft curly hair that covered it, but for some strange reason, her caress seemed to be having no effect on him. His stomach tightened at the realization. "All I know, Paul," she said as she continued touching him lightly, "is that I love you, and we're to be married in August, yet since your sister's arrival we haven't even discussed the wedding plans. It's as if I don't even exist anymore. Everything centers about her. Why shouldn't I be jealous?"

His mouth tightened irritably, yet he knew she was right. He couldn't blame her for feeling hurt. He sighed uncomfortably. "All right, I get the message," he said softly, controlling his anger at himself. "I promise I won't neglect you anymore," and he looked deep into her eyes, hoping for something to happen, but it didn't. Well, by God, he'd make it happen.

Her lips parted, inviting him, and his mouth covered hers in a long, drawn-out kiss; then he held her close while she whispered in his ear about all the plans she was making for the wedding. He pretended to pay attention, but he didn't hear, not really. He was remembering the dashing cavalier who was being so attentive toward Gigi, and as Lenore's lips brushed his ear, he remembered how differently Gigi had felt when he'd held her close like this, and he winced. He tried to push the thought to the back of his mind and blot it out, but it was no use.

He inhaled sharply, interrupting Lenore's voice with an agonized groan, and furious with himself, he kissed her again, savagely this time, hoping to feel something, anything, and it took her breath away. But for him, for Paul, there was no warmth, no passion in the kiss, only fury, because the whole while he was kissing her, he was wondering what it would be like to kiss Gigi like this, and he cursed to himself, an empty, sick feeling in the pit of his stomach, and Lenore had no idea that the arousal she felt pushing hard against her had nothing to do with his feelings for her.

Meanwhile, Gigi and her cavalier were heading toward the refreshments.

"Since you know my name, sir," Gigi asked, "don't you think it proper I know the rest of yours . . . André?"

"André Diego de los Reyes, at your service," he answered smiling.

"But you're not from New York."

"Sí, señorita. You're right. I'm from below the border. Not far from your own western state." He sipped at the cup of punch he'd accepted from the waiter.

"Your home's in Mexico?" she asked.

"Sí. It's a marvelous place to live. The weather's always warm, the trees like no others, and some of the mountains have snow on them all year round. Your home, your west, Texas especially, is much the same."

"It sounds enchanting." She sighed. "I wish I could remember."

"Perhaps someday you will, señorita," he said. "But someone as lovely as you are needn't worry. Men will always be at your command, and with someone to love you . . . that's all a woman really needs."

"You exaggerate, Mr. de los Reyes," she said. "As yet, no men are swarming after me."

"It's not that they don't want to, señorita, I'm sure," he said, glancing about the ballroom, then back to her. "I've seen it in their eyes. They're, shall we say, conservative, where I . . . I haven't the conventions, not the restrictions. Please, may I call on you, Señorita Gigi?"

Gigi blushed. This was something new. He was good-looking, but for some reason something about him made her uneasy. She glanced across the floor as Lenore and Paul came in from the balcony and walked toward the refreshment table. They spotted her and walked over.

"Here's my . . ."—she hesitated a moment, as if unwilling to use the word—"my brother Paul, now with his fiancée," she said to André, who still stood beside her.

"Ah, *sí.*" André reached his hand out as Paul walked up. "Señor Paul Larrabee, may I introduce myself," he said confidently. "I'm André Diego de los Reyes, at your service, señor."

Paul shook his hand, then introduced Lenore. "My fiancée, Miss Lenore Van Der Linden."

Lenore smiled. "How do you do, Mr. de los Reyes."

"*Por favor* . . . please, everyone's to call me André," he insisted. "My mother was French, my father Spanish, and as my friends, I wish you'd call me André. 'Señor' is much too formal."

Gigi looked at Paul. "André's from Mexico, Paul," she said.

"I was telling your sister how beautiful the western states are, since she doesn't remember," he replied.

Paul frowned. "You know about her amnesia?" he asked.

"*Sí.*" André's dark eyes smoldered beneath his thin black mask. "I know a great deal about Señorita Gigi, Señor Larrabee," he said. "I've made it my business to know as much as possible about her, and I've asked permission from her to pay a visit. If that's all right with her family, of course," he said.

"And if she'll spend the rest of the evening with me, I'll be more than happy to see her to her door."

Lenore smiled broadly. "Oh, Paul, isn't that lovely," she exclaimed, relieved. "Now you won't have to worry about Gigi."

But Paul took a longer look at this man who'd suddenly burst into their lives. He was handsome enough, and tall, with thick black hair, thin mustache, and dark eyes that flashed hungrily whenever they rested on Gigi. His dusky olive complexion only tended to enhance the muscular frame beneath the silver-embroidered suit he wore. Yet, there was something about him . . . maybe the glib way he spoke such flattering phrases, or the fact that he was from Mexico, or maybe it was simply his interest in Gigi that bothered him.

"Mr. de los Reyes," he said slowly, "if Gigi'd like you to call, that's up to her. I'm sure my father'd be agreeable, and if she cares, you can spend the rest of the evening with her. But as to escorting her home . . ." He shook his head. "I have to say no. My father isn't here tonight, and she's my responsibility. She'll leave with us."

André shrugged. "As you wish, señor," he replied, disappointed. "I was hoping . . ." He straightened, glancing at Gigi. "But at least I may be with her until the ball's over. Appropriate, isn't it," he said to her, his eyes suddenly glistening, "that we should both be dressed in my native costume? It's as if we were meant for each other, don't you think?" and he smiled broadly.

Paul was annoyed with his brashness. "Tell me, Mr. de los Reyes," he said, changing the subject. "How long have you been in New York?"

"How long? Oh, a few days . . . long enough to learn my way around the city."

"Then it's your first trip here?"

"Sí, señor. I've been to Washington, D.C., many times, but never New York."

"You have friends here?"

"Sí." He turned to Gigi as the music started up again. "Shall we dance?" he asked abruptly, and she looked at Paul, shrugged her shoulders lightly, then entered André's arms and they glided across the room together.

Lenore's eyes narrowed as she and Paul stood watching. "Now what's wrong?" she asked as she saw the troubled expression on Paul's face.

"There's something about that man I don't like," he said, watching the comfortable way André de los Reyes held Gigi in his arms.

"Hmff. You wouldn't like anyone who tried to romance Gigi, would you?" she grumbled.

He scowled. "That's not it, and you know it," he answered. "There's just something . . . I can't put my finger on it. . . ."

She put her hand on his arm. "Why don't you forget it for now, Paul, please," she begged. "I'd like to enjoy the rest of the evening for a change. You promised."

He drew his eyes reluctantly from Gigi, then looked at her, embarrassed. "That's right," he said, his hand covering hers where it rested on his sleeve. "I did promise not to neglect you, didn't I? And here I am doing it already." He pulled her around into his arms, and they glided out onto the ballroom floor.

The unmasking was at midnight, and Paul made sure he got a good look at André's face minus the mask before the ball was over, but it did little good. All it confirmed was that he was a ruggedly handsome Latin, as he'd known from the start.

On the way home, he questioned Gigi, but she knew little more than what he'd told them all when they were together.

"He embarrasses me," said Gigi as they rode along in the carriage. "Always calling me 'lovely lady,' and being so outspoken in front of others. But I guess that's the way Spaniards are."

Lenore smiled. "He's a Latin, Gigi," she encouraged her. "I hear tell Latin men are fantastic lovers. When I was in Europe, women clamored for their attention, and I hear they're quite select with their women, so you should feel flattered."

Gigi flushed. "I suppose you're right, but there's something about him that makes me uneasy."

"You felt it too?" asked Paul.

She nodded.

"I think you're both being foolish," said Lenore disgustedly. "I think it's wonderful someone doesn't seem to be intimidated by Gigi's background. And I think your father'll be pleased that, in spite of everything, at least one gentleman hasn't shied away, and has been man enough to declare himself. Now, if Paul doesn't discourage him . . ."

"Why should I do a thing like that?" he asked.

She looked straight at him, her eyes studying his face intently. "That's what I've been asking myself," she said, and
was still staring at him as the carriage pulled up in front of
the door to her elaborate home.

Gigi waited in the carriage while Paul escorted Lenore to
the door. Bruce and Rose had come in separate carriages
with their companions, so after Lenore was dropped off, Gigi
and Paul were alone.

Paul signaled the driver on. Gigi was exceptionally quiet as
they made their way home. It was the wee hours of the
morning, and Paul thought perhaps she was tired.

"What's the matter?" he finally asked when he could hold
back no longer, and she moved restlessly, shifting her position
in the seat.

"I'm afraid, Paul," she said softly, "but I don't know why."

"Of what?"

"André de los Reyes."

"André . . . ?"

"Yes. His eyes look at me so strangely. As if . . ." She
shrugged. "Oh, I just can't explain it."

Paul knew exactly what she meant. He'd seen it too. The
man was obviously attracted to her, yet he was rather secretive and unwilling to volunteer much information about himself. Maybe that's why Paul insisted on bringing Gigi home
himself. For all of André de los Reyes' Latin charm, there
was something almost phony about him. But if so, why would
he single out Gigi? That was the puzzle. Of all the women in
New York, why Gigi? Unless it was really Jason's wealth that
attracted him, or maybe Gigi had known him before. He had
thought of that too. Sometimes André looked at her in such a
familiar way. Was he part of the past she couldn't remember?
Paul's eyes darkened as the thought crossed his mind.

They were about three miles from home, moving along
slowly, uneventfully, when suddenly Paul heard the driver
start shouting. He cursed, wondering what was going on, and
stuck his head out the window just in time to see a carriage
coming straight for them, trying to block their path, the
driver using a whip on the horses, and before he had a
chance to duck his head back inside, Tuttleby, the driver,
swerved, avoiding a sure collision.

Their carriage hit the side of the road, bounding out across
a ditch. Gigi screamed, hitting the side of the coach, then
suddenly she fell hard against Paul, who was thrown back-

ward, and they both landed on the floor as the carriage hit a rock, came to a crashing stop, and turned on its side, the axle broken. They sat for a moment dazed, staring at each other. Then: "Are you all right?" he gasped breathlessly, reaching up, straightening her black lace mantilla and helping her pull down the skirt of her dress as he started to get up.

She nodded, breathing heavily and trembling as Tuttleby stuck his head down through the window. It was so dark he could hardly see, because the moon was screened by a cloud. "Are you all right?" asked Tuttleby shakily.

Paul nodded. "I think so," he said. "But give me a hand, will you? We'll get Gigi out of here."

He boosted her up through the window with Tuttleby's help, then climbed out after her. The other carriage was out of sight already, and Paul cursed as his feet hit the ground.

"How are the horses?" he asked.

Tuttleby shook his head, upset. "The horses are fine, Mr. Paul," he said. "But the carriage isn't much good for anything."

Paul could barely see in the dark. Not only was the axle broken, but one of the wheels was shattered, and the tongue ripped off. "About how far are we from the house, Tuttleby?" he asked.

The man answered slowly, "About three miles. Give or take a few steps."

"Good. Then since the horses seem to be all right, unhitch them and we'll ride the rest of the way bareback," he said. "It's better than walking," and he tried to help Gigi straighten herself and make herself presentable once more.

"Yes, sir," Tuttleby said, and went to unhitch the horses. "Mr. Paul, could you come here a minute?" he said, trying to be nonchalant, and Paul walked over to see what he wanted, leaving Gigi standing by the battered carriage.

"What is it?" he asked.

"Look ahead about five or six feet, sir, but be careful."

Paul walked up slowly, then peered off into space.

"You know where we are now, sir?" asked Tuttleby.

Paul knew, and he breathed a sigh, his face pale. It was the ravine. As a boy he used to come and climb the hill, pretending he was climbing mountains. The road skirted it about thirty or forty feet away, then went down a sloping grade before going up the other side, but the ravine itself was a sheer drop of some two hundred feet. If the carriage hadn't hit the rock and turned over, stopping the horses, they probably would have ended up at the bottom of it, crushed inside the carriage.

Paul shuddered. "That was close," he said, then glanced back at Gigi. "Don't mention it to Gigi. It'll only frighten her more, and she's had enough of a scare for one evening," he said, then glanced again quickly at Tuttleby. "Tell me, Tuttleby," he said, pondering thoughtfully. "Do you think that other carriage did this on purpose?"

Tuttleby frowned, then shook his head. "I don't think they meant for us to go over the cliff, sir, no, if that's what you mean," he said. "But I do think they were hoping to stop us. Maybe thieves? Robbers? I think things got out of hand."

"Hmmm," said Paul, then shrugged. "Well, as I said, don't tell Miss Gigi," he cautioned him again.

Tuttleby nodded. "Yes, sir," he said, and he unhitched the horses for them.

He rode one, and Paul sat Gigi on the other, then climbed on behind, and they headed toward Larrabee Manor. Anyone who had seen them would probably have thought they were ghosts, what with Paul's gleaming white shirt and sword, Gigi's fluttering mantilla and Spanish clothes, and Tuttleby's high hat with his flowing cape covering him like a shroud.

"I'd hate to meet anyone tonight," said Paul as they rounded a bend in the road. "We'd probably scare the wits out of them," and that's just what happened moments later when Harvey Redding's carriage came into view and the driver reined up abruptly, his eyes wide with fright. Harvey'd escorted Rose home and was on his way back to the city.

"Good heavens, Paul! What happened?" he exclaimed as he stuck his coonskin-capped head out the window and recognized them when the coach came to a stop. He was still in costume and had dressed as Daniel Boone, although his glasses and frail stature made a mockery of the man he was pretending to represent.

"Some drunken bum ran us off the road," answered Paul as his arm tightened about Gigi. "The carriage is back there torn apart."

"Do you know who it was?" asked Harvey.

"Afraid not. It was too dark to see."

"Well, I'm glad you're all right," he said. His head was sweating in the warm night air, and he pulled off his hat. "Would you like a ride back to the house? I wouldn't mind."

"No, thanks," said Paul. "The horses'll get us there safe enough."

"I don't know who it might have been," mused Harvey, frowning. "No one passed me on the road."

"That's strange."

"Maybe not," said Harvey. "I left your house only a few minutes ago, they might have already been ahead of me." He wiped the sweat from his brow with a handkerchief and thrust the hat back onto his head. "Well, I'm glad everyone's all right. Now I'd better get going, it's late, take care," he said, and motioned for his driver to start, then leaned back comfortably, and the carriage pulled away.

Gigi watched it leave, then turned back and looked up to see Paul's eyes looking directly into hers. His arm moved caressingly on her waist as he gently nudged the horse in the sides and as they moved away, down the road, her head tilted back, and she leaned against him, secretly enjoying his nearness, even though she knew it was wrong.

When they reached the house, Jason was in the foyer waiting for them. He'd been watching for them from the drawing-room window and had seen the unusual trio as they made their way up the drive, filtering in and out among the tree shadows as the moon came out from behind the clouds.

"What on earth happened?" he asked as they stepped inside.

Paul was surprised to see him. "An accident on the way home," he explained, wishing his father hadn't waited up.

"Where's the carriage?"

"Down the road."

"How did it happen?"

Paul helped Gigi off with her fringed Spanish shawl. "Some drunk, driving like a madman," explained Paul. "He ran us off the road. The carriage is ruined, but thank God we're safe, except for a few bumps and bruises."

Jason shook his head angrily. "I don't understand, Paul. Who would be driving like that on these roads at this time of night?"

"I told you, Father," Paul insisted. "It was a drunk, I'm sure. Only a drunk would attempt going that fast after dark. He probably never even saw us."

"You're sure?" asked Jason. "I've never known of anything like this to happen before."

Paul assured him. "There's always a first time."

Jason looked at Gigi. "You're sure you're all right, my dear?" he asked.

Gigi nodded. She was still shaken, but the ride with Paul had calmed her considerably, at least in some ways. In other ways it had disturbed her even more than the accident. "Yes, I'm all right," she replied.

"Good," he said. "Then I'll ask you about this young man they said you spent the evening with."

"They?" questioned Gigi.

"Rose and Bruce."

"Oh." She might have known they'd have brought the news right home. "His name is André Diego de los Reyes, and that's about all any of us know about him," she said.

Jason frowned. "Where's he from?"

"Mexico."

"Mexico?" That took him by surprise. "What's he doing in New York?"

"He didn't say," she said. "But while we were dancing, he did mention that he was a friend of the ambassador from Mexico."

"Hmmm!" Jason seemed displeased. "I'd like to meet the man before you spend much more time with him," he said.

"I assure you, Father," interrupted Paul, "Gigi wouldn't think of entertaining him without your permission."

Jason nodded. "Good." He reached out and took Gigi's hand, his steely gray eyes possessive. "I wouldn't want anyone to sweep you off your feet just yet, my dear," he said forcefully. "I want to have you around for a while. I'm enjoying your company too much to have you snatched away so soon."

She smiled. "No need to worry, sir," she said. "I'm not sure I even like Mr. de los Reyes."

"Oh?"

"I guess I'm not used to so much flattery and attention."

He smiled back. "I'm glad. Now, since it's late, and I assume you all had a good time at the ball, I suggest we call it a night." He dismissed the servants, called for Ahmed, and they went to their rooms.

5

Gigi was sore and bruised when she woke the next morning, and she lay on the bed, letting Bridget rub her generously with liniment.

"Gracious!" Bridget said as she massaged Gigi's arms and legs. "You really are lucky you're not hurt worse, you know."

"I know," agreed Gigi. She'd been so stiff all morning.

"I heard Mr. Tuttleby telling Mrs. Sharp you were lucky the carriage hit that rock and turned over, or you'd have been at the bottom of the ravine," said Bridget, putting pressure on the back of Gigi's thighs as she stroked vigorously.

"What ravine?" she asked, swiveling her head to look at Bridget, and Bridget hesitated with her massaging, then splashed some cologne over the liniment to help mask its strong medicinal smell.

"There's a ravine and a cliff, with a sheer drop right where the carriage was headed," she said as she rubbed. "I hate to think what would have happened if you'd gone over."

Gigi frowned. "Strange . . . Paul never said a word." She turned over and let Bridget splash the cologne on her knees, stroking it to her ankles. "He surely must have known last night."

"He probably didn't want you any more upset than you already were," said Bridget as she finished. She helped Gigi from the bed, helping her get into her petticoats. "Now, what are you doing today?" she asked. "A lawn party? Tennis matches?"

Gigi shook her head. "I'm staying home today for a change and resting, thank God. So if you'll help me pick out a dress to wear, I'll go have breakfast," and Bridget picked out a beautiful soft pink embroidered muslin for her to slip into, then they left the room.

It was early afternoon: Gigi had spent most of the morning in the library reading. Now she was just finishing lunch on the terrace, when Biddy came out and told her she was wanted on the telephone. She followed the small maid into the foyer where the telephone hung between a Gainsborough and Titian.

Evidently Gigi had never heard of telephones before coming to the Larrabees', and they fascinated her. She stared at it for a minute, then held the receiver close to her ear, speaking loudly into the mouthpiece attached to the brown box on the wall. "Hello? Hello?"

The voice came back louder than she'd expected, and she could hear the accent clearly. *"Buenos días, señorita.* I was hoping you'd be home."

"Mr. de los Reyes?"

"Sí, sí, little one. Will you be home this afternoon?"

"Yes," she blurted into the mouthpiece, then wished she hadn't.

"Bueno," came his enthusiastic reply. "Then may I keep my promise and come for a visit?"

She hesitated. She didn't really want to see him again, but knew it'd be rude to say no. Especially since she'd already told him she'd be home. Besides, Jason wanted to meet him, and Jason wasn't going to be too busy today.

"If you'd like," she answered.

"I'll be there within the hour," he promised gaily.

"All right. I'll see you then," she said. "Good-bye."

"Hasta luego, señorita. Until then," and she heard the other end of the telephone go dead.

She gazed at the receiver rather curiously, then hung it up and went toward Jason's quarters to let him know Mr. de los Reyes would be there soon.

André arrived as he said, within the hour. Well, at least he was prompt. She was surprised to see him in more conventional clothes. He was very good-looking, his face a bit broad, forehead high, but unmistakably attractive, the thin mustache bringing out his Latin features. He wore a plain dark blue velvet suit, jacket ending at the waist, with a white shirt, a dash of red in the thin cravat at his throat. Somehow, dressed like this, a flat-crowned, broad-brimmed hat in his hand, he lost some of the mysterious qualities he'd held for her last night. She wasn't afraid of him now, except for those eyes. They still seemed so intense, almost cruel at times.

Jason received him in the drawing room. "My family told me about the mysterious gentleman who was so attentive toward my daughter last evening," he said. "How do you do, Mr. de los Reyes."

André smiled charmingly. "At your service, señor."

"Tell me," said Jason. "Just where are you from in Mexico, sir?"

"Just north of La Mariposa near the Sabinas River, Señor Larrabee." André's dark eyes flashed. "My hacienda's beautiful. We call her Flor de la Montaña, Flower of the Mountain, because she was built in the foothills of the Sierra del Carmen, in the north country of Coahuila."

"You know our American west?"

"*Sí.* I've been to your west many times, señor."

"I see. And what brings you to New York, Mr. de los Reyes?" Jason asked as Gigi sat listening to them.

"A holiday. I have friends here, and I've been wanting to visit them for some time." He looked at Gigi. "Now I'm glad I came. I never expected to meet anyone as lovely as your daughter, señor."

Jason frowned. "I'll warn you now, Mr. de los Reyes—"

"*Por favor,* please, señor, the name is André."

"André, then. As I was saying, I hope you won't become too serious about my daughter. I don't intend to lose her so quickly after having just found her."

André's face fell. "Ah, señor, I'm disappointed naturally," he said sadly. "But I can be patient for one so exquisite." His eyes sought Gigi's, and she flushed. "For her I'd wait an eternity," he went on, and once more that hungry, yearning look crept into his dark eyes. "May I take her riding some afternoon, señor?" he asked. "I'd enjoy seeing the countryside on horseback."

Jason nodded. "Why don't you go now? We have a stable full of excellent horseflesh, and the afternoon's sunny."

André's eyes lit up. "Ah, you're a man after my own heart, Señor Larrabee. If Gigi will say yes?"

She stared at him for a moment thoughtfully, then smiled apprehensively. "I'll go change and be right down," she said, and she went up the staircase to her room, leaving them in the drawing room talking.

As she reached her bedroom door, she realized that they

still hadn't learned anything about the man. He'd told Jason
as little as he'd told the rest of them. Oh, well, Jason seemed
satisfied, and at least André was a diversion. He was the first
man who'd seriously treated her like she was something other
than a loose woman. And he was decidedly attractive. Perhaps it wouldn't hurt to be nice to him. It was a way to keep
her occupied so she wouldn't think of Paul so much. That
was something she didn't like. Not at all. These strange
feelings she had toward Paul. It was insane, and the worst
part was that she knew Paul felt them too, even though both
of them tried hard to ignore it. She could tell by his eyes
sometimes when he looked at her, and sometimes by the
things he said.

She had to rid herself of these feelings once and for all,
and maybe André was the answer. She'd play up to him.
Maybe she'd forget how Paul's arms had felt that day on the
terrace, and last night when he'd held her tight as they'd ridden home together on the same horse. There'd been warmth
and desire in his eyes when she'd glanced back at him.
Damn! She cursed herself, then flushed at her own actions.
Well, the only way to forget one man's arms was to let another man hold her. At least that sounded sensible. She'd have
to wrap her thoughts around someone else, and it might as
well be André. After all, he was handsome, and he was attentive. What more could she ask? Maybe she'd even fall in
love. Who knows?

Bridget helped her into a pair of black riding pants, the
latest creation from Paris. Actually it was more of a skirt
with a separation between the legs so she could ride astride
instead of sidesaddle. Her boots were black, like the skirt,
with a white long-sleeved blouse and a small black jacket and
hat trimmed with black velvet braid. She and Paul had gone
riding often along the riverbanks, and she always wore this
outfit, and she remembered the approving look in Paul's eyes
when he looked at her. You stupid fool, she told herself now
as she stared into the mirror, letting Bridget pull her hair
back and tie it with a velvet ribbon, he's your brother, get
him out of your mind!

She turned to Bridget when the girl had finished. "Do you
think André will approve?" she asked, forcing her thoughts
from Paul.

"Oh, Miss Gigi," said Bridget, her brown eyes resting ad-
miringly on her young mistress. "Any man who doesn't

should have his head examined. Here . . ." She reached over and picked up a perfume flask from the dresser and pulled out the stopper. "Just a dab in case he decides to come close," she said, and she touched the stopper on each side, just below Gigi's ear. "Now you're truly beautiful." She sighed wistfully, putting the perfume flask back.

Gigi reached out and took Bridget's hands, squeezing them affectionately. "Bridget, you've been so kind to me," she said. "You draw my bath, take care of my clothes. You do so much, how can I ever repay you?"

Bridget smiled. "I'd rather do this than scurry about the kitchen with Mrs. Sharp at my heels," she said, and pulled her hands from Gigi's, primping her honey-blond hair. "Besides," she said, "this job gives me more time to spend with my beau."

The thought of Bridget having a beau hadn't occurred to Gigi, but it should have. After all, the girl was sixteen and nice-looking; naturally the boys would like her. "Your beau?" She smiled. "Have you known him long?" she asked, pleased Bridget shared this confidence with her.

"Since I've been here," she said. "He works in the stables taking care of the horses."

"You mean Jamie, Mr. Tuttleby's son?"

Bridget blushed. "How did you know?"

"He's the only one of the boys down there who'd have a right to look at you, Bridget," said Gigi. "He's handsome, that's for sure, and he'll do well for himself someday, I can tell," and Gigi felt she was right. Jamie Tuttleby wasn't like most of the lazy boys at the stables. He was always there when needed, and always busy doing something. And she hadn't lied. He was quite nice-looking, and very masculine in a rather disheveled way, with his hair askew, his hands calloused from work, and the trace of a beard shaved from his once smooth cheeks.

Bridget was so proud of him. "Do you really think he'll be somebody someday, Miss Gigi?" she asked. "He wants to, you know. He wants to have a stable of his own someday and rent out horses. And we plan to get married, but not until he can provide for me. We're both young yet, so we can wait."

Gigi was so happy for her, she gave her a hug. "Why don't you go see him while I'm out riding?" she said, releasing her to grab her riding crop. "I won't need you for a while."

Bridget smiled thankfully. "Oh, thanks. Now, if I can manage to sneak away from the house without being seen. Mr.
Larrabee doesn't like any of the girls hanging about the
stables."

"I wouldn't want you to get in trouble, Bridget," said Gigi,
frowning; then: "I know," she said. "You take a walk, and
I'll be down at the stables, I'll tell Jamie to meet you by the
river, at the picnic grove."

"Would you? Really?" asked Bridget.

"Just don't let Biddy or anyone else know," cautioned Gigi.

Bridget shook her head. "Never," she said. "No one will
ever know, only us."

They left the room and went downstairs, Bridget through
the music room and Gigi to the drawing room.

André was captivated by her loveliness, at least that's what
he kept telling her, and Jason followed them to the door,
shaking hands with André before they left to go to the
stables. The stables were in back and to the side of the house
some distance, and the walk down the drive was invigorating
in the warmth of the afternoon sun.

While André and the groom picked out two horses, Gigi
found Jamie and gave him Bridget's message, then joined
André as the groom finished tightening the cinch on her
horse. It was a beautiful roan with a white blaze on its face.
A horse her father'd given her when she'd first arrived.

They rode off toward the river and the rolling hills beyond,
and Gigi was determined to center all her attention on
André. To flirt and cajole him in an attempt to push her
feelings about Paul to the back of her mind.

The afternoon went well. But one thing was certain. Jason
Larrabee didn't trust André as fully as he led the man to believe, for everywhere they rode, a red-turbaned figure on a
big black horse accompanied them, just far enough away to
barely be seen now and then through the trees.

"It's been a wonderful afternoon, *querida*," said André as
they made their way back toward the stables sometime later.

She smiled coyly. She'd been charming and gracious all afternoon. "Perhaps you'll stay to dinner, André," she suggested. "That is, if you've nothing more pressing."

"More pressing? *Válgame Dios!* What could be more
pressing than having dinner with the most beautiful woman
in the whole of New York?" he answered breathlessly. "I'll
stay. I'll be delighted to stay."

She smiled, not at all surprised at his answer.

Rose and Bruce were the ones who were surprised to see André at the dinner table, and although they plied him with as many questions as Jason did, his answers were always rather vague and they still knew little more about him when they left the table, except that he was charming, witty, and very much smitten with Gigi. Paul was absent from the table this evening, having accepted a dinner invitation from the Van Der Lindens.

After dinner they retired to the music room, where Rose played for them, and much to Gigi's surprise, André picked up the guitar from its case in the corner of the room and serenaded them with a medley of Spanish love songs.

It was sometime later, well after ten o'clock, when André and Gigi stood on the terrace near the fountain, alone at last.

André's dark eyes flashed moodily. "I'll say one thing for you, Gigi," he said, sighing. "You may not have a duenna following you about as do the women in my country, but you're still the hardest person to be alone with."

She smiled seductively. "We're alone now," she said.

He reached out in the darkness and drew her to him, his eyes smoldering, warm with desire.

"You're so lovely," he whispered softly. "So very lovely," and his mouth began to descend on hers, when they heard the French doors open and footsteps.

"*Madre de Dios!*" muttered André under his breath, as Paul walked toward them, and he dropped his arms from about her, releasing her, his eyes flashing angrily in disappointment.

Paul stopped suddenly and stared at them both, only it was too dark for Gigi to see the fury in his eyes. "Sorry, I didn't realize you were out here," he said coolly. "I didn't mean to interrupt." Yet he made no move to go back into the house.

André walked back toward the lawn furniture where Paul had seated himself in one of the wrought-iron chairs, and he sighed, exhaling loudly. "Perhaps it's time for me to be leaving anyway, señor," he said reluctantly, realizing it looked like Paul was here to stay, for he'd made himself quite comfortable. "It's late." He looked over at Gigi. "I'll be back again," he assured her, gazing into her blue-green eyes.

She glanced at him sheepishly. "I'll see you to the door," she offered, but he raised his hand, stopping her.

"No. It's all right," he said softly. "I'll let myself out, but

I'll be back. I'll call you." He took her hand in his, squeezing her fingers lightly. *"Adiós, querida,"* and he kissed the tips of her fingers. "Good night, Señor Larrabee," he said to Paul, then left the terrace, going into the foyer to retrieve his hat, and on to the front door.

She watched through the French doors as he took his hat from the rack, opened the door, and went out. He hadn't even sent anyone to get his carriage, so he'd have to walk all the way to the stables for it. Well, maybe the walk would soothe him some. She knew he was irritated by Paul's interruption, and in a way, so was she.

"You had to walk in just then, didn't you?" she said, turning to Paul, her eyes unsettled.

He stood up, his jaw tightening. "Maybe it's best I did. He was going to kiss you!"

"Did it ever occur to you that maybe I wanted him to?"

He was taken aback. "Maybe you . . . ?" He frowned. "You wanted him to?"

"Maybe I wanted to see what it would be like to be kissed, Paul," she said, lowering her voice so that only he could hear. "After all, I can't remember anything. I don't know if I've ever been kissed or not, and how will I know if I like it, if no one ever kisses me?"

His eyes blazed. "But you don't go around kissing just anyone who comes along just to see if you're going to like it!"

"André isn't just anyone!"

"Oh, isn't he?" He looked down into her upturned face, soft and vulnerable in the moonlight. "I'll tell you who he is," he said. "He's some Casanova who probably has a woman in every city from here to Mexico, that's who he is! We know nothing about him except that he has his eye on you."

Her head tilted defiantly. "Is that so bad?" she asked belligerently. "Maybe I would've liked his kiss."

Paul's face was one of torment as he gazed down at her. "Gigi, you're not going to fall in love with him, are you?" he asked softly.

She looked up into his eyes, steely gray in frustration, the moonlight gently dancing on his dark hair. She could clearly see the solid outline of his chin, his eyes searching her face anxiously.

"I don't know, Paul," she said softly. "I don't know if I can fall in love. I don't know what love is like, I don't even know what it is." She looked deep into his eyes. "What is love, Paul?" she asked breathlessly. "Tell me what love is."

"Love . . . ?" His voice was deep, husky, his face close to hers, his heart pounding. "Love is wanting to be with one person more than anything else in the world," he whispered softly, his breathing erratic. His eyes bored into hers. "And wanting to tell that person just how you feel . . . love is melting inside when your eyes meet . . . wanting to take her in your arms and kiss her and never let her go . . . wanting someone so badly you ache . . ." His voice broke as he realized what was happening. "Oh, my God, Gigi," he groaned passionately. "Do I have to tell you what love is . . . don't you know?"

She saw the pain in his eyes and felt the torment in her own body, and she began to tremble. "Oh, Paul!" she cried weakly, realizing what she'd done. There was no excuse. "I'm sorry, I'm sorry!" she cried, trying to make amends. "Please . . . forgive me!" and she whirled abruptly, running from the terrace, tears welling up in her eyes.

Yes, she knew what love was. She'd been fighting it too long these past weeks. It was ridiculous! Insane! Women didn't go around falling in love with their own brothers. The two of them had different mothers, true, but . . . this was madness! She should never have come to New York. Oh, God!

She reached the upstairs hall and slowed down, trying to compose herself. She had felt it that first day when he'd walked into her bedroom at Mrs. Thornapple's. The wonderful sense of pleasure she derived just from looking at him. He did things to her she couldn't explain. She had sensed it even then, yet tried to deny it. Well, she couldn't deny it any longer, and she knew it was hopeless.

Bridget was waiting when she reached her room, yet she never said a word about the tears Gigi wiped away as she walked through the door, and later that night as Gigi lay tossing and turning in bed, she suddenly remembered Biddy's words and she felt ashamed. She should have heeded the warning and left, she knew that now, but it was too late. There could only be heartbreak for both herself and Paul. Nothing could change the fact that he was her brother, and yet nothing could change the fact that she loved him with all her heart. That night, Gigi, tormented beyond reason, cried herself to sleep.

The next day she avoided seeing Paul all morning, but at lunchtime it was impossible.

"Have you made any plans for the wedding, Paul?" asked Jason as they all sat around the dining-room table finishing their dessert.

"No," he answered quietly.

"Good heavens," Jason said. "It's only a few weeks away. Surely you and Lenore have the guest list made up and the invitations ready to send."

"I don't know." His eyes were intent on his food.

"You don't . . . I've been asking questions about the wedding for the past week now, and every time I ask, you don't know," Jason said. "What the hell's the matter with you anyway, Paul?" He was upset.

Paul's eyes shot to his father's face. "Maybe I'm sick and tired of being quizzed all the time!" he snapped angrily. "Maybe I think it's time everyone minded their own business! If you want to know about the wedding," he said, "why don't you ask Lenore? She's making all the arrangements!" and they all stared as Paul stood up abruptly, leaving the table, his dessert half-finished.

"Well, what's gotten into him?" said Rose. "It isn't like dear brother Paul to be so touchy."

Bruce snickered. "Maybe he's getting cold feet. He's been avoiding marriage a long time. Maybe he's having second thoughts."

"Paul? Nonsense!" exclaimed Jason. "He and Lenore have always been a natural. The families expect it."

"Maybe that's the trouble," said Bruce. "Has Paul expected it? Maybe he wanted to choose his own wife."

Jason blustered. "He did choose her. Nobody told him he had to marry her."

"Not in so many words, no," agreed Bruce. "But as you said, it was expected, and he knew it."

"Don't be silly, son," Jason assured him. "Paul's always been in love with Lenore, since they were children."

"I don't know, Father," interrupted Rose, her pale brown eyes amused at her older brother's discomfiture. "Maybe Bruce is right. Maybe he is having misgivings."

Jason's hand slammed the table beside his plate, rattling the silverware, and Gigi jumped, startled. "I won't have it!" he yelled furiously. "I won't have it, do you hear! Paul asked Lenore to marry him, and he's not backing out." He calmed momentarily, the fingers on the hand that attacked the table suddenly twitching nervously as he pondered. "I'd better have a talk with Paul," he said suddenly, and he took a deep breath. "If he's having doubts, he'd better forget them. I'll not let anything spoil this wedding. Nothing!"

"Well, something's wrong with him, that's for sure," said Bruce. He turned to Gigi, who'd been listening to them, her face pale, dessert forgotten. "You and Paul spend a great deal of time together, Gigi," he said aggressively. "Did he say anything to you?"

Her face flushed crimson as she glanced at Bruce, wishing she could ignore his question. She knew what was the matter. How well she knew. She fought back the tears. "He didn't say a thing," she said meekly. "Now, if you'll excuse me, I promised to help Bridget with something," and she left the table while Rose stared after her, a strange expression in her eyes.

Jason didn't seem to notice it, however, and continued fussing and fuming over Paul's unusual behavior. As soon as he was through eating, Jason went looking for Paul, and found him in the business library and office going over some work he'd been neglecting lately.

"Ah, there you are," said Jason as Paul looked up from the large mahogany desk.

This room was different from the other library. The other library in the other wing of the house was furnished with plush furniture and reading lamps. This library, along with its shelves of books, had filing cabinets, office furniture, and a business atmosphere. It was really Paul's office, where he took care of the business end of Larrabee Enterprises for Jason.

Paul laid his pen down as his father wheeled his chair over to the desk.

"If you don't mind, Paul, I'd like to have a word with you," he said briskly.

Paul toyed nervously with a paperweight. "About what?" he asked. He was noticeably on edge.

"About you and Lenore."

"What about us?" Paul's eyes masked his feelings.

"Are you in love with her?" his father asked. He'd always been a blunt man, but now the question rankled Paul.

"We're getting married, aren't we?" he answered.

"That's not what I asked."

Paul's jaws clenched, and he slammed his fist on the desk.

"Look, Father, we're getting married, the whole thing's been arranged," he said bitterly. "Everyone will be happy. So why don't we just leave it at that!"

"You don't look very happy, Paul."

He sighed. "Well, I am!"

"And you don't act it, either." Jason knew his son well. Something was definitely wrong. Could it be possible? Could Rose and Bruce be right? Or maybe . . . Could there be another woman? He hadn't thought of that. Maybe Paul . . . "Paul, is there someone else?" he asked slowly, watching the expression on his son's face, but it changed little, only the eyes darkening savagely. "You've been away from the house quite a bit lately. I never questioned that you weren't with Lenore."

Paul stood up, turning his back on his father, walking over to the window, staring out, watching the birch trees blowing in the wind that had stirred up outside. Dark clouds were heaving about the sky, and it had been threatening rain all day.

How could he answer? There wasn't any answer. He couldn't let his father know how he felt about Gigi. Ever since he'd first seen her sitting in that big four-poster at Mrs. Thornapple's, with those soft blue-green eyes and warm mouth . . . Oh, God! If things could only be different, but they couldn't. She was Gigi Rouvier, his half-sister. A part of his flesh, and because of it, she was forbidden to him.

He could never hold her in his arms and feel the warmth of her soft skin beneath his fingers, never kiss her mouth and feel her lips surrender as she gave herself to him. He could never make love to her as he wanted, and he began to ache physically as a storm broke inside him. A storm of fury toward the man who'd fathered his heartache.

"Don't worry, Father," he said bitterly, his voice hard and cold as he turned to face him. "I'll marry Lenore. I'll marry her and we'll have children, and I'll be an ideal husband, and she'll never have to worry about me going astray, and we'll live happily ever after."

Jason flinched. "But you didn't answer my question, Paul."

"And dammit, I won't! I can't!" he said acidly. "There's nothing more to be said. Now, will you let the matter drop? For God's sake, forget it!" and he turned his back again, thrusting his hands in his pockets.

Jason saw the set of his son's shoulders and knew it wouldn't do any good to question him further. Maybe Bruce and Rose were right. Maybe it was just the jitters. He'd had them too before he'd gotten married. Then he remembered something and felt a sickening, guilty feeling in the pit of his stomach. He hadn't been in love with his wife. It had been a marriage planned for profit. Was he doing the same thing to Paul? He shook his head thoughtfully. No! Paul had chosen Lenore himself. No one had pushed him, but for the moment he'd better leave him alone.

Paul heard the wheelchair move across the floor, then heard the door shut behind his father, and he sighed.

When he'd asked Lenore to marry him, it had seemed the natural thing to do. He was almost twenty-nine now, and it was time he settled down. Besides, Jason had been after him to get married and give him grandchildren. Everyone expected his final decision to be Lenore, he knew. She was beautiful and they were both of the same social standing. They were used to each other, from being together so much as children, and it never occurred to him that the fondness he felt toward her wasn't love—until he met Gigi, that is; then suddenly he knew. Lenore was something comfortable and secure, a way of life his social status had become accustomed to, but love? Lenore had barely aroused him. He had no desire to touch her or fondle her, and her kisses left him empty. Love was far different. It throbbed through your veins like a horse surging at the bridle, ready to be let free. It was moments of torment and ecstasy rolled into one fell swoop that knocked you down and never bothered to set you back upright again. It left your knees weak and your mouth dry, and your insides tied up in knots, and not to be able to fulfill the desires it brought with it was torture beyond anything he'd ever known, and it made him break out in a cold sweat.

"Oh, God," he prayed softly, "give me the strength," and he closed his eyes as a clap of thunder broke the stillness outside.

It threatened rain all afternoon, but held off. Paul left the house shortly before dinner to go to the Van Der Lindens', and the early evening was uneventful. For once Jason had made no plans for them to go out.

It wasn't quite dark outside when Gigi, in a dress of frothy blue organza, stood on the portico off her bedroom, watching the storm clouds still piling up in the sky. She had seen a man ride up to the door a few minutes before, and now he rode off again into the growing darkness, but she hadn't given it a thought until a few minutes later, when Bridget entered the room.

"Miss Gigi?" she asked furtively.

"Out here on the balcony," she called, and Bridget came out, holding an envelope toward her.

"Here," she said. "This just came, and the man said to give it to you personally. It's probably from your Latin gentleman friend."

"Now, what makes you say that?" asked Gigi, taking the letter from her outstretched hand.

"Just a guess," said Bridget.

Gigi stood staring at the envelope.

"Well, open it, read it," Bridget said hurriedly.

Gigi smiled. "You're too anxious, Bridget," but she opened the envelope and unfolded the note inside. Her blue-green eyes narrowed as she read it, and Bridget saw her expression change to one of perplexity.

"What is it, Miss Gigi, bad news?" she asked.

She shook her head slowly, hesitantly. "I don't know," she said softly, bewildered. "It's so strange."

"Strange?"

She nodded, then looked straight at Bridget, frowning. "If I tell you, will you promise not to tell anyone?" she asked.

Bridget crossed her heart. "On my honor, Miss Gigi," she said solemnly. "You know I wouldn't say anything."

Gigi handed her the note, and Bridget shook her head, puzzled, as she read it. "But you can't go to Central Park at this time of night," she protested. "It's dangerous."

"Isn't that where we went to see Mr. Sousa's band?" she asked. "I know where it is."

Bridget pursed her lips. "That's beside the point," she protested. "How do you know this note's right. Who'd send such a thing?"

"I don't know, but it says if I go there at that particular spot, I'll learn all about my past and who Gigi Rouvier really is."

"But you're Gigi Rouvier."

"I know. But what was I before I came to New York? Before the train wreck? Don't you see, Bridget, I have to go."

"How?"

She stood for a minute thinking. "I know, we'll find Jamie and have his father hitch up the coach," she said hurriedly. "But you mustn't tell a soul. Mr. Tuttleby can take me, and no one will be the wiser."

She went to the closet, took out a royal-blue velvet cape with a huge rose beaded and embroidered on the back and smaller roses on the hood, and slipped it on.

"Aren't you going to tell anyone else you're leaving?" asked Bridget.

"No. The note says to come alone. They'll think I'm in my room, so we'll just leave it at that."

Bridget scowled unhappily, shaking her head. "I don't think you should go alone," she protested. "You should have Mr. Paul go with you."

"Paul's at Lenore's."

"They have a telephone."

She shook her head. "No. I'm going alone. Don't worry, I'll be all right. Tuttleby will be with me."

Bridget didn't like it. It was too late for Gigi to go wandering about Central Park or anywhere else alone. By the time she got there, it would be pitch dark, but there was no way she could make her change her mind. Gigi was determined.

They left the room and managed to sneak from the house unnoticed. The air had cooled due to the threatening rain. Gigi felt a drop or two as they walked toward the stables, and Gigi waited while Bridget went to the door and knocked. Mrs. Tuttleby opened it.

"May I see Jamie a minute?" asked Bridget, and Mrs. Tuttleby opened the door wider for the girl to enter.

A few minutes later Mr. Tuttleby came outside. He was a big man with white bushy sideburns and a kindly face. "Come in the house, miss," he said. "No need to stand out here."

She shook her head. "There's no time, Mr. Tuttleby," she said quickly. "We have to leave at once."

He scratched his head. "I don't know, miss. I shouldn't go without Mr. Larrabee's permission."

"If he finds out, I'll tell him it's my fault," she pleaded. "Please, Tuttleby, it means so much . . ." She lifted her head, determined. "If you don't take me, I'll saddle a horse and go alone," she said stubbornly, and he shrugged.

He couldn't have that, and he was sure she meant it. That's one thing he'd learned about the young lady since she'd come to Larrabee Manor, she was willfully independent. Just like the old man. "All right," he said, sighing. "Wait'll I get a cloak." He went back into the house, and was followed back out by Bridget and Jamie. They helped hitch the coach; then Gigi made Jamie promise to walk Bridget back to the house, and they were on their way.

Lightning and thunder still flashed and rolled intermittently across the sky, but the storm hadn't come yet. It was sometime later that Tuttleby reined the horses in at Central Park and got down from his perch. They'd brought the closed carriage because of the impending rain, and he opened the door for her.

"Do you know where to go?" he asked, helping her down.

She nodded. "I'm to go to where the bandstand is set up and wait. They'll contact me."

"I should go with you," he said, but she shook her head.

"No. It said alone." She put her hand on his arm. "Don't worry, I'll be only a short distance away. I can see the outline of the bandstand over there," and she motioned off into the darkness toward the vague outline of frame and wood that could be seen through the windswept trees and shrubs.

As he watched her closely, she moved off in that direction, toward the bandstand, being careful to watch where she was walking. There was no moon tonight because of the storm, only the streetlights to see by, and the wind whipped about, blowing the trees, making a dreadful noise, the branches casting eerie shadows about.

She reached the bandstand and looked around. No one was about. She stood for about five minutes, then suddenly heard a noise behind her. As she whirled around, two men reached out and grabbed her arms. She let out a shriek and started struggling, but they were too strong. A hand covered her mouth, and she started to kick. Then, just as she heard Tuttleby join the ruckus, she wrenched free, only to fall and hit her head against a corner of the bandstand, and everything around her went black as she drifted into unconsciousness.

6

Bridget and Jamie were in a stew. They both had misgivings as they watched the coach disappear down the drive.

"She shouldn't have gone alone," said Bridget, and Jamie agreed.

They talked of it apprehensively as they headed slowly toward the house, then finally Bridget made up her mind. It took some time to reach Paul at the Van Der Lindens' and get him to the telephone. Their maid had strict orders not to disturb the family, because an important guest was being entertained. The Duke of something-or-other. Some pompous English-sounding place. It wasn't until Bridget told her it was a matter of life and death that she relented and finally went to get Paul.

"Mr. Paul, it's Bridget," she blurted anxiously into the mouthpiece, then took a deep breath. "It's awful important."

"What is it, Bridget?" His voice deepened fearfully. "Has something happened? Is Gigi all right?"

She held the receiver tightly, her hand sweaty, as Jamie kept his eye on all the halls to make sure they weren't overheard. She didn't want Jason Larrabee to know.

"As far as I know, Mr. Paul," she said cautiously. "But I think she's in danger." She explained the note and told him exactly where Gigi had gone, and for a moment there was only silence on the other end of the line.

"I shouldn't have let her go, should I, Mr. Paul?" she said, breaking the silence.

"Never mind that," he said anxiously. "It couldn't be helped. She'd have gone regardless. Don't worry, Bridget," he assured her. "If I leave right away, I can get there about the same time she does. Thanks for letting me know. And

. . . oh, yes," he added hurriedly, "don't tell my father. Do you understand?"

"Yes, Mr. Paul. I won't," she said.

"Good girl. And don't worry, I'll take care of everything." He hung up, turning from the telephone, only to discover Lenore staring at him.

She was wearing a dress of mauve silk embroidered with plum-colored flowers about the skirt, and yards of mauve gauze shirred and draped about the bodice and sleeves, giving her blond beauty a fragile look. But her pale blue eyes were far from echoing the same fragility. "Now what?" she asked coldly.

"I have to leave, Lenore," he said. "It's quite urgent."

"That sister of yours, no doubt," she said disgustedly. "Honestly, Paul," she exhaled angrily. "What's she done now?"

"It isn't anything she's done, Lenore, it's . . . You wouldn't understand, and it'd take too long to explain. I'll tell you about it tomorrow," and he headed toward the front door.

"Don't I even deserve a good-bye kiss?" she asked, then glanced up at his head. "And you're forgetting your hat." She took it from the hat rack, holding it out to him.

He took the hat from her and kissed her lightly, then went out the door.

"I wonder what it is someone isn't to let his father know about Gigi," she asked herself curiously, and she walked to the telephone, lifting the receiver. It might be interesting to find out, and she waited for the operator to come on the line.

Paul rode as fast as he could. The night was pitch dark, threatening rain momentarily, and the streets were deserted, so he made good time. He was almost there when the rain finally hit. At first there were only a few drops at a time, but big ones, splattering him in the face. He wiped the rain from his face and spotted the coach, heading toward it just as he heard Gigi's screams.

She was over by the bandstand, and he spurred his horse faster, off the road, onto the park grass, reaching the bandstand as he heard Tuttleby shouting and saw him grappling with two men by the steps. But Tuttleby was in trouble.

Paul lunged from the saddle and charged into the men whom Tuttleby was trying to keep from dragging Gigi away.

His fists connected, startling them, and they dropped their burden, letting her collapse against the bandstand as they tried to defend themselves, but Paul's assault was vicious as he waded in.

The two men broke free, stumbling and diving into the bushes, then they took off running deeper into the park.

Tuttleby stopped, straightening, gasping, catching his breath, breathing deeply as he recognized Paul in the darkness. "Good Lord, sir," he gulped, winded. "Where'd you come from?"

Paul wiped a trickle of blood from the side of his mouth. "Where's Gigi?" he asked abruptly, and both men looked about, searching in the dark.

"Here, over here," said Tuttleby, kneeling by the steps of the platform as the rain started coming down harder. "She must have hit her head when they dropped her. She's out cold."

Paul knelt down beside her still form and felt her pulse to make sure, then breathed a sigh of relief. "Thank God," he said, and picked her up in his arms. "Bring my horse and tie it to the back of the carriage, Tuttleby," he said. "I'll ride inside with her. We're going home."

They hurried to the coach, and Tuttleby opened the door. Paul climbed in, holding her tenderly in his arms, and the carriage moved slowly forward as rain started falling more heavily, drowning out the beat of the horses' hooves on the road.

Paul tried to lean her head back gently against the side of the carriage, and she started to stir, her body twisting back and forth violently.

"No! No!" she cried hysterically. "No, Gigi! The train . . . we're falling! Look out! The train! The train! No!"

Paul shook her gently, and she opened her eyes wide. Only one small lantern was lit inside the carriage, its flickering flame casting faint shadows, and she could just barely see. "Gigi, it's all right," Paul said, looking at her anxiously. "It's all right."

Then suddenly she saw he was there, and she clung to him desperately, sobbing, her hands clutching at his coat as she stared at him in the faint light from the lantern.

"The train wreck, Paul, I remember the train wreck. I remember falling and seeing another girl falling, and I tried to stop it. I tried to help her, but I couldn't. Oh, Paul, it was horrible."

"It's over now, Gigi. Everything is all right," he soothed, brushing her dark hair away from her face. "It's all over."

After a few minutes her sobbing slowly subsided. She stared at him apprehensively, her blue-green eyes misty; then suddenly, self-consciously, she moved away and leaned her head back against the side of the carriage again. For a long time they rode along, neither one saying anything, yet each very aware of the other's presence in the dimly lit coach.

"How did you know to come?" she finally asked softly, glancing at him.

His eyes sifted over her. "That's my secret."

She sighed. "I know," she said breathlessly. "Bridget told you." She lowered her eyes momentarily, then glanced back up at him sheepishly. "I'm glad she did now," she confessed. "Only, I'm sorry."

"For what?"

"I dragged you away from Lenore's."

"I was having a boring time."

"Oh . . ." There was silence again except for the sound of the rain hitting the carriage; then: "Paul," she said softly, "who am I really?"

His voice was strained. "You know the answer to that, Gigi," he said.

"Do I?" She looked directly into his warm gray eyes, a sob in her voice. "Oh, my God, Paul," she pleaded shamelessly. "You know the way I feel about you! I know you do. A woman doesn't feel that way about her brother, and you know it. You can't be my brother, Paul . . . please. You can't be." Her breath caught passionately. "Please, Paul. Tell me you're not my brother!"

She moved on the seat, the movement sensuous, inviting, and he couldn't fight it anymore.

He reached out hesitantly and touched her face, his hand shaking, then slowly swept her into his arms, drawing her close against him, holding her as he gazed into her eyes.

"Tell me, Paul," she whispered breathlessly, her body trembling. "Tell me who I really am, please!" and her eyes searched his, questioning.

He stared at her, unwavering, his eyes devouring her, then slowly his quivering lips covered hers, and all the passion he'd been restraining surged wildly to the surface. He kissed her deeply, sensuously, over and over again, his head spinning, the blood in his veins pulsing like liquid fire.

Gigi moaned beneath his smoldering lips, her body yielding, her loins throbbing, and each kiss became more passionate than the last, until they were both intoxicated, their bodies begging for release.

She eased her lips reluctantly from his, her eyes wild with desire. "Paul," she moaned breathlessly, her mouth against his. "Oh, Paul . . ."

His mouth touched hers again, closing over it, and he groaned deep in his throat as hot flames shot through his loins. He kissed her deeply, then drew his lips from hers, burying his face against her neck, his lips nibbling her ear, sending chills down her spine, and Gigi felt sweet, savage sensations bursting deep within her. She never dreamed it would be like this.

"Oh, my God," he moaned hoarsely, his eyes caressing her, his hands beginning to move across her soft, firm breasts, bringing her body to life. He wanted her more than he wanted life itself.

She melted against him eagerly, responding to his passionate lovemaking as the carriage moved along in the darkness. His hands claimed her, arousing the passion he'd always known was hidden just beneath the surface.

Then suddenly he straightened, his hands reluctantly easing their burning caresses, his lips searing a last kiss across her quivering mouth. "Gigi, it's no good," he whispered softly, unsteadily, as his lips left hers, and she let out a sob, clinging to him desperately.

"Paul, no . . ." she begged, but his eyes hardened.

"It has to be, Gigi. You know I'm right." He moved her head over, resting it back against the seat, and stared at her, not wanting to let it end, but knowing it had to. "I'm your brother, Gigi," he whispered softly.

She shook her head. "No!"

"Yes! We have to accept it." His jaw tightened savagely. "We have no choice!"

Tears sprang to her eyes, and she gulped back deep sobs.

"It has to be, Gigi," he whispered, his hand touching her face lovingly. "There's nothing for us."

"Why?" she cried in despair. "Why did this happen to us, Paul?"

He shook his head. "I don't know. I only know it's wrong,

all wrong." He wiped a tear from her cheek with his finger, then cupped her face in his hand. "Gigi, we can't ever let anyone know this happened," he said passionately. "If anyone found out . . ."

She nodded, sniffing in, her eyes clouded. "I know," she replied bitterly. "I know." She reached up and touched his cheek, then shuddered. "I'm all right, Paul," she said finally, composing herself. "Don't worry. I'm all right."

He reached up to slide back the little window that separated them from Tuttleby. He pulled the panel back, then glanced at her one last time as she straightened her clothes and moved away from him on the seat.

"When we get to the house, Tuttleby, pull around to the kitchen and we'll try to get in without being seen," he said, masking the turmoil he felt. "The less Father knows about our little venture tonight, the better," and Tuttleby acknowledged.

Paul slid the panel back into place, then reached over, pulling the cloak about her, trying to ease some of her misery. "We'll go through the kitchen and try to get upstairs without being seen," he said patiently. "I don't want Father to know about your little escapade if I can help it."

"But what if someone does see us?"

"Then let me handle it." He touched her face lovingly. "I'm sorry, Gigi," he said passionately. "I love you, but I have to let you go. You know that." He whispered softly, "There's no future for us. There never was," and she stared at him, on the verge of tears, knowing he was right and cursing because she didn't want to accept it.

"What if I'm not your sister, Paul?" she said suddenly. "What if we find out we've been wrong?"

"Don't make it worse for us, Gigi," he said. He shook his head. "We both know it's only wishful thinking. I'm your half-brother, and there's no way we can change it, no matter how hard we try."

Gigi flinched, gazing into his eyes, knowing he was right, and she leaned back against the seat, listening to the rain hitting hard against the sides of the carriage as Tuttleby turned into the long drive at the front of the house.

A few minutes later there was a knock on the panel just above Paul's head. He slid it back.

"We're home, Mr. Paul," said Tuttleby. "But you'll have to hurry, it's really a downpour."

"You open the door for me, Tuttleby," Paul said, "and I'll carry Miss Gigi in." While Tuttleby was climbing down to open the door, Paul met Gigi's eyes once more. "You're sure you're all right?" he asked.

She nodded, unable to speak, her heart in her throat.

He tried to smile, but it was useless, so instead he frowned angrily, his blood simmering at the thought of what his father'd done to them. The door opened and he stepped out into the drenching rain, then reached up, sweeping her into his arms, heading for the kitchen door.

They were soaked by the time they reached the house, and Paul hurried into the warmth of the spicy kitchen, running smack into Mrs. Sharp.

"Land sakes! Where have you been?" she exclaimed as he stood just inside the door, water dripping from them both, and Paul stared at her guiltily.

"We were out for a ride," he said, and saw the disbelief in her eyes.

"On a night like this?" She laughed.

"On a night like this," he said. "At least that's what you're to tell anyone who might happen to ask, understand?"

She shrugged. "If that's the way you want it, Mr. Paul," she answered.

His eyes darkened. "That's the way I want it."

He was about to start for the hall door to take Gigi upstairs, when it opened wide and Jason came wheeling in with Ahmed in tow. They were the last people he'd wanted to see. His eyes narrowed irritably.

"Well, where the hell have you been, and what's going on?" Jason asked as he stopped just inside the room, staring at them. "I've been worried sick!"

Paul took a deep breath. He hadn't expected this. He was hoping to sneak in quietly. "Now, don't get excited, Father—" he began, but Jason interrupted.

"What's this Lenore says about something happening to Gigi?" he asked.

Paul clenched his teeth angrily. Lenore! It would have to be Lenore. He might have known. "If you don't mind, Father," he said, trying to keep control of himself, "there's been an accident and Gigi had a pretty bad bump on the head. I'd like to get her upstairs before she gets sick. She's wet and cold."

Jason looked at Gigi anxiously, eyes alert. "All right,

hurry, get her upstairs, then come down to my quarters. I want an explanation. I'll be waiting for you." He moved aside so Paul could get through, his eyes on Gigi's wet, disheveled appearance as Paul swept past him and on out of the room.

Bridget was waiting for them in Gigi's room, and as Paul reached down and turned the knob, swinging the door open, she jumped from the chair to greet them.

"I didn't tell them anything, Mr. Paul," she blurted as he stepped inside. "Honest. He asked, but I never said a word."

Paul smiled wearily as he kicked the door shut behind him. "I know," he said, and walked to the chaise longue, setting Gigi down gently.

"But, Paul, I'm soaked," she cried as her wet clothes began to seep onto the velvet cover.

He sat beside her, oblivious of his own wet clothes. "It'll dry out," he said. "Now, I forgot to ask in the carriage. How's your head?"

She touched it lightly. "It smarts, but I have the strangest feeling, Paul. I suddenly remember a large room, and a lot of people dressed in strange clothes."

He frowned. "Can you remember anything else? When you remembered the train wreck, you said you could see another woman. Do you know who it was?"

She shook her head. "No . . . my mind's a blank."

"It must have been the blow on the head. You may start remembering everything now." His eyes were intent on her face.

She took his hand and squeezed it. "Oh, Paul, I'm frightened."

He squeezed her hand back, then turned to Bridget. "Fill a tub with hot water so she can soak," he ordered. "She's going to need warming up and drying out."

Bridget nodded, disappearing into the dressing room, and Paul's hand tightened on hers.

"You're going to have to forget what happened in the carriage tonight, Gigi. You know that, don't you?" he whispered.

She sighed. "Can you?" she asked softly.

His eyes turned a stormy gray, his generous lips drawing into a thin line. "Yes." He released her hand.

"I don't believe you."

He shrugged. "That's up to you, but right now I have to go down and try to soothe Father, and we'd better have our stories straight."

"What will you tell him?"

"You were out for a ride. Some robbers jumped the carriage. Tuttleby fought them off, but you were hurt in the struggle."

"Why don't you tell him the truth?"

"Can you imagine what he'd do if he knew somebody had purposely set a trap for you?"

She frowned. "That's what puzzles me, Paul," she said, studying his face. "Why did they do it? Were they trying to abduct me? If so, what was their reason?"

He shook his head. "I wish I knew." He stood up and walked to the French doors, staring out at the rain, wondering.

Was she right? Were they trying to kidnap her? If so, what did they want with her? What was the reason for it all? It didn't make sense.

Suddenly Bridget came in and shooed Paul out so she could get Gigi into the hot tub, and Paul went reluctantly downstairs, still wondering.

Jason was waiting for him in his quarters. The main room in his wing was overly large, but contained few chairs or sofas, making it easier for him to move about in his wheelchair. The plush surroundings were typical of his expensive and somewhat flamboyant taste, including a concealed liquor cabinet in one corner, and plush red carpeting.

Ahmed was nowhere in sight, and Paul assumed he was in the bedroom preparing things for the night.

"Would you care for a drink, Paul?" asked Jason, glancing at Paul's drenched clothes. "You look cold."

Paul nodded. He did need a drink, in more ways than one. "A small one," he said. Maybe it would help. "Make it brandy."

"Now, what's this all about and where has Gigi been?" Jason asked anxiously, as he poured the drinks and handed Paul his.

Paul straightened. "She said she just felt like getting out of the house for a ride," explained Paul, trying to be casual. "So instead of disturbing anyone, she talked Tuttleby into taking her." He held up his hand as Jason made a move to protest. "Don't worry, I've reprimanded Tuttleby for it already, so you don't have to do it again." He tried to soothe him. "Evidently someone spotted the carriage as belonging to the Larrabees and figured it'd be easy pickings. To make a long story short, when they discovered Gigi was alone, they started roughing her up, but Tuttleby wouldn't stand for it. In the ruckus, he managed to scare them off, but Gigi suffered a blow to the head that rendered her unconscious. Tuttleby put her in the coach, drove to the nearest house with a telephone, and called me for help. He didn't want to drive her all the way home alone. That's all there was to it."

Jason eyed his son skeptically. "You're sure that's all that happened?"

Paul gestured irritably. "You saw for yourself."

"Lenore said she heard you talking on the telephone, and whoever you were talking to, you persuaded them not to tell me." He scowled, disturbed. "You were going to keep it from me?"

Paul's lips tightened. "Why have you worry? The danger was over."

He shook his head. "I don't like it, Paul," he said. "I'm going to have to caution Gigi about going out alone. We can't have things like this happening."

"I'm sure she knows better now," Paul said as he finished the drink and set the empty glass down. "By the way, Father," he continued, "I'll be gone all day tomorrow. I'm leaving at daybreak and may not be back until late afternoon. If I'm not, make my excuses, will you?"

Jason eyed him curiously. "May I ask where you're off to?" he asked.

Paul frowned. "It's personal business. I'd rather not say, if you don't mind."

Jason's eyebrows arched, surprised. "I do mind, Paul." His eyes narrowed shrewdly. "But then, you're a grown man now. I guess I have no right to demand an accounting of your time." He hesitated a moment; then: "Does it have anything to do with what we spoke of earlier today?" he asked suspiciously.

Paul saw the meaning in his father's words. "In a way," he said as he turned to leave. "Good night, Father."

Jason called to him as he reached the door, "Paul?"

Paul turned.

"Break it off gently, Paul," he said. "Don't leave any reminders about like I did. Don't leave any Gigi Rouviers to haunt you and Lenore in later years, all right, son?"

Paul frowned as he looked at his father's face. He'd guessed right. His father thought he was going to say one last good-bye to his ladylove. The woman he thought Paul was seeing on the sly. If he only knew that the woman Paul loved was under this very roof, and that he loved her far more than his father had loved the first Gigi Rouvier, and it was killing him inside . . .

"Good night, Father," he said again bitterly, and closed the door behind him, leaving Jason wondering.

The next morning was July 4. Paul rose before daybreak, ate breakfast in the kitchen while Mrs. Sharp was baking the day's bread, then took off on horseback before the sun came up over the river. It was a long ride to Mrs. Thornapple's, only he'd make it faster than he and Gigi had done in the carriage. As he rode along, oblivious of the people who passed him, he thought of all that was happening.

He remembered now, when he'd first met Gigi, she said she felt strange being called Gigi. That she didn't feel like a Gigi Rouvier, and his own feelings had made him wonder too. From the very first he'd been attracted to her. It was a body chemistry he couldn't explain. It was something that didn't happen between sister and brother, at least it shouldn't. Then, last night, when she was coming to, she had called out her own name. She had done it just once, but it had been enough to start him thinking. Maybe there had been another young woman on the train. Gigi said she'd seen one when she remembered the train wreck. Maybe she really wasn't Gigi Rouvier. Yet, if she was someone else, why did she look exactly like the first Gigi Rouvier? His father had found a small picture of the original Gigi and had showed it to them, and the resemblance was uncanny. If she wasn't Gigi Rouvier, then who was she, and why was she wearing the brooch, and why was the letter found in her handbag? He had to know the answers for certain.

He spurred his horse harder the more he thought, and the more he thought, the more nothing made sense. One thing was a fact, however: someone was after Gigi. Whether to kill her or not, he didn't know. But it had to be someone who knew about her past. He didn't like leaving Gigi alone. He'd have to try to get back as soon as possible, and he spurred his horse even faster.

He arrived at Mrs. Thornapple's shortly before lunch, cutting the time it had taken them in the carriage in half. When Mrs. Thornapple opened the door, she was surprised, and didn't recognize him for a minute in his riding clothes.

"Good gracious," she finally said, admiring the handsome figure he made, "yes, I remember you. It was some months ago. You're the young gentleman who came after the young lady from the train wreck. The one who couldn't remember who she was."

Paul nodded. "May I have a few words with you, Mrs. Thornapple?" he asked. "It's quite important."

"I do have a visitor," she said, taking the straight pins from her mouth. "But come in. We can talk anyway, if it's all right with you. I'm working on her costume for the parade this afternoon."

She led him to her parlour, where a woman stood waiting, the hem in her red-white-and-blue dress only partly pinned up.

"This is Mrs. Fair, the former Miss Warren, whose wedding dress you confiscated that evening," she said as she introduced them.

"Mrs. Fair?" he said. "I'm glad to see it didn't deter the wedding, and I'm much obliged for the use of the dress." He was sure now, after seeing Mrs. Fair, that the dress was far more becoming on Gigi than on this thin, hawk-faced woman in front of him.

"What is it you wanted to know?" asked Mrs. Thornapple as she got down on her knees and began to work on the hem again.

Paul cleared his throat. "I'm hoping you can tell me if there were any other young women in the train wreck. One who might have been killed, perhaps, and not identified."

"Don't tell me you made a mistake about the young lady," she exclaimed, looking up at him apprehensively. "Oh, sir, that would be dreadful. And her so young and pretty."

"No," he said briskly. "But we think perhaps she may have had a traveling companion," explained Paul. "If there was some way to find out . . ."

"I sent the other gentleman to Constable Cagan," Mrs. Thornapple said as she looked back again at the hem. "Why don't you try him? He should know."

Paul stared at her, perplexed. "What other gentleman?" he asked abruptly.

She kept working on the dress as she talked, the pins shifting between her lips. "Oh, there was a foreign gentleman who stopped by, asking about lady passengers from the train wreck," she said, sticking pins in the hem. "He asked about someone matching Miss Rouvier's description."

"Did you tell him about her?" asked Paul.

"Why, yes, sir. He even wanted your name. Said he'd stop by and pay you a visit."

"You explained about Miss Rouvier's amnesia?" asked Paul.

"Yes, sir. But he didn't seem to care."

Paul frowned. "You said he was foreign?"

"Oh, yes," she said definitely. "He had a terrible accent. And he kept calling me 'señora.' And when he left he said '*adiós*'. Isn't that Spanish, sir?" she asked.

It certainly is, thought Paul. He nodded. "Can you give me a description of the man?"

Her eyes narrowed. "Let's see." She rested back on her heels. "He was shorter than you," she said thoughtfully. "But husky, thick through the middle, and going bald. Had a huge mustache and bushy eyebrows, yet strutted around as if he was somebody." She concentrated on her sewing again. "Scared me a bit, he did, with his deep, booming voice."

Paul sighed. He'd thought she was going to describe André de los Reyes, but the description she just gave was decidedly not his. He thanked her, then asked for the directions to the constable's office, and left, headed toward the center of town. The constable was right where she'd said he'd be, not in his office, but helping get ready for the holiday parade scheduled for late afternoon.

Paul watched for a few minutes as the constable helped put the finishing touches of crepe paper on a horse-drawn beer wagon, then Paul sauntered forward, leading his horse.

"Constable Cagan?" he asked, and the man swiveled around.

He was heavy-jowled, red-faced, and robust. "At your service, sir," he said, stuffing what was left of a roll of crepe paper into the hands of a young lad, who promptly scooted off with it to the other side of the wagon. He squinted in the late-morning sun. "Something I can do for you?" he asked.

Paul's eyes rested momentarily on the shiny badge pinned to the man's shirt pocket. "I'd like some information, if you don't mind," he said, and the constable eyed him curiously.

"Might be able to help," he said. "What's the problem?"

"It's about the train wreck back in the spring. I was wondering if there's any way I can guarantee a positive identification of one of the survivors."

Constable Cagan rubbed his chin, then exhaled noisily. "You wouldn't be referrin' to that young lady who couldn't remember who she was, would you, sir?" he asked.

Paul nodded. "She still can't remember," he explained. "And at times, well . . . there are times when she says she's certain there has to be some mistake."

The constable sighed, then shook his head. "Don't see how," he said firmly. " 'Course, there's no way to know who else was in that coach, except for the charred bodies we found, and there were, I think, three unidentified young women tangled in the mess. But your young lady was holding that little pink handbag so tight we had to practically pry her fingers loose. They were wound around the straps, and that pretty pin with the jewels on it was pinned to her shawl. Now, why would she have them if they weren't hers?"

"What of the other women who weren't identified?" Paul asked. "Did they have any personal effects? Any belongings that weren't burned?"

"I'll tell you what," Cagan said, making sure they didn't need him anymore for parade preparations. "I'll take you over to the office and you can look through what we got. If it'll help any . . . I don't know."

Paul thanked him, then followed him across town to his office, tethering his horse at the hitching post out front.

It took almost an hour to sort through the assorted remnants, and Paul felt an odd sense of the macabre as he studied each piece. There was a partially burned jeweled metal hair comb, assorted lockets, watches, and other jewelry, with names and initials engraved on some, all blackened from the heat. Bits and pieces of charred clothing, shoes and boots, but nothing to link anyone to Gigi Rouvier.

"I'm sorry," said the constable as he saw the disappointed look on Paul's face. "But it's like I told that Mexican fella. The lady who was at Mrs. Thornapple's had to be Gigi Rouvier."

Paul looked up from the items scattered about the constable's desk. "Mrs. Thornapple told me about the Mexican," he said anxiously. "Did he tell you who he was and why he was looking for Miss Rouvier?"

"Well, he wasn't exactly looking for Miss Rouvier," the constable explained. "He said he was looking for a young lady, and the description he gave me matched Miss Rouvier."

"Her name?"

He shrugged. "He never gave me her name, only the description. Said he was a colonel in the Mexican Army. Colonel Alvarez, or something like that. Said the lady he was looking for may have been on the train. I told him about Miss Rouvier, since the description he gave me fit, and he took down your address in New York."

Now Paul was really baffled. Why would a colonel from the Mexican Army be looking for Gigi, and why hadn't he contacted them? It didn't make sense.

He put all the things back in their small leather bags, thanked Constable Cagan, then left, heading back for New York City. He didn't like it. Not at all. Especially after what had happened to Gigi last night.

Last night! He thought back to last night, and his heart was heavy as he rode along. He'd hoped to find something, anything, to ease his conscience. What happened last night between himself and Gigi should never have happened. Yet he had to face the truth. He'd wanted it to happen ever since the first moment he'd gazed into those beautiful blue-green eyes of hers. There was something about her that he'd never found in any other woman. She had the power to turn his insides to jelly with just one look from those smoldering eyes.

If there had just been something, even the slightest indication that she wasn't the real Gigi Rouvier, but he had to face that fact too. His morning's ride, instead of relieving the situation, had only made it worse. The proof had been even more binding, and there was no way he could try to deny it. He cursed, digging his horse in the ribs, the bright holiday suddenly weighing heavily on him, darkening his mood.

Gigi stretched and sat up in bed, staring at Bridget, who had woken her only a few minutes before.

"How's your head?" asked Bridget as she set out the clothes for her, then went into the bathroom, leaving the door open so she could talk as she filled the tub.

Gigi felt her head. It was sore and tender, but the ache was gone. "I'd almost forgotten about it," she said. And she had. Her thoughts had been about Paul, and so had her dreams, but she couldn't let Bridget suspect.

She slipped from the covers and hurried through her bath,

then let Bridget help her into a gold dress with puffed sleeves, draped bodice, and a neckline edged in Irish lace.

"What are your plans for today?" asked Bridget a short time later as she began to fix Gigi's hair.

Gigi frowned. What were her plans? Then she remembered. It was the Fourth of July. She'd promised to go riding with André in the afternoon, then she, Jason, and Paul were to meet Rose and Bruce and their companions at Lenore's for a formal party that evening with fireworks. This morning held nothing special.

She told Bridget her plans, then ended with a casual remark, wondering what Paul was doing this morning, and was surprised to learn from Bridget that Paul had left the house on horseback barely at daybreak, and no one seemed to know where he'd gone.

She frowned, watching Bridget as she pinned up her hair.

"Miss Gigi," asked Bridget, setting the curls in place, securing them, "I know it's not my place, but you did show me that note . . . what do you think those men were trying to do last night?"

Gigi saw her worried look, and tried to smile. "Oh . . . who knows?" she said softly. "There's been so much publicity in the papers lately. They probably figured Mr. Larrabee has a great deal of money. It wouldn't be the first time someone was kidnapped and held for ransom."

Bridget shivered, then set the last curl in place. "It's frightening," she said, watching Gigi in the mirror.

"Then again," said Gigi, contemplating thoughtfully, "it might have something to do with my past." She turned to face Bridget as the girl finished. "After all, Bridget," she reminded her, "I have no idea what Gigi Rouvier was. She could have robbed banks for all I know."

Bridget's eyes sparked. "Miss Gigi, don't say such things," she said. "It's nothing to make light of. You could have been hurt bad."

Gigi nodded as she stood up and walked over to the French doors, breathing in the warm clean air that filled the room, feeling the sun on her face. "Well, I wasn't hurt," she said. Then felt the bruise on her forehead. "Well, not badly anyway," she corrected herself, then turned back toward Bridget. "Did my cape dry out yet?" she asked.

Bridget shook her head. "I doubt it. I took it outside this morning to dry in the sunshine, but I hope it's not ruined. It's such a beautiful cape, and cold rainwater isn't exactly the best thing for velvet."

Gigi hesitated. She hadn't thought of that. She'd watched Bridget's eyes last night while she helped her on with the cape. It seemed to fascinate her, with its delicate beading and embroidered rose design. "You like that particular cape, don't you, Bridget?" she said.

Bridget blushed. "I think it's the most beautiful thing I've ever seen." She sighed, and her eyes softened as she thought of it.

"Then it's yours," Gigi said suddenly.

Bridget gasped. "Mine?"

Gigi took a quick last glance at herself in the mirror. "Why not?" she said firmly. "Why shouldn't you have something pretty to wear too? And here," she said, turning to her closet, pulling the door open, reaching inside. "You're about the same size I am." She shuffled through the rack of dresses and pulled out a blue one with lace and frills, holding it out toward the girl. "And take this," she said anxiously. "You have to have something fancy to wear with the cape."

Bridget's eyes widened. "I . . . I can't take that," she stammered, but Gigi insisted.

She walked over and shoved the dress into the girl's arms. "I insist," she said stubbornly. "They're my things, and I can give them to you if I want. Besides, every girl deserves something frilly and frivolous."

Bridget shook her head, speechless, as she stared at Gigi, the dress clutched hesitantly in her hands.

"And I won't take no for an answer," said Gigi as she watched the girl. "Now, why don't you try it on to make sure it fits, while I go downstairs and have breakfast."

Bridget didn't know what to say as Gigi walked up to her and helped her hold the dress in front of her to see how it would look.

"Go ahead, try it on," coaxed Gigi, then gave Bridget a hug. "I want you to have it."

Bridget sighed. "I don't know what to say," she said, fingering the delicate, filmy material. She shook her head. "I just don't know what to say."

Gigi smiled. "Then don't say anything." She was pleased with herself. "Just make sure you wear it, and don't just hide it away to look at." She was still smiling as she left the room.

Bridget stood for a long time staring at the dress in her

hands, knowing she shouldn't accept it, yet wanting to so badly. Then: "Why not?" she whispered softly to herself, and held the dress close against her body as she sauntered slowly toward the full-length mirror on the closet door. "Yes, why not!" and suddenly she laid the dress down on the bed and began to unfasten the front of her plain gray work dress.

When she reached the dining room, Gigi was surprised to find Jason and Rose still at the breakfast table, and she couldn't help but overhear the last of their conversation as she crossed the hall from the music room and entered.

"And I'm sure we won't have to worry about any more nonsense as far as he and Lenore are concerned," Jason was saying.

Rose glanced up and saw Gigi, then looked at her father. "I wouldn't be too sure about that, Father," she said, eyeing Gigi curiously, and Gigi frowned as Jason sensed her presence and turned.

"Well, Gigi," he said happily. "Come in, come in." He motioned for her to join them. "I was hoping you'd come down before I finished. It always brightens my day to visit with you at the breakfast table."

Gigi glided into the room and let Ahmed emerge silently from the shadows to pull the chair out for her, thanking him as she sat down. She was used to his presence now, and thought little of it, as he often assisted her when the other servants weren't about. In fact, it was almost becoming a habit to rely on him for little things like helping her into the carriage and pulling out her chair at the table. She glanced at Jason. "I didn't mean to sleep so late," she apologized. "But I was so exhausted."

Jason reached over, taking her hand, squeezing it affectionately. "No need to apologize, my dear," he said, then glanced at her forehead. "How's your head this morning?"

She extricated her hand from his and reached up, touching the bruise. "I hardly know it's there."

Jason motioned to Ahmed, who reached out and pulled the bell cord so she could order breakfast, then he went on talking.

"Well, I'm glad you're all right," he said solicitously. "I only hope you'll remember from now on not to go out alone. By the way," he changed the subject readily, "your Mr. de los Reyes called already this morning to make sure you hadn't forgotten that you were to go riding with him this afternoon."

She sighed. He was the last person in the world she wanted to see today, especially after last night, but she had promised. "I haven't forgotten," she said unemotionally. The thought of listening to him trying to charm her was irritating. She had to admit he seemed nice enough, but he did absolutely nothing for her emotionally.

"He said he'd be here shortly after lunch," said Jason, then motioned for Ahmed. "Now, if my two lovely daughters will excuse me," he went on, "I have some things to do in my quarters. Holiday or no, the business still goes on."

Gigi watched him leave, noting the animated way his face moved as he talked to Ahmed about some merger he was planning, and she realized once again how much Paul resembled him.

Rose glanced at Gigi with disdain. "Father seems to think things are all right between Lenore and Paul," she said quietly, then suddenly added, "What do you think, Gigi?"

Gigi shrugged as she looked at Rose. Rose was wearing a white piqué tennis dress with a sailor's collar, huge bouffant sleeves, snug at the wrist with red and blue satin braiding, and the hem of the skirt was trimmed with the same braiding. Large white pearl buttons held the low-cut bodice together, and streamers of red-white-and-blue ribbon were woven through the light brown curls on top her head, ending in bows above her right ear.

"I never thought one way or the other about Paul and Lenore," Gigi said, studying her half-sister. "I think what they do is their business."

Rose smirked. "Oh, come now, Gigi," she said, wiping her mouth on the napkin as she finished eating. "You and Paul spend so much time together. Surely he's confided in you."

Gigi glanced over as the maid came in carrying a tray with bowls and platters of fresh food on it, holding them so Gigi could choose what she wanted, and she was grateful for the distraction. She was unable to look at Rose right now, afraid her face would give away her feelings.

"What's the matter, Gigi?" teased Rose, noticing the slight flush to her cheeks. "Does talking about Lenore and Paul bother you?"

Gigi straightened as she finished filling her plate and set it in front of her, then swallowed hard and faced Rose, trying to keep her voice calm. "Bother me?" She laughed lightly. "Why should it bother me?" she asked, beginning to eat.

Rose's eyes narrowed. "That's what I'd like to know," she said, then rested her elbow on the table, her chin in her hand, leaning on it as she studied Gigi, watching her beginning to pick at her food. "Biddy's been telling me ever so many things lately, Gigi," she said coyly, trying to read the look on Gigi's face. Her eyes were intent on her. "She sees a lot more than the rest of us, you know. . . . Why, she said you were in Paul's arms the day after you got here."

The food caught in Gigi's throat, and she reached for the water glass, washing it down the rest of the way as she tried to stop her heart from pounding. She set the glass down carefully. "If you mean that day on the terrace when he tried to comfort me. . . ."

"Oh . . . is that what you call it?" Rose's brown eyes danced wickedly. "Why, I bet he comforts you a lot lately, doesn't he, dear sister!" she said sarcastically.

The color drained from Gigi's face as she set her fork down, staring angrily at Rose, seeing the hatred in her eyes. "Just what are you insinuating, Rose? What are you trying to say?"

"Say? I'll tell you what I'm trying to say," she said furiously, unable to hold her tongue any longer. "It's been obvious ever since you came here. I've seen the way he looks at you when he doesn't know anyone's watching. Biddy warned us when you first came that you'd be just like your mother. She said there'd be trouble, and she was right!"

Gigi stared at her, her face pale. "I don't know what you're talking about," she said.

Rose took a deep breath, then went on unhindered. "You don't know? Little Miss Innocent, I suppose," she purred viciously, her gold-flecked brown eyes sifting over Gigi contemptuously. "Even Father's noticed the change in Paul," she went on angrily. "Only, he has no idea it has anything to do with you."

"Me?" Her voice broke.

"Yes, you. You think I haven't seen it? Whenever you're in the room, Paul can't keep his eyes off you, and I've seen the way you look back at him. I've watched the two of you for a long time now. Don't you know what you're doing, Gigi?" Her eyes blazed, voice lowering ominously. "You're destroying Paul," she cried, trying to keep her voice low. "No matter how much you want him, you can't have him, and he can't have you. Don't you understand? Don't you know it's against the law? It's against everything holy. It's sacrilegious." Her voice trembled. "He's your brother, Gigi. Your brother! It's degenerate and perverted. They have a word for it." Her lip curled viciously. "A nasty word."

"Stop it!" cried Gigi, her face livid. "Stop it! You don't know—"

"Don't I?" continued Rose venomously. "What's the matter, don't you like the word, Gigi? Does it catch in your throat and choke you? Or maybe you've never heard it. Poor, innocent girl who's lost her memory," she cooed. Then her voice became sharp, brittle again. "Didn't you ever hear of incest, Gigi?" she asked heatedly. "Because that's what it'll be if you succeed in what you're doing. Keep on with Paul and see where it'll lead you. You can't marry him! You're his sister, remember? You're only dragging Paul into the gutter with you. You'll destroy him!"

Gigi stared at Rose, her face ashen, eyes haunted. Oh, God! She couldn't listen. Rose's words cut her heart like a sword thrust, gouging deep into her, ringing in her ears. How could she fight back? She couldn't.

Slowly, as if in a daze, she pushed back her chair and stood up, biting her lip, her eyes hollow and empty. She was determined not to break down. Setting her napkin down mechanically, she turned and walked from the room without saying another word, head held high, without even trying to retaliate. Any words she might have hurled at her half-sister were caught in her throat and would have done little good if she'd released them.

It wasn't until she was across the hall, into the music room, that a sob wrenched its way from deep inside her, and she grabbed her skirts, beginning to run, and she didn't stop running until she reached her bedroom, hurling the door open, leaning back against it once she was inside.

Gigi had forgotten about Bridget, and as she stood now leaning against the closed door, trying to hold back the sobs, she stared at Bridget, who was still parading in front of the mirror in the frothy blue dress she'd been trying on.

"Miss Gigi!" exclaimed Bridget as she whirled around, aghast at the sight of her. Gigi's face was white and drawn, filled with agonizing torment. "What is it?" the girl asked. "What's the matter?"

Gigi shook her head, trying to still the nausea that fluttered in her stomach, wiping the tears away with her fingers, trying to make her heart stop racing. "It's . . . it's nothing, really," she murmured quickly. "I . . . I just never realized Rose hated me so much, that's all!" she said breathlessly.

Bridget shook her head as she walked over to the bed and slipped hurriedly from the blue dress, putting her plain gray cotton back on, then trying to comfort her. "Oh, shucks. If that's all that's bothering you . . . good gracious, Miss Rose doesn't like much of anybody," she said matter-of-factly, trying to make Gigi feel better. "I wouldn't go letting anything she said bother me, if I was you." Bridget went to the dresser and took a handkerchief from the top drawer. "Here, dry your eyes," she ordered affectionately, handing it to her mistress. "And remember one thing when Miss Rose starts her nasty ways. She's jealous, Miss Gigi, just plain jealous. Why, before you came, she had everything all to herself, including her father and brothers, and she set great store in being known as the only daughter of Jason Larrabee. Now she has to share the prestige and she don't like it. No, ma'am, not one little bit does she like it."

"Prestige?" Gigi gulped back a sob. "What prestige is there for someone like me?" she asked, sinking down on the edge of the bed, twisting the lace-edged handkerchief in her hands. "Prestige!" She said it bitterly. "Oh, yes, I'm Jason Larrabee's daughter, all right. But if it weren't for his money and influence . . . You can't imagine the torture I've been through since I came here, Bridget," she said softly. "I didn't want to be Jason Larrabee's daughter. I don't want to be now. Oh, God! I wish that I could change it all!"

Bridget knelt beside Gigi and put her hands over her mistress's. Gigi's hands were as cold as ice. "Please, Miss Gigi," she whispered, trying to warm Gigi's hands. "Please, don't let her get to you. You're the best thing that's ever happened to this family, and you know it," she said. "Don't let Miss Rose's jealousy rob you of what's rightfully yours. Don't pay no attention to her ravings, because that's all they are." She squeezed Gigi's hands, then pulled her to her feet. "Now, dry your eyes and don't let it worry you no more. I know what you've been through and what you're going to keep going through. Remember, I was born out of wedlock too. I know what people think."

Gigi blew her nose, then stared at Bridget. "Do you know what the sons and husbands of these wealthy socialites talk about when they get me alone at parties and gatherings?" she asked, sniffing in angrily. "I've never told anyone else, but I've had men make such embarrassing advances to me. Not only the eligible men in New York, but some not so eligible. That's the kind of prestige I enjoy."

Bridget nodded. "I know," she said. "And it's not right. And it's not right for Miss Rose to make you feel miserable like this either. She shouldn't be allowed to insult you like she does."

Gigi studied Bridget, then felt a tug at her heart. If only she could tell her what Rose's accusations had been, and why they'd hurt her so. But there were things Gigi could never tell Bridget, things she could confide to no one. She shuddered, remembering Rose's vindictiveness. That's one thing Bridget had never been accused of, being in love with her brother. And the worst part of it was that it wasn't a lie. It was true. God in heaven, it was true! She was in love with Paul, and she hated herself for it.

Slowly she dried her eyes, walking over to look in the mirror, hoping her eyes would lose some of their redness.

Bridget watched her. "You just hold your head up with the best of them, Miss Gigi," she said, watching her try to cover the redness with a little face powder. "That's what my Jamie told me." Her face flushed. "He knows all about me. I felt it only right to tell him, and he says it don't matter where you come from, but what you are that counts."

Gigi turned to look at her rather wistfully. "It matters where you come from too, Bridget," she said. "At least it does where I'm concerned. But then . . . you wouldn't understand." She tried to put Rose's heated words from her thoughts. "You didn't say," she said, sniffing in, changing the subject, afraid she'd start crying again if she didn't, "how do you like the dress?"

Bridget gazed at it where she'd set it on the lounge. "Oh, I love it," she said enthusiastically.

Gigi forced a smile. "Will you promise me to wear it tonight when you meet Jamie down by the river?" she asked.

Bridget smiled back. "I promise," she said hopefully. "That is, if I get to sneak away."

"You will," said Gigi. "The Van Der Lindens are having a party, and I won't be needing you, once I'm dressed."

Bridget was pleased, yet she frowned. "Are you sure everything's all right now?" she asked skeptically.

"Everything will never really be all right," Gigi answered

dejectedly, her eyes soulfully wistful. "But please, Bridget, don't worry."

Bridget was stubborn. "Well, I don't want you crying anymore, especially over Miss Rose. That Biddy has a wild imagination and a wilder tongue. I imagine she's been filling Miss Rose's head with all sorts of ravings. I should tell Mr. Paul when he gets back. That's what I should do," she said.

"Oh, no!" cried Gigi, grabbing Bridget's arm as she headed for the door with her dress. "Please! Don't say anything to Paul, Bridget," she said. "I'll make sure I tell him myself," she assured her. "Please."

Bridget nodded. "Well, all right, but you make sure you tell him. It isn't right for Miss Rose to get you upset like this."

She assured her once more that she'd tell Paul, and Bridget left. Gigi sighed, staring at herself in the mirror of the vanity, brushing a stray strand of hair back from her forehead.

"You're a fool, you know that, don't you, Gigi Rouvier?" she said to herself as she stared into the mirror, tears once more welling up in her eyes. "A stupid fool!" and she could hold back no longer, letting the tears fall free, her heart broken in little pieces. What a holiday! She threw the hairbrush, stood up, and flung herself on the bed and cried until there were no more tears left.

7

André was on time again, as usual, which frustrated Gigi, because Jason frequently remarked that people who were on time were usually responsible and trustworthy, and she didn't want André to be responsible and trustworthy. She wanted him to be hateful and mean so she could despise him. But except for the way his dark eyes studied her with an intensity that was sometimes frightening, he was the epitome of what a man should be. Thoughtful, charming, handsome, loving. Then why couldn't she love him? Why did his claims of undying devotion and declarations of love leave her unmoved and empty inside?

She'd cried herself out shortly before lunch, but ate in her room alone. Now, wearing a new fancy riding suit of deep turquoise to match the color of her eyes, which had finally lost their redness, she descended the stairs in the drawing room to meet him.

André's dark eyes pored over her as she approached. Sunlight, streaming through the windows behind her, caught her dark hair, turning it iridescent, like the feathers of a raven, and her face, the blue-green eyes hauntingly brilliant, reminded him of a painting he had once seen of the Madonna. He was sure he'd never seen anyone more beautiful, and told her so, watching her blush.

He kissed her hand, then straightened, studying her, remembering regretfully how irritated he'd been when they'd first ordered him on this assignment. If he'd known she was going to be so sensuously beautiful, so warm and vivacious, he would have accepted the orders cheerfully, instead of grudgingly. He'd never dreamed the compensations would be so rewarding. His fingers caressed her hand sensuously as he tucked it in the crook of his elbow, and they turned toward Jason, taking their leave.

As they left the house, Gigi squinted, the bright afternoon sun hurting her eyes in spite of the wide crown on the softly feminine hat she'd been carrying in her hand and now set on her head. She felt little like riding, but had to forget somehow. The memory of last night was still too vivid in her mind, and Rose's accusing words still echoed loudly in her ears.

She turned to André, forcing a smile to her full lips, wondering if he was really the answer to her dilemma, and somewhere in the distance, a firecracker exploded. "What do you think of our Fourth of July?" she asked, trying to make conversation as they walked toward the stables.

He smiled, white teeth flashing beneath the dark mustache. "It reminds me of home," he said. "The parades, fireworks, crowds, like one of our fiestas."

Gigi frowned, suddenly realizing that the day before, when her father had been talking about the Fourth of July celebration, and about going to the Van Der Lindens' for a party and their private exhibition of fireworks, she had had no idea what it was all about and had to ask Bridget to tell her about it. She had found out that July 4 was a holiday, a day for celebration, but she couldn't ever remember celebrating it. Why? She remembered other things. It was like that day at Coney Island when she and Paul had seen the couple swimming. It had been a shock. Somehow she knew she'd never seen or worn a bathing suit before. In fact, the idea of a woman baring herself that way in public seemed disgraceful. It was the same way now. Somehow she just knew she'd never celebrated the Fourth of July before, but why?

"What's the matter, *mi querida?*" André asked softly, seeing her frown. "Don't you enjoy fiestas?"

"I . . ." Her frown deepened, and she flushed. "I don't ever remember celebrating the Fourth of July before," she said slowly.

His eyes softened. "Is that so strange?" he asked. "After all, there are many things you can't remember."

"But I should think I'd remember this. It's supposed to be the biggest holiday of the year, next to Christmas."

"But you have amnesia."

"I remember Christmas, though."

"You do?" His eyebrows raised, and she paled, kicking a

pebble from the dusty drive as they walked, her eyes suddenly fixed on the stable door some yards in the distance.

"I do," she said, but didn't elaborate. "I . . . I remember a
few things." She left it at that, reluctant to tell him for some
reason. And that was strange too. Why didn't she want to tell
him? It didn't make sense.

But she did remember. Suddenly she remembered guitar
music, and glowing candles, and a Nativity scene glistening
like gold, and most of all the *piñata*. She remembered
watching it burst open, the presents inside flying in all directions. She closed her eyes abruptly, then opened them just as
quickly again as they reached the stable doors, shaking the
image from her mind as she greeted Jamie, who was waiting
for them with her horse already saddled.

André helped her into the saddle, then mounted his own
horse, which he'd ridden out from the city and left with
Jamie on his arrival; then they headed toward the path that
wound along the riverbank, riding side by side, enjoying the
warm afternoon sun.

Bridget stepped from the harness room of the stables and
joined Jamie by the stable door and watched them ride off.

"Did you saddle Ahmed's horse too?" she asked as she held
her hand above her eyes to shield them from the sun as she
watched.

Jamie nodded. "Just like Mr. Larrabee ordered," and they
both turned as Ahmed emerged from one of the stalls, leading a sleek black stallion. He wore dark pants tucked into
black boots, and a dark shirt, yet the ever-present red turban
still covered his head. He led the horse outside, then mounted
easily, without even looking at them, his eyes riveted toward
the river; then he headed stealthily after the disappearing
couple.

Gigi and André had been riding for quite some time. The
ground was wet and soggy, and in some places closer to the
riverbank, it oozed with mud, and they steered their horses
away from it.

André had noticed from the start that she'd been moody.
Usually she was animated and lively, her conversation quick
and witty, but today something was on her mind. She was
restless, irritable, even though she tried hard to hide it. He
glanced back toward the trees they'd emerged from a few
minutes before and caught a glimpse of red through the
leaves and cursed to himself. Ahmed. He was like a leech. He

turned back to Gigi, trying to ignore the silent servant. "You enjoy the river, don't you?" he said.

She nodded. "I often walk to the picnic grove near the edge of the river in the evenings," she remarked. "The air's so fresh and clean." And Paul's usually with me when he's home, she thought to herself, then frowned. This was ridiculous. She had to forget Paul, put him out of her thoughts once and for all. Her jaw tightened stubbornly as she glanced ahead and caught a glimpse of a tumbledown barn way up ahead some distance from the riverbank. At one time it had been used to store hay. Now it was abandoned, the roof falling in, the door off.

"I'll race you to the barn!" she cried suddenly, her eyes coming alive, and André was taken by surprise as she threw her head back recklessly and dug her heels in her horse's ribs, shooting forward, throwing clumps of mud as she galloped across the field.

He hesitated, but only a second; then his eyes too took on a new depth, and he reined his horse after her, leaning low in the saddle, catching up to her, and they raced side by side.

They reined up at the barn together, horses prancing excitedly, and Gigi leaned back in the saddle, breathing hard. "Nothing like getting the cobwebs out, is there?" she gasped breathlessly, and he grinned broadly as he leaped from his horse and held his hands out for her.

She laughed to keep from crying, and leaned over, falling toward him.

André watched the light in her eyes warily. It was too quick, too vibrant. She was upset, and he wished to God he knew why. Had she discovered who he really was? Had she begun to remember? What then?

But no! Her eyes weren't accusing, or even afraid, they were sensuously alive, inviting, yet passionately intense. He caught her, letting her fall against him, and he held her there, his body tense, alert. He could feel the stirring inside as usual, only deeper this time, gnawing and twisting in his loins. God, she was lovely.

"You should have let me win!" she whispered breathlessly, looking up at him, and his dark eyes caressed her.

"I did," he whispered softly. "Your prize, *querida*," and he leaned forward, pulling her closer in his arms, his mouth covering hers.

Gigi tried to respond. She wanted to respond. Oh, how she

wanted it, but although her lips moved beneath his, there was no fire, no warmth, no strange tingling deep in her loins, only a slight flush of warmth that crept over her.

She pressed closer to him, praying to feel something, anything other than this weak response, but there was nothing.

André felt the solid warmth of her slight body against him, as his lips took hers; then he drew his head back slowly. *"Mi querida, tus besos son como vino dulce,"* he whispered passionately, and she answered him, protesting weakly, in his own language.

"No, por favor, no podrás," she said without thinking, then suddenly opened her eyes wide and stared at him dumbfounded while he still held her against him.

She frowned, staring hard into his dark eyes, a weird feeling down deep inside, and he spoke to her softly again in Spanish, and strangely she understood him, but didn't answer.

"Gigi?" he said again, this time in English. "Please, you're so lovely. Don't look so shocked. You know I've wanted to kiss you since the first night we met."

She shook her head slightly, her eyes bewildered, a frown creasing her forehead. "I . . . it isn't that. It isn't the kiss." Her frown deepened. "I understood you," she said slowly, her eyes intent on his, all remembrance of his kiss pushed to the back of her senses. "Don't you understand? You spoke Spanish, and I understood you."

He returned her frown. "So?"

"Don't you see?" she said, pushing herself back farther to look full into his face, yet still letting him hold her. "I know what you said. You said my kisses were like sweet wine."

"And I meant it," he replied softly, trying once more to kiss her, but she pulled back, wrenching clear of his arms.

"André," she said, irritated. "Be serious, please." Her eyes were intense, troubled. "How did I know?" she asked.

He sighed, gazing at her. "It's simple, *querida*," he said slowly. "Your father told me you came from a small convent close to the Mexican border. It's only natural you'd understand and be able to speak some Spanish. Almost everyone in Texas, New Mexico, and Arizona does. It's no surprise to me."

She stared at him, listening to every word of his heavily accented English, then slowly nodded. "You're right, I suppose," she said hesitantly. "I'd forgotten. They said I'd lived at . . . I believe they called it Las Hermanas del Sagrado

Corazon de Jesus—the Sisters of the Sacred Heart of Jesus or some such name."

"*Sí*," he answered. "And it's about thirty miles or so from the border of Mexico."

Suddenly she felt foolish for making such a fuss. But at the time . . . Since she'd first met him, André had said a few words here and there, and it never occurred to her that she'd understood that "*Sí*" meant "yes," and "*querida*" meant "sweetheart." It wasn't until he'd begun to make love to her in Spanish that the truth suddenly dawned on her, but now . . .

"I feel ridiculous," she said, blushing, but he smiled, and she realized how tall and muscular he was.

His body was like a fine sculpture, well-disciplined and taut. His hips slim, shoulders broad, the clothes he usually wore—tight pants, silk shirts, and embroidered jackets common to his country—accentuating them. He had the same forceful, self-assured stride Paul possessed, but his walk was brisk, alert, not as casual as Paul's, and every movement was well-calculated, even when he tried to appear at ease. It was as if he were playing a part. But then, maybe he was. After all, it must be hard to try to make your way in a strange country. Especially one so different from his own.

Gigi reached over and patted her horse's soft, velvet nose. "André, just what are you really doing in New York?" she asked suddenly, tired of guessing.

The corner of his mouth twitched as his eyes held hers. "I was wondering how long it'd be before you came right out and demanded to know," he said, then answered, "I work at the Mexican consulate here. I'm what you'd call a courier perhaps, or an aide to Presidente Díaz. I'm on a special assignment for my government." He shrugged. "I wish I could tell you more, *querida*, but I'm sorry, I'm not at liberty to discuss my work."

"Oh." She smiled saucily, continuing to play the temptress, forcing her thoughts away from Paul. "Shall we ride farther?" she said, reaching for her horse's reins, and André stepped to her side as if to help her mount.

She reached a hand out for him to steady her while her foot moved toward the stirrups, but instead of helping her onto the horse, he swung her abruptly into his arms once more, his husky laughter falling gently on her ears.

"You didn't really want to ride more, did you, *querida?*" he asked intimately as he gazed into her eyes.

Gigi sighed. "Not really," she said, lying to herself, forcing herself to play along with his banter, and once more his lips found hers.

This time the kiss was even more sensuous than before, and although it took Gigi's breath away, and brought a response that surprised her, she felt empty inside when it was over, and she looked into his dark eyes. "We'd better go." She sighed, disappointed, but André didn't seem to notice her disappointment.

Pleased with himself, he cupped her chin in his hand and kissed her again quickly, full on the lips, then released her and helped her to her horse, watching out of the corner of his eye to where Ahmed hung back in the shadows of the trees, keeping an eye on them.

André's hand covered hers as she held the reins, and he gazed up at her attentively. "Tonight, Gigi?" he said, his long tapered fingers caressing hers. "Do you have plans?"

She nodded. "Father made plans some weeks ago, André. I'm sorry," she said. "Perhaps another time."

"Tomorrow night?"

She hesitated, then smiled. "All right. Tomorrow night."

"The theater?"

"The theater will be fine."

"Good." He squeezed her hand, then released it and mounted his horse, and by the time they returned to the stables, he'd made plans not only for tomorrow night but also for the night after, and the night after that. He was playing right into her hands.

Later that evening as Gigi sat in front of her dressing table and let Bridget fix her hair, she thought over the afternoon ride and her promise to spend more time with André. It was the only way. If she was to forget Rose's accusations and her feelings toward Paul that had kindled the accusations, André was as good a man as any to use.

Bridget finished Gigi's hair, and Gigi stood up, appraising herself in the mirror. Her dress of red velvet had a heart-shaped neckline, cut rather low in front, pushing her full young breasts up, making them seem even more voluptuous. The girdled waist pulled her in tight and small. She studied herself critically for a moment, then reached into the jewelry box on the dresser and took out the diamond-and-ruby brooch that spelled her name and fastened it on the front of the dress between the soft curves of her breasts. There, that looked better; then she inserted small diamond-and-ruby teardrops in her earlobes to make her toilet complete. Satisfied, she dismissed Bridget, then started downstairs.

Paul had returned quietly that afternoon, shortly after she and André had returned from their ride, but she hadn't seen him as yet, and he'd mentioned to no one where he'd been.

They were all seated at the dinner table when she entered the dining room. Jason, Bruce, and Paul were in white tie and tails, and Rose was in a frothy concoction of sapphire-blue chiffon, accented by sapphires in her earlobes and gracing her long neck. Rose and Bruce were invited to the Van Der Lindens' too. However, Bruce would leave himself to pick up Natalie, and Harvey Redding was to pick up Rose.

Jason smiled. "Well," he said, his eyes devouring Gigi, "you look exceptionally lovely tonight, my dear."

Gigi blushed as she sat down. "Thank you."

"And how was your ride with Mr. de los Reyes?"

"Fine," she said; then, for the first time since entering the dining room, she glanced directly at Paul. He wasn't looking at her. His eyes held a rather troubled stare, and he was studying the floral centerpiece on the table. She glanced back to Jason. "We rode along the river most of the way," she went on. "Then stopped for a while by the old abandoned barn."

Jason's eyes sparked. "I know," he said testily. "Ahmed informed me."

Gigi flushed a deep crimson. Good old Ahmed. She glanced back behind Jason's chair to where Ahmed stood stoically watching them eat. "I figured he would," she said quietly.

Now suddenly she did feel Paul's eyes on her, and when she glanced his way, into them, the pain was so intense, it was like a knife being forced into her breastbone. It was an actual physical pain that made her wince, and she quickly looked back to Jason.

"I don't know as I like him kissing you like that," said Jason angrily, not seeing the perturbed look that crossed Paul's face as he spoke. "If he's made any improper advances, or forced himself on you, I'll see he never comes again!"

Gigi's blush deepened even more, and she shook her head. "Oh, no . . . please. It was just a little kiss. I didn't mind, really," she said, embarrassed. Her face was as scarlet now as her dress. "I . . . I guess he likes me."

"But whom do *you* like?" asked Rose abruptly, and Gigi's eyes faltered hesitantly as she turned to Rose, wishing she were dead.

"Why, I—?"

"Don't be silly," Jason interrupted, making it unnecessary for Gigi to continue trying to answer. "Gigi hasn't been here long enough to become attached to any one man yet, Rose. Have you, my dear?" he said, patting Gigi's hand. "Give her time." He looked directly at Gigi, noting the high color in her face and unusual brilliance of her blue-green eyes. "Besides," he went on, "I want her to take her time before falling in love, because I'm going to be very particular about the man she finally chooses."

Rose looked straight at Gigi, her eyes hard and cold, then back to her father. "Perhaps you won't approve of the man Gigi falls in love with, Father," she said. "Has that ever occurred to you?"

Jason shook his head. "Nonsense. Gigi has good taste. She'll pick a real man." He glanced about the table. "Someone like her brother Paul, here!" he said boisterously, and Rose choked, sputtering uncontrollably as the white wine she was sipping suddenly went down the wrong way.

Paul's eyes met Gigi's, and he gave her a questioning look that wasn't lost on Bruce as Jason tried to help Rose.

"Are you all right?" asked Jason, and Rose finally composed herself, swallowing unhindered.

"I'm fine," she gasped, breathing heavily, making sure no wine had spilled on her gown, and they were all distracted, the conversation forgotten, as the servants began bringing in the food. The conversation at the table for the rest of the evening was meaningless and trite.

They were just finishing dessert when Jason suddenly turned to Paul. He'd been picking at his food during most of the meal, and once Paul had even asked him if he was feeling all right, but he'd assured him he felt fine.

"Paul?" he said now, resting his spoon easily against his dessert dish, his hand shaking slightly. "I'm afraid you were right." His eyes had lost much of their luster, and his mouth looked drawn and pale. "My stomach's a little upset," he said. "And I don't feel quite up to it." He set down his napkin. "Would you mind too much giving my best to Katrin and Nels?" he asked. "Tell them I just can't make the festivities tonight."

"Are you sure it's not serious?" asked Bruce, watching his father closely. "You look pale, Father."

Jason shook his head. "It's nothing, really. I think I've just been going too much lately and eating too much good food. I'm not as young as I used to be, you know."

"Are you sure this whole business hasn't been too much for you, Father?" asked Rose snidely. "It has been a bit much."

He continued to shake his head stubbornly. "Nonsense! I've been enjoying every minute." He smiled at Gigi. "I'm just tired." He rubbed his brow. "And I've eaten too much, that's all." He gestured, and Ahmed was with him immediately, pulling the wheelchair from the table.

"See that he gets to bed right away, Ahmed," said Paul as the red-turbaned servant turned the wheelchair around. Ahmed nodded.

"Don't be silly," protested Jason as Ahmed headed for the door. "I'll just rest a little." He looked back over his shoulder at Ahmed. "Paul's just being fussy, Ahmed. I'm all right," he assured him. "Just a little under the weather, that's all," and he smiled as he bid them all good-bye while Ahmed maneuvered the wheelchair through the door into the hall.

They finished eating quickly, with little conversation, most of it centering around Jason's health; then Paul pulled the bell cord and one of the young girls came in from the kitchen.

"Tell Mrs. Sharp to have Tuttleby meet us around front with the carriage, and send up for Miss Gigi's wrap," he instructed as the girl stood waiting. "We'll be leaving shortly."

She nodded, then left.

He stood up and came around, helping Gigi with her chair, trying to keep himself composed. They had weathered the meal fine, addressing each other as little as possible, only their eyes communicating, and all evening Gigi sensed anger in Paul. Now her heart stood still in her breast as she realized they'd be riding to the Van Der Lindens' in the carriage alone.

"If you'll excuse the two of us," Paul said to Rose and Bruce as he took Gigi's arm. "Lenore asked if I'd get there early. We'll see the two of you there later, at about eight-thirty?"

They both nodded, muttering in agreement to his question, and Rose gave Gigi a penetrating, forceful look that Paul couldn't fathom. It wasn't a look of hatred or anger, but a smug look that seemed to say: I told you so.

He shrugged, frowning as he escorted Gigi from the dining room to the foyer, where they met Bridget at the front door. She helped Gigi on with her black velvet cape, and they left the house.

Usually July evenings were hot and humid, but for some reason the past few days had been stormy and exceptionally cool. Now, tonight, a chill still clung to the air. Tuttleby arrived in front with the closed-in carriage as they descended the steps. It was dark out, and Paul held Gigi's arm, helping her into the coach. The flesh on her bare elbow where his fingers rested tingled at his touch.

He turned to Tuttleby. "The Van Der Lindens'," he said, then climbed inside and sat down beside her, closing the carriage door behind him.

They sat quietly side by side, neither one talking, yet very aware of each other as the carriage began to move down the drive; then suddenly Paul straightened angrily, his jaw tightening.

"You let him kiss you?" he asked furiously, and Gigi held her breath momentarily, not knowing what to say.

So that's why he was upset. "Does it matter?" she said slowly, wanting to hate him. "Does anything really matter anymore, Paul?" she cried.

"You know it does!"

"It shouldn't!"

"Don't you think I don't know that?" He turned to her reluctantly, knowing that when he looked into her eyes like this the battle to keep from kissing her was all the harder to fight, yet he couldn't help himself. He had to know what she felt. "Just the thought of him holding you . . ." He looked away again hurriedly, not trusting himself. "I went to Mrs. Thornapple's this morning," he said.

"Why?"

"Why?" He shrugged. "I don't really know." He frowned, looking back into her eyes, his face revealing the fight he was close to losing. "I guess I had some crazy notion that maybe you were someone else . . . at least I was hoping."

"And?"

He looked away again. "Nothing. Everything there only confirms it. One thing, though," he said, and this time when he looked at her, his eyes were puzzled. "Do you happen to remember a Colonel Alvarez?" he asked curiously. "Rather fat, big mustache, deep voice?"

She shook her head slowly. "No." Her voice lowered. "Only, I did learn something today, Paul," she offered hesitantly, glad to talk about something less hurtful. "I can understand and speak Spanish fluently. At first it frightened me, but André said it's because the convent I was in is near Mexico. What do you think?"

He thought for a minute. Could it be? Or was there some connection with Alvarez and André? Had they both known her before? He didn't want to scare her needlessly, yet they had to find the answers somewhere. In her memory? Perhaps.

"He's probably right," he said, and the lines in his forehead creased into a deeper frown. "But it does seem strange, because the colonel I mentioned was at Mrs. Thornapple's looking for a woman of your description, and he's a member of the Mexican Army."

"The Mexican Army?" She shook her head, baffled. "What would I have to do with the Mexican Army?"

He sighed. "I don't know, but I'm certainly going to try to find out."

They rode along in silence again for a short time, once more aware of the tension between them, and this time it was Gigi who spoke first.

"I'm sorry," she said softly, in answer to the first words Paul had spoken earlier. "I thought if I let him kiss me and make love to me, I'd be able to forget what happened last night, like you told me to," she said.

Paul didn't answer. There was no lantern lit in the coach tonight, but Gigi could see his profile framed in the window. His lips were tight, jaw firm, head erect, staring straight ahead.

"You did say to forget, didn't you?" she asked.

"Yes!"

"Have you?"

He sighed, then suddenly turned toward her, and all his resolve was forgotten. He couldn't help it. She was like a breath of air to him, and he was drowning in her nearness, his whole body vibrating with emotion. He reached out slowly and pulled her to him.

"You knew last night that I could never forget, didn't you?" he whispered huskily, and she sighed, melting against him.

His lips found hers in the darkness, and once more they clung to each other, afraid to let go. It was madness, insanity, and they both knew it, yet he kissed her passionately, his hands caressing her soft warm body, the sweet heady fragrance of her perfume making his head reel.

He smothered her with kisses, his lips caressing her eyes, her throat, tingling against her ears as he whispered her name, bringing her body to life, and she responded to him fervently, offering in return the passion and ecstasy he pleaded for.

Suddenly he stopped kissing her, his lips only inches from her ear. "I can't go," he whispered huskily as he held her close. "I can't. Not tonight. I can't take you to Lenore's."

She gasped, drawing back to look into his face. "We . . . we have to go. They're expecting us," she murmured breathlessly.

"No!" His answer was vehement, filled with the passionate storm that raged within him. "I won't be in the same room with you and not be able to touch you," he said. "Not tonight." His voice was deep, husky. "I know it's wrong, but I want to be alone with you, just the two of us. I can't bear the thought of trying to be nice to Lenore when what I really want is to be with you. I've put in enough evenings watching men making passes at you. I couldn't stand that, not now. I have to have one night to remember for the rest of my life. Let's forget who we are and what we are, only for tonight, Gigi. Let's go where we can be alone, just the two of us."

She sighed, knowing it was wrong, but unable to help herself. "Yes . . . oh, yes," she whispered.

He reached up and slid back the panel above his head. "Tuttleby?"

The voice came back loud and clear as Tuttleby stuck his mouth close to the panel. "Yes, Mr. Paul?"

"Take us to Central Park, Tuttleby," he said.

Tuttleby was taken aback. "Yes, sir," he said hesitantly, then added, "But, sir, the Van Der Lindens'?"

"To hell with the Van Der Lindens tonight, Tuttleby," Paul yelled up to him, his face flushed with excitement. "Gigi

and I are going to Central Park. We have our own way of
celebrating the Fourth of July," and his voice had a ring to it
Tuttleby had never heard before. "Now, on to the park."

Tuttleby shrugged, shaking his head. He didn't like it. No,
sir, he didn't like it at all. "Yes, sir," he said reluctantly,
straightening in his seat.

Paul closed the panel, then reached out and cupped Gigi's
face in his hand. He could barely make out the soft, warm,
blue-green eyes and voluptuous mouth.

"What will you tell them?" she asked suddenly, and he
stared at her as if mesmerized.

"I'll think of something." He kissed her lightly, his lips
barely brushing hers. "Right now I don't care," he whispered
against her mouth. "Right now all I want is to be with you,"
and he kissed her deeply this time, with all the urgency the
moment demanded, and Gigi felt the glow spread through
her, making her body throb.

The ride tonight took longer than Paul thought it would,
but they didn't care. Even when crowds blocked the streets
and children threw firecrackers at the horses, spooking them,
making Tuttleby curse, neither Paul nor Gigi seemed to
mind.

Everyone in New York City was out tonight, and there
were numerous neighborhood festivals, parties, and street
dances. In spite of the coolness of the evening, spirits were
high and the general air of celebration seemed to reach everyone.

At the crowded entrance to the park, Paul gave instruc-
tions to Tuttleby that he could do as he wished, only pick
them up back here after the fireworks display. Then he and
Gigi melted into the crowd.

The night air was warmer here away from the windswept
river, and the milling crowd radiated its own heat. They
moved along slowly with the crowd, holding hands, making
their way along one of the paths, stopping occasionally to
watch something interesting, moving haphazardly past trees,
shrubs, and benches until they finally came to an open area
where people were dancing on a special platform built just
for tonight. There was a railing built around the platform,
draped with red-white-and-blue bunting, and a small orchestra sat in one corner of the platform. The music was loud
and exuberant, and the people even louder as they whirled
around the floor to a rousing polka.

They leaned against the railing for a long time watching the dancers; then Paul caught Gigi's hand in his as the musicians started playing a slow waltz. "Shall we?" he asked, motioning toward the dancers, his gray eyes intense, and she nodded.

They left the railing and joined the others on the low platform. Some of the couples looked at them rather curiously as Paul took Gigi in his arms, and she felt self-conscious.

"They're staring at us," she said furtively.

He smiled. "I don't imagine they see many men in white tie and tails," he said.

Gigi frowned. "What if they recognize us?"

Paul glanced about quickly, then looked back at Gigi. "I don't suppose any of them read the society pages, so we should be safe."

She watched the other dancers furtively for a few minutes. Paul was right. No one was paying the least bit of attention to them anymore. They were too busy enjoying themselves.

The waltz should have been light and gay, with violins and piano so they could lose themselves in its strains, but instead, it was brassy, the band composed of horns, accordion, and drums, ruining the tempo with its harshness. They tried, but it just wasn't the same, and the music lost some of its magic in the process.

Paul's jaw tightened irritably as he held her close in his arms. Something wasn't right. It was as if the brash music was mocking them, revealing to the whole world the sordid taint that haunted them. He inhaled suddenly as the music ended. "Let's get out of here," he whispered hoarsely, his lips brushing her hair, and she pulled back, gazing up at him.

She saw the pain in his eyes as his hand found hers and he led her through the bustling crowd. They stepped off the platform and walked away as the band began another rousing polka and the dancers again started stomping the floor.

"I'm sorry," he said as they strolled side by side, moving out among the grass and trees, beginning to lose the strains of the music behind them as the other sounds of the almost carnival-like atmosphere mingled with the polka. "I didn't know it'd be this noisy."

She kicked at a blade of grass at the side of the trail with the toes of her red satin slipper. "It's not noisy here," she said, and he looked around.

She was right. They'd reached a quiet area of the park,

dark and secluded, where the noise of the crowd and band music were only a jumble of distant cacophony on the night breeze. Even the trails were almost deserted.

"So I see," he said, and smiled. "Come on."

He took her hand, pulling her off the main trail, and she followed silently for some time, stumbling erratically between the trees and bushes, trying to keep up with his long stride. Then suddenly, as she realized they were in a deserted spot deep in the park, he stopped.

"Where are we?" she asked breathlessly, looking up at him.

He pulled her into his arms, his lips nuzzling her neck. "Who cares?" He sighed huskily. "What's important is that we're alone at last," and his mouth covered hers in a long, searing kiss that fused her nerves together into an explosive charge tucked deep in her loins.

"Oh, God, Paul," she whispered as he drew his mouth from hers. "I love you so much!"

His fingers touched her cheek, brushing a stray strand of hair from her lips as he looked down at her, and he kissed them, lightly this time, teasingly, and she trembled.

"You're cold?" he asked.

She shook her head. "No."

"Frightened?"

"A little."

"Of me?"

She sighed. "Of myself. I don't think I've ever felt so strongly about anything before as I feel about you," she said. "I couldn't have, and it scares me."

"I know." She was so small, so fragile. Almost lost in his arms. He cupped her head in his broad hand, his fingers buried in her hair.

"Paul?" Her eyes grew misty. "What do we do tomorrow, Paul?" she asked. "And the day after that, and the day after that?" but he kissed her lips, stopping her.

"We don't talk about tomorrow," he said, his mouth against hers. "Dammit, Gigi, I'm only human!" He drew his lips away and looked deep into her blue-green eyes, watching the moonlight begin to dance in them as it rose above the trees behind him. "We made a promise, remember?" he said. "Tonight's ours. It may be the only night we'll ever have, but it's ours, and no one or nothing will ever take it from us. Remember?"

She stared up at him, her eyes caressing his ruggedly handsome face, looking into his warm gray eyes, moving over his sensuous mouth. Yes, she'd promised him. Tonight would be theirs. Something to have for always, even though they could never truly have each other. She sighed, accepting the fact that when morning came it would never be again. Not for them.

"I remember," she said through tears. "Only, I wish I could hold back the sun, because I don't know if I'll be strong enough when tomorrow comes."

A long agonized groan wrenched itself from deep inside Paul, and he held her even closer. "I love you, Gigi," he whispered softly, almost angrily. "It's wrong, and indecent, and immoral, and I know it, and I've cursed myself a thousand times for it, and yet I can't help myself. I love you!" and with this cry he pulled her with him onto the soft, cool ground, nestling her back against a small clump of grass, where they were unseen by anyone who might happen to wander by.

He took the cloak from her shoulders, rolled it into a pillow, and tucked it beneath her head, watching the moonbeams play in her dark hair and about her face.

"You're so lovely," he said softly as he settled on his stomach beside her, leaning on one elbow, looking down, and she reached up, running her finger down his prominent cheekbone and across his firm chin.

"What are you going to tell them back at the house?" she asked.

He shrugged. "The truth."

Her eyes widened. "The truth?"

"After we left the house, I decided to take you to see what it's like to be in Central Park on the Fourth of July. Father knows they always have a big celebration here, with dancing and fireworks."

"How about the Van Der Lindens? We didn't let them know we weren't coming."

"It's simple," he said. "There were too many crowds, and I couldn't get to a telephone."

"You think they'll believe it?"

"Father will. After all, you're my half-sister."

"But what of the rest of the family?" She suddenly remembered Rose. Her voice lowered. "What will they think?"

He smiled wickedly. "Who cares?" He leaned over and kissed her.

Oh, God, she thought, letting his kiss flow through her like liquid fire. She was so ashamed. She should tell him about Rose, about Rose's suspicions and accusations. She should push him away and put an end to this whole affair, but she couldn't. Here in his arms, with his mouth on hers, his hand caressing her, moving deftly to release her breasts from the confines of her bodice, she was lost. There was nothing to do but surrender.

She gulped back tears as his mouth left her lips and trailed its way down her throat to her breast, his tongue tracing the outline of her nipple as it hardened, and a sigh escaped her lips. "Please, Paul," she whispered softly. "We mustn't!"

His breath was warm on her skin, his heart pounding as his lips traced the path of his tongue back up, then moved once more to her mouth.

"Don't worry, I'm not," he whispered gently, after kissing her once more. "I'm not that crazy, not yet. I only wanted a little. A taste of what might've been, if circumstances were different." His eyes grew stormy and passionate as they looked into hers, and somehow she knew no man had ever looked at her like this, or aroused her like this. "I wish to God I could give you more, Gigi," he said softly. "I wish I could give you the love you should have. To feel the warmth of your body next to mine, and the ecstasy I know we could give each other. But I won't. I'll ache like the devil, I know, but I still have some sanity left."

"Oh, Paul! My darling Paul!" she moaned softly, reaching up, sinking her hands in his dark hair, ruffling it, pulling his head down so his face was buried in the cleft between her full breasts, and he kissed them passionately, then once more sought the comfort of her mouth, his tongue parting her lips, exploring its sweetness as an owl hooted somewhere out in the park, and overhead the moonlit sky suddenly erupted into a myriad of sparkling colors.

8

Bridget waited until Jason retired to his quarters, Bruce left to pick up Natalie, and Harvey Redding arrived to escort Rose to the Van Der Lindens'; then she grabbed a pitcher of warm water and hurried to her room in the servants' quarters above the kitchen. All day she'd been thinking of the dress and cloak Gigi had given her. She'd never had anything so beautiful to wear before in her life.

She closed the door to her small room hurriedly, and sighed, setting the pitcher on the water closet, then slowly moved to the armoire in the far corner and took the dress and cloak out, laying them neatly across the bed. She stared at them for some time, hardly able to believe that they were really hers, then slowly began to undress. Tossing her gray uniform at the foot of the bed, she let out a furtive giggle, then poured the water in the basin and started washing.

This finished, she slipped on two more petticoats, then carefully lifted the dress and pulled it on over her head, fastening the pearl buttons up the front as she stared at herself in the mirror above the dresser. The material felt sensuous against her fingers, soft and sheer, and suddenly she felt so different. She was no longer a clumsy girl or an inexperienced young lady's maid, she was a grown woman. The dress seemed to change her. She stared at herself studiously, tilting her head this way, then that, noting the graceful curve of her cheekbone. Yes, the dress definitely made a difference.

Even her skin took on a glow, as did her smile. And her eyes. She leaned closer to the mirror. She never realized how brown they were. The pale blue of the dress made them look like pools of dark coffee. And her hair! She straightened again, lifting it gracefully from her neck, holding it atop her head, and the transformation was astounding. Why, dressed like this, she was even prettier than Miss Rose.

She picked up the hairbrush, brushed her hair to a glowing sheen, then twisted it, fastening the heavy coil atop her head with hairpins. The effect was much better than just plopping it up any old way. She made sure it wouldn't fall, then went back to the bed and picked up the cape, fingering the beading, running her hand across the rich blue velvet.

She twirled it around, nestling it onto her shoulders carefully, then fastened it at the neck. Now the transformation was complete. She liked it. She glanced quickly at the uniform crumpled on the bed, then back to the mirror, and sighed, pulling the cloak tighter about herself, feeling its luxurious satin lining against her flesh where it was fastened.

Satisfied that there was nothing more to be done to make herself look any lovelier, she turned the lamp down low and left the room, closing the door softly behind her.

The stairs from the servants' quarters came down into the kitchen next to one of the huge fireplaces, and she crept down them cautiously, hoping on hope that no one would be about. All the way down, she'd smelled the aroma of cinnamon buns baking and coffee perking, but when she stepped into the kitchen, not even Mrs. Sharp was in sight. She straightened, listening, afraid, but hearing nothing except the bubbling sound of the coffee as it brewed on the stove.

Gingerly she made her way across the room to the back door, opening it easily so it wouldn't click, then quickly slipped outside. It was pitch dark, the moon still hidden behind trees on the horizon. She had promised to meet Jamie at a quarter to nine down by the river at the old picnic grove some distance from the house, and she was late.

Moving swiftly, she hurried down the sloping lawn, holding up her skirts so as not to trip, her eyes squinting into the darkness. She reached the edge of the lawn in minutes and skirted it, finally finding the path that led through the small grove of trees and bushes that separated the picnic grounds from the house.

As she stepped off the lawn onto the path, she stopped abruptly and hesitated, dropping her skirt, straightening it, then readjusted the cloak on her shoulders. She had to look just right. Just like a lady, because that's how she felt tonight, like a lady. A real honest-to-goodness lady. Jamie would be so proud.

Her head went up, nose thrust into the air sedately, and after taking a deep breath, determined to look as womanly as she felt, she began walking carefully down the dark path.

Usually she and Jamie met behind the stables, but tonight she knew she'd be late so she'd told him to go on ahead and she'd meet him at the river. Now, suddenly, as she moved farther along the path, she began to wonder if it had been such a good idea. Not only was it exceptionally dark, but the moon that was rising couldn't reach in here among all the trees, and it made it even darker. She could barely see her hand in front of her face.

A chill ran through her, and she stopped hesitantly, reaching up, pulling the hood of the cloak up over her head. She hadn't realized when she'd left the house that the night air was so cool. It must be because she was closer to the river now. She stood quietly for a minute, listening to the night sounds, then took a deep breath and started out again. A few steps farther, she stopped again. This time her ears pricked up and she held her breath.

What was that? The usual sounds seemed to be magnified all around her. Suddenly a twig snapped somewhere close by, and she inhaled sharply, every nerve alert, straining her ears, her eyes trying to pierce the darkness. She stood motionless, listening, but heard nothing more. Only the constant chorus of crickets and tree frogs.

Swallowing hard, she tried to admonish herself for being so foolish. Telling herself it was probably just a rabbit, or field mouse, or even one of the cats from the stables prowling about, she moved again, beginning to walk once more, slowly this time, and with far less abandon than when she'd left the house. She'd gone only a few steps when suddenly her heart fell to her stomach, and this time she knew it had been no mistake. She stopped, whirling around, listening, her mouth dry. Behind her on the path she could hear footfalls. Not loud, but soft, as if someone was trying not to be heard.

"Who's there?" she gasped breathlessly, hoping to hear Jamie's welcoming voice, but instead the footsteps stopped, and only the night sounds went on. "Who's there?" she repeated again, louder. Still nothing.

She bit her lips, wondering what to do. Her knees were shaking now, her eyes misting. If it had been Jamie, he'd have answered. He'd never frighten her like this. But since it wasn't Jamie, then who? It was so terribly dark.

She turned again and moved a few feet further, listening apprehensively. Once more the footsteps moved with her.

Oh, God! Who was out there? Her heart was pounding as fear gripped her, and her feet suddenly began to move faster along the path. She no longer thought of the dress and cloak she wore, or of being a lady, or anything else. Her only thought was to reach the picnic grounds and Jamie.

Suddenly, as she stumbled along in the darkness, she realized whoever it was was no longer trying to be quiet, and that her pursuer was quickly closing the distance between them. She broke into a run as the footsteps grew louder.

Her cloak caught on bushes, and the uneven ground slowed her down, but she plunged forward anyway, the steady beat of her racing heart thudding in her ears along with the crashing, pounding footsteps that echoed behind her.

She was almost there. Just a little farther. If only . . . Quickly she glanced back. The footsteps seemed to be on top of her now, and as she continued to run, anxiously watching the path behind her, a huge figure loomed out of the darkness so quickly she had barely enough time for a strangled sob to escape her lips, then strong arms imprisoned her, one arm working like a vise across her throat, and she felt the air being cut off.

She gasped, choking, pulling and clawing at the arm that was cutting off her wind, trying to get air in her lungs as a voice close to her ear whispered hoarsely, "Well, señorita, so we meet again, eh?" She could feel his hot breath on her ear, the faint smell of garlic filling her nostrils. "There's no use struggling, you know," he went on. "You're going with us this time whether you want to or not," but before he could get her fully subdued, she began to kick and flail at him, trying to break his hold.

His arm tightened, pressing harder against her windpipe, and Bridget felt the world begin to reel. She tried to keep on fighting, tried to breathe again, but it was useless, and her lungs felt like they'd explode, as a cold blackness engulfed her, carrying her into oblivion.

Jamie sat on top of the picnic table waiting. He'd already been waiting for quite some time, and was getting impatient. He tugged at the sleeves of his good suit coat and smiled to himself, pleased. Bridget was sure in for a surprise. She had no idea he had the buggy waiting by the stables and was planning to take her for a ride. Maybe they'd even get to see fireworks somewhere. He smoothed a callused hand through unruly brown hair and glanced toward the path again, sighing.

She said she'd be late, but this late? It wasn't like Bridget. Not at all. She was up to something. He leaned forward, looking out over the river, where the moon had just cleared the trees. It was light enough here at the picnic grove, but terribly dark in the woods. Frowning, he glanced once more toward the path, eyes straining. Maybe he ought to go meet her. After all, it'd be the gentlemanly thing to do, and it wouldn't hurt. She might be afraid in the dark.

Shrugging, he slid his lanky frame from the table and straightened, then suddenly tensed. What the hell! A strangled cry broke the stillness, and the hair on his neck prickled. He swallowed cautiously, a lump in his throat. Bridget!

His heart dropped to his stomach, and he raced across the picnic grounds to the path, plunging into the woods, lanky legs adjusting quickly to the uneven ground as he ran. He could hear struggling now, and muffled sounds as the darkness seemed to swallow him up. His eyes were just getting used to the dark when he saw them up ahead. There were two men, vague, dark shadows on the path. One was holding Bridget in what looked like a headlock, and the other was doing something at her feet.

He saw her body suddenly slump, and he let out an enraged bellow that echoed through the woods, startling them as he lunged forward, grabbing the man who was holding Bridget. The man was paunchy and fat, his breathing labored. One of Jamie's hands landed across his face, fingers digging into his flabby jowls, while Jamie's other hand reached around, pulling the man's arm from Bridget's throat, twisting it around to meet his back.

The man grimaced, grunting something unintelligible, and released his hold. Her support gone, Bridget slid forward, landing directly on the other man, who'd been trying to tie her feet together with a rope. The man's hands clenched on the rope harder when she knocked into him. He tried to keep his balance, but couldn't, and sprawled on the ground, Bridget's unconscious body a deadweight on top of him.

He gasped, heaving air into his lungs, then shoved hard, pushing her still form off, while Jamie and the other man continued struggling. Regaining his feet, the thinner of the two men sized up the situation quickly. The intruder was younger and taller than his partner, with less flesh to hamper him, the strength in his arms reinforced by anger. His partner didn't have a chance. The rope still in his hands, the thinner man rushed in to help, trying to swing it over Jamie's head, to catch it around his throat, but Jamie was too quick.

He released the fat man, shoving him to the ground, grabbed the rope as it tried to snake about his neck, and spun the man with the rope around, slamming him into a nearby tree.

The man let out a yelp and slid down the trunk, the wind partially knocked out of him, as his partner stared from the ground in disbelief. Cursing, spluttering like a madman, the man with the rope gained his knees, then straightened all the way again, breathing heavily as he stared at the intruder, who was like a young bull. Long, wiry, and all muscle. There wasn't a chance in a million.

Hating to admit defeat, but hating more the idea of getting caught, the man motioned for his partner to stay put, then dropped the rope and reached down, pulling a knife from its sheath, waiting.

Tears filled Jamie's eyes. He hated to fight, hated it with a passion, but these men had hurt Bridget. They had to pay. He felt a new surge of strength flow through him.

The fat man was still on the ground, but the man he'd slammed against the tree was coming at him again, this time slowly, gauging his moves. It was so dark Jamie could barely see him. He stood his ground, wincing, wishing the man would just turn and run, wishing they'd both leave so he could find out if Bridget was all right. She lay so quiet and still. He glanced quickly at his feet, at Bridget's motionless body, and it was then the other man made his move.

He sensed Jamie's concern for the girl lying on the ground, and saw the faint movement of his head as he inclined it downward. A quick lunge brought him in close enough, and he swung his arm upward.

Jamie didn't see the knife, but he felt it as he grabbed, trying to fend the man off. The knife tore into his shoulder, ripping deep into the flesh, spilling blood all over his good suit, burying itself to the hilt, and the realization of what was happening was a shock. He gasped, astounded, feeling the pain as the knife sank deeper and deeper; then his bewilderment and pain turned into violent fury.

With no thought to how much he was hurting, he lifted the man into the air bodily, and flung him at the fat man, who was moving toward them now, intent on helping his partner. The man crashed into his partner hard, and the impact hurled them both into the underbrush, where they rolled onto the ground, broken branches from the bushes scraping their skin.

Jamie stood for a minute dazed, then his hand went to his shoulder, and he felt sticky blood oozing between his fingers. My God, he'd been stabbed! Still in shock, he pulled the knife out, tossing it aside as he inhaled sharply and stared in the direction he'd thrown the man, his breath coming in deep sobs. Damn, it hurt! He'd never felt pain like this before. It weakened his knees and made his head spin.

The fat man moved cautiously, staring at the young man before them, then reached out, shaking his partner to make sure he was conscious. "Ramón!" he whispered breathlessly.

"*Sí, mi coronel!*"

"Let's get out of here," he said.

Ramón clenched his teeth as he started to get up. "But the girl?"

"Forget her. *Vámonos!*" He reached out, helping him, and quickly, covered by the darkness, they moved cautiously away through the woods, keeping close to the edge of the path, leaving Jamie standing alone.

Jamie squinted, straining his eyes. His shoulder hurt like hell, but they were going to come at him again, he knew. He had to stay up. He had to protect Bridget. Instinctively he straightened, trying to get his eyes to focus in the darkness, but everything looked the same. Fuzzy. Now, where had they gone? They had to be around somewhere.

His head moved from side to side, searching. It was suddenly so quiet. Too quiet. He stood motionless, listening. Even the crickets and tree toads weren't chirping anymore. All he could hear was the faint rustling of the leaves overhead and his own breathing. He inhaled, trying to keep his head from spinning, but it wasn't any use. The pain in his shoulder was suddenly overpowering, filling his whole body with a strange warmth that made him feel sick. He couldn't pass out. Not now. But as he hit the ground, the last thing he saw before darkness replaced the pain was Bridget beside him, still as death.

How long Jamie lay there, he didn't know, but his head

was pounding and his shoulder throbbed. Even his arm and leg muscles ached as he stirred, trying to remember where he was and what had happened. Dried blood was encrusted on his upper lip. He was surprised. He hadn't even felt the blow. It must have happened when he was struggling with the fat man. He licked it with his tongue, feeling the swelling, then forgot about it quickly as his eyes fell on Bridget's still form only inches from him.

Only, it wasn't Bridget. Or was it? The dress wasn't Bridget's. He leaned closer, trying to see better. The dress looked like Gigi's. One she'd had on just last week. He reached out and felt the material. Silk. Bridget never had a silk dress in her life. He reached up, touching her hair. It was soft and long, piled atop her head. His hand touched her face, and she stirred, strange gurgling sounds coming from her throat.

"Jamie?" she moaned. "Jamie?"

It was Bridget!

"Bridget!" he cried, his hand stroking her cheek, fingers caressing her, and she let out a raspy cry.

"Oh, God, Jamie!"

His head fell to her shoulder as tears flooded his eyes, and he swallowed hard. "Bridget, are you all right, honey?"

She gasped for air. Her throat was on fire, and she could hardly swallow. "He choked me," she gasped, her voice raspy and breathless.

"But you're all right? Otherwise you're all right?"

Her hand moved to his head where it was cradled on her shoulder. "Yes, I'm all right."

"Thank God."

He still lay against her, unable to move, and suddenly she tensed.

"Jamie? Jamie, are you all right?" she asked.

He didn't answer.

"Jamie? I asked you, are you all right?"

He didn't want to tell her. He felt so damn useless. "It's my shoulder," he finally said, his breath warm on her cheek. "It was dark, and I couldn't see. One of them had a knife."

She inhaled, moving quickly, sliding out from under him as best she could, helping him to sit up. "I've got to get you back to the house," she said, her voice barely above a whisper. "Has it stopped bleeding?"

She reached out, touching his shoulder, feeling for the

wound. It was still bleeding, and she winced. Putting his other arm over her shoulder, she helped him to his feet.

"Come on," she said stubbornly. "We've got to get help."

He stood for a minute, his knees weak, insides tied in knots. "I'm gonna be sick," he said suddenly, and let go of her, leaning against the nearest tree, and lost his supper. The force of the vomiting made his head hurt worse.

Bridget wouldn't give up. When Jamie at last straightened up, she placed his arm about her shoulder again, and once more they staggered along the path toward the house. Stepping out onto the open lawn, they stopped momentarily and gazed across it. The moon was up full now, the sky clear, and the house looked miles away.

At the Van Der Linden estate, Lenore stood in a corner of the huge parlor of her gracious home, blue eyes glistening furiously as she noted the time on the gold-faced clock that graced the marble mantel over the fireplace. It was almost nine-thirty already, and still no sign of Paul. Where on earth was he? This was ridiculous. It wasn't bad enough he'd called last night and canceled the picnic she'd planned for earlier today. Now this! Ever since Gigi'd arrived on the scene, it seemed he was always busy with one thing or another, and his explanation was always that his father counted on him. Well, so did she.

She straightened, adjusting the stiffened white lace that framed her bare shoulders, smoothing the sheer chiffon that draped across the bodice and white silk skirt of her evening dress, ending in layers of froth that floated to the floor. Except for a small sprig of lily of the valley placed at the deep neckline, her only other hint of coloring to offset the stark white of the dress was more lily of the valley twined amid the curls atop her head. Even her jewelry was heirloom pearls, and she reached up, fingering them nervously as she once more looked across the room in expectation.

She'd made sure she looked extra special tonight. A little reminder to Paul of how lovely she was going to look in her wedding dress. She could hardly wait for him to see it. It was an original Doucet. Nothing but the best. She sighed, letting her thoughts concentrate fully on Paul, and what it was going to be like to be Mrs. Paul Larrabee. She said the name over slowly to herself. Mrs. Paul Larrabee.

He was the best-looking man in New York society, and its

most eligible bachelor, and already, as his fiancée, she was
the envy of all the other women. She'd often seen the envious
looks shot her way when she was with him, and she'd overheard more than one woman lament the fact that he was no
longer available. That was their misfortune. Her chin tilted
stubbornly.

If they'd only known how long she'd prayed that someday
she'd be Mrs. Paul Larrabee. From the first time she'd set
eyes on Paul, it was what she'd wanted. He was ten and she
was five, and besides being handsome and rich, he was the
only boy she'd ever met who didn't make fun of her because
she was so tall, her skin so fair, and her hair so light that her
eyebrows didn't show. Even then all the other girls made eyes
at him. She watched quietly, biding her time. For years she
watched while he got older, and taller, and handsomer, and
she got older, taller, and filled out in the right places, and
during those years their families became closer and closer
friends.

Their families spent summers together at Newport, holidays at each other's homes, and growing up together had
given her an edge the other girls hadn't had. Yet it hadn't
been easy to snare Paul. He'd been elusive for a long time,
never seeming to be interested in any one woman, yet spending time with them all, until after her return from Europe.
When her father had first sent her, she'd died a thousand
deaths, afraid she'd lost him for sure. But he'd still managed
to avoid the altar.

Maybe it was her absence those two years that helped him
make up his mind, or maybe he finally realized she'd grown
up. Whatever it was, her return to New York brought about
the results she'd been waiting for so long. He began spending
more and more time with her, and then suddenly they were
talking about marriage, and before he could even think of
changing his mind, she'd picked out the ring and set the date.
She wasn't about to let him get away. Not now. Not with
what she wanted so close. Mrs. Paul Larrabee! She sighed
again, glancing once more at the clock, then tensed with agi-
tation.

It was nine-thirty, and still no sign of him. She glanced
about, catching sight of Rose across the room. Reaching
down, she lifted her skirts gracefully and made her way
through the crowd, nodding politely to people here and there,
asking if they were enjoying themselves, and making hurried

excuses for Paul's absence when asked, although every time she had to, her irritation grew.

Finally, her face flushed, she stopped in front of Rose. Rose was alone, having left Harvey talking politics with some of the men.

"I thought you said Paul and Gigi left half an hour before Harvey picked you up?" Lenore said as she gazed at her future sister-in-law.

Rose shrugged. "They did. And his last words were, and I quote, 'Lenore wants me to get there early, so we'll see you there about eight-thirty, all right?' Bruce and I agreed, and they left."

"Well, it's after nine. Where are they?"

Rose tossed her head haughtily, the sapphires dangling from her ears glistening in the light from the crystal chandeliers overhead. "How should I know?" she said. "But then, Gigi's with him. What can you expect?"

Lenore stared at her curiously. "Just what do you mean by that?"

Rose was amazed. "You mean you don't know? You honestly don't know?" Surely Lenore wasn't serious. After all, it was the little remarks Lenore had made from time to time that had gotten her to wondering and caused her to start watching Paul more closely. "Oh, come on, Lenore." She looked amused. "You're not that naïve."

Lenore held her breath as she stared at Rose, at the young woman who'd someday be her sister-in-law; then her eyes narrowed shrewdly. She was insinuating that . . . Paul and Gigi? He'd spent a good deal of time with her, true. But . . . Paul and Gigi? God, no, she was his sister! Even Paul wouldn't stoop to something like that. Yet . . . there were the looks. Sometimes she'd caught them staring at each other so strangely. And Paul was overly protective of her. But . . . Oh, it was insane. It was only that his father insisted he take care of her. Gigi and Paul? No, never! She breathed deeply, trying to keep her voice subdued.

"If you're hinting at what I think you're hinting at, Rose, I think you'd better forget it," she said solemnly, disliking the thought of the scandal that could be caused if anyone overheard Rose. "Paul's got more sense than that."

Rose's mouth twisted cynically. "Does he really?" Her brown eyes grew intense, gold flecks sifting through them. "He's a man, Lenore, and a virile one at that. If he were my

future husband, I certainly wouldn't want him spending so
much time with another woman, even if she was his sister."

She saw the doubt begin to creep into Lenore's eyes again.
Oh, this was fun. Wouldn't Paul have ten fits. What a won-
derful way to get even with him. "What's the matter,
Lenore?" she asked calmly. "Did I say something wrong?"

Lenore wrung her hands together, trying not to lose control. She couldn't lose control. Lenore Amelia Van Der Linden never lost control of her emotions, and she wasn't about
to start now. She stared intently at Rose, her mouth dry,
stomach tightening. In the first place, Paul was too level-
headed and in control of himself and his life to do anything
like Rose was accusing him of. She said he was a man, a virile one, but Rose didn't know Paul, not the way she knew
him. True, he was a bit of a rebel as far as society was concerned, but he never got carried away like some men who
were unable to control themselves. No. Paul was always
calm, cool, and collected. Even when he kissed her, he knew
just when to stop. He never got carried away. A frown
creased her forehead. Of course, there was that night on the
terrace. The night of the masquerade ball. But then, that was
the only time he'd ever lost control the least little bit. The
frown disappeared. That's one of the things she liked about
Paul. He wasn't all hands and never tried to take liberties.
No. Paul and Gigi? Never!

Why, in the first place, Gigi had no class, no breeding. She
was outspoken, unsophisticated, and earthy. Even with
Jason's money to back her, she'd proved herself beneath them
socially. Paul knew better than to even consider such a thing.
She studied Rose. She knew Rose hated Gigi. So did she, but
this was uncalled-for.

"I think you're overstepping yourself this time, Rose," she
finally said, the doubt once more pushed aside. "Oh, I agree,
Paul seems to dote on Gigi's every whim. Even I'd like to
claw her eyes out at times. But what you're intimating . . .
no, Rose, not Paul. It's a novelty for him, having another sister, that's all. Believe me, Paul has more sense than to let a
stupid thing like that happen."

Rose smirked. She hadn't expected to be successful, but
then, she wondered if Lenore even cared. Sometimes she was
sure that Lenore was more obsessed with the idea of being
Mrs. Paul Larrabee than she was with Paul himself, and if

this were so, she'd never admit to anything that might jeopardize her dreams.

"Well, all I know is, if he were my fiancé," she said slowly, "I think I'd keep a better eye on him."

Lenore started to answer, but at that moment one of the maids interrupted. "Excuse me, Miss Lenore," she said, touching Lenore's arm to get her attention. "But Mr. Larrabee's on the telephone asking for Mr. Paul. Says it's an emergency, and I don't know what to tell him. I haven't been able to find Mr. Paul."

Lenore glared at her. "Mr. Paul isn't here yet," she snapped irritably, then turned to Rose.

"Maybe I'd better talk to Father," suggested Rose. "I hope he isn't worse. He looked so pale earlier at dinner."

Lenore agreed, and both women picked up their skirts, following the maid from the room.

The Van Der Lindens' house was large and ostentatious, with marble floors in most of the downstairs, a circular staircase in the entrance hall, and gilded pictures gracing the walls. Silks and velvets in rich deep tones of gold and burgundy were overly abundant, and the furniture was carved and ornate. The plain wood telephone box and black telephone looked out-of-place on the wall in the foyer.

Rose lifted the receiver as she leaned close to the speaker. "Father, it's me, Rose," she said loudly, her voice echoing in the room. The foyer was deserted now except for herself and Lenore. Everyone else was at the other end of the house in the huge parlor. "What's wrong?"

She heard a muffled grunt on the other end.

"Father?"

"Where's Paul?" Her father's voice was anything but weak. He was booming into the mouthpiece.

She had no answer. "He's not here."

"Not there? What do you mean, he's not there? Where'd he go?"

She glanced quickly at Lenore. "He didn't go anyplace, Father," she said. "He and Gigi never got here. I was just about to call and see if you knew where they were." There was silence; then: "Father, what's the matter?" she asked again.

This time his voice was tense. "Tuttleby's son, Jamie, has been hurt," he said quickly. "It seems he and that . . . that young girl who took over as Gigi's maid have been having clandestine meetings behind our backs. They were down by

the river tonight at the picnic grove having an assignation,
when some men attacked them. One of them had a knife."

"Oh, no!"

"Jamie's alive, but we've had to get a doctor and send for
the police, and I don't like the sound of the whole thing. The
young woman's throat was injured some, and she's been having a hard time talking, but from what she says, the men evidently thought she was Gigi."

"Gigi? Why would they think that?"

"Because she was wearing Gigi's clothes." There was a
slight pause; then Jason continued, disgruntled. "She said
Gigi gave them to her."

"Why would she do that?"

He cleared his throat. "Well, now, how should I know?" he
retorted. "Really, Rose, you can ask the dumbest questions
sometimes." She could tell he was more than a little upset.
"You say Paul never got there?"

"That's right, Father," she answered, and heard him exhale
disgustedly.

"Let me talk to Lenore," he said.

She handed the telephone to Lenore, shrugging her shoulders as she did so. Jason told Lenore the same thing he'd told
Rose, then asked if she had any idea at all where Paul was.

"No, Mr. Larrabee," she said, her voice tinged with rage.
"I don't know any more than you do."

"But he left hours ago."

"So Rose said."

"Well, if he shows up or calls, tell him to come home right
away, will you?" he asked.

She was the epitome of sweetness, her voice warm and co-
operative, yet her eyes were cold and hard. "I certainly will,"
she said, then asked, "Did you want to talk to Rose again?"

"No," he answered. "Just tell her to come home right
away. Both Rose and Bruce. I want them here!"

"All right," she said, then said good-bye and hung up.
"Your father wants you and Bruce to go home right away,"
she said, and saw Rose's eyes darken.

"Oh, jolly," Rose complained loudly. "Just because some
servant's gotten himself stabbed, I have to miss out on the
rest of the party. And what do I do with Harvey?"

"Why don't you have Harvey take Natalie home?" suggested Lenore. "It'd save Bruce having to escort her home first.
Besides, why should Harvey and Natalie have their evening

ruined. That way they can both stay and see the fireworks
display."

Rose tucked a stray strand of hair that had fallen onto her
neck back into place, trying not to dislodge the rest of her
curls in the process. "How about helping me find Bruce?" she
said heatedly as they started toward the back of the house
again, where the party was in full swing. "Maybe it'll help
keep your mind off Paul."

Lenore frowned. Right now nothing could take her mind
off Paul, and after talking to his father, she didn't know
whether to worry or get mad. One thing for sure. He was going to have some tall explaining to do, and she set her jaw
firmly as she joined her guests once more, trying to look calm
and unshaken.

Jason sat in the drawing room, his hands clasped tightly on
the arms of his wheelchair, the knuckles white as he stared
hard at Rose and Bruce. They looked every inch the typical
well-bred young society couple, yet the words Rose had just
uttered had left him momentarily speechless.

It was after ten. They'd been home less than fifteen
minutes, and during that time they'd managed to shatter every vestige of control he possessed.

He finally found his voice again, and this time it exploded
across the room. "How dare you!" he shouted at Rose, the
veins in his neck standing out like ropes. "How dare you accuse your brother of such a lecherous thing? I won't hear of
it, do you hear? I won't hear of it!"

Rose stood her ground. She swallowed hard, praying to
make him understand. She and Bruce had arrived home only
minutes ago to find the whole house in an uproar. Not only
had Jamie been stabbed and Bridget hurt, but Paul and Gigi
were still missing and Jason had been unable to track them
down. It had taken Rose only minutes to realize this was the
opportunity she'd been waiting for. However, she hadn't
counted on so much opposition, and Bruce's silence wasn't
helping any.

"Oh, yes, you will listen, Father," she said. "You'll listen
because it's the truth," she threw at him. "Where do you
think they are now, Father, your precious son and daughter?
They're together somewhere making love, that's where they
are. Probably in some secluded place where they won't be

disturbed." She shook her head. "Are you that blind, Father? Haven't you seen it? Why, it's so obvious it's sickening!"

See it? See it? My God, he'd never even looked for such a thing. How could he see it? Paul and Gigi? My God, she was his sister! Dammit! Rose and Bruce had let their jealousy and spite go too far this time. He'd have no more of their accusations. No more!

He turned on them viciously. "Stop it!" he cried. "I said I won't hear of it!" His voice lowered, but his face was livid. "You'll go up to your room, Rose, you and Bruce both," he said furiously, "and you'll think over what you've just said, and you'll see you've been wrong. Do you understand?" He paused, then went on more calmly. "Because if you don't, if I ever hear either one of you utter one more word on the subject, one more accusation, this night or at any other time, I'll disown you both. Do I make myself clear?"

Rose stared at him in disbelief. He wasn't listening, not to a word. He was shutting the truth out! She wanted to cry. To scream. To show him how wrong he was, but she knew it was hopeless when he was like this. Paul had always been his pet. His favorite. Paul could do no wrong. And Gigi . . . well, the sun rose and set on Gigi. She should have known he wouldn't believe them. What was the use?

She glanced quickly at Bruce standing beside her. His face was white. Even if she stood up to her father, Bruce would never back her up. He didn't have the backbone. Well, fine. She sneered. Let Gigi and Paul have their little clandestine meetings. Let them get themselves in deeper until it was too late, then she'd throw it in her father's face and see who had the last laugh. He wouldn't believe them—fine, then let him try to pick up the pieces.

She looked at her father, biting her lip nervously, trying not to enrage him further, then took a deep breath. "All right, Father," she finally said, her voice subdued. "I'll go to my room like a good little girl, so will Bruce," she said, and glanced at her brother, then back to Jason. "And I won't say one more word on the subject, I promise, not one more word. But just remember one thing. Someday, Father, we're going to be able to say, 'I told you so,' and when that day comes, both Bruce and I expect an apology from you. Good night!" and she turned to Bruce and grabbed his arm, pulling him toward the door.

"You'll get no apology from me, young lady," he shouted

as they walked away. "Never!" and he shook his fist at their retreating figures as they left the drawing room; then he slowly lowered his fist, staring after them.

He hadn't wanted to hurt them. He never wanted to hurt Rose and Bruce. He loved them. But they were so much like their mother. So ready to see faults in others, while they ignored their own. He'd put up with their coolness toward Gigi these past months, even let them beg off going places and doing things with her, but he couldn't ignore what had just happened. It was one thing to resent someone, but another to make accusations of such base behavior, such degradation.

Paul and Gigi in love? He shook his head, his gray eyes darkening as he motioned for Ahmed, who'd been standing silently, blending into the shadows of the room, and asked him to go fix him a drink; then he wheeled himself to the front window, staring out.

Paul and Gigi? Again the names rang in his head, sifting through his thoughts, and he remembered the look on Rose's face and her accusing words. "They're in love, Father. Don't you understand?" she'd said calmly as she stood in front of him only moments ago. "They're in love. Paul and Gigi are lovers."

In love . . . in love! The words kept ringing in his ears, and he shut his eyes, trying to keep them from finding a resting place, but it was useless. He opened his eyes again and stared out at the night, remembering the talk he'd had only yesterday with Paul. Could it be? Was Rose right? He remembered the look on Paul's face when he'd asked him if he loved Lenore, and then later when he'd brought Gigi home wet and hurt. There'd been something about the way he'd looked at her as he'd stood in the kitchen holding her in his arms. Something about the way her arms were fastened about his neck while she gazed up at him. He couldn't quite put his finger on it; yet, Rose had said it was obvious. Could it be true? Had he been blind? After all, he'd thrown them together perhaps more than he should. Oh, my God, what if she was right?

He tried to dismiss the thoughts that crowded in on him, tried to brush them aside and pretend they didn't exist, but it was no use. The more he tried to rationalize everything, the more confused he became, and by the time Ahmed handed him his brandy, he'd already made up his mind to wait up and have a long talk with Paul and Gigi when they returned. *If* they returned. There was a feeling of dread inside him as he realized there was a great number of things that needed answering.

9

André was restless. He sat in the overstuffed chair in front of the huge window, watching the city below as it celebrated the Fourth of July. His rooms were on the top floor of the Mexican consulate, giving him a full view of the street, and he leaned forward, trying to get a better look at the celebrants. Gas lights gleamed everywhere, and occasionally a firecracker sent sparks flying, scattering people on the sidewalks. He squinted into the crowd intently, hoping perhaps to recognize two familiar faces, but nothing.

The colonel and Ramón had left before he'd arrived back at the consulate. That was hours ago, long before dinner, and they'd left no message as to where they were going. If they'd gotten into trouble . . .

He stood up, jamming his hands into the pockets of his tight-fitting blue velvet pants, then turned away from the window and began to pace the room, gauging his steps along the edge of the Persian rug that covered the floor.

Bumblers, that's what they were. Why Rubio had sent them to back him up, he had no idea. The plan was to get the young woman back to Mexico any way they could, but preferably peaceably. Both the colonel and Ramón seemed to have forgotten that last word, "peaceably," and were determined to get her there by any means, fair or foul. They'd already bungled two attempts at kidnapping. The fools!

He'd told them there was only one way to get her there. Even Rubio agreed his plan was the best. It took longer, yes, but involved no danger, no suspicions. And besides, he thought to himself, straightening arrogantly, he enjoyed the prospect.

At first he'd been apprehensive. After all, it wasn't easy to make love to a woman who was unattractive, and he'd had

143

no idea what she looked like beforehand. But one look at her and he knew he had nothing to worry about. She was beautiful, sensuous. There was an earthy quality about her that made him tingle deep down in his loins every time he looked at her. And she liked him, he could tell. Not love yet, perhaps, but with time . . . After all, there was no big hurry. They had until the Christmas holidays to stop El Verdugo. Rubio said he wanted it done right. That's why he'd been chosen. The young woman had been raised in a cloistered convent and had had no contact with men since she was a child. So it would take the right sort of man to woo her. A man who knew about women, yet one that few women could resist.

He stopped for a minute and gazed across the room into the mirror on the wall above the sofa, studying himself. Straightening crisply, he tugged at the tails of the blue velvet suit jacket he wore, its short bolero length making his shoulders seem broader. As he raised his eyes, resting them on the face that stared back at him from the mirror, he was pleased. *Sí*, he was as good-looking as any man. His smile had even been called disarming, and what was it that one woman had told him? That his dark eyes had depths in them she longed to explore, that they were wickedly alive? He smiled, amused. Ah, yes, more than one woman had found him attractive. Why not this one?

He licked his lips, remembering earlier in the day when he'd held her in his arms and kissed her. Yes, she was aware of his virility, very much aware, and he was sure that it wouldn't be long before his conquest was complete. It just took a little time, a little charm, and a lot of planning.

He smiled knowingly, then turned from the mirror, startled, as the door suddenly burst open and the colonel and Ramón hurried in.

They looked tired and bedraggled as they half-stumbled into the room, cursing to each other over their misfortune; then both of them stopped short as their eyes fell on André.

"*Madre de Dios!*" exclaimed André, his hands moving to rest arrogantly on his hips as he watched them. "Where the devil have you two been?"

Colonel Alvarez, in dress uniform, hefted his gunbelt higher onto his hips, sucking his stomach in the best he could as he answered. "We have been trying to do what you refuse to do, Major," he said angrily, trying to ignore the shabby ap-

pearance he was making with his uniform scuffed and soiled.
"We have been here for weeks already, and all you can do is
kiss the lady's hand, send her flowers, and take her riding.
You accomplish nothing."

"And you're accomplishing more?" he asked, his dark eyes
flashing. He gestured at their disheveled appearance, and the
colonel's face reddened behind the huge mustache and busy
brows.

"At least we're trying," he boomed back.

"Ah, *sí*, you're trying," André continued, this time in
Spanish. "And the next time it's apt to be you who's caught
and not she. Then what will you do? Señor Larrabee holds
much weight in this city, his word is powerful. You two
could find yourselves cooling your heels in jail for a long
time if you keep this up."

The colonel snorted disagreeably as he strolled over to a
liquor cabinet on the inside wall and helped himself to a glass
of Madeira, trying to ease some of the pain from the
scratches on his face and hands and the bruises on his shins.

He downed the wine hurriedly, then sighed, turning to
André. "Major de los Reyes, it seems to me that you have
forgotten momentarily who holds the rank here," he said, his
voice a low growl. "I am the colonel, not you, and it is I who
give the orders around here, not you. Is that understood?"

André half-smiled, only his eyes showed no amusement.
They were dark, threatening. "Ah, but no, *mi coronel*, no, no,
no. You misunderstand," he reprimanded, watching the expression on the colonel's face change. "When you and your
aide, Lieutenant Chavez here, were chosen to escort me to
New York, there was no mention made whatsoever that you
were in charge. Don't you remember? You, sir, are part of
the regular army. You were sent along merely as an extra
protection, an extra precaution. I . . ."—he put his hand on
his chest—"I am one of the Bravi." He emphasized the words
slowly, meticulously. "One of Señor Romero Rubio's elite.
Therefore, my rank, although, as you reminded me, is only
that of a major, it takes preference over yours, and always
will, because I am one of the Bravi. It is I who was given the
order to take the lady back to Mexico with your help, not
you with my help. And there is only one way the young lady
will go, and that's willingly, and I'm the only one who can
accomplish that, understood? We are in the United States, not
Mexico, and this must be done with finesse."

The colonel's eyes narrowed. He didn't like this young hidalgo. He was too arrogant, too sure of himself. He stared at Major de los Reyes. The man was too handsome, too charming, too expert with the ladies, and he resented the muscular body that filled out the suit he wore. He had money, charm—everything Alvarez lacked—and André seemed to enjoy lording it over them.

André watched the colonel's eyes come to grips with the envy inside him and he interrupted his thoughts. "All right, what happened?" he finally asked as his gaze moved to Ramón Chavez's thin frame. He stared into his pinched face. Ramón's nose was thin, his chin pointed, and his lips a narrow line, making him look sinister even though he tried not to.

Ramón took a step toward the colonel, wincing, one hand moving up, rubbing his back as the colonel handed him a drink; then the colonel answered André. "The *Santo Domingo* sails tomorrow, Major," he said slowly. "Or had you forgotten?"

"No, I hadn't forgotten, Colonel."

"Then you remember that Señor Rubio suggested perhaps it would be easier to sail than go overland when he discovered the woman had left Texas for New York?"

André studied him intently. "I remember," he said.

"Good, then you will agree that if we had been able to capture the young lady tonight and put her aboard the *Santo Domingo*, our job would have been completed. She would have sailed to Mexico with no one the wiser. The mission would have been accomplished with time to spare, and we could have headed home."

"But you didn't capture her, did you?" he taunted, and the colonel reddened. "I asked you what happened, Colonel," he said more firmly, and this time the colonel downed another glass of wine before turning to face the younger man.

His face was distorted with anger and frustration. "It would have worked if it hadn't been for that young giant who showed up."

"What are you talking about? Start at the beginning."

Colonel Alvarez sighed, then walked toward the window, watching the crowds below. "We saw her leave the house shortly after dark, wearing the same blue cape she wore last night," he explained slowly. "She headed for the woods down by the river, so we followed." He paused momentarily, then went on. "There was no one about. It was perfect." He turned back to face André. "Our horses were in the woods down the road a piece, and all we had to do was grab her, tie her up, wrap her in a serape, and take her to the harbor where the ship waited. It was all very simple."

André studied him intently as he talked. "If it was so simple, then what went wrong?" he asked again.

The colonel swallowed hard, his large bloodshot eyes darkening. "We caught up with her and were in the process of tying her up, when suddenly some wild man tore into us from out of nowhere. *Madre de Dios!* He was taller than both Ramón and I. I don't even know where he came from, but he was all over us. There was nothing we could do. Nothing." He shook his head as his eyes lowered from André's face, and he continued reluctantly. "We dropped the girl and tried to defend ourselves, but it didn't do much good. He was as strong as an ox."

André stared at him hard now, his body tense, eyes alert. "But you're here?" he questioned suddenly, a feeling of dread in the pit of his stomach.

Colonel Alvarez' eyes met André's once more, and he straightened stubbornly. "We're here because Ramón can still use a knife," he answered, and saw André's eyes darken.

"A knife!" He threw up his hands. "A knife! You fools!" he cried, staring at them in disbelief. "You blundering idiots! Of all the stupidity!" He shook his head, running one hand through his dark hair, his jaw tightening. "That's just what Señor Rubio was afraid of. That's the very reason he said peaceably, if at all possible." He confronted them angrily. "Don't you think I could have tried the same thing?" he asked as the two men stared at him belligerently. "Violence was to be used only as a last resort, because there's too much chance of something going wrong, like tonight, and ending up not only without the girl, but maybe dead, or sitting in an American jail somewhere. If they trace you to the consulate . . ." He exhaled disgustedly, then closed his eyes momentarily, trying to control his temper. He opened his eyes, straightening again as he stared at them. "Is the girl all right?" he asked anxiously, and both men glanced quickly at each other, then back to André, their faces chagrined.

The colonel shrugged. "We have no idea," he said hesitantly. "Ramón used his knife on the man, and the girl fainted, I think. At least she fell to the ground when he attacked me and I lost my hold on her. I assume she fainted."

André's dark eyes snapped. "Then you have no idea whether the man is dead, the girl all right, or anything?" he asked.

Colonel Alvarez set the wineglass down and tried to suck in his stomach, straightening, trying to look as impressive as André. "Major de los Reyes," he answered, "I realize Ramón and I are peons as far as you are concerned. That we have not had the good fortune to have a rich father and an aristocratic mother as have you, but we are not stupid idiots, as you are so fond of calling us, and I resent the accusation. I did not become a colonel because of my good looks and charm." He sneered as he said it, knowing it was a deliberate insult to the major. "I became a colonel because of my abilities. I have been in enough battles and led enough campaigns in my lifetime to know that when the objective is as valuable as the young woman in question, that nothing is done to harm her in any way. We merely tried to kidnap her, not kill her. The young lady, I'm sure, is probably at home now, shaken perhaps, and telling everyone about her narrow escape. But as to her condition, I think I can safely say that no harm has been done."

André stared at the colonel, wishing fervently that Señor Rubio had let him come alone. "I certainly hope so," he offered, then sighed. "Well, we won't really know until tomorrow, will we?" He walked to the cabinet and poured himself a drink, holding the glass up after setting back the decanter, watching the clear deep burgundy liquid through the side of the delicately carved goblet. He inhaled, lowering his hand briskly, and took a quick sip, then turned to the colonel. "Perhaps, Colonel, now, since you've discovered that it doesn't pay to risk our mission on chance, you'll be content to leave the young woman alone and let me continue to do this in my own way. As Señor Rubio said, we have until the holidays." He eyed them warily. "Do I have your assurance that you'll make no more foolhardy attempts at taking her captive? No more harebrained schemes?"

Colonel Alvarez glanced quickly at Ramón, then back to André. He hated to admit it, but perhaps the major was right this time. Perhaps it was best to leave the whole thing in his hands. After all, things hadn't been going well for them, like tonight. But letting André have his own way didn't sit well with him. He frowned, staring at the younger man, then sighed. "All right, Major, for now the young lady will be solely in your hands. Ramón and I will merely wait, in case you fail. As you say, we have until the holidays."

André nodded as he watched the other man's eyes. "Good," he said more cheerfully. "And I promise you that if I fail to win her heart with a promise of marriage within three months, I'll not only give my consent to transporting her to Mexico forcibly, but I will help you both. Is it a bargain?" He stared at the colonel, his eyes glistening greedily.

The colonel smiled, pleased. "Done," he agreed heartily, pouring himself another drink, and they sealed their bargain in a toast to Mexico and the completion of their mission.

Gigi stirred in Paul's arms, her body warm and weak from his kisses. She wished the evening didn't have to come to an end. She stared up into his eyes, letting his hands caress her breasts. It seemed such a natural thing to let him do, and each caress filled her with tingling sensations that exploded deep inside her.

"Paul," she whispered softly, her lips still burning from his last kiss. "Paul, what's wrong with me?" she asked suddenly.

His eyes shifted uneasily as they continued to devour her. "What do you mean?"

Her face reddened faintly and she hesitated momentarily before going on. "Well," she finally murmured, "when you kissed me . . . I thought your lips would still the ache inside that I always felt when you're near, but instead, it's gotten worse. I hurt so inside. Oh, Paul, I'm so dumb. I've heard of men lusting for women, and I know that when a man makes complete love to a woman he possesses her body by joining her to him somehow, some way, and I think I know what that way is, and I know it must be a sinful act because it's always whispered about so secretively, but I'm not sure what it really is, and yet I feel as though it wouldn't be a sin and that I'd want it with you. To be a part of you . . . is it wrong?"

His hand moved from her breast to caress her neck, and suddenly he frowned. How foolish he'd been. His father said she'd been raised in a convent, where she probably had never heard anything about making love except what the girls whispered about when the sisters weren't around. He should have realized what was happening to her. She knew just enough to know something was missing, but she could only guess at what it was.

He cupped her chin in his hand, kissed her mouth tenderly, then explained it to her, letting the words sink in and find meaning now, when her body could understand because of its torment.

"So you see, my love, there's nothing wrong with you," he said huskily as he finished. "Or with love. It's the most natural thing in the world. Your body is only crying to be fulfilled. And, oh, God, how I wish I could do that for you."

A tear made its way to the corner of her eye, then rolled down the side of her face. "If you did, would it be called incest?" she asked hesitantly, and he stiffened, watching her intently, his eyes suddenly darkening.

"Where did you hear that word?" he asked.

Another tear fell from the corner of her eyes. She didn't want to tell him. She stared at him apprehensively. "This morning," she finally said. "Rose accused me of being in love with you. She said it was incest. I looked the word up in the dictionary in the library, but I still couldn't understand what it meant. I do now. I don't think anyone has ever spoken to me of the things you told me, and I didn't know. I had no idea." She shook her head. "Oh, Paul, what are we to do?"

His fingers touched her lips, stilling her as a physical pain tore through his breast. What was there for them to do? Nothing. Absolutely nothing! They couldn't go on like this, and he knew it. They had tonight, but tonight couldn't last forever.

He swallowed hard, his heart twisting inside him. "Rose is right, Gigi. For me just to love you isn't incest, but if I were to make love to you and let you become a part of me, then it would be incest."

"And incest is the lowest form of degradation a man can fall into, isn't it?" she said. "At least I think I heard someone say that once, a long time ago. Now I know what they meant."

Paul reached down slowly and gently lifted the bodice of her dress so that it once more covered her breasts, then let his fingers slowly fasten the hooks as another cannonade of fireworks exploded overhead. This time longer and louder than any that had filled the sky so far.

"It's over, darling," he said huskily, his fingers fumbling as he replaced the brooch between her breasts, and Gigi shivered, letting even more tears roll quickly onto the cloak that was rolled up and tucked beneath her head.

"Everything's over, isn't it?" she said bitterly, trying to hold back the tears, and he sighed, looking down at her. She looked so beautiful, her blue-green eyes glistening with tears.

"Not everything, my love," he whispered. "No matter what happens to us, I want you to know that I'll love you always."

"And I love you."

He stared at her a minute longer, drinking in the fragrance of her perfume, and the remembrance of the love they shared; then he looked away quickly and stood up, reaching his hand out for her to take, helping her to her feet.

She stood beside him, so small and fragile, yet so alive and vibrant. Just once more. He had to feel her in his arms just once more, with no restraints, and he pulled her to him, holding her close.

By the time they walked back to the park entrance where Tuttleby waited, the glow had left their eyes and a sad melancholy filled them both. They tried to smile and laugh for Tuttleby's sake, so he wouldn't be suspicious, but the smiles were forced, the laughter false, and all the way home in the carriage, although his arm was about her and her head rested on his shoulder, there was no joy for them.

Only as the carriage made its way up the drive did they finally give themselves up once more to the carefree abandon that had filled their hours together, and the kiss was filled with all the love they shared, ending for them both with a half-strangled sob of despair.

Paul was solemn as he reached up, taking her hand, helping her from the carriage, and his eyes scanned the house quickly as they started up the steps. There was a light on in the drawing room as well as the foyer, and when Ahmed silently met them in the foyer, nodding knowingly toward the drawing room, Paul tensed.

Jason's mood was black as he waited for them. He'd been unable to forget Rose's accusation, and the thought had sickened him physically. He'd watched the carriage come slowly up the drive, and now as he waited for Ahmed to bring them to him, his hands were wet with perspiration, his heart pounding.

Paul was well-composed as he came through the door, ushering Gigi ahead of him, and Jason stared at them fiercely.

"Father," said Paul easily, "what . . . why on earth are you still up?"

"Why . . . ? Paul, where the devil have you two been?" Jason exploded.

Paul stopped, staring at him, then forced a disarming smile to his lips. "Now, before you get all worked up and end up making yourself sick again, you could let me explain," he said.

Jason frowned, straightening stubbornly in his wheelchair. "Explain, then."

Paul avoided looking at Gigi, keeping his eyes on his father. "When we left here, we got to talking, and one thing led to another. I decided Gigi'd seen enough of fancy parties and balls. I wanted to show her something different." He shrugged. "So I took her to Central Park."

"Central Park!"

Paul looked chagrined at his father's surprise. "What's wrong with that? She'd been there for the band concert, but the Fourth of July's different. The dancing, the whole atmosphere. You know yourself what it's like there on the Fourth."

Jason glanced at Gigi. She flushed and looked uncomfortable. He confronted Paul again. "There are no telephones between here and Central Park?" he asked.

"None that were free." Paul tried to be nonchalant. "The crowds were thick," he explained. "I couldn't get within ten feet of a telephone."

Jason studied him intently. It was logical, and he could understand Paul's motives. Paul was forever looking for entertainment outside his social realm, and so had he at Paul's age. That's how he'd met Gigi's mother. He turned to Gigi. "Did you enjoy yourself, my dear?" he asked.

Her eyes lowered self-consciously. "Yes," she answered hesitantly. "It was much different than I expected." She glanced briefly at Paul, then back to her father. "There was so much noise, but the fireworks were beautiful."

Jason inhaled, glancing quickly from one to the other. There was something . . . He brushed the thought aside momentarily, then addressed Paul again. "We've had some trouble tonight," he said quickly.

Paul, who'd begun to feel uncomfortable too beneath his father's scrutiny, frowned. "What kind of trouble?"

Jason told them of Jamie's brush with death while rescuing Bridget, and for a few minutes both Gigi and Paul forgot their own problems.

"Are you sure they're both all right?" asked Gigi.

Jason nodded. "Both of them are fine. But there are a few questions I'd like you to answer, my dear," he went on. "Did you give the young girl one of your dresses and your cloak to wear?"

Gigi stared at him, puzzled, then became embarrassed as she remembered. She blushed, "I . . . I hope you don't mind, sir. Yes, I did," she said. "But what does that have to do with what happened?"

Jason's eyes met Paul's; then he looked back at Gigi. "The girl said she was sure the man who attacked her thought she was you," he explained. "And I can see why. She was wearing the clothes you'd given her. And it was the same cloak you'd worn last night."

Gigi felt Paul's eyes on her, and she looked at him, bewildered, remembering the narrow escape she'd had the night before. "But why would anyone want to kidnap me?" she asked.

Jason snorted irritably. "Why? Doesn't this house and the fact that you're my daughter explain why?" he asked. He looked at Paul. "I've been thinking, Paul," he said. "Perhaps the trouble she had last night that you thought was unimportant is more important than we give it credit for."

Paul's frown deepened. His father was right, but he didn't want to have to tell him. Jason looked pale. He shouldn't even be concerning himself with all this. He was getting too upset.

"Father," suggested Paul, "why don't you go to bed and get some sleep and let me handle it for you? There's really no need for you to be upset—"

"No need!" Jason had been watching the two of them closely as they talked. There was an intimacy between them. The way their eyes caressed one another. He hadn't wanted to confront them with it, but it was no use. He couldn't forget. Dammit! He just couldn't forget. "I didn't just stay up to tell you about the servants, Paul," he finally said, his fingers drumming nervously on the arms of his wheelchair. "There was another, much more pressing matter that kept me awake."

For the first time in his life Paul was unable to gauge the mood his father was in. "Oh?" he said slowly, and Jason swallowed hard, sighing.

His brooding eyes lowered momentarily; then he raised

them, tilting his chin up stubbornly at the same time, his fingers clenching nervously on his lap robe. "I heard something about you tonight, Paul, that I didn't want to believe," he said finally. "Something so base that I was sure it was a lie. Now, after thinking it over, I'm not so certain anymore."

Paul glanced at Gigi apprehensively. "Perhaps Gigi had better say good night then, Father," he said. "If it's so terrible. I'd hate for her to hear me being accused of anything low and vile."

Jason shook his head as Gigi made a move to leave the room. "No, stay here, my dear," he insisted sternly, stopping her; then his voice lowered, became more resonant. "After all, this also concerns you."

Gigi hesitated, standing motionless, staring at Jason, her feet rooted to the spot. She couldn't move now if she'd wanted to. Her legs were shaking too much. "It . . . it concerns me?" she asked softly, one hand nervously fingering the diamond-and-ruby brooch.

Jason nodded. "Yes." Then he turned to Paul. "What I heard is sickening, Paul, and I've been trying all evening to shut it from my mind, but now, looking at the two of you . . . I have been blind, haven't I?" he said.

Paul grimaced. "What do you mean, blind?"

Jason was through toying. His deep gray eyes were no longer brooding, but hard, demanding. "You're in love with her, aren't you, Paul?" he asked abruptly.

Paul's eyes grew guarded. "In love?" He straightened, a sickening feeling gripping his insides. "In love with whom, Father?" he asked.

Jason's eyes narrowed. "Don't pretend with me, Paul. It won't work," he cried bitterly. "You know damn well what I'm talking about. Now I know why the short temper, restlessness. You're in love with Gigi, aren't you, Paul?" he asked furiously, and his eyes moved to rest on Gigi as he spoke, and he saw her tremble.

Paul stood rigid for a moment, staring at his father. How could he deny the words? His heart was in agony as he too turned to look at Gigi, who'd suddenly become very pale. He couldn't let anyone do this to her. Not even his father. He had to deny it. "Who told you a lie like that?" he asked, his voice firm and steadier than he'd thought it would be, but Jason wasn't appeased.

"Never mind who told me," he said. "The point is that it's true." His eyes bored steadily into Paul's. "Isn't it?"

"No!" Paul's jaw tightened as the anger began to well up inside him. "No, it's not true," he went on. "Not a word of it. It's a damn lie!"

"A lie?" Tears filled Jason's eyes as he stared at his elder son, then glanced at the lovely young woman he'd fathered so many years ago. "Then if it's a lie, why do I feel in here"—he struck his breast forcefully—"that it's the truth? That Gigi's the woman you haven't been able to get out of your system? That she's the reason you've been neglecting Lenore so shamefully? Why?"

"Who knows why. Maybe because you loved her mother. Maybe because you know we're so much alike, you and I. How should I know why!"

Jason's voice rose in volume as he looked once more at Gigi. "You, Gigi. If he won't tell me, then maybe it'll have to come from you. Gigi, I'm asking you to tell me the truth," he demanded. "What is it between you? Are you in love with Paul?"

Paul saw the tears in her eyes and her trembling hands. "For God's sake, Father," he shouted, "leave her alone! She doesn't have to listen to your accusations!"

"Doesn't she? She's in this house, isn't she? She's under my roof! I brought her into the world, and, by God, now I have a right to know!" He squared off once more at Gigi, his face livid, certain now that his worst fears were true. "Gigi, I demand you tell me," he yelled stubbornly. "Are you in love with Paul?"

She stared at him transfixed, the tears that had slowly been forming earlier suddenly springing to her eyes. How could she deny her heart? She tried. She opened her mouth and tried to speak, but the words just wouldn't come.

"Oh, God!" she moaned helplessly as she suddenly burst into tears, and Jason knew.

Now he knew the answer as Paul turned abruptly and watched Gigi lift her skirts and bolt for the stairs, running up them as fast as she could while tears streamed unchecked down her cheeks.

Gigi knew Jason and Paul were watching, and she knew that her outburst had been the same as a declaration, but she didn't care. Suddenly it didn't matter anymore, because she was numb inside. As she turned on the upstairs landing, heading down the hall toward her room, Jason's voice once more echoed in the drawing room downstairs.

"My God, Paul, how could you let something like this happen?" he cried passionately as he stared at his son.

Paul turned to face him, his gray eyes blazing. "Me? How could *I* let it happen? You brought her here, Father, not I!"

"But I didn't bring her here for you to seduce!"

"I didn't seduce her!"

"What did you do to her, then, Paul? My God, she's your sister! What have you done?"

He shook his head. "Nothing! I've done nothing!"

Jason pointed toward the stairs. "Nothing made that child run from the room in tears?"

"She's not a child, Father. She's a woman," he said bitterly. "Or hadn't you noticed!"

"She's barely out of her teens, Paul. The product of a convent. What does she know of men and their ways? If you've ruined her . . . ?"

Paul's jaws clenched. "I told you, I didn't touch her."

"Then what did you do? Something happened!" Jason's fist came down on the arm of his wheelchair. "I want to know, Paul, and I want to know now. I have to know what went on between you, do you hear?" His eyes were stormy, darkening to a steely gray. "I want to know, are you in love with her, Paul? Answer me!"

"All right! All right!" yelled Paul, his body taut with anger, his control held by a slim thread; then his voice lowered passionately, his breathing erratic as he towered over his father. "Yes, I'm in love with her," he answered slowly, his eyes hard and cold as they watched his father's face. "I fell in love with her the first time I saw her propped up in that big four-poster bed." He turned from his father and walked to the fireplace, staring into the cold, dead ashes, but not really seeing them. His mind was miles away on a lonely spot in Central Park with fireworks exploding overhead. "I fell in love with her smile, her warmth, her vibrant zest for life," he went on. "Just to look at her is like . . . like . . ." He suddenly whirled to face his father once more. "We had one night together, Father. Tonight! One night out of our lives. I know it was crazy, insane, we both did, but we had to have something."

Jason's face looked sallow and gaunt. "What happened, Paul?" he asked again, his voice barely a whisper.

Paul flinched. "Nothing," he answered, his anger of moments ago held in check. "It's the truth, Father," he went on. "Nothing more happened except a few stolen kisses."

Tears welled up in Jason's eyes again as he stared at Paul, wishing this whole nightmare would end. "But she's your sister, Paul," he pleaded unsteadily. "My God, son," he gasped, "she's your own flesh and blood."

Paul straightened, his tall frame trembling. "Don't you think I don't know that?" he cried. "Don't you think I haven't thought of it every waking moment? Do you think it's fun being in love with a woman I can't touch? My God, Father, it's torment! It's a living hell!"

He turned again toward the fireplace, leaning against the mantel, gazing once more into the empty grate as Jason stared at him.

Jason watched him for a long time, and the silence in the room was deadly; then he spoke. "There'll be no more, Paul," he said, his hands clenching the arms of his wheelchair so tightly the knuckles were white. "There'll be no more nights like tonight. This unnatural thing between you and your sister will be no more. It's ended here and now, do you understand?"

Paul didn't answer, he couldn't, his insides were tied in knots, his mouth dry.

Jason went on, determined. "There's only one way out of all this as far as I can see," he said grimly, grasping for something to hang on to. "Your wedding's set for the twelfth of August. We'll move the date up. Instead, you and Lenore will be married a week from Saturday, on July 15. I'm sure that'll work. I'll leave the arrangements up to you. You can talk Lenore into it. Use some sort of excuse. You're in a hurry, can't wait . . . you can come up with something. If I know Lenore, she'll probably welcome the change."

Paul clenched his fists, lifting his head, gazing across the room. "I imagine she will," he said wearily.

Jason shook his head as he stared at his elder son. "Paul, it's no good," he admonished. "I know how you must feel, but it's unhealthy, and if anyone found out . . ." His eyes settled on Paul's ruggedly handsome face. "I never dreamed you were capable of something like this, Paul," he said. "Never in all my years." He looked bewildered. "I trusted you with that girl, Paul, and you broke that trust. I hold you and you alone responsible for what happened, do you understand?"

Again Paul was silent, staring across the room at nothing. He understood only too well.

"But the damage has been done," Jason went on, exhaling nervously. "What matters now, Paul, is that we have to rectify it." He was hoping to capture his son's attention once more. "Paul, someone has to explain to Gigi. Someone has to try to make her understand," he said. "What must the poor girl think, having you kissing her, trying to make love to her. No wonder she's in tears. My God, Paul, how could you!" he cried.

"Because I'm in love with her!" Paul yelled, and Jason flinched.

"Well, I won't have it, Paul. Not in this house. I won't!" he demanded. "It has to end here and now. This very minute."

Paul straightened to his full height, his eyes no longer brooding, but dark and forbidding, his face drawn into an unfeeling mask of cynicism. He remembered the tears in Gigi's eyes, and the youthful innocence that betrayed her as they lay together in the grass. He remembered the kisses and caresses, and the words of love, and his heart turned over inside him. It was over; he had had his night. A night he'd never forget. A night that could never be again, and he knew it. Responsible? Maybe he was responsible, he didn't know. He turned to face his father.

"Don't worry, Father, it's ended," he said huskily, his voice vibrant with emotion. "It ended tonight. We knew it couldn't last, that it should never be, and we made a promise to ourselves that we'd try to forget what we feel for each other. What happened was really not of our doing, you know. It was just something . . . I can't explain it. I don't think Gigi could either. You can't really explain and rationalize feelings. They're too elusive." He tilted his head back momentarily and closed his eyes, then opened them again and looked once more at Jason. "Don't worry, I haven't gone completely mad," he said. "You're right. It can never be, and I know it," he went on as he walked slowly toward Jason. "I'm not about to shout to the world that I'm in love with my sister, Father, nor will Gigi care to admit to anyone her feelings for me. We both know how hopeless it is and that there's no future together for us. We knew it months ago."

"Months ago?" Jason frowned as his son came closer. "You mean the affair's been going on that long?"

"Affair?" Paul stopped abruptly, staring at his father. "Who said we were having an affair?"

"Rose said—"

"Rose said?" He sneered, realizing now who'd done the first accusing. "I might have known," he said. "For your information, Father, we weren't having an affair," he explained. "There's been nothing more between us than words and a few embraces."

"But you don't understand, Paul," said Jason. "If Rose could see what's been going on, then so could others." He looked up into his son's face. "I only hope to God that we're not too late, Paul," he went on. "That no one else has seen what Rose saw, what I've been too blind to see."

"They didn't," Paul insisted. "There's been nothing to see. We've been very discreet, and there'll be nothing more for them to see, Father," he said slowly. "There'll be no reason for anyone to say a thing, because it's over. I'll be the perfect brother, epitome of decency, there'll be no scandal, no need for any more accusations. You're right, of course. I'll marry Lenore and forget Gigi. That is, I'll try to forget."

Jason flinched. "Paul?"

Paul's eyes found those of his father, and Jason felt a physical pain shoot through him at the look in his son's eyes. Paul looked defeated.

"I'm sorry, Paul," he apologized. "I wouldn't have had this happen for the world, and you know it."

A cynical half-smile pulled at the corners of Paul's mouth as he stared at the man who'd caused him so much heartache. "I know," he answered softly. "But isn't there a place in the Bible where it says the sins of the father are passed on to the children?"

Jason's eyes filled with tears as he realized Paul was blaming him. "Forgive me, Paul, please," he pleaded. "Please, son, forgive me," but Paul was in no mood to grant forgiveness.

It would take more than a few empty, lifeless words to take the chill from his heart. It would take more than an apology to still the ache inside him, because he knew that no matter what, even though he did as his father wished and married Lenore, his life would never be the same again. He couldn't forgive his father, at least not yet, not with the pain so new and unbearable.

He sighed. "Maybe someday, Father," he finally said as he stared down at him bitterly. "Maybe someday. But not now. Good night." He turned, walking to the staircase, and Jason sat below, with tears in his eyes and an ache in his heart that couldn't be stilled, and watched him ascend.

10

Gigi stirred restlessly in the huge satiny surroundings of her bed. The soft pink and dove-gray brocades and satins that had once felt luxurious and sensuous against her bare skin now felt cold and impersonal. She shook her dark, curly head. It felt two sizes too big, and her mouth was dry, like cotton. She'd cried herself to sleep last night, and now her eyes hurt too. She'd been lying on her stomach, and turned over now, curling onto her side, staring unhappily across the sunlit room.

Her red velvet dress lay crumpled in a heap on the floor where she'd stepped out of it, her petticoats were strewn half off, half on the vanity seat, and the diamond-and-ruby brooch glittered from where it lay on the carpet near them. She exhaled wearily, having remembered throwing it across the room last night as she'd tearfully undressed, not caring where it landed, only wanting to get rid of it.

She punched at the pillow beneath her head, then rubbed her temple gingerly, remembering everything that happened. Her evening with Paul, the quarrel with Jason. It wasn't fair! The whole thing wasn't fair. She should never have let herself fall in love with Paul. It was impossible. And what they'd done last night was unforgivable. But how did you tell your heart not to care? She'd tried. Lord, how she'd tried.

Now Jason knew, and she wondered what had happened after she'd left them last night. Had Paul told his father everything? Even if he had, though, it didn't matter. Not anymore, because last night was not only the beginning but also the end. One night to last a lifetime, they'd agreed. And now it was over. Everything was over.

She sighed, pushing herself into a sitting position, shoving the unruly curls from in front of her blue-green eyes, trying

161

to get enough gumption to get up. She was just about resigned to the fact that she'd have to dress herself this morning, when she heard a noise and looked up. Bridget stood in
the doorway to the powder room, hands on hips, staring at
her. She must have come into the room while she was still
asleep. That's why the drapes were drawn already. They'd
been closed last night. It was the morning sun streaming in at
the French doors that had wakened her.

She swung her feet to the floor and stared intently at
Bridget, momentarily forgetting her own miserable plight.
"Bridget, are you all right?" she asked anxiously as she sat on
the edge of the bed frowning.

Bridget's usual smile softened the corners of her mouth,
but this morning it wasn't as broad, and her voice was raspy
as she spoke. "Yes, I'm all right, Miss Gigi," she said. "But
Jamie's still pretty bad. Although the doctor said as how he'll
get better."

Gigi shook her head as Bridget walked over and took a
blue lace dressing gown from the closet, bringing it to her.
She stood up and slipped it on, covering the matching lace
nightgown she was wearing.

"Father told us what happened when we got home last
night," she said, fastening the buttons on the dressing gown.
"He said you told him you thought whoever attacked you
thought you were me."

Bridget glanced at her nervously, nodding. "I'm sure of it,
Miss Gigi," she offered. "Just as he grabbed me, he said,
'Well, so we meet again, Señorita.' I've never met anybody
who talks like that, but I know I've heard Mr. de los Reyes
call you señorita."

Gigi's eyes suddenly grew wary, and she gazed thoughtfully
across the room. André? Could he be mixed up in this? A
tingling sensation coursed up her back, making the hair at the
nape of her neck prickle.

"Bridget, it . . . did you recognize the men?" she asked
hesitantly.

Bridget sighed. "Don't worry, Miss Gigi. It wasn't Mr. de
los Reyes," she assured her. "I thought of that too. But I
know it wasn't him."

Gigi was relieved.

Bridget walked over and picked up the brooch, looking it
over absentmindedly, then set it on the vanity and began to
gather Gigi's clothes up from the floor. "I know Mr. de los

Reyes' voice," she went on. "These men sounded rough. You know, like the difference between a man who's a gentleman and one who ain't. Like Mr. Paul. Now, he's a gentleman."

Gigi's face paled suddenly at the mention of Paul's name, but Bridget didn't notice. She was too busy picking up the clothes.

"I knew I should've come up and helped you last night," she continued as she shook out the red dress, trying to straighten the folds that had creased it as it lay on the floor overnight. "I told Mr. Larrabee I was all right, but he insisted he'd have Biddy help you." She shook her head. "I can tell from this mess, though, that nobody helped you, did they?"

Gigi exhaled, walking toward the French doors, staring out at the day that was warmer than the past few days. "I guess we got home too late," she explained, once more remembering her helpless situation.

She let Bridget pick the things up and put them away while she stood leaning against the doorframe. Last night! It was still so vivid in her mind, yet something . . . She tried to remember. Paul had revealed so much to her, things he'd thought at first she'd known. And that was something else. Why hadn't she known? Didn't all grown men and women know these things? Rose seemed to. Why not her? She scowled, rubbing her forehead, trying to reach somewhere into the past for an answer, trying to catch a glimpse of what her life might have been. They said she'd been raised in a convent. Then why couldn't she remember? There was nothing.

The things Paul had done to her, the caresses, the way he kissed her and made her feel, were new to her. Somehow she knew no man had ever touched her as Paul had, and the pleasure had been almost unbearable. This was the love that people talked about. And it was the first time she'd ever remembered experiencing it. She closed her eyes and covered them with her hand, trying to force her thoughts back to before the train wreck, but it was useless. Whatever was there, was just beyond her reach.

She sighed, straightening as Bridget called that her bathwater was ready, and during the bath, as she stroked the washcloth across her full breasts, down her trim legs, and between her thighs, she wondered what it was like to be fulfilled as Paul had explained to her, wondering what it would be like to be a part of him, and she trembled more than once at the thought.

Bridget laid out her clothes while she bathed, and now she slipped into her underclothes and petticoats, then put on the apricot-colored cotton, its skirt embroidered with delicate white flowers, their green leaves trailing haphazardly around the bottom of the skirt. The bodice too was embroidered in larger white flowers, the huge sleeves with white lace inserts puffing out at the shoulders, leaving her arms bare. Bridget fastened the dress up the back, then draped a plain gold chain about Gigi's neck, letting the fire opal at the end of it, surrounded by delicate gold filigree, rest comfortably on the bare skin above her generous bosom. The matching earrings were placed in her ears after her hair was secured atop her head so the curls cascaded as far as the nape of the neck.

"There," said Bridget, satisfied at last. She and Gigi had talked the whole while Gigi was dressing, and Gigi had managed to worm the story of exactly what happened the night before out of the young girl, and Bridget had also managed to discover about Paul and Gigi's excursion to Central Park, although the reason for it, and what happened while they were there, were omitted in the telling.

Gigi stared back at her reflection in the mirror as Bridget set the last earring in place, and her insides suddenly began to constrict. She was all ready to go down to breakfast, to start a new day, only she didn't want to. How on earth was she going to face her father? She had no idea what he and Paul had said after she'd left them. What if he ordered her out of the house? Where would she go? What would she do? What if he wouldn't even let her talk to Paul again?

Her hands began to perspire, and her fingers twitched nervously. What if Paul told him about the things they'd said about the things he did? How could she face Jason? And what of Paul? Last night it had seemed so natural to be with him and let him touch her. This morning, now, in the clear light of day, she wasn't so sure. She was so mixed up. What would he say when he saw her again?

A few minutes later her worst fears were laid to rest as she entered the dining room and joined the rest of the family for breakfast. But now another fear gripped her. Not only was she able to face Paul, but his manner toward her was so casual and offhand that for a moment she wasn't even sure last night had ever happened.

His clothes this morning were casual. White pants, deep blue Prince Albert frock coat, striped shirt. Even his cravat was tied at a rakish angle that was unusual for Paul, and he treated her no differently than he'd treated her any other time the past few months. In fact, one might say he even seemed less concerned with her presence than usual, although he was charming, considerate, and quite civil, throwing in remarks now and then about the picnic he and Lenore were going on this afternoon.

Jason too acted as if nothing had happened, although she did notice the dark shadows beneath his eyes that hadn't been there the night before, and a sad droop to his mouth that spoiled his handsomely distinguished face. Even his hair seemed to have a little more gray in it this morning, and his eyes were more intense than usual. Other than that, however, his words were the same usual morning banter about business and his own social world.

Even Rose, who was always making snide remarks, seemed less concerned with annoying Gigi this morning, and she and Bruce kept up a lively chatter about the holiday parties they'd attended.

Gigi ate slowly, quieter than usual, listening to them, a feeling of dread in the pit of her stomach. She had been afraid to face them, afraid they'd accuse her again, afraid of the consequences of what she'd done, but instead, all of them were acting as if nothing had happened. As if last night had never been. Not one word was mentioned. No reference to the fact that they'd missed the Van Der Lindens' party or to Central Park. Nothing.

Even Paul. Had it meant so little to him that he could forget so quickly? She knew they'd both made a vow to forget, but vows were so easy to say, harder to keep. Had his been easy to stick to because he really hadn't cared? Had he meant what he said last night about loving her always, or had he only been playing her for a fool?

She swallowed hard, trying to ease the lump in her throat as she listened to the conversation around her. And as Paul stood up, excusing himself, explaining that he had work to do before going out, she looked directly into his eyes, and the lump in her throat sank to her stomach. His eyes were hard and cold, unfeeling, and she clenched her teeth bitterly. Well, what more had she expected? He'd said it was over. At least he could forget, and she attacked her eggs Benedict with a vengeance. If he could forget, so could she, and she forced a determined smile to her lips as she finished her breakfast and one of the maids came in, announcing that André de los Reyes was waiting to talk to her on the telephone.

A few minutes later she stood alone in the huge entrance hall. She straightened her skirt deliberately, put a stray strand of hair back into place, then picked up the receiver from where it dangled beside the big brown box on the foyer wall.

"Hello?" she said unsteadily, her mind made up to forget Paul, her heart crying against it.

"Good morning, Gigi." André sounded quite anxious. "Did you have a happy holiday?" he asked.

She tried to sound nonchalant. "As well as can be expected. We went to Central Park," she said, her voice strained, using the "we" so he wouldn't have any suspicions about her and Paul going alone. This way he'd have no idea who might have been included.

"Central Park?" He sounded a little surprised. "I thought you were staying at home last night."

"We were going to go to the Van Der Lindens', but changed our minds." She stared at the floor, watching the tip of her white patents. There was a speck of dirt on the toe, and she lifted her foot, wiping it off on her petticoat, then inspected it again, making sure it was gone. She tucked her foot back beneath the edge of her dress, concentrating once more on André. "Did you have a nice holiday?" she asked.

"It wasn't a holiday for me, Gigi, remember?" he reminded her. "The consulate was closed in observance, but I had things to do."

"You worked last evening then?"

"Sí. But tell me"—his voice was warm, vibrant—"are you still going to the theater with me this evening?"

Her breath caught in her throat. That's right, she'd forgotten. She'd asked Jason when she and André had returned from their ride the afternoon before, and he'd consented. On one condition, that is. That Paul and Lenore make it a foursome. After last night, though, maybe things had changed.

"I am as far as I know," she said; then her voice lowered unsteadily. "I hope you don't mind that Father insisted Paul and his fiancée come along."

"No . . . not at all," he replied. "I guess I can hold your hand when your big brother's not looking. One duenna's as bad as another. At least he doesn't intimidate me as much as that silent servant of your father's does, *querida*," he said. "Sometimes Ahmed looks at me as if he thinks I'm going to eat you."

She half-laughed. "Oh, André, really."

"It's not funny, *querida*," he said unhappily. "It's true, and it's not the easiest thing in the world to make love to a woman under those circumstances, you know." He went on, his voice lowering, registering a note of latent passion. "But then, if that's the only way I can see you, *mi querida*, I don't care if a hundred Ahmeds are lurking in the shadows. Just so I can be with you."

She didn't answer. She couldn't. She just held the receiver, staring into the mouthpiece, remembering yesterday afternoon when they'd gone riding.

"Tonight, then, Gigi?" he asked softly, and she sighed.

"Tonight," she answered.

"Bien! Hasta luego."

"Good-bye," she said, and hung up, her emotions in a turmoil.

What was it about André? She wasn't in love with him, she knew. But there was a certain charm, a magnetism about him that was exciting and at the same time almost frightening. Although his kisses yesterday had not had the same effect on her that Paul's kisses had, she had to admit that they did arouse some feelings in her. Feelings deep in her loins similar to the ones she felt last night as she lay on the sand, letting Paul caress her breasts. Why?

Was it a natural way to feel that had nothing to do with love? What that why Paul was acting the way he was today? Was he aroused last night simply because he was a man and she was a woman? Could she feel the same way with André without love?

If only she had someone to talk to, maybe she could understand. But there was no one, and she turned quickly, heading for the library, hoping perhaps to find an answer somewhere in the myriad of books lining the walls.

Paul sat in his office staring at the papers in front of him, unable to concentrate on anything. All he could see were her bright blue-green eyes gazing at him, bewildered, beseeching him, waiting for a sign, anything to show that he cared. He had given her none. To have done so, to have let his guard down, would have been his ruin. As it was, treating her no differently than he treated Rose, acting as if he didn't care, was the hardest thing he'd ever had to do in his life. She'd looked so lovely this morning. So provocatively sensuous, the dress she wore clinging lusciously to every curve, her eyes alive and warm.

He pushed the papers from in front of him and stood up, walking to the window, shoving his hands deep into his pockets, staring out at the beautiful summer day. Here along the Hudson the beauty of the land was all one could ask for, with its rolling hills, fertile valleys, and cool forests. That's why his father had built here. Most of the other prominent New York families, like the Van Der Lindens', built in town on the boulevard. He'd have none of it.

But now, looking at the brilliant sky and gently sloping landscape, Paul remembered the early-morning rides teaching Gigi how to handle a horse, her fresh young mind grasping everything so quickly. She'd been so eager to learn and seemed sometimes to remember another time when she had ridden, so riding had come easily to her.

He cursed softly to himself, his jaw tightening, and tried to rationalize his feelings. He hadn't wanted to fall in love with her. He hadn't even realized it was love until that night on the terrace after André had left. At first he'd kept telling himself it was merely brotherly concern. But when he'd held her in his arms, then tried to tell her what love was . . .

He closed his eyes, pressing his fingertips to the bridge of his nose. It was over. What was the use of even thinking about it? He straightened stubbornly. One thing for sure. Brooding and conjuring up old memories was no way to forget. The best way to forget was to concentrate on another woman. After all, he still had Lenore. She was stunning, sophisticated, and any man would be happy at the prospect of having her for a wife. Hadn't he proposed to her because he'd been unable to find any other woman who possessed all the attributes he'd always considered necessary for becoming Mrs. Paul Larrabee? And he'd escorted enough women around to be able to pick and choose. He should be happy. Why wasn't he? Why couldn't he be content with Lenore? She was everything he'd always told himself he wanted in the woman he loved. That's why this whole thing had him so baffled.

If he was going to fall in love, then why wasn't it with one of the women who'd wandered in and out of his life over the years? They'd all been enchanting, sophisticated. He'd been the envy of other men because of the women he knew, and even now, with his engagement to Lenore. Then why had he fallen in love with an unsophisticated girl, barely out of the cradle? Paul Larrabee, man-about-town, brought low by a winsome smile and a pair of innocent blue-green eyes, but the worst blow of all was that they should belong to his half-sister. Damn!

He turned abruptly from the window, pulling a watch from his pocket, checking the time, then headed for the door.

Lenore sat in the Van Der Lindens' library, her mind far from the book she was reading. Paul had called earlier, requesting to see her, and she'd invited him for the picnic lunch they'd had to cancel the day before. Today was Wednesday, and she knew he wasn't used to taking time off from work during the week, but if he could always find time for Gigi, he could do the same for her. He hadn't protested. She waited impatiently, going over what she was going to say and how she was going to act toward him. His explanation had better be a good one. The toe of her blue kid shoe tapped nervously on the marble floor.

Things were awkward and strained between them when Paul arrived, and they said little to each other except the usual greetings; then the small buggy, driven by Paul, pulled away from the house and moved on down the road. But later, settling down in a meadow on the banks of the river, spreading the tablecloth out, Lenore knew it was now or never. She had to know. She'd been cool toward him on the ride, the few words between them stilted.

She slipped from her suit jacket and sat down, spreading her deep blue satin skirt about her, fluffing the huge leg-o'-mutton sleeves on her white silk blouse, billowing them out. Then she reached up and took the elaborate hat from her flaxen hair. It was an extravagant little piece of blue felt with satin bows, white velvet rosettes that resembled flowers, and dainty ostrich plumes. She set it aside, glancing at Paul as she did so.

He dropped to the ground beside her and began opening the picnic basket, oblivious of the grass stains he was getting on the knees of his white flannel pants. Removing his dark blue frock coat, he tossed it aside next to his straw hat, took off the cravat, and loosened the collar of his shirt, then rolled the sleeves up and started removing the things from the picnic basket.

"Are you ready to explain yet, Paul?" she asked miserably, trying to hide her annoyance.

He stopped, a bottle of wine in his hand, looking at her hesitantly. "Are you ready to forgive me?" he countered.

She pursed her lips. "It all depends on what there is to forgive."

His cool gray eyes met her angry blue ones, and he stared at her for a long moment. "Maybe we'd better eat something first," he said.

She shook her head. "I couldn't, not just yet."

"All right." He put the bottle back in the basket, then sat back, gazing at her. She was doing a magnificent job of holding her temper in check. He had to give her credit. "It was a rotten thing to do, wasn't it?" he said.

The blue in her eyes deepened. "Why, Paul?" was all she asked, and he watched the anger tightening her jaw.

"Because once in a while I get fed up with the artificial life we lead," he confessed. "I wanted to be with the other half for a change, show Gigi what a good time really is. So we went to Central Park."

"Central Park?"

"That's right. But not the Central Park you know. Not the bridle paths or just to ride through in a fancy carriage showing off. We walked around through the crowds. There's always a big celebration there on the Fourth of July, with dancing and fireworks."

She frowned. "Do you go there often just to walk around?"

"Once in a while."

"But never with me."

"You wouldn't like it, Lenore, and you know it," he said. "It's just not for you. At least not where I go. I mix in with the everyday people. People you'd consider riffraff. It's a place where I can relax without the pressures of being Paul Larrabee. Where I can lose myself in the crowd and just be a person. Sometimes I have to get away, and there are times when Gigi feels the same. So last night we did."

She watched his eyes as he spoke. They were hard, uncompromising, as if waiting for her to challenge him, and if she did, she was sure she'd lose him. Paul Larrabee wasn't the type of man to cater to a woman just to keep peace. He had a mind of his own. You didn't tell him to do anything, you asked him, then hoped you asked in the right way. He could be maneuvered just so far, but the reins had to be kept loose, giving him room to breathe. Central Park!

"You could have at least called," she admonished irritably. "Good heavens, Paul, everyone kept asking where you were, and I felt like a fool not knowing. What was I to tell them?"

"I'm sorry," he said. "I tried to get to a telephone, but there aren't that many booths around, and the ones I did see were too crowded."

"I suppose I should understand, but I don't," she replied. "I had so much planned yesterday. The picnic, and last night . . . nothing went right." She avoided his eyes momentarily, hoping her voice didn't sound too demanding or whiny. "So help me, if I didn't know better, Paul, and if Gigi wasn't your sister"—she looked at him again, this time her blue eyes intense—"I'd swear there was something going on," she said.

Paul caught his breath, and his insides tightened as their eyes met. She couldn't know. He stared at her, unwavering, then reached out, half-laughing as he took her hand in his, pulling her closer. "What on earth are you talking about?" he asked huskily, and she swallowed hard, staring at him as he pulled her the rest of the way into his arms so her head was cradled on his shoulder.

"Paul, you do love me, don't you?" she asked suddenly.

His smile was disarming. "Don't be foolish, Lenore," he whispered. "You know I do."

"Then why have you been so distant lately? Paul, I'm frightened." She toyed with the collar of his shirt. For the first time since he'd known her, Paul saw uncertainty in Lenore's clear blue eyes. "Paul, if anything happened to us, I think I'd die," she went on. "I've never told you this, but being Mrs. Paul Larrabee means more to me than life itself. I've always loved you, Paul, for years and years," she said. "And just the thought that something might happen . . . that you might change your mind . . ."

Paul's hand moved up to caress her cheek. The skin was soft, very fair. His fingertips touched her earlobe, and he felt her tremble. He studied the line of her jaw as it reached the hairline, noting the soft hollow in her cheek, the classic bone structure of her face. She was like a Dresden doll, cold and unemotional. At least that's the way she'd always seemed, but now, suddenly, her eyes held a depth that went beyond her porcelain exterior.

"How would you like to make certain I don't change my mind?" he asked softly.

She frowned. "What . . . ?"

"Let's get married right away, Lenore," he pleaded, taking advantage of her emotional state. "Let's not wait any longer. Why we decided to wait until August anyway, I'll never know. We can get married a week from Saturday. What do you think?"

She was staring at him curiously, her eyes wide, mouth agape in disbelief. "A week from Saturday?"

"Why not?"

"But, Paul. All our plans . . ."

He cupped her face in his hand, his other arm tightening, holding her firmly against him. "Darling, we've waited too long already," he whispered. "Besides, plans can be changed."

"But a week from Saturday!"

He leaned forward and kissed her softly, hoping he hadn't lost his power of persuasion. "Please, Lenore, say you will." His lips moved from her mouth to her ear, and his breath, warm on her neck, made her shiver. "Please, love," he continued to plead. "I can't wait until August. Being with you so much and not being able to touch you has been torment. Say you will, Lenore. It's what you've always wanted, darling, what we both want."

Lenore swallowed hard, then pushed against Paul, and he lifted his lips from her neck where they'd been caressing her. His eyes locked with hers, and for a moment he thought he'd lost; then she sighed.

"You're serious, aren't you, Paul?" she said softly.

He breathed deeply. "Very serious," he answered.

She continued to stare, feeling his arms holding her, remembering the touch of his lips on her neck, and remembering the night of the masquerade ball, when he'd kissed her and she'd felt his arousal. If she said yes now there'd be no more fear of losing him.

"All right," she replied passionately, her eyes radiating the inner happiness she felt. "If you insist, we'll be married a week from Saturday, but after we're married, no more Central Parks, please, Paul," she begged. "At least not without me."

He sighed, a dull ache settling in his breastbone. "No more Central Parks ever, I promise," he said firmly. "There'll be no need for any," and she smiled.

"Then kiss me, Paul," she said, and his lips came down on
hers brutally, taking her breath away, and Lenore was the
proudest, happiest woman in the world. She'd played her
cards right. If she'd bucked him, if she'd shown her anger,
she might have lost him. As it was, in less than two weeks
she'd be Mrs. Paul Larrabee.

Gigi stood in front of the full-length mirror scrutinizing
herself. She was wearing the same deep turquoise dress she'd
worn that night so long ago when she'd first gone to Delmonico's with Jason and Paul and met all of Jason's friends and
business associates. The tiny seed pearls glittered here and
there where they were scattered about the skirt and bodice of
the dress. It was one of her favorites, and she watched the
lace about the bottom of the skirt swish as she turned from
side to side, examining herself, to make sure she looked all
right.

Bridget had fixed her hair away from her face, the curls
nestled firmly in place atop her head, and delicate pearl earrings hung from her earlobes, matching the strands of pearls
that embellished her throat.

André should be pleased, she thought, and inadvertently
wondered what Paul would think. But then, Paul didn't matter, did he? She fought back tears that threatened to filter
into her eyes. She had managed to sneak a few words with
Paul earlier in the day before he'd left for Lenore's, and he'd
reluctantly told her about the argument he and Jason had
had, and Jason's reaction when he'd learned the truth. And
he'd also told her of his promise to his father that it was
over, that what had existed between them was dead, and he
tried to make her believe it too, treating her with angry indifference and bitter words, and it had hurt her terribly. Now
she was trying to think of him indifferently as a defense
against her real feelings. Paul had left immediately after their
talk and been gone all afternoon, and as far as she knew, he
still wasn't back. She wondered if he'd get back in time for
the theater. If he didn't, that was his problem. Jason said he'd
made arrangements with Paul and that he'd reminded him;
besides, being alone with André tonight might be just the
remedy she needed to get over Paul. After all, yesterday afternoon had proved more than interesting. What might
tonight bring?

Satisfied that she looked all right, she turned, snatching up the fancy cape that matched the dress, and went downstairs. She left the cape in the foyer, and proceeded to the dining room, surprised to see that Paul had returned, changed clothes, and was just sitting down to dinner.

"Well, Gigi," said Jason, concern mirrored in his eyes. "We have seen hardly anything of you all day, and when you were late coming down, I was about to ask one of the servants to see if everything was all right."

"I'm fine," she said unsteadily as she let Ahmed pull the chair out for her, then sat down. She could feel everyone's eyes on her, especially Paul's, but she was unable to look at him, afraid of what she might see in those cool gray eyes. She smoothed the skirt of her dress, clearing her throat, trying to act normal. "I've spent most of the day in the library," she said. "There were some things I wanted to look up. I didn't mean to be late for dinner."

"You're not really late, my dear," said Jason congenially. "I shouldn't have said anything. After all, Paul just arrived too."

"But he has an excuse," said Rose, butting into the conversation. She glanced at Paul. "Why don't you tell Gigi about your news, Paul?" she urged coyly. "I'm sure she'd love to know, wouldn't you, Gigi?"

"Know what?" she asked, watching the self-satisfied look on her half-sister's face.

"Tell her, Paul," Rose urged again. "She might even like the idea. Who knows?"

Paul's mouth set stubbornly as he stared at Rose, wishing he could strangle her.

Gigi composed herself and looked at Paul, her eyes curious, wondering. "What news do you have, Paul?" she asked softly, trying to keep her voice steady.

Paul's eyes darted from Rose to Bruce, then to his father, finally resting once more on Gigi. "Lenore and I are getting married a week from Saturday instead of in August," he finally said. He watched Gigi's eyes, and the pain he saw in them made him curse silently to himself.

"Perhaps you'd like to be in the wedding party too, along with me," said Rose, rubbing it in, and Paul frowned at her tactless offer; then he went on hesitantly, hoping to soothe Gigi's pain, trying to make her feel more at ease. "I'm sure Lenore won't mind, if you'd like to," he said.

Gigi took a deep breath, then tried to smile, but couldn't,

so instead she straightened stubbornly, determined to show them it didn't matter.

"I'd love to," she said calmly. "And may I invite André to the wedding reception?" she asked. "You are still having the reception, aren't you?"

Paul's eyes bored into hers, but she couldn't read the meaning behind them. They seemed to be both questioning and angry. "We'd be delighted to have him," he answered. "In fact, we can ask him this evening," he said. "On the way to the theater."

Gigi forced a smile. "Lovely," she said, and at that moment the girls brought in the food and the awkward situation was more easily bridged, although the wedding was not forgotten and aspects of it were discussed off and on during dinner, making Gigi more than a little uncomfortable, because still no one else, only Paul earlier in the day, had made any mention about last night's affair.

André arrived on time just as dinner ended, and Paul watched jealously as he helped Gigi on with her cape and escorted her to the waiting carriage, while he followed close behind, trying to look unconcerned. He was sure the evening was going to be a disaster, at least for him. All the way to Lenore's he had to listen to André's rich, deep voice, the heavy Spanish accent remarkably sensuous as he talked to Gigi.

By the time they reached the Van Der Linden's, Paul's composure was badly shaken, although he tried not to show it as Gigi, who'd been practically ignoring his presence, paid rapt attention to her escort. She smiled seductively at André's whispered endearments, letting him hold her hand furtively beneath the folds of her cloak, where he was sure she thought he couldn't see. Then occasionally they'd even lapse into Spanish. When this happened, Paul frowned, wondering once more if perhaps André may have known Gigi before, and also wondering if maybe he'd had something to do with the attack on Bridget, although the girl insisted that neither of the men could have been André.

Lenore seemed quite content as she joined them. Happy to see André so attentive toward Gigi, and exuberant, if Lenore could ever be called exuberant, over the recent change in their coming nuptials. She looked exquisite in green satin and emeralds that clashed with her brilliant blue eyes, filling them with green flecks. Her dress had enormous bouffant sleeves, the waist small, skirt full and bustled, but it showed off her statuesque proportions beautifully.

Gigi was always jealous whenever she saw Lenore. There was an air about her that was unmistakably social register, and Gigi felt intimidated. Tonight, watching her clinging to Paul even more possessively than usual was even worse, although Gigi appeared unperturbed.

Outwardly, the evening was a complete success. Everyone was cordial and charming. Paul and Lenore invited André to the wedding; Gigi confirmed that she'd be glad to be in the wedding party; André, through subtle questioning, discovered the events of the night before concerning Ramón and the colonel's little adventure; and they all seemed to enjoy the play. But inwardly, against all appearances, the evening was as Paul predicted, a total disaster, at least for him. And for Gigi too, although he had no way of knowing it. Although Paul seemed to be overly attentive toward Lenore, subconsciously, his every thought was on Gigi. He knew every time she looked into André's eyes, every time she smiled at him, and every word that passed between them.

And Gigi, although seemingly caught up in André's charming attentiveness, saw every gesture Paul made toward Lenore, every concern he gave her, and it tore at her heart, making her reactions toward André more reckless than they should have been, causing Paul even further anguish.

By the time Paul said good night to Lenore and kissed her at her front door, returning promptly to the carriage, he was in a foul mood. And the fact that when he returned to the carriage and seated himself across from them, he instinctively sensed that André had been kissing Gigi, didn't help matters. How could he not show how he felt? He wanted to kill the sniveling Latin, but instead he tried to ignore him, and stared out the window irritably as the carriage rolled on toward Larrabee Manor.

"I hope you don't mind, Paul," said Gigi, interrupting Paul's thoughts as the carriage pulled up at the front steps of the stone mansion, "but I've asked André if he'd like to come in for a nightcap. It is all right, isn't it? I mean . . . you don't think Jason will mind?"

Paul glanced at André, noting the gleam in his dark eyes, then looked back at Gigi, frowning. "I'm afraid I do mind, Gigi," he said sternly. "I wish you'd asked me first. I don't think it would be wise this evening. Father wasn't feeling too well, and it is rather late."

She frowned back at him, turning toward André apologetically as the carriage stopped. "I'm sorry," she said, but he assured her it was all right.

Paul listened to her apology as he stepped from the carriage, then turned to help her down, but it was André who emerged next, and Paul's jaw set angrily as, instead, he watched André hold up his hand to help her. He had to admit as he studied André, the man was good-looking, whether wearing his usual native costume or the white tie and tails he had on tonight. Was it any wonder Gigi found him attractive? Paul watched sullenly, then turned abruptly and headed for the door, with André and Gigi close behind.

He hesitated at the door, waiting, and André glanced at him curiously. "It is all right, my walking her to the door, isn't it?" he asked, noting the threatening looks he was getting from Paul. "After all, I did ask her to the theater. It's only natural I see her to the door."

"Then your mission's accomplished, isn't it?" said Paul. "We happen to be at the door."

André glanced casually up at the huge oak door as Paul turned the knob and swung it open; then his eyes flashed stubbornly. The American was worse than a duenna. Well, that was his problem. André straightened to his full height, turning to Gigi, reaching out, taking her hand, oblivious momentarily of Paul standing watching. If he didn't have the courtesy to let him say good night in private, he concluded, then he'd just have to watch.

He moved closer, resting her hand on his chest, his own hand covering hers, looking down into her eyes, taking in their warm blue-green depths. "I'll call you tomorrow, *querida*," he whispered softly. "Until then . . ." and before she could protest, he bent to meet her lips in a lingering kiss that took her by surprise. "*Adiós*," he whispered softly as his mouth left hers; then he turned to Paul, nodding good night, and strode arrogantly back to the waiting carriage, climbing in, closing the door firmly behind him.

Paul stood at the door with his hand still on the knob, his eyes glazed with anger as he watched the carriage move down the drive; then he turned slowly toward Gigi, who was still standing motionless, her feet seemingly rooted to the spot.

She hadn't expected André to kiss her. Not in front of Paul. Slowly her hand moved to her mouth, and she touched her lips gingerly where André's lips had held them only moments before; then her head snapped quickly as Paul spoke.

"Well, are you going to stand there all night mooning over his kiss?" he asked irritably, and she dropped her hand hurriedly, then stepped on into the house.

The door closed hard behind her, and she whirled around, angry because she wished it had been Paul kissing her and not André, and there was nothing she could do about it. "I wasn't mooning over his kiss," she said, staring at him. "Besides, if you didn't like watching, why didn't you go in the house?"

"And leave you alone with him?"

"Why not?"

"And have him make love to you again like he did in the carriage!" Paul's eyes blazed as they bored into hers. "I'm not a fool, Gigi. I know what went on between you two while I was walking Lenore to the door."

"Oh, aren't you smart. And I suppose you didn't kiss Lenore."

"That's different. She's my fiancée."

"That's right. She's your fiancée, Paul. Lenore belongs to you, I don't. You have no right to tell me whom I can and can't kiss."

He straightened, clenching his fists, towering over her, his face livid. "Gigi, be sensible. Do you know how hard it was for me to sit there listening to the two of you?" he whispered huskily. "Trying to pretend I don't care? My God! Do you have to play up to him like that?"

"Play up to him? Is that what's bothering you? Well, what about me? Do you think I enjoy seeing Lenore hanging on your arm," she cried, "knowing that in less than two weeks she'll be sharing your bed? Am I to stand by watching you and Lenore together, knowing you're making love to her, and expect it not to hurt? I have to have something to ease the pain, Paul, and as long as André's willing, I'll let him."

"No!"

"Yes!"

"I won't let him touch you!"

Gigi straightened, her eyes intent on his face, lips trembling. "Oh, I see," she said furiously. "It's all right for you to have Lenore, but I can't have André. Well, that's not the way

I see it, Paul. You have no say-so in the matter. None. I'll do as I want. I'm the one who'll decide what man will touch me, not you!"

Their eyes locked in fiery combat, neither giving in as Gigi waited to see what would happen. The silence between them hung heavy as they stood in the foyer staring at each other; then slowly Gigi felt the beginning tears starting to surface as bittersweet pangs of longing began to eat at her insides. She wanted Paul. Oh, God! How she wanted him.

Suddenly she wrenched her eyes from his and turned to go, her back to him as she headed purposefully toward the drawing-room hall.

"Gigi?"

She stopped at the sound of his voice, her back still to him, refusing to turn around.

He followed, stepping up behind her, so close she could feel the strength of his body, the warmth of his breath on the back of her hair. "Don't do it, Gigi," he pleaded softly, his voice low and vibrant. "Don't make a sham of what we had last night, please."

She flinched, trembling, then swallowed hard. "Last night is over, Paul," she whispered quietly, her back still to him. "Last night should never have been, but it was. You gave me a taste of what might have been, and someday I hope maybe I can find what we've been denied. Since I'm not allowed to find it with you, then I'll have to find it in someone else's arms. I'm sorry, Paul, that's the way it has to be. You can't ask me to live without it. You have no right." She paused momentarily, then sighed. "Good night, Paul," and she walked away, leaving him standing alone in the huge foyer, staring after her, wishing he were dead, because he knew she was right.

The next week and a half literally flew by, even though there was very little for Gigi to do. Bridget accompanied her to Redfern's, where she ordered a few new gowns, at Jason's suggestion; then they lunched in a quiet, out-of-the-way place before going home. But there were few places she was allowed without a proper chaperon, and since Paul begged off, being too busy with wedding plans, most of her days were spent trying to keep herself occupied at the house.

Rose and Bruce still avoided her whenever possible, so sometimes she'd embroider, read, or take walks down by the river. The bicycling craze was on, and she did take up the pastime. But Jason wouldn't let her ride alone, and Rose and Bruce let her know they disliked her company when she tried to join them. So eventually the bicycle Jason bought for her sat most of the time collecting dust.

In the evenings she welcomed André with relief. He called every day and came over every evening. Since Jason could think of no other suitable chaperon for her, he and Ahmed accompanied them when they went into the city to dine or to the theater or minstrel shows. But André seemed to dislike crowds, so those times were few.

Most of their evenings were spent at the manor house just talking or playing games. Even though they weren't entirely alone, Gigi looked forward to his coming. Their favorite pastime was to take an early-evening canter along the river to the abandoned barn, where they'd tether their horses and stroll along the bank. They both knew Ahmed was ever present somewhere in the shadows of the trees, but at least here they felt as if they were really, finally alone. And as each day went by, Gigi felt drawn more and more to André for the comfort and attention she'd once craved from Paul, and the kisses and caresses shared with him were a balm to her.

Paul had thrown himself into his work and the plans for the wedding, letting both monopolize his time. Even inventing things to be done to keep himself occupied when there was nothing more to do. Rarely was he at home, and when he was forced to spend time with the family, he held himself apart, his mood varying from unpleasant to indifferent or downright rude, and whenever he entered a room where Gigi was, she sensed his unspoken anger toward her, so she purposely tried to stay out of his way.

There were times, however, when she couldn't, and moments when she ached inside because of the looks he gave her. Sometimes they were looks filled with warmth, passion, and longing, but they were looks that could never be fulfilled. Then at other times his eyes held condemnation and reproach because of André, and when this happened, she'd lash out at him whenever the opportunity arose, just to get even and try to ease the hurt some.

Jason thought it unusual to see them suddenly so much at odds with each other, the words between them sharp and bruising. But he accepted it as a sign that the unhealthy alliance between them had merely been a passing fancy and sighed in relief, thinking the affair had finally passed. Little did he know that the anger they vented on each other was a defense against giving in to the love that still haunted them.

The evening wedding was to be at St. Thomas Church, with the reception held at the Van Der Lindens' estate. Gigi fidgeted nervously now as she stood in the room at the church waiting for the organ music to begin. It was early Saturday evening, July 15, the night of the wedding, and she'd cried herself to sleep the night before and most of the morning. Now she was hoping no one would notice the slight puffiness that was still visible about her eyes.

She stared across the room to where Lenore waited, head held high, the veil cascading from her blond hair sweeping the floor. It was gossamer sheer, with tiny diamonds sprinkled here and there, the tiara that held it encrusted with diamonds and pearls. Her dress of white satin was trimmed with Irish lace about the bodice and bouffant sleeves, the skirt caught up here and there, draping gracefully from small clusters of diamond-and-pearl orange blossoms. It was exquisite and ex-

pensive, and Lenore's golden hair and gentian eyes brought
an even more delicate aura to its fragility. Even though she
was taller than Gigi, her body statuesque, like that of her Vi-
king ancestors, her fair coloring softened her looks, making
her appear delicate and extremely feminine.

Gigi watched Lenore's lovely smile, the graceful way her
hands moved as she accepted the bridal bouquet of orange
blossoms and white orchids from her father. There wasn't a
hair out of place on her head. Always the immaculate
Lenore. Gigi swallowed hard, turning away, smoothing the
skirt of her own dress, brushing a stray strand of hair up off
the nape of her neck where it had begun to tickle.

As one of the bridesmaids, she'd been unable to pick her
own dress, but had to wear the dress Lenore picked out, and
she stared down at it now, hating it. There were nine bridesmaids. Rose wore salmon pink, and the other young women
were in yellows and pale shades from blue to green. Lenore,
at Rose's insistence, had suggested that Gigi wear pale lavender. Gigi suspected it was because, with her dark hair and
brilliant blue-green eyes, Rose probably thought the color
would look washed out and lifeless on her. And it probably
would have, too, if Gigi had been anyone other than Gigi.
But on her, with her dark hair and lively beauty, the plain
dress, with its high lace collar, bouffant sleeves, and full billowing skirt below a pinched-in waist, looked more like the
frosting on a delightful cake, and the nosegay of violets and
baby's breath she carried put just the right dash of color in to
complete the picture. And although Gigi felt inferior, gazing
at the other young women enviously, she had no way of
knowing she looked every bit as enchanting as the bride.

She smoothed her skirt as the strains of the organ filtered
into the room, then sighed. There was no going back, nothing
she could do. Paul was really getting married. She gripped
the nosegay tighter, her hands clammy with perspiration, then
adjusted the wide-brimmed lavender picture hat that sat atop
her head and took her place in line behind Lenore. She
wished they'd placed her farther toward the end of the line.
As it was, Lenore's cousin was maid of honor, Rose next in
line, then Gigi, and she was close enough that she'd be able
to hear the whole ceremony.

She didn't want to hear it. She couldn't bear the thought of
listening to Paul saying the words that made Lenore his wife.
She'd block it from her mind somehow. She'd think of other

things. Of Coney Island or Central Park. No, not them. She'd think of André and forget all about Paul. She had to. For her sake and Paul's too. She tilted her chin up stubbornly, holding back the tears that fought to be free. She could do it, she would do it.

The music grew louder, and Lenore took her father's arm, smiling at him graciously, then walked slowly, leaving the room with her attendants, including Gigi, in slow procession behind her.

The huge church was jammed with people. The Van Der Linden-Larrabee wedding attracted society's elite, and for the past week the society pages of the newspapers had been filled with stories that covered the prenuptial parties and preparations.

Paul frowned as he stood tall and erect in white tie and tails at the front of the church waiting, organ music pounding in his ears. If he could only shut it off. His jaw tightened. He was here, actually going through with it. They should give him some kind of medal. He should leave, walk out, join the Foreign Legion. Anything except marry Lenore.

He glanced down the center aisle of the church, his eyes resting on his bride as she slowly walked toward him. His bride! Well, he'd asked her to marry him, hadn't he? His eyes pierced the veil that covered her face, and he studied her features thoughtfully, trying to convince himself that he wasn't making a mistake. What had he expected to feel like standing here, ready to commit himself to a life with her? Happy? What a farce. He knew he'd never love her, not the way he loved Gigi. What he was doing was expected, and he was going to have to live up to the demands that went with it. And one of those demands was to forget Gigi.

As he met Lenore's soft blue eyes beneath the veil, and saw the proud smile on her face, he realized any other man would've been ecstatic. She was truly lovely, and he should be grateful that he could turn his thoughts to someone else to try to forget Gigi, but it wasn't that easy. Without thinking, for a split second his eyes left Lenore's and he glanced behind her to Gigi, and as Lenore stepped up to stand beside him, his eyes stopped on Gigi's, holding their blue-green warmth for barely a second before the minister's voice began and he looked back once more to Lenore. Taking her hand in his, he faced the front of the church. Well, he was committed. There was no way to stop it. No going back.

Gigi tried to forget the pained look she'd caught in Paul's
eyes barely moments ago, tried to shut out what they were
saying, but it was impossible, and she heard every word loud
and clear, and each word was like the blow of a hammer
sealing her heart up forever. By the time the ceremony was
over, she was numb, beyond feeling anymore.

The wedding dinner was held in the pink-and-marble ban-
quet room at the Van Der Linden estate, while stringed in-
struments serenaded everyone. Jason, with Ahmed on one
side, Katrin and Nels on the other, watched over everything
with delight.

Gigi had avoided both bride and groom since the ceremony. Now she sat next to André at the lavishly spread table,
barely picking at her food. Occasionally she'd glance toward
Lenore and Paul where they sat at the head of the long ban-
quet table, warm flushes pulsing through her as they were
toasted over and over again. Then later, after the wedding
cake had been cut and they all retired to the ballroom, she
watched agonizingly as the couple moved onto the floor,
starting the festivities by dancing the first dance alone, circling the room slowly to the strains of a waltz.

When the first dance was finally over and the music started
up again for everyone to join the newlyweds, André leaned
forward, taking Gigi's hand, pulling her toward him.

"Come, *querida*, the first dance is mine," he said softly,
and Gigi forced a smile as his arm went about her and they
circled out onto the floor that was beginning to fill with
guests. "You look too sad for a member of the wedding,
querida," he whispered as they waltzed slowly toward the
French doors at the far end of the ballroom. "What's the
matter? You've been so touchy all week long."

"It's nothing," she answered. "It's . . . it's just that sometimes I wish I could remember." She shook her head. "Never
mind, André. I'm just so glad you came tonight."

"So am I." He held her tighter against him, motioning his
head toward the French doors. "It's been a busy evening, and
it's rather stuffy in here. I could use some fresh air. How
about you?"

She let him lead her from the floor, across the room
toward the doors, then outside onto the long expanse of lawn
and gardens. They walked for a few minutes, then stopped
beside some shrubs that screened them from the house and

the other couples who'd also drifted outside. She stood for a long time gazing out into the night, and he silently watched her, studying her face for a long time, noting the melancholy look.

Her moods all week had been disturbing. In fact, from the first night he'd met her she'd been hard to understand, but the past few days had been even worse. He'd often watched her go from carefree gaiety to fiery anger without a moment's warning. Her eyes were expressive and disturbed, yet revealed little of what she was really feeling inside. She was restless, edgy, quick to anger. Especially with Paul. He frowned. Paul? He brushed the ends of his mustache with the back of one finger, and his dark eyes studied her in the moonlight, watching it play on her ebony hair, free now from the cumbersome hat she'd worn earlier, the dark curls vivid in the moonlight.

Suddenly an uneasy feeling began to creep over him. Paul! He hadn't thought. Paul was getting married. Paul and Gigi had been practically inseparable the past few months, ever since her arrival. Could it be? Could she have been falling in love with him? His frown deepened as he watched her close her eyes, tilting her head back, breathing in the warm night air, and he remembered watching her during the ceremony, seeing the tears that edged her eyes. Once more the uneasy feeling tightened into a knot in the center of his stomach, and the reality made him catch his breath in surprise. *Madre de Dios!* That had to be it! It was logical as all hell. He hadn't even thought of it before, but he should have. After all, she wasn't really Paul's sister, even though she didn't know it. The attraction could be there without her realizing it. My God! If she thought she was in love with her brother . . .

As she opened her eyes again and turned to him, the pain he saw in them was so intense he wished for a moment he could tell her who she really was, that she wasn't Paul's sister, that she had every right to love him, that nothing else mattered but her happiness; then abruptly his better judgment took over and he remembered who he was and why he was here, and he straightened, knowing his task was going to be harder than he thought. Yet, he was confident of his charms.

He reached out, pulling her toward him, his arms enfolding her, and he felt a stirring deep inside. "Gigi, my lovely Gigi," he whispered, and she looked up at him wistfully.

"Am I really lovely, André?" she asked.

"So lovely it takes my breath away." He leaned forward and kissed her passionately on the mouth, his arms tightening about her. When he finally drew his lips from hers, he sighed. "Gigi, you must know how I feel about you," he whispered softly. "You can't be blind. Ah, *mi querida,* I'd be so honored if you'd be my wife."

She stared up at him, taken completely by surprise. His dark eyes were warm, yet so intense. She hadn't expected this. André just didn't seem like the marrying kind. She half-smiled apologetically, not quite sure she believed what she'd heard. "Your wife?"

"*Sí.*"

She shook her head slowly. "Oh, André," she said. "Please don't spoil it. Not so soon."

"Soon? What is time where the heart's concerned?" He reached up, touching her cheek, his strong tapered fingers running seductively down her jawline to beneath her chin. "I don't need any more time to know I love you."

"But I need time," she said, and reached up, taking his hand from beneath her chin, holding his fingers to keep them from any more sensuous wanderings. "It's too soon for me, André," she went on. "I like you . . . I like you very much, but marriage? It's so permanent." Her eyes suddenly fell before his gaze, and she sighed. "Not yet, André, please. Not just yet."

"I'll ask again."

"I know."

"And someday you'll say yes."

"Someday maybe, but not now." She glanced about. "Now I'd like to dance some more if you don't mind?"

He smiled, undaunted by her first refusal. "As you wish, my love," he said, and ushered her back to the ballroom.

Paul rarely drank more than two or three drinks during an evening out, but tonight was different. He needed something to keep going, to dull the pain. He'd just finished his fourth or fifth drink—he hadn't kept count—and accepted the hearty teasing from some of his friends, when he spotted André and Gigi dancing together across the ballroom floor. He'd watched them off and on during the course of the evening, and always it was the same. André was holding her close, whispering in her ear, smiling at her with dark eyes, and she seemed perfectly contented.

Paul stared at them for a long time, toying with the empty glass in his hand, only half-listening to the conversation of the men he was with, and it suddenly dawned on him. He hadn't spoken to Gigi all day, nor yet this evening. About the only time he ever saw her anymore was during meals, and he'd left the house early this morning purposely to avoid her, knowing that it must be as hard for her as it was for him.

Now, as he stared at her across the room, noting the intimate way André was holding her, watching the man's hungry eyes caress her and seeing her response, he felt a surge of anger run through him, and suddenly excused himself, heading across the crowded floor.

Lenore had called in special decorators, and the Van Der Linden-Larrabee wedding reception was already being talked about for its extravagance. In the center of the huge ballroom was an exact replica of a fancy gazebo made with the petals of thousands of white flowers, and around it was a wide, mirror-bottomed moat fed by delicate sprays of water coming from the base of the gazebo. Beautiful white swans swam in the moat, and its outer edges were hung with thick curtains of white gardenias and camellias that cascaded all the way to the floor while silver and crystal clouds hung suspended from the high ceiling, and soft blue incandescent lights from above reflected off the extravaganza. In the center of the gazebo sat the string band, their access to it across a flower-festooned bridge. The effect was striking, but Paul didn't seem to care, and paid little attention to it now as he skirted it, then made his way to where André and Gigi were. He tapped André lightly on the shoulder.

The couple stopped dancing, and turned abruptly, staring at Paul, André continuing to hold Gigi close.

"Do you mind?" asked Paul, nodding toward Gigi, but refusing to look at her just yet. "It seems my sister's the only one who hasn't had a dance with the groom yet this evening."

André smiled reluctantly as his arms eased from about her. "My pleasure," he said congenially, letting his hand drop from her waist. "Perhaps I'll go see if I can find the bride," and he glanced at Gigi quickly before walking away.

Gigi stared hard at Paul, and he took a deep breath as he finally looked at her, then stepped forward, his arm encircling her waist, and he felt her tense beneath his hands.

"You don't mind, do you?" he asked.

She was looking directly at him, her eyes challenging.
"Should I?"

He fought back as he pulled her closer, and began to lead
her across the floor to the strains of the music. "You've been
avoiding me all evening," he said. "You could have at least
had the decency to wish us well."

"Oh, is that what it is? Decency?" She half-laughed. "I
guess I'm not a very decent person."

His arm tightened. "Gigi!"

"Well, I'm not, am I, Paul?" she asked, still looking into
his troubled gray eyes. "I could scratch her eyes out!"

"I know."

"I hate her!"

"I know that too."

They were at the far end of the ballroom, near the French
doors, and for the second time tonight Gigi was propelled
through them, out to the moonlit gardens.

"Paul!"

"Don't argue," he said firmly, and he waltzed her toward
the far end of the garden to a secluded spot where no one
would see, then stopped, his arm still about her waist. He
tucked her other hand close against his chest, looking deep
into her turquoise eyes, and she stared at him curiously.

"You've been drinking," she said.

He smiled, that disarming smile that always left her weak.
"Why not? I need a little bolstering." He saw the look on her
face. "Don't worry, I'm not drunk," he assured her. "Not yet,
anyway, but I wish I were." His voice deepened. "I wish I
could get drunk enough to pass out, then I wouldn't have to
worry about my wedding night. I could postpone it for at
least another day. But that's not the way Paul Larrabee does
things, is it?"

She forced her eyes from his and started to squirm, trying
to extricate herself from his arms, but he was too strong.

"No!" he said forcefully. "Don't!" His arm about her waist
held her like a vise, and he caught her wrist, his fingers
pressing hard against her flesh. Then slowly, as his smoky
gray eyes locked with hers, he drew her hand to his mouth
and kissed the palm, sending shivers through her.

"Paul, please!" she cried breathlessly. "It's hard enough.
Don't make it worse!"

He pressed her open palm against his cheek, and a warm

flood went through him, settling in his loins. "What's the matter?" he asked cynically. "Don't you like it?"

She stared at him, bewildered, her eyes searching his face, but it didn't seem to lessen his determination.

He leaned forward, burying his face against the warm flesh of her neck, his lips burning wherever they touched her skin.

"No!" she gasped, but his lips moved to her ear, and she felt his breath warm and sensuous against it.

"Why did you let me marry Lenore?" he asked passionately.

She answered in a half-choked sob, "There was no other way!"

"I could have left New York. Gone away, to Europe, anywhere." He raised his head, his eyes gazing into hers, searching them with a bittersweet pain. "It would have been better than this."

"You couldn't have gone, and you know it," she whispered breathlessly. "Jason needs you."

"And what of my needs? They mean nothing?"

Her eyes fell before his smoldering gaze. She knew well what he meant. "You'll have Lenore."

"And pray how do I tell my body that there's no difference between you and her when in my heart I know too well there is?" His face darkened as his anger at being denied the one thing in the world he wanted more than anything else began to surge once more through his veins. "What do I do when I take her in my arms and nothing happens, Gigi? What do I do?"

She toyed with his tie, this time trying to avoid direct contact with his eyes, because they made her feel warm and giddy inside. "Oh, Paul, don't be absurd," she said. "She's a beautiful woman. No man could be indifferent to her."

"No man except one who'd held you in his arms first." She felt his body tense, sensing his bitter anger. "You have no idea what you've done to me, have you?" he asked.

Once more her eyes raised stubbornly to meet his. "I've done nothing!"

"Haven't you?"

She stared hard at him, her body aching with the torment of his nearness, her insides gripped with the agony of her own needs. She loved this man with all her heart and soul, and yet she had to send him to another woman, because the world said it was wrong.

"I have only loved you . . ." she gasped, sobbing out the last words barely above a whisper, "like any sister should!"

His eyes darkened as her words thrust home, reminding him that there was nothing left for them. "I hate you!" he cried huskily, but instead of releasing her, his mouth sought hers hungrily, in a kiss that seared them both.

After long moments, when both their bodies responded heatedly to the passion that filled them, his mouth reluctantly eased from hers, and he looked deep into her eyes, misty now with glistening tears.

"I wish you well, Paul," she whispered.

He swallowed hard. "I think I'm going to need another drink." He trembled, and his arms unwrapped themselves from about her.

She reached out, touching the front of his shirt lightly as he started to walk away. "Paul?"

He hesitated.

"Don't hate me, please, Paul," she begged.

He tried to smile, but it didn't quite come off; instead, his voice was deep, unsteady as he spoke. "You didn't think I really could, did you?" he asked, and her hand dropped as he walked away, leaving her standing alone.

He had to get away from her. Had to think. He'd wanted to hurt her for André and for what she'd done to him, but it was no use, because to hurt her was to hurt himself, and he was hurting too much already.

He stopped just outside the French doors, looking back toward where he'd left her. She stood alone, quiet and still in the moonlight, looking so small and fragile. Something tugged at his heart. It wasn't her fault. How could he blame her, any more than he could blame himself? Neither of them had wanted this, neither of them had asked for it, and now they were both looking for a way out. He didn't want her to be with André any more than she wanted him to be with Lenore, but they both had to accept it.

He turned back, hesitated a moment, then retraced his steps until he was once more beside her. "I guess I don't really want that drink, after all," he confessed sheepishly.

She turned to him slowly, tears glistening on her long, thick lashes. "I'm glad."

He held his breath momentarily, then forced himself to go on. "I'm sorry, Gigi, truly I am," he said. He paused, studying her face in the moonlight, then continued. "I'm not going about this the right way, am I?"

She stared up at him, frowning.

"You see," he went on, "I'm having a hard time with it. Seeing you all the time like this, knowing there's nothing I can do . . . I'm going to have to get used to it, though, I know, so I may as well start now. It won't be easy, you understand, and sometimes I may treat you a little badly, but I won't really mean it. Like a few moments ago." His voice deepened. "I didn't mean to hurt you."

She swallowed hard. "I know," she said, still looking up at him. "Sometimes I want to hate you too."

He hardened his heart to how lovely and vulnerable she looked, then straightened, his mouth curving into what he hoped looked like a more brotherly grin. "Well, now that we've settled that," he said, trying to be nonchalant, "shall we finish our dance?"

"Why not?" she said, taking a deep breath, and they headed back toward the French doors, together this time, both resigned to their fate and trying desperately to accept it as graciously as they knew how.

Lenore stood at the side of the ballroom, finally having a moment to herself. She gazed across the floor, watching, as Paul danced with Gigi. She had seen them come in from outside only moments before, and at first she'd become irritated, but then she was determined that nothing was going to spoil her wedding day. Nothing! Not even Paul's preoccupation with his sister.

Her brilliant blue eyes followed them closely as she suddenly remembered that it was the first time she'd seen them together all evening. That was strange, because usually wherever Paul was, Gigi was right by his side. Tonight had been different, though. Much different in so many ways. In fact, the past week and a half, ever since the day Paul had asked to change the date of the wedding, things had been different. Almost every free moment Paul had, had been spent with her. Even in the evenings. Whereas before, she and Paul, or just Paul, had escorted Gigi about New York, now Jason and Ahmed took over the chore as chaperons. Was it strictly because of the preparations for the wedding? She wondered, and suddenly all the little insinuations Rose had thrown at her since Gigi's arrival began to take root in her thoughts.

She watched closely as Paul smiled down at Gigi, noting the warmth and feeling in his eyes. And he was holding her so close. Lenore frowned, her eyes shifting to Gigi's face, and suddenly a chill went through her. Gigi was staring back at him, directly into his eyes, with such passionate intensity that it was shocking.

The music stopped, and for a moment the two just stood staring at each other as if mesmerized; then, as if startled by a sudden loud noise, Paul laughed, trying to look unconcerned as André claimed Gigi once more for the next dance. Lenore watched the brief conversation among the three of them, until Gigi and André danced away; then she studied Paul's face. He was no longer smiling, but somber, his eyes hard and cold as he watched André glide away with Gigi in his arms.

Rose's insinuations on the Fourth of July became all too clear to her. Paul had spent the evening of the Fourth alone with Gigi, and he'd asked her to marry him the very next day. Could it be? Oh, God! Could it really be possible? She suddenly felt sick.

Her fists clenched, and she turned, holding the train of her dress up so as not to trip, making excuses to the people who were once more beginning to converge on her, and she headed for the powder room, which was down the marble-floored hall from the ballroom. All along the way she had to keep making excuses as to why she couldn't stop; then, when she opened the door to the powder room, it was so crowded. She shut it quickly again and turned back, staring down the hall, aware of the couples lounging around. She had to be by herself to be able to think clearly. She couldn't talk to anyone while she was so upset. No one must ever see her upset like this, and Rose's terrible, damning words kept nagging her, forcing their way to the surface. She had to conquer them.

Making her way down the hall again, she moved past the ballroom door and started for the main part of the house, when Paul's voice made her suddenly turn around. "There you are," he said calmly, and she lifted her eyes to meet his as he approached. "Father wants to know what time we're going to be leaving," he said.

"Leaving?"

He frowned. "On our honeymoon." His frown deepened as he saw the uncertainty in her eyes. "What is it, Lenore?

What's the matter?" he asked, seeing the slight trembling to her lips.

"The matter? Why, nothing," she said, trying to be casual. "I just . . . well, it seems like I daren't even have a minute to myself, Paul," she said. "Everyone's been crowding around so. We haven't even been able to be alone."

His eyes flickered over her face, then moved to her bosom, where her full breasts moved rhythmically with every breath. They lingered on her generous curves, then caressed the slim waist, hoping to ignite a spark, anything to help, but he felt nothing. She was a bride, entitled to more than what he felt he could give, yet he had to make her believe he cared. Really cared.

He reached up, touching her face, then letting his fingers play with her earlobe and stroke the nape of her neck. Thank God, at least she was beautiful. As beautiful as any of the women he'd bedded over the years. But that was before Gigi. He tried to force Gigi from his mind, concentrating only on Lenore. On the soft body beneath the virginal white wedding dress, and the part of her that had no face, only the means of stopping the ache in his loins. If he could think of nothing else but the physical side of it, maybe he could see it through.

His arms went around her, and he pulled her close, ignoring the guests in the hallway who'd begun to stare at them and smile furtively at one another. "We could leave now," he suggested anxiously. "The train isn't due to pull out until one o'clock in the morning, but I know where there's a little hotel we could check in to for a few hours until it's time."

She blushed. "Paul, really," she whispered, hoping the others hadn't heard. "What would people think."

"They'd think we wanted to be alone."

"But a hotel, and for only a few hours!"

"That's all it takes, Lenore, only a few hours." He smiled as he saw her discomfiture over his statement. "What's wrong? We are married, you know."

She stared into his gray eyes, surprised at his candor. "It . . . well, really, Paul. We haven't even . . . I've never been . . ."

"Well, I should hope not," he countered, pretending indignation, and her face turned crimson.

His smile suddenly faded and his eyes took on a hungry look as he continued to stare at her. She was a woman.

Breasts round and firm, her legs long and supple. Only a fool
would turn away. He needed release because of the torment
Gigi had kindled in him, and Lenore would give it to him.
Not the woman he wanted, true, but the one he could legally
possess.

"If you won't go to a hotel, then let's go to the station. Our
private car's ready and waiting for us. I need you now,
Lenore," he said huskily. "I've waited long enough."

"You're serious, aren't you?" she asked.

He sighed. "Yes."

"You really love me that much?"

"Yes," he lied, and she swallowed uneasily as a warm
feeling spread through her.

She must have been wrong before. Crazy to think that
Rose had been right. What a fool she'd been to let her imagination run away with her like that, to let Rose's remarks get
to her. Why, he was looking at her now with such longing.
She shoved any doubts she might've had to the back of her
mind and promised him he could tell his father that the bride
and groom would be leaving the reception earlier than
planned; then she smiled at him apprehensively, sure she'd
done the right thing, yet wishing she could have prolonged it
for a while longer. To kiss Paul was one thing, but climbing
in bed with him . . .

The private railroad car had been lit dimly when they
stepped in, the atmosphere conducive to intimacy, and now,
as Paul finished taking off his clothes, setting aside his pants,
wearing only his underwear, he glanced toward the screen
where Lenore was undressing.

"The reception went well, don't you think?" he said, trying
to put her at ease.

She answered from behind the screen, "Everyone said it
was the most dazzling affair in over twenty years and that the
gazebo was every bit as spectacular as the decorations at the
Lukemeyer ball at Delmonico's back in 1873, when they had
a small lake with swans on it right in the middle of the ban-
quet table," she said. "Father was such a dear to put up with
the expense. Of course, he said there was nothing too good
for a Van Der Linden."

"You're not a Van Der Linden anymore, Lenore. You're a
Larrabee," Paul reminded her.

She sighed. "I know. Isn't it wonderful?" and she slowly
stepped out from behind the screen.

Paul held his breath as his eyes fell on her. She looked truly lovely. All white and pink and sensuous. Her hair was still pinned up, and the dim light in their elaborately furnished railroad car turned it to deep gold atop her head. The white satin nightgown, plunging to her waist in front, was trimmed with the same Irish lace that had graced her wedding dress, her firm, high breasts barely concealed by it, and it clung to her seductively, accentuating every curve.

She was enough to make any man's blood heat in his veins, but unfortunately, Paul wasn't just any man. He was a man in love with another woman. He stared at her transfixed, his eyes moving over every curve, every wayward movement, but instead of appreciating the body displayed before him, he began to wonder what Gigi would look like with the same gown caressing her creamy, velvet skin. She'd be smaller, yet every bit as sensuous, her curves even more devastating. Her dark hair would bring out highlights in the white satin, and her delicately tantalizing curves would accentuate every line. She'd be alive beneath the smooth satin, bringing life to the gown that covered it. Something Lenore could never do. So different from what he stared at now.

He was brought back to reality by the realization that the woman standing before him, posing like a Greek goddess, belonged to him. Although every line and curve cried of sensuality, and her smile was meant to convey an invitation, there was something about the perfection of the moment that made him hesitate. It was as if she were only to be looked at, but not touched.

Hell, this was crazy. He watched her, his cool gray eyes steady on her face, then moving to take in her hair. Why didn't she take it down? Let it fall where it may, so she didn't look quite so immaculate.

He kept watching as she smiled at him, then reached over, pulled back the covers on the bed, and climbed in between the cool sheets, settling down. She glanced up at him self-consciously as she smoothed the gold brocade bedspread across her breasts, trying to pull it a fraction higher.

"Your nightshirt's probably in the drawer," she suggested softly.

He half-smiled. "I don't wear a nightshirt."

"Oh?"

He walked around the foot of the bed to his side, then slipped in beside her. "I hope you don't mind," he said, moving close. "But I never wear a nightshirt, I always go to bed like this."

She glanced quickly at his underwear as he pulled the covers up; then she looked into his gray eyes, not quite sure what she saw. Amusement? Love? Or was it something else? Something that frightened her with its intensity. Paul had never looked at her like this before.

She fidgeted nervously with the covers as she gazed up at him.

Without another word, he bent over her, trying to will his body to want her. He needed something, anything, to ease the pain inside. His head moved down, his lips caressing her throat, his hand moving into her hair.

She let out a small moan. "Paul . . . you're messing my hair!"

"I'm what?" He raised his head, looking down at her again.

Her blue eyes were passionless, filled only with irritation. "I said, you're messing my hair," she repeated. "It took me so long to get it like this."

He stared at her, frowning, not quite believing what he'd just heard, then sighed. "Is it really so important?" he asked.

"Well, after all, I don't want to look like some frump."

He stared at her, unable to answer, tossing thoughts about, trying to understand. He was trying to make love to her, and she was worried about her hair?

Her voice was low, sultry, barely above a whisper as she spoke again. "You know I can't stand it when my hair's messy, Paul," she said. "Really!"

His frown deepened as he continued to stare at her, trying to look into her eyes, but she avoided looking directly at him. What was the matter with her anyway? She'd never been cold like this. Reserved perhaps, and inhibited, but never so unfeeling.

She looked away, staring toward the dimly lit lamp on the wall, and he reached down, continuing to watch the expression on her face as he touched her breast, letting his fingers slide over the satin material that encased it, until he felt bare skin; then his fingers searched beneath the material, caressing her nipple softly.

She squirmed beneath him, slowly at first, then more violently. "Paul, what are you doing?" she cried, her eyes finding his again. "You're pawing me!"

This time there was no mistaking the tone of her voice, nor the look of disgust on her face.

"Look, Paul. Why don't you just forget all the nonsense and get it over with?" she went on. "For heaven's sake, I'd rather have that than be pawed all night."

He was at a loss. His fingers hesitated. "I thought you enjoyed making love," he said, trying to make some sense out of what was happening.

She gazed up into his eyes, her own eyes softening. "Oh, but I do," she exclaimed. "I love it when you kiss me."

"For God's sake, Lenore, marriage is more than just a few kisses," he countered.

She tried to laugh and make light of his words, but her heart began pounding so hard it made her breathless. "I know," she answered. "I know. That's why I'm telling you . . . go right ahead, Paul, I'm ready. I know what's expected."

His mind raced quickly as he watched her lips curve into tremulous lines and the expression on her face change from fearful to resigned. Oh, yes, she knew what to expect, all right. What was that his father had said of her parents? Their lives had never been complicated by passion? Evidently Lenore's wasn't going to be either. Yes, she'd tolerate him. She'd let him make love to her, fulfill his male needs, and she wouldn't even respond. She wouldn't do a thing to help, and would probably hate every minute of it.

Well, dammit, he was going to take her anyway, whether she liked it or not. He'd planned to be gentle, pretending to love her and not just possess her, but not anymore. Not now. He was hurt and angry.

Once more his head dropped to her neck, and he began to kiss her, not only messing her hair, but his hand began to knead her nipple vigorously, breaking the thin shoulder strap of her nightgown, baring her breast.

She squirmed again, moving violently beneath him as his mouth sucked at her white throat, and the sweet fragrance of her perfume filled his nostrils, arousing in him an even more bitter rage.

"For heaven's sake, Paul," she gasped helplessly. "What are you doing?"

He gritted his teeth, then jammed his mouth against her ear. "I'm making love to you," he blurted angrily, and she cringed, clenching her fists, body tense.

"Then do it!" she cried breathlessly. "My God! Get done with it," and his eyes closed as his lips moved once more against her skin, sliding down her throat until they reached her taut nipple.

Then suddenly, it wasn't Lenore he saw before him. With his eyes closed like this, he could once more see Gigi's full breasts overflowing her bodice as he lay beside her in the grass. And as his mouth touched Lenore's nipple, it wasn't Lenore's nipple beneath his lips, but Gigi's. The more he thought of her, the more she was there with him, and before long, his movements gentled, and it wasn't Lenore he was making love to, it was Gigi, in his mind and heart. Gigi with her warmth and vibrancy. Gigi with her love. Gigi with her irresistible body that could do things to him no other woman could.

And as he moved over Lenore, his heart racing, body ready to be fulfilled, it wasn't Lenore he plunged into, but Gigi, and he didn't even hear Lenore's muffled cry and the sobbing whimpers that followed it as she gritted her teeth and clenched her fists, accepting his entrance with loathing. He was lost in thoughts of Gigi, and only Gigi.

He let his release come quickly, and as quickly his body relaxed, his head buried against the soft flesh of Lenore's neck. She lay beneath him panting, slow tears seeping from the corners of her eyes, her mouth moving, but no words coming out. She never dreamed it would be this bad. She felt sickened, defiled. The closeness of Paul's body pressing down on her, his spent maleness still against her, made her stomach churn. She could even feel the slimy moisture of his seed between her legs, its warmth covering her soreness.

She let out a sob. "Oh, Paul," she gasped, her voice breaking. "I never dreamed it would be like this!"

He raised his head apprehensively, looking down at her, finally pulling himself from his dream, to the world of reality. "Like what?" he asked.

She avoided his eyes, her face pale. "I don't know, I just can't explain it," she said. "I feel . . ."

"What do you feel?"

She looked dismayed. "Empty . . . dirty . . . unclean!"

He inhaled sharply, then abruptly rolled off her, stood up, and grabbed his underwear from where he'd tossed it. Walking over, he grabbed a towel, cleaning himself off. He set the towel down on the chair and grabbed a clean one, throwing it at her where she still lay on the bed.

"Here, clean up," he said as he pulled his underwear back on.

She reached out gingerly, biting her lip as she used the towel, then handed it back to him and pulled her nightgown down over her exposed body, trying unsuccessfully to keep the side of her nightgown with the torn strap up over her breast.

"Don't worry about it. There's no one to see it but me," he said as he walked over, blew out the light, then returned to the bed. "You can fix it in the morning."

She didn't answer as he climbed in beside her and stretched out. She knew he was angry, that she'd upset him, and she could hear him breathing heavily.

"I'm sorry, Paul," she finally said softly. "I had no idea . . ." Her voice trailed off.

He took a deep breath, staring into the darkness. "I know" was all he could muster.

She moved timidly, moving closer to him, touching his bare arm, her fingers caressing his taut biceps affectionately. "I do love you, Paul. Please, you must believe that," she whispered. "It's just that . . . Mother said it would be all right, that it would hurt a little, but that . . . I never expected . . . I'll get used to it. I will. Please . . ."

Paul closed his eyes, once more smelling the sweet fragrance of her perfume, letting the soft strokes of her fingers linger on his arm as she moved closer to him. Damm it! Why couldn't he just ignore her, treat her as coldly as she'd treated him? But he couldn't. Something in her voice filled him with shame and embarrassment. Maybe she was right. After all, many women were frightened at first. Maybe with time . . .

"Please, Paul, don't be angry with me," she pleaded. "I'll try to do better next time. I promise I will. Don't be angry with me."

"I'm not angry with you," he said huskily, raising his arm for her to come closer, and she snuggled against him, resting her head on his shoulder. "It's my fault. I should have been more understanding."

"Oh, no," she said, her breath warm against his neck. "You had every right. It's my duty, and I'll just have to get used to it. After all, how else can I have a son for you?"

"You want to have a son for me?"

She moved against him, more contented in his arms now that the ordeal was over. "Yes, I want to have a son for you," she said, and kissed him softly on the neck.

"But you don't like making love."

"If what we did is making love, Paul, then no, I don't like it," she said. "I don't know what you got from it, but I got nothing."

"Maybe that's because you've never tried to feel."

"Oh, I felt, Paul." Her body tensed momentarily as she lay against him. "I felt a great deal. It's just that I'm not sure what I felt. . . ." Her voice dropped to a whisper. "I . . . I guess I felt violated."

She felt his arm tighten about her, but he didn't answer, and she held her breath, waiting for a response.

"I'm sorry," he finally said. "I hope I never make you feel that way again," and his lips brushed her hair. "You're my wife, Lenore . . . perhaps you're right, in time . . ." His voice trailed off as Lenore snuggled closer.

It would be all right. She just knew it would. Even if she never got used to it, it would be all right. She could put up with it, and she would, and she'd even try to pretend she liked it. It was a small price to pay for being Mrs. Paul Larrabee. "I love you, Paul," she whispered softly.

He swallowed hard. "I love you too," he lied, and held her close, cradling her in his arms, and suddenly they heard the clang of the coupling outside on the railroad car, then listened as the engine belched loudly and began to move, the jerk of the car telling them that they were on their way to Niagara Falls.

This was it. His wedding night. Oh, God, he wished he could have gotten drunk. Maybe it would have been better.

"Well, I guess we'd better say good night," he said softly.

She reached up and touched his face. "Yes, Paul, we'd better. Good night."

He pulled her closer in his arms, trying to show a semblance of love, listening to the rhythmic click of the wheels as they picked up speed. With their ever-present click to help mesmerize him, and the gentle motion of the train, after a good deal of soul-searching he finally was able to fall into a restless sleep. But all night long he was haunted by dreams. Dreams of the beautiful young woman he loved and had left behind. A woman who could never belong to him.

12

During the next two weeks, while Paul and Lenore sent cards from the International Hotel in Niagara Falls, the Palmer House in Chicago, and the White Sulphur Springs Hotel in West Virginia, with cards and letters from a number of small towns en route, Gigi tried to live a normal life.

Jason seemed to have forgotten her past indiscretions with Paul completely, still treating her as the daughter he should have acknowledged years before. And not once since that miserable evening when he'd accused her of being in love with Paul had he even mentioned it. Evidently he blamed Paul more than he blamed her. He was kind and affectionate, even went out of his way being nice to André, who spent more and more time at the huge mansion.

In fact, the more André came to the house, the more Jason began to trust him, often letting him spend time alone with her. The bicycle that had been collecting dust the past few weeks was once more brought into use, as Gigi, desperate for something to fill her hours, persuaded Jason to let her join the Michaux Club, explaining that she wouldn't be alone. There were dozens of people she could ride with, and often she could be seen, full bloomers catching in the wind, as she wore the latest cycling fashions from Paris and joined the other cyclists through Central Park.

After a great deal of urging on her part, André began to accompany her too, marveling at the maneuverability of the cycles, and laughing uproariously as he wondered what his fellow countrymen would think if they could only see him. It was great fun, and helped the time pass, as well as helping keep her mind off the newlyweds, and Gigi began to laugh again.

One afternoon Jason even let André take her, unchaperoned, to the Rockaway Hunt Club polo games. And since that day turned out well, a few days later he let him escort her to a horse show, then dinner and the theater, just the two of them.

It was obvious he felt André's presence more and more acceptable, and André and Gigi were getting along beautifully.

But the days went slowly, and with each day the hurt inside Gigi scarred deeper into her heart. Especially when Paul's name was mentioned or there was some reminder that he and Lenore were alone together on a honeymoon. Oh, how she wished that honeymoon could have been hers.

She stood in front of the mirror in her room a week after the wedding and stared long and hard at her reflection. "You're a fool, Gigi," she whispered aloud to herself as she studied her face. "A stupid fool. Mooning over a man you have no right to even consider loving, and making yourself miserable in the process."

She brushed a stray hair from her forehead and stood up, straightening the deep blue jacket of her new riding suit. Well, no more. After all, she thought, I'm going through this life only once—why should I brood and make myself sick? I still have André. So she clenched her jaw stubbornly, then left her room, determined to crush and destroy any feeling she might have for Paul. It shouldn't be that hard. Besides, it would be easier with Paul so far away.

She was smiling as she joined André for their canter along the river, and later, when he kissed her and held her close, she kissed him back with a passion resurrected out of loneliness and hurt, hoping it would make her feel better, but it didn't. And that night, alone again with her memories, she cried herself to sleep.

She knew she had to get Paul out of her system one way or another, and the worst part of it was that when he and Lenore returned, they'd be staying at Larrabee Manor. Jason had insisted. He said he couldn't do without having Paul close by, because of business. Paul was like his right arm. He knew the workings of Larrabee Enterprises inside and out, and it was essential that he stay available at a moment's notice. That meant instead of Paul moving out, Lenore would be moving in, and they'd all be under the same roof.

Paul and Lenore were due back on August 2, and during the wait for their return, André proposed three more times. Although his kisses tried to persuade her to say yes, she still couldn't let her heart forget the memory of Paul. Not just yet, so she declined.

But at least she wasn't brooding anymore. By the time the day before their arrival home rolled around, she had accepted things as they were and decided to pretend it didn't matter. It really wasn't that hard if you once put your mind to it. You just hardened your heart so you couldn't feel. And you didn't smile from inside anymore, because if you did, the hard shell would begin to crumble and all would be lost. You smiled only from the outside, never really feeling it. All real emotions were packed tightly together and stored away where they couldn't hurt anymore.

Even with all this, however, she discovered she wasn't as prepared for their arrival home as she thought when the private railroad car the newlyweds had left in brought them back a day early, Tuesday evening, August 1. They arrived at the house unannounced in a rented carriage, bag and baggage, shortly before dark, after having eaten dinner in town.

Jason, Bruce, and Rose were there to greet them. Gigi wished she had been home too, because maybe then, with a lot of people around, the shock of seeing Paul again would have been lessened. But she wasn't. She was out with André when they arrived, and had no idea they'd come home.

It was almost midnight when André brought her home, said good night, and she entered the house. They had seen the lights on in the drawing room when he'd walked her to the door, but neither had been in a mood for petty conversation with anyone. She'd just refused another of his proposals, and the thought of trying to carry on a conversation with Rose or Bruce, or being questioned by Jason, was anathema.

She stood for some time in the foyer, leaning back against the door, wondering why she couldn't bring herself to say yes to André, and wondering how she was going to react tomorrow when the newlyweds arrived home, when she suddenly tensed. Someone had stepped into the foyer from the hallway that led to the drawing room, and had stopped in the shadows, watching her. She had no idea how long the person had been there.

"Ahmed?" she asked hesitantly as she straightened, unfastening the clasp on her turquoise satin cloak, then let it slip from her shoulders.

The figure hesitated, then stepped out of the shadows into the light cast from the fancy wall sconces that graced the foyer walls. As the dim light fell on him, Gigi gasped. "Paul!"

He moved toward her slowly, trying to ignore the disturbing reaction his body was having at the sight of her. She looked enchanting, and it was devastating. How the hell was he going to live normally in the same house with her?

Gigi tried to stop her heart from dropping to her stomach as his eyes caught hers and held.

"We got home a day early," he explained. "I didn't think it necessary to wire ahead."

"I see." She bit her lip, knees trembling. "I hope you don't expect me to ask if you had a nice trip," she said, still trying to catch her breath from the shock.

His face was grim. "I don't."

"Good." She turned away reluctantly, knowing that if she didn't, she might walk right into his arms. "Where's Lenore?" she asked unsteadily as she hung her cloak on the hall tree, since there seemed to be no servants about.

"I'm right here," said Lenore from the other side of the foyer, and both Gigi and Paul turned abruptly in surprise.

Neither had seen or heard her enter. She'd stepped from the hallway into the foyer as Gigi turned to hang up her cloak, missing their earlier exchange of words by seconds, but neither of them knew it and both watched her apprehensively. Now she approached them languorously, the skirt of her green silk traveling suit leaving a soft rustling in her wake.

She still looked the same, thought Gigi. Every hair in place, clothes immaculate, her walk graceful and sedate, and as usual, Gigi felt intimidated.

Gigi had worn her hair loose tonight, held back on each side with pearl-trimmed combs, and small strands of it had fallen, curling haphazardly about her forehead from the slight breeze that had caught it while André walked her to the door. On top of that, her turquoise satin dress was rumpled from the ride in the carriage, two of the seed pearls missing from its bodice, having come loose when André's embraces had become too exuberant during the ride. Her jaw tightened stubbornly as Lenore took Paul's arm.

Gigi tried to think of something to say as she stared at this beautiful woman who was now Paul's wife, but could think of nothing. It was Lenore who broke the awkwardly strained silence.

"Well, what a surprise," she said. "We heard the carriage, and your father sent Paul to make sure it was you, since he already excused the servants for the evening. I was wondering what was taking him so long."

Paul inhaled sharply, putting his hand over Lenore's where her arm was tucked through his, her hand resting on his forearm. "We were getting ready to retire," said Paul as he continued to stare at the delectable young woman in front of them, at the same time conscious of Lenore's cool, smooth hand beneath his. "I think Father was worried because you got home so late. Isn't André coming in?"

"He has an early appointment in the morning." She straightened her skirt self-consciously, then pushed the stray strands of hair back to where they belonged before going on, her voice still unsteady, although she tried not to let it show. "You'll have to excuse me," she finally said. "But I . . . well, we didn't expect you home until tomorrow. I'm still a little surprised—"

"We had a simply glorious time," cut in Lenore, looking pleased. "But Paul ran into a business associate while we were in West Virginia, and decided we'd better not chance staying away that extra day. Something about stocks and gold certificates or something, wasn't it, darling?" she asked.

Paul nodded. "But it's nothing to worry about. Just something I felt shouldn't wait."

Lenore smiled radiantly. "Oh, White Sulphur Springs is marvelous, Gigi," she cooed softly. "Picnics, balls, the whole atmosphere's so romantic. It's the ideal place for a honeymoon." She glanced quickly at Paul, then back to Gigi. "But then, Chicago was marvelous too. Of course, nothing can compare with Paris, and I'd have loved to go there, but Paul explained that he couldn't be gone that long this year. He did promise, though, that we'd go next year. That is, unless I'm in the family way by then. We do so hope to have a family right away," she said.

Gigi stared at her hard. For some reason, she just couldn't imagine Lenore being pregnant. Not meticulously groomed Lenore. How in the world would she ever walk gracefully with her stomach sticking out in front of her, and what would she do when she couldn't see her feet anymore? The thought was provokingly funny, only Gigi felt too miserable to laugh.

"How nice," she remarked, trying to be cordial and sisterly. "But I didn't know you were fond of children, Lenore."

Lenore's face flushed slightly as her haughty eyes stared Gigi down. "One isn't fond or unfond of children, Gigi," she replied. "It's every woman's duty to have children. And I intend to give Paul at least one son, and it's logical that the sooner it's accomplished, the better."

Gigi saw the flicker of distaste in Lenore's eyes, and decided that the lady's words were braver than her actions. Suddenly she wondered too if perhaps Lenore was as cold and impersonal in bed as she was out, or had Paul been able to thaw her reserve? Paul! Her eyes shifted to his, and suddenly Gigi's knees felt weak. Paul in bed with Lenore, Paul caressing her, wanting her. Oh, God! She had to stop. Had to think of something else before she lost control completely. She took a deep breath. "Are you two the only ones up?" she asked, changing the subject.

Paul caught the slight trembling of her lips. "No," he said, trying to help ease the awkward situation. "Rose and Bruce are home tonight too, and Father insisted we all stay up until you arrived."

Gigi started to move toward the hallway, and Lenore and Paul turned with her. "I suppose he's waiting for a report on my evening with André," she said, trying to keep the talk on a more comfortable subject, at least for her, as they accompanied her from the foyer toward the drawing room. "Father's been quite lenient lately where André's concerned," she went on as they walked through the hallway. "I do believe he's beginning to like him."

"You're still seeing him often, then?" asked Paul.

"Almost every day." She tried to smile casually. "Can you imagine, I even talked him into going cycling with me." Remembering the sight of André on a bicycle for the first time brought a genuine smile to her lips, and her eyes shone impishly as she momentarily forgot her heartache. "I don't think I've ever seen anything funnier—" she laughed softly— "than a Spanish gentleman, used to riding a magnificent stallion, trying to master a pair of handlebars and two skinny wheels. It's quite the sight."

"You mean he actually went cycling with you?" asked Lenore.

Gigi's smile broadened as she relaxed a little. Maybe if she could keep things between them neutral, it would work. She sighed. "He did," she answered as they moved beneath the arches into the drawing room. "And Father let us take the sailboat up the river. I'm not much for sailing, though, and neither is André, so we took Ahmed along for moral support that day." Gigi turned from Paul and Lenore, greeting her father as they entered the room, and she walked over, kissing him on the cheek. "Father, you shouldn't have stayed up. It's so late," she said.

Jason squeezed her hand as she kissed him, his eyes caressing her beautiful face. She looked so like her mother. He glanced at Lenore and Paul as Gigi straightened, planting herself defensively beside his wheelchair, her hand resting on Jason's shoulder.

"She's right, you know. It's late," said Jason. "And I imagine you and Lenore are tired from the long ride, Paul. Perhaps we should say good night."

Gigi followed his eyes as he addressed Rose and Bruce, who were watching her stoically from where they sat on the sofa. Rose's eyes were steady on Gigi, her lips pursed disagreeably, as her hands nervously smoothed the skirt of her pink cambric dress, and Bruce looked stilted and uncomfortable as he followed suit, his eyes sifting over her disapprovingly, while his finger tried to loosen the knot in his ascot tie where it evidently was irritating his Adam's apple, turning his face almost the same shade of deep purple as his Prince Albert frock coat.

"You two are going up too now, aren't you?" he suggested. "After all, we have had a rather exciting evening. I think it would do us all good to get a good night's rest."

Ahmed emerged from the shadows, as usual, as everyone started saying good night, and for once Gigi was thankful Rose and Bruce were around as Ahmed disappeared with Jason into his private quarters. At least with Rose and Bruce along, she didn't have to walk upstairs alone with Lenore and Paul. The conversation as they went to their rooms stayed light and impersonal, and she was glad.

It was still hard for Gigi, however, after saying good night to them, to watch Paul disappear into his room down the hall with Lenore on his arm, knowing that within minutes she'd be lying beside him in bed. She was almost in tears, so it was a relief when she entered her own room and discovered that Bridget had waited up for her. Bridget could always make her forget for a while, and it wasn't until later, when the lights were out and the moon filtered silently in through the open French doors, that she began to cry softly before finally drifting off into a dream-filled sleep.

The next few weeks were a war of nerves for both Gigi and Paul. Although they tried to avoid each other whenever possible, there were times when it just couldn't be. She'd bump into him alone in the hallway, or outside. She even rose earlier than usual one day to avoid having to face him at the breakfast table, only to discover he'd done the same.

While Paul and Lenore had been away, Jason had gotten the brilliant idea to have Gigi straighten out Paul's filing cabinets one afternoon when she'd been wandering around looking for something to do. Now Gigi realized she should have refused, because Paul was always having to call her in to find something for him that she'd managed to file away under a different heading, according to her personal filing system, and the atmosphere in Paul's combination office-library was rather conducive to quiet intimacy. Soon, in order to survive, the two began sniping at each other again in defense whenever the going became too rough to take.

Rose still ostracized Gigi, as did Bruce, but both of them accepted Lenore into the fold. Rose however, never really accepted anyone who tried to run the household and take the prestige from her. So although she accepted Lenore as Paul's wife, she never relinquished her position. If Lenore so much as dared to infringe on what Rose assumed were her rights as Jason's daughter, she brewed up a storm.

But Lenore didn't seem to mind. Instead, she enjoyed her leisure hours doing as she pleased, without any demands being made on her. Her life was comfortable and she was pleased with it. At least she would have been if it hadn't been for one thing. Ever since their arrival home, Paul had become quiet and exceptionally irritable. And she began to realize that he was even more so when Gigi was around.

The air between Gigi and Paul was almost explosive, as if they were silently battling each other. And there were times when Lenore would discover them standing alone together talking. They'd act so guilty. Once she'd finally managed to convince herself that she was only letting Rose's uncalled-for remarks get to her because of the earlier insinuations, then her mind had been changed abruptly when she'd caught them staring at each other across the dinner table with that same soulful look she'd seen on their faces on the dance floor the night of the wedding reception, and her fears once more emerged, haunting her.

Rose's remarks didn't help either. She still hinted that something was going on. It was maddening. Every night when she crawled in bed beside Paul, Lenore tried to convince herself that it wasn't true. That it was only her imagination. She even tried to force herself to enjoy his lovemaking, in the hopes it would still the pain her suspicions aroused and make Paul love her all the more. She was Mrs. Paul Larrabee, and nothing was going to spoil it for her. Nothing!

The days moved into weeks, and it was hot, even for August. Sometimes the temperature soared into the nineties, and no one could seem to find relief from it. André still courted Gigi, and her near proximity to Paul, and frustration over her suppressed desires, made her even more reckless where he was concerned. Once, when they'd been alone on a picnic, she'd even let him caress her as she'd let Paul, hoping to recapture what she'd found in Paul's arms. His hands had been gentle, his kisses passionate, words tender and loving, and it had felt good, bringing some of the familiar feeling back to her loins. But it wasn't the same, and she felt empty inside as she stared up into his dark, compelling eyes, cursing Paul for what he'd done to her, and cursing herself for having come to New York.

She'd changed so much since her arrival. The last time she'd looked into her mirror she'd realized that there was little resemblance now to the naive young woman who'd sat cross-legged in the big four-poster bed at Mrs. Thornapple's and wondered who she was. Her eyes were no longer innocent, but held a depth of passion that marked her as a woman. Oh, God, that she could go back. That she didn't have to be Gigi Rouvier anymore.

It was the end of August. The thirtieth, to be exact. Jason, with Ahmed at his side, accompanied by Bruce, Rose, and Lenore, was at the Van Der Lindens', where they'd been invited for a small dinner party. Paul had been invited too, but had declined, having to attend a business meeting in town in Jason's place.

Gigi hadn't gone along to the Van Der Lindens' either. Instead, she'd been to the theater that evening with André, but had made him bring her home early. She'd used the lame excuse that she had a headache. The real reason was that he'd proposed again, only this time, instead of asking for an answer right away, he'd insisted she wait until tomorrow.

"Maybe it'll be better when you have time to think it out, *querida*," he'd insisted, and had kissed her passionately, declaring his undying love.

He'd been serious, much more so than in his earlier proposals, and it had upset her. She had to be alone to think. So she declined his offer to attend a party after the theater, and had him bring her home.

On reaching her bedroom, she let Bridget help her into a pink lace nightgown, then took the pins from her hair, letting it fall, and brushed it vigorously while Bridget hung up her clothes.

What could she tell him? How long would André hang around waiting for an answer? She stared at her reflection in the mirror. Maybe he was right. Maybe she did need time to think about it more, instead of just saying no so quickly. Was André the answer? She cared for him. At least she thought she did. They had fun together and seemed to get along well. True, there were things about him that puzzled her at times. Sometimes he seemed so distant and reserved, and at others so warm and generous. Almost as if he were acting a part. If only she could be sure. One thing she was definitely sure of: she couldn't have Paul. What to do?

She set the hairbrush down, saying good night as Bridget left to go back to her room in the servants' quarters; then she climbed into bed, leaving the lamp on. She'd just read for a little. She picked up a book from the stand, settling back, bunching the pillows beneath her head, and relaxed.

It was close to midnight when she finally looked up from the book, stretching against the satin sheets, trying to ease the tension from her body. She hadn't really been absorbed in the book, only reading the words. They hadn't penetrated. Her eyes had read them, but nothing much had registered.

She glanced up at the lamp, frowning. It was getting dim. Oh, drat! The maids must have forgotten to fill it. Too bad they lived too far out for gas lights. It would be a lot easier if all they had to do was turn a knob instead of worrying whether they were running out of kerosene. Oh, well, maybe soon those newfangled electric things everyone was talking about would be available for everyone.

She watched the lamp as it got dimmer and dimmer, then went out completely, plunging the room into darkness. She shrugged, setting the book aside. She wouldn't bother anymore tonight. But she could use a bite to eat. She thought of the pastries Mrs. Sharp always had down in the kitchen, and her mouth began to water. Why not? She could go down the servants' stairs. Who'd see her?

She slipped from the bed and moved through the room, using the moonlight streaming in at the French doors that led to the balcony for light. She made her way to the chair where Bridget had draped her matching dressing gown and began putting it on, slipping her arms in the sleeves as she headed for the door.

Downstairs, Paul had just reached the house after stabling his horse. One of the downstairs maids met him at the door, took his hat and gloves, then informed him that the others weren't home yet.

He sighed as she went back toward the kitchen; then he made his way slowly toward the drawing room. He was glad no one else was home. The thought of facing Lenore right now was upsetting. It had been a long time since he'd ridden home at night alone in the moonlight, and it reminded him of another night when he'd ridden home with Gigi on the horse in front of him. He could even remember the smell of her hair and the soft, gentle curve of her body as it nestled against him.

The situation here was impossible. How could you stop loving someone simply because you were told to? He reached the staircase, ascending slowly, his thoughts miles away. Maybe he could get to bed and asleep before Lenore got home. He kept trying to put off making love to her, but she was so obsessed with the idea of getting pregnant so she could have a son. Sometimes he wished she would get pregnant, then maybe he wouldn't have to touch her. Not so often, anyway. It was obvious she still didn't enjoy his invasion of her body. She'd stiffen and tense, pretending it was all right, yet dreading every moment, and she thought he couldn't tell. If she wasn't such a beautiful woman with such an exquisite body, and if he weren't so starved for Gigi, he probably wouldn't be able to do a thing. But as it was, she always managed to arouse him. He was getting tired of the empty act, though. It meant nothing to him but a physical release, and tonight he just wanted to be alone with his thoughts. He almost hadn't even come home, only he decided getting drunk and staying out all night wasn't the answer.

Maybe he could talk his father into letting them leave to find a place of their own. At least that would help. He wouldn't have to see Gigi every day.

He reached the landing and started down the hall, shedding his suit coat, loosening his tie, but as he reached the door to Gigi's room, he stopped, not quite knowing why. She was still out with André, and his heart lurched at the thought. He hated the man for no other reason than his interest in Gigi. Jason had checked him out and discovered that he was exactly who he claimed to be. André Diego de los Reyes, the cousin of General Reyes, commander of President Díaz's northern Mexican forces. And André also happened to be the son of a wealthy landowner. He was special aide to President Díaz, and attaché to the Mexican consulate in New York.

Paul stood in the dimly lit upstairs hallway, his suit coat slung across one arm, staring at the door to Gigi's bedroom, when suddenly it burst open and Gigi stood there, one arm plunged into her dressing gown, the other searching for the remaining sleeve.

She stopped stark still, mouth gaping, and stared back at him, forgetting completely that the lace nightgown she had on revealed more than it should. She hadn't heard him come home.

Paul couldn't take his eyes from her. He'd purposely tried to avoid explosive situations; now suddenly one was thrust on him with no warning, no time to set up any barriers. His eyes fell on her dark hair curling riotously onto her shoulders, touching the creamy skin that was bared beneath only a bit of narrow satin cording. Every line, every curve of her body was exposed beneath the lace, one nipple showing deep rosy pink amid the delicate design that revealed more than it covered. She looked warm, tousled, and inviting. Her eyes shone, lips parting, but no words came from her.

"Gigi," he whispered huskily, staring into her blue-green eyes, and he unconsciously took a step toward her, as if drawn like a moth to a flame.

They hung, balanced there, staring into each other's eyes, neither moving nor uttering another sound as the air about them became charged with the ecstasy of a moment caught in time and space.

Then suddenly he was over the threshold, the door was closed behind him, his suit coat lay on the floor beside her dressing gown, and she was in his arms, her mouth hot against his, the searing passion fusing them together.

He lifted her in his arms and carried her to the bed, divesting her of her nightgown as he gently laid her down; then his hands traveled the length of her small fragile body, exploring every precious curve, every soft hill and warm valley.

There was only moonlight in the room now, but it was enough to see her by, and he'd never seen anything so exquisite before in his life. Her waist was small, hips well-rounded, breasts full and sensitive. As he touched them, the nipples surged up hard and firm in answer, and she moaned, her hands moving up to caress his neck, then slipping lower to where the buttons of his shirt restricted their movement.

"I need you, Paul," she whispered breathlessly, her mouth against his, and he straightened, almost ripping the shirt from his body as he hurriedly undressed.

He sank onto the bed and rolled against her, and not even the cold satin sheets could cool the heat that ran through him. Her skin was like velvet against his, her mouth like intoxicating wine, and he drank his fill as she responded.

Gigi was on fire. Her body ready to explode. Every nerve was alive, waiting.

Paul kissed her, then let his lips trail down to the pulse at the front of her throat, sending shivers through her. His hand moved from her breast to her hip, then across her, burying itself in the patch of dark hair, where his fingers probed, beginning to stroke her gently.

"Oh, Paul, I love you," she cried against his ear, and he raised his head, gazing down into her blue-green eyes.

"You know what we're doing is wrong, don't you?" he asked.

"Yes!" She shook her head. "But I don't care. I can't go on like this, Paul. It's driving me crazy. I have to know. Paul. I have to know what's it's like. I have to stop the ache inside."

He stared at her, drinking in her loveliness, the promises he had made to his father, to himself, and to Lenore all forgotten.

"And so you shall," he whispered against her mouth. "I'll make you forget everything, my darling, everything but this," and his mouth took hers once more, urging her to a violent response that shook the foundations of her soul until only the moment mattered.

When he moved over her and entered, the movement was

so quick, the passion so strong, the need so great, that Gigi felt nothing but a slight pain, quickly gone and replaced by a profound ecstasy and rapture. He thrust into her over and over again, and it was heavenly as he brought her to a peak of pleasure that made her cry out. She gasped, clinging to him desperately, and Paul knew her release had begun. His heart was full as he felt her body arch eagerly against him, taking all he could give, wanting every inch of him and reveling in it. He wanted nothing more than this beautiful woman. Had wanted her for so long. He held her close, and as he plunged deep, his heart soaring, his body shook in an agony of pleasurable sensations that ripped his soul from inside him, fusing it to hers, and they were one.

His lips softened against hers, the trembling over, and he inhaled as he raised his head. He'd never felt like this before in his life. Never had his release been so strong, so overpowering. Never had his heart felt like it was bursting inside him.

"I love you," he whispered softly against her mouth. "I love you," and he kissed her again.

She trembled as his kiss went through her; then he raised his head again, and she looked up into his warm gray eyes. "What do we do now, Paul?" she asked softly, afraid of his answer.

He lay above her, still inside her, his body a part of her, and touched her cheek lightly, running his finger down until it reached the corner of her mouth. "I wish I knew," he said. "I know I love you and I'm not allowed to, and it's killing me."

She moved her head so her lips touched his finger, and she kissed it softly. "Is there an answer, Paul?" she asked. "Somewhere in this crazy world of ours, is there really any answer for people like us, or do we go on all our lives loving each other and feeling guilty about it?"

He moved slowly, slipping from her, and as he did so, he pulled her close in his arms, letting her head rest on his shoulder, but the moment was lost as he suddenly strained his ears.

"Listen!" he cried softly, and as they held their breaths, the sound of a carriage, horses, and harness creaked and clopped on the drive beneath the portico out front, the noise drifting in through the French doors. "My God! They're home, Gigi!" he cried softly, and raised up on his elbows, his face pale.

"Paul, you've got to go!" she whispered anxiously. "If

Lenore finds you in here . . . if Father finds out . . . My
God, Paul!"

He reached out, cupping her head in his hands, kissing her
quickly, then jumped from the bed, rummaging around in the
dark for his clothes.

She left the bed and helped him, bumping into him in the
dark, and he stumbled against the furniture, cursing his care-
lessness as he struggled into his underwear.

She shoved his suit coat, shirt, and pants at him as he
picked up his shoes and stockings, hesitating for a minute,
looking about in the moonlight to see if he'd forgotten anything.

"Hurry!" she urged. "Oh, Paul, do hurry."

He reached for the door, and glanced out, relieved to find
the hall still empty, and started to leave, when she stopped
him.

"Your cufflinks!" she cried. "Wait!" She ran back into the
room and grabbed them off the stand where he'd left them,
shoving them into his hand as he stepped out; then she hurriedly closed the door behind him. But as she did so, neither
of them saw or heard one of the cufflinks drop to the hall
carpet and wedge itself under the edge of the door, where it
lay barely visible.

Paul bunched the clothes in his arms and ran down the
hall, wearing only his underwear, yanking the door to his bedroom open and stepping quickly inside. He closed the door
behind him and sighed, then moved rapidly about the room,
setting the stage. He flung what he thought were both cufflinks on the dresser, his shirt, pants, and suit coat haphazardly onto the chair, then pulled back the covers on the bed
and jumped in, settling down, trying to slow his breathing so
it sounded as if he'd been asleep, or at least dozing, and
waited for Lenore.

Lenore would have been pleased with the evening if it
hadn't been for Rose. More and more as the days went on,
she'd begun to resent Paul's sister, and she could understand
some of his anger with her over the years. She was vicious
and vengeful. Just because she hated Gigi was no reason she
should keep insinuating that something was going on between
Gigi and Paul. She'd kept it up all evening, every chance she
had.

Really, it was too much. Paul was in love with her. Hadn't
he told her so dozens of times already since the wedding?

And she was going to have Paul's baby. She just knew it. Maybe she'd even discover she was pregnant before the month was over. God knows she'd been trying hard enough. She abhorred the thought of being pregnant and having to be disfigured for so long. But it couldn't be helped. A son would cement her marriage and ensure her position as Paul's wife. Every man wanted a son. Even her father had wanted a son, and the fact that he'd never had one had always been a disappointment. Well, she wasn't going to disappoint Paul. Much as she hated it, she'd have his son, and he'd have no reason ever to stop loving her, because she'd be a dutiful wife. Gigi! Rose was impossible.

Lenore had left them all in the drawing room, going upstairs right away when she'd learned Paul was already home.

"And Miss Gigi came home early too. About an hour before Mr. Paul." the maid had said.

Lenore had caught Rose's sly look as they'd listened to the maid's words, but she brushed it aside, trying to forget it as she reached the top of the stairs, straightening the skirt on her deep violet dress. The low, tucked bodice of the dress was embroidered with small delicate flowers, and set off to advantage the huge amethyst that graced her throat and ornamented her earlobes. Her hair was still in place, her back erect as she started walking down the upstairs hall, but her thoughts were miles away. She was thinking about Paul, and her honeymoon, and when they'd ever have a place of their own.

Suddenly she frowned, her steps slowing as she stopped in front of Gigi's bedroom door, cocking her head to one side, trying to see better, and she squinted, staring at the floor. Something was stuck beneath the door, sparkling off and on as the light in the wall sconce fell on it. She'd noticed it as she walked down the hall. It had obviously wedged there when someone shut the door.

She sighed absentmindedly and bent down, running her fingers beneath the edge of the door, pulling the object, pressing it into the carpet to loosen it, then yanking it free.

She stood up, held it in her hand, then suddenly came to life as she stared in disbelief, swallowing hard, her stomach tightening. Paul's cufflink. It was Paul's cufflink! Now, what on earth was it doing wedged beneath his sister's bedroom door?

A strange sensation began to creep up her spine, raising

gooseflesh on the nape of her neck, and she bit her lips. Gigi and Paul? Was Rose right? No! She shook her head, tears beginning to well up in her eyes. She didn't want to believe it. There had to be some other explanation. Maybe it fell as he was walking down the hall. But if it had, it wouldn't have been wedged under the door, would it?

Her troubled eyes moved up from her hand, and she stared at the closed door before her. What if Paul was in there? A wave of nausea swept over her. The maid said Gigi came home early. She had to know. Had to find out. Her fingers wrapped tightly around the cufflink, she reached up, her hand trembling, and knocked.

Gigi was back in bed again, trying to still her pounding heart. She held her breath when she heard the knock. "Come in!"

Lenore opened the door gingerly and stepped in, leaving the door open behind her, adjusting her eyes in the darkened room. She could barely see Gigi's vague outline on the bed. She was alone, and Lenore sighed, relieved. Now she had to think of some sort of reason for disturbing her.

Gigi was unnerved. Still flushed and warm inside from Paul's lovemaking. The shock of being torn from him so abruptly had given her the sensation of suddenly being plunged into ice water. She was pale and trembling as Lenore stared at her.

"I'm sorry, Gigi," Lenore began, "but the maid said you came home early because you weren't feeling well. I thought I'd drop by to make sure you're all right."

"I'm fine," she muttered softly, curious about Lenore's concern. "Only a little headache. Nothing to worry about."

Lenore glanced quickly about the moonlit room just to make sure, then apologized and left, closing the door firmly behind her. She stood stock-still, one hand holding the doorknob, the other still clutching the cufflink. Paul wasn't there, no, but he had been, she was sure of it. She could have sworn she'd caught the faint masculine odor of him as she stood inside the door. He used a special highly scented soap and toilet articles. It was the smell she always associated with Paul and no one else, and there was no logical reason why the odor should have been in Gigi's room. None, unless he'd been there.

She straightened, tilting her chin up stubbornly. No! There had to be another explanation. Maybe she was imagining it, letting Rose's hints and innuendos cloud her senses. She stared down the hall, determined to let nothing mar her happiness with Paul. He did love her. She was certain. He had to love her—he'd married her, hadn't he? She headed down the hall.

She hesitated, then opened the door to the bedroom she and Paul shared, and stepped in. The room was dark, and as she glanced toward the bed, she vaguely made out Paul's long form. Was he asleep, or just pretending? She walked to the dresser, set the cufflink down, picked up a match, struck it, then lit the lamp on the dresser, setting the chimney back on.

She was ready to turn toward the bed again, when she glanced at the top of the dresser, to where she'd set the cufflink. There directly next to the one she'd set down, was its mate, big as life. Her heart sank. That meant Paul had been wearing them tonight.

Her eyes moved to the chair next to the dresser, to the shirt where it lay beneath the suit coat and pants. She frowned. How strange that the shirt should be under the suit. Wasn't it logical that as Paul undressed, the shirt would be taken off last, and be on the top of the suit?

She exhaled nervously, then pursed her lips. But then, maybe when he undressed he had set his clothes on the bed, tossing them onto the chair afterward. It was possible. She turned. "Paul? Are you asleep?"

He moved slightly. "Not fully." Then he stretched, pretending to have been dozing. "I didn't hear you come in."

"We just got back." She came over and sat on the edge of the bed with her back to him, hoping her voice showed no signs of hostility. "Will you unfasten me?"

He blinked, squinting as he adjusted to the light. He hesitated, but only for a moment, then reached over and began unhooking the back of her gown.

"The maid said you got home not quite an hour ago," she said. "Did you know Gigi came home early too?"

He thought back to what the maid had told him when he'd come home. She'd said the others hadn't returned yet; he'd assumed she'd meant Gigi too, and he remembered how surprised he'd been when she opened her bedroom door. "No, I didn't," he replied. "She wasn't downstairs when I came in."

"She's in bed with a headache. At least, that's what she says." Lenore sighed as he finished unfastening her; then she stood up and began to undress. "I think it's just an excuse, though," she said, slipping from her dress, laying it across the chair for the maid to hang up in the morning. "I think maybe she might have had a quarrel with André." She kept talking as she finished getting ready for bed. "Did you notice how unsettled André seemed earlier when he came to take her to the theater?" she asked. "I think he's been trying to decide whether to ask her to marry him or not, and wondering if your father will approve."

Paul watched Lenore as she stepped from her underthings. There was no mistaking the fact that she was lovely. But she was so different from Gigi.

She pulled on a filmy nightgown of pink organza. This done, she walked over to blow out the lamp. For a fraction of a minute he saw her look down, staring at something on the dresser by the lamp; then she blew the lamp out and returned to the bed. Climbing in, she cuddled close, forcing him to put an arm about her.

His body was still satiated from Gigi's lovemaking, and he instinctively pulled Lenore close, basking in the afterglow and the balm of contentment her nearness afforded as a substitute for Gigi.

"I missed you tonight, Paul," she whispered softly, and he drew in a sharp breath.

Not that. Lord, not that. He could hold her like this, but make love to her after what he'd just been through? Never!

"The meeting was hectic," he answered huskily. "And exhausting. I didn't even take time for a nightcap before coming to bed. I hope you don't mind if we go to sleep right away, Lenore. I'm really exceptionally tired tonight."

She ran her cheek along his arm, then buried her lips against his shoulder. She loved kissing him and having him kiss her. It felt warm and good. Made her tingle all over. It was just the pawing she didn't like, and the other degrading surrender that filled her with loathing. This she reveled in. The soft feel of his skin against her lips, the flush that went through her when their lips met. She breathed in deeply, then suddenly stopped, holding her breath. That smell on his skin. That sensuous fragrance mingling with the scent of his soap.

She sniffed in again, trying not to be obvious, then tensed, resting her head back onto his shoulder. The smell was unmistakable. It was the fragrance that always clung to Gigi. Oh, God! What now? He had to have been with her. Did she dare say anything. The cufflink, the scent of him in Gigi's room, now this! If something was going on, how far had it gone?

Suddenly she felt sick, her mouth dry. Paul loved her! Or did he? Her mind was racing. Could it be possible? Had Paul married her to cover it up? Or perhaps hoping the marriage would put a stop to it? But then, he'd asked her to marry him long before Gigi'd come to New York. Her jaw clenched stubbornly. No! That wasn't the answer. He did love her, not Gigi. This was probably something else entirely and had nothing to do with love. Something like what Jason had done years before. Men couldn't always help themselves with women like Gigi. Even men like Paul. But, my God, this was even worse than what Jason had done. Well, if it had happened, it wasn't going to happen again. If anything was going on, it wasn't Paul's fault. It was the fault of that wretched dark-haired witch his father had brought into the house.

Lenore made her decision with misgivings, but with no idea of what else she might do. For now she wouldn't say anything. She was just going to watch, keeping her eyes and ears open. Maybe Rose was right and had seen something the rest of them had been blind to. If so, she'd deal with it somehow, some way. The thought of Paul committing incest was preposterous, yet what had happened tonight couldn't be ignored. It was obvious that something *had* happened. Maybe not incest, but that could be next. She couldn't let it happen. If Gigi thinks she's going to seduce Paul away from me, she's sadly mistaken, she told herself stubbornly. Paul belongs to me now.

She looked over at the outline of his face close to hers. How many years she'd loved him and longed to be Mrs. Paul Larrabee. Oh, Paul, she whispered softly to herself, how could you let something like this happen? How could you? Gigi's your sister! Suddenly the thought that he might have touched Gigi, even kissed her or, worse, made love to her, made her skin crawl, and she moved slowly, hesitantly to her own side of the bed.

"I'm glad you're tired tonight, Paul," she finally said as she made sure there was absolutely no contact between them, "because I am too. Terribly tired." He was surprised as she plumped the pillow up, then rested her head back on it, making sure she didn't mess up her hair. Tomorrow she'd watch.

Tomorrow and the next day, and the next, until she had definite proof, then she'd put a stop to Gigi, even if she had to force Jason to send her away. She closed her eyes. "Good night."

Eventually she fell into a fitful, frightening sleep, while, beside her, Paul frowned, unable to relax, wondering why Lenore had suddenly decided to forsake her obsession with trying to become pregnant.

Unless . . . Maybe she thought she was already pregnant and was just waiting for confirmation. His frown deepened as he lay in the dark, thinking. My God! Gigi could get pregnant too. He cursed softly to himself. What a fool he'd been, and what on earth would they do if she did? This time when he vowed to keep hands off, the promise was made with more conviction than he'd ever felt before in his life, and he went to sleep with a memory of her he knew would have to last a lifetime.

Down the hall, Gigi still sat up in bed, staring in the darkness toward the door Lenore had closed only a short time before. The scent of Paul, from where he'd lain beside her, drifted up from the satin sheets, and a hollow, empty feeling crept through her. Lenore knew, or at least suspected. She was sure of it. Something in her eyes had betrayed her suspicions, and she'd looked on the verge of tears.

Slowly she pushed back the covers and climbed from the bed, making her way across the moonlit room to where she could stand beside the French doors and look out. There had to be an answer somewhere. There had to. She couldn't go on like this. She could never again be the young woman from Mrs. Thornapple's, she knew. There was no going back to start over again,. But she had to find some solution, because to keep moving in the direction she was moving was nothing short of disaster.

She mulled over everything that had happened in the past few months, and only one thing seemed clear. There was only one answer to her problem, to everything. She didn't want it, not really, but it was the only thing she could do. She stared out into the hot summer night, listening to the crickets with their lilting serenade, and made one of the hardest decisions she'd ever had to make.

Moments later, when she climbed back into bed, she prayed to God it wouldn't be the wrong one and that she hadn't made it too late, yet even though her decision had been made with a clear head and sensible reasoning, her pillow was wet, and dawn was just beyond the horizon when she finally fell asleep.

13

Gigi was surprised. She had slept until well past the noon hour, and no one had come to see how she was. No one but Bridget, that is. However, Gigi hadn't been aware of her visits. Every time the young girl checked on her she'd been sleeping. The night before, the maids had reported that Gigi had asked André to bring her home early from the theater because of a headache, so everyone assumed she was merely suffering from a minor ailment that would soon be slept off.

Only Paul knew the real reason for her procrastinations, but he dared not give himself away. Instead, he buried himself in his office, pretending to keep busy while he raked his conscience over the coals. Hating himself for what he'd done to her, yet remembering her lovemaking with reverence.

When Gigi finally did emerge from the pink satin covers, with her eyes slightly swollen from crying and her head really aching, Bridget was there to greet her. "Good morning," she said softly. "Or should I say good afternoon?"

Gigi squinted as she tried to adjust her eyes to the bright sunlight that was streaming in at the French doors. "Bridget?"

Bridget reached down and touched Gigi's forehead, making sure there was no fever. "How do you feel?"

"Terrible." She closed her eyes again, then turned over onto her back. "My head feels like a balloon."

"You look like you've been crying."

Gigi flushed. "I guess I have."

"Can I help?"

She opened her eyes and stared at the ceiling. "Not with the crying, but you can get me something for this head. No laudanum, though. I've slept enough for one day."

223

Bridget left and came back a short time later with a water glass half-full of a pale amber liquid.

Gigi scowled as Bridget handed it to her. "What's this?"

"It's only hot water, cider vinegar, and two teaspoonfuls of honey."

"You expect me to drink it? And on an empty stomach?"

"It isn't that bad, really, Miss Gigi," she said solicitously. "It soothes the nerves and helps. Drink it down while it's still hot, and I'll go get you something to eat. I told Mrs. Sharp to fix you a tray."

Gigi wrinkled her nose in distaste as Bridget once more left the room. She leaned forward, sniffed the tart-smelling brew, then sighed.

Ten minutes later, when Bridget returned, the glass was empty, and Gigi was propped up against the pillows, anxious for a bite of something, anything, so she could get the taste out of her mouth.

"That was horrible," she told Bridget as the young girl set a bed tray in front of her. "I hope Mrs. Sharp fixed me something strong enough to take away the taste."

The tray was on legs, so it rested like a bench across Gigi's lap, and she began lifting lids to see what she'd brought. "Chicken soup?" she asked as she glanced at Bridget.

"Well, you slept through breakfast, and it *is* the best thing for an upset stomach," the girl replied.

"It wasn't my stomach that was upset."

"It's good for your head, too," insisted Bridget, and walked to the powder room, disappearing inside.

Gigi heard water running. "I don't feel like a bath. Not right now," she said, loud enough to be heard in the powder room. "Later."

The water stopped abruptly, and Bridget emerged once more, tossing her long honey-blond hair back away from her face as she stared at her mistress. "Your father wants to know if you still want Mr. André to come for dinner tonight," she said, smoothing the skirt of her gray uniform dress. "Will you feel up to it?"

Gigi tasted the soup, then nodded. "Certainly. I'm not really sick. Not seriously, anyway," she said as she stirred the soup. "I'll be fine by the time André arrives. Besides, I have an announcement to make tonight at dinner."

Gigi was feeling much better and looked lovely in a pale lemon dress of sheer organza, the bouffant sleeves and full skirt trimmed with delicate lace, the shirred bodice clinging low, emphasizing her full bosom. Instead of piling her hair atop her head, she'd simply pulled it back and tied it with a yellow ribbon. The effect made her look young and innocent as she faced her father, who sat at the head of the table staring at her in shocked disbelief following her casual announcement.

"I said, last night André proposed," she repeated softly as all eyes rested on her, "and I've decided to accept." Her face was flushed. "I don't know why you're all looking so surprised," she went on self-consciously as they stared at her. "Surely you must have guessed how we feel." She forced herself to look at André, dressed in one of his silver-trimmed suits, seated by her side. He was eyeing her intently, no less surprised than everyone else.

For weeks now he'd done everything he could think of to persuade her to marry him. And last night when he'd proposed, he'd even hinted that he might have to leave New York soon, but she'd seemed even more distant than before. He was about ready to concede to the colonel that his idea was losing ground. Now, here she was suddenly presenting him with the whole thing on a silver platter. He searched her eyes for an answer, for some clue to why she had suddenly changed her mind. There was none. Had she really, finally, fallen in love with him? After all, it wasn't an impossibility. Her beautiful blue-green eyes were, as always, unrevealing. Yet they stared into his forcefully.

He lifted her hand and kissed the tips of her fingers, his voice low and breathless. "*Mi querida,*" he whispered softly. "Giving me my answer like this . . . *Madre de Dios,* if you only knew how happy you've made me."

She forced a smile. "I do know," she said softly, and he squeezed her fingers.

"Well, it doesn't make me happy!" yelled Jason from the far end of the table as the full impact of her words sank in. "I won't hear of it!"

Gigi's flush deepened. She'd expected opposition from Jason. But not quite so demonstrative. Her eyes wavered momentarily, but she wasn't about to give in. She had to be firm. "You object?" she asked quietly.

He studied her openly. "That's putting it mildly. Whatever

possessed you to think I'd let you marry Señor de los Reyes here?" he went on. "Or anyone else, for that matter?"

She bit her lips, then straightened stubbornly. "I didn't think I needed your permission."

"You mean you thought you could just do whatever you wanted? Marry whomever you pleased?"

"That's what most people do, isn't it?"

"You are not most people, young lady," he ventured.

"Oh, I know that," she said bitterly. "I'm your daughter."

"That's right. And as my daughter, you'll marry when I say so, not before."

"I see." She licked her lips nervously as she tried to stare him down. Her fingers tightened on André's hand. "Then for convenience' sake, shall we say you're not my father?" she said impertinently.

He fumed. "What the hell are you talking about?"

She leaned forward. "I'm talking about this," she said slowly. "I've just remembered who I really am," she went on boldly. "I've had amnesia, remember? I haven't been able to remember anything. Well, I suddenly remember it all, and I'm not your daughter. You told me I was your daughter. I didn't say it. I didn't ask to be brought here."

"No one will believe you."

"Wouldn't they? Oh, I think they would, and you'd be surprised what I can remember if I want to. And if I remember rightly, I should be over twenty-one. I wouldn't need your permission to get married, would I?"

"That's preposterous!"

"Is it? Well, it's no more preposterous than what you presume. And I don't think you'd like the notoriety, either. Even if people found out I was lying, I think they'd want to know why, and I don't think you'd care much for the publicity."

Jason's eyes blazed, the tendons in his neck so taut they were like ropes as he stared at her. "You'd do that to me? After all I've done for you?"

"All you've done for me?" She half-laughed. "What have you done for me?" she cried. "Caged me up in this house like a prisoner, made me the laughingstock of everyone in New York. Oh, yes, you've given me beautiful clothes, and a roof over my head, and I'm grateful for that, but I could have gotten the same thing by letting one of your fine friends keep me, as they so delicately put it. And I'd have had as much freedom and been looked at with about the same amount of respect, too. For months now I've played the part, I've been what you wanted me to be. Now, please . . ." Her voice lowered, and tears filled the corners of her eyes. "I have to do this, Father, I have to do something for me. Just for me." She was almost afraid of the lie she was about to utter. "I love André, Father," she said nervously. "Last night after he asked me to marry him, he said he may soon be leaving. He's expecting to be called back to Mexico for a while. I can't let him go without me."

Jason's face fell. He was losing her as he'd lost her mother. "No!"

"Yes! It's what I want, Father."

"I found out this morning that I'll be leaving on Saturday," André said quickly, grasping at the opportunity. "We can be married at my parents' hacienda near La Mariposa." He hoped the bewildered look on Jason's face was a sign he was weakening. "I know it's short notice," he said. "But I'll take good care of her, Señor Larrabee," he went on. "You can be assured of that. And it isn't permanent. In a few months I'll be back in New York, and you can see Gigi whenever you want."

"Please, Father," begged Gigi, spurred on now by the knowledge that she could get away sooner than she dreamed. "You have to say yes. I want your blessing, please!"

Jason studied their faces. There were tears in Gigi's eyes, and her lips trembled. Did she really love this man that much? He assessed André. What was it about the man that disturbed him? It was obvious by the gleam in his eyes that he was pleased with Gigi's announcement. At the moment he looked every bit the dashing, love-stricken suitor. It was those other times that bothered Jason. The moments when he'd catch him off guard. At those times André's eyes held an intensity that was alarming, as if he were calculating every move, even his thoughts controlled to the point of being without emotion. Which was the real André?

Jason breathed heavily, his hands gripping the arms of his wheelchair until the knuckles were white. He didn't want to lose Gigi. Not yet. He'd just found her. God, she was a fiery little thing, just like her mother. So determined, so independent. His anger began to ease, and his resolve wavered. He glanced about the table. "You really want this?" he asked reluctantly as he looked once more at Gigi.

"More than I've ever wanted anything."

"But it's so sudden."

Her eyes softened. "I don't want to hurt you, Father," she said, "but if you say no, you'll leave me no choice."

"You'd be leaving . . ."

"Only for a little while. I'll come back to visit whenever you want."

Jason's eyes locked with André's. "You'd take good care of her?"

André's arm went about Gigi's shoulder protectively. "I'll guard her with my life, señor," he said.

Jason scowled. He wasn't one to admit defeat gracefully. But what could he do? It was what she wanted. Besides, Rose was still throwing about her little insinuating remarks regarding Paul and Gigi. What if someone realized what her double-entendres meant?

"You say you'll be married at your father's hacienda?" he asked suddenly. "If I give my consent, why can't you marry her before leaving?"

"*Por favor*," said André. "Please, Señor Larrabee, let me explain," he said. "It's the custom in my family. Every de los Reyes for generations has married in the chapel at Flor de la Montaña. My parents would be mortified if I did otherwise. I want them to accept Gigi. As it is, they'll be displeased because we won't be able to be married at the altar." He saw the questioning look on Jason's face, and went on. "I'm a Catholic, señor. Gigi isn't. I didn't ask her to accept my religion, therefore we can't be married directly at the altar or receive the sacraments. And then, there's the question of her birth."

"Her birth?" Jason looked puzzled.

"*Sí*." André smiled apologetically. "Forgive me, Señor Larrabee, but she was born out of wedlock. This alone will be hard to explain to a family that holds parentage in such high esteem. For myself, I wouldn't care if she'd been spawned by the devil himself, but my saintly mother will be hard to win over. If I were to marry her first and explain later, we'd never be able to convince her that Gigi was worthy of becoming a de los Reyes. She'd never accept her."

Jason was vexed. "Of all the conceit!"

"Conceit?" André straightened. "Not conceit, señor. Pride perhaps. The de los Reyes are descended from Spanish royalty." André's eyes flashed knowingly. "You too have your pride, Señor Larrabee," he said smoothly. "Your son Paul's marriage proves that." He glanced at Paul, who had been staring at him steadily since the conversation began. "Isn't that so, Paul?" he asked. "You must agree with me that your choice of a wife was ruled greatly by her social standing."

Paul didn't answer, but his jaw clenched ominously.

André once more addressed Jason. "So you see, Señor Larrabee, much as we all hate to admit it, pride in one's family is important." His arm tightened about Gigi's shoulder. "Let Gigi come into my family with my parents' blessings, and with yours, señor, please," he said.

If he could, Jason would have moved both heaven and earth to have avoided this scene, but it was no use. Gigi was a beautiful woman, and headstrong. He sighed. "I'll give my blessing on one condition," he said hesitantly. "That Paul accompanies her to Mexico with you and takes my place at the wedding, giving the bride away."

Gigi's heart sank to her stomach, and she felt sick. She wanted to go away from Paul, not take him with her. Oh, God!

"I'd say that's a reasonable request," said Paul quickly. He didn't trust André. There was a fierceness to the triumphant way his eyes shone as he looked at Gigi. It was unnatural.

"And I'll go with Paul," suggested Lenore, studying her husband's face before turning to her father-in-law. She wasn't about to let Paul go all the way to Mexico with Gigi. André or no André. Anything could happen. "It's ideal," she told Jason. "Gigi will need a woman along, there'll be so much to do."

"But we can't drag Paul away from his work," Gigi protested nervously. "Maybe there's some other way. Maybe you could come yourself, Father. I'm sure you could."

André shook his head. "I'm afraid your father would find the journey too rough, *mi querida*," he said. "The train ride itself is long and tiring, then we have to take a wagon and horses to the hacienda. It's about a hundred miles or more. The journey would be too much."

She frowned. "There's no other way to get there?"

"None." He patted her hand. "Don't worry, Gigi, I'm sure if your father insists that Paul come, there'll be no problem. My parents will be pleased to meet your brother and his wife."

"I know that," she said. "It's just that . . . well, I felt that
Father needed Paul here."

"On the contrary," said Jason. "I'd worry the whole while
if Paul weren't with you. I'm not pleased with this, you
know, my dear," he said, looking deep into her blue-green
eyes. "I hate the thought of losing you. It hurts. But since it's
what you want, I'll give in. My only restriction is that your
brother substitute for what I'm unable to do myself. Is that
agreed?"

Gigi held her breath, feeling the warmth of André's hand
on hers as he continued patting and stroking it; then she
glanced quickly across the table at Paul, whose eyes were like
a darkened sky on a storm-swept afternoon, and she agreed.
Paul would accompany them to Mexico.

"And I'm going with you, Paul," insisted Lenore later in
the evening as she and Paul stood facing each other in their
bedroom, ready for bed. "I know you don't like the idea. I
could tell by the look on your face, but you're not going to
talk Jason out of letting me go. I won't hear of it."

She was wearing a nightgown of blue satin that matched
the gentian blue of her eyes, and the light from the lamp on
the dresser shadowed her face strangely, making it gro-
tesquely cynical, distorting her high cheekbones into gaunt
lines, making the corners of her mouth seem to droop.

"I haven't thought of trying to talk him out of it," he said,
watching the play of shadows on her face. "Besides, you're
my wife, not his. He really hasn't any say in the matter."

She sighed. "Good."

"But there is something that's bothering me."

"Oh? What?"

"When we were on our honeymoon, you did nothing but
complain about how much you hated trains. It seems strange
now that you'd suddenly volunteer for such a long ride on
one."

She glared at him, then turned quickly and climbed into
bed, pulling the covers to her chin. She ought to tell him. She
should shout at him, let him know that she knew what was
going on, why Gigi had suddenly decided to marry André,
but she couldn't. If she did, he might walk out, and she'd die
before she'd let him do that. She couldn't let him go. Not
ever.

Instead, she mustered all her courage and looked him
straight in the eye. "Will you please turn off the light, Paul,"

she said softly, "and come to bed," and moments later, as Paul once more climbed in beside her, he wondered again why she seemed to have lost interest in becoming pregnant, even to the point of staying so far to her own side of the bed that not one part of their bodies was touching. Oh, well, women were strange creatures.

He said good night and turned over, contemplating Gigi's decision and the long trip ahead of them.

André was elated as he returned to the consulate. Everything he'd worked for all these months was coming to fruition. He took the stairs to the second floor two at a time, happy in the knowledge that two days hence they'd be on their way.

There was no need to knock on the door to the sitting room; he knew what he'd discover inside. He swung the door wide, revealing the colonel and Ramón sitting at a small table with a deck of cards momentarily between them. The colonel looked up from his cards momentarily, then perused them once more.

"*Dos,*" he said to Ramón as he discarded two cards, and Ramón dealt two off the top of the deck.

André closed the door behind him, then stood for a few minutes watching them play. When the hand was over, the colonel raked in his money and Ramón began to shuffle again. André grew impatient. He strolled to the liquor cabinet and poured himself a brandy. "You're not curious as to why I'm smiling?" he asked as he turned toward them, sipping the brandy.

"Why should we be?" snorted the colonel sarcastically. "What did she do, let you feel her up again like before, or maybe she let you bed her this time, is that it?"

André's eyes narrowed as he stepped forward.

Suddenly the colonel felt his shirt constricting him from the nape of his neck, and he glanced up to where André stood towering above his left shoulder. He flinched.

"I have slit men's throats for far less, *mi coronel,*" André said viciously. "I told you before, and I will remind you. Just because the young lady is the daughter of El Verdugo does not mean she's also a *puta.* She's a lady. Don't you forget that."

Colonel Alvarez choked as André's fingers tightened on his shirt. "*Madre de Dios,* Major, I'm on your side, remember?" he gulped.

André's smile was sinister. "How could I forget?" he answered, then pushed the colonel away so he fell against the table, spilling his cards. "For your information," said André, standing tall and erect, looking down at them arrogantly, "the young lady will be leaving New York with me on Saturday morning, heading for Mexico, where she thinks we'll be married. Now, did I or did I not do what I said I'd do?"

Both men stared in disbelief.

"It's true?" asked Ramón.

"It's true," answered André, brushing one finger along his mustache, pleased with himself. He straightened, taking another sip of brandy. "However, there's one fly in the ointment, so to speak," he said cautiously. "Señor and Señora Paul Larrabee are to accompany us."

The colonel grinned. "How far?"

"As far as I say." André grinned back. "That, Colonel, will be your job," he went on. "We'll take the train to Eagle Pass on the Texas border. From there we'll hire wagons and men. You'll leave tomorrow, both of you, and see that the right men are available. I want men who know how to use guns, yet men who'll keep their mouths shut for the right pay. Once across the Rio del Norte into Mexico, the trap can be sprung. Not until we're far enough from the border, however, so she can't attempt an escape. When she's safely in our hands, we'll send word to her father, and he'll have to surrender. What choice will he have—his life or hers?"

The colonel's dark, greedy eyes rested uncomfortably on Major de los Reyes. "And if he refuses to surrender?"

"He won't."

"But if he does?"

André's eyes narrowed. "We'll deal with that problem if and when it arises," he answered, but the colonel wasn't so sure.

"You will kill the girl?"

"I said we'd deal with it if and when we have to." His jaw tightened. "For now, get your things packed. Your train pulls out first thing in the morning. I didn't want to stall and take a chance that she'd change her mind. I felt the sooner we left, the better. It won't give you much time, but it's the best we can do. You'll leave tonight so that no one sees you leaving the consulate, and in the morning, before your train pulls out, you'll send a wire to Romero Rubio telling him I'm on my way home to be married. He'll understand, and his men will contact you when you reach Eagle Pass. You know the rest of the plan by heart. I wish you luck."

The colonel glared at André, then gathered the cards together, shoving the pesos he'd won back into his pockets. Within half an hour he and Ramón were packed, leaving the consulate, heading toward a sleazy hotel where they'd spend the night before going to the depot.

André stood at the upstairs window of his suite in the consulate, watching them melt into the shadows. He breathed a sigh of relief, then frowned. What the devil was the matter with him anyway? He'd accomplished what he'd set out to do, so why did it suddenly leave a sour taste in his mouth? Why did he have this tight ache in the pit of his stomach? Perhaps because of all the women he'd made love to over the years, she was the most beautiful and sumptuous. He could close his eyes even now and look into hers, drowning in their blue-green depths. And her mouth, so exquisite, like the petals of a rose just opening, soft and velvety. The arch of her brow, deep contours in her cheeks, small nose, and delicately rounded chin. To think someone so lovely might have to die just because of an old man. What a waste. Could he let it happen?

He took another sip of brandy, wondering. If he didn't know better, he'd swear he'd fallen for the girl. Hell, maybe he did like her more than he should, but there was no law to say he couldn't. Besides, there was also no law that said he couldn't make the most of the time left to him. Once across the border, they could get rid of Paul and Lenore, and he could have her all to himself. After all, Señor Rubio said nothing about what was to be done with her after her father's surrender—or before, for that matter.

André smiled, his swarthy face taking on a new glow of confidence. "Ah, *mi querida*," he whispered softly to himself, "soon I'll have you all to myself, then I'll show you what real lovemaking is." He downed the rest of the brandy and headed for bed, satisfied that all was going well.

It was Friday morning. Gigi woke up earlier than usual, unable to sleep. Now she stood in the stables dressed for riding, letting Jamie help her mount.

"I'm glad your shoulder healed so well, Jamie," she said as he gave her a boost into the saddle.

He smiled. "So am I." He was relieved. "For a while I

thought maybe I'd never use the arm again, but it's almost as good as new already."

She started to move toward the stable door.

"I still think you should wait for Ahmed, Miss Gigi," he said thoughtfully. "I don't think it's such a good idea for you to go roaming around alone."

She smiled wistfully. "I won't be long, Jamie," she said. "Just a short ride along the riverbank."

She spurred her horse through the stable door as Jamie watched skeptically. He didn't like it. Not at all. He headed for the house.

Gigi had been riding for almost half an hour when she realized she wasn't alone. She frowned, turning her horse off the path, moving into the bushes, hoping she hadn't been seen, then waited, listening to the oncoming hoofbeats.

Paul laughed. "I hope you don't think you're hiding," he called out, amused, as he approached. "The burgundy riding suit you're wearing clashes beautifully with the green leaves on that bush."

She sighed, exasperated, pulling her horse back onto the path. "Why didn't you call out or something so I'd know it was you?" she said. "You scared me half to death." She straightened, eyeing him dubiously. "What are you doing here anyway? It's barely dawn, the sun isn't even up yet. You haven't ridden this early for a long time."

He leaned forward, resting comfortably in the saddle, his brown pants and deep green riding coat blending in with the trees that were half-hidden by the early-morning mists.

"Jamie got worried and came to the house," he explained. "I happened to be the only one up besides Mrs. Sharp. You don't mind, do you? Jamie was right, you shouldn't ride alone."

"You mean I'm safe with you? Oh, that's really funny." She nudged her horse in the ribs, and they moved along the path that wound along beside the river. "You're the last person in the world I should be riding with alone."

"Jamie didn't know that."

"How unfortunate."

Paul reached over and grabbed her horse's reins, stopping her, looking into her eyes. "Why, Gigi?" he asked suddenly. "Why did you accept André's proposal?"

"You don't know? You really don't know?"

"I know you don't love him."

"You don't love Lenore either."

"Gigi." He let go of her reins and dismounted, then walked over, reaching up to take her from her horse. She let him set her on the ground, but his arms stayed around her. "Gigi, if you'll change your mind, if you stay, I'll promise never to let it happen again."

She stared up into his handsome face, so dear to her. "You really think you can keep that promise?"

He held his breath, gazing into her eyes, then touched the side of her face lovingly. "No . . . I guess I can't," he finally said. "But why do you have to marry him? Don't make the same mistake I made. Leave, go to Europe, anywhere, but don't give yourself away like this."

"I have no choice, and you know it, Paul," she said. "Father would never consent to letting me go away by myself." She sighed. "That's why I'm going to Mexico. It's no good, Paul," she went on softly. "What we've done is wrong. It's sinful, and we could be arrested if anyone found out. We've no right to love each other, so it has to end. I only hope it's not too late. But if it is, then I'll hope the child's all right. If I marry André right away, if what happened to us the other night reaps a harvest neither of us wants, then only you and I will ever know the truth. I'll raise the child as André's and hope no one ever finds out."

He bent down, his mouth covering hers, and kissed her softly. "How can I bear to let him have you?" he whispered softly against her mouth.

She reached up, touching his face, her fingers trembling as she traced his jawline, etching his features on her mind for all time. "Kiss me good-bye now, Paul, a kiss to last forever," she whispered softly. "Because even though you'll be with me always in my heart, there can be no more between us, ever again. I'm to be Mrs. André Diego de los Reyes. It's the only answer. The only sane way out of all this. And once I get to Mexico, I'll never be around to tempt you again."

He kissed her long and hard, and held her close, remembering a night that should never have been, and by the time they returned to the stables, there were no more words that could be said between them. There was nothing more to say.

Gigi watched Lenore fuming as she sat opposite her, gazing out the window of the train as it sped through the countryside. Lenore had been irritated enough because they had

only one day to prepare for the trip, but that could be overlooked, since servants did all the packing. However, the real
blow had come when she discovered there were no private
cars available on such short notice, and they'd have to travel
in a common coach. Her one compensation was that they had
curtains, enabling them some privacy.

She sat now, shoulders tense, face grim, not even making
any pretense of enjoying herself.

Paul looked over at her for a moment, wondering why she
had even bothered to come. He was sitting beside her, and
suddenly Gigi felt his eyes on her. "Are you sure you don't
mind watching where we've been, Gigi?" he said. "I could
trade seats with you."

She shook her head. "No, that's all right. It's fine." She
smiled. "Besides, I enjoy seeing where we've been." She
glanced out the window, only to shiver, a sense of something
vaguely familiar flitting across her mind. What she felt was so
strange, so different, it was hard to grasp. She had been
pulled from the train wreck months ago, yet suddenly the
clouded memory of a different railroad car, an old-fashioned
one crowded with people, kerosene lamps burning to light the
darkness, crept through her mind. She tried to hold it, to
hang on, but it was no use. As fleetingly as it had begun to
emerge, it faded, and once more she was staring at only the
landscape as it slid by.

"Are you cold?" asked André. He was sitting next to her
and felt her shiver.

She shook her head. "No. I . . . for a moment I thought I
could remember something," she said, then frowned as both
men looked at each other, their eyes locked.

Paul saw André tense. Why? He'd watched him closely
ever since they'd left New York a few hours ago. He seemed
nervous, almost too anxious for things to go well. Paul
watched now as André looked away, turning toward Gigi,
once more talking to her, his voice so low this time that it
was barely a whisper in Gigi's ear. What was it about the
man that rubbed him the wrong way? It wasn't just his atten-
tions toward Gigi. It was something more, something intangi-
ble. It was the cruel, sinister look that often crept into his
eyes when he thought no one was looking, the sharp ominous
tremor in his deeply accented voice when things didn't seem
to be going his way. Was it simply a clash of personalities?
Or were Paul's instincts right? Was there more to André Di-

ego de los Reyes than what showed on the surface? He wondered.

Gigi glanced up and caught Paul's eyes on her. His expression was identical to the expression that had been on
Jason's face just before he'd said good-bye at the station and
had Ahmed wheel him from the boarding platform to where
he could wave to them. It had been a questioning look, filled
with apprehension, only Jason's eyes had been filled with
tears. For a few unguarded moments Gigi wished she hadn't
had to say good-bye. She hated leaving everyone behind, including Bridget. Jason had offered to let the girl go along.
But Gigi couldn't take her away from Jamie. It wouldn't have
been fair. However, they had been so close, and the parting
had also been a tearful one. Yet she knew it was for the best.
She had to go. It was the only way out of a horrible situation.

She drew her eyes from Paul's face, looking at André, responding mechanically to the tender words of endearment
he'd whispered into her ear. So far Paul and André had been
cordial to each other. She only hoped the rest of the trip
would be accomplished without too much fuss, and she
smiled at André, then Paul, hoping to inject a little warmth
and friendliness into the atmosphere that was often more
uncomfortable than it should be.

They ate in the dining cars, and slept on the train, riding
straight through, stopping only to change trains when necessary. At times the endless stretches of countryside became
monotonous, and the towns and cities along the way were a
relief on the landscape.

Paul and André kept up a continuous facade of friendship,
often playing cards with some of the men in the parlor car,
and discussing railroads, politics, and whether or not it was
wise to invest in the new horseless carriages everyone was
talking about. "After all, look what Edison's electric lights
have done for the country," explained Paul. "And at one
time people thought it was a joke. Someday every city across
the nation will be bright with lights."

They rode through Pittsburgh, Cincinnati, St. Louis, then
dropped south to Little Rock, Dallas, Austin, and San Antonio, where they boarded a train with even less attractive accommodations. When they finally were ready to disembark in
Eagle Pass, a week after their departure from New York,
they were tired and weary, not only from the constant riding

but also from Lenore's incessant complaints about the food, her comforts, and the people they were forced to associate with during the trip.

Eagle Pass was a small town on the Texas border, situated alongside the Rio Grande. At one time it had been the site of an army post. Now those days were long gone, but the atmosphere still hung on. The fort was still standing about four miles upriver, and the town, with its raw courage, clung to the countryside, hoping for better times, the influence of its close Mexican neighbor widely apparent. For directly across the Rio Grande from Eagle Pass was the Mexican town of Piedras Negras, a railroad bridge across the river, which the Mexicans called the Rio Bravo del Norte, connecting the two places.

The railroad itself continued down into Mexico, to Monterrey and eventually Mexico City. But André said his father's hacienda was west of Eagle Pass in the foothills of the Sierra Madres, north of La Mariposa, where no railroad had yet been built, so they'd hire men and wagons and traverse the last part of the land on horseback.

The train stopped, and Gigi gazed about thoughtfully as she raised the skirt of her green silk traveling suit, stepping onto the platform, using André's hand to keep her balance. It was late afternoon, and a few people stood about. Some had been waiting for the train, others just loitering. One man in particular caught her eye, although she tried not to let it show. Maybe it was the way he was dressed that made her so conscious of him, or the way his eyes narrowed when he looked at her, but something made her unusually aware of him, and a little uneasy at the same time.

He was tall, lean, dark-skinned, and wore a mustache. Mexican, no doubt, but his clothes were unlike most of the other men's. He wore a black suit, white shirt with a black necktie, and a bowler hat atop his head. He would have looked more at home on the streets of New York than in this small border town.

She felt his eyes on her the whole while they made arrangements to have their trunks transported to the local hotel. He never raised his head, but as he leaned against the building, slouching lackadaisically, his eyes followed her every move, alert, as if waiting. She tried to brush aside the nagging fear that had begun to grip her, but couldn't. Why would a complete stranger stare at her so? And that was another thing. Was he a stranger? The more she became aware of him, the more she realized that there was something vaguely familiar about him.

She tried not to make him aware that she'd noticed him, and smiled, taking André's arm, letting him escort her to the edge of the railroad platform and they accompanied Paul and Lenore down the main street of Eagle Pass toward the hotel.

It was a small hotel with unglamorous accommodations, which brought another rise of ire from Lenore, who for the first time in her life looked less than immaculate. The absence of servants and lack of proper toilet facilities on the trip had taken its toll on her, and Gigi noticed that she actually had more than one hair out of place on her head and that the skirt of her rich brown velvet traveling suit, with its gold-braid trim, was rumpled and creased from having to sit so long in one spot without moving. There was also a spot of gravy on the limp ruffle of her pale gold blouse. For the first time in months, Gigi wasn't intimidated by Lenore's presence. In fact, she felt she'd weathered the long trip far more easily than Lenore, and she could tell by the glances of the men as she walked toward the hotel that she still looked attractive enough to command an audience.

"You mean that's all you have available? I can't even have a sitting room?" Lenore complained as they stood in the lobby of the hotel.

The clerk shook his head. He was a short, balding man with muttonchops and a nose that seemed to be spread all over his face. His mouth drooped at the corners, and as he listened to Lenore's tirade, his pale blue eyes shifted first to Paul, then André, then settled on Gigi, where they suddenly widened in surprise, although he tried to conceal it.

Gigi watched curiously as his face reddened self-consciously when she caught him staring. He was embarrassed, and his calm, assured manner disappeared. He fidgeted nervously with his pocket watch, then shoved the register toward Paul. "If you'll sign please, sir," he said quickly.

Paul signed for him and Lenore, then let André and Gigi sign for themselves. The clerk handed them the keys, then turned the hotel register around so he could read it while they headed for the stairs. His eyes scanned the page, then stopped abruptly, and he grew pale as he read the name neatly written below that of Mr. and Mrs. Paul Larrabee. It couldn't be! But it was. He glanced up quickly, watching the young woman ascending the open staircase on the arm of the handsome gentleman who'd escorted her into the lobby, but as he stared, he was unaware that Paul had noticed his discomfiture and was now watching him furtively, wondering why Gigi's presence had disturbed him.

The clerk watched as the strangers disappeared into the upstairs hall, then called hurriedly to someone in the back room to keep an eye on the place and bolted out the front door, not even bothering to grab his hat on the way. He scurried along the sidewalk, nodding to friends here and there, walking sprightly, tipping an imaginary hat when necessary, then slowed as he reached a saloon a few streets down from the hotel. He straightened his vest, but instead of going in the front way, he ducked down the alley, circling to the back, and slipped in the back door.

The back room was dark and musty, a set of stairs off to the left. He ascended them, then knocked on the first door he came to. Judah should be in his room. He was always in his room this time of day. A gruff voice called out, and the desk clerk reached down, opening the door.

Judah Parsons' office never failed to amaze Hank Wattle. It was neat, clean, the beautiful mahogany desk highly polished, Persian rug on the floor immaculately swept, and the richly upholstered furniture should have been out-of-place, but wasn't. It blended in well with the other furnishings. The door to an adjoining bedroom was standing open, and even in there the furnishings were velvets and brocades.

The desk clerk faced the man who sat at the desk going over some papers, his head of thick gray hair turning silvery gold as the rays from the afternoon sunlight streaming in the open window behind him fell on it. Hank stared.

"Something I can do for you, Hank?" Judah asked, putting down his pen, reaching for a cigar. He was a solid man in his early fifties who liked to think that he ran the town of Eagle Pass, although some of the more prominent citizens would be quick to argue the point.

Hank shuffled his feet nervously, then sighed. "It ain't right, Judah. Something's wrong somewhere," he said hurriedly. "It just ain't right."

"What ain't right?"

"Over at the hotel." He pointed back over his shoulder excitedly. "There's a young woman, came in on the train this afternoon with some other folks. She signed the register as Gigi Rouvier. But, Judah, she ain't Gigi."

Judah had started to light his cigar; now suddenly he forgot to puff, blowing out the match as he stared at Hank. "What do you mean, she's not Gigi?"

"Just what I said." He emphasized the words. "She ain't Gigi Rouvier!"

"Then who . . . ?"

"That's what I figured you'd wanna find out."

Judah Parsons, owner and operator of the Red Dog Saloon, a man whose living was made with liquor, cards, women, and investments that had questionable overtones, fidgeted hesitantly with the cigar in his fingers, contemplating Hank's news, then tossed the still-unlit cigar aside. "What does she look like?" he asked slowly.

"That's just it," said Hank, puzzled. "She's real pretty. Looks more like she could be Gigi's daughter than young Gigi herself. Fact is, she looks like Miss Rouvier probably looked some twenty years ago."

Judah frowned, then scratched his head. It didn't make sense. Gigi Rouvier had worked for him at the tables for about ten years, migrating here from California's Gold Coast with her young daughter. She'd been a beautiful woman when she arrived. Disillusioned by men, fed up with the kind of life her daughter was always exposed to. But Eagle Pass had been no better. She knew no other way of making a living, so she stuck it out, hoping if she saved enough money, maybe she could chuck it all and her daughter wouldn't have to live the same way.

It was inevitable that she turn to Judah, and for years she had been his mistress, as well as the best faro dealer he had. It wasn't until the last two years, when her health began to fail and she grew worn and emaciated, that Judah realized how much she meant to him. If he could have married her, it might have been different, but Gigi would never have consented, even if he'd been free to marry instead of tied down to Elsie. He'd married Judge Bascomb's daughter Elsie for appearance' sake and political gain when he'd first settled in Eagle Pass years before. The marriage had been a sham from the start, and more of his nights were spent at the Red Dog than at home, but Elsie refused to give in, and held on like a leech, pretending she didn't care.

If it hadn't been for Elsie, he'd have taken care of Gigi's

daughter himself when Gigi passed away, but Gigi refused to let him, even if Elsie hadn't protested. People talked enough as it was. She wanted better for young Gigi. So she'd written to the girl's father, made arrangements, and the day after her mother's funeral, young Gigi Rouvier left Eagle Pass, heading for New York.

Judah frowned, remembering the day the young girl left, the expectant light in her soft gray eyes. She was young, not quite twenty, and he'd been glad to see her leaving this sort of life behind. He'd only hoped it hadn't been too late. Maybe for Gigi it hadn't, because she wasn't a very pretty girl. Nothing like her mother, and the men paid little attention to her. Besides, her mother had tried so hard to protect her, refusing even to let her inside the Red Dog.

He sighed, worried. If the young woman who checked into the hotel now wasn't Gigi, who was she, and what had happened to Gigi? His eyes narrowed. "When can I see her?" he asked Hank.

Hank bit his lips, thinking, then straightened. "I know. They'll probably wanna know where to eat. I'll recommend the Steak House, and you can go there and see for yourself."

Judah picked up the cigar again and fumbled in the pocket of his silk-lined gray frock coat, then checked his pocket watch before shoving it back into place, tugging at the front of his ruby-red brocade vest. He struck the match and lit his cigar, letting the smoke curl up to the ceiling.

"I'll stroll over that way in about an hour," he said. "If they're not there, I'll be down to the hotel to find out what's going on. If you learn anything new, let me know." He leaned back in his chair, eyeing Hank suspiciously. "Do you think anyone else knows what's going on?" he asked.

Hank shook his head. "I think they came straight from the depot. But I'm tellin' you. If she keeps walkin' around town, folks are gonna start noticin', and maybe some'll even start askin' questions, and I think you oughta know the answers, Judah, b'fore they do."

Judah nodded. "Thanks, Hank." He dismissed the little man, then sat at his desk gazing off into space. Gigi had confided in him about young Gigi's father, making him promise not to tell anyone in town. She'd even done all she could to hide her true circumstances from Jason Larrabee, going so far as to tell him she'd been living in a convent up closer to San Antonio. She even had her mail sent there, where someone—he had no idea who—sent it on to her at Eagle Pass. It was a small deception, but one she felt necessary for her daughter's sake. She didn't want Jason Larrabee to know what she had turned into, or that his daughter had been raised in such disreputable surroundings.

He scowled as he remembered the day he'd put young Gigi on the train, making sure she had the brooch and the letter. What could have happened? Where was the girl? Well, he was sure as hell going to find out. He stood up, checked his watch again, then began to gather his papers up into a neat pile at the corner of his desk, wondering who this young woman was who was calling herself Gigi Rouvier.

14

In another part of town, closer to the river, Miguel Hernandez grabbed the bowler hat from atop his head and tossed it onto a lumpy cot before grabbing a chair and pulling it up to the table.

"I told you she was coming right behind them, amigo," he said to the man sitting opposite him at the table. "Now, aren't you glad we left New York when we did? This way Pedro kept an eye on her while we got things all set down here. It was the best way."

His companion scowled. "So you said," he replied. He was also Mexican. His white shirt and baggy buckskin pants were half-covered by two broad ammunition belts worn hanging from each shoulder and crisscrossed across his chest. Over the border, in Mexico, they were called bandoliers, and the man, his craggy face lined from the harsh dry weather, black hair shining in the late-afternoon sun that streamed in at the glassless window, was called a *bandido*. His name was Juan Fuerentes, and he'd been waiting patiently for Miguel's return from the depot.

He snapped back the barrel of the gun he was cleaning, then shoved it back into its holster. "You're sure it's her?" he asked.

"*Sí*. It's the same girl we saw with de los Reyes in New York," said Miguel. "De los Reyes wouldn't make a mistake, his superiors would hang him, and besides, the description fits. I know it's been a long time and people change, but it has to be her."

Juan nodded. "*Bueno*. Then I will have to ride, and ride hard. I should be back later tonight. If for any reason she leaves town, follow her. Tell Maria at the cantina, and I'll find you. Otherwise, just hang around and keep an eye on her." He eyed his friend curiously. "And *por favor*, get rid of those clothes. They were all right while we were in New York, but you are about as conspicuous in them around here as a rattlesnake would be in the middle of a street in Brooklyn."

Miguel glanced down at his black suit, touching it lovingly. He'd never had anything quite like it before. He straightened, his long body wiry beneath the city clothes. "*Sí*," he said reluctantly. "If I have to." He moved to the back of the small shanty that was no better than a broken-down shed and pulled out a large worn carpetbag, extricating from it a set of clothes identical to those worn by his companion, including bandolier and pistols.

Since he and Juan had arrived in Eagle Pass, following Rubio's henchmen Colonel Alvarez and his aide Lieutenant Ramón Chaves from New York City, they had been taking turns hanging about the depot, knowing that Major de los Reyes would not be far behind. They had been informed by inside sources that Major de los Reyes had been assigned the task of locating the daughter of El Verdugo and returning her to Mexico. Now that he was this close, they had to act fast. While she was in New York, things were at a standstill. As long as she stayed there as the daughter of Jason Larrabee, where Miguel and Juan could keep a furtive eye on her, she was safe. Most of the time anyway. Of course, there was the incident of the runaway carriage, and the attempt in Central Park. Fortunately, Paul Larrabee had been on hand both times and they hadn't had to show themselves, and evidently Major de los Reyes had squelched any more attempts by them to capture her after the knifing incident. They never did hear what really happened that night, but then, that was understandable, since they'd followed Paul Larrabee and Gigi Rouvier to Central Park, and the papers had reported little about it, but they surmised that the colonel and Ramón were responsible.

Now, however, they had to know what to do. Their orders had been to follow de los Reyes and find the girl and watch over her. Were they to watch now as she crossed the border right into the hands of her father's enemies?

Miguel shuddered as he stripped off the black suit, setting it aside, then once more donned the clothes he wore as an aide to the outlaw El Verdugo.

At the hotel, Gigi checked one last time in the mirror to make sure she looked all right, then turned, glancing about the room. It certainly wasn't luxurious. There was a bed, bare floor, except for one hand-woven rug, a straight-backed chair, dry sink with a basin and pitcher in it, a small wardrobe for hanging clothes, and the dresser with its mirror. She smiled to herself, wondering how Paul was holding up under the verbal outburst Lenore was undoubtedly in the middle of. The poor man. It seemed strange that before their marriage Lenore always agreed with him on everything, even though it was obvious she disliked some of his suggestions and decisions. It was only after the wedding that she made her feelings known. It was as if she no longer felt it necessary to be agreeable. Her congenial nature had certainly soured. Of course, maybe it was the trip. After all, Lenore was spoiled. Used to the best. Servants to wait on her hand and foot, and people catering to her every whim. It was unlikely she'd be happy in these surroundings.

Gigi walked over to the bed and picked up her handbag. All the rooms in the hotel had clocks on the walls, and she checked the time, then left the room, heading downstairs. Paul had told her to be in the lobby by six-thirty, and they'd locate someplace to eat. She was still wearing her green silk traveling suit, but had changed hats and was wearing a small black-velvet-trimmed hat of green felt, with tiny black feather plumes lying across the tilted brim. She felt it made her look more chic and sophisticated than the green silk bonnet she'd worn on the train.

Naturally, as she entered the lobby, she noticed right away that Lenore had changed, either with Paul's help, or, if she knew Lenore, she'd probably insisted Paul hire a girl to wait on her while they were in town. André did say it would probably take them a day or two to arrange for the wagon, supplies, and horses, so it was logical Lenore would demand as many comforts of home as possible.

Gigi looked Lenore over carefully. Once more she was immaculate, right down to the golden hairs at the nape of her neck that were tucked neatly into the tight chignon. But her street dress of deep blue brocaded satin, with bouffant sleeves trimmed in embroidered ivory satin to just below the elbow, was far too ostentatious for an evening out in a town such as Eagle Pass. Lenore wasn't aware of it, however, and held her head high, the hat adorning it, a concoction of blue and ivory satin ribbons with embroidery that matched the dress, resting neatly atop the blond head as she watched Gigi approach.

Gigi's eyes moved from Lenore to Paul, then to André and back to Paul. Such a contrast. Paul wore the simple gray suit he'd worn on the train, his deep burgundy cravat neatly tied over a white shirt. André wore one of his velvet suits. Black, with silver embroidery that graced the lapels of the waist-length jacket and ran rampant down the side of the tight-fitting pants. His shirt was white, with ruffles to the waist, a narrow black ribbon tied in a bow at the throat. Paul's hat was a gray felt with wide, rolling brim; André's was broad-brimmed black velvet with silver trim and a flat crown. The two men were so different, each handsome in his own way, but it was Paul's compelling gray eyes that warmed her and made her feel strange and weak inside, and she turned to André for rescuing, holding her hand out to take his arm.

"There's a restaurant a block from here," said Paul as Lenore took his arm. "The hotel clerk said it's about the best around."

André opened the door for Gigi, and she took his arm, letting him escort her outside, while Paul and Lenore followed. The early-evening air was still muggy. It was September already, but this part of Texas was still hot, the days long and sultry.

Gigi had paid little attention to the town earlier on the way to the hotel; now she looked about curiously. There seemed to be as many Mexicans loitering around as Americans, and the town was extremely small compared to New York City. There were no large ten-story buildings or grand boulevards. Only facaded storefronts, wooden sidewalks, and not even a semblance of streetlamps. It was still light out, but shadows were beginning to appear here and there, deepening as they walked, and she knew that by the time they were through eating it would be dark out.

The Steak House was a quiet place that specialized in what was called western food and home cooking. They were ushered to a table in the back by a friendly waitress who, much to Gigi's surprise, stared at her rather curiously after she'd seated them. The waitress was a young woman, perhaps in her early twenties. A little plump and unpretentious, she wore her brown hair in one thick braid down her back, her brown eyes flashing excitedly at the obviously rich customers. She never said anything directly to Gigi, only looked puzzled while she took their orders, as if trying to remember something.

The food was surprisingly delicious. They all had grilled steaks, baked potatoes swimming in butter, cabbage salad, glazed carrots, and apple pie. Gigi, André, and Paul ate heartily, while Lenore picked at her food. complaining that the steak was too rare, the potato too old, the salad too sour, and the carrots too sweet. Only the pie seemed to satisfy her.

Paul was halfway through the meal when he suddenly felt an uneasy prickling at the nape of his neck, as if someone was staring at him. He set his fork down, reached for his cup, and as he slowly sipped his coffee, looked around at the other tables.

There was a couple at the table near the door enjoying each other's company, two men at another table arguing while they ate, two ladies near the front window who were deep in conversation, a man engrossed in cutting a steak at one of the other tables. But over Lenore's right shoulder his eyes suddenly locked with those of a formidable gray-haired man who was sitting alone at a table in the corner, toying with his food, his generous mouth drawn into a severe line. The man stared into Paul's eyes, his own dark blue eyes blazing with curiosity.

Paul frowned and glanced away, then looked back quickly in time to see the man's eyes settle on Gigi. Paul watched his every move. He wasn't eating, he was just staring, and his eyes seemed to devour Gigi with their intensity. Paul set his cup back down and continued eating, pretending to be oblivious of the man, but every chance he had, he glanced his way, and the man was still looking at Gigi. Paul said nothing to the others, but later, when the meal was over and they were leaving the restaurant, he drew the waitress aside, asking her who the man was.

She glanced quickly toward the man in the corner, then flushed, lowering her voice so he'd be unable to hear. "Why, that's Judah Parsons, sir," she answered. "Everybody in town knows Judah. He owns the Red Dog Saloon a few doors down. Doesn't eat here often. Lives at the edge of town with his wife." She smiled.

Paul thanked her, made a mental note of it, then joined the others after taking one last hurried glance at Mr. Parsons.

Gigi was reluctant to go back to the hotel right away, and for once Lenore agreed with her. There was nothing to do at

the hotel but sit and look at four walls, so they strolled about
town, taking in the sights, which weren't much. There were
small stockyards near the depot, with a livery and feed close
by. A freight office, gunshop, hardware, telegraph office, two
banks, various saloons, a general store, and the usual other
small businesses needed to keep life going so far from the big
cities. But almost everything at this hour of the evening was
closed. Someday perhaps Eagle Pass would be a fairly good-
sized city, but for now it was simply the last stop before the
Mexican border.

For the first time in days Gigi relaxed as they walked
about town, unaware that Paul was far from relaxed. Even
André seemed oblivious of the fact that everywhere they
went, the few people they passed stared furtively at them,
their eyes on Gigi especially. Sometimes their faces showed
signs of puzzled recognition. Other times they looked bewildered, as if they should recognize her, but couldn't. By the
time they returned to the hotel, Paul was twice as determined
to try to find out what was going on.

Gigi had decided to go to bed early, tired from the long
train ride, and André said he was going to see if he could locate a man with a wagon, so Paul had escorted Lenore to
their room, then informed her he'd be going out for a while.

She stared at him as he headed for the door. "I suppose it's
necessary?" she asked as he reached for the doorknob.

He turned, trying to ignore the sarcasm in her voice. "If
you must know, I'm going to the Red Dog Saloon," he said
calmly.

"The Red Dog Saloon?" She shuddered. "You mean that
disgusting-looking place we passed a few blocks from the hotel?" She looked at him in repulsion. "Good heavens, Paul,"
she exclaimed, exasperated. "If you must drink, can't you just
have a bottle sent up here! Do you have to go slumming with
that riffraff?"

He straightened. "I'm not going there to drink, Lenore. I'm
going there to try to get some answers to some questions that
have been bothering me."

"What kind of questions?"

He sighed. "I'll tell you all about it when I get back." He
turned again to leave.

"Just like that you're going out?" she cried angrily. "Not,
'Lenore, do you mind if I go for a walk and leave you here
all by yourself?' or not even a 'Would you like to come along,

darling, so you won't have to sit here all alone?' " When he looked back at her again, her eyes were blazing. "Just a flat 'I'm going out awhile, I'll be back'? Paul, what's the matter with you?" she asked. "All evening your mind's been miles away. And the way you stared at that man in the restaurant. It was positively embarrassing."

"I didn't know you were aware of it."

She frowned. "You stared a hole right through him."

"I only did it because he was staring at Gigi."

"Aha!" she cried triumphantly. "The magic words. It's your dear sweet sister you're worried about, isn't it?" She shook her head. "I should have known."

"Now, what's that supposed to mean?"

She inhaled sharply, her eyes clouding with uncertainty. She hadn't meant to say that. Not really. She'd been doing things all wrong lately. She hadn't meant to say anything. She'd been trying not to let the shock of his apparent betrayal reach her, but it had, making her vulnerable in so many ways. She picked at him and everyone else constantly, even though she knew it was wrong. The anger and frustration inside her continued to rebel at the thought of her husband's horrible sin, only she couldn't let him know. Not now. She couldn't risk losing him. So far, she had only suspicions. Nothing had actually been proven. She'd have to watch her tongue more closely.

She relaxed, her eyes softening as she looked at him more casually. "As I said once before, Paul," she said, her voice less harsh, warmth for him once more trying to creep into it, "your sister comes first, the rest of us second, thanks to your father." She waved her hand as if dismissing him. "Oh, go, go on. You'll go anyway, whether I want you to or not. So go right ahead."

Paul stared long and hard for a moment, paying special heed to the way the light on the dresser fell across her breasts, remembering the well-rounded hips that were hidden beneath the folds of blue satin she was wearing. It had been well over a week since he'd made love to Lenore. Not since the night before he'd made love to Gigi. Lenore had complained about being too tired getting ready for the trip before they left New York, and it had been impossible to do anything on the train. Was that why she seemed so edgy? So irritable and quick to criticize? It wasn't like her. It wasn't that he really wanted her. Not the way he wanted Gigi. But he'd been fighting Gigi's nearness all week, and every time he looked at Gigi. his loins groaned with frustration. He looked straight into Lenore's blue eyes. They looked lost, apprehensive. Maybe they both needed release.

He let go the door handle, straightened, and walked toward her, taking her slowly into his arms, his gray eyes searching hers. "I'm sorry, darling," he said softly. "It's just something I have to do." His hand moved up to caress her neck, and he touched her face. "Why don't you just relax, get ready for bed, and I won't be long."

Her lips parted, and she almost spoiled it, but then held her tongue. "Promise?" she whispered.

"Promise." He kissed her lightly. then released her and headed for the door. Once more she stopped him with his hand on the knob.

"Paul?" He turned, and her eyes sought his. "I'm sorry I've been so miserable lately."

He nodded. "I know."

She smiled. "Hurry back."

He returned her smile, then left. As he stepped into the hall, his smile faded completely as he thought of the years ahead and the mess he'd made of things. He hurried past the door to Gigi's room, went on downstairs, and headed for the saloon.

Judah was standing on the balcony above the main floor of the saloon, contemplating whether to just march over to the hotel and confront the young woman with his revelation, or ask Mr. Larrabee, or what, when Paul walked in.

The saloon was fairly crowded, it being Saturday night, but it wasn't crowded enough that he had to elbow his way in, so Paul sauntered to the end of the bar, where he could get the bartender's attention.

"Yes, sir," the man said as he wiped the bar in front of Paul.

"I'm looking for Judah Parsons," he asked casually.

The big, burly man nodded toward the back and upward with his head, and Paul's eyes narrowed as he glanced across the room to the balcony overhead. Judah was relaxing against one of the support posts, his eyes on Paul, and Paul straightened uneasily. He'd probably been watching since he stepped inside.

"Thanks."

He strolled toward the back, ascended the stairs, and introduced himself. "Mr. Parsons, Paul Larrabee, New York City," he said, holding out his hand.

Judah straightened to his full height and hesitated momentarily, then shook hands. "My office?" he said, gesturing toward a door behind him.

Paul nodded.

Judah's office was fancier than Paul expected, and he could see that the adjoining room was furnished with a large four-poster bed. He remembered the waitress telling him that Mr. Parsons lived at the edge of town with his wife. Evidently he believed in the old saying about too much work and no play . . . There was another door on the far wall, and Paul assumed from where it was located that it probably led downstairs to the back alley. There was always a back way out in a setup like this. He turned as Judah spoke.

"Well, at least that's one decision I don't have to worry about making anymore," Judah said as he headed for the brandy decanter on his desk. "Care for a drink?"

"A small one." Paul watched him pour. "You know why I'm here?"

"I might."

Paul accepted the drink. "What's your interest in Gigi?" he asked bluntly.

Judah took a sip of brandy. "Who is she?" he countered.

"What do you mean, who is she? You evidently know very well who she is," he said. "She's my half-sister, Gigi Rouvier."

Judah shook his head. "No, she ain't, fella," he said irritably. "No siree. She may be calling herself that, but she's no more Gigi Rouvier than I am."

Paul's face went white. He swallowed hard, his fingers tightening on the glass he was holding, and he stared dumbfounded, as if he was going to fall over. "What are you talking about?" he murmured breathlessly, almost incoherently.

Judah finished his brandy, then set the glass down forcefully, his dark blue eyes steady on Paul. "I said she's not Gigi Rouvier."

"But that's impossible."

"Is it? Well, not to me. You see, six months ago I helped Gigi Rouvier bury her mother, then made sure the young lady was safely on a train headed for New York City, where she was to meet up with her real pa, a Mr. Jason Larrabee. That young lady over at the hotel, sir, is not Gigi Rouvier. I sure as hell don't know who she is, Mr. Larrabee, but I aim to find out. So I think you have some answers to give me. Now, where is the real Gigi Rouvier?"

Paul stared, bewildered, then gulped the last of his brandy, trying to fortify himself, his hands trembling. "My God!" he blurted, then suddenly confronted Judah. "Do you know what you're saying?" he asked huskily. "You're sure?"

Judah's eyes flashed. "I've known Gigi Rouvier for a good ten years, fella," he said. "And that young woman ain't her."

"Then who is she?"

"You don't know?"

Paul frowned. This was unbelievable. "How should I know? I thought she was my half-sister." He set his empty glass on the desk, took out his handkerchief, and wiped the beads of perspiration from his brow. "Maybe you'd better tell it from the beginning," he said breathlessly.

Judah offered him a chair, fortifying him with a refill of brandy, then sat in his own chair behind the desk and lit a cigar, pouring himself another brandy.

"Gigi Rouvier's mother carried the same name," he began slowly. "She and I'd been pretty close ever since she came to Eagle Pass some ten years ago with her little girl. Times were rough, and she had a hard time findin' a job. She started as just one of the girls, then ended up at the faro table. But she watched over her kid like a hawk. Wouldn't let her hang around the saloon or nothin'. Tried to keep her away from this sort of life. It was hard, though. She was a stubborn kid, and although when she grew up she wasn't too pretty, she really filled out and her ma used to worry about her all the time." He hesitated, glancing studiously at Paul. "Yeah, I can see where you could be related," he offered. "Same bone structure, same gray eyes. Gigi didn't look nothin' like her ma. Guess she took after her pa." He flicked an ash off his cigar, then leaned forward across the desk. "To go on, last summer Gigi's ma got real sick. She'd been losing weight, and . . ." Paul could swear he saw tears in the man's eyes, but Judah swallowed, then went on. "When she knew she was dying, she wrote to the girl's pa, then made me promise to see that she went to him. Now, I know I probably should have gone with her, but I knew how bad her ma didn't want the girl's pa to know what kind of a life she was leadin'. So I let the kid go alone. Now, tell me, Mr. Larrabee. Gigi Rouvier left this town for New York City back in April—where is she?"

Paul was flabbergasted. "I don't know." He told Judah about the train wreck, the brooch, and the letter. "And when my father saw her, he said there couldn't be any mistake. That she looks just like the original Gigi Rouvier."

"That's just the trouble," said Judah, agreeing with Jason. "She does. But why? Who is she?"

Paul shook his head. "I haven't the faintest . . ."

Both men were at a loss. They went back over both stories but could find no answer.

"And she doesn't remember anything?" asked Judah.

"Not a thing." Paul was in a turmoil. The shock of Judah's revelation had torn him apart inside. If Gigi wasn't his sister—rather, if the woman at the hotel wasn't Gigi . . . But how, why, who? It didn't make sense. The full realization of it began flooding through him, and his nerves tingled expectantly, his stomach swirling, muscles tightening. He stood up and paced Judah's office, then stopped by the window, gazing down into the alley below. "The convent!" he whispered absentmindedly, then turned back to Judah. "What about the convent?" he asked. "Maybe someone there knows something. My father's correspondence with Gigi Rouvier was sent to the convent of the Sisters of the Sacred Heart of Jesus. Someone there forwarded it here. Maybe they know something."

"It's worth a try."

"Do you know where it is?"

"It's about twenty or thirty miles northeast of here, near Elm Creek. You'll have to take horses. The railroad doesn't go anywhere near it, and from what I hear, it's cloistered."

"Then how did Gigi Rouvier manage to have her mail sent there?"

Judah half-smiled. "You have a point."

Paul studied him thoughtfully, then asked, "Will you ride up there with me?"

Judah took a slow sip of brandy.

"I need somebody who knows his way around," explained Paul, "and since you already have an interest in all this . . ."

Judah straightened, frowning, and chewed on his cigar. "When do you intend to go?"

"First thing in the morning."

Judah puffed on the cigar while contemplating, then took it from his mouth. "Are you sure you really want me along?"

he asked. "What about that fancy Mexican who was stickin' so close to your lady? Where's he come into this?"

Paul's jaw flexed. "My wife and I are escorting her to Mexico, where she's to marry him," he said. "He thinks she's Gigi Rouvier too."

"Then he'll be along?"

"I imagine."

Judah's eyes narrowed. "I don't like his looks."

"Well, now, neither do I, Mr. Parsons," said Paul defensively. "But I'm not the one who accepted his proposal, she did."

Judah tamped the cigar out in an ashtray on his desk, then finished his brandy, his dark blue eyes amused. "The name's Judah, Mr. Larrabee," he said gruffly. "And I'd be glad to go with you. I got my own horse. I'll meet you out front here at dawn tomorrow, if that's all right with you."

Paul reached out his hand, and Judah shook it. "And my name's Paul," Paul said as he felt the man's firm handshake. "Maybe between the two of us we can find out what the hell this is all about."

Judah released Paul's hand. "You sure you wouldn't care for another drink, Mr. Larra . . . Paul?" he asked, but Paul declined.

"Enough," he said. "I'd better get back to the hotel. I'll see you in the morning." He picked his hat up from the desk and left the room, while Judah frowned, watching him go, then followed him to the office door. He stood on the balcony watching Paul until he left the saloon, then shrugged. Strange man, Paul Larrabee, he mused to himself. He'd have sworn the man looked like he could use another drink. And his eyes when he learned about the woman who was supposed to be his sister—for a brief moment they'd been so vibrantly alive, as if a storm had been unleashed inside him. Weird. Oh, well, maybe he'd find out what was troubling the man tomorrow. He sighed, then turned and went back into his office.

Paul jammed the hat on his head as he left the saloon, almost colliding with a couple of dusty cowboys who looked like they'd just come off the trail. They stared at his tailor-made suit and fancy hat, then backed away, making sarcastic remarks, but Paul paid no attention; he was too busy trying to sort things out in his mind.

His feet moved reluctantly toward the hotel, but the closer he came, the more hesitant he was. He couldn't go in now.

Not yet. Lenore had said she'd be waiting. What should he do, tell her what he'd just found out? Should he tell André the truth, or just make up some excuse for going with Judah in the morning and tell André when he returned? Or maybe he should tell Gigi. But she wasn't Gigi. He swore under his breath, then turned abruptly, heading away from the hotel, his feet taking him along a street that led toward the river.

He slowed as he moved through the main street of town, walking deliberately, shoving his hands in his pockets, his thoughts miles away. If Judah was right, if Gigi wasn't really Gigi, if she wasn't really his sister, then they hadn't done anything wrong. The love they shared was as natural as that of any man and woman. And Judah had insisted he was right. Paul could think of no reason why Judah would lie. He remembered the look in Gigi's eyes just tonight when she'd joined them in the lobby, and he shivered inside. Then suddenly a helpless feeling of rage began to stir within him. It was too late. Damn! Even if she wasn't his sister, it was too late. He was tied to Lenore.

For the next half-hour, as he made his way to the edge of the river, then stood staring into it, he fought with himself, trying to find an answer for his feelings and the mess he'd made of things. After a tremendous amount of soul-searching, in which he decided he was solely to blame for everything, he realized there was little he could do about the situation, at least not right now.

He'd been sitting on the riverbank, and stood up now, taking one last look across the river toward the faint lights of the Mexican village that stood on the opposite bank, then headed once more for the hotel.

He couldn't figure out what it was that made him stop. Ordinarily others' affairs were their business, but maybe because tonight was so explosive, everything was registering indelibly on his mind. As he walked back, passing an old shed a few hundred yards from the river, he stopped as the conversation of the men inside penetrated his thoughts.

"And how do we get her alone?" Miguel asked thoughtfully, his deeply accented voice carrying out the broken window. "She's always with de los Reyes or Larrabee. We can't take them on."

Paul froze, his ears alert, his mind suddenly cleared of the turmoil that had racked it. He inhaled sharply, then moved slowly closer, his back to the side of the hut, his head close to the window, where he could hear better as the men kept talking, unaware of his presence.

"Whatever we do, we must do quickly, amigo," said Juan. "The señorita still does not remember who she is, so she will not come willingly."

Paul pressed even closer, listening to the conversation intently, turning his head ever so slightly, hugging the wall so he could use a corner of the window to peek in. There were two men in the room. One tall, lean, with a thin mustache, his face still young, but with an expression grown old from living the life of a fugitive. The other man was shorter, stocky, his weather-beaten face lined from the elements, his expression intense, unsmiling. Paul studied their clothes, noting the bandoliers slung across their chests. He scowled, puzzled. Now, why the hell were a couple of bandits hiding in a broken-down shack on the Mexican border talking about kidnapping Gigi? Because that's exactly what they were doing.

He stood outside the small hut for a long time, fascinated, drawing as close as he could, listening to Juan and Miguel arguing over the best way to capture her, and it wasn't until a dog came sniffing about, whining, and both men lapsed into Spanish, that Paul slipped from the building and darted quickly away, melting into the shadows.

He took a deep breath as he plunged into a copse of trees some yards from the shack, then hesitated, looking back to see if anyone was following. He flattened himself rigidly against a tree, holding his breath as one of the men, the tall one, appeared in the dimly lit doorway, then stepped outside, gun in hand, calling the dog, petting him affectionately as he gazed about, looking to see if anything was in the shadows. The Mexican circled the hut, then knelt by the door, petting the dog, talking to him softly as he continued to survey his surroundings closely.

Paul continued to hold his breath, not daring to move, hoping the dog would be content having his back scratched by the bandit whom the other man called Miguel, and he sighed, relieved, when the bandit finally shrugged, seemingly satisfied, and stood up, slipping the gun back in his holster, returning once more to the conversation inside the shack.

The breath eased from Paul slowly. His mouth was dry, like cotton, his heart racing. That was close. He stared at the tumbledown shack, then frowned. Now what? Go gack to the hotel and . . . What? His jaw clenched stubbornly as he straightened, then turned and made his way out of the tangle of trees, brushing twigs and dirt from his gray suit.

There was only one man he could think of who might possibly know what was going on—at least he'd give it a try—and a few minutes later he again pushed his way through the swinging doors of the Red Dog Saloon. This time, when he confronted Judah, the big man was seated at his desk just finishing some tally sheets on the night's winnings, since the tables had closed half an hour before, and only a few stragglers were left downstairs, finishing the last of their beers.

"Well, well, Paul, I thought you'd be over at the hotel in bed already," said Judah as Paul stepped through the door to his office. "It's past midnight, and we have an early start in the morning."

"I've got a new problem," said Paul, tossing his hat on the chair as he stared at the man, and he told him about the shack and the two men and the conversation that had brought him here.

Judah listened quietly, engrossed in Paul's story, his fingers drumming softly on the desk. When Paul was finished, Judah took a deep breath and scowled. "Well, I'll be damned!" he murmured. "You're sure you heard right?"

"There was no mistake."

Judah pushed his chair back and stood up, and Paul suddenly realized that Judah wasn't as big as he'd first thought. They were both six feet, but Judah seemed bigger because of his massive shoulders and broad face. Even his hands were larger than Paul's, the fingers thick and blunt. Not the hands of a gambler. Paul watched him go to a small cabinet in the corner and return with a new box of fresh cigars, setting them on the desk; then Judah sat back down again.

"I suppose you think I know something about it, right?" asked Judah, lighting a cigar, puffing on it ceremoniously.

Paul leaned forward, his gray eyes curiously alive. "Do you?" he asked.

Judah exhaled, letting the cigar smoke curl to the ceiling. "All I know is that sometimes we get Mexicans from across the border. Most of them aren't really bandits. They're probably some of El Verdugo's men."

"El Verdugo?"

Judah watched the question in Paul's eyes. "The Executioner," he explained. "You see, President Díaz isn't too well liked in Mexico, and there are some Mexicans who think the country would be better off without him. El Verdugo's one of them. Word from across the border is that he's threatened to kill Díaz on New Year's Day, and so far, everybody he's threatened has died. That's why they call him the Executioner. Of course its his style too that helps give him his name. He usually holds a mock trial, then carries out his death sentence in military fashion, with blindfold, firing squad . . ."

Paul was amazed. "But who is he?"

"Who?" Judah shrugged. "Who knows? A disgruntled citizen, one of Díaz's own men who turned against him, maybe even an American. The rumors fly thick, but I think Díaz probably knows who he is." Judah leaned back in his chair. "You see, as long as El Verdugo's men conduct themselves civilly on this side of the river, there's nothing we can do, so they go back and forth at will. That probably explains the men you saw."

Paul's eyes hardened. "But what about Gigi? I mean . . . well, you know what I mean . . . why would they want her?"

Judah straightened, taking the cigar from his mouth, leaning on the desk. "Now, that's a question." He paused, then went on. "This Mexican she's supposed to marry. I never did ask his name."

"It's André. André Diego de los Reyes. Says his family has a hacienda near the sierras somewhere, north of a place called La Mariposa. That's where we're headed."

He saw Judah's eyes light up. "Aha, maybe that's it," he mused. "The man who's head of Díaz's army in Coahuila in the north country is General Reyes. I bet they're kin. If so, then El Verdugo may figure it'd be worth his while to get his hands on the bride so he could put a bit of a squeeze on the general. Stranger things have happened."

Paul's scowl deepened. If Judah was right, why hadn't André said something? And where was he now? He'd left the hotel, supposedly to find a wagon for hauling the trunks and baggage. Had he returned?

Paul stood up and paced the room impatiently, trying to put the pieces together. Should he tell André, or should he tell anyone for that matter, until he found out what the devil was going on? But then, he had to protect Gigi in some way. He had to go to the convent tomorrow—there was too great a chance that someone there might know something—yet he didn't dare leave Gigi alone. He could leave her with Lenore, but what protection would that be? Lenore wouldn't be able to fend off two men. He could leave her with André, but then, he wasn't sure now whether to trust even André, the way things were going. Besides, as he had told Judah before, André probably would want to go with them. And what if André was upset when he discovered Gigi wasn't who she was supposed to be? It was too complicated! And what of Judah? The man seemed honest enough. It was Judah's voice that brought him back to reality.

"You're going to wear out that carpet, Paul," he said gruffly. "Why don't you come sit down. I think I have a solution to part of the problem."

Paul stopped in the middle of the Persian carpet. "What's that?"

"I know why you're so upset. You're worried about the young woman. Look, why don't you bring her over here? No one will know. Come in the back way, it's always unlocked downstairs, but I'll give you both of the keys to my office here. She can spend the night here and stay in the room all day tomorrow. It's Sunday, and the place is closed. Nobody'll bother her. Only you and I'll know she's here. If you want, you can tell your wife and have her bring some food for her tomorrow. We should be back by late afternoon, and maybe by then we'll have some answers."

Paul stared at him hard, his mind going over the suggestion, weighing the possibility. "What about you?" asked Paul.

Judah glanced toward the adjoining room, where the bed was clearly visible. "I guess I'll have to spend a night at home for a change," he said. "I was going home anyway to tell Elsie I'd be out of town tomorrow. She might even appreciate having me spend the night. Who knows?" He half-smiled, then went on. "I'm afraid my wife and I don't get along too well, Paul," he said thoughtfully. "I guess we live in two different worlds." He stretched and put out his cigar as he stood up. "Well, have you made up your mind?"

Paul watched Judah unhook a ring with two keys on it from his watch chain, then sighed. "Thanks, Judah," he said softly. "I'm going to trust you. I don't know why, but I am. Maybe because we both want an answer to all this. I don't know. But thanks."

Judah tossed the keys to Paul. "Bring her up here now. I'll be gone by the time you get back. Come up the back way. I'll leave the lights on, but be careful nobody sees you. And tell her to make sure she doesn't open either door unless she knows who's on the other side."

Paul thanked him again, promising to see him in the morning, and this time Judah ushered him down the stairs to the back alley. By the time Paul reached the hotel, even the desk clerk was snoozing on a cot in the back room, and he crept upstairs as quietly as possible, hoping he wouldn't meet anyone on the way. For a second he contemplated seeing if André was awake, then changed his mind and instead stopped at Gigi's door, the full realization once more hitting him as he knocked lightly. She wasn't Gigi, but who was she?

Gigi stirred, half-asleep, not quite sure she'd heard right; then she heard it again. She slipped from the bed, put on a wrapper, and tiptoed quietly to the door. "Who's there?"

"It's Paul."

"Paul?"

"Gigi, I have to talk to you. Open the door, please."

She hesitated, remembering their last encounter under similar circumstances, then realized he sounded extremely anxious. Wanting to keep as quiet as possible, she opened the door without further argument, and Paul stepped into the darkened room.

"Don't light the lamp," he said, whispering. "I don't want anyone to know you're stirring about."

She rubbed the sleep from her eyes, frowning. "What is it?"

He turned staring at her. All he could see was her vague outline, but he could tell that her hair was down, cascading about her shoulders. His heart grew heavy. "I found something out tonight," he said slowly, his voice low and husky. "It's going to take a lot of explaining, but I can't tell you here." He hesitated, then went on. "I want you to put on your clothes and come with me, but bring along your nightclothes. It's going to be impossible for you to stay here in this room."

"But why?"

"I'll explain later." He could sense her reluctance, even in the dark. "Please, Gigi, I'll watch out the window while you change. You can get dressed in the dark, can't you?"

She nodded. "Yes, but I don't understand."

"I know. Just trust me."

She moved to the armoire and took down her green traveling suit, feeling about in the dark as she slipped from her

nightgown and into her clothes. All the while, Paul stood at
the window, his back rigid, eyes alert for anything down in
the street below that looked suspicious. He saw nothing, and
when she was finished, he helped gather her nightclothes, then
quietly opened the door and they crept down the stairs. The
night clerk was still sleeping as they opened the door and
stepped outside, and Paul breathed a sigh. So far, so good.

In minutes he was opening the back door to the Red Dog
Saloon and escorting Gigi up the back stairs. True to his
word, Judah was gone, but the lamp was still lit, casting
warm shadows through the office as he ushered Gigi inside.

"Well, here we are," he said as he closed the door behind
them, locking it.

Gigi whirled around, puzzled. "Here we are where?" she
asked.

Paul walked over to the bedroom door and swung it wide,
stepping inside, and tossing her nightclothes on the bed.
"You're to stay here tonight and all day tomorrow until I get
back," he said firmly. "And you're to let no one in except
Lenore when she brings you something to eat, understand?"

"Understand? Am I a prisoner, Paul? What's going on?
Where are you going?"

She'd followed Paul into the bedroom and stood facing
him. Her eyes were still heavy from sleep, and she looked all
soft and warm. "No, you're not a prisoner," he whispered.
"But I want you here where you'll be safe."

"You said you'd tell me what this is all about," she reminded him as she watched the indecision in his eyes.
"Please, Paul."

How to tell her? He took a deep breath. "First of all, this
place belongs to a man named Judah Parsons," he said.
"They're his private rooms at the Red Dog Saloon."

Her eyebrows raised, but he continued.

"Second . . ." He paused, his voice breaking. "Second," he
said again slowly, hesitantly, "you're not my sister, Gigi. I
discovered tonight that you're not Gigi Rouvier."

Her eyes widened, mouth trembling as she stared at him,
trying to comprehend. She shook her head slowly in disbelief,
but he went on.

"Judah knew the real Gigi Rouvier," he explained, his
voice heavy with emotion. "He knew the woman who was my
father's mistress, and he knew the daughter she brought into

the world, my half-sister, and he said you're not Gigi Rouvier, and everyone in this town knows it."

She gazed at him incredulously, her eyes shining, not daring to believe what he was saying. "There's no mistake?" she asked, her voice tremulous.

He shook his head, his voice lost momentarily in the lump in his throat.

"But who am I?" she asked breathlessly.

"I don't know. That's where I'm going tomorrow, to see if the sisters at the convent up near Elm Creek can shed some light on this whole thing."

Gigi flushed as she stared at Paul, and suddenly a warm glow swept through her. "Paul?" she whispered, her voice almost lost in the large bedroom. "Paul, do you realize what this means?"

He straightened, his face tense as his eyes met hers. "It means I'm still married to Lenore, Gigi," he said bitterly. "Goddamm it! I should've gone away. I should've done anything but marry her!"

Tears welled up in Gigi's eyes. He was right. She was no longer his sister, but Lenore was still his wife. No matter what he found out tomorrow, he was still a married man. Oh, God!

"It's hopeless, isn't it, Paul?" she cried unhappily.

He reached out. He only meant to touch her face, wipe the tears away, but suddenly she was in his arms, and all the longing of the past days caught up with them.

His lips clung to hers passionately, and she kissed him back with a fervor that made up for their days of denial.

He drew his mouth from hers and looked deep into her eyes. "Why do I feel like this?" he whispered softly.

"Like what?"

"Whenever I held you in my arms before, there was always something, a feeling deep inside that warred with me, turning my joy to a bittersweet sorrow, and it hung heavy on my heart, but now . . . just knowing that you're not my sister, that the love we share is no longer tarnished or forbidden, I feel free, exhilarated, like a little boy who's discovered he can fly."

"And Lenore?"

"Don't spoil it, Gigi. Let me love freely, if for just a little while," he whispered, his mouth barely inches from hers. "Let me enjoy what should have been mine but for a quirk of fate.

Tonight there's no Lenore, no André. There's just you and me."

His hands moved as he spoke, beginning to unfasten the back of her dress. She didn't stop him. She couldn't, because she wanted him as much as he wanted her. Instead, she helped loosen his cravat and unbuttoned his shirt, her fingers running through the thick hair on his chest as he carried her to the bed. He laid her down gently, then stretched out beside her, and they were both transported to a world apart from reality.

His hands worked their miracle, bringing her body to life, and she loved him in return with a passion that knew no bounds. As he thrust into her over and over again, slowly, sensuously, reaping the harvest of their mutual love, she arched to meet him with a violence that made them truly one, and they climaxed together, bringing them a rapture sweet with memories.

Paul gazed down into her soft blue-green eyes, warm and satiated with love. "We'll work something out," he said hoarsely, still trembling from the wonder of his release. "Now that I know we have every right to love each other, I don't intend to let anything stand in the way."

"But Lenore will never give you up without a fight, Paul," she whispered sadly, and reached up, touching his face, running her hand down his strong cheek, letting her fingertips caress the corners of his mouth.

He sighed. "I know, and I don't want to hurt her. I never did, but I want you so badly it's killing me."

"You have me, Paul," she murmured softly. "I'm yours now and forever, you know that. But until we can figure some way out of this mess, some way for us to be together always without destroying everyone around us, no one else must ever know. Promise?"

He looked deep into her eyes, his own filled with passion. "Promise," he agreed, and kissed her hungrily, then let his mouth move fleetingly over her breasts as he slipped off her, taking her into his arms to hold her close. "My God," he said. "I just remembered I told Lenore to wait up for me. She's probably wondering where the hell I am."

Gigi snuggled close, breasts tingling, loins throbbing, the feel of him next to her warming her deep inside; then she frowned. "Paul, you didn't tell me why you brought me here," she said, and he hugged her tightly against him and told her of the two men in the hut.

It was then she told him of the man at the depot, and he fit the description of one of the men, except for the clothes. "I finally remembered tonight, just before I went to sleep, where I'd seen him before," she said as she lay with her cheek resting on his arm so she could look up into his face. "I was going to tell you in the morning. It was in New York. I hadn't thought of it at the time, not until I saw him on the platform here at the depot, but he was always in the crowd somewhere whenever I'd go someplace, especially with André. I guess I got so used to seeing him that he became part of the landscape. But down here he seemed so out-of-place."

"Well, after what happened in New York, with Jamie getting hurt and all, you're to stay right here where you'll be safe," he said as he brushed a stray strand of hair from her face. The dim light from the lamp on the dresser made soft shadows dance across the room and brought out the highlights of her dark hair spread on the pillow beside him and down across his arm. "Oh, darling, I wish I could stay with you like this forever," he whispered. "But if I do, I'll never get any sleep." He pulled her to him again, and once more began to kiss her, and before he left, he made her his again, merging their bodies in a love that made him ache inside later when she was no longer near for him to touch.

15

Lenore stood upstairs in front of the window of their room the next morning, watching Paul and André down the street as they reined their horses up in front of the Red Dog Saloon, where they were met by a man she assumed was Mr. Parsons. Her brilliant blue eyes were anything but tranquil. She'd tried to keep the anger from showing while Paul was present, but now rage flashed strikingly from her eyes, making them even brighter.

Paul had been unaware last night when he came home so late that she'd been watching through a crack in their partially open door earlier in the evening and had seen him and Gigi sneak from her room and leave the hotel. Lenore had closed the door quickly, hurried to the window, opened it, and put her head out and had seen them moving furtively in the shadows as they made their way to the Red Dog Saloon.

He'd been there with Gigi for over two hours, and it was close to three in the morning when he'd finally returned to the hotel. That had been another shock. When he returned, he'd told her that Gigi, or the woman they called Gigi, wasn't really his sister. That Mr. Parsons, who owned the saloon, knew the real Gigi Rouvier, as did everyone in Eagle Pass, and that in the morning he and this Judah Parsons were riding north to some convent where the original Gigi Rouvier had received her mail from New York, to try to discover just who Gigi really was. Oh, that was the clincher, all right. That did the whole evening up royal.

Tears flooded to the surface of Lenore's eyes, and she straightened her bouffant sleeves on her pink satin dress, then ran a hand over the tiny waist. The dress was getting tight already. Good. Soon everyone would know, and soon she'd tell

Paul, but not yet. Not until that dark-haired witch was out of the picture.

She clenched her fist, feeling the sharp nails against her palm. She should scratch her eyes out. But no, that wouldn't be ladylike.

She bit her lip as she watched the three men disappear down the road. They made an unusual trio. Mr. Parsons in his western garb, André wearing one of his elaborate Spanish outfits, and Paul in his riding clothes with the highly polished boots that was more suited to the bridle paths in Central Park. She wondered how Paul had broken the news to André. He'd said he was going to wake him early, tell him about Gigi, and ask him if he wanted to go along. She wondered if André was still as eager to wed Gigi now that he knew she wasn't really Jason Larrabee's daughter. The little bitch was probably just pretending to be Jason's daughter so she could take advantage of all his money. Oh, how she hated her, and now she had even more reason. Now she was sure. The look on Paul's face last night revealed everything. The haunted, hungry look was gone from his eyes when he returned. He was relaxed and contented, so different from earlier in the evening.

She had dozed off and on while waiting up for him until she'd heard the slight noise when he and Gigi had slipped from Gigi's room. And afterward, for the rest of the evening, she was unable to even doze, but sat up in bed fuming while she waited. Paul hadn't even cared. He'd forgotten all about his promise to come back to her, and when he did show up, he'd climbed in bed without even bothering to give her a good-night kiss. She was the one who had to remind him, and even then, his kiss was cold, unfeeling. He'd given it all to Gigi, even the kisses that should have been hers.

She turned from the window and took a deep breath, wiping the tears from her eyes. Paul had explained to her about the men he'd overheard planning to kidnap Gigi and why he'd taken her to Mr. Parsons' quarters; then, this morning, before leaving, he'd had the nerve to ask her to take Gigi some breakfast. Well, fine, it was the chance she'd been waiting for. She put on her brown felt hat with the pink satin ribbons, grabbed a pair of pink gloves that matched her dress, and left the room.

She ate breakfast alone at the Steak House, a situation she detested, then asked for some food to take out, if that was possible. The waitress brought her two sweet rolls and a pint of milk in a small sack. She paid for her meal, then left, looking about to make sure she wasn't being followed. Paul had specifically made it clear that no one was to see her take food to Gigi. She strolled along the boardwalk, crossed the next two side streets, then ducked quickly down the alley to the back of the Red Dog Saloon, positive no one had seen her. Then she opened the back door and stepped inside. Since it was Sunday, few people were wandering about, and complete silence greeted her as she stood in the back hall. She found the stairs on the left and ascended slowly, knocking on the first door she came to, disgusted at having to be in what she considered a wretched, despicable place. Bad enough they had to stay at that hotel; then he made her come here. She knocked again.

Gigi had slept later than she'd planned. Since there was really no reason for her to get up, she'd enjoyed the warmth and comfort of the big bed, remembering a few hours ago when Paul had shared it with her. After dozing off and on, she'd finally crawled out and put on her clothes, then spent the next few minutes making the bed. She'd just finished, when she straightened, startled. Someone was knocking on one of the doors to the office.

Leaving the bedroom, she walked into the office, listening closely, then moved to press her ear against the door that led down the back stairs as the knock came again.

"Who's there?" she whispered.

"It's Lenore. Paul said to bring you something to eat."

Gigi walked over and took the key from the desk, then came back, opening the door, and Lenore stepped in.

"I think this is absolutely ridiculous," she said as she watched Gigi hurriedly lock the door again behind her. "Paul must be out of his mind. I can't think of any logical reason why anyone would want to kidnap you."

"Nor can I," replied Gigi. "But after some of the things that happened in New York, I can see where he'd worry."

Lenore handed Gigi the small paper bag. "Here, I hope this is enough. I didn't want to be conspicuous bringing a tray or anything."

Gigi put the key in the pocket of her green silk skirt, then took the bag to the desk, looking inside as she walked. She set it on the desk, then turned back to Lenore. "It's fine," she said. "I'm not hungry right now. I'll eat it later." She studied

Lenore carefully, noting once again that she looked stunning.
Gigi's hand moved up to her own hair that was pulled back
and tied with a ribbon to keep it from swirling all over her
head. She'd found toilet articles on the dresser in the bedroom and at least had been able to brush it, but once more
Lenore looked like she'd just stepped off the pages of *Harper's Bazaar*, and Gigi felt deflated.

"Did Paul tell you why he went away?" she asked Lenore
timidly, wondering if he'd said anything about her not being
his sister.

Lenore glared back at her contemptuously. "He told me,"
she retorted. "As if it'll make any difference."

Gigi frowned. "Any difference? What do you mean?"

"Oh, come now, Gigi." Lenore's eyes were suddenly wild
and savage. "Don't play the little innocent with me," she said
viciously. "It doesn't really matter what he finds in that convent, now, does it? Whether you're really his sister or not
doesn't matter anymore at all, because you see, regardless of
what he discovers, he's still my husband, and he's going to
stay my husband. Now, do you understand?"

Gigi paled as she stared into Lenore's eyes.

Lenore laughed cynically. "You didn't think I knew, did
you?" she said coolly. "Oh, I'm not as dumb and naive as
you think, Gigi, believe me. Not at all. You and Paul think
you've put something over on me. Well, you haven't. You
think I never saw the way the two of you were with each
other? The sly looks, whispered conversations. No one could
be under the same roof with you two and not see it." She
straightened arrogantly and looked down her nose at Gigi as
if she were looking at a small, annoying insect. "You know, I
rather suspected it before we were married, but then I
thought Paul had more sense. That something so evil and sordid was beyond him. And then, too, I wasn't about to let annoying suspicions spoil things. You see, marrying Paul was
my one dream in life." Again her eyes flashed with hatred,
and her voice became harsh and brittle. "But I wasn't wrong,
was I?" She saw Gigi clutch the side of the desk as she tried
to keep her knees from buckling, and knew she was right.
"From the day we returned to Larrabee Manor after the honeymoon, I could see it in both your eyes." She was enjoying
watching Gigi squirm, and Gigi had no recollection of ever
having seen anyone look at her so viciously and with such
hatred. "Rose knew, didn't she? She tried to warn me, only I

didn't listen. I didn't think I had to. Then, last week, the day
before your momentous decision to marry André, you had
your chance, didn't you? Tell me, who seduced whom?"

Gigi tried to talk, wanting to deny all of it, but was unable
to "I . . . we . . ."

"Oh, don't bother trying to justify yourself," Lenore exclaimed hurriedly, waving away her feeble attempt at an answer with a quick gesture of her gloved hand. "I wouldn't
expect either of you to admit it. But you see, I know Paul
was in your room that night, Gigi, the scent of him was unmistakable, just as it's probably in there right now on the bed
where you slept last night." She gestured with her hand
toward the open bedroom door. "And Paul reeked of your
cheap perfume that night too, just like he did last night when
he came back to the hotel trying not to look guilty." She
paused, letting the words sink in. "Oh, yes, I know Paul made
love to you last night, Gigi. I know. He didn't even try to
hide the fact that something had taken that lustful, yearning
look from his eyes. You see, earlier, when he left, he'd
promised to come back to me. He needed me last night, and
would have been content with me, if it hadn't been for you."

"Please, Lenore!" Gigi finally found her voice, unsteady as
it was. "It isn't like that at all. We never wanted anything to
happen."

"Then why didn't you leave him alone?"

"I tried. Oh, God, how I tried. I tried to stop loving him. I
didn't want to love him. I even promised to marry André to
get away, because I knew it wasn't right, but now . . . I'm
not his sister, Lenore, now there's no reason we can't love
each other."

Lenore stared at her wide-eyed. "No reason?" she asked incredulously. "What do you think I am, nothing?"

"That's not what I meant."

"But it's what you said." Her eyes blazed. "If you think
I'm just going to step aside and give Paul a divorce, or let
him get an annulment so you can have him, you're sadly mistaken, my dear," she said fiercely. "Paul's mine. I made up
my mind years ago that I was going to be his wife, and now
that I have him, I don't intend to relinquish him to you or
anyone else."

Gigi bit her lip nervously. "Even if he doesn't want to
stay?"

"Oh, he'll stay." She sneered. "You'll see. He'll stay, be-

cause I'm afraid the alternative would ruin him both socially
and financially, and his father as well. You see, I can play as
dirty as you. How long do you think Larrabee Enterprises
would last if Jason's business associates discovered his son
committed incest?"

"He hasn't!"

"But he thought he had. Both of you thought you had, yet
it didn't stop you, did it? You still kept right on. Wouldn't
the world love to know that you fell in love thinking you
were brother and sister. I can just see the headlines."

"That's not fair. When they discover we're not related,
they'll understand."

"Will they? You think so? You don't know New York society very well. An affair is bad enough, Gigi, but something
like yours and Paul's . . . He'd never live it down, and
besides, Jason would never let Paul divorce the woman who's
going to give him his first grandchild."

Gigi's heart sank with despair, and she felt sick. "Oh, no!"

"Oh, yes." Lenore smoothed the waistline of her pink satin
dress. "I wasn't quite sure at first, but I am now. There are
too many signs. I haven't told Paul yet. I was going to tell
him last night, but then . . . You see, I don't think Paul will
think it proper to divorce a pregnant wife, Gigi. On top of
everything else, it would just add fuel to the fire. Believe me,
Gigi"—her eyes glowed with satisfaction—"I don't think
Paul's quite that callous."

Gigi turned away. She couldn't look at her any longer. Everything she'd said was right. Last night she and Paul thought
maybe there was a way out somehow, that some way, now
that they knew they weren't related, maybe they could sort
things out and find an answer, but there was no answer. It
was as simple as that. Paul was married to Lenore, and
Lenore was prepared to fight for him. A fight that would ruin
both Paul and his father. It seemed hopeless, yet Gigi
couldn't completely give up. Instinct, something, told her to
fight back. She couldn't give Paul up that easily.

She stared out the window into the deserted alley below,
then slowly turned back to face Lenore, her eyes filled with
pain. "You'd use a child to hold him?" she asked.

"I'll use anything I can."

"Then I pity you. Because Paul doesn't love you and never
has," Gigi said. "He married you because Jason insisted, not
because he loves you."

"He told you he doesn't love me?"

"He loves me!"

Lenore straightened confidently. "Gigi, Paul asked me to marry him before he even knew you existed," she said slowly.

"But he doesn't love you!"

"Oh, Gigi, for heaven's sake." Lenore sighed, hoping her voice sounded convincing. "How many men have done the same thing? A pretty face, a woman who's willing . . . Gigi, you're a diversion for Paul. Nothing more," she said. "Like Gigi Rouvier was for his father. You think because he's told you he loves you that it makes it true? How stupid and naive can you be? He's told me hundreds of times since our marriage that he loves me, just like he's told you, and he's made love to me too, Gigi, the same as he has you." She was fighting to keep Paul any way she could. Her jaw tightened. "Do you think I got pregnant all by myself? You're not that innocent, Gigi." She glanced surreptitiously at Gigi, then continued. "I knew when I married Paul that he might have a roving eye, but I decided I could handle it. You see, that part of our marriage isn't the most important part. The important thing is that regardless of how many times he might stray, he'll always come back to me. I'm the one who'll have his children—his wife. Regardless of what he's told you, he does love me—he proved that by coming back to me last night, and he's proved it by the child I'm carrying. So you might as well go right ahead with your plans to marry André, because no matter what Paul finds out, no matter who you really are, Gigi, I'll never give him up. Never, and you might as well accept it."

Gigi stared at her, tears glistening in her eyes. Lenore was lying; Paul didn't love her. Yet she was right. Gigi could fight for him all she wanted, but it wouldn't do any good. Lenore was his wife, and she had no right to him. Yet, something inside made her continue to rebel. She fought back the tears, swallowing hard, and reached in her pocket, taking out the key, then walked over and unlocked the door. She kept her back to Lenore as she opened it, then took a deep breath. "If you don't mind, I'd rather be alone," she said stubbornly. "We'll discuss the matter when Paul returns."

Lenore snorted irritably. "It won't change a thing," she said heatedly. "Not a thing. Paul belongs to me."

Gigi turned, her face livid, eyes blazing and wet with tears.

"Get out!" she gasped furiously. "Get out now before I forget who you are!"

Lenore's eyes bored into hers steadily, and for a few reckless moments the air between them bristled dangerously; then her head tilted haughtily, and she took a deep breath. "Gladly," she spat at Gigi as she headed toward the door, and she flounced out with an air of superiority that left Gigi trembling.

Gigi watched her disappear down the steps, then shut the door, locking it, stuffing the key in her pocket, then leaned against it, her heart pounding. What was she to do? It was bad enough discovering she wasn't Jason's daughter. The mystery of who she might be had haunted her all morning. Now this! Did Paul really love her, or was Lenore right—was she just a diversion? No! It couldn't be. What she and Paul had together was more than that. He did love her. This was only Lenore's way of hanging on, of hurting her. She felt miserable as she turned from the door and walked to the desk, staring down at the paper bag Lenore had brought, wondering where Paul was and what he might have discovered.

The sun was hot, beating down on the parched earth where it reflected up at the three men as they rode along. Paul glanced down at his city clothes that were so out-of-place here, brushing dust off his riding breeches, pulling the wide-brimmed hat down a little more to shade his eyes. They'd been riding for hours.

He glanced over at Judah, marveling at the man's stamina. He might spend a good deal of time at the gaming tables, but he was also no slouch when it came to the saddle, and he seemed to know the area like the back of his hand. He'd changed from the fancy clothes Paul had seen him wearing last night to Levi's, leather vest, blue linen shirt, ten-gallon hat, and high-heeled boots, and he looked at home in them. He was even wearing six-shooters. A necessity, he'd pointed out to both Paul and André before they'd started out, explaining that the territory was infested with rattlers. Paul had been right the first time. Judah was no ordinary gambling man. He watched now as André moved closer to Judah and said something, pointing off toward some hills in the distance, and Judah nodded; then André moved back to his position at Judah's far left.

Paul frowned, glancing at André as he reined his stallion away from Judah, his eyes on the hills up ahead. Something had been bothering him ever since he'd confronted André this morning with the bizarre news that Gigi wasn't Jason's daughter.

For some strange reason, André didn't seem too surprised. Oh, he put on a good act, pretending shock and registering concern about who she might be, but his eyes showed no alarm, their depths contradicting the confusion that his words implied. The farther they rode and the closer they came to the convent, the more he was convinced that André knew all along that she wasn't the real Gigi Rouvier, but there was no way he could satisfy his suspicions. At least there wasn't without perhaps putting Gigi in more danger, because he still felt uneasy about de los Reyes in other respects. There was still an air of mystery about him that couldn't be ignored. So he rode along, one eye on André, the other on the trail, praying to God he'd find an answer at the convent.

It was noon by the time they reached the sunbaked walls of the cloistered convent and rang the huge bell that stood outside the wooden gates. Some fifteen minutes later, after much arguing and pleading, they were finally ushered into the office of the mother superior, a short woman, roundly built, with a solemn face that stared at them curiously from her neatly tailored black habit.

"I'm sorry you had to wait outside so long," she apologized, her pale blue eyes studying them. "But visitors are unwelcome here. I wished to refuse your plea, but Sister Theresa said you stated it could be a matter of life and death."

Paul straightened, apologizing for their dusty appearance and their insistence that they couldn't leave without talking to someone, and the men nodded as she studied them, her eyes resting exceptionally long on André.

"Then what is it you wish?" she asked.

Paul glanced at André and Judah, then back to the nun. "We'd like to have some questions answered if we may, ma'am," he said. "Some time ago some letters were sent here addressed to a Miss Gigi Rouvier." He hesitated, wondering if his eyes were deceiving him, because he'd have sworn he saw the nun tense, yet as he stared at her hard, there was no further sign. He went on. "Someone here evidently

readdressed the letters to Miss Rouvier and sent them on to
Eagle Pass. We'd like to know who that someone was."

The nun licked her lips, then pretended to relax, although
her eyes were still sharp, alert. "I'm the one who readdressed
the letters," she said casually, and Paul was surprised.

"You?"

"Why not me?"

"But how did you know Miss Rouvier?" he asked, startled.
It was obvious Gigi Rouvier was a lady of questionable vir-
tue, and the idea that she'd be friends with a nun didn't add
up.

"I didn't know her," she explained. "Not intimately. Occasionally she and her daughter would stop by the convent here
and visit with some of the sisters. I think perhaps Miss Rouvier wished her life had been a different one. Then one day a
Mexican gentleman—or should I say a man, that would be
more appropriate—came to the gates and left a letter. It was
addressed to me. There was some money in it, a letter, and in-
structions. I was to send the accompanying letter, then read-
dress any answering mail to Miss Rouvier in Eagle Pass. The
donation was acceptable, so I complied." She frowned. "Was
it unlawful? Did I do something wrong?"

Paul shook his head, then glanced at André and Judah
again before going on. "Well, can you answer me something
else?" he asked.

"I'll try."

He reached into the inside pocket of his green riding coat
and took out an envelope, opening it, slipping what looked
like a newspaper clipping from inside, and began unfolding it
as both Judah and André watched curiously; then he held it
out for the nun to see. It was the newspaper clipping telling
of Gigi's arrival in New York and her identity as the daughter of Jason Larrabee; the picture was clear, easy to recognize.

"Do you know, or have you ever seen, this young
woman?" he asked the nun, and for a moment he saw something in her eyes. Was it fear? "Do you know her?" he asked
anxiously.

Her jaw flexed nervously, and she held her mouth rigid.
"I've never seen her before," she said, and glanced furtively
at André as she said it, as if watching his reaction.

Paul was puzzled. It was obvious by the look on her face

that she was lying, but why? And why would she be so conscious of André's reaction to her denial? It didn't make sense.

"You're sure?" he asked.

"Quite sure," she said, handing the clipping back to him.

Paul was frustrated as he stared at the picture of Gigi.
"But there has to be an answer somewhere," he said.

"What kind of an answer?" she asked.

This time Judah spoke, telling her of putting Gigi Rouvier
on the train to New York, and the young woman back in
Eagle Pass now who thought she was Gigi Rouvier, but
couldn't remember who she was.

"She's to marry Señor de los Reyes here," he said hopefully, gesturing toward André. "But I think we should find
out who she really is first, and too, we have to find out what
happened to the real Gigi Rouvier."

The mother superior looked anguished, as if she wanted to
speak but couldn't, and shook her head sadly. "I'm sorry. I
wish I could help," she said. "But I can't."

"Can't or won't?" asked Paul.

It was the wrong thing to say. The nun's eyes suddenly
turned cold, her back stiff as she straightened, giving the bell
cord behind her a pull, then excused herself. "Sister Theresa
will see you out," she said sternly, and left the room, using a
different door than the one they'd used to enter.

"You really fixed that one," said Judah a few minutes later
as they left the gates behind and headed back toward Eagle
Pass. "If she did know anything, she wasn't about to relent
and tell us after what you said."

"She wasn't about to tell us either way," countered Paul.
"It was obvious she knew something, but what?" He glanced
at André. "How about you, André? Any ideas?"

"Ideas?" He shook his head. "I think this whole thing is for
nothing," he said irritably. He hadn't wanted to come along,
but was forced to. Coming here was only delaying them. The
sooner Gigi was in his complete control, the better. Then he
could relax. "I've got a wagon all set, supplies ready, and
within another two weeks Gigi will be Señora de los Reyes,
so what does it matter who she was or is?" he said.

"You don't care?"

He straightened in the saddle, pulling the brim of his fancy
embroidered sombrero down to cover his dark eyes from the
late-afternoon sun. "Not especially," he said, moving easily
with the slow gait of his stallion. "Gigi's a very beautiful

woman. Perhaps someday she'll remember who she is, I don't know. But I don't much care, either. I didn't fall in love with a name, señores, I fell in love with a woman."

"You're not even curious?"

"Sí, yes, I'm curious. Who wouldn't be? But whoever she might be won't change the fact that I still intend to marry her, so I don't see why we have to go through all this. It's a waste of time."

Paul's eyes narrowed slightly as he dug his horse in the ribs and moved closer, pursuing his conversation with André. "Just how do you intend to marry a woman without a name?" he asked cautiously.

André glanced sideways at him. "What do you mean?"

"It's obvious she can't use the name she's been using. If she marries you using the name of Gigi Rouvier, the marriage would be invalid."

"Then perhaps we can find another name for her to use. The name matters little. With all due respect to your family, Paul," he said, "I'd say the matter is out of your hands now. It's up to Gigi, or whatever her name may be. I'm sure the fact that she's not Gigi Rouvier hasn't given her a change of heart, so I don't intend to change my plans. Everything's arranged for tomorrow morning—horses, wagons, even some men to ride escort because of the *bandidos* in the hills."

Paul bit his lip. Ah, yes, the bandits. He had told André about Gigi's identity, but had neglected to inform him of the two bandits in the hut by the river, who were planning to kidnap her. Now, why hadn't he told him? Judah and Lenore knew, and Paul had even sworn them to secrecy. Maybe it was instinct that made him cautious. Whatever it was, he was glad now that André had been kept in the dark, because the man's whole attitude just wasn't normal. If he really loved Gigi, if he really cared, he'd be willing to go through hell itself to help her discover her real identity. No, there was too much about André that still bothered him.

"I'm afraid the wagons are going to have to wait," he finally said, and watched André's eyes flash unexpectedly. "She may not be a Larrabee, André," he went on, "but she's still my responsibility, and I don't intend to cross into Mexico until we try a little harder to find out who she really is. Even if we have to go back to New York."

"*Madre de Dios!* You can't mean that," cried André, alarmed. "I've everything arranged. I even sent a telegram to

my parents." He blustered irritably, his cocksure attitude of
only moments ago suddenly gone. "You can't be serious."

"Dead serious," said Paul. "A young woman's disappeared
somewhere between here and New York, and another
woman's taken her place. I think maybe when we get back to
Eagle Pass it's time we talked to the authorities, and I think
Mr. Parsons will agree." He glanced at Judah. "How about it,
Judah?"

Judah had been listening to the conversation between the
two men; now he moved closer, reining his horse next to
Paul. "I think the man's right, Señor de los Reyes," he agreed
congenially, his eyes on André's handsome face. "Young Gigi
was like a daughter to me, and I don't intend to let it just
drop."

André's stomach tightened. *Caramba!* Of all the damn
luck. So close, and now this. Maybe he ought to tell them
about the real Gigi Rouvier, but if he did, he'd have to explain how he knew, and the whole thing would be over. He
clenched his teeth angrily, smoothing the edges of his
mustache, trying to appear calm and nonchalant. He couldn't
fail. He had to find a way. "*Muy bien,*" he finally said after a
few moments, his voice harsh, unyielding. "If you insist. But
no matter what you discover, señores, and no matter how long
it takes, I still intend to make her my wife, remember that!"

"If she still wants it," said Paul.

André half-smiled. "She will." As they quickened their
pace, dodging wrinkled cactus and dry grass that crackled in
the hot afternoon breeze, he kept his mind working. He
wasn't about to be thwarted now. Trying to kidnap her from
New York would have been foolhardy, but from Eagle Pass?
The border was only a few hundred yards away, and once
across . . .

Paul glanced over at André as they rode, noting his preoccupation with his thoughts, and so did Judah, and as they
shortened the miles between themselves and Eagle Pass, neither knew that the other had the same misgivings every time
their eyes fell on the Mexican, both wondering apprehensively just what he was up to.

Miguel had been watching the back door of the hotel all
morning and had now become impatient, his lazy gaze moving from the hotel door to Juan, who was sitting on the steps
of the general store across the street from the hotel. He

strolled toward Juan. "It isn't fair, amigo," he said cautiously as he settled in beside him, leaning against the porch rail. "We have seen nothing of her all day, and she was not there this morning before dawn when we went to her room. The door was unlocked, the room empty. You saw for yourself."

"And I still say she was in the other room with the Señor Larrabee and his wife."

"Ha! You saw in New York. Señor Larrabee's wife looks at her with hate in here," and he pointed to his heart. "Why should she spend the night in their room?"

Juan threw up his hands. "How should I know?" Both men had their bandoliers and guns hidden beneath serapes as they pretended to lounge about, keeping an eye on the hotel. It wasn't quite noon, and they'd been trying all morning to figure out a way to find out where the young woman calling herself Gigi Rouvier could have disappeared to.

Suddenly Juan smiled, straightening, eyes alert as he saw the blond woman, Señor Larrabee's wife, pull back the curtain of her hotel-room window and glance down the street. "I know that has to be it," he said hurriedly. "It has to be." He looked up at Miguel. "We both saw Señor Larrabee and Major de los Reyes leave town this morning with Judah Parsons, right?"

"Sí." Miguel continued to look uninterested, and relaxed as he leaned against the rail.

"And we know only the two women are in town, right?"

"Sí."

"We don't know where one is, but we do know where the other is, and I just know I'm right. They are both together. Only Señora Larrabee comes to the window, but that doesn't mean the other one is not in the same room. Only Señora Larrabee goes to breakfast. Perhaps the other one didn't care to eat. It's the only answer. Maybe they discovered something. Maybe the señorita has finally remembered who she is, or maybe she has discovered who de los Reyes is. Whatever, she has to be with Señor Larrabee's wife. Come on." He stood up, and Miguel caught his arm.

"Where are you going?"

"To knock on the door to Señor Larrabee's room."

Miguel's eyebrows raised. "Knock?"

Juan smiled, his tanned face wreathed in creases as he stared at his friend. "How else to get her to open the door, amigo?" he said. "Now, *adelante!* Come along, all is not lost," and they headed toward the hotel, then skirted around to the back, using the back stairs.

Lenore had been in a dither all morning. Her confrontation with Gigi hadn't gone well at all, although she was sure her statements had borne more truth than what Gigi wanted to admit.

She turned from the window and walked to the dresser, staring at herself in the mirror. She studied the line of her jaw, the arch of her brow, and the golden sheen of her blond hair. She was beautiful, there was no way to deny it. And how many times Paul had told her so. Then why?

Her fists clenched savagely. Why had he gone to that tramp? That . . . that . . . What was the fascination? Because that's what it had to be. He couldn't really love her. He couldn't! She was his wife, and he'd made love to her too many times. Oh, God, how she hated Gigi, or whoever the devil she was.

She jerked abruptly from the mirror, startled by a knock on the door, then turned, staring at the door apprehensively. It was too early for Paul to be back.

"Who's there?" she called. No one answered.

The knock came again, harder. She moved to the door.

"Who's there?"

"A message for you, Señora Larrabee," a deeply accented voice said, and she froze.

"What kind of a message?"

"A telegram."

She hesitated, then sighed. It was probably from Jason. "Put it under the door," she said cautiously, but the voice on the other side of the door wouldn't comply.

"You have to sign for it, señora," he said. "Please, it will take but a minute. The telegrapher said it was important."

She shrugged, disgusted. Oh, this was silly. Paul had said Gigi had to keep hidden; he didn't say that she had to stay in her room and keep the doors locked. After all, he even made her promise to take Gigi some food. She was being overly cautious.

She reached down and unlocked the door, then began to open it slowly, and was taken completely by surprise as two Mexicans pushed their way quickly in, pulling guns from beneath their serapes, pointing them directly at her.

"Shut the door quickly," Juan ordered as he waved his pistol at Lenore.

Miguel closed the door behind them while Lenore backed away toward the other side of the room, her face pale, eyes wide with fright.

"What do you want?" she cried breathlessly.

Juan frowned as he gazed about the room. "Where is she?" he asked.

Lenore shook her head, her voice unsteady. "Who?"

Miguel's dark eyes caught her as he moved up behind Juan, leaning over his friend's shoulder. "The señorita who calls herself Gigi Rouvier," he said softly. "Where is she? She is not in her room"—he glanced about—"nor is she here." His eyes locked with hers again. "What have you done with her?"

"I . . . I didn't do anything with her," she said, trying to compose herself as she stared back at him.

"But you know where she is?"

Lenore forced herself to calm down and tried to think rationally, studying them both. They were obviously the two men Paul had told her about last night, and they were looking for Gigi. She frowned, wondering what it was all about.

"Yes, I know where she is," she finally said as an idea began to form. "Why do you want her?"

The men looked at each other, then back to Lenore. "We intend her no harm," Juan said, watching her closely. "Our only wish is to get her out of Eagle Pass to where she'll be safe."

"Safe?"

"*Sí.*" His eyes narrowed. "Right now, señora, the señorita is in much danger for her life."

Lenore was taken aback. "I don't believe you."

"Believe what you will, but the important thing is that what's to be done must be done today, now." He raised his gun a little higher. "Now, if you will kindly take us to the señorita . . ."

Lenore looked down the barrel of his pistol and swallowed hard, her palms clammy. What should she do?

"Señora?" asked Miguel, his pistol moving up beside Juan's, and Lenore bit her lip, her eyes moving to the taller of the two Mexicans.

If Gigi was gone when Paul returned, he'd be furious. Yet, what was she supposed to do—get killed because of her? Because of that tramp? Besides, if these men took her away . . . They said they weren't going to hurt her. . . . Paul would never know whether she'd told them willingly or by force. She licked her lips nervously, once more looking down the barrel of Juan's gun. It was the answer to her prayers.

"You're sure you don't intend to hurt her?" she asked anxiously. She wasn't about to get involved in any murder, although she'd give almost anything to get Gigi out of her life forever. Actually, at first, she'd thought of killing Gigi herself, but the thought of getting caught made her change her mind. She wasn't about to end up rotting in prison somewhere for murdering Gigi and still not have Paul. There were other ways to put Gigi in her place, and it looked like one had been plunked down right in her lap. But she didn't want to appear too anxious. She had to make it look like she was reluctant, just in case.

She wrung her hands nervously. "Oh, dear," she said, looking directly at the guns in their hands. "You'd really shoot?"

"There are other ways to persuade you to tell us where she is," said Juan, grinning broadly; then his grin faded, replaced by a dour look. "But I was hoping perhaps these would be persuasion enough," and he moved his pistol slightly to indicate what he was referring to.

She took a deep breath, taking in the strong, ropelike hands that held the pistol. The knuckles were scarred. He was a frightening man, strong, formidable. So was his partner. Neither of them made her feel comfortable.

"Señora, where is she?" asked Miguel again.

Lenore trembled. "All right," she said, trying to keep her voice steady. "She's at Mr. Parsons' saloon."

"The Red Dog?" Miguel frowned. "It's closed today. It's Sunday."

"Yes, I know," she explained. "But she's in Mr. Parsons' private quarters, with orders to open the door only for me."

Juan nodded, his face breaking into a grin. "Ah, sí, we should have thought of it before, since Judah Parsons rode off with Señor Larrabee." Once more his pistol moved, this time directly into her vision, only inches from her face. "And since, as you say, she will open the door only for you, Señora Larrabee, then I suggest you come with us. *Andale!*" and minutes later Lenore was leading the way down the back stairs, accompanied by the two Mexican bandits, their guns out of sight beneath their serapes, but still trained directly on her.

Gigi sat at the desk, her head in her hands. She'd been trying all morning to try to remember. She'd thought back over everything that had happened since she'd come to months ago in Mrs. Thornapple's big four-poster bed. Nothing helped. She sighed and stood up, turning to look out the window, as a knock echoed through the room. She glanced at the clock on the wall. It was only eleven-thirty; it couldn't be Paul yet. He said he wouldn't be back until late afternoon.

She moved toward the door that led to the stairs and the back alley, and leaned close, listening as the knock came again. "Who is it?"

There was silence; then: "It's Lenore."

Gigi's jaw tightened. "What do you want?"

"Paul said to bring you something for lunch too."

"I'm not hungry."

Lenore glanced quickly at the two bandits standing beside her with their guns drawn. She had to think of something, some way to make Gigi open the door.

"Please, Gigi," she said anxiously. "I have to talk to you."

"Not until Paul returns."

She was getting desperate. "It can't wait until Paul returns. Please," she begged. "Open the door, Gigi. I'm sorry I spoke to you the way I did. Please, open the door just for a minute."

Gigi hesitated. Maybe she should. After all, it must be important if Lenore had the gumption to say she was sorry.

"All right," she murmured slowly, and reached in her pocket, pulling out the key, and put it in the lock. She turned it slowly, reluctantly, then began to open the door, only to have it pushed in quickly, startling her.

She let out a cry and backed away as the two Mexicans pushed Lenore aside and burst in, but there wasn't time to think. She turned, bolting for the open door to the bedroom, darting through, and tried to close the door behind her, but the men were too strong. They pushed against the door hard, and when she knew she couldn't hold it any longer, she let go, scrambling toward the bed, both of them at her heels.

She started to scream as the taller of the two men grabbed her, but his hand stopped her scream in flight, covering her nose and mouth at the same time, and she fought frantically for air. Her arms flailed, and she kicked wildly, catching the other man in the face with the heel of her shoe.

"*Caramba!*" he cried, trying to grab her legs, and all the

while Lenore stood in the bedroom doorway watching complacently.

The man's hand slipped from Gigi's nose to cover only her mouth now, and her eyes stared into his face fearfully as she sucked air into her lungs through her freed nostrils. It was the man from the depot. She began to squirm, jerking her body wildly, and as she started to slip from the man's grasp, he tried to tighten his hold. She wrenched her head from his hand so her mouth was free, but the movement was too quick and she couldn't stop herself in time, and the last thing she felt as she opened her mouth again to scream was her head hitting something solid, a sickening crunch bringing quick tears to her eyes. She tried to hang on, but the pain was unbearable. She tried to finish the scream that had been tearing from her throat, but nothing came, and as voices reeled around her, trying to come into focus, she slipped slowly into a deep dark pit, into blackness where there was nothing to fight anymore.

....
....
....
....

16

Paul was furious as he stood in the bedroom of Judah's private quarters and stared at Lenore, who was sitting on the edge of the bed, rubbing her wrists to get the circulation back in them.

It had been a lucky accident that had rendered Gigi unconscious, because Lenore was sure the two men wouldn't have been able to get her out of the building otherwise. She stared at Paul now, her eyes blazing. He didn't seem to be worried about whether she was all right or not. It didn't matter that her mouth felt like cotton, the edges of it sore and chafed where the gag bit in. No, all he cared about was that his precious Gigi was gone.

The bandits had said it was necessary to tie her up too so she wouldn't warn anyone, and she hadn't protested, figuring it would look better when Paul arrived, but there'd been no reason for them to pull the ropes so tight. Nor had there been any reason for the gag in her mouth, although she had to admit it had been more impressive. When Paul and Judah broke the door down and found her trussed up on the bed, they had quite a shock. She rubbed the edge of her mouth with her fingers gingerly.

"Well, what was I to do?" she yelled at Paul as she glared at him. "Let them shoot me? Because that's what they would have done, you know, shot me. Or broken my arm or something just as horrible if I hadn't told them."

"Dammit, Lenore, you could've thought of something!"

"What?"

Judah had gone back into the other room, and came back with a glass of brandy, handing it to her. "Here, take a sip, it'll make you feel better," he said.

She looked up at him, her blue eyes edged with tears. "Thank you."

Paul was still holding the rope he'd taken from Lenore's ankles and wrists, and he curled it about his hands as he turned and walked to the window, staring out. "What I'd like to know is, how did they get her out of town?" he murmured, half to himself.

"They used a wagon," said Lenore as she sipped at the brandy, and Paul whirled around. "At least that's what I heard them saying while they tied me up," she went on self-consciously. His gray eyes seemed to bore into hers. "One of the men, the one called Miguel, went after a buckboard while the other one tied me up and kept an eye on Gigi. They tied her up and gagged her in case she came to, and I heard them say something about putting her in the back of the buckboard and covering her with a tarp until they were out of town and could use horses."

Paul glanced at Judah. "Do you think they'll cross the border?" he asked.

Judah nodded. "If they're El Verdugo's men, they'll not only head for the border, but go straight for the mountains." He looked at Paul intently. "How are you going to explain this to Señor de los Reyes?"

Paul shrugged. "I don't know." He scowled. They'd left André back at the hotel. Judah had accompanied Paul to his room, where they'd discovered Lenore missing, then both men had rushed to the Red Dog Saloon, breaking the door in when there'd been no answer to their knock. Now Paul was going to have to try to explain to André why he hadn't told him about the bandits.

Lenore emptied the brandy from the glass and handed it back to Judah, then tried to stand up. Her knees were still shaking a little, and Judah helped her. In a way she was glad the Mexicans had been so rough on her afterward, because it made her story to Paul more plausible. If he knew she'd simply stood by and watched them take Gigi without even attempting to go for help . . . But then, there was no need for him ever to know. She straightened, thanking Judah, brushing the wrinkles from her pink satin dress. "Well, I guess that settles that," she said. "If she's across the border in Mexico, there isn't much we can do, is there?"

Paul frowned as he stared at her. "Nothing we can do? What the hell's the matter with you?" He looked at Judah.

"Do you know anybody around who's good at tracking?" he asked.

A slight smile played about the corner of Judah's mouth, and somehow Paul knew what he was going to say before he said it. "I'm the best there is," he answered. "Before settling down in Eagle Pass, I think I roamed every inch of land on both sides of the Rio Grande. You plan to look for her?"

Lenore cringed, cutting Paul off before he had a chance to answer. "You can't!" she cried helplessly, and both men were startled by the ferocity of her plea.

Paul's face darkened, his eyes stormy. "Lenore, for Christ's sake," he yelled. "Do you expect me to just sit back and do nothing? They might kill her!"

"Well, I wish they would!" she cried, and tears welled up in her eyes. "I hate her!"

Paul turned crimson.

"I think I'd better leave," said Judah diplomatically as his face flushed, embarrassed. "I'll be out in the other room," and he left the two of them in the bedroom alone, shutting the door behind him.

Paul straightened, pulling savagely on the rope he was still holding as he stared at Lenore. It was the first time he'd ever seen her so unnerved. "All right, now that Judah's gone . . . what's this all about?" he asked, and she paled.

She'd said too much already, far too much, but there was no going back now. Well, he might as well know. "What do you think it's about?" she said through her tears as she tried to stare him down. "I know all about you and your so-called sister."

"She's not my sister."

"Oh, I know that. And aren't you glad?" Her mouth curled into a cynical sneer and she sniffed in, wiping her eyes with her fingers, wishing the tears would stop. "You and your precious Gigi. I know you've slept with her," she went on tearfully. "Last night, and the night before she decided to marry André. I know all about you two, and I wonder, Paul . . ." She gulped back the tears, swallowing hard. "I wonder if your father and friends would think so highly of you if they knew about your disgusting affair."

His eyes narrowed, and she straightened, composing herself some, knowing that she was hitting him where it hurt, and she went on. "And you had no idea she wasn't your sister then, either, Paul, did you? Not until yesterday. Believe me"—her voice grew harsh, brittle—"the scandal would rock New York as well as the foundations of Larrabee Enterprises, and you know it."

"You bitch!"

"Me, a bitch? Oh, come now, I'm the wronged wife, Paul. Good heavens, you're my husband, not hers," she said; then her voice lowered again viciously, and she added disgustedly, "Although watching you, sometimes it's hard for people to tell."

His eyes blazed as he stared at this beautiful woman he'd promised to love. A woman who despised the very act. "I could kill you!" he said furiously.

"Why don't you? Then you'd never have her," she laughed, mocking him.

He moved quickly, grabbing her wrist, his eyes like molten steel, the fire in them strengthening his dark good looks, making him even more desirable, and Lenore shuddered.

"You think it wouldn't be easy?" he whispered brutally, his face so close to hers that his breath fell hot on her cheek. His fingers tightened on her wrist until it hurt. "Dammit, Lenore, don't tempt me!"

She stared back at him, suddenly feeling the magnetism he radiated, the virile masculinity that he always exuded, and realized once more why women found him so attractive. Why she'd loved him all these years. She couldn't lose him. Not now. What would people think? What would they say? She had to keep him, use her head, and she had to be strong. Stronger than she'd ever been before in her life. He belonged to her and she wasn't going to let him go. Not for anything or anyone.

"Paul, please," she said, her voice unsteady. "Do you think it's easy for me to see her taking you from me? I love you, Paul. I always have, and I always will."

He stared at her forcefully, but his fingers eased on her wrist.

She wrenched her wrist from his hand and straightened, smoothing her skirt, composing herself, then went on. "I meant what I said, Paul." Her voice broke. "If you go after Gigi, if you bring her back, I still won't give you up. Never!" she said bitterly, and once more tears came to her eyes. "Regardless of what's happened, you're mine, and you always will be."

He stared at her hard, his breathing heavy, fists clenching

angrily. Oh, how he'd like to hit her, but he wouldn't give her the satisfaction. It would be only another thing she could chalk up against him. Instead, he took a deep breath and turned, heading for the bedroom door.

"Paul?" she yelled after him.

He stopped with his back still to her, his hand on the knob.

"If you go after her, I'll never forgive you!" she yelled. "I mean it. You'll be sorry!"

He swung the door open, ignoring her threat, and stepped outside, and as he slammed it behind him, her voice became only a muffled jumble, then quickly died away.

Judah was sitting at his desk pretending to go over some papers as Paul stepped into his office. When he saw him, he stood up, shoving a cigar in his mouth. "Are you ready?" he asked, taking special note of the fury still in Paul's eyes and his flushed face.

Paul nodded. "Let's go," he answered, heading toward the back door, hanging splintered on its hinges. "I guess we'd better find de los Reyes and let him know what's going on," and he stepped carefully through the broken doorway and started down the steps, followed closely by Judah.

André wasn't at the hotel. After a fifteen-minute search they found him outside the freight office, where he'd been checking on the wagon and driver he'd hired for the trip in the morning, and the look on his face when Paul told him about Gigi was electrifying. His face turned livid, and his dark eyes held a fury that was frightening.

"You knew those men were in town last night and said nothing?" he questioned Paul heatedly, but Paul wasn't easily intimidated by André or anyone else.

"Going over what I did or didn't do won't get Gigi back," he said with equal vigor. "I came because I felt you should know what's happened, not to stand here listening to you trying to blame me for it."

André stared at him, fire in his eyes, his fists clenched as he spoke. "If you'd just told me." He shook his head in disgust. "Are you sure the men who took her are the ones you heard talking? The ones who talked about El Verdugo?"

"That's another thing," said Paul, ignoring the question. "You accuse me of not telling you everything. Why didn't you tell me about this El Verdugo? Surely you knew about him before this. And why didn't you tell me there was a chance he'd try something like this because of your relation to this General Reyes Judah was telling me about?"

André straightened arrogantly, staring at the two men. So that's what they thought. That El Verdugo had kidnapped Gigi in an attempt to intimidate General Reyes. Well, fine, let them, so much the better.

"Because I never dreamed it would matter," he answered cautiously, going along with their conclusion. "I didn't think the man would stoop so low as to do something like this, but I should've known, been more careful."

Paul watched his eyes. They weren't the eyes of a man who'd just discovered the woman he loved was in danger. They were the eyes of a cunning man, a man who was both angry and cautious, weighing every word before it left his mouth.

"We're going after her," he told André, looking for his reaction, but to his surprise, André agreed.

"I'll go with you," he said firmly. "Whether you want me to or not, but I suggest we travel light, take only what's necessary. If they're El Verdugo's men—and you said they were—they'll head straight for the mountains. Perhaps if we leave right away, we can catch them." He brushed some dust from the pants of his elegant black suit with its silver trim, and Judah noted the muscle control the man had. Earlier, he'd also noticed the way he rode a horse, the easy gait yet erect posture. He'd have sworn it was the mark of a military man. He frowned, watching André closely as Paul answered him.

"I have to get some things from the hotel," said Paul. "And we'll need supplies."

"I'll get supplies," said Judah, finally taking his eyes from André. "I've been this route before. It's not quite five o'clock, so we have a couple of hours before dark. If we can pick up their trail tonight, it'll make it easier in the morning. If we wait too long, we might not even find anything. As it is, they have a pretty good head start."

André brushed the edge of his mustache. "I'll meet you both at the hotel in half an hour, then," he said thoughtfully. "I have something to do before we leave."

"Anything we can help you with?" asked Paul.

He shook his head. "No. Nothing. It's something I have to take care of. And I'll cancel the wagon, too," he replied, and turned, going back into the freight office.

Judah watched him leave, then turned to Paul. "Why is it I just can't like that man?" he said. "There's something about him that don't ring true."

"I feel the same way you do," agreed Paul. "But there's nothing I can do about it except keep my eyes open. Now, let me help you get those supplies before I get my things from the hotel."

Judah nodded, and they walked off together.

A short while later, as they stood in front of the general store fastening the supplies onto a packhorse Judah had acquired, Paul suddenly looked up, then caught Judah's attention.

"Look what just came out of the telegraph office," he said as he fastened down a canvas bag, pulling the ropes secure to tighten it.

Judah looked up in time to see André heading toward the hotel, his long stride unmistakable, the late-afternoon sun glittering off his fancifully embroidered clothes.

"Wonder who he got in touch with," mused Paul as they watched him disappear into the hotel.

"You want to find out?"

"How?"

"Come on." Judah finished tying down the last bundle, then hitched up his Levi's, motioning for Paul to follow, and in minutes they were standing in the telegraph office.

Judah winked at Paul, then turned to the telegrapher. "Hey, Sam," he said jovially, "you know that ten dollars you owe me?" Five minutes later they left the telegraph office.

"Now, what do you make of that?" asked Paul as they walked toward the hotel.

Judah hunched his shoulders, stuffing his hands in his pockets as he thought over the message. André had sent a telegram to Romero Rubio, who besides being Minister of the Interior and head of the dreaded Bravi was also President Díaz's father-in-law. The message had been in Spanish, and Judah had translated it for Paul. It read: "El Verdugo's men have bride. Will rendezvous as planned at San Rodrigo and proceed from there." He'd signed it simply "André."

"As I said before," said Judah when they reached the hotel steps, "I don't trust the man. Rubio's the head of the Bravi, Díaz's secret police. I think perhaps there's more to the mystery of Gigi Rouvier than either of us realized." They stopped, and he glanced quickly at Paul. "Be careful, my friend," he said suddenly. "Damn careful."

Paul nodded. "Thanks, Judah. Now, bring the horses around as soon as you can. I'll go up and see what I need."

Paul watched, frowning as Judah turned and sauntered off toward the packhorse that was still tied up in front of the general store; then he turned and went into the hotel. He hurried upstairs, but hesitated before the door to his room.

Lenore was undoubtedly in there. She probably had come back while they were looking for André. Well, what the hell, he couldn't avoid her. After all, as she kept reminding him, she was his wife.

He opened the door and stepped in, shutting it hurriedly behind him, then stared across the room. Lenore stood by the bed, wearing a dark brown riding skirt, short-waisted matching jacket with gold buttons, and tan silk blouse, her blond hair braided neatly and fastened into a coronet atop her head. She was stuffing some clothes into a small carpetbag.

"What are you doing?" he asked as he headed for his suitcase in the corner to get a few things he'd need.

Her blue eyes hardened as she watched him. "I'm going with you."

"Oh no you're not!" He plunked the suitcase on the chair.

"Oh yes I am." She was just as determined. She straightened, fastening the clasp on the carpetbag in front of her. "Because if I don't go with you, I'm going to send a telegram to Jason telling him all about you and your precious sister."

"You wouldn't dare!"

"Try me!"

He swore under his breath.

"I'm not going to have you out there alone with her," she went on as she watched him fume. "I won't sit back here wondering if you're ever coming back, wondering what's going on. I'm going."

He sighed. What was the use of arguing? He shrugged as he finished gathering the things he needed, then grabbed a small bag from on top of one of the trunks, dumping the contents of soaps and paraphernalia onto the floor, stuffing his clothes inside. This done, he reached down among the things on the floor, grabbed a bar of soap, his razor, and a few other things, wrapped them in a towel, and put them in on top of the clothes, then shut the bag.

"Come on, then. If you're coming with me, let's go," he said. "Judah said we have only a couple of hours until dark." He headed for the door.

Lenore grabbed her bag, shoved a broad-brimmed hat on her head, and followed him out.

Judah wasn't any too pleased about her joining them, but one look at her face told him she'd never change her mind. So they waited while he found a horse for her and added a few more supplies, and at half-past five they were heading out of Eagle Pass along the winding river, where Judah discovered that a lone wagon, accompanied by two men fitting the description Lenore had given them, had traveled earlier in the day.

Paul glanced at the scabbard on his saddle, at the Winchester Judah insisted he take along, then let his eyes settle on the mother-of-pearl-handled silver pistol André wore on his hip in a beautifully tooled gunbelt. He wondered, would they really need them? He drew his eyes from the gun and glanced at Judah, unsmiling.

Judah nodded back. "Don't worry, Paul, we'll find her," he assured him. "There ain't nothin' can hide from me out there," and he hitched his own six-shooters more comfortably onto his hips, then spurred his horse forward, leading them northwest along the banks of the Rio Grande.

Gigi was coming to. Her head hurt something fierce. She tried to swallow, then realized there was a gag across her mouth. Breathing heavily, she managed to drag air into her lungs, only it hurt. And, oh, her head. The pain was excruciating. Her hands were tied behind her.

She opened her eyes slowly. All she could see were the gray, weather-beaten sides of a wagon. She was being hauled somewhere. Suddenly, as she stared at the old boards, feeling the jostling of the buckboard as it bumped along the road, a weird sensation filled her, and she frowned, her eyes puzzled.

She moved her head, looking up at the sky, watching the occasional passing of a tree overhead, and the realization slowly crept through her, making the flesh on her skin crawl. Suddenly the whole thing was clear. She could remember! Oh, God, she could remember! The past came flooding into her memory like a dam bursting. She knew, at last she knew!

Tears welled up in her eyes as the past and present all jumbled together in a haze of memories that left her breathless.

She blinked, then shut her eyes again, letting the full impact hit her as she rode along. She wasn't Gigi Rouvier! My God, Judah Parsons was right. She wasn't Gigi Rouvier! Suddenly her forehead creased into a deep frown, and with it, with the realization of who she really was, the danger of the moment became more frightening. Where was she, and what were they going to do with her?

Opening her eyes again, she tried to roll over into a better position, the tarpaulin covering her almost completely off, and she froze as the wagon suddenly stopped. She lay helpless, wondering what was going to happen next, moving her head into a better position, where she could see the back of the head of the man who was driving. He sat on the wagon seat, talking in Spanish to someone she couldn't see. She strained her ears, listening, then held her breath. There couldn't be any mistake. It had to be.

She started moaning, grunting beneath the gag, trying to get their attention, and Miguel turned, looking down at her, then climbed over the seat into the wagon bed.

"She's come to," he called to Juan, who quickly left his horse and joined him.

He climbed into the buckboard, and they knelt beside her, gazing down into her blue-green eyes, and Miguel laid his hand on her brow. "At least she's not feverish," he said in Spanish.

She tried to move. She had to let them know somehow. She tossed her head about, trying to make them understand, holding her mouth toward them, hoping they'd get the idea.

Miguel glanced back over his shoulder at Juan. "What's the matter with her, do you think?" he asked, still talking in Spanish.

Juan frowned. "Why don't you take the gag from her mouth and find out?"

"Poor little one," Miguel said as he reached down, and she stopped tossing her head about as he lifted it, turning it to loosen the cloth, then let the gag fall.

She turned her head slowly. It was still cradled in Miguel's large tanned hand, and she gazed up at him, tears forming in the corners of her eyes. "Miguel?" she whispered hoarsely, her voice breaking, and both bandits' eyes widened in sur-

prise. "Miguel . . . it is you, isn't it?" she gasped breathlessly.
She smiled through the tears. She hadn't seen either Miguel
or Juan for at least six or seven years. The mother superior
had said it was for the best. "You were in New York
watching over me, weren't you?" she asked. "Both you and
Juan," and she glanced over Miguel's shoulder to the other
man who was staring down at her.

"You remember?" asked Juan.

"*Sí.* I remember," she answered.

Miguel let go of her head and reached down, turning her
over to reach the ropes that held her wrists bound, then
yanked the tarpaulin the rest of the way off her and untied
her ankles. While he did this, Juan rolled the tarpaulin up
into a ball, then handed it to Miguel when he was through,
and they put it beneath her head as a pillow.

"We did not want to tie you up like this, little one," he
said affectionately. "But with your memory gone . . . we
couldn't take a chance that you might cry out or try to get
away."

She moved slightly in the hard wagon bed, trying to get the
circulation moving more freely in her arms and legs again,
and reached up to touch the back of her head. Dried blood
was encrusted on a small cut that hurt like the devil. "What
did I hit?" she asked.

"One of the bedposts." Miguel flushed. "I tried to avoid it,
but you are surely your father's daughter, Señorita Gia, you
fight like a tiger," he said, and his mouth broke into a grin
beneath the dark mustache that adorned his upper lip.

Her hand dropped from her head, and she tried to sit up.
"Where are we?"

"We're up near the old fort, about four miles from Eagle
Pass. Juan feels it's better to cross the border up here where
we're not as apt to be seen by the border guards. Besides, the
water is shallow here, and we weren't sure just how soon you
could sit a horse."

She sat up all the way now that her wrists and ankles were
free. Her head was still hurting, but beginning to clear. The
sensation of memory after so long a time was strange, almost
heady. She remembered not only the past but also the
present, and suddenly she shuddered.

"What is it, little one?" asked Miguel as he saw her
tremble.

"I think I'm remembering too much," she murmured bitterly and put her hands over her eyes. Paul's face rose before her in the blackness beneath her palms, and all the memories of everything they'd shared together filled her. A bittersweet ache settled deep in her loins. How much she loved him, but it was hopeless. Lenore was pregnant, and she'd never give him up without a horrible fight. The scandal would destroy Paul and probably kill Jason.

Her hands slid slowly from her eyes, and she looked at Miguel. "I almost ruined everything, didn't I, Miguel?" she confessed hesitantly, remembering why she had come to Eagle Pass. "André is in on it somehow, isn't he?" she asked.

She remembered André's dashing personality and dark good looks. He was the perfect Latin, experienced with women, and just the man to charm a naive young girl.

Only she wasn't a naive young girl anymore. Paul had changed all that. No wonder she had known nothing of life and love when she'd arrived in New York. Her life since the age of nine had been spent in the convent of the Sisters of the Sacred Heart of Jesus. She remembered it all now. The danger and intrigue. The years of frustration, being shut off from the world. She wasn't Gigi Rouvier. No, she was Gia María d'Alessandro, daughter of General Maximilian d'Alessandro, who was of Spanish and Italian heritage, and his wife, the former Genia Rouvier, twin sister to the original French actress Gigi Rouvier. No wonder she had looked so much like the portrait Jason had of Gigi. Gigi Rouvier had been her aunt. Genia had died when Gia was only eight, and for almost a year afterward she and her father had stayed at the hacienda in Monterrey, enjoying each other's company, comforting one another. She bit her lip remembering all the times they went riding in the hills together, and the beautiful palomino horse he'd bought for her that year on her birthday, and the Christmas celebration with the *piñata* and songs. Her father had loved to play the guitar, and often played while they sang together.

She sighed. Those days were gone forever. They'd been wrenched from her viciously with the confiscation of her father's lands. She hadn't known what it was all about at the time, only that her father was no longer a wealthy man, and that his life was in danger, and that in order that he might live, she had to go away. It was only later, as the nuns taught her of the treachery of President Díaz, that Gia knew the full extent of her father's ostracism. He was an outlaw, living in the mountains fighting for the poor people of Mexico with every weapon God gave him.

El Verdugo! The Executioner! How far he'd come from being one of Díaz's favored generals. Of course, that was before Porfirio Díaz, dictator, decided that he was God's gift to Mexico with virtual authority over its people.

She gazed up at Miguel. Kind, faithful Miguel. And Juan. They had been with her father for years, and had worked at the hacienda before all the trouble began. It was Miguel and Juan who had journeyed north with her and taken her across the border that dark, stormy night years ago, leaving her at the convent. It was Miguel and Juan who had brought the occasional letters from her father, until the journey had become too dangerous. It was Miguel and Juan who had brought Aunt Gigi and cousin Gigi from California to Eagle Pass so they could visit her occasionally so she didn't feel quite so abandoned.

Even after all these years she had recognized them. She took Miguel's hand and squeezed it. "Exactly what was André's plan?" she asked him.

"He was to get you across the border willingly, if possible, then once into Mexican territory, where there was no chance for escape, the soldiers would miraculously show up and take you into custody. Your father thinks much of you, little one," he said. "If he didn't turn himself in, they were to threaten to kill you."

"Oh, no. And I went right along with it, thanks to the train wreck."

"Ah, but no. The wreck was a blessing for you in one way, little one," explained Juan. "Major de los Reyes' mission was to return you to Mexico. He managed to trace you to the convent and to Gigi Rouvier. If there hadn't been a train wreck, and if you hadn't taken the place of the real Gigi Rouvier, it would have been so easy for him to abduct you in New York and smuggle you aboard a ship heading for Mexico. After all, who would cry if the daughter of a Mexican outlaw disappeared? But Jason Larrabee would have raised hell if his daughter had disappeared. Because of the train wreck, it became too dangerous for them to kidnap you. Although his foolish henchmen tried twice." He bowed his head humbly. "I feel bad about your cousin, though, Gia."

Tears rolled down Gia's cheeks. She and cousin Gigi had become close over the years, and now, remembering the train

wreck and the horrible death that had taken her life
wrenched at her heart. But she straightened stubbornly. It did
no good to dwell on these things. Just as it did no good to
think of Paul anymore and the love she knew could never be
hers. She'd changed so much since the day she'd left the convent and joined Gigi in San Antonio for the trip to New
York. She'd been excited, innocent, yet frightened a little. But
the world hadn't changed, and she was back in the same
cruel world.

There were still men trying to kill her father, and Gia
Maria d'Alessandro was still a fugitive from her native land.
For just a moment she wished she could be Gigi again, but
she had to leave that life behind, and that meant leaving Paul
behind too.

She brushed the tears from her eyes and moved about
more, setting her muscles into play. In a way, it was good to
be Gia again, although her life as Jason's pampered daughter
was going to leave more scars than she really needed.

"Did Father tell you to bring me to him?" she asked, trying to keep her mind on the present as she stood up, shaking
the dust from her clothes.

Both men got to their feet beside her, gazing about to
make sure they weren't being watched. The road had been
fairly deserted, and when they'd heard her coming to, they'd
pulled off it into a maze of trees.

"Sí," said Juan, answering her question. "We have a horse
and clothes ready." He motioned toward the green silk traveling suit she was still wearing, with its abundance of petticoats and fancy satin trimming. "We knew you could not ride
in those."

He jumped from the wagon bed and strode to one of the
horses, taking a bundle from the back, while Miguel got
down, then lifted his arms and helped her down. She took the
bundle from Juan and cautioned them to keep watch while
she changed, then hid behind some bushes and shed the fancy
street clothes, pulling on a pair of baggy leather pants and
white shirt like those worn by the two Mexicans. Although
they had belonged to a young Mexican boy back in Eagle
Pass, on Gia there was plenty of room, and she frowned as
she glanced down at herself. But at least they had remembered to bring her something for her feet, and she slipped off
her black kid shoes and put on the Apache moccasins.

She came out from behind the bushes, tossed the rumpled

green suit into the wagon, then reached up, touching the
goose egg on her head.

"Here," said Miguel, handing her a sombrero he'd had on
the seat beside him. "Put this on."

She set it on her head gingerly, then slipped the bead up
on the ties until it reached her chin, so it wouldn't fall off.
"Well, I guess I'm ready," she said finally, after straightening
her clothes a little.

They helped her into the saddle, then unhitched the horse
from the buckboard, tied some supplies onto his back, and
within half an hour were wading the Rio Grande in an iso-
lated spot even farther upriver.

Gia pulled her wet horse up onto the bank in Mexican territory and glanced behind her at the long expanse of water
known as the Rio Grande. It was behind her, the life she'd
grown accustomed to and the man who had made that life
worthwhile. Tears began to seep into the corners of her eyes.
She bit them back, clenching her teeth stubbornly. She
couldn't let it get to her, not now. Things had changed so
much since the moment she'd opened the door to let Lenore
into the room again, and there was no going back, ever. It
was better like this anyway. She'd be out of Paul's life.

As Juan and Miguel joined her on the riverbank, she
whirled her horse around, then spurred him forward, gal-
loping off, her dark hair flying, the wind in her face. It had
been years since she'd ridden like this, so wild and free. She
had never ridden during her years at the convent, and in
New York she'd had to ride prim and proper, but here she
could feel the sandy soil flying at her horse's feet and breathe
in the nostalgic smell of the sunbaked earth. For a few moments anyway it was good to be Gia again and forget the
ache in her heart as she let out a cry, challenging the world
about her and the two Mexicans who tried to keep up.

Hours had passed. They were riding slowly now and had
been riding steadily, with Miguel in the lead, stopping only
long enough to check the trail. They were avoiding the main
roads, following half-hidden trails the Apaches and Coman-
cheros had used during the years they had terrorized the set-
tlers. Trails now used only by outlaws, bandits, and anyone
else trying to avoid the ever-present soldiers that patrolled the
area.

When night came, they camped in a small grove of trees
near a stream, sleeping out under the stars. Gia spent a rest-

less night, waking often from dreams of Paul, the train wreck, and all the memories of her life jumbled together.

When morning came, she was still tired and dragged herself from her bedroll. There was little ceremony at breakfast, only a tin of coffee and plate of beans eaten over a low fire; then they moved on. When lunch came, it was more of the same. After a day and a half more of extremely hard riding and sleeping out again under the stars, they followed a narrow path in the foothills of the sierras that led to her father's camp. It was hidden well, and as she rode in, looking about at all the men, rifles close at hand, their faces showing the effects of being hunted, the tears finally came in full force. She was going to see her father again for the first time in ten years, and she wondered how much he had changed.

17

They had picked up the trail just before dark, finding the abandoned buckboard in a grove of trees near the river, Gigi's rumpled clothes still in it.

"I bet they crossed just the other side of the old fort," said Judah as he studied the hoofprints.

They moved on, pressing hard, trying to beat the darkness that was slowly beginning to descend. Judah was right. They found the tracks of the horses leading into the river at a shallow spot just beyond where Judah said the old forty-niners' trail crossed the river—a spot, he explained, logical for them to use, because border patrols on both sides were scarce in this area, riding through only every few days. The river was long, desolate miles, and it was hard to keep watch on every place where anyone could cross. Even now there was no sign of any border patrol.

As they moved forward and waded their horses into midstream, Paul frowned. The river was still higher than usual because of the fall rains, and it looked so far across. He glanced at Lenore. She was holding up well so far, but they'd been on the trail only a few hours. It would be dark by the time they reached the other side of the river, and he wondered how she was going to manage sleeping all night in a bedroll out under the stars.

When they finally reached the other side, wet and tired, it was so dark Paul could barely see his hand in front of his face. They made camp a few hundred yards from the edge of the water, and Paul watched Lenore's face closely as she kept her eyes on Judah while he built a fire. She hadn't even started to take care of her horse. She was just standing there holding on to the reins quietly, watching what was going on.

Suddenly he felt sorry for her. He hadn't wanted to hurt

301

her, and when he'd asked her to marry him, he'd never dreamed he ever would hurt her. How could he guess when Gigi came into their lives that things would become so complicated? He'd cooled down some since their argument earlier in the afternoon, and he finished taking care of his horse, then walked over to where she was standing. "Give me the reins and I'll settle him for the night," he said.

Her head tilted arrogantly. "Why?"

"Look, I'm sorry," he said, taking the reins from her hands, moving over to pat her horse's nose. "That wasn't fair of me this afternoon."

"Don't be ridiculous, Paul," she said. "You meant every word, and so did I, so why this sudden concern?"

"You're still my wife."

"How nice of you to remember."

"Lenore, we've a long way to go, and it won't help if you keep that attitude," he said. "You're not used to this sort of thing. I can help make it easier for you."

"Don't put yourself out."

"Will you stop that!" He looked directly at her, searching her eyes. "I meant it when I said I was sorry. I don't like what's happened any more than you do," he said. "Don't make it even harder." He tensed. "I admit I've acted abominably. I've been the worst husband a woman could have. I've committed every sin in the book, but I'm still your husband, Lenore, and from what you've said, and the stubborn look in your eyes, it'll be a long time before the situation changes. So whether you like it or not, I'm still responsible for you."

He started to walk away with her horse, but she stopped him. "Paul?"

He turned, hesitating. "What is it?"

"There's something you should know, Paul," she said slowly, then bit her lip. Her voice lowered to barely above a whisper. "I'm pregnant, Paul," she said softly.

He stared at her dumbfounded. "You're sure?"

"Yes."

"Damn!" His jaw clenched as he saw any prospect of ever getting his freedom tossed to the winds. How could he even think of trying to divorce a woman who was carrying his child and still hold his head up? He studied her thoughtfully, wondering if maybe she might be lying. "You came on this trip knowing you were pregnant?" he asked. "Knowing you could lose it?"

"You wouldn't care," she snapped.

"Wouldn't I?" His eyes hardened. "You're going back," he said, straightening stubbornly, but she shook her head.

"I won't go."

"You'll go if I say so."

"I won't go, Paul," she repeated, her eyes rigid, unyielding. "Don't worry, I won't lose the baby. My mother went riding every day when she carried me, at least until she couldn't fit on the horse anymore."

"Your mother rode sidesaddle in Central Park," he reminded her. "She wasn't chasing someone halfway across the country."

"So what's the difference? I had Nordic ancestors who probably did worse. Besides, why should you care?"

He exhaled irritably. "You know better than that, Lenore," he said. "You know very well this changes things."

Her mouth curved sardonically. "It does?" She looked deep into his eyes. "I didn't realize . . . What does it change, Paul?"

She knew very well what it changed, that's why she hadn't told him earlier in the day. She'd been letting him hope, giving him enough rope to hang himself before tightening the last screw. She knew very well that no matter how much he wanted out of the marriage, he'd never leave her under these circumstances.

"Don't play with me, Lenore," he said bitterly. "I don't like games. You know I can't divorce you now."

"Then that means you've come to your senses and decided she isn't worth it?" she asked viciously.

Paul's eyes darkened. "It means I'll stick around and play the dutiful husband and father, but that's all I'll do," he said angrily. "If you want more, you'll have to go somewhere else for it."

"Oh, no, Paul. This is going to be on my terms, not yours," she countered, her eyes blazing. "And I refuse to have you make me a laughingstock in front of my friends. You'll not only play the dutiful husband, but you'll play the faithful husband too, do you understand? Because if you slip just once, Paul, the whole world will learn about your precious sister. Make no mistake, Paul, you're mine, and as I said before, I don't intend to ever give you up."

He stared at her intently. How deceiving she could be. The flames from the fire Judah had started cast their warm light on her, animating her face, softening the severe lines of her hair, making her look soft and lovely, and anyone gazing at her would swear she was all sweetness and warmth. Too bad he could see beyond the beauty, too bad he knew the woman beneath the sweet veneer.

"And to think I felt sorry for you! All right," he said resentfully. "The terms are yours, my dear, because as you've reminded me, this whole thing is my fault. But I'll warn you now, Lenore, since you'll allow me no freedom to vent my lusts elsewhere, the next time you crawl in bed with me, you'd better be ready to respond instead of lying there like a limp rag. Do I make my point?"

"You wouldn't dare!"

"Wouldn't I? Don't push me!"

Lenore fidgeted nervously as she stared at him. "Will you give her up, Paul?" she asked anxiously. "Will you tell her to go ahead and marry André?"

His eyes were wild, burning. "Yes," he said softly. "On the condition that you never tell a living soul what happened between her and me. Agreed?"

She smiled triumphantly. "Agreed," she said. "And don't worry about the baby, Paul, we Van Der Lindens are a strong breed. I intend to have this baby, make no mistake. And, oh, Paul, thanks for taking care of my horse," she said confidently. "And when you're through there, you can throw my bedroll down beside yours. I wouldn't think of sleeping by myself out here."

His eyes were like granite as he turned and walked away, his grip on the horse's reins so tight his knuckles were white. She'd won. Lenore had won. She knew that a baby was the one thing that would hold him, that would hold any man of conscience. Was that why she'd been so eager to get pregnant since their wedding? Damn her anyway! He glanced back at her for a moment, then fastened her horse beside the others and started to loosen the cinch.

Lenore watched Paul walk away, a feeling of satisfaction winging through her. She was going to make him pay for what he'd done. Oh, how she'd make him pay. She sighed, then turned to walk toward the fire, almost bumping into André.

"Oh, excuse me," she said, flustered. "I didn't know you were there."

"*De nada,*" he said softly, making sure he wasn't in the

way. "You and Señor Paul, something's the matter?" he asked suddenly, his eyes intent on her face.

She straightened haughtily, brushing some of the afternoon's dust from her riding skirt as she glanced over at Paul, then back at André. "Why, no, André, nothing's the matter. Why do you ask?" she said.

He frowned. "You both seemed rather quiet on the trail, and just now I could have sworn I saw fire in your eyes, señora."

She pursed her lips. "A minor disagreement," she ventured reluctantly. "Nothing serious."

"*Bien*," he offered. "I'd hate to think the two of you weren't getting along well. Tell me, did Paul tell you about Gigi last night and about the two *bandidos?*" he asked.

She gazed at him curiously. "Certainly. Why?"

"I was just wondering. It seems strange he was so reluctant to tell me about the two men." He glanced over at Paul, who had taken the bedroll from Lenore's horse and unrolled it beside his own. "Has he told you why he didn't tell me?" he asked.

Lenore frowned. He hadn't. "No."

"Hmmm. Ah, well, perhaps he has his reasons," he mused, then straightened, the puzzled look on his face replaced by one of expectancy. "Shall we see if our guide has any coffee started?" he asked, using his inborn charm, and Lenore let André escort her to the fire, where Judah was watching a pot of coffee bubbling away.

It was late. The night was quiet except for the noises of the gently flowing river, and occasionally a night animal wandered through, sniffing about. Paul had a hard time sleeping. For one thing, it was hard to sleep fully dressed, and all he could think of was the godawful mess he'd made of everything. Time after time he'd glance over at Lenore, her head close to his, and study her face in the moonlight, wanting to hate her, but unable to. He didn't love her, but he didn't hate her either.

When morning finally came, he was tired and irritable, and Lenore, sensing it, didn't cross him. After a quick breakfast cooked by Judah over the rekindled fire, they set off northwest across the plains. The tracks they were following stuck close to the road at first, while the land was fairly level; then, a little before noon, when the landscape became more scenic, with rocky, bush-covered knolls cropping up now and then to replace the cactus and sand, Judah began to lead them from the road into the rocky hills toward trails long forgotten by most Mexicans.

Paul noticed the nervous fidgeting André had begun to do shortly after they'd left the main road, and he kept a furtive eye on him. André kept looking around, studying the landscape, craning his neck as if looking for something.

Finally, shortly before lunchtime, they dropped down near the roadway again, following close to it until they reached the banks of the San Rodrigo River. The river was shallow here, and Judah explained that the road forded it about half a mile upstream from where they were crossing, and once on the other side, they took to the hills again before finally stopping to eat. As they munched on their beans and dry bread and drank their coffee, taking a short break from the saddle, André stretched, setting his plate down. "How far is the main road from here, Señor Parsons?" he asked casually.

Judah had found a clearing for them to stop in, and now he was resting his back against a small boulder, using the shade of a scraggly bush. He squinted as he glanced up at André. "About a mile," he answered.

"In which direction?"

"Now, why do you want to know that?"

"I have my reasons, Señor Parsons, *por favor?*" he said, straightening his jacket arrogantly.

Judah nodded his head toward a break in the rocks off to his left. "Straight that way."

André sauntered toward his horse, then mounted, turning to address them. "While you all finish eating, I'm going for a short ride," he explained, pulling his horse about, moving in the direction Judah had pointed. "I won't be long," and while they sat silently watching, he maneuvered his horse among the rocks until he was out of sight.

"I hope he gets lost," said Paul.

"He won't," remarked Judah. "He knows right where he's going." He glanced at Paul. "Remember that telegram?"

"Yeah."

"I got a good look when we were at the top of that last hill, and I think he did too. There's a whole passel of soldiers on the road back there by the river. They weren't moving. Looked more like they were off their horses waiting for someone. That telegram said, 'rendezvous at San Rodrigo.' Well, that river's the San Rodrigo. That's why I decided to stop here to eat. I could see de los Reyes was getting edgy, and wanted to see what he'd do."

"You think those men are waiting for him?"

"They sure weren't sitting around just enjoying the scenery. They've got soldiers patrolling these hills and the river, I agree, but they're few and far between, and usually not more than two or three at a time at the most. I got a glimpse of close to a hundred or more men down there."

Paul frowned as Lenore listened closely to their conversation. "What do you think it's all about, Judah?" he asked.

"I think maybe we're in the middle of a rat's nest, my friend," he said quietly. "And I don't think I like it."

Lenore's stomach began to churn as she looked at the beans on her plate, then glanced at Judah. "What do you mean, a rat's nest, Mr. Parsons?" she asked warily.

Judah's frown deepened. "I mean I think we're leading President Díaz's secret police right into El Verdugo's stronghold, and we're going to be right in the middle."

She grimaced. "Who is this El Verdugo anyway?" she asked. "I've heard all of you mention him before."

Judah explained.

"Then why don't we go back?" she asked when he'd finished.

He glanced at Paul. "Are those your sentiments too, my friend?"

Paul's jaw tightened. "We came after Gigi." He looked quickly at Lenore. "I won't leave until we know she's safe."

"Paul, be sensible," she said, trying to keep her voice down in case André was within earshot. "We can't get mixed up in this."

"We're already in it, Lenore," he retorted. "You don't think they're going to let us just leave, do you?"

"But—"

"There's only one thing I don't understand," said Judah, contemplating. Paul questioned him with his eyes. "de los Reyes sent that telegram yesterday afternoon, late," Judah explained. "Now, I can see if a few soldiers showed up from Piedras Negras across the river from Eagle Pass, maybe ten or twelve, but I could bet that was a whole platoon I saw down on that road. They had to have been close by waiting for orders. They could never have ridden up from Monterrey or anywhere else in so short a time. And if they were waiting here, what were they waiting for? Why were they going to

rendezvous with de los Reyes in the first place? He was coming to Mexico to get married, not fight El Verdugo." He
looked at Paul intently. "There are too many questions, my
friend, without any answers."

Paul stared at the plate of beans in front of him as he
thought over what Judah had said. Judah was right. Why had
André planned to meet those soldiers? And why was he being
so secretive about it? The whole thing smelled. He set his
plate down and stood up, walking in the direction André had
ridden out. The land was rocky here, with scrub mesquite
clinging to the sides of the hill.

He moved cautiously across the dry, rock-strewn ground,
climbing away from them, up the hill quite a distance, working his way until he looked back and had a clear view of the
road below. He stood for a long time, partially hidden by
some bushes, and watched the activity below. Every muscle
in his body was taut as he shaded his eyes, watching, the
newly acquired tan on his face creasing deep wrinkles into his
forehead.

Finally, after a quarter of an hour, he broke his stance and
climbed down from the small ridge he was on and joined
Lenore and Judah again at the fire. They'd been quietly
watching him, and it was Judah who asked the question
they'd been waiting to hear the answer to. "What's happening?"

Paul's eyes narrowed as he spoke. "He's on his way back
with the whole damn lot of them," he said.

Lenore stood up quickly, brushing the dirt from her riding
skirt. "Paul, let's get out of here," she said hurriedly. "I don't
like it."

"It's too late," he said. "Ask Judah. He'll tell you we
wouldn't have a chance of getting away."

Judah finished the beans on his tin plate. Lenore cringed,
watching him as he wiped it clean with some sandy soil and a
rag, since water was scarce. "Paul's right," he said, standing
up, walking over to put the dish away on the packhorse.
"Besides," he went on, "if we slipped out of here, we'd never
find out what that sneaky Mexican's up to, now, would we?"

Lenore didn't care. She was already tired of riding. Her
muscles were stiff and sore, her seat tender, and she felt filthy
from head to foot. Even when she licked her lips she could
feel dirt and grit, and it got inside her mouth, crunching
against her teeth. She argued heatedly with Paul about the fu-

tility of the whole trip, and it wasn't until he reminded her, with little sympathy, that he'd told her not to come that she shut her mouth stubbornly and left him be.

Seconds after the last heated words passed between them, André rode back through the break in the rocks, followed closely by a number of men. All of the soldiers couldn't ride comfortably into the clearing on the side of the hill. Most of them were strung out in single file halfway down the trail. However, two men rode forward with André. One was a tall, thin Mexican with sharp features and eyes that snapped alertly, missing nothing. The other was a man of medium height, stocky, with a fairly good-sized paunch that hung over his gunbelt. He had a large mustache, heavy jowls, and slow eyes that looked things over very carefully before moving on.

"We're in luck," said André as he alighted from the saddle, followed by the two officers. "I ran into Colonel Alvarez and his men down near the main road. He told me they've been searching the hills for days trying to find El Verdugo, and when I heard that, naturally I offered to help." He introduced them around, and when he did, Paul felt his stomach swirl apprehensively. The Mexican André was casually introducing to them as Colonel Alvarez was the man who'd stopped at Mrs. Thornapple's shortly after the train wreck and questioned both her and the constable about a young woman of Gigi's description. He wondered just what the hell was going on.

Paul glanced quickly at Judah, who returned his glance, winking furtively; then Judah looked at André. "Help how?" he asked after acknowledging the introduction but refusing to shake hands.

"Why, señor, we've been following El Verdugo's men for miles," André said, surprised that Judah hadn't understood. "I thought since there are only three of us, it would be wise to have help, and since the trail we're following is tangible and will no doubt lead us to the man's main encampment, it would be smart to offer our services. The colonel and his men have been roaming the hills for days looking for some sign of the man."

Judah glanced at Colonel Alvarez, looking him over thoroughly, then let his eyes linger on the men who followed him. Actually, if he didn't know better, he could believe it. None of them looked smart enough to pick up the trail of anything. Except for the two officers, Colonel Alvarez and the one

André introduced as Lieutenant Ramón Chavez, the soldiers looked like what they were, an assortment of farmers and peons conscripted against their will into the military by the Mexican government. They looked ill-trained and unaccustomed to fighting. No wonder El Verdugo had remained hidden for so long.

Judah felt Paul's questioning eyes on him, but had to play the game anyway, hoping Paul would understand and hold off any objections he might have until later. "I don't rightly mind them comin' along," he said slowly, his Texas drawl a little more pronounced than usual. "But I can't guarantee he's goin' to find El Verdugo at the end of the trail. I never took time to learn that Spanish of yours, Señor de los Reyes, so make sure your colonel knows what we're doin'. We're goin' after the girl, remember, and that's all we're doin'. If we reach her before they reach El Verdugo's hideout, that's as far as I go."

André's eyes narrowed slightly as he studied the man. Was he hedging or was he simply stating fact? He nodded. "I think the colonel understands." He turned to Colonel Alvarez. "Está bien, satisfactorio, Coronel?"

The colonel nodded. "sí." Then he spoke to André at length in Spanish while all three Americans showed ignorance of what was being said.

Lenore and Paul didn't have to pretend. They knew very little Spanish except "hello" and "good-bye," but Judah had all he could do to keep his expression impassive as he listened. Paul knew Judah had been lying when he'd told André he didn't know Spanish, and now he watched Judah's face as André and the colonel talked. Only his eyes revealed that he knew what the two men were saying, and Paul suddenly understood why he feigned ignorance. Judah acted quite nonchalant and strolled over to the fire, kicking sandy soil onto the flames, putting it out, but making sure he stayed within earshot of the two men. Paul watched him furtively.

When the fire was out and the men through talking, Judah picked up the rest of the tin plates and cups, cleaned them off as he had his own, then bundled them back onto the packhorse. This done, he turned to Paul, who was checking out the cinch on Lenore's horse. "Are you ready to ride?" he asked.

Paul nodded, helping Lenore into the saddle, then mounted his own horse quickly. André, the colonel, and Ramón fol-

lowed suit. Minutes later, as they wound their way up the
side of the hill, then over the top and down the other side,
moving along overgrown trails that Judah seemingly discovered out of nowhere, Paul wondered what the hell this whole
thing was all about and what Judah might have heard that reflected so ominously in his eyes. But he'd have to be patient.
Judah would tell him in his own good time.

The late-afternoon sun was hot as they rode along, and
Lenore could feel the perspiration trickling between her
breasts, making her clothes stick to her, and the sunburn on
the end of her nose was beginning to hurt. She didn't dare
complain, though, since she'd insisted on coming. She gritted
her teeth as her rear end hit the saddle again, and she bit back
the pain. She should have done more riding in New York, instead of lying in bed in the mornings; then at least she'd have
been used to it.

She glanced over at Paul. He was so determined. Well, at
least she had one consolation. Even when they did find Gigi,
there was nothing he could do but turn her over to André,
unless he wanted to create one of the worst scandals of the
century, and she knew that wasn't Paul's way. She smiled
smugly, hating every mile they covered, yet glad she was going to be on hand when Paul told Gigi it was over. Her
smiled broadened as she glanced back at the soldiers following along the trail. It was almost a surety that with them
along there'd be shooting when they finally reached the outlaws, and stray bullets were often known to pick their targets
indiscriminately. Wouldn't it be sheer luck if Gigi caught a
bullet? Then she'd be out of their lives forever. Lenore
gripped the reins tightly and spurred her horse faster to catch
up to André, who was following directly behind Judah. Was
it too much to hope for? she wondered.

Paul watched Lenore ahead of him on her horse. He knew
she was in misery, but she was stubborn. She looked well in
the saddle, even under those circumstances. Tall and statuesque. But her fair skin was taking brutal punishment, and
he saw her pull the broad-brimmed hat she was wearing farther down in front to cover the tip of her nose where it had
burned red.

It seemed strange to think she was carrying his child. He
stared at her back, watching the easy way she was letting the
saddle hit her rear. He bet she was sore. Served her right.
Then he took it back. No! He shouldn't think that way. What

if the ride was too much and she lost the baby—how would he feel then? Damn her! Why had he asked her to marry him anyway? He had nobody to blame but himself, so he might as well accept his fate. He scowled, fighting vainly with his conscience, his eyes moving past his wife to André, riding ahead of her.

André kept his eyes on Judah, moving slowly along the trail, following the tracks of the outlaws. With each mile, they were heading deeper into the foothills of the sierras, and the going became rougher. At times Judah had to leave the saddle and check the terrain when the trail moved over bare rock.

At first André had been irritated because Judah had pushed his way into Paul's confidence, but now he was glad. André was a military man. So were Alvarez and Chavez, and not one man with the troops could have followed the trail Judah Parsons was following. He'd been heartsick when Paul told him Gigi had been kidnapped, but now maybe it was going to be a blessing in disguise. For years the patrols had tried to locate El Verdugo's main camp. Now, with Judah's help, they were going to walk right in. Señor Rubio would be delighted. This was even better than originally planned. There would be no guesswork, no wondering. It would be just a matter of strength, and the strength was on his side. He had almost a hundred men with him, and enough arms to blow El Verdugo sky-high. He smiled, pleased with himself as he pulled his eyes from Judah, looking back at the packhorses and long line of soldiers threading their way along the trail.

Judah stretched as he straightened from the fire. They had camped in an arroyo with steep hills on each side, guards posted at intervals. He stood for a minute watching the guards as they rested at ease, looking about. The sun had finally dipped beyond the horizon, but it was still light enough to see fairly well.

Ever since they'd set up camp, he'd been waiting for an opportunity to talk to Paul alone. Now it looked like he was going to get his chance as Paul sauntered over, leaving Lenore and André to finish the conversation the three of them had been having.

"Any idea how close we might be?" Paul asked Judah as he stepped up beside him.

Judah shrugged. "Nope, except our trio seems to be moving faster now. Might mean they're getting closer." He turned abruptly, his eyes locking with Paul's. "There's somethin' I got to tell you, Paul, that you ain't goin' to like," he said as his eyes hardened. "And when I tell you," he went on, "you got to try to act like I ain't tellin' you nothin' more excitin' than the time of day. Understand?"

Paul nodded.

"Okay." Judah took a deep breath, then began again. "That fancy dude de los Reyes ain't what he's supposed to be," he said slowly.

Paul frowned, his eyes boring into Judah's. "My father had him checked out."

"Somebody was covering for him. He's a major in Rubio's Bravi, those secret police I was telling you about," he explained. "Colonel Alvarez is Mexican Army, Lieutenant Chavez is his aide. I've listened to them talking off and on all afternoon. De los Reyes was sent to the United States to kidnap the daughter of El Verdugo."

"Daughter?" Paul looked momentarily shocked, and Judah cautioned him to take it easy and not look so surprised, then went on.

"Seems his daughter spent the past ten years at the convent of the Sisters of the Sacred Heart of Jesus near Elm Creek, but when de los Reyes sent Alvarez to the convent to locate her, she'd left. Somehow they got wind she was headed for New York." He stopped, his eyes searching Paul's. "Does that give you any ideas, Paul?" he asked.

Paul frowned, trying to fit the pieces together. "Gigi?" he asked hesitantly.

"The woman we're following, the one calling herself Gigi Rouvier, is really the daughter of one of Díaz's ex-generals, Maximilian d'Alessandro, otherwise known as El Verdugo, the Executioner. Her name is Gia Maria d'Alessandro."

"But where does the real Gigi Rouvier come into it?"

"That's what I haven't found out yet," he said, and glanced toward André. "But maybe I'll learn that too before this is over."

"What do you think is going to happen, Judah?" he asked anxiously.

Judah sighed. "I wish I knew."

"We can't let them attack that camp, you know that," he said. "Gigi could get killed."

"You mean Gia." Judah nodded. "I know. I have no love

for Díaz and his regime, and I'm in sympathy with these men in the hills—they're fighting for a good cause—but I also know that de los Reyes is smart enough to know if I tried to double-cross him by leading him on a wild-goose chase. At least now."

"What do you have in mind?"

Judah turned, heading toward his horse, untying his bed-roll, and Paul followed. They were still far enough away from André or any of the soldiers to be heard.

"I've got a plan," he said furtively. "Don't know if it'll work or not, but we can't afford not to try it."

"Go on." Paul pretended to relax, watching the soldiers but lounging about as if he and Judah were merely passing the time of day.

"Well, I figure we're moving much slower than our quarry is, with all these men," he said, motioning with his head toward the soldiers. "Now, it's logical Gia and the two men with her will reach El Verdugo's camp before we do, and it's also logical that they'll have guards watching to signal our approach. If I can catch any of those signals, I might be able to know when we're getting close. If not, they'll let us know. I'm sure they ain't goin' to let us just walk right in." He glanced around quickly to make sure no one was close enough to overhear. "I thought when we got close enough, maybe once these toy soldiers get set for whatever they're planning to do, when nightfall comes, we'd sort of slip off to El Verdugo's camp and have a little parley with him and find out how the young lady's doin'."

"You think he's going to be happy, us leading them in?" asked Paul as he looked again toward the soldiers.

Judah shrugged. "That's the chance we have to take. Besides, maybe the young lady we're goin' to see will put in a good word for us, since she's obviously his daughter."

"Then what?" asked Paul.

"Then, my friend, we decide whose side we're going to be on. Theirs . . ." He glanced at the soldiers again. "His . . ." He looked off toward the mountains ahead. "Or ours."

"What do you mean, ours?"

"I'm hoping our side can sneak away when and if the fighting starts. I've been takin' inventory. We've been movin' northwest for the past four or five hours. We're somewhere in the Serranías del Burro. Now, if he's holed up where I think he's holed up, it's only about fifty miles from the Big Bend, maybe less. That means only fifty miles from the border instead of the almost hundred we've already gone. We won't be anywhere near Eagle Pass, but we'll be just downriver from the Boquillas Canyon, and I don't think de los Reyes' men'll follow us into American territory."

"If they do?"

"That's the chance we'll have to take."

"When do we make our move?"

"I'll let you know." He glanced across the camp to where Lenore was sitting staring into the fire Judah had started for them to cook supper over. "Only one thing's botherin' me, Paul," he complained. "What about your wife? I don't think she's goin' to like the idea of ridin' into the outlaw camp."

Paul frowned, his eyes moving to watch Lenore. Judah was right. Lenore would refuse to go. Unless . . . "Suppose we don't tell her where we're going," he said cautiously, looking back to Judah "Suppose we wait until it's time to leave, then I'll try to think of some explanation. Maybe I'll tell her we're giving up, that we discovered who Gigi is and there's no need to worry about her anymore."

"You think she'll believe you?"

"We have to take her with us, so it's the only thing we can do." He glanced at Lenore once more. "I think she'll go along with it. Especially if you try to convince her I'm telling the truth."

Judah smiled. "You think I can do a better job of convincing her?"

"Let's put it this way," said Paul, watching the curious look in Judah's eyes. "I think she'll believe you quicker than she would me. As you probably noticed, we haven't exactly been getting on too well."

"I noticed." Judah frowned. "Anything I can do to help?"

"Nope," said Paul. "But thanks for the offer." Paul straightened, stretching as André strolled toward them from the other side of camp.

"I'll let you know when," said Judah quickly, then changed the subject, greeting André casually as he joined them.

For the next three days they moved on slowly through the desolate countryside. The weather stayed hot, the land inhospitable. There were no signs of any villages—or even any other human beings, for that matter. Their only sign of anyone ever having been in the area was the tracks they were

following and an occasional abandoned mine—abandoned
years before, when they'd played out. Even these were few,
though, and were almost unrecognizable by the growth of
brush around them.

Now Paul began to understand why the land was so desolate and uninhabited. They rode through deep arroyos where
raging rivers once wound their endless ways. They had dried
up over the centuries and left nothing but sand, gravel, and
dust in their wake. Then the group climbed up hills that grew
into mountains as they moved farther into the sierras. Mountains covered with chaparral, pine, and firs that grew in spite
of the rocky soil, leaving the palo verde, yucca, and century
plant behind near the dry washes. And where there had once
been water, willow and cottonwood trees shaded the
saltbushes of the alkali sinks. The land changed so quickly
with each elevation, sometimes bringing cool breezes among
the firs, but always bringing incessant heat as the trail
brought them slowly down once more into the arid sunbaked
arroyos that could stretch for miles, with steep cliffs on each
side.

It was near sundown the sixth day after they'd left Eagle
Pass when Judah saw the telltale signal he was looking for up
ahead. El Verdugo's men were using mirrors to signal their
approach, and he figured they had to be close. He slowed his
pace, getting off his horse more often than usual to study the
ground, wasting as much time as he could, until finally, about
half an hour before dark, he told André it was getting too
dark to see and they'd better make camp.

He'd made it a habit every night to sleep as far from the
soldiers and André as possible, having Paul and Lenore join
him near his bedroll. And they'd also made it a habit to keep
their horses saddled and tethered close by in case of any trouble, so André suspected nothing as Judah built the fire. They
talked a little, and the evening moved along as usual; then everyone began to settle down for the night.

Judah unfastened his bedroll as he stood next to Paul, his
eyes furtively watching a group of soldiers not too far away.
"Tonight's the night," he told Paul. "That's why I picked this
spot to bed down."

Paul looked around. They were halfway up the side of a
sloping hill that leveled off partway, then dropped again at a
steep grade before reaching the flat ground below. Judah had
told André and his colonel that it would be cooler up here on

the side of the hill than near the radiating heat of the sandy arroyo below.

Judah set his bedroll down close to the edge of the steep slope, then motioned for Paul to put his and Lenore's bedrolls beside him. Their horses were tethered not ten feet away.

"So far, so good," said Judah. "Now, warn your wife. Tell her I told you we're getting close to the outlaw camp and I don't like what's goin' on. Tell her the story you thought up, and add that we're goin' back down the trail we came up earlier today, where we'll be safe. I don't think she'll know the difference in the dark, once we get started."

Paul nodded and left Judah, joining Lenore, who was standing by the fire alone. "Do you still want to get out of here?" he asked quickly, keeping his voice down.

She stared at him, surprised. "Why?"

"Don't ask questions, just answer. Do you still want to go back to Eagle Pass?"

She eyed him suspiciously. "And not go after Gigi?"

"Shhh," he cautioned her. "Keep your voice down. Do you want to go or don't you?"

"Why the sudden change of direction, Paul?" she asked. "You were willing to risk your life to go after her before."

"That was before I found out who she really is."

"Oh?"

"I thought she was in danger, that the men who kidnapped her would harm her. Now I know they won't."

"What makes you so sure?"

"She's the daughter of El Verdugo. That's why she was taken," he explained. "They were only taking her to her father. She'll be safe, and there's no reason for us to go on."

She eyed him skeptically. "You're lying."

"Why should I?" he half-whispered. "Now, look. I'm leaving. If you want to go with me, fine. If not, you can stay here and play the deserted wife for André and take a chance on getting shot. I don't care."

"How did you find out about Gigi?" she asked.

"Never mind how I found out, I just did," he said angrily, still trying to keep his voice down. "Now, are you coming with me or not?"

"You're sure you're not going to that outlaw's camp to try to rescue her?"

He stared at her hard. "I told you she doesn't need rescuing."

She licked her lips, feeling the dust that still clung to them. It was such a long ride back. Yet . . . She gazed at Paul suspiciously. It wasn't like him to ride off and leave Gigi. "Why are you doing this?" she asked slowly.

"Because it's the sensible thing to do. As long as Gigi's safe with her father, there's no point in going on. We could all get shot. André will never be able to find the outlaw camp without Judah's help, so if we leave, there won't be any fighting. We'll be safe, Gigi will be safe, and nobody will have to worry about getting shot."

She frowned. "But André's planning to marry Gigi."

"Lenore, look, André's not planning to marry Gigi," he said firmly. "I'll explain the whole thing later. But for now, please, are you going with me or aren't you?"

She took a deep breath as she looked at him. "Was there ever any question, Paul?" she said confidently. "I don't intend to let you out of my sight."

He exhaled. "Good," he said, then cautioned her not to let on to André or the soldiers that anything was going on. "If you do, we'll never get out of here alive," he cautioned her. "They need Judah to find the outlaw camp for them." Then he took her elbow, ushering her toward their bedrolls.

The camp quieted down earlier than usual. Probably because the weather had cooled considerably after sundown, making for comfortable sleeping.

Lenore felt a shiver run through her as she lay next to Paul in her bedroll. She tried cuddling farther into it to get warmer, but still trembled. "Paul?" she whispered quietly, gazing over at him in the dark. "I'm cold, Paul."

He sighed, then held his arm out. She squirmed from her bedroll into his and cuddled close, savoring the warmth from him, and her trembling stopped.

"I'm glad you've come to your senses, Paul," she said softly. "We'll have a good life together, you'll see." She tucked a stray strand of hair into the coroneted braids that were still atop her head. Only twice since leaving Eagle Pass had she been able to take her hair down and brush it out, then rebraid it into long golden coils, putting them back on top of her head. The last time had been three days ago, so her hair was pretty unruly. It seemed like there was never enough time, and she was too tired even to attempt it again.

And she hadn't had a sponge bath for days, either, only managed a superficial wash each time they came to a stream or trickle of water. She felt dirty all over, yet at the moment she was content, because for the first time in days Paul hadn't turned from her. "I've missed being close to you like this, Paul," she said softly.

He sighed She felt warm against him, her supple, long-legged body molding against his intimately. A wave of revulsion washed over him. He didn't want to be with her, yet knew there was no way out. She was his wife, and in spite of everything, she wanted him to treat her like a wife. He forced himself to pull her closer, pretending an intimacy he neither felt comfortable with nor wanted to share.

"I'm sorry, Lenore," he whispered huskily, realizing there was no use dreaming or even wishing things could be different. Knowing there was no use fighting the years ahead. He could live those years arguing with her constantly, growing to hate her with every day of his imprisonment, or he could accept the inevitable and try to make the most of a bad situation. He didn't want to hate her. As angry as he was over the situation, it hadn't been her fault. She was going to have his child, had married him in good faith. She deserved better than what she was getting. At least he could do that much for her. He held her close, letting her face press against his neck, feeling her breath warm on his flesh. "I'm sorry for everything that's happened," he went on slowly. "And it'll never happen again. When all this is over, we'll go back to New York and the baby will be born and everything will be as it should be. As it was meant to be."

She kissed his neck. "Oh, Paul, I'm so glad." She sighed. "And you'll forget about this ridiculous infatuation for . . . for her?" she asked.

He swallowed hard. "It's over," he whispered softly.

"Paul, kiss me," she pleaded.

He hesitated.

"If it's over, Paul, then kiss me," she demanded again, her voice barely a whisper.

Her face tilted up to his, and he hesitated again. Then slowly his arm tightened about her, pressing her closer, and his lips found hers and he kissed her long and hard while his heart was tearing to pieces inside him, and he knew it would always be like this.

It was two hours before daylight when Judah nudged Paul

on the shoulder, making sure he was awake. Paul put his hand over Lenore's mouth as he woke her, so she wasn't startled at his touch, because she'd fallen asleep in his arms. She had tried to stay awake until it was time to leave, but after a few passionate kisses she'd become warm and contented and had given in to her drowsiness.

She stared at Paul, puzzled at first, then remembered what was going on and nodded. He released her and motioned with his head toward the horses. Judah was already standing beside his horse.

There was no moon, the fire had died almost completely, and it was so dark you could barely see your hand in front of your face. Paul and Lenore worked quickly and quietly, rolling up their bedrolls, staying crouched low, hugging the ground. This done, they crept on all fours to where the horses were. Judah had untied all three and was waiting silently for them to join him. No one said a word, afraid their voices would carry in the cool night air. Paul tied Lenore's bedroll down and fixed his own, then looked at Judah.

Judah motioned with his hand for them to stand stock-still, then took one last quick look about the camp. Everything was still peaceful and quiet. The soldiers who were on guard had their backs to them, and everyone else was still asleep. A finger went to his lips, and he cautioned them about noise, then motioned them forward. They took their horses' reins and took three or four steps cautiously, heading for the edge of the hill; then Judah glanced again quickly behind him. So far it was going well. They had only a few feet to go. They held their breath and continued walking, still leading the horses. When they reached the edge of the hill, Judah sighed. They were going to make it.

He took one last careful look, then straightened and stepped over the edge, starting slowly down the incline with Lenore and her horse beside him and Paul on the other side of Lenore. Within minutes they'd dropped below the ridge above, where they were out of sight of the camp. Judah still moved cautiously, however, slowing some when the hill became a little steep, then moving faster when the footing was more sure, and Paul and Lenore kept up right beside him.

Occasionally they scared up a small animal or had to go around a clump of bushes, but the hill was mostly bare of obstacles. Some ten minutes after leaving camp, Judah finally stopped, his heeled boots grating on the fine gravelly sand of the arroyo, and he heaved a sigh. "Well, we made it," he whispered softly. "So far, so good." He motioned for them to get into the saddle, and Paul helped Lenore mount.

By the time the sun reached the horizon, spreading a warm golden glow over the countryside, they were well on their way deeper into the arroyo, leaving behind them an encampment that rang with André's curses as he blamed the guards for their stupidity and vowed he'd never rest until the treacherous gringos were once more in his hands.

18

Gia sat cross-legged on the hard cot, her eyes studying the man who sat going over some papers at a table on the other side of the large room that was furnished with crude handmade furniture and Mexican ingenuity. It was early yet, the sun having risen less than an hour before. She leaned back against the adobe wall behind her, toying with the front of her old shirt as she stared at him. He was so different from the man she remembered.

His hair had been black and wavy the last time she'd seen him, and had been meticulously groomed. Now it was peppered with gray, thick and bushy, falling carelessly to his collar, and the sideburns growing far down on his chin were joined by a huge mustache that almost hid his mouth. His dark eyes had once been enhanced by thick lashes that made them seem even larger, and so warm. Now they were adorned by crow's-feet and sun-weathered wrinkles that narrowed them slightly and made them hard and cold. That night so long ago when he'd said good-bye to her he'd been wearing a beautiful suit of deep blue velvet with silver trim that made him look so handsome and elegant. Now he wore an old military uniform that had seen better days, his only adornment a six-shooter resting on his hip. Even his boots were creased and worn, the hat he usually wore grease-stained.

She watched creases play across his brow as he studied the map before him, and she felt a tug at her heart. What had happened to him over the years? She'd arrived two days ago, and from the moment of her arrival she knew he'd changed in more than just appearance. Gone was the laughing, warmhearted father she'd known in her youth. The handsome caballero and dashing officer who'd kissed her good-bye that day and instructed her to go with Juan and Miguel had been

replaced by a bitter man whose heart was weary and whose
head was filled with killing and vengeance. Oh, he had a
cause, yes. She knew the plight of those under Porfirio Díaz
only too well. The mother superior at the convent had made
sure of that. His cause was just, but in accepting it he'd killed
the man he'd once been, and a new one had been born. A
savage man with a goal that made her shiver. He was no
longer her father, he was El Verdugo, the Executioner, with
blood on his hands, coarse curses on his lips, and a mistress
who shared his bed.

That was another thing hard to get used to. Her father had
been every inch the gentleman and had adored her mother.
Genia d'Alessandro had been such a lady. She'd been small,
enchantingly lovely, with the same blue-green eyes that were
now staring from Gia's face, and after her death Maximilian
d'Alessandro had mourned her heartbreakingly, vowing never
to love again. What a shock it had been on her arrival to see
Dolores hanging on his arm so possessively. Dolores was
voluptuous and earthy, with dark flashing eyes, a generous
mouth, uproariously hearty laughter, and a way of moving
that was an open invitation to enjoy her wares. Her hair was
long, black, and straight, jaw square, cheekbones prominent,
and she had large work-worn hands. Yet Maximilian
d'Alessandro treated her with an intimacy that shocked Gia.
Miguel and Juan should have warned her, but they'd said
nothing. Now Gia stared at her father, wishing the years
could be rolled back and life could be different for them
both.

She turned abruptly as Dolores came in, chattering angrily
about something one of the other women had done. There
were always camp followers, and El Verdugo's camp was no
different.

Gia watched them together. Watched the intent look on
her father's face as he listened to Dolores' complaint, then
saw his eyes soften as he talked to her, trying to soothe her
ruffled feathers. His arm went about her waist and he looked
up at her with an appreciative glint in his eyes. It wasn't a
look of love, but a look of need. An intimate look that told
Dolores she belonged to him. Gia was expecting to be asked
to go for a walk any moment now.

She smiled cynically to herself. A year ago she'd have been
innocent of the look that passed between her father and Do-

lores. Now, she not only recognized it but also understood it, and a deep restless ache settled in her loins as she remembered Paul's lovemaking. She straightened, starting to move toward the door voluntarily so they wouldn't have to ask her to leave, but her father stopped her.

"Where're you going, little one?" he asked gruffly in Spanish.

She hesitated, then turned back to face them, answering him in the same language. "I was going to go for a short walk," she said quietly. "I get tired of sitting here doing nothing."

He laughed. "I think you were going to be discreet. Am I mistaken?" he asked, and saw her flush. "Come here, child," he commanded, but she stood her ground.

"I'm not a child anymore, Father," she said.

His eyes roamed over her. No, she was right, she wasn't a child anymore. His gaze rested on the full breasts barely concealed beneath the plunging neckline, moving down, taking in the vague outline of the hips beneath the baggy pants she had on; then he looked intently at her face. She was the image of her mother, and his heart turned over inside him. Those days were so long ago. A tear threatened at the corner of his eyes.

"No, *querida*," he said huskily, his voice deep with emotion as he remembered the past. "You're not a child anymore," and his arm tightened about Dolores' waist, but before he could say more, a noise out front distracted them and all three stared toward the door.

Gia backed up, returning to the cot as Miguel hurried into the room. "*Jefe!*" he cried as he burst in, then apologized quickly for not having knocked first.

"Miguel, it's all right," Maximilian said to his old friend. "It's all right, just tell us what it is," he said.

Miguel took a deep breath. "The men are bringing some people in," he answered excitedly. "They're almost here."

Maximilian d'Alessandro's arm dropped from about Dolores' waist and she moved away from him as he shot to his feet. "Where are they now?" he snapped.

"About a quarter-mile off, coming down the hill."

El Verdugo hitched his gunbelt higher on his hip, his hand caressing the butt of his six-shooter. "I'll meet them outside," he said, then turned to Dolores. "It's a long time since we've had strangers here," he said. "Tell the women to stay under cover until I give the word." He looked back at Miguel. "Signal the men," he said, then turned his attention to Gia as Miguel left. "You'll stay here," he commanded sternly, his dark eyes flashing.

She nodded, then moved to the window of the adobe, pulling back a corner of the rough dark green cloth that covered it so she could see out. She watched as her father joined his men and they stood waiting for the arrivals.

Paul stared down into the valley ahead of them. Unlike the dried-up arroyos they'd been moving through for the early part of the morning, the valley they'd entered was greener and more fertile, with a stream running through it, fed by a natural spring. They'd moved up out of the last arroyo and climbed some distance, then ridden through a rocky pass and begun to drop to the valley, and he realized it was part of the mountain itself. It was a dimple in the mountain's surface, which, although nothing like the mountain valleys of the east, could be considered lush next to its surroundings.

It wasn't this, however, that made him gawk as they rode down into the valley, led by the two bandits who had accosted them about an hour earlier. It was the fact that men had begun to emerge from everywhere. They were only small moving blurs at first when he'd seen them from a distance, but as they left the ridge that circled the valley and drew closer, he began to make out their features, and it was then he realized where they were coming from, and he stared in awe, as did Lenore and Judah.

From above, as they'd descended down the slope, the valley had looked like any other valley. A little less sand and rock and much greener in places, but that was all. Now, here, riding into its midst, Paul could only marvel at what had been done. No wonder no one had ever found El Verdugo.

The adobe buildings that housed the outlaw's men, the barns and sheds that hid his horses and equipment, were all hidden beneath the rocks and greenery that lay on the valley floor. Dirt and stones had been carried to the rooftops and piled against the outside walls of every building, and bushes had been planted there. Now, years later, vegetation covered almost everything, making natural caves of the buildings. From a distance it was completely concealed. Now, up close, Paul shook his head in amazement.

He nudged his horse in the ribs as he moved up beside

Judah at the insistence of one of their guides, and Lenore followed suit, so the three were riding abreast of each other,
with Judah at Paul's left and Lenore at his right, the bandits
one ahead and one behind.

There was a small clearing up ahead, grasses giving way to
some sandy soil. Paul could see that the area was used more,
the grasses worn, paths here and there, but these smaller details had been undetectable from above. As he watched, the
men in the clearing ahead moved aside, and one man walked
toward them, his stride confident, stature solid, unyielding.

He yelled something in Spanish, and the men escorting
them motioned for them to stop. Paul reined up, leaning
toward Lenore's horse, calming the animal, which seemed to
sense her upset and was jittery as she tried to bring him to a
halt.

Lenore had thrown a fit when the bandits pounced on
them, and she'd accused Paul of maneuvering the whole
thing. "You knew we were going the wrong way, didn't you!"
she'd yelled at him. "You did it on purpose. I know you. You
had to see her! You just had to see her!" She'd straightened
then, realizing Judah was witness to her outburst, and her
voice lowered, more controlled. "Well, you can see her all
you want, Paul," she'd said through clenched teeth. "But I'm
still holding you to your promise, do you understand?"

He'd looked directly into her eyes, his own eyes smoldering.

"I mean it," she'd repeated viciously.

"I know. I said before, I won't ever leave you and the
baby, Lenore. I promise." His voice was flat, stilted. "We
only want to make sure Gigi's going to be safe with André
and his men out there," and as the outlaws brought them the
rest of the way into the valley, he'd finally explained to her
who André was and why they couldn't just run off.

Lenore was still upset, but she'd listened; now she stared
angrily at Paul as he helped quiet her mount.

Maximilian stood directly in front of Judah's horse, legs
apart, feet planted firmly, and stared up at him. He spoke in
Spanish, and Judah answered, while Paul and Lenore
watched. Then the man, known to Paul as El Verdugo,
turned to him and chose his words carefully. His English was
quite good, although heavily accented. "You're Señor Larrabee?" he asked.

Paul nodded.

"Then it's you to whom I owe much for the care of my daughter, am I right?" he asked.

Paul shook his head. "To my father," he answered.

"Ah, *sí*." El Verdugo smiled, white teeth glistening beneath his huge mustache. "Then I welcome his son to my camp." He raised his hand to shake Paul's, but Paul stared at him, embarrassed.

"But, señor . . ." he began and turned to Judah hesitantly. "Judah, didn't you tell him about the soldiers?" he asked.

El Verdugo's smile faded, but he still extended his hand to Paul, moving it even closer to Paul to take. "*Sí*, he told me about the *soldados*," he said firmly, still holding his hand out. "But that doesn't mean I can't welcome you. You didn't bring them here because you wanted to."

Paul relented and grasped the man's hand. It was strong, firm, and his eyes missed nothing.

"I think perhaps I'm as much to blame for the *soldados* being here as you, *mi amigo*," he said. "It was I who had Juan and Miguel bring Gia here. It was my men who left the trail that brought you here. So I too am to blame. If I hadn't brought her here . . ." He shrugged.

"If you hadn't brought her here, she'd be in the hands of Major de los Reyes' men by now and things could've been far worse for you and her," Judah reminded him.

El Verdugo nodded. "*Sí*, you're right, señor," he said. "That's why I blame no one. At least here, both she and I have a chance."

"How is she?" asked Paul.

"She's fine," he said, straightening proudly. "She's been here two days, and already she's becoming one of us."

Paul frowned. Gigi a bandit? His frown deepened, and suddenly Maximilian understood.

"Ah, *sí*, I understand," he said, staring at Paul. "But my Gia knows who she is now," he said, trying to put Paul's fears to rest. "She knows she's not your sister now, Señor Larrabee," he said. He glanced at Lenore. "Isn't it marvelous she remembers everything?" he went on. "And she's told me she wants to forget all about New York, that she's happy here with me in her own land."

"And if the soldiers attack?" asked Paul.

El Verdugo's face hardened, his eyes blazing hotly. "Then my men will make short work of them," he snapped.

"I hate to sound pessimistic, señor," said Judah, interrupting him. "But de los Reyes has a whole platoon of men out there, and I've a sneaking feelin' he's learned enough on this trip to maybe follow our tracks right on in here. It was dark when we left his camp, and we didn't get a chance to cover our tracks."

This time El Verdugo didn't look quite so sure. "I'll send some men out to hit and run, try to divert them," he said seriously. He scowled. "If they should find their way here, señor, then I'm afraid we're in more trouble than I thought, if he does have a whole platoon. I'm not at full strength, most of the men are out on raids." He straightened. "But all isn't lost," he said optimistically. "The battle's never over until the last shot's fired, and there's every possibility they won't find us. Now," he addressed them all, "if you'll leave the horses to my men, I'm sure Gia'll be glad to see all of you."

Gia had been watching from the window, and the sight of Paul had set her heart racing. He couldn't be here! Not here in the middle of nowhere. Not Paul! She watched him talking to her father, hoping in one way her father would send them all away so she wouldn't have to talk to him again, yet wishing she could hear his deep, rich voice just once more. Then she saw them dismount and knew her wish had been granted. She stood still, watching them approach, then bit her lip as her father called for her to come out.

She dropped the corner of the curtain that covered the window and straightened, smoothing the neckline of her shirt, hitching up the oversize pants. She licked her hand and wiped a dark hair back into place off her forehead. She'd combed her hair when she'd first gotten out of bed this morning, but it was always unruly. She looked a mess. Oh, well, it was now or never.

Her head was high, eyes squinting slightly from the bright sunlight as she stepped from the camouflaged adobe hut. She walked slowly, her moccasins moving easily on the dusty path. Her eyes avoided them, and she used one hand to shade them, but knew it wouldn't do any good; sooner or later she'd have to focus on something, on Paul, and the pain would come.

She stopped, staring at the ground, then slowly looked up. It was no use. She couldn't avoid it. Her eyes locked with Paul's and she inhaled, a shock running through her, weakening her knees.

Maximilian saw the strange, passionate look in his daughter's brilliant blue-green eyes as she looked at this man who only a few days ago she'd thought was her brother, and he cringed. It was the look her mother, Genia, had given him so often. A look of love so savagely passionate the air seemed charged with electricity, and as he gazed at Paul, he could see he was returning the look with the same vibrant emotion.

He laughed, trying to ease the situation, realizing now why Gia had avoided talking about her stay in New York. Why she'd wanted to forget it. Then his eyes moved to the tall blond woman standing beside Paul Larrabee. His wife! Maximilian d'Alessandro tried to save the moment for his daughter, and his arm went about her shoulder protectively, helping her break the hold Paul's eyes had on her. "Here, I told you she's fine," he said affectionately. "And see . . ." He gestured to her clothes. "She's already one of us."

Lenore watched the flush on Gigi's face deepen. Only she wasn't Gigi. She wasn't Paul's sister. What was it that outlaw called her? Gia? Her name was Gia, and Paul was looking at her as if he could devour her, as if she were the only other person on the face of the earth. Lenore clenched her jaw rigidly as El Verdugo invited them all into his quarters.

The adobe was large inside, and cool because of the cave-like atmosphere the camouflage gave it. Gia moved over to her cot on the far wall and sat down, feeling Paul's eyes on her, pulling her legs up beneath her because they wouldn't reach the floor if she sat on the edge of the bed. She avoided looking at Paul, and instead watched quietly as Dolores moved about the room finding chairs for everyone; then Gia frowned as Lenore, who was about to sit down, suddenly gasped loudly, a hand moving automatically to her abdomen.

Lenore held her breath, grinding her teeth as a sharp pain coursed through her, cramping her insides, and Paul drew his eyes quickly from their conquest of Gia and let them settle on his wife. "What is it?" he asked, seeing her flinch.

She shook her head. "I don't know. I . . . I had a few small pains earlier, shortly after we started down the hill," she gasped breathlessly. "But not this bad."

"My wife's pregnant," said Paul, explaining to everyone. "Do you suppose . . . ?" He addressed El Verdugo. "Is there a place she could lie down?"

Dolores came to Lenore's side and put an arm about her, trying to help. "I'll take her into our bedroom," she said, glancing at Maximilian, who nodded his approval; then she turned Lenore toward a curtain hanging over a doorway at one end of the hut.

Lenore started to move slowly, as if every movement was painful, and her face revealed the agony she was in. Paul watched, but only for a brief second; then he walked over, picked her up, and Dolores held the curtain aside while he carried her into the other room and laid her on the bed.

Four hours later, Lenore, with Dolores at her side and Gia helping, lost the baby she had wanted so badly, while outside the adobe hut, in the surrounding hills, Major de los Reyes, his soldiers following close behind, stumbled onto one of the secret passes that led to the hidden valley.

At first André didn't see it. He'd been following the tracks of the horses since daylight, then lost them in a rough area where there was an abundance of gravel and rocks. He probably wouldn't have seen it then either if it hadn't been for the button. He'd been riding back and forth for some ten minutes, trying to figure out which way they could have gone.

He had tracked men before, but not like this. This kind of tracking, in these hills, was the kind a man like Judah Parsons thrived on. It took an expert, and even then he'd have trouble. André had never realized the good job Judah had been doing until now. Damn the man anyway! He should have known they were up to something. The way they were acting, keeping to themselves, letting conversations die when he came around. And now the three of them had been joined by two more horses. Probably guards from El Verdugo's camp.

Could they have discovered who he really was or who Gia really was? This whole thing was becoming impossible, and would all have been so simple if that *puta* Gigi Rouvier hadn't died and decided to send her daughter to New York. If she hadn't died, Gia wouldn't have decided to go with her cousin, she would have stayed at the convent and been there when Colonel Alvarez and Ramón went after her, and it would have been such a simple task to get her across the border. By now they'd have had El Verdugo in their hands, André would have had Gia all to himself, and this whole mess would have been over. Instead, everything was getting botched up.

He dismounted and dropped the reins, gazing about, looking for something, anything. Then he saw it, something shining, the sun glinting off it as he moved his head. He stepped forward and bent down, then grimaced. It was one of the buttons off the brown jacket Lenore was wearing. The jacket to her riding suit had a double row of tiny gold buttons down the front, and she had evidently lost one. He glanced about, noticing a few broken twigs on a small scrub oak near two huge boulders, then realized there was a large space between the boulders. He glanced down, then knelt, examining the ground carefully, seeing the faint outline of hoofprints in the dirt.

He straightened, walking back to his horse, then mounted quickly, signaling to the colonel and Ramón to get the men, and within minutes they were moving through the wide crevice behind the bushes. Once the branches of the scrub oak had been pulled aside, the space between the boulders was even wider than it had first looked, and the men could easily ride through two at a time. André never would have found it if it hadn't been for the button, and he smiled as he watched the men spreading out behind him, wondering if El Verdugo's men had alerted him yet. He was sure they must have been watching, because they had been harassing the line of soldiers off and on all morning.

That was another thing. To the untrained eye, the land he saw below him now that he'd reached the other side of the pass would have been nothing more than an innocent-looking valley hidden away in this mostly arid land. But to the experienced eye of a soldier, one with military training, it took only a short time to realize that the brush-and-rock-covered hills in the valley below were not just haphazardly formed by nature, but were set at intervals exactly like those found in military forts. And it didn't take long for his trained eye to notice that the supposed wild horses cavorting on the floor of the valley were really being kept in by split-rail fencing that was hidden beneath thick growing bushes forming their corral. He grimaced. The place was so well-hidden. Even if someone stumbled on the trail between the boulders, he wasn't likely to look at the valley with more than an appreciative eye.

There were no tents, no usual signs of an outlaw camp. Even the gardens that fed El Verdugo's small army of men weren't planted in rows, but were planted haphazardly here and there to appear not to be gardens. He'd hidden here in these mountains for some six or seven years now, and it was evident why he was able to stay hidden. The man was clever, all right. But not clever enough.

André had moved a little closer down the slope, and he glanced back occasionally, watching the soldiers above him filtering along the high ridge that rimmed the valley. He studied the terrain, looking about for places that could be used best to his advantage, while below, Maximilian d'Alessandro stood outside the entrance to his headquarters, watching through binoculars as the thin line of men made their way across the ridge about a mile distant. They looked like small ants scampering about.

He squinted in the late-afternoon sun. The men he'd sent out earlier to harass the soldiers had returned only a few hours later with the news that the ploy hadn't worked and that the small army of men was still moving on and had, in fact, found one of the hidden entrances that led to the valley. He put the binoculars to his eyes again and watched as the soldiers began to move off the ridge and his men prepared for the fight that was inevitable.

"How many men do you have?" asked Judah from beside El Verdugo as they stood near the door to his headquarters.

Maximilian frowned. "Enough, perhaps," he said slowly, then took the binoculars down once more and turned to Judah. "But I'd feel better if the rest of my men were here." He stretched, hitching up his gunbelt. "Where's your friend from New York, amigo?" he asked, gazing about.

Judah nodded. "He went in and talked to his wife for a few minutes, then came back out and took off walking."

"He should have known better, letting her make this trip," Maximilian offered. "A ride like that in her condition . . ." He shook his head.

"I don't think Paul had much of a choice, General," replied Judah. "From the way the two of them were acting on the way out, I don't think he knew she was pregnant when we left Eagle Pass."

El Verdugo frowned, staring at the powerfully built man next to him. "You know Señor Larrabee well?" he asked.

Judah shook his head. "Not as well as I'd like. I only met him when they showed up in Eagle Pass."

"I wonder what this is between him and my Gia?" asked Maximilian.

Judah sighed. "You saw it too?"

"I saw it and I don't like it." He was restless, and shifted his gunbelt again. "I think perhaps my Gia has grown up too soon," he said, watching closely as the men prepared to defend the camp. "I think perhaps this man has broken her heart, señor," he said slowly. "What do you think?"

Judah remembered the look on Paul's face when he learned Gia wasn't his sister. He nodded. "I think perhaps you're right, General," he said. "But I don't think either one of us can do anything about it, can we?"

Maximilian's eyes darkened. "No, I suppose we can't." He straightened. "By the way. Have you seen my Gia?" he asked.

"I think she went for a walk too," said Judah. "Said she needed some fresh air."

Maximilian frowned, then was distracted as shots were heard in the distance and one of the men called to him. He left the doorway hurriedly, with Judah at his heels.

Paul hadn't strolled far. Sporadic fighting was already starting at the fringe areas of the camp, but at the moment he couldn't seem to concentrate on anything. All he could think of was his own miserable predicament. He kicked at the gravel in the path as he absentmindedly watched some outlaws putting up a barricade of wagons, boxes, and whatever they could get their hands on. He glanced back toward El Verdugo's headquarters. The adobe hut he used was built against the side of the mountain, which was small as mountains go, and the land behind it sloped up to the rocky timberline some couple of hundred feet above it. To the right of the headquarters were the stables, and beyond that was the first blockhouse. There were four blockhouses, and an uneven wall of rock and stone ran from each blockhouse, except for the spot directly in the center of the crescent-shaped fortifications, where it had been left open as a gate. It was here the barricades was being thrown up.

Living quarters for the men were scattered here and there in the half-circle that made up the camp, with the corrals and gardens between them and the irregular stone wall. It was like a small village, but there were no children. El Verdugo had allowed some of his men to bring women, but wives and children were left behind in the various villages scattered across Mexico, so the women were few.

Paul watched as one group of outlaws pulled a wagon over to the opening to fill one of the gaps, turning it on its side, starting to shove it into place; then suddenly he hesitated, his eyes caught by a slight figure pushing on the farthest end of the wagon. She had an ammunition belt slung across her left shoulder, covering her baggy clothes, the holster hanging onto her right hip, and her hair was pulled back, tied with a leather thong at the nape of the neck.

He straightened, cursing, walked over as the wagon began to slide into place, and grabbed her arm, pulling her back, whirling her to face him. "Gigi, my God, what the devil are you doing?" he asked.

She stared at him, startled at first; then her eyes flashed with emotion as she wrenched free. "What does it look like I'm doing?" she said, putting her shoulder back to the wagon, pushing again. "These are my people, and I belong here."

He stared at her for a second, then put his shoulder next to hers, helping her push. "You don't belong here, any more than I do," he said as he strained against the wagon.

"Paul, please," she said. "It's no use." The wagon slipped into place, and they started to straighten, then both hit the ground, Paul's body half-covering hers as a volley of shots splattered into the wagon bed beside them.

"Are you all right?" asked Paul as the men around them returned the fire, and Gia nodded as she moved from beneath him and lay on her stomach beside him in the dirt.

"That was close," she said breathlessly, and she peeked around the corner of the wagon.

"And they're going to get closer," he said angrily. "Gigi, you can't stay here."

"Paul, I'm not Gigi," she said, correcting him. "It's Gia, remember? We left Gigi back in Eagle Pass. She is no more."

His eyes bored into hers. "Oh yes she is. The name is different, but the woman is still the same."

"Paul, don't!"

"I have to." He reached for her, and she tried to pull away from him, but he was too quick and caught her, rolling her onto her back beneath him. She lay, her head on the ground, looking into his stormy gray eyes, his mouth only inches from hers. "You can't stay here, Gia, I won't let you," he said huskily. "Let your father fight his own battles. You're not a part of it. You never were."

She shook her head. "It's too late, Paul, don't you understand?" she said. "It's too late for everything. There's no way out of this valley except past those soldiers, and they're not about to let anyone leave. And even if we did get out of here, Paul, there'd be nothing for us, ever. Don't you see that? It's better this way."

"How can you say that?"

"Because I was there, Paul, you weren't." She bit her lip, her eyes misty. "I was with Lenore when she lost her baby, Paul. I listened to her screams, her pleading. I saw what she went through. Paul, she loves you! Whatever else she's done, your wife loves you. You're her whole life. As important to her as the air she breathes and the food that keeps her alive. You're her whole reason for living. Being married to you has become an obsession with her. When she knew she was losing the baby, she became hysterical because she was so afraid of losing you. I should try to take that from her? I can't, Paul. I can't fight her. She's lived for only one thing, Paul, ever since she was a little girl, to be your wife. Now she has you and she'll never give you up, and I can't blame her!"

Another volley of bullets tore into the wagon, and once more Paul's body shielded her. The men around them returned the shots again, and Gia slid from beneath Paul, moving onto her knees, propping herself against the wagon.

"What are you doing?" he asked as she leaned over again, peeking out from behind the wagon.

She reached down, pulling the gun from its holster at her hip, and Paul gasped, startled. "You're not going to shoot that thing?"

Her teeth clenched viciously. The gun was heavier than she'd realized. She'd had Miguel get it for her, but she'd never fired one before in her life. It felt hard and cold, her small hand barely reaching around the butt. "I have to, Paul," she said stubbornly, trying awkwardly to lift it, then using both hands. She swallowed hard as tears welled up in her eyes. "I'm an outlaw, Paul," she said shakily. "I'm El Verdugo's daughter, and I'm expected to kill or be killed. That's what I'm here for, remember?" and she tried to point the gun toward where the soldiers were hiding in the rocks and brush.

"You're crazy!" he said, and reached for the gun, trying to pull it from her grasp.

"No!" She struggled with him. "No, Paul, please! Don't you see," she cried helplessly as she hung on to the gun.

"This way you won't have to worry. You and Lenore and Judah are Americans, André will let you go. You can go back with Lenore and have a life together in New York, where you belong. I never was a part of your life, I never could be."

She managed to wrench free and try to point the gun again, but this time, instead of trying to take the gun from her, Paul stood up quickly, crouching, then leaned down and grabbed her arm, pulling her to her feet, breaking her aim, and he dragged her away from the wagon, running hard with her as she stumbled along behind him, the gun dangling from her hand. Shots were spitting all around them as he ran a zigzag pattern toward her father's headquarters, pushed open the door, and ducked in, pulling her in after him, whirling her around to face him.

"Now, let's get this straight," he said breathlessly as he stared at her hard. "If anybody's going to use that gun, it's going to be me, not you, do you understand? You can't even shoot the thing."

Her hand hung limply at her side, but she shook her head stubbornly. "I have to, Paul," she pleaded. "I'm his daughter. It's expected of me. Besides, if I'm killed, it'll only be so much the better, because it'll be quick and painless, not tortured like the years without you will be. I can't live without you, Paul . . . I know that. I don't want to."

"You can and you will!" He took the gun from her hand and set it on the table. "You're going to live, and somehow we're going to get out of here, and this whole nightmare's going to be over."

She stared at him, shaking her head. "It's hopeless."

Suddenly Judah flew into the room with a couple of bullets close behind that embedded themselves in the thick door as he shut it behind him. He ducked to one side, then stood staring at the two of them. There were tears in Gia's eyes, and Paul's face was flushed.

"Sorry, I didn't mean to interrupt anything," he said as he straightened, moving quickly toward the cot beneath the window, where Gia slept.

"You didn't interrupt anything," said Paul, and he noticed Judah was carrying a couple of rifles.

Judah stared hard at Gia for a second, then looked at Paul, hefting one of the rifles toward him. "Here, I brought the Winchester from your saddle," he said. "Thought maybe you might need it." His blue eyes studied Paul. "You know how to shoot it, don't you?" he asked.

Paul nodded as he took the rifle from Judah. "But I thought we were going to be on *our* side, Judah," he reminded him.

"That was before your wife decided to lose her baby, and before I saw the layout of this camp. Hell, I thought it would be like any other outlaw camp. A few tents. I never thought it would be a fortification like this, with only one way out. D'Alessandro built this place like a military fort."

Paul looked at Gia, and their eyes held; then she looked quickly at Judah. "Mr. Parsons, if you and Paul stay out of the fighting, André and his men won't be able to hold you, will they?" she said. "After all, you're Americans."

"Half an hour ago you might have been right, honey," he said, and his mouth was grim. "But it ain't goin' to work like that, Gia. Not now. I already made my mark out there, and I aim to go back out. But I'm still hoping maybe I can find some way to sneak out of here. Maybe up over the back of this here place when it gets dark. I don't know, but I saw Paul drag you in here, and I came to tell you your pa said to stay inside and stay put. He don't want you gettin' any crazy notions about helpin'. He saw you wearin' that gunbelt," and he let his eyes rest on her haphazard uniform. "I also thought maybe Paul might want to help out some," he said as an afterthought.

Gia glanced at Paul, his face hard, unsmiling as he stared back at Judah. "You're right," he said slowly. "I guess I'd better earn my keep." Then he turned to Gia. "Stay in here and take care of Lenore," he said. "We'll be back in a little while."

Judah started for the door, with Paul behind him, and Gia watched them leave, a heavy ache in her heart. "Be careful, Paul," she called.

He waved as he went out, crouching, and she prayed he'd be all right.

The fighting went on all the rest of the afternoon, and as night settled in, so did the soldiers. The outlaws stayed in their positions ringing the uneven wall, and the women, including Gia, took around food and water, making sure they kept down, using the cover of darkness to hide them.

"How's Lenore?" asked Paul as Gia handed him a drink.

She tried to sound normal. "She's doing fine. Dolores has her sitting up in bed. She said Lenore's lucky she's so healthy. The miscarriage was thorough, and she's not hemorrhaging or anything." Her eyes fell before his smoldering gaze. "She's been asking for you."

"I can't go see her again, not yet," he whispered. "Is she scared?"

"Not of André or the soldiers, only of losing you."

He handed the tin cup back to her as Judah joined them, and the subject was subtly changed.

The night seemed to drag on. Gia and the other women kept up their work, tending the wounded and feeding the men. It was hot and humid, the moon barely a slit crescent in the sky as the men tried to catch a few winks of sleep, alternating with each other while repelling the occasional outbursts of fire from the enemy. Paul and Judah stayed side by side, dozing when they could, taking an occasional potshot at the movement far out in the brush, while Maximilian walked among his men giving encouragement, trying to weigh the odds on their chances of getting through the siege alive.

In the adobe hut nestled against the side of the mountain, Lenore spent a restless night, cringing with each new volley of shots that broke the stillness, hating Gia for getting them in this predicament, and praying that Paul was safe.

When the sun finally rose again over the horizon, it brought with it a renewed attack, and Paul and Judah found themselves in the middle of a battle that was slowly being lost. It was late afternoon when Judah glanced around at all the wounded and dead, wondering what the devil was keeping him and Paul alive and unhurt, then suggested Paul take a break and go see Lenore, since he hadn't seen her since the shooting had started.

"You're sure you'll be all right?" asked Paul. He was becoming fond of Judah. The man was a good friend to have around.

Judah laughed. "Just make sure you're all right," he said lazily. "It's goin' to take some doin' just to make it back to the hut. They've been pickin' us off like flies."

Paul took a deep breath and looked around. Some of the soldiers were in vantage points on a slight rise the other side of the wall, where they were hidden behind some rocks, and

El Verdugo's headquarters was a clear target for them. He clamped a hand on Judah's shoulder affectionately. "Okay, cover me," he said, then took off on a zigzag run toward the hut, some hundred yards away.

19

The air was stale, and it was dark and musty in the bedroom inside the adobe. Its only window was half-covered with trailing vines that obscured the late-afternoon sunlight and kept out the heat, and Lenore was glad of that. But she hated being stuck away here in this miserable room, not knowing what was going on. She turned over onto her stomach, pushing herself up onto one elbow, listening to the staccato sounds of the battle being waged outside, then pursed her lips angrily. Damn Paul anyway! It was all his fault. He'd lied to her, told her they were going back. She should've known he'd never leave that little tramp. Her teeth clenched and her hands balled into fists, and she hit the pillow with a violence that almost tore the worn casing; then wearily she let her head fall into the dent her fist had made, tears of anger glistening in her eyes.

A few minutes later she raised her head from the depths of the pillow and stared toward the door that led to the other room. And that was another thing. Paul had come to see her right after she'd lost the baby, and Gigi—no, her name was Gia—had poked her head in once in a while to make sure she was all right, but other than that she hadn't seen another soul since she'd been in this filthy room, except for that dirty Mexican woman who could speak only a few words of broken English. Why didn't someone besides that scroungy woman and Gia come to see her? Why hadn't Paul come? Why?

Well, if he wouldn't come to her, she'd go to see him. She wasn't going to stay in this room not knowing what was going on, having no one to talk to, not knowing where Paul was and whether he was with Gia or not. Just the thought that he might be with her brought a new flood of tears to her eyes.

Had Gia spent last night in Paul's arms? The thought made her furious, and she sniffed back the tears.

She rolled over again angrily, yet gingerly, shoving the covers aside, and pushed herself up easily, sitting at the edge of the bed. Strange that she wasn't sicker. She was a little dizzy at first as she raised her head, and her legs felt a little weak, but all in all she felt better than she expected. Maybe because she had been only a few weeks along. Even the bleeding wasn't heavy, and as she stood up, reaching for her blouse on the chair next to the bed, she felt the uncomfortable padding wadded between her legs.

The Mexican woman had undressed her, all but the chemise, then put her underdrawers back on after she'd lost the baby, so she slipped the tan blouse back on, letting her thoughts wander as she buttoned it. Her clothes were filthy, having been worn for a week, but it was all she had. She'd had no idea when they left Eagle Pass that they'd be gone this long, and had brought along only a couple of changes of underclothes. Well, it couldn't be helped. She picked up the soiled riding skirt and stepped into it, grabbing the edge of the bed when she almost lost her balance, then straightening as she fastened it at the waist. She reached for the jacket, then changed her mind. She didn't really need it. It was hot enough without it. Besides, she'd lost a button somewhere. It was bad enough having to wear dirty clothes, let alone clothes that were falling apart.

She pulled her short leather riding boots from beneath the chair and put them on, shaking them out first, as Paul had always cautioned her, to make sure nothing had crawled inside. She didn't know what they'd done with her stockings, because she couldn't find them, and the boots felt hot and sticky on her feet, but she wasn't about to wander around on the hard-packed dirt floor of the adobe in her bare feet like that Mexican woman did.

She sat on the edge of the bed, running her hand up the back of her neck to the messy braids that were still coroneted atop her head. The pins were secure, but strands were poking out here and there, and she tried to push them back into place. Tears filled her eyes as she thought of the beautiful clothes back in her hotel room in Eagle Pass, and the servants that had always made life so easy for her back in New York. How she hated this filthy place, and they wouldn't even be here if it weren't for Gia. How she hated her!

She sighed, holding back the tears, and stood up again, using the chair to steady herself for a second, when her knees started to buckle. She took a deep breath and straightened stubbornly, letting her eyes move to the door, staring hesitantly at the ragged curtain covering it. Now that she was up, she wasn't quite sure she was doing the right thing. Someone was in the other room, she knew, because she'd heard shuffling noises a few minutes ago.

If her luck was running true to form, it was probably that Mexican woman, or maybe that pompous outlaw. They said he was Gia's father, but she couldn't stand the sight of him. His clothes were dirty, and he'd made her feel so uncomfortable the way he'd stared at her when Paul introduced her to him when they'd first ridden into camp. His dark penetrating eyes had made her flesh crawl, as if he could look right into her soul.

She shrugged, her stomach tightening, then pursed her lips resolutely, and headed slowly for the doorway, determined to find out what was going on, She pulled back the curtain, then hesitated, staring into the other room.

Her brilliant blue eyes fell on Gia, who was standing near the fireplace, her back to the bedroom door, putting things into a pot that hung down over the fire. Lenore watched silently, the knuckles on her hand white as she clenched the green curtain that separated the two rooms, studying Gia as she moved about.

Gia was still wearing the same oversize clothes she'd had on the day before, and they were just as soiled, and her hair was pulled back, tied at the nape of the neck with a leather thong, but to Lenore's surprise, Gia's hair looked clean and shiny, natural curls wisping about her face. She must have found time to wash it someplace. Lenore's free hand instinctively moved to her own disheveled hair that hadn't been combed out and rebraided for days.

She watched Gia closely, her eyes narrowing as her mind began to wander. She tried to fight it, but couldn't, and she began to imagine Paul making love to Gia, kissing her, molding his body to hers, touching her lovingly, caressing her, and sour bile worked its way to her mouth and her stomach began to churn. She continued to stare at Gia's back, letting her thoughts fly erratically, hate building up in her until she trembled, shuddering with the violence of it; then slowly she straightened, pulling herself together, forcing her hands to quit shaking, and stepped into the main room, the raging hatred inside her masked by a false calm.

Gia had been trying to block out the sound of gunfire from outside as she made her way about the room fixing a pot of beans so the men would have something to eat. They were tired and weary, she knew, and maybe this would help raise their spirits a little. She tried not to think of Paul and what was in store for them, but it wasn't easy. If only he hadn't come. It had served no purpose except to make her heart shatter even more, because he couldn't leave Lenore, ever, and she knew it. How could she take her happiness at another woman's expense? It wasn't right. She had put him out of her life when she'd crossed the Rio Bravo del Norte, the river the Americans called the Rio Grande. Why hadn't he stayed on the other side?

She stirred the beans absentmindedly, then jerked her head abruptly at a noise behind her. She whirled around, then stopped, the spoon still in her hand. "Oh, you scared me," she said, relieved, her voice low and husky, then composed herself as she watched Lenore move farther into the room. "You shouldn't be up yet," she said, setting the spoon down on the table while Lenore glanced about, making sure Gia was truly alone.

"How long did you think I'd stay in there by myself, not knowing what's going on?" Lenore snapped sarcastically as she looked again at this young woman who'd managed to change her life so thoroughly. "That Mexican woman who keeps running in and out can hardly speak a word of English, and I guess no one else cares whether I'm all right or not."

Gia frowned unhappily, wishing she could avoid a confrontation with her. "It isn't that," she said self-consciously. "Paul just didn't want you to be worried."

"Paul?" Lenore's eyes narrowed curiously. "Where is he?"

Gia motioned with her head toward the door. "Out there fighting."

"The fool!" Lenore's mouth set in a grimace, and she walked further into the room, moving toward the window that was above the cot where Gia slept. She reached out, moving the edge of the tattered curtain that covered it, then suddenly dropped to the cot gasping in shock as Gia shouted a warning and a volley of shots tore through the curtain.

Gia hit the floor, and Lenore lay back against the hard-

packed adobe wall, trembling as she stared up at the cur-
tained window.

"I tried to warn you," Gia said, getting up from the floor,
dusting off her baggy pants.

Lenore's eyes were wild. "We'll all be killed!" she cried
hysterically.

"We will if you do that again," said Gia, brushing the
loose dirt from her clothes. "But don't worry. Earlier today
Father told me he thinks there's a way for the three of you to
leave, only you can't go until after dark. As long as you stay
alive until then, you'll be all right."

Lenore studied her suspiciously. "And you?"

Gia flushed. "He insists I go too," she said softly.

Lenore's eyes flashed as she stared hard at Gia. My God,
did this always have to happen? Couldn't things go her way
just once? First the baby, now this? If Gia went with them,
there'd never be an end to it. She saw the way Gia and Paul
had looked at each other when they'd ridden in yesterday. So
had everyone else. It was disgraceful. No woman should be
allowed to look at another woman's husband like that. She
frowned, her eyes vindictive as she stared at Gia. How she
loathed the very sight of her. Why didn't Gia just stay here
and be killed with the rest of them? If she went with them,
Paul would be lost to her, and she knew it. Even if there was
no divorce, he'd find a way to see Gia. She'd always be there
somewhere, and Lenore would never have any peace. As long
as Gia was alive, Paul would never truly belong to her. He
might even be willing to try to survive the scandal of a divorce if he thought Gia would be waiting to comfort him
when it was all over. Lenore's eyes darkened fiendishly as she
stared at Gia, and a strange morbid thought crossed her
mind, bringing with it a weird sense of exhilaration. Her eyes
grew shrewd.

What if Gia wasn't here? The thought was intriguing. She
said she'd be going with them. What if she wasn't alive to go
with them? Lenore's jaw clenched savagely as she suddenly
turned from Gia and let her eyes stray toward the foot of the
cot she was sitting on, to the ammunition belt Gia had been
wearing the day before. It was slung over the wooden post at
the foot of the cot, but the holster was empty. Where was the
gun?

Her thoughts already dangerously alive, she began to gaze
slowly about the room, taking in every detail, while Gia

watched her for a few minutes, wondering what she might have on her mind that made her eyes look so wild and strange; then Gia shrugged, turning away once more to start looking for something in the wooden cupboards at the left of the fireplace. At the moment, Lenore was the least of her worries.

Lenore's blue eyes moved from one piece of furniture to another, resting only long enough to see that there was no gun or weapon of any kind. Then her eyes moved over to the mess on the table. Just maybe . . .

She stood up again and sauntered slowly toward the table, acting as nonchalant as possible, while Gia, ignoring her, continued to search the cupboards, mumbling something about chili peppers and herbs. Lenore's heart was aflutter, leaping into her throat as her eyes fastened on the table. It was there! The gun was there. It was big, a monstrous thing with a mother-of-pearl handle, and it was wedged between a tin cup and some empty bowls.

She stared at it, her stomach churning nervously. It would be so simple. Afterward she could go back into the other room, crawl back into bed, and no one would know the difference. They'd think Gia had been hit by a stray bullet coming through the window. But murder? Could she do it? She drew her eyes from the gun and looked once more at the figure of the young woman who had stolen her husband's heart, and again the hate came flooding back, blinding her conscience, anger driving her. Yes! She *could* do it. She clenched her teeth together stubbornly. She had to. No one would do it for her. She couldn't let Gia go on living. Not now. It was always Gia, Gia, Gia! She couldn't let her go back to Eagle Pass, and she wasn't going to lose Paul.

Her lips twisted nervously as she glanced once more at the gun, shuddering in anticipation. Moving slowly, she inched closer to the table, her eyes on Gia's back, watching her moving canisters and jars about, muttering to herself because she couldn't find what she wanted; then finally Lenore stopped, reaching out hesitantly, making sure not to touch anything else.

Her heart was pounding, echoing loudly in her ears, and her face was flushed. She wrapped her fingers gently around the butt of the gun and started to lift, then realized it was too heavy. Keeping a furtive eye on Gia, she leaned closer to the table and used both hands.

The gun felt cold and bulky, and she bit her lip, her hands trembling; then she straightened stubbornly, composing herself, convincing herself there was nothing wrong with what she was doing. That she was justified. After all, she rationalized, Paul was her husband, she had to save him from this wicked, evil woman. She squared her shoulders, body tense, and aimed the gun directly at Gia's back, then took a deep breath.

"Gia?" she called softly, and Gia hesitated, disgusted because she hadn't found what she wanted.

"What is it?" she asked irritably, not angry at Lenore, but angry at herself for wasting time searching for something that obviously wasn't there, and she turned abruptly, brushing a stray curl from her forehead, then froze, startled as her eyes fell on the gun Lenore had trained on her. "Wh-what the devil are you doing?" she gasped in astonishment.

Lenore swallowed hard, her face pale as she stared at Gia. She licked her lips. The decision was made, and now there was no going back. She was glad. She wanted Gia dead, and this was the only way. Her jaw tensed. "What does it look like I'm doing?" she asked bluntly.

Gia scowled, one hand moving to her throat nervously as she stared back at Lenore. She was serious. Lenore was dead serious, she could see it in her eyes. "Put the gun down, Lenore, please," she begged breathlessly, realizing Lenore was irrational.

But Lenore shook her head, her blue eyes wild, glittering unnaturally. "No," she answered emphatically. "No, I won't, and I won't let you take Paul from me, either, do you hear?" she cried. "He's mine, Gia, not yours. Mine!"

"Oh, Lenore," Gia cried anxiously, her eyes wavering toward the gun barrel, then lifting to see the hatred in Lenore's face. "I'm not going to take Paul from you. I told him I couldn't . . . that I couldn't do that to you."

"Liar!"

"Lenore, please," she pleaded. "No, please, I'm not lying. Ask Paul. He'll tell you. I love him, yes, but I can't take my happiness at your expense." Tears filled Gia's eyes. "Lenore, please, don't do this!"

Lenore straightened, stronger now, gathering courage, exhilarated by the fear in Gia's eyes. Oh, this was wonderful.

"It won't do you any good, you know," she said, sneering, her eyes intent on Gia. She was enjoying this, watching her squirm. It was such a pleasure to know she was suffering for a change, as Lenore had suffered. "Even if you promised never to see Paul again, I wouldn't believe you," she said. "Or him either. Why should I? He's lied to me before. He's lied to me all along because of you." She raised the gun higher, securing her aim, and Gia held her breath. "I can't take the chance, Gia, I just can't," she went on. "You understand that, don't you?" Her voice was pitched too high, the intonation close to hysteria. "I've lost the baby, and it was the only thing that was keeping Paul from leaving me, and I can't take the chance that he'll change his mind, so we're going to let them think a stray bullet hit you. Don't you think that's clever? It'll be easy, and they'll never know."

"My God, Lenore, you're crazy!" Gia cried. "You don't know what you're doing." Gia continued to plead. "You can't do this . . . you just can't." Tears rolled down Gia's cheeks as she stared at Lenore, watching the angry frustration in her face, her finger tightening on the trigger, her troubled mind already beyond logical reasoning, and Gia suddenly knew it was too late. There'd be no use pleading, no more trying to reason with her. She watched Lenore's finger flexing, the muscles tensing on the trigger, her eyes suddenly glazed and frenetic.

"No!" Gia screamed helplessly. "Lenore, please, no!" but it was too late.

Lenore let out a strangled sob, and as her finger squeezed hard on the trigger, the door suddenly burst open, a draft of air gusting into the room, waving the curtains that hung above the cot, and once more a volley of bullets from outside ripped through the tattered curtains, their noise echoing and blending with the shot that left the gun held in Lenore's hands as Gia ducked sideways, letting the bullet from Lenore's gun, that was meant for her, ricochet harmlessly off the fireplace.

Lenore felt the jolt of the pistol in her hands, but she felt something else too. As she stared transfixed at the horrified look on Gia's face, reveling in the thought that Gia would no longer exist for Paul to love, a numbness ran through her arm and chest, and she felt as if she'd been kicked by a horse. Then suddenly a searing pain gripped every nerve in her body, and she gasped, her knees turning to jelly. She tried to catch herself, but couldn't. The air coming into her lungs hurt, and all that came out when she tried to scream for help

was a raspy croak. She watched, terrified, unable to believe
what was happening as her fingers grew numb and useless,
the gun slipping from them, crashing onto the dishes on the
table, and the last thing she heard before sinking limply to
the floor was Paul's voice shouting in disbelief.

Paul had stood frozen in the doorway, watching the terrible tableau being played out before him, shock paralyzing
him momentarily at the sight. Now suddenly he came to life,
sickened by what he'd seen and jolted cruelly by it.

"Lenore!" he yelled, lunging forward into the room, slamming the door behind him, oblivious of the bullets trying to
cut him down as he stood there. They were smashing into the
wooden door now as it shut behind him, but he paid no heed.
One knee hit the floor, and he stopped abruptly beside
Lenore, staring incredulously into her still face.

"Lenore?" he cried again hesitantly, but this time it was no
more than a hollow gasp, and his stomach tightened convul-
sively as his eyes followed the trail of blood that was oozing
from the fatal wounds in her arms and chest, streaking her
tan silk blouse. "Oh, Lenore, my God!" he whispered softly.
"I never . . . I never wanted this." He reached out to her
face, touching a strand of hair that had fallen across her
eyes, brushing it back affectionately, then lifted her hand,
feeling for a pulse. "She's dead," he said softly, then drew his
eyes from Lenore's face and looked up at Gia. "My God,
Gia, she's dead," he exclaimed again.

"She tried to kill me," gasped Gia breathlessly.

Paul flinched. "I never thought . . ." he began; then his
eyes moved once more to the still form on the floor. "She
didn't have to," he said bitterly, then stood up and looked
directly at Gia. "Didn't you tell her?" he asked, bewildered.

Gia nodded. "She didn't believe me," she said, trembling,
her hands shaking as her eyes met his. "I told her that even
though I loved you I'd never let you leave her, but she called
me a liar. She was out of her head with jealousy. Oh, God,
Paul, she wanted me dead."

He nodded. "I know, I saw . . ." He stared down at
Lenore sprawled on the floor, her once beautifully coiffured
hair dirty and disheveled. She resembled little the sophisticated woman he'd married only a few months ago, and he
tried to sort out exactly what he felt as he stared at her lifeless body. His feelings were all crazy and mixed up, and the

most he could say was that he felt sorry for her and sick to think she had resorted to murder.

Gia wiped the tears from her eyes as she watched Paul's face, realizing he was going to blame himself for what had happened "Don't Paul, please," she whispered huskily, her voice breaking. "Don't blame yourself, please." She shook her head emphatically. "You couldn't have changed it if you'd wanted to, because even if I had gone away, out of your life, she'd never have believed there wasn't still something between us."

"But why?" he asked angrily. "Why would she think she had to resort to murder?"

"The trip, losing the baby . . . I think it was all too much, Paul," Gia explained, trying to make him understand. "Lenore was strong physically, yes, but she couldn't take failure. She always had her own way in everything. I realized that when I first met her. She looked down on others around her because by doing so it made her even greater in her own eyes. Nothing she had was second best, and you'd become an obsession with her. She loved you, yes, but you were one of her possessions- -the most important one perhaps, but a possession. When Lenore lost the baby and thought she'd lost you, I think her mind snapped. She wasn't herself."

Paul frowned, then shut his eyes, trying to compose himself. Gia was right. She had to be. Lenore had always been in such complete control of her emotions, the only explanation for something like this was that when she finally did give in to them, she'd been unable to handle them. And there was no going back, no way he could change things. Suddenly the thought that the body sprawled on the floor might have been Gia instead of Lenore made him shudder. He opened his eyes and looked fully at Gia for a brief moment, letting his eyes caress her hair, the beauty of her face, the warmth in her turquoise eyes, and he said a silent prayer, thanking God for preventing Lenore from carrying out her plans and asking God's forgiveness for driving Lenore to the lengths she'd gone to because of her love for him.

He was about to step over Lenore's body and take Gia in his arms to comfort her, when the outside door flew open again, waving the curtains, at the window once more, and this time it was Paul who moved quickly, realizing what was happening. He lunged toward Gia, slamming both of them against the fireplace as another volley of shots tore through the curtains, chipping hard adobe mud off the wall opposite the window, above the table. They both held their breath.

Judah hit the floor as he came in, rolling sideways, heaving the door shut behind him, then leaned against the wall, listening to the shots pounding against the thick adobe hut.

"What the hell's going on?" he asked when the firing stopped, stunned as he stared at the strange scene before him.

Paul straightened, helping Gia, who was thrown off balance when he'd crashed into her ducking the shots; then he faced Judah apprehensively. He glanced quickly at Lenore lying near the table, then took a deep breath as he realized Judah was staring at her too.

"She's dead," he said grimly. "When I came in, the same thing happened that happened just now, and she was hit."

Judah winced as he stood up, straightening, then squared his shoulders, walking over, looking down at Paul's dead wife. He glanced quickly at the window, then to Paul and Gia, then back to where Lenore lay, and he nodded. "It's a dangerous game we're playing, Paul," he said roughly. "Too bad she never understood." He chewed his lip; then his jaw set stubbornly. "The general sent me to tell you there may be a way out of here for us if we want to take the chance, but he says it's dangerous."

Paul scowled. "How dangerous?"

"Not as dangerous as it is if we stay here," he said. "Only, he insists Gia goes with us, but then, I don't think you'll mind that, will you?"

Paul's gray eyes deepened as he stared at Judah.

Judah shook his head. "Now, don't get all put out, Paul," he said. "I know how things are and I ain't one to condemn one way or another, and I guess I can understand how things got fouled up. You thought Gia was your sister. That'd scare any man into doin' things wrong." He glanced at Lenore's lifeless body again, then looked once more at Paul. "But your wife's dead already, and we've got a decision to make. You want to take that chance the general's ready to give us, or stay here and face the same thing?"

Paul looked down at Gia, his heart in his eyes. "If there's even the slightest chance of getting Gia out of here alive, we're going," he said firmly, then turned back to Judah. "Did he say what it was?"

"No. Only that we'd have to wait until after dark." He motioned toward Lenore's body, still on the dirt floor between them. "I'll put her in the other room," he said. "Then I'll go tell the general what happened, if I can get back out there without getting hit."

"No," Gia said quickly, her hand on Paul's arm. "The sun's already starting to go down." She looked at Judah. "Stay here, Mr. Parsons," she said. "My father will be here as soon as it's dark. If you try to go out there again, you'll never make it."

Judah glanced at the door, splintered by bullet holes, and the shredded curtains at the window, then stared at Lenore, so still in death. "Maybe you're right," he said, changing his mind, and he looked toward the fireplace. "Seems to me I remember as how you've been fixin' us somethin' to eat," he said, sniffing the air, his nose twitching. Then he walked over, picked up Lenore's limp body, and went toward the other room.

Paul stared at Judah, not knowing quite what to do, feeling that somehow he wasn't doing the right thing; then he straightened, his broad shoulders erect as he followed behind Judah, holding back the curtain separating the two rooms, watching as Judah laid Lenore on the bed, crossing her arms over her breasts, and pulled the blanket up, covering her from head to toe. This done, Judah turned, caught sight of Paul watching him, and frowned. "I know how you feel. Don't know whether to laugh or cry, huh, friend?" he said, and Paul was taken by surprise.

"I told you before," said Judah, slapping Paul on the shoulder as he reached him, turning him around, leading him back into the other room, "I can sympathize with you. I married Elsie for prestige, because it was convenient, and if somethin' happened to her, I'd be in your shoes. I wouldn't know whether to cry or cheer. It ain't that she's all that bad, you see. Elsie's Elsie. I don't hate her and I don't love her. But now, Gigi . . . That was different." He motioned for Paul to sit in one of the chairs at the table, then scuffed up the bloodstains in the dust of the floor with his boots as he went on. "Now, when Gigi died," he said, his voice lowering affectionately, "I think I cried for three days. At least it felt like it."

"I didn't want Lenore dead," said Paul slowly.

Judah sighed. "Hell, I know that," he said, then sat down opposite Paul. "So does Gia. But look at the facts, Paul, before you go feelin' guilty about bein' glad that she ain't goin'

to be around to spoil things anymore." Judah reached out
and took one of the clean bowls from the table, handing it to
Gia for her to fill, and she took it hesitantly as he turned
again toward Paul. "I watched the two of you on the way out
here," he went on. "Been watchin' you ever since we left Eagle
Pass. That lady of yours was a tyrant, Paul, and she'd have
made your life miserable. Every chance she had, she tried to
cut you down, and she'd have kept right on doin' it until even
the little you did feel for her turned into hate. I saw the way
she treated you, like you owed her the world on a silver platter."

"That's just it, Judah," interrupted Paul, his voice deep and
vibrant with emotion. "She married me in good faith. She
had no idea the mess I was in."

"Did you ask to fall in love with Gia, Paul?" asked Judah.

"No."

"Did you ask Lenore to step in front of those bullets?"

"No."

"Then for Christ's sake, friend, instead of castigating yourself for it, be glad God's given you a chance to have what
you really want out of life. Feel bad because she's dead if
you want, that's your right, but don't go blamin' yourself or
feelin' guilty because you've got a chance now at a little happiness. Take it, grab hold, and don't let go, because, believe
me, Paul, this world can be mighty cruel, and there isn't everybody gets a second chance. I know."

Paul's eyes grew hard, intense, as he stared at Judah. The
man was right. He let his eyes move from Judah to Gia,
watching the way her small frame moved across the floor
when she went to the pot of beans to dish up some for Judah.
Her figure was still hidden beneath the baggy old clothing,
but he knew every line of it, every sensuous curve. As he
watched her, his heart ached with longing, and suddenly he
remembered the sickening feeling that had hit him when he
opened the door and saw Lenore aiming that deadly gun at
her. The horror he'd felt had been only too real, and in that
split second before the bullets hit Lenore, he'd wanted to kill
her himself.

His jaw tensed as Gia came back to the table, setting the
bowl of beans down in front of Judah.

"Here, eat," said Judah, shoving the bowl over toward
Paul.

"I'm not hungry," he said huskily.

Judah shook his head. "You'll be all right, friend," he mused. "It just takes a while. But right now you'd better get some food under your belt. You too, Gia," he said, gazing over at the beautiful dark-haired young woman who'd been the cause of so much of their misery. "Because I have a feelin' what we eat tonight might be the last thing we get to eat for a long while. Even if we get out of here, we're about fifty miles from the border, and we're bound to do some hard ridin'. Besides," he went on, his eyes still on Gia, "you never did get a chance to tell us what happened to the real Gigi Rouvier, and I said I wasn't goin' to leave here until I found out. Now, we got a little time before your father gets here, and since he didn't want us out there helpin' no more, you might's well let us in on it so's I can put my mind at ease."

Gia studied him for a minute. He was big, gruff, and a little overbearing in a likable way. He sort of took hold and figured right from the start that he was boss. She liked Judah. He was honest and straightforward, at least with his friends, if not with his wife, and she liked him for that.

She filled another bowl, bringing it back to the table, then watched Judah shoving things aside to make room for it. When he picked up the pearl-handled gun, looking it over curiously, wondering what it was doing on the table, her eyes met Paul's and she held her breath, knowing he was thinking the same thing she was. Neither of them had said a word to Judah about Lenore's attempt at murder. Had they been wrong? Paul's eyes warmed as he looked into hers, and he reached up, taking the bowl from her hand, letting his fingers caress hers affectionately. No, they hadn't been wrong. It would stay between them. No one else would ever have to know. Lenore had died as she'd intended Gia to die, violently. It was over.

Gia flushed, giving Paul his answer by her silence, then turned back to the pot of beans, filling a bowl for herself. And as shadows began to filter into the trees and valleys, and the battle still raged outside, Gia sat at the table and told them how she'd been accompanying her cousin to New York because her father sent word his enemies had discovered her whereabouts. And how, on the train ride, she'd borrowed the diamond brooch to hold her shawl together because she'd been cold and it kept slipping off her shoulders, and how Gigi Rouvier had dropped something on the floor only moments before the train wreck and had shoved her handbag in Gia's lap to hold so she could retrieve it. That's why she'd been clutching the pink silk handbag when they found her. And since her mother and Gigi's mother had been identical twins, and since Gia looked like her mother, it was no surprise the mistake had been made.

Gia told them all about her cousin, and her own years at the convent and her father's troubles with President Díaz, and as the shadows grew deeper, leaving only flames from the fireplace to see by, Judah and Paul finally learned all the answers.

20

Maximilian leaned against the side of the stone blockhouse he and his men had built many years before. It was so dark now that he could hardly see. His left shoulder felt like it was on fire, as if a thousand devils were tormenting it, and he held his hand over it, knowing the wound was bad. Dolores had managed to stop the bleeding seconds before a bullet had cut her down, and he cringed, tears at the corner of his eyes, remembering the startled look on her face and the love in her eyes as she'd died in his arms.

They were losing the battle, and he knew it. He had hoped maybe, even though the odds were against them, that perhaps the soldiers would make the mistake of trying to rush the fortifications, but their leaders were smart. Instead, they dug in, picking men off one at a time, content to wait it out. *Madre de Dios*, if only the rest of his men were here. He'd sent out three bands of men only a week ago, south to Durango and west to Chihuahua and Sonora, on raids to bring back ammunition and supplies that were sorely needed. Now he could use not only the men but also the supplies. Ammunition was running dangerously low, and the men were discouraged. There was only one thing left for them, but first he had to try to get the *americanos* and Gia to safety.

He tried to straighten, then slumped against Miguel, who was standing beside him waiting for his decision. "Let's get back to my place," he said quietly. "I think it's dark enough now that we don't have to worry about getting shot at. Then I want you to go get the four horses and bring them, like I told you."

Miguel nodded. *"Sí, Jefe,"* he said quickly, and helped his leader, letting him lean on him for support while they worked their way back toward the hill where the adobe hut was nestled. Miguel tried to keep Maximilian in the deepest shadows, avoiding the open ground where there was a chance their dark forms would be seen against the bare earth.

When they finally reached the adobe, Miguel propped Maximilian against the outside wall, moving toward the doorway. He leaned close, his cheek pressed to it.

"Amigos?" he whispered hoarsely, knocking lightly on the door. "Ho! Amigos?"

The three people inside the hut were still sitting at the table deep in conversation, and it was Judah who looked up in response to Miguel's knock. He cautioned Gia and Paul to listen, then got up and walked to the door.

"*Sí?*" he said hesitantly.

"It's Miguel," the man on the other side of the door said anxiously. "Tell me, is the fire still going in the fireplace?"

Judah glanced back toward the fireplace, where red coals glowed, relieving the darkness in the room. "*Sí,*" he answered quickly.

Miguel's voice came back, muffled but audible. "Put it out," he said. "*El Jefe* is with me, and if we open the door without putting the fire out first, we will be excellent targets for the snipers on the hill, who have been enjoying themselves all day at our expense."

Judah took a deep breath. Miguel was right. He moved hurriedly, grabbing a wooden bucket from the floor near the fireplace, using the dipper in it to toss water onto the flames, extinguishing them.

As the room was suddenly plunged into total darkness, Paul reached across the table, his hand tightening hard on Gia's, and Judah straightened, stumbling across the floor in the dark toward the door.

"It's clear," he said, and seconds later the door opened and Miguel ducked inside, backing in as he came, helping Maximilian as best he could.

An occasional shot rang out behind them from some lone marksman who was sure he could see in the dark, but other than that, the mountain valley was fairly quiet for a change.

Gia strained her eyes, watching closely as the vague figures of the two men moved inside. Then she realized something was wrong. "Father?" she questioned hesitantly, and let go of Paul's hand, getting up from the table, moving swiftly toward the dark form of the man who was slumping onto the cot beneath the window.

"It's nothing, just a scratch," he said in the darkness.

She inhaled stubbornly. "There's a candle on the table, Paul," she said firmly. "Will you get it?"

"First let Miguel leave," her father protested quietly. "He has an errand to run," and he squeezed his friend's hand, then watched as he slipped back outside.

When the door was shut again and the candle was finally lit, Maximilian gazed up behind him toward the windows. Earlier, shortly before dark, Judah and Paul had stretched a thick blanket, hanging it across the window to cover the tattered curtains. Now even the flickering candlelight couldn't reveal the presence of the window. He sighed. *"Bueno,"* he said, glancing at Judah. "I was worried about that. Those snipers on the hill have been enjoying themselves too much today. No need to make it easier for them now. Besides, I want my Gia safe."

"Paul's wife was already hit," offered Judah, and saw Maximilian's eyebrows knit together.

"How badly?"

Judah motioned with his head. "Her body's stretched out on the bed in there. There was nothing we could do."

Maximilian studied Paul for a minute, then glanced at his daughter, seeing the turmoil in her eyes, and he looked back at Paul. "I'm sorry, señor," he said, but then added, "but now you will take care of my Gia for me, *sí*, señor?"

Paul's eyes grew intense as he stared at the man. He knew. Somehow General Maximilian d'Alessandro knew how he felt about his daughter. "Yes, I'll take care of Gia, always," he said softly.

Maximilian nodded. *"Bueno!* Now, I will tell you what you will do," he said as Gia reached out and began to check his wound to see that it was still bound tight enough that it wasn't bleeding. He looked at Judah. "You, go over to the cupboard, please," he said.

Judah stared at him for a moment, then complied. When he was standing in front of the cupboard, Maximilian instructed him to lift his hand and grab the edge of the large cumbersome cupboards that filled the wall next to the fireplace.

"Now, pull!" he commanded sharply, and Judah pulled, holding tight, trying to pull the cupboards toward him as best he could. At first they didn't want to move; they seemed stuck, and he looked back at El Verdugo, perplexed, but the man insisted. Then slowly, as Judah strained, pulling harder, he could feel them begin to give, and he straightened eagerly, pulling with all his might this time, his fingers working their way behind the edge of the boards.

Paul, who had been sitting at the table all this while, stood up hurriedly and joined him, slipping his fingers in beside Judah's, and the two of them began to pull, using all their strength. Slowly, as the whole wall of cupboards began to move farther out into the room, opening like a door, Paul and Judah could do nothing but stare. For behind it was an empty, dark tunnel reaching deep into the side of the mountain.

Maximilian nodded. "Fine, *muy bien*," he said.

Gia looked at him, startled. "What is it?"

He smiled a strained half-smile. The wound in his shoulder hurt terribly, but he didn't want them to know. "It's an abandoned mine," he explained as he gazed toward the dark tunnel. "When we first came here, we were going to use it as an escape route if necessary, but over the years the shoring's fallen, parts of it have caved in, and I don't even know if it's passable anymore. But there's a chance. The tunnel's big enough for not only men but also horses—we know that—but it's been a long time since anyone's been in it. However, Miguel's on his way here now with your horses. That's why we had to wait until after dark. We'd never have gotten the horses in here in the daylight. I want you"—and he looked at Judah—"to take my daughter and Señor Larrabee and leave by way of the mine. It won't be easy, amigo. In fact, it'll be quite dangerous, but to stay here means certain death."

"What of you, General," asked Judah. "And your men?"

"If at all possible, before dawn we'll make a break for the hills. Many of us, I'm afraid, won't make it, but it's our only chance."

"You can't ride!" protested Gia. "You're wounded."

"This isn't the first time," he said, glancing toward his shoulder.

"But perhaps the worst?" she retorted.

He reached out with his good arm, his hand on hers, holding it tightly. "It has to be this way, little one," he said softly. "If I make it, I'll join my men in the south and we'll find a new stronghold."

She eyed him intently. "If you make it!"

"Gia's right," interrupted Judah. "You don't have a chance

in hell with that shoulder the way it is." His eyes lit up
shrewdly. "But I have an idea, General, one I think will not
only work, but perhaps might drive Major de los Reyes a
little crazy in the process."

Paul stared into the black tunnel; then his eyes rested on
Judah, as did Gia's and her father's.

"It's simple," said Judah, explaining to them hurriedly.
"We'll all go through the mine, every one of your men out
there, then the last ones through scatter the dirt on the floor
to erase our tracks, shut the cupboard behind them and leave
de los Reyes to wonder where we went."

All three stared at him for a long time, the idea rolling
over in their minds.

"It just might work," said Paul.

"What if the tunnel is blocked?" asked El Verdugo hesitantly.

"We've got shovels. We can dig our way through. Besides,
even if it's blocked, we can hide until de los Reyes and his
men leave." He studied the general. The man was weary and
weakening fast. "If you and your men try to ride out of here,
you'll be cut to ribbons, and you know it," he said. "It's the
only thing left for all of us."

Paul agreed, and so did Gia, but Maximilian took a little
more persuading.

It wasn't until after Miguel's return with the four horses
that Maximilian finally realized the sense in Judah's suggestion. With Miguel's persuasion and Gia's pleading, he finally
wavered and gave the orders to move out.

It was an exceptionally dark night, the moon obscured by
clouds, and Judah was glad of it. If there had been even a
sliver of a moon, as there had been two nights ago, they'd
have been in trouble. But as it was, El Verdugo's men were
able, one at a time, to leave their places of concealment,
sneak into the stable where the horses were kept, then make
their way quietly to El Verdugo's headquarters without being
detected by the soldiers.

Occasionally a shot would ring out in the darkness, and
someone from the camp would answer in turn, but only to
put de los Reyes' men off guard.

Judah was the first man into the tunnel, followed closely
by Paul, and behind Paul Gia moved stealthily, leading not
only her own horse but also her father's horse, with him in
the saddle. The wound had weakened him too much, and

they had all insisted that he ride. Behind Gia the men were
strung out, moving into the mine one at a time. Judah carried
a lantern, but didn't light it until he was far enough into the
tunnel so the light wouldn't shine back into the room, giving
them away. It was hard working in the darkness, and he was
relieved when he was finally able to strike a match.

The tunnel was musty, the strong smell of earth filling his
nostrils as he lit the lantern and held it forward to see. Cobwebs filled the space ahead, and he brushed them away with
a gloved hand, moving forward gingerly, testing the ground
as he walked, to make sure there were no sudden drop-offs or
hidden shafts they could fall into.

As the group moved deeper into the tunnel, one by one the
men left their posts and followed, until only Miguel and Juan
were left. Before entering the tunnel themselves, they made
their way furtively through the camp, setting sombreros in
strategic places, propping up empty guns they were unable to
take with them, so that when morning came de los Reyes'
men would think the camp was still occupied. This done, they
moved into the general's headquarters, closed the huge oak
door for the last time, put their horses inside the tunnel and
lit the candles, then used whatever they could find at hand to
obliterate the tracks on the hard-packed dirt floor, so that de
los Reyes couldn't follow. When they'd completed this, they
lit the last lantern and set it inside the tunnel, blew out the
candle, and entered the mine themselves, pulling the door
shut behind them.

Up ahead, Judah was picking his way along the abandoned
mine shaft, stepping over broken shoring, stopping when
necessary, while he and the rest of the men relied on the
shovels to widen the passage that had caved in partway years
before.

They had been moving for well over an hour. Paul
watched Judah ahead of him as he stopped and reached
down at his feet, picked up a stone. Then he watched him
throw it ahead of him into the darkness beyond.

"Listen!" he called, and Paul strained his ears. For a long
time there was only silence; then a hollow kerplunking sound
echoed back to them. Paul shuddered.

Judah held the lantern as high as he could and leaned forward. "It's a shaft about fifty feet deep," he said, then
glanced about, trying to find a way around it. There was
none. He stood for a long time contemplating, then remem-

bered they'd passed a pile of lumber some yards back. He called for the men to bring up planks, and in a short time he'd laid a makeshift bridge across the shaft.

"You expect us to use that?" asked Paul as he stared at the rickety structure.

Judah stood with hands on hips and looked at the planks. "It's either that or go back, and I don't think any of us wants that." He took out a pocket watch and checked the time. "I don't know how much farther this tunnel goes, Paul," he said anxiously, "but I'd like to get through before dawn if we can, just in case de los Reyes should get wise, so I'll go first." He put one foot on the plank and stomped. It seemed fairly solid. Satisfied, he reached over and grabbed his horse's reins from Paul's hand. He took a deep breath, tested the thick boards once more, then walked across, leading his horse after him, the lantern lighting his way.

Paul watched Judah cross the planks, an uneasy feeling in the pit of his stomach. One wrong step and he'd end up at the bottom of the shaft, but he didn't. He reached the other side and breathed a sigh of relief as he looked around. He was in a large underground room, probably the main shaft room. He glanced up. There had once been a shaft overhead. All that was left now were a few broken beams. He turned, motioning Paul across.

Paul glanced back at Gia and swallowed hard, then held tight to his horse's reins and started across himself. He could feel the planks shake with each step, and held his breath, finally letting it free as he reached solid ground again.

Behind him Gia looked up at her father atop his horse, then at the narrow plank bridge that crossed the mine shaft. How was she to get him across?

"Bring your own horse across," instructed Judah as she neared the edge of the planks. "After you're across, I'll go back and bring him across."

Gia wasn't sure she liked it, but it was the only way. There wasn't room for two horses side by side on the planks, and her heart was in her throat as she and her horse moved across; then she watched her father and Judah's progress, praying the planks would hold and the horse's footing would be sure and her father wouldn't slip. Because even though he was hugging the saddle horn, there was no guarantee; if he started to slide, he'd carry the horse and Judah down the shaft with him.

By the time they reached the shaft room, Maximilian's wound was bleeding again, and Judah let Gia take time to have him hauled from the horse's back, then let her re-bandage it while he watched the rest of the men make their way across the makeshift bridge. The shaft room was large enough to accommodate them all, and by the time the last man finally moved across the planks, Gia had Maximilian ready to move on. At least as ready as he'd ever be.

Judah and Paul helped him back into the saddle, and they started out again, with Judah once more in the lead, his lantern lighting the way into the dark recesses of the tunnel.

Two hours before dawn, after taking two wrong turns and having to backtrack, bypassing two more deep shafts, barely missing ending up at the bottom of them, Judah finally smelled a whiff of fresh air. And fifteen minutes later, he and Paul were battering down the boards at the end of the tunnel, stepping out into the night air.

Gia followed them out, stepping across the fallen boards, letting the air refresh her as she looked quickly about. This side of the mountain leveled off a little here near the mouth of the mine, then dropped again about two hundred feet away to a dry arroyo below. It was still dark, but she could make out the vague landscape. A light breeze was blowing, and it felt good on her face as she took a deep refreshing breath of air, then led her father's horse to one side, looking up at him, tethering her own horse on a nearby bush. Even though it was dark, she could see the agony on his face. Judah had tried to remove the bullet before they left the adobe, but it was buried too deep, and he'd told Gia that it would require a surgeon's skill. She stared at her father apprehensively.

"Father, you can't ride far like this," she said, touching his arm affectionately as she looked up at him.

Maximilian's eyes were on the mouth of the tunnel, and he strained them to see in the darkness as he watched his men emerging one at a time; then he looked down at Gia. "I have no choice, little one," he said softly, pain visible in his eyes and audible in his voice. "My men will ride back to their villages and south to warn the others not to come back, and we will have to find a new place to call our home. I must go with them."

"Why?"

His hand covered hers on his arm. "Why?" He shook his head. "You still don't know why?"

"Oh, I know why you're fighting, Father. I've always known that," she said. "I just want to know why you have to go with them now. You need medical attention, a doctor. It's over two hundred miles to where you could find help."

"She's right," said Judah, interrupting their conversation as he and Paul stepped over to stand beside Gia. "If you try riding south with your men, in the condition you're in, you won't last more than a couple of days, if even that." He hitched up his gunbelt, his massive frame dwarfing Gia. "It's only about fifty miles to the river at the most, General," he went on. "And once across, we can find a doctor and get you patched up."

He shook his head weakly. "I can't leave my men."

"General, they'll move faster without you," Judah reasoned, but Maximilian was stubborn.

It wasn't until Miguel and Juan emerged from the tunnel and joined Gia, Judah, and Paul in their persuasions that he once more gave in to them. An hour before dawn, they separated, the outlaws, some thirty men who were left, riding hard toward the south to lose themselves in the villages until they could reunite again, while the four riders that were left reined their horses northward toward the Rio Grande.

André stood in El Verdugo's abandoned headquarters, the expression on his face one of both anger and bewilderment. As dawn crept up over the mountain, he'd been ecstatic with anticipation of what was ahead. By dark the night before it was apparent that El Verdugo's men were in trouble. Not a shot was being wasted, and there were fewer men returning his soldier's fire. He and Colonel Alvarez had planned an all-out attack for morning, expecting little resistance from the outlaws, but when the attack finally came at dawn, he was flabbergasted to watch Colonel Alvarez' men ride in with no resistance at all. Not a shot was fired.

He'd quickly mounted his horse and spurred him forward, entering the outlaws' stronghold with a look of disbelief on his handsome, swarthy face. Dead men had been propped into position to make it look as if they were defending the site, and battered sombreros were also placed about, adding to the deception, but except for a few horses left in the stables, not another living thing remained in the camp.

The whole place had been quiet as he rode in, almost eerie as the cool night mists began to lift, making room for the brilliant shafts of sunlight that filtered through it.

Now André cursed as he glanced about the main room of the adobe that was El Verdugo's headquarters. A dirty kettle that had once held beans hung over the cold, dead ashes in the fireplace, dirty dishes were on the table, and a heavy blanket had been hung over the only window. He ripped the blanket down angrily, letting the early-morning sunlight filter in through the tattered curtains that still covered the window; then he glanced toward the door, splintered haphazardly by the bullets Colonel Alvarez' men had sunk into it during their siege.

He took a deep breath, letting his fingers caress the rough blanket in his hands as he stared toward the curtain separating the adjoining room. Wherever they had gone, one thing had been left behind. The body of Señor Larrabee's dead wife had been discovered on the bed in the next room, covered with a blanket similar to the one he'd pulled down from the window. She'd been shot. André frowned, wondering whether by accident or intentionally, and his eyes narrowed as he remembered the looks that had passed between Gia and her so-called brother.

His hand tightened into a fist as he drew his thoughts from their perusal of the body in the other room and let his eyes fall on Colonel Alvarez, who was silhouetted in the doorway, his face as filled with shock as André's had been.

"Well, don't just stand there, idiot!" he shouted angrily in Spanish, his face livid with rage. "They couldn't just disappear into thin air! Find them!"

The colonel shifted his gunbelt more firmly onto his hips, then tugged at his uniform jacket. "We have looked, Major, until there is nowhere else to look," he said defensively. "There is not a sign of them." His dark eyes flashed in his tanned face, the huge mustache twitching above taut lips. "Only one thing is strange, Major," he said, explaining quickly. "We have noticed that there are a great number of horse's tracks leading from the stables to here, as if they were brought to the door just outside. Then the tracks disappear."

André frowned, his eyes narrowing curiously, jaw set in stubborn anger. He straightened, throwing the blanket onto the cot beneath the window, then grimaced. "Show me!" he ordered furiously, and Colonel Alvarez stepped aside, gesturing to the ground outside the door.

André studied it thoughtfully, eyes intent on the hard-packed earth that was covered with a fine powder of loose dirt. There were so many tracks that one set seemed to obscure the other and they all jumbled together. But one thing was apparent. The tracks ended facing one way, toward the door of the adobe that served as El Verdugo's headquarters. None of the tracks led away; yet, from the door on, the only tracks on the floor in the powdery dirt were his own and those of Colonel Alvarez. Not another boot track was even visible.

André's frown deepened. He moved back into the main room and stood for a long time, studying the floor, then exhaled angrily. He left the door open wide and reached up, yanking the tattered curtain from the window to let in more light, then motioned for the colonel to stay where he was standing near the door while he moved slowly about the room, his eyes intent on the floor.

It was too clean, too clear of tracks. Someone had taken pains to scrape up the hard-packed dirt, then brushed it with perhaps a tree branch, or broom, or some other similar object to obliterate even the footprints.

André scrutinized the floor for a long time, looking about carefully for some sign, some reason for someone to have so carefully removed any traces of anyone's having been there. He was about to give up, when he noticed a strange mark on the floor that had been missed by whoever had swept it. He moved nearer, bending close; then his eyes narrowed shrewdly as his hand reached out and lightly brushed aside some of the loose dirt. The rounded curve of a hoofprint was still discernible, although most of it had carefully been scuffed up. He ran his fingers over it, staring at it, puzzled, then glanced up in the direction it was headed. The hoofprint was less than a foot from the wall of cupboards that had been built beside the fireplace. He stared at the cupboards for a long time, looking first at them, then occasionally glancing down toward the hoofprint. Suddenly he stood up forcefully, his eyes blazing as he turned toward Colonel Alvarez, who was still standing near the doorway watching him.

"Get some of your men in here, pronto, and have them bring tools so we can tear that cupboard apart," he shouted furiously. And in a short time, with the help of two of the

soldiers, André was standing in front of the tunnel that led
into the abandoned mine in the mountainside, a look of consternation on his handsome face.

"Are you going to go in there?" asked the colonel, who
was standing beside André, staring after him into the
darkness.

André stuck his head in as far as he could, determining
only that there were signs of horses and men inside; then he
turned back to the colonel. "No, I'm not going in," he said.
"But we are going after them." He brushed the dirt from his
clothes and shifted his gunbelt to rest easier on his hips as he
spoke. "Get some of your men," he commanded, ordering the
colonel about. "Enough for a small squad. The others will
stay here and guard the place in case any of El Verdugo's
men decide to come back. Bring the rest of the men with us."
He walked to the door of the adobe and stared outside into
the early-morning sun. "If that tunnel was used for an escape
route, then it's got to have an exit somewhere on the other
side of this mountain," he explained. "And I intend to find
it." His shoulders straightened arrogantly as Colonel Alvarez
watched him step outside, and a short time later André was
heading out of the camp with Colonel Alvarez and Ramón
accompanying him, a small contingent of soldiers close on
their heels as they made their way toward the other side of
the mountain.

André gazed down momentarily into the arroyo below as
they moved steadily along this side of the mountain. It was
far down, sunlight bleaching the sandy bottom almost white.
His eyes roamed up once more to the land ahead of him.
They'd been working their way steadily around the mountain,
alert for any change of landscape, anything out of place that
would reveal an exit to the mine. So far, they'd found nothing. Then suddenly he stopped, stretching in the saddle to see
better, one hand shading his eyes.

Colonel Alvarez reined up beside him. "What is it?"

"Wait here," cautioned André, and he rode his horse into
the shade of some boulders, dismounted, handing his horse's
reins to the colonel, then took off on foot. He climbed over
an outcropping of rocks, then walked along the edge of a
level area that stretched out before him, his eyes glued to a
dark area heavy with scrub brush. He was right; he took a
deep, satisfied breath as he neared, then stood with hands on
hips, surveying the scene.

Loose boards lay about the dark entrance to the mine, and he could tell they'd been thrown aside recently. As he looked down, he could see that the ground had been churned up by dozens of horses. He cursed. This was going to make it harder.

He began to circle the area, looking for tracks, trying to understand what the ground was telling him as easily as Judah had, but his skill fell far short of the American's. It took almost half an hour of diligent searching and deciphering to come up with the conclusion that all but four riders had headed south into the mountains again, probably to lose themselves in the villages, where they'd never be found. But it was the four other riders he was interested in. Two of the horses would belong to the *americanos,* the third to Gia. The fourth? Since Lenore Larrabee was dead, who else but El Verdugo? And what better way to elude capture than reaching the American border?

Once onto the scent, André managed to find their trail more easily as it wound its way down the side of the mountain into the arroyo. And as the sun began to climb higher into the sky, promising another warm day, Colonel Alvarez and his soldiers headed up the arroyo toward the Rio Grande, with André doggedly leading the way, following the tracks of the four horsemen.

Gia was exhausted. They'd been riding for hours. It might not have been so bad if they'd had something decent to eat, but supplies had been low when the siege started, and they could take little with them except some jerky and dried cornbread. Even so, they hadn't been able to stop until well after dark, and they had had no sleep the night before. Judah was sure André and the colonel wouldn't be able to follow their trail at night, even if they discovered the mine with its exit, but he was still uneasy when they stopped, his eyes constantly searching the darkness.

The fire he built was small, only big enough to keep away animals that might get too close, and Gia sat in front of it now, gazing into the flames, trying to keep her eyes open. She wanted to sleep and had even tried curling up next to her father, but nightmares and restlessness had brought her back to the fire once more.

She pulled her knees up and wound her arms about them, then leaned her head back and stared up at the sky. It was

still moonless, only a few stars in view, and since the sun had
set earlier, a crisp coolness had begun to fill the air. She
shivered slightly as the warmth from the flames penetrated
her thin clothing. She was still in the horrible-looking baggy
pants and shirt and still wearing the moccasins. The sombrero
she'd been wearing was near where her father was sleeping,
but she didn't need it now.

She reached up and touched her hair. After taking food to
the men the night before their escape, she had made her way
to the stream a short distance from the adobe and washed it,
and it had felt so refreshing. Now it was dirty again from the
day's long ride, and she wondered if she'd ever feel clean
again. She took the leather thong off it and ran her fingers
through it like a comb, feeling the silken curls, then untied
the ends of the leather thong and began to fasten it around
her hair again to hold it back.

"No, don't," said Paul from behind her, and she let her
hands stop in midair, staring up at him as he sat down next
to her so close she could feel the warmth of his body through
the thin material of her old clothes.

He reached out and took the leather thong from her fingers, twisting it in his own as he let his hand move into her
hair. "I love your hair long and loose," he said softly,
caressing it.

The blue-green of Gia's eyes took on the color of the
flames, turning a deep reddish gold with hints of blue-violet
running through them, and Paul watched them, entranced.
She stared at him openly, and once more he was reminded of
the young woman he'd first seen in the big four-poster bed at
Mrs. Thornapple's. But the innocence was gone from her eyes
now, replaced by a depth of passion that left him weak.

It was the first they'd been alone since their escape. Judah
was taking first watch and was a short distance away at a
vantage point where he could watch the trail behind them,
and Maximilian was asleep on the other side of the fire. Gia
had checked his bandages again when they stopped for the
night, and she was glad he was getting a chance to sleep, because he'd been getting worse. He'd lost more blood and had
begun to act feverish at times, and she hoped he'd be able to
make it. But at the moment her father's welfare was the farthest thing from her thoughts as she stared into Paul's warm
gray eyes, golden in the firelight. The flames, casting shadows
on his tanned face, made his ruggedly sensuous features more

prominent than they normally were, and she felt a stirring deep inside. She held her breath, her heart pounding.

"What happens to us now, Paul?" she asked breathlessly.

His eyes held hers for the longest time. "You heard Judah," he whispered softly. "He's right. I've punished myself all day for Lenore, I've cursed myself a thousand times over, but I can't go back and make it right, it's too late. So if we get out of here alive—and God help us, I hope we do—I intend to make up to you for all the unhappiness this horrible nightmare has given you. It may be too late for Lenore, but I pray to God it's not too late for us."

Her eyes softened as his hand cupped her head, and she leaned back, letting her head rest against his palm, the touch of him reassuring her. "It isn't," she whispered. "We'll make it, Paul," she went on. "All I need is a little rest."

He smiled that crooked unnerving smile that always made her insides warm and weak, then pulled her to him, cradling her head on his shoulder as he stretched out next to the fire, holding her close against him.

"But Judah . . . ?" she protested as he held her tightly.

His jaw clenched stubbornly, his eyes darkening possessively. "Judah understands," he said, his lips against her hair as he cradled her in his arms. "Now, get some sleep." She sighed wearily, cuddling close, feeling his unshaven stubble of beard against her hair as she closed her eyes, and she didn't care. Whatever tomorrow brought, life or death, for just a little while, for tonight she was content, so content and so tired that when it was Paul's turn to take the watch, she never even felt him roll her from his arms into the warm blanket that surrounded her, but just kept right on sleeping.

They had been riding hard since sunup, and it was well past noon the second day after their escape. Gia had spent the night before in Paul's arms again, and neither Judah nor Maximilian was surprised. In fact, in one of his more lucid moments Maximilian had made Paul promise never to leave her side.

Gia was more worried about her father than she'd let on. They had wanted to tie him to the saddle, but only as a last resort. He refused, and now she glanced ahead of her, watching him hang on desperately as they rode along, heading toward Big Bend country. The day was hot again, and

Gia's clothes were sticking to her. The land they were going through was desolate and barren.

They were out of the high mountains and deep arroyos, moving across wide stretches of land broken occasionally by cactus, yucca, and mesquite, with only an occasional hill or valley. Lizards scurried from their path, and other animals made themselves scarce as the riders came through, and still they moved on.

Gia's stomach was already growling as she reached over, grabbing the piece of jerky Judah handed her. "Father's pretty bad, isn't he?" she asked as he started toward Paul, who was bringing up the rear.

"It isn't good," answered Judah, easing his horse up beside her. "But I think he just might make it. We've got about an hour's ride, maybe less."

"Where are you planning to cross?" she asked anxiously.

He glanced up ahead. "Near Boquillas Canyon."

"Boquillas Canyon? Father'll never be able to take those cliffs."

"We won't cross at the canyon itself," he explained as he turned in the saddle, his eyes on the ridge some distance behind them. "There's a place about a mile downriver from the canyon. It's only a narrow pass, but there are no cliffs, and once on the other side, it's about two miles to the nearest town. It's rather hard to find, and not too well-known, but it'll serve its purpose."

"You've been there before?" she asked curiously.

He smiled broadly. "Me and every other outlaw and Comanchero south of the border," he said. Then his smile faded abruptly, to be replaced by a deep scowl. "Paul!" he shouted, and Paul, who'd also been turned slightly in the saddle, watching the horizon behind them, spun around and spurred his horse forward. "Are those riders in the rear?" he asked as Paul reined in close, frowning.

"I was about to ask you," he said.

Judah shaded his eyes and studied the horizon; then his jaw tightened viciously, nostrils flaring. "The damn bastards followed our trail," he said disgustedly. "And they're close!"

Paul glanced hurriedly at Gia, then to her father, who was still managing to stay in the saddle somehow. "Can we make it?" he asked Judah.

Judah chewed his lips thoughtfully. "We'll sure as hell try." He spurred his horse forward and grabbed Maximilian's horse's reins. The wounded man glanced at him glassy-eyed, the fever working on him again, and to Judah's dismay, he was laughing, as if it were a joke, probably reliving some past adventure. For once, Judah was thankful for his delirium. He was evidently recalling a time when he'd had to ride long and far, and he was hanging on for dear life.

Judah could only hope he wouldn't let go as the four of them swept across the dry plains with nowhere to hide from their pursuers, who they knew had already spotted them.

Gia was scared as she leaned forward in the saddle. They'd been pushing their horses almost past the limit for well over an hour, and still the soldiers were gaining ground. Every muscle in her body ached, and the dirt and sand that flew about them as they galloped made her mouth dry and gritty. Then suddenly, as a shot rang out behind them and she realized they were almost within the soldiers' shooting range, they topped a small rise, and up ahead, stretching out from the jaws of Boquillas Canyon in the distance, was the river, like a long curving ribbon on the landscape.

Judah let out a shout as he started down the incline toward the Rio Grande, about a mile distant, but his shout was drowned out by the sound of gunfire behind them.

Maximilian wasn't even sitting in the saddle anymore, he was bent forward, one arm wound around the saddle horn, his head resting on it, only the strength in his legs against the horse's sides keeping him astride. But he was scared. Not for himself; for Gia. He could feel his legs weakening, the muscles becoming rubbery. If he fell now, if he let go and she stopped to help him, the soldiers would overtake them and she'd never be free again. As the daughter of an outlaw, her life would be over too, and she'd spend the rest of her years in prison, or worse, at the mercy of Romero Rubio's men. He had to make it, had to hang on. He tried tightening his grip on the saddle horn, but it was no use. As they neared the river, the jarring of the horse and loss of blood were too much.

Judah's eyes were on the water some fifty feet ahead of him, sandwiched between a heavy grove of white thorn trees on the right and some flint-rock cliffs on the left. The pass in the cliffs hadn't been discernible from a distance, but now relief showed in Judah's eyes as he spurred his horse toward it, keeping the rein on Maximilian's horse twined around his left hand.

He glanced back hurriedly as his horse came to the edge of the water and plunged in; then Judah pulled rein, his horse skidding to a stop a few feet into the water as he realized Maximilian was slipping. In seconds Judah was out of the saddle, but it wasn't quick enough, and the general hit the ground, his head barely inches from the water. Judah knelt, helping to ease him into a better position, as Gia and Paul, who were close behind, dismounted just as quickly, hurrying forward to the fallen man.

Gia's knees hit the ground beside her father, her eyes misty, face streaked with dirt. "Father, please, we're almost there!" she yelled, but he didn't hear her. He didn't want to.

His blood had been flowing freely for the past few hours, and Gia gasped as she realized his shirt was dripping with blood, as were his pants. Suddenly Maximilian felt strangely at peace. "I'm . . . I'm not going to make it, little one," he said, gasping. "But you will. You have to," he said.

"And what of you, Father?" she pleaded. "What of your cause?"

"My cause?" He tried to laugh, but the laughter was drowned in the blood that gushed into his mouth. He spit it out, then tried again. "My cause will go on," he said hesitantly, the effort almost too much. "There are others who will keep it alive, and somewhere, sometime, someone will succeed where I have failed. Even now, somewhere in this land there is probably a man who will someday bring freedom to my people, but for now, my time is over."

"No!" Gia's fists clenched as she stared down at the man who'd once been so young and handsome, who'd kissed her good-bye those many years ago and sent her north to safety. "You can't die," she whispered softly. "I've just found you again."

But General Maximilian d'Alessandro wasn't listening anymore. His eyes were glazed, his breathing shallow, and he saw Paul through a hazy mist. "You promised?" he said softly.

Paul nodded. He knew what the outlaw meant. "I promised," he answered.

Maximilian smiled weakly, his eyes once more caressing Gia as he took his last breath.

There was no time now for sentiment. No time even to take a few seconds to say good-bye, as a shot rang out, closer this time. Gia dropped her father's hand, letting Paul pull her to her feet. There was only time to get back into the saddle, spur their horses about, and plunge ahead again, into the river, wading their horses into the shallow water that barely reached to the horses' bellies.

From behind them, André watched the trio splashing their way across the water, and cursed, trying to shoot from the saddle, but losing his accuracy. He hadn't wanted only El Verdugo; he had wanted the Americans too, and the woman for himself. He had dreamed for a long time of the day when Gia would be his. If he could have, he would have made her his while they were in New York, but it was impossible. Now . . . From the moment he'd laid eyes on her in New York, he'd wanted her, and the thought that he was losing her made him livid. He had been so sure of everything. So sure it would turn out in his favor, and the taste of defeat was sour in his mouth.

He stared down at the dead body of El Verdugo, where Colonel Alvarez' soldiers were clustering, then spurred his horse to the water's edge, where he reined in hard, waving his gun in the air.

He could cross, but it would do no good, because the colonel and his men wouldn't cross with him. The army's orders were to stay out of American territory, and if he went alone, there'd be no one to back him up. He aimed his gun and fired at the riders as they reached the other side and scrambled from their horses, hiding behind an outcropping of rocks, grass, and trees some ten feet from the edge of the water. Then he turned, straightening in the saddle as he watched the soldiers roll the general's body into a blanket and tie it on his horse. All the while he watched them, he knew he was being spied on from the opposite bank, and he sat arrogantly erect in the saddle, throwing them a silent challenge, but they didn't accept it.

Tears ran down Gia's cheeks as she watched the soldiers roll her father's body up in the blanket and sling it across the saddle of his horse, tying it down. "Well, they have him," she said, sniffing as she wiped the tears away, mixing the dirt on her face with them. "I hope André's happy."

Paul grimaced, watching Major André de los Reyes astride his horse on the other side of the riverbank. Happy? He certainly didn't look happy, and Paul was sure he knew why. Although he'd been sent to capture El Verdugo, he'd been intent on capturing his daughter too, and his strategy hadn't worked. Thank God.

Paul glanced at Judah. "So what will he do now, Judah?" he asked.

Judah shrugged as they lay prone on the ground, watching the activity across the river. "I imagine he'll report back to Romero Rubio," he said prophetically. "And get a promotion for bringing in El Verdugo." He raised his head higher, then stood up slowly as the soldiers, with André and the colonel leading them, began to reorganize and file away from the river, leaving the pass the way they came. "But then, I don't think he's ever going to forget that he almost had us too." He watched for a long time, until the soldiers disappeared from view, then turned, walking toward where his horse was nonchalantly grazing on some grass, resting after the ordeal behind him. "You two coming?" he called back over his shoulder.

Paul looked at Gia, sighing. "Well, are we?" he asked.

She stared at his unshaven face, the ache in her heart over her father's death slowly replaced by a warmth of passion for this man who had risked his life for her. He was used to being a leader in his own world, yet he'd come into her world, letting Judah lead because it was a world alien to him in every respect. He'd known nothing of the danger and intrigue he'd been subjected to, yet had accepted it because of his love for her. How she adored him. Her father was dead, and so was Lenore, but she and Paul were alive, and the world went on.

"Yes, we are," she said emphatically, and let Paul pull her to her feet, into his arms. As his lips came down on hers, kissing her passionately, Judah looked back, wondering what the devil was taking them so long.

He smiled, then turned back toward his horse, patting him on the nose. "You know, fella," he said pensively, glad Major de los Reyes hadn't decided to press the advantage and cross the river, "I don't think either one of us is really needed anymore, do you?" and he was humming a quiet tune as he climbed into the saddle and took one last glance at Gia and Paul locked in each other's arms.

Epilogue

On Sunday, October 1, 1893, the remains of Lenore Larrabee were turned over to the American authorities in Eagle Pass, Texas, with a statement that she'd been killed by El Verdugo and his men, who had captured both her and her husband, Paul Larrabee, son of multimillionaire industrialist Jason Larrabee, while the two were on a trip from New York to Mexico. Paul Larrabee had escaped, but the body of Lenore Larrabee was found in the outlaw's abandoned camp.

Of course no one made any effort to explain to the newspapers how Paul Larrabee managed to escape, nor was there any explanation as to what happened to Jason Larrabee's illegitimate daughter, Gigi Rouvier, who had accompanied Paul and Lenore Larrabee to Mexico, along with her new fiancé. Nor was there any explanation as to why her supposed fiancé suddenly showed up in Mexico City a week later, acting as if the engagement had never been announced.

On October 10, as the leaves on the trees in Central Park began to change their summer greens to gold and crimson, Lenore Larrabee's body arrived in New York City, accompanied by her husband and the woman the world had once thought was his sister, but who, Jason Larrabee revealed, was really Gia Maria d'Alessandro, a cousin to the young woman he'd fathered twenty years before. But no comment was made of the relationship between Miss d'Alessandro and General Maximilian d'Alessandro, the man the Mexican newspapers were denouncing as the notorious El Verdugo, who had died defending the same camp where Lenore Larrabee was killed.

Then, on Saturday, October 21, 1893, only a few days after the funeral of Lenore Larrabee, New York society was once more agog as Paul Larrabee quietly married Gia Maria d'Alessandro and left on his honeymoon.

About that same time, south of the border, a young man of sixteen, Doroteo Arango, heard the accounts of the death of El Verdugo, listened to the unhappy cries of his friends and neighbors, watched the agonizing outrages perpetrated against his fellow countrymen, and a burning flame of vengeance began to smolder within him. And because of the bitter anger that was kindled in Doroteo's heart, Maximilian d'Alessandro's last words spoken to his daughter as he died became prophetic. For that young man, Doroteo Arango, was destined someday to be known as Pancho Villa.

About the Author

The granddaughter of an old-time vaudevillian, Mrs. Shiplett was born and raised in Onio. She has been married to her husband for twenty-eight years and they have lived in the city of Mentor-on-the-Lake for twenty-three years. She has four daughters and two grandchildren and enjoys living an active outdoor life.

Praise for Keri Arthur

Winner of the *Romantic Times*
2008 Reviewers' Choice Awards
for Career Achievement in Urban Fantasy

**"Keri Arthur's imagination and energy infuse
everything she writes with zest."**
—**Charlaine Harris**

Darkness Devours

"Prepare for intense action and sexual attraction to take center stage. . . . Arthur writes stellar action scenes. . . . I absolutely cannot wait to read what happens next in this indomitable story. *Darkness Devours* is bloody good with its provocative heroine and killer plotline."
—Joyfully Reviewed

"An intricate and thrilling urban fantasy filled with sensuality, violence, and imagination . . . mesmerizing."
—Night Owl Reviews

"Reminiscent of the early Anita Blake books, Arthur's third Dark Angels book is an action-packed and highly sensual urban fantasy. . . . If you're a fan of Arthur's Riley Jenson Guardian series, you won't want to miss reading this spin-off."
—All Things Urban Fantasy

"Action-packed and loaded with hot guys (yummy!), this third installment has Risa running for both her life . . . and her heart."
—The Book Swarm

"[Arthur's] ability to raise the stakes in each book never ceases to amaze me. . . . I give *Darkness Devours* a resounding five-star rating. Arthur sure knows how to keep the reader coming back for more!"
—A Book Obsession

"Risa is becoming a fierce heroine. . . . The series keeps picking up steam and this is the strongest installment yet."
—*USA Today* Happy Ever After

continued . . .

Darkness Unbound

"Keri Arthur has blown me away again. Her worlds are so complex and 'real.' . . . Risa makes readers fall in love with her. . . . I highly recommend Arthur's books."
— *USA Today*

"Must read! I love, love, love it! Arthur's . . . kick-ass action and indelible heroine left me enraptured. Risa Jones is one of a kind; she is the next generation's paranormal superheroine!"   —Joyfully Reviewed

"Risa is an amazing character; she most certainly kicks butt."   —Serendipity Reviews

Darkness Rising

"You will fall hard for [Keri Arthur's] Dark Angels series."   —Coffee Time Romance & More

"A highly imaginative world with memorable characters . . . everything a fan of romance and urban fantasy would enjoy. There is a cosmopolitan mix of supernatural creatures: werewolves, vampires, and witches . . . an exciting new series!"   —Night Owl Reviews

Full Moon Rising

"Keri Arthur skillfully mixes her suspenseful plot with heady romance . . . sexy vampires, randy werewolves, and unabashed, unapologetic, joyful sex—you've gotta love it. Smart, sexy, and well conceived."   —Kim Harrison

"Deliciously sexy . . . [it] pulls you in and won't let go. Keri Arthur knows how to thrill! Buckle up and get ready for a wild, cool ride!"   —Shana Abé

"Will remind many of Anita Blake, Laurell K. Hamilton's kick-ass vampire hunter. . . . Fans of . . . Charlaine Harris's Sookie Stackhouse vampire series will be rewarded."   —*Publishers Weekly*

"Well-done and entertaining."
— *The Sunday Oklahoman*

"Sexy and fast-paced." — *The Davis Enterprise*

"Hot werewolves, sexy vampires, a huge amount of butt kickin', and no-holds-barred sex. If you like a twist to your paranormal romance, you'll love this book."
— Fresh Fiction

Kissing Sin

Finalist for the 2008 Fantasm Award
for Best Werewolf Romance

"Strong world building, vivid personalities, and the distinctive cultures of each of the various paranormal strains combine for a rich narrative, and Arthur's descriptive prose adds texture and menace." — *Publishers Weekly*

"The second book in this paranormal Guardian series is just as phenomenal as the first. . . . I am addicted!"
— Fresh Fiction

Dangerous Games

Finalist for the 2008 Fantasm Award
for Best Urban Fantasy Romance

"By far one of the best books I have ever read."
— Coffee Time Romance & More

"[An] absorbing read." — SFRevu

"This series is phenomenal! It keeps you spellbound and mesmerized on every page. Absolutely perfect!"
— Fresh Fiction

Embraced by Darkness

"Positively one of the best urban fantasy authors in print today." — Darque Reviews

"Arthur's characters inhabit a dark, sexy world of the paranormal." — *News and Sentinel* (Parkersburg, WV)

Also by Keri Arthur

The Dark Angels Series

Darkness Unbound
Darkness Rising
Darkness Devours
Darkness Hunts

DARKNESS UNMASKED

A DARK ANGELS NOVEL

KERI ARTHUR

A SIGNET SELECT BOOK

SIGNET SELECT
Published by the Penguin Group
Penguin Group (USA) Inc., 375 Hudson Street,
New York, New York 10014, USA

USA | Canada | UK | Ireland | Australia | New Zealand | India | South Africa | China

Penguin Books Ltd., Registered Offices: 80 Strand, London WC2R 0RL, England
For more information about the Penguin Group visit penguin.com.

First published by Signet Select, an imprint of New American Library,
a division of Penguin Group (USA) Inc.

First Printing, June 2013
10 9 8 7 6 5 4 3 2 1

ISBN 978-0-451-23713-2

Printed in the United States of America

I'd like to thank the following people:

my editor, Danielle Perez; copy editor Penina Lopez;
and the man responsible for the fabulous
cover, Tony Mauro.

A special thanks to:

my fabulous agent, Miriam Kriss; my talented and
funny crit buddies—Mel, Robyn, Chris, Carolyn, and
Freya; and finally, my lovely daughter, Kasey.

Chapter 1

The office phone rang with a sharpness that jolted me instantly awake. I jerked upright, peeled a wayward bit of paper from my nose, and stared at the phone blankly. Then the caller ID registered and I groaned. The call was coming from Madeline Hunter, the bitch who was not only in charge of the Directorate of Other Races, but was a leading member of the high vampire council, too. She was also the very last person in this world—or the next—who I wanted to hear from right now.

Unfortunately, given that she was now my boss, she was not someone I could—or should—ignore.

I hit the vid-phone's ANSWER button and said in a less-than-polite voice, "What?"

She paused, and something flashed in the green of her eyes. A darkness that spoke of anger. But all she said was, "I have a task for you."

A curse rose in my throat, but I somehow managed to leash it. "What sort of task?"

But even as I asked the question, I knew. There was only one reason for her to be ringing me, and that was to track down an escapee from hell. She had not only the Directorate at her command, but a stableful of Cazadors—the high council's elite killing force—and they dealt with all manner of murderers and madmen on an everyday basis.

I even had one following me around astrally, reporting my every move back to Hunter. Trust was not high on her list of good traits.

Not that I think she had all that many good traits.

"A close friend of mine was murdered last night." Her voice held very little emotion, and she was scarier because of it. "I want you to investigate."

Hunter had friends. Imagine that. I scrubbed a hand across my eyes and said somewhat wearily, "Look, as much as I absolutely adore working for you, the reality is the Directorate is far better equipped to handle *this* sort of murderer."

"The Directorate hasn't your experience with the denizens of hell," she snapped. "Nor do they have a reaper at their beck and call."

So I'd been right—it *was* an escapee from hell. Not great news, but I guess it *was* my fault that these things were about in the world. It might have become my task to find the three lost keys that controlled the gates to heaven and hell, but the only one I'd managed to find so far had almost immediately been stolen from me. As a result, the first gate to hell had been permanently opened by person or persons unknown, and the stronger demons were now coming through. Not in great numbers—not yet—but that was thanks only to the fact that the remaining gates were still shut.

Of course, given the choice, I'd rather *not* find the other keys. After all, if no one knew where they were, then they couldn't be used to either permanently open or close the gates. But it wasn't like I had a choice, not anymore. It was either find them or die. Or, when it came to the choice given to me by my father—who was one of the Raziq, the rogue Aedh priests who'd helped create the keys, and also the man responsible for having them stolen—watch my friends die.

"Azriel isn't at my beck and call," I said, unable to hide the annoyance in my voice. "He just wants the keys, the same as you and the council."

Not to mention the Raziq and my goddamn father.

"*This* takes priority over finding the keys."

I snorted. "Since when?"

That darkness in her eyes got stronger. "Since I walked into my lover's house and discovered his corpse."

I stared at her for a moment, seeing little in the way of true emotion in either her expression or her voice. And yet her need for revenge, to rend and tear, was so strong that even through the vid-phone I could almost taste it. That sort of fury, I thought with a shiver, was not something I ever wanted aimed my way.

Yet, despite knowing it wasn't sensible, I couldn't help saying, "I'm betting the rest of the council wouldn't actually agree with that assessment."

I think if she could have jumped down the phone line and throttled me, she would have. As it was, she bared her teeth, her canines elongating just a little, and said in a soft voice, "You should not be

worried about what the rest of the council is thinking right now."

The only time I'd stop worrying about the rest of
the council was when she achieved her goal of su-
preme control over the lot of them. Until then, they
were as big a threat to me as she was.

But I wasn't stupid enough to actually come out
and say *that* to her. "Hunting for your friend's killer
is going to steal precious time away from the search
for—"

"And," she cut in coolly, "just where, exactly, is
your search for the keys?"

Nowhere, that was where. My father might have
given me clues for the next key's location, but deciphering *those* was another matter entirely. We figured it was somewhere in the middle of Victoria's
famous golden triangle, but given *that* particular
region encompassed more than nine thousand square
kilometers of land, that left us with a vast area to
explore. It was fucking frustrating, but all Azriel
and I could do was keep on searching and hope that
sooner or later fate gave us a goddamn break.

"It's probably in the same place as your search
for my mother's killer."

The minute the words left my mouth, I regretted
them. Hunter really *wasn't* someone I needed to
antagonize, and yet it was her damn promise to
help find my mother's killer that had made me
agree to work for her and the council in the first
place. And while I'd kept my end of the bargain, she
hadn't.

For several very long seconds, she didn't reply.

She simply stared at me, her expression remote and her eyes colder than the Antarctic. Then she said, voice so soft it was barely audible, "Tread warily, Risa dearest."

I gulped. I couldn't help it. Death glared at me through the phone's screen, and she scared the hell out of me.

I took a slow, deep breath, but it really didn't help ease the sense of dread or the sudden desire to just give it all the fuck away. To let fate deal her cards and accept whatever might come my way—be that death at Hunter's hand or someone else's.

I was sick of it. Sick of the threats, sick of the fighting, sick of a search that seemed to have no end and no possibility of our winning.

Death is not a solution of any *kind,* Azriel said, his mind voice sharp.

I looked up from the phone's screen. He appeared in front of my desk, the heat of his presence playing gently through my being, a sensation as intimate as the caress of fingers against skin. Longing shivered through me.

Reapers, like the Aedh, weren't actually flesh beings—although they could certainly attain that form whenever they wished—but rather beings made of energy who lived on the gray fields, the area that divided earth from heaven and hell. Or the light and dark portals, as they preferred to call them.

Although I had no idea whether his reaper form would be considered handsome—or even how reapers defined handsome—his human form certainly was. His face was chiseled, almost classical in

its beauty, but possessed the hard edge of a man
who'd fought many battles. His body held a similar
hardness, though his build was more that of an ath-
lete than a weight lifter. Distinctive black tats that
resembled the left half of a wing swept around his
ribs from underneath his arm, the tips brushing
across the left side of his neck.

Only it wasn't a tat. It was a Dušan—a darker,
more stylized brother to the lilac one that resided
on my left arm—and had been designed to protect
us when we walked the gray fields. We had no idea
who'd sent them to us, but Azriel suspected it was
my father. He was apparently one of the few left in
this world—or the next—who had the power to
make them.

Of course, Azriel wasn't *just* a reaper, but something far more. He was one of the Mijai, the dark
angels who hunted and killed the things that broke
free from hell. And they had more than their fair
share of work now that the first gate had been
opened.

*If you ask me, death is looking more and more the
perfect solution when it comes to the keys.* My mental voice sounded as weary as my physical one. I
wasn't actually telepathic, but that didn't matter
when it came to my reaper. He could hear my
thoughts as clearly as the spoken word.

Unfortunately, it wasn't always a two-way street.
Most of the time I heard his thoughts only when it
was a deliberate act on his part. *If I'm not here to
find the damn things, then the world and my friends
remain safe.*

He crossed his arms, an action that only emphasized the muscles in his arms and shoulders. *Death is no solution. Not for you. Not now.*

And what the hell is that supposed to mean?

His gaze met mine, his blue eyes—one as vivid and bright as a sapphire, the other as dark as a storm-driven sea—giving little away. *It means exactly what it says.*

Great. More riddles. Another thing I really needed right now. I returned my attention to Hunter's death-like stare. "How did your friend die?"

"He was restrained, then drained."

"Drained? As in, a vampire-style, all-the-blood-from-the-body draining, or something else?"

She hesitated, and just for a second I saw something close to grief in her eyes. Whoever her friend was, they'd been a lot closer than mere lovers.

"Have you ever seen the husk of a fly after a spider has finished with it?" she said. "That's what he looked like. There was nothing left but the dried remains of outer skin. *Everything* else had been sucked away."

I stared at her for a moment, wondering whether I'd heard her right, then swallowed heavily and said, "Everything? As in, blood, bone—"

"Blood, bone, muscle, intestines, brain. *Everything.*" Her voice was suddenly fierce. "As I said, *all* that remained was the shell of hardened outer skin."

A shudder ran through me. I did *not* want to meet, let alone chase, something that could do *that* to a body.

"How can human skin be hardened into a shell?

Or the entire innards of a body be sucked away? It had to be one *hell* of a wound."

"On the contrary, the wound was quite small— two slashes on either side of his abdomen." She hesitated. "He did not appear to die in agony. Quite the opposite, in fact."

"I guess that's some comfort—"

"He's *dead*," she cut in harshly. "How is that ever going to be a comfort?"

I should have known I'd get my head bitten off if I tried sympathy on the bitch. "Where is his body? And is the Directorate being called in on this?"

If they were, it could get tricky. Uncle Rhoan worked for them—he was, in fact, second in charge of the guardian division these days—but he had no idea I was working for Hunter and the council. And I wanted to keep it that way, because the shit would really hit the fan if he and Aunt Riley ever found out. They'd always considered me one of their pack, but that protectiveness had increased when Mom had died. They'd kill me if they knew I'd agreed to work with Hunter—although I now suspected I couldn't have actually *refused* to work with her—and once they'd dealt with me, they'd track her down and confront her. And *that* was a situation that could *never* end nicely.

I'd already endangered the lives of too many people I cared about by dragging them into this mad quest for the keys—I didn't want to make the situation worse in any way.

"Yes, they are," she said. "But Jack has been

made aware of my wishes in this and will ensure you get first bite at the crime scene."

Amusement briefly ran through me, although I doubted her pun had been intentional. "That really doesn't help with the problem—"

"Rhoan Jenson will not get in the way of this. You are a consultant, nothing more, as far as he is concerned."

I snorted. "A consultant you're using to hunt and kill."

"Yes. And you would do well to remember that you remain alive only as long as the council and I agree on your usefulness."

"And," Azriel said, suddenly standing behind me. His closeness had desire stirring, even though I had little enough energy to spare. "You would do well to remember that *any* attempt to harm her would be met with even more deadly force."

Hunter smiled, but there was nothing pleasant about it. "We both know you cannot take a life without just cause, reaper, so do not make your meaningless threats to me."

"What I have done once, I can do again," he said, his voice stony. "And in this case, as in the last, I would revel in a death taken before its time."

Azriel, stop poking the bear. I've already antagonized her enough.

That is a somewhat absurd statement, given she is clearly vampire, not bear.

Amusement slithered through me again, as he'd no doubt intended. He'd grown something of a sense of humor of late—which was, according to him, a consequence of spending far too much time in flesh form. Whether that was true or not, I had no idea, but I certainly preferred this more "human" version to the remote starchiness that had been present when he'd first appeared. *You know what I mean.*

Surprisingly, I do. He touched my shoulder, the contact light but somehow possessive. *But her threats grow tedious. She must be made aware it gains her nothing.*

Hunter laughed. The sound was harsh and cold, and sent another round of chills down my spine. "Reaper, you amuse me. One of these days, when I'm tired of this life, I might just be tempted to take you on."

And she was crazy enough to do it, too.

"However," she continued, "that time is *not* now. I will send you my friend's address, Risa. The Directorate will arrive at his home at four. Please be finished with your initial investigation before then, and report your impressions immediately."

I glanced at my watch. She'd given me a whole hour. Whoop-de-do. "Where does he live, and what sort of security system has he got in place?"

"I've just sent you all his details."

My cell phone beeped almost immediately. I picked it up and glanced at the message. Hunter's friend—who went by the very German-sounding name of Wolfgang Schmidt—lived in Brighton, a very upmarket suburb near the beach. No surprise there, I guess—I certainly couldn't imagine her slumming it with the regular folk in places like Broad-meadows or Dandenong.

I read the rest of the text, then looked up at the main phone's screen again. "Is the security system just key coded?"

"Yes. Wolfgang is—*was*—a very old-fashioned vampire. He saw no need for anything more than a basic system."

And maybe, just maybe, that had gotten him killed. While there was no electronic security system on earth that would actually *stop* a demon, it wasn't beyond the realms of possibility that something other than a demon had killed her vampire friend.

I mean, no one could ever be one hundred percent right all the time. Not even Hunter—although I'm sure *she'd* claim otherwise. And really, what sane person would argue the point with her when she wasn't?

Certainly not me.

And yet you do, Azriel commented, a trace of amusement in his mental tone.

I think we've already established I'm not always sane. To Hunter, I added, "You're not going to be there?"

"No."

I frowned. "Why not?"

"Because I have"—she hesitated, and an almost predatory gleam touched her gaze—"a meeting that needs to be attended."

If that gleam was any indication, the so-called

meeting involved bloodshed of some kind. After all, the council—and Hunter—considered it perfectly acceptable to punish those who broke the rules by allowing them to be ripped to shreds by younger vampires.

Still, it seemed odd that she wasn't hanging around to garner my impressions, especially if she cared for the dead man as much as I suspected.

Like many who have lived for centuries, she has strayed from the path of humanity, Azriel commented. *For her, emotions are fleeting, tenuous things.*

But not all those who live so long find that fate. Uncle Quinn's not far off Hunter in age, and he's as emotional as anyone. Although he could also be as stoic and cold as any of them when the urge took him.

He is one of the few exceptions. It is very rare to live so long and hang on to humanity.

I glanced at him. *Does that apply to reapers as well?*

Reapers are not human, so we can hardly hang on to what we do not have.

But you are capable of emotions.

Again a smile touched his thoughts, and it shimmered through me like a warm summer breeze. *Yes, we are, especially if we are foolish enough to remain in flesh too long.*

In other words, I wasn't to read too much into what he said or did while he wore flesh, because when all this was over, we'd both go our separate ways and life would return to normal.

I wanted that. I really did.

But at the same time, it was becoming harder and harder to imagine life without Azriel in it.

He made no comment on that particular thought, and I returned my attention to Hunter. "Once I've checked out the crime scene, what then? Are you going to tell me more about him, or am I expected to work on this case completely blind?"

"Impressions first," she said, and hung up.

"Fuck you and the broom you rode in on," I muttered, then leaned back in my chair. "Well, this totally sucks."

"An unfortunate consequence of agreeing to work with someone like Hunter is being at her beck and call." He spun my chair around, then squatted in front of me and took my hands in his. His fingers were warm against mine, his touch comforting. "But there is little we can do until your mother's killer is caught."

I snorted softly. "Even if we *do* find her killer, do you really think she's going to let me go?"

"We both know the answer to that. But once the killer is caught, we will be in a better position to deny her."

"Maybe." And maybe not. After all, Hunter wouldn't have any qualms about threatening the lives of my friends if it meant securing long-term obedience.

"It does not pay to worry about things that may never happen."

"No." I leaned forward and rested my forehead

against his as I closed my eyes. "I guess we'd better get moving. I want to be out of that house before the Directorate gets there."

"Do you wish me to transport us there?"

His breath washed across my lips and left them tingling. Half of me wanted to kiss him, and the other half just wanted him to wrap his arms around me and hold me like he never intended to let go. Unfortunately, neither was particularly practical right now.

And it was a sad statement about my life when desire gave way to practicality.

"It'll be faster if you do." While I could shift into my Aedh form and travel there under my own steam, my energy levels were still low and I really didn't want to push it. Not yet, not for something like this.

He rose, dragging me up with him, then wrapped his arms around me.

"Wait." I broke from his grasp and moved around the desk, striding out of my office and down to the storeroom at the other end of the hall. We kept all of RYT's—which was the name of the café I owned with two of my best friends, Ilianna and Tao— nonperishable items up here, which meant not only things like spare plates, cutlery, and serviettes, but also serving gloves. It was the latter I needed, simply because the last thing I wanted was to be leaving fingerprints around Wolfgang's house for the Directorate and Uncle Rhoan to find. I tore open a box, shoved a couple of the clear latex gloves into the pocket of my jeans, then headed back into the office. I grabbed my cell phone from the desk and let myself be wrapped in the warmth of Azriel's arms again. "Okay, go for it."

The words had barely left my mouth when his power surged through me, running along every muscle, every fiber, until my whole body sang to its tune. Until it felt like there was no me and no him, just the sum of us—energy beings with no flesh to hold us in place.

All too quickly, my office was replaced by the gray fields. Once upon a time the fields had been little more than thick veils and shadows—a zone where things not sighted on the living plane gained substance. But the more time I spent in Azriel's company, the more "real" the fields became. This time, the ethereal, beautiful structures that filled this place somehow seemed more solid, and instead of the reapers being little more than wispy, luminous shapes, I could now pick out faces. They glowed with life and energy, reminding me of the drawings of angels so often seen in scriptures—beautiful and yet somehow alien.

Then the fields were gone, and we regained substance. And though it involved no effort on my part, it still left my head spinning.

"You," he said, expression concerned, "are not recovering as quickly as you should."

"It's been a hard few weeks." I stepped back to study the building in front of us, even though all I really wanted to do was remain in his arms. That, however, was not an option. Not now and certainly not in the future. Not on any long-term, forever-type basis, anyway.

Which, if I was being at all honest with myself, totally sucked. But then, I had a very long history of falling for inappropriate men. Take my former Aedh lover, Lucian, for instance.

"Let's not," Azriel said, voice grim as he touched my back and then lightly waved me forward.

Amusement teased my lips. "He's out of my life, Azriel, and no longer a threat to whatever plans you—"

"It is not the threat to *me* I worry about," he cut in, voice irritated.

I raised my eyebrows. "Well, he can hardly threaten *me*, given he and everyone else wants the damn keys."

"His need for the keys did not stop his attempt to strangle you."

Well, no, it hadn't. But I suspected Lucian's actions had been little more than a momentary lapse of control—one he would have snapped out of before he'd actually killed me. Although, to be honest, I hadn't actually been so certain of that when his hands had been around my neck.

I opened the ornate metal gate and walked up the brick pathway toward the front door. Wolfgang's house was one of the increasingly rare red-brick Edwardian houses that used to take pride of place in the leafy bayside suburb. The front garden was small but meticulously tended, as was the house itself. I pulled out the gloves as I walked up the brick pathway toward the ornate front door, then said, "Lucian is no longer our problem."

"If you think that, you are a fool."

And I wasn't a fool. Not really. I just kept hoping that if I believed something hard enough, it might actually come true. I slipped the gloves on and switched the discussion back to my health. It was far safer ground.

"You can't expect me to recover instantly, Azriel. I'm flesh and blood, not—"

"You are half Aedh," he cut in again. His voice was still testy. But then, he always did sound that way after a discussion about Lucian, whom he hated with a surprising amount of passion for someone who claimed it was only his flesh form that gave him emotions. "More so, given what Malin did to you."

Malin was the woman in charge of the Raziq, my father's former lover, and a woman scorned. My father had not only betrayed her trust by stealing the keys from under her nose, but he had also refused to give her the child she'd wanted. Instead, for reasons known only to himself, he'd gone to my mother and produced me.

"Meaning what?" My voice was perhaps sharper than it should have been. "You never *actually* explained what she did."

And I certainly couldn't remember—she'd made sure of that.

He hesitated, his expression giving little away. "No. And I have already said more than I should."

Because of my father. Because whatever Malin did had somehow altered me—and not *just* by altering the device the Raziq had previously woven into the fabric of my heart, which had been designed to notify them when I was in my father's presence.

My sigh was one of frustration, but I knew better than to argue with Azriel—at least when he had *that* face on. "It doesn't alter the fact that a body— even one that is half energy—can run on empty for only so long."

A fact he knew well enough—his own lack of energy was the reason he'd been unable to heal me lately. Of course, reapers didn't "recharge" by eating or sleeping or any of the other things humans did, but rather by mingling energies—which was the reaper version of sex—with those who possessed a harmonious frequency. Unfortunately for them, such compatibility wasn't widespread, and Azriel's recharge companion had been killed long ago while escorting a soul through the dark portals. The good news was that he *could* apparently recharge through me—though *why* he could do this when I wasn't a full-energy being, but rather half werewolf, he refused to say. Just as he'd so far refused to recharge. Up until very recently, he'd been more worried about the threat of assimilation—which was when a reaper became so tuned to a human, their life forces merged and they became as one—than the lowering of his ability to heal me.

All that had changed when I'd almost died after a fight on the astral plane. Because, as I'd already noted, without me, no one could find the keys. My father's blood had been used in the creation of the keys, and only someone of his blood could find them.

Of course, making the decision to recharge and actually doing it were two entirely different things. Especially when I barely had enough energy to function, let alone have sex.

Which was another sad statement about the state of my life.

I punched the security code into the discreet system sitting to the left of the doorframe. The device beeped, and the light flicked from red to green. I opened the door but didn't immediately enter, instead letting the scents within the house flow over me.

The most obvious was the smell of death, although it wasn't particularly strong and it certainly didn't hold the decayed-meat aroma that sometimes accompanied the dead. Underneath that rode less-definable scents. The strongest of these was almost musky but had an edge that somehow seemed . . . alien? It was certainly no smell that I'd ever encountered before, although musk was a common enough scent among shifters.

Was that what we were dealing with, rather than a demon? I had to hope so, if only because I then had more of a chance of diverting the search to the Directorate.

The hallway that stretched before us was surprisingly bright and airy and ran the entire length of the house. Several doorways led off it from either side and, down at the very end, double glass sliding doors led out into a rear yard that contained a pool.

Like the front yard, both the hallway and the rear
yard were meticulous—there didn't appear to be a
leaf out of place, and there certainly wasn't even the
slightest hint of dust on the richly colored floorboards. Whoever looked after this place—be it
Wolfgang or hired help—was one hell of a house-
keeper.

I took a cautious step inside, then stopped again,
flaring my nostrils to define where the death scent
was strongest.

"The body lies in the living area down at the far
end of this hall," Azriel said. He was standing so
close that his breath tickled the hairs at the nape of
my neck.

I eyed the far end of the hall warily. Why, I had
no idea. It wasn't like Wolfgang's husked remains
would provide any threat. It was just that smell—
the oddness of it. "Does his soul remain?"

"No. The death was an ordained one."

This meant that a reaper had been here to escort
him to whichever gate he'd been destined for. It
probably would have been comforting news to anyone but Hunter. "Does that also mean whatever did
this isn't a demon? If this death was meant to be,
then surely it can't be an escapee from hell?"

He touched my back and gently propelled me
forward. My footsteps echoed on the polished
boards, the sound like gunshots in the silence. Azriel was ghostlike.

"Whether this death was the result of an attack
from a demon has no bearing on it being ordained

or not. If death is meant to find you, there is no avoiding it."

"Which doesn't actually answer the question of whether or not a demon did this."

"It could be either a malevolent spirit or some kind of demon, thanks to the first portal being open."

And *it* was only open thanks to me.

"*That* thanks belongs to us all," he corrected softly. "It is a blame that lies with everyone who was involved in that first quest."

But in particular, with one.

He might not have said the words, but they hung in the air regardless. And while it was now very obvious that Lucian had an agenda all his own when it came to the keys, I didn't think he was responsible for snatching the first one. He'd been as furious as we'd been over its loss.

Of course, I'd also been sure that he'd never harm me, and his strangulation attempt had certainly proven that wrong. Yet I still believed he didn't want me dead. Not until the keys were found, anyway.

I frowned. "I thought you said malevolent spirits were of this world rather than from hell?"

"They are."

"Then why would the opening of the first gate affect them in any way?"

"Because the dark path is a place filled with dark emotions and, with the first gate open, these emotions have begun to filter into this reality."

"Meaning what?"

I slowed as I neared the living area and trepidation flared, though I still had no idea what I feared. Maybe it was simply death itself. Or maybe it was just a hangover from the hell of the last few weeks. Between escapee demons, malevolent spirits, and psycho astral travelers, I'd certainly been kept on my toes.

Or flat on my back, bleeding all over the pavement, as was generally the case.

"Meaning," Azriel said softly, "that it feeds the darker souls, be they human or spirit."

"So, basically, it's the beginning of hell on earth?" Two steps and I'd be in the living room. My stomach began twisting into knots. I flexed my fingers and forced reluctant feet forward.

"Basically, yes."

"Great." As if the weight on my shoulders wasn't already enough, I now had the sanity of the masses to worry about.

I entered the living room and saw the body.

Or rather, the body-shaped parcel.

Because Hunter had left out one very important fact when she'd described Wolfgang's death.

Not only had he been sucked as dry as a fly caught by a spider, but he'd been entangled in the biggest damn spiderweb I'd ever seen.

Chapter 2

"Oh god," I said, and immediately backed away. Unfortunately, I couldn't retreat far, because Azriel was right behind me. I might as well have backed into a concrete wall. "She could have mentioned some kind of spider got him. I *hate* spiders."

"Whatever was responsible for this death was something more than just a spider," he commented, a slight trace of amusement in his voice.

I scowled up at him. "You *think*?"

He obviously didn't catch the sarcasm, because he added, "Either that, or this was the work of a multitude of spiders, and the pristine nature of this house precludes that possibility."

A multitude of spiders . . . A shudder went through me at the thought. I rubbed my arms and forced my feet forward again. Wolfgang had died lounging comfortably on the well-padded leather sofa that wrapped around the corner of the room. He was fully clothed, though his shirt was undone to his belly button, and his tie and shoes lay on the floor near the coffee table. His feet were crossed at the ankles, and there was a dreamy, relaxed expression frozen on the remains of his face. He'd obviously died totally unaware that anything untoward was happening.

The web that encased him was anchored to the floor near his feet, then spun up his legs and along the entire length of his torso, enclosing his arms and his body in a fine, transparent filament. Two tears on either side of his belly button indicated the puncture site and, if the size of those wounds was anything to go by, we were dealing with a *damn* big spider.

Another shudder ran through me. I took a deep breath that did little to ease the growing sense of horror, then stopped near his feet and flared my nostrils, drawing in the air and sorting through the scents. That odd, alien aroma was stronger here, but it didn't appear to be coming from the body itself but rather the surrounding air. It was as if the scent of the creature had so heavily perfumed the room that it lingered long after it had gone.

I hesitated, then tentatively prodded the silvery casing with a stiffened finger. It wasn't sticky as I'd expected, and felt a little like plastic—almost as if it had hardened in the air. I leaned a little closer to inspect the wounds. Other than a slight discoloring around the edges of the punctures, there was little blood, but the wounds themselves suggested the creature's fangs were at least as thick as my fist.

It was going to take more than one can of fly spray to get rid of *this* damn spider.

I closed my eyes, took another deep, shuddering breath, then said, "What do you know about spider-like spirits or demons?"

"I believe there is a spirit known as the Jorōgumo, but I know nothing about them." Azriel moved around the coffee table, then stopped opposite me, his eyes slightly narrowed as he studied Wolfgang's remains. Power shimmered through the air, sharp and almost bitter in the stillness. It died just as quickly, and his gaze met mine. "There is no brain left in this body, so I cannot read what memories might have remained."

"Hunter did say everything had been sucked away." My gaze rose to Wolfgang's face, which was free of the transparent net. "Is there any way you can find out more about Jorōgumos? I mean, I can Google them, but I can't imagine Google being a reliable source of information when it comes to facts about spirits."

"I can ask, but Mijai fight demons, not spirits."

Meaning I'd probably have to rely on earth-bound resources. Perhaps the Brindle witches could help. I frowned. "Why hasn't his body collapsed in on itself?"

"I cannot say. I am not an expert on spirits, let alone spiders."

"And when it comes to spiders, my knowledge stops at either avoiding them, or killing the fuckers on sight."

I glanced at my watch. Ten minutes gone and, so far, we'd discovered nothing Hunter hadn't already known. I looked around the room, hoping there was something that jumped up and screamed clue. As usual, fate wasn't being overly helpful.

I spotted his jacket flung over one of the kitchen

chairs and walked over to pick it up. His keys were in the left front pocket, and his wallet was in one of the inside ones. Opening the latter revealed his driver's license, several platinum credit cards, and at least five hundred dollars in cash. Robbery obviously wasn't a motive—which was an odd thought when related to spiders or spirits, but perhaps not if we were dealing with some sort of shifter.

Frowning, I put his wallet back and went through the rest of his pockets. The only other thing to be found was a business card for some place called Dark Soul. I flicked it over, but the back was empty. God, I thought, this had better not be another fucking blood whore club. I'd had more than enough of them lately to last a lifetime. I placed the card back where I'd found it, then did a search of the rest of the house. As I expected, I found absolutely nothing.

This was useless—and I told Hunter as much when I went outside to call her back.

"I do not care what you think in regards to the viability of this task," she snapped. The vid-screen had been turned off at her end, and I couldn't help but be a little thankful for that. I had the distinct impression her expression would not have been pleasant. "I merely want your impressions of the kill."

I couldn't see the point of that, either, given my impressions were unlikely to be any different from hers, but I took a deep breath and said, "He was killed by something that appears to have spiderlike tendencies. There's a musky scent in the air that is not dissimilar to the musk of shifters, but if it *is* a

shifter, then it's one I've not come across before."
My voice was as sharp as hers, which probably
wasn't wise given all the shit I'd said earlier, but
then, she *was* on the other end of the phone rather
than in person, so she could hardly smack me down.
Not immediately, anyway. "I didn't find anything
that hinted at who or what else might have been
here, but Azriel said there are spider spirits known
as Jorõgumos, so it's possible we're dealing with
one of those. I did find a business card for someplace called Dark Soul."

"That is—*was*—one of his favorite music venues.
He'd been planning to go there last night."

"Why was he carrying one of their business cards
if he went there regularly?"

"I don't know."

Color me shocked, I wanted to snap, but wisely
resisted the urge. "So he might have picked up his
killer there?"

"Possibly. Dark Soul is not a vampire venue. It
caters to all races who enjoy alternative music."

"Well, it wasn't a human who killed him." Not
unless Spider-Man was fact rather than fiction.

"Of course not," she said coolly. "Wolfgang was
a powerful vampire. He would not have been taken
easily by anyone—or any race."

And yet he'd sat there and allowed himself to be
bound by a web and then sucked dry. I rubbed my
arms against the chill that stole across my skin.
How could anyone—powerful or not—allow something like that?

"Which means either he was drugged, or there

was some form of magic involved." And if it was the former, was there enough of him left to find a trace of it?

"Yes." Hunter's voice still held little emotion, yet it hinted at a fury so deep it scared the hell out of me. "Which is why I wanted you to investigate. Whatever did this was *not* of this world. I'm sure of it. I want you to hunt it down, but do *not* kill it. *That* pleasure I reserve for myself."

Well, I wasn't about to argue over *that* particular order. "If we can find this thing, it's all yours."

"Oh, you had better find it, trust me." She paused, as if waiting for a comment, but what the hell was I supposed to say to a threat like that? After a moment, she continued. "I will arrange for you to talk to Dark Soul's owner and view their security tapes. Perhaps we can identify who—if anyone—he was there with."

"They're hardly likely to talk to me, given I'm not anything official—"

"That will be fixed," she cut in. "Keep me informed."

She hung up again. My fingers clenched the phone so tightly, my knuckles went white, and it was all I could do not to throw the damn thing and then stomp all over it in frustration.

Azriel plucked it from my fingers. "Temper tantrums, as I believe you would call such an action, will do no good. And it may well destroy a perfectly usable device."

I raised an eyebrow. "Have you ever had a good temper tantrum?"

Amusement lurked in the rich depths of his mismatched blue eyes. "No. But I do believe that the longer I reside in your presence, the more it becomes a possibility."

I snorted softly. "You could be right. And for future reference, a well-timed temper tantrum is a very good form of stress release."

"Meaning, I'm wrong in believing there might be more pleasing alternatives than throwing a tantrum?"

I arched an eyebrow and stepped a little closer, but any reply I might have made was cut short as my phone rang. A quick look showed that it was Stane — Tao's cousin, and a black marketer who just happened to be able to hack into any computer system ever created. It was an ability I'd made full use of when it came to Hunter's cases as well as the search for the keys. I half thought about ignoring the call just to continue the gently teasing conversation with Azriel, but I knew Stane wouldn't be ringing unless he'd uncovered something important.

"Hey," I said, by way of greeting. "What's the latest?"

"Well, let's see," he said, the rich tones of his voice more gravelly than usual. He'd obviously been hitting the online gaming hard again. "My mother is insisting I meet the daughter of her best friend and has in fact arranged a double date for this evening. And I believe I have found that storage locker you were looking for."

I blinked at the dual information and decided to tackle the juicier one first. "A double date?"

"Yeah, the mothers are coming. Won't that be fun?"

His voice was dry, and I chuckled softly. "Oh come on, she might actually be *nice*."

"She's taking her mother on a *date*. What does that say about her?"

"Hey, your mother will be there, too, remember."

"Yeah, but my mother has become a conniving witch who plots incessantly to get me married."

"What makes you think her mother isn't?"

"Because," he grumbled, "it was apparently her idea, not her mother's. Besides, the word from the pack is that she doesn't approve of wolf clubs. Hates what they represent."

"She's a werewolf, isn't she? How the hell can she disapprove of the clubs?"

"Who the fuck knows? Maybe she's a prude."

Was it even possible to be a werewolf *and* a prude? It certainly wasn't a likely combination. "If you think it's going to be that bad, don't go."

He snorted. "My mother will make my life hell if I don't go. Trust me."

I grinned. Stane was afraid of his mother. Imagine that. "And the storage container?"

"Oh. Yeah." There was a brief whoosh of sound, and I had the mental image of him scooting from one screen of his massive computer "bridge" to the other. "I couldn't find anything listed under John Nadler's name, but I did find one under Genevieve Sands."

Who was one of Nadler's heirs, according to the information I'd gotten from a ghost. Nadler was the man behind the consortium that had been buying up the land all around Stane's shop. Not that he wanted the land, per se; he just wanted to control what lay underneath it—a major ley-line intersection. Such intersections were places of great power and could be used to manipulate time, reality, or fate. But they could also be used to create a rift between this world and the next, and we very much suspected that whoever had stolen the first key had used the power of the intersection to access the gray fields and find the gates.

Which, in turn, meant that John Nadler was either involved with the sorcerer, or was the sorcerer himself. Unfortunately, he was also a face-shifter, and it was damnably hard to track someone who could alter their facial features at will. Of course, I was *also* a face-shifter, but that didn't make it any easier for me to spot others of my kind.

This particular face-shifter had assumed the identity of the real John Nadler after he'd killed him—a fact we were sure of only because the body of the real Nadler had turned up just as we were getting closer to pinning down the fake. We suspected that at least one of the three people named in Nadler's will was in fact the face-shifter, but so far we'd yet to track any of them down.

"You want to send me the address?" I said. "I might go check it out."

"Just sent you that. I've also hacked into their security cams so we can screen who might be coming and going. But is there anything else you need done?"

I couldn't help smiling at the hint of desperation in his voice. "Haven't we already given you enough?"

"No. I mean, I have a double date I need to get out of, remember."

I chuckled softly. "Think of your mother's wrath, and—as they say in the classics—suck it up, princess."

"Some help you are," he muttered. "The rates are going up next time you want me to do something."

"You'd be bored to death inside a week if we weren't bugging you."

"That," he said grimly, "is undoubtedly true. Think of me suffering while you're off enjoying yourself somewhere tonight."

"Tell you what—I'll send a bottle of Bollinger for you to drown your after-date sorrows in."

"At least *that* would give me something to look forward to." His sigh was overly dramatic. "Chat to you later."

He hung up. Two seconds later, my phone beeped, an indication that Stane's information had arrived. The storage locker was located in Clifton Hill and wasn't all that far away from Stane's shop. I shoved the phone back into my pocket, then locked the front door of Wolfgang's house and met Azriel's gaze. "Can you take us there now?"

He stepped close again and wrapped his arms around my waist. I resisted the temptation to snuggle deeper into his arms, and a heartbeat later we were zipping back through the gray fields.

We reappeared near the intersection of Hoddle Street and the Eastern Freeway exit. The self-storage premises couldn't be missed—it was a three-story brick building that had been painted in orange and blue stripes, with a huge white lock on the front of it.

"How do you plan to access this locker?" Azriel said.

I scanned the building and noted the cameras placed strategically around the perimeter. Undoubtedly, it would be a similar story inside, and that meant it might be wise to indulge in a little face-shifting. If Genevieve Sands *was* connected to Nadler, then they might be keeping an eye on who went near their storage locker. It wouldn't be hard to do—anyone with the right sort of knowledge would be able to hack into the security system. The last thing I wanted was for them to see how close we were. We didn't need another possible lead closing down before it led to anything—or anyone.

"I guess how we approach it depends on who is at the desk," I said eventually. "If it's male, I'll flirt. If it's female, you flirt."

He raised his eyebrows. "The last time we did something like that, you stomped out in what I believe you would call a snit."

"It wasn't a snit," I replied, amused. "It was mere annoyance. You were flirting with a stranger at a time you were refusing to do *anything* with me."

"I am still not doing anything with you."

"That's true." I gave a mock sigh. "God, it's been so long, I can hardly even remember what a kiss is, let alone sex."

"Then perhaps," he said, and stepped closer, "I should remind you."

His lips met mine, and though the kiss was little

more than a tease, it was also the sweetest damn thing I'd ever experienced. It made me feel higher than a kite and warmer than the sun, cherished and oddly alive all in one quicksilver moment. And I sighed in frustration when he pulled back.

"Damn it, Azriel—"

He pressed a finger against my lips, silencing my protest. "What you desire and what your body is capable of are two very different things right now." He gave me a lopsided smile that was oddly endearing. "I want what you want, believe me, but I am not willing to tax your strength any more than necessary. And, right now, that's what we would be doing."

"The whole point of sex *is* to be taxed," I replied, exasperated. "If you're not boneless and replete afterward, then you haven't put enough effort into it."

"What effort can you put into it when you are all but exhausted?" He raised an eyebrow, expression amused. "Trust me, given the risks involved, I want nothing more than your maximum."

I laughed softly, then rose on tiptoes and dropped another quick kiss on his lips. "Believe me, when you give in—and you will give in, reaper—I'll give you one hundred percent, exhausted or not."

"A promise I will hold you to."

"As long as you *do* hold me, I don't care." I reluctantly returned my attention to the building in front of us. "Can't you just pull the information about the storage locker from the mind of whoever is manning the reception desk?"

"I could, but our sorcerer appears to have telepathic abilities, remember, and while it is unlikely he would sense any psychic intrusion on my part, it is a risk we should not take, given he is most certainly aware of my presence on this quest."

I frowned. "Does that mean clouding her perception is out?"

"No. Clouding is more a sensory intrusion than a mental one, and therefore it is safer."

"Then I guess you'd better make whoever is inside think we're cops."

"That I can do." He placed his fingers under my elbow and lightly guided me across to the thick shrubs that lined one side of the nearby parking lot. "If you wish to alter your facial shape, you will not be seen here by either the cameras or those driving by."

"Good idea." While Azriel might be able to stop people from noticing his comings and goings, the last thing we needed was some poor driver spotting what I was doing and having a freak-out. While humanity was as aware of shape-shifters as they were vamps and werewolves, very few knew of the existence of us face-shifters.

I flexed my fingers, then closed my eyes and pictured my own face—from the silver of my hair, the lilac of my eyes, the slight uptilt of my nose and defined cheekbones, to the fullness of my lips. Then I replaced it with more rounded features, thinner lips, and very short black hair. A black so rich it shone blue in the sunlight.

Once that image was frozen in my mind, I reached for the magic. It exploded around me, thick and fierce, as if it had been contained for far too long. It swept through me like a gale, making my muscles tremble and the image waver. I frowned, holding the image fiercely against the storm. Power began to pulsate, burn, and change me. My skin rippled as my features altered, and my hair suddenly felt shorter and somehow finer. As the magic faded, my knees buckled, my legs suddenly weak.

Azriel gripped my arm and saved me from falling.

"Damn," I muttered, leaning against him briefly. "That never seems to get any easier."

"Given you continue to function barely above exhaustion, it is unlikely to."

"It's not like I can do a whole lot about that," I muttered, and forced my knees to lock. "What I need is for the bad guys to stop creating havoc for a month or so."

"A situation that is unlikely. I am actually amazed that your father has let the lack of progress on finding the second key slide for as long as he has."

"He could hardly force me to look when I was all but dead in the hospital. Even he isn't that callous."

"I would not be so sure of that."

Actually, I wasn't. My father had shown a decided lack of parental care up until this point, and I had no doubt that lack would continue.

"Ready to go?" Azriel added.

I took another of those deep, steadying breaths that really didn't help all that much, then nodded. He touched a hand to my back again and guided me toward the front door, his fingers spearing warmth into my spine despite the thickness of my sweater.

A deeper, more resonant energy swirled as we entered the building—Azriel, touching the receptionist's mind to alter her perception.

So what will she see us as?

Police, as you wished.

Good. There were no cameras in this particular area, so the lie wouldn't immediately be uncovered.

The receptionist gave us a cheerful smile. "And what can I do for you both on this rather chilly autumn morning?"

"I'm afraid we're here on official business." Azriel stopped in front of the desk and gave her a warm smile.

Her smile grew. So much for him not flirting. "And what business would that be?"

"We need to know if there's a Genevieve Sands renting a storage unit here."

"Just a moment, and I'll check." She glanced down at her computer, quickly typing, then said, "Yes, she is. It's one of the larger ground-floor units."

"Would we be able to look at it?"

She frowned. "I'm afraid I can't let you in without a search warrant—"

"That's okay," I said, noting with amusement— and perhaps a touch of annoyance—that she barely even glanced at me. "We just want to inspect its location for the moment."

"I can't see the harm in that." She half shrugged. "It's unit G-18. I'll buzz you through the security door; then follow the corridor down and around to your right."

"Thanks, Maggie." Azriel gave her the sort of smile that would have melted the iciest heart. This poor woman had no hope whatsoever, and practically puddled on the seat. "It's appreciated."

"You're very welcome," she all but stammered.

Amusement glittered in Azriel's bright eyes as he turned away. I followed, knowing I probably could have danced around naked and she wouldn't have even noticed. I shook my head in amusement. *You, reaper, are incorrigible.*

He glanced at me, one eyebrow raised, and the laughter I'd caught earlier was now richer in the depths of his eyes. *And why would you say that?*

Because every time you have to cloud the mind of a pretty woman, you flirt.

On the contrary, I am merely polite.

I snorted softly. *Polite doesn't come in the form of a high-wattage, sexy-as-hell smile.*

His amusement deepened, and it shimmered inside me, warm and enticing. *So you think my smile is sexy?*

I rolled my eyes and nudged him with my shoulder. *Fishing for compliments, are we?*

No. I merely ask a logical question. The security door buzzed as we neared it. He caught it with his fingertips, opening it and then ushering me through. *It is the resonance of energy that attracts reapers rather than anything as fleeting as an expression.*

I followed the receptionist's directions, making a mental note of the regularly spaced security cameras, then glanced at him with raised eyebrows and said, *Does that mean you don't think my physical form is attractive?*

Who is fishing for compliments now?

I grinned. *Hey, it's not like you throw them around with great abandon.*

No, he agreed, and touched my back again, his palm still light against my spine yet somehow oddly possessive. Or maybe that was merely wishful thinking on my behalf. *And yes, I find your physical form attractive. But it is the being within that flesh, the timbre and music of all that you are, that is the most dangerous to someone like me.*

Because of the threat of assimilation. It was a sobering reminder of the risk we were taking, and I had to wonder whether it was actually worth it.

But how could I be around him and not want him? That seemed as impossible to me now as it would be to stop breathing.

"Indeed," he agreed softly. Almost grimly. Then he motioned with his free hand. "The locker we seek is just ahead."

I slowed as we neared it. It looked like every other unit in this area in that it was fronted by a double-sized roller door that was padlocked at either edge. I'm not sure why I'd been expecting something else—but maybe it was simply the fact that Nadler didn't seem to do *anything* that could be considered ordinary.

Of course, Genevieve Sands might *not* be connected to him in any way—but I seriously doubted that was the case.

"There is magic here."

Azriel stopped in front of the unit and crossed his arms. His expression gave little away, but blue fire flickered down the sides of his sword, radiating an energy that was oddly tense. Valdis—the name of the demon trapped within the sword, giving the steel a life and energy of its own—was as ready for action as her master.

I had a similar sword strapped to my back, but Amaya was shadow-wreathed and invisible. The only time anyone was truly aware of her presence was when I slid her dark blade into their flesh—although she did have a tendency to scream for bloodshed, and generally at the most inappropriate times.

"But what sort of magic? Good or bad?" I stopped beside him and eyed the roller door dubiously. I couldn't feel anything, but then, I wasn't always sensitive to magic.

"Neither. In fact, it is almost Aedh-like in construction."

I frowned. "The only Aedh we know who play around with magic are the Raziq, and I seriously doubt they'd be involved on *any* level with Nadler."

"There is Lucian."

I frowned. "Yeah, but he isn't capable of magic."

"That we know of."

True. But surely to god *he* wasn't linked to Nadler. Surely to god I hadn't been *that* gullible.

Azriel, perhaps wisely, made no comment about that particular thought.

I studied the innocuous-looking door for several seconds, then carefully raised a hand. As my fingertips neared the metal, energy began to flow across them. As Azriel had said, it didn't feel evil or dark, just wrong. It was also oddly similar to the magic in the circle of stones that had formed a protective barrier around the gateway Jak—my ex, and a reporter who was helping us—and I had discovered underground when we'd been searching for Nadler's base of operations in West Street. And that certainly suggested I'd been right in suspecting a link between Genevieve Sands and Nadler himself. According to Ilianna—who wasn't only my best friend but an extremely powerful witch—every spell was as individual as the person creating it. Two spells having the same sort of feel could only mean the same person was behind both.

"We need to get in there," I said. "We need to uncover what they might be hiding."

"I do not think that would be a wise move."

I frowned. "Why?"

"For one, the magic involved prevents me from entering, and two, I would think crossing the threshold would notify Sands, or Nadler, or whoever else might be the true owner of this container."

My frown deepened. "So is the spell reaper specific, or is it more generally aimed at energy beings?" Because if it were the latter, it would also prevent me from entering.

He hesitated, and his energy slithered around me as he carefully tested the boundaries of the magic. "Reaper specific, by the feel of it."

"Meaning whoever is behind this is more than a little familiar with your presence?"

"Yes." He glanced at me. "Lucian."

"You can't blame him for every bit of evil we come across just because you don't like or trust him," I said, irritated.

"He is Aedh, he was your father's *chrání*, he spelled you, and he is sexually involved with a dark sorceress. Why would he not be a suspect?"

Chrání was the Aedh word for a student or protégé, and it meant that even if Lucian hadn't been involved with the making of the keys, he most certainly knew a whole lot more about them than he'd ever let on. And while he'd been using me to keep track of everything we did to locate the keys—had, in fact, placed a *geas* on me that had made it next to impossible for me to resist him sexually, which was important given he could read my mind only during sex—my father had been keeping track of *him* through me. Blood called to blood, and that apparently meant he not only knew where I was at any given time, but he could read my thoughts from a distance.

"Look, I'm not denying he's involved. I just don't think he's responsible for this." I waved a hand at the door and, as I did so, my fingers brushed the unseen magic. Light danced across them, warm and almost welcoming. Which was decidedly odd. "It seems to react to touch, too."

"That is only logical. If whoever owns this had been hiding the real Nadler's body in a freezer within, then he or she would not wish to risk anyone breaking in."

"So why not ward against Aedh as well?"

"I do not know."

Neither did I, and it piqued my interest. "I've got to get in there. This could be the break we've been looking for."

"I do not think—"

"I know," I cut in. "And I'm going to try regardless."

Irritation swirled down the link between us, thick and sharp. I might not be able to catch his thoughts and feelings unless he wished it, but every now and again emotion got the better of his control. And while that could be a dual-edged sword—especially when it generally happened only when he was really angry over something I'd said or done—I wasn't about to wish it away. I actually liked getting glimpses of what was going on in my generally stoic reaper's mind.

I glanced toward the end of the hallway and studied the security camera. If I was going to get into the storage locker, I'd have to do it in Aedh form—and the last thing I needed was the transformation being caught on tape. "Can you do something about those things?"

"A well-placed blow from Valdis would do a good job of destroying them."

"I was hoping for something a little more discreet than that."

He contemplated the camera for a moment, then said, "Perhaps the woman at the desk can be convinced to turn them off temporarily."

"I'm sure you could sweet-talk the sun out of the sky if it suited you, reaper."

He frowned, though amusement creased the corners of his bright eyes. "That is an illogical statement."

"Which doesn't mean it's not true." I waved a hand. "Go sweet-talk. I'll wait here."

He turned and left. I contemplated the battered roller door for several seconds, then turned my attention to the doors on either side. Would it be worth breaking into them on the off chance there was some form of ventilation between the two rooms? In Aedh form I was little more than mist, so even the smallest of cracks would give access. With any sort of luck, the magic that protected Genevieve's locker was concentrated at the entrance rather than being all-encompassing. A long shot, granted, but surely some sort of luck *had* to fall our way eventually.

I contemplated the door for a few more seconds, then retreated to the other side of the hall to wait. Azriel returned a few minutes later. "The cameras at either end of this hall have been turned off."

I pushed away from the wall and handed him my phone. "I'm going to try entry from one of the other lockers. Hopefully, whoever set the spell might not have considered that eventuality."

"Unlikely. The magic feels encompassing."

"Meaning floor and ceiling, as well as walls?"

He hesitated. "Oddly, not the floor."

"Then maybe that will play in our favor."

"And maybe you just waste your time."

"Maybe. I'm still going to try."

"Of course you are."

He said it with resigned acceptance, and I couldn't help smiling. Then I took a deep breath, releasing it slowly as I called to the Aedh within me. Despite the sheer level of fatigue that still assailed me, she answered swiftly, and with such force, I gasped. It tore through me, a whirlwind of magic that rendered flesh and muscle and bone apart, until I was little more than particles of energy amassed in the air—a being who could see and hear, but not speak. I turned and headed for the locker to the right of the one registered to Genevieve Sands, sliding in through the small gap between the concrete and in the roller door. The area beyond was dark and crammed full of all sorts of boxes and antique-looking furniture. I swung around, scanning the wall that divided this locker from the other, but couldn't see anything that might give me access. But if there was going to be a gap, then it would more than likely be where the wall met the floor or roof, not in the actual wall. I rose up but couldn't see any access points along the joint between the wall and ceiling. Maybe Azriel was right—maybe this *was* a waste of time. But that didn't mean I was about to give up—not before I'd checked all options, anyway.

I made my way back down, slipping between a couple of the old boxes that were crammed along the base of the wall. Dust, cobwebs, and god knows what else fell around me, the bits clinging annoyingly to the particles that were my body. It meant that, at best, I'd be as itchy as hell when I re-formed and, at worst, I'd be brushing bits of debris from my skin for days.

There were lots of skeletal bits of spiders and bugs along the joint between wall and floor, as well as flashes of living things that skittered away as I approached them. I'd always thought being in Aedh form meant I was invisible to things that weren't either energy beings or in some way connected to them, such as the Razan, who were the human slaves of the Raziq. Obviously, I was wrong.

I slipped through another gap between the boxes, but drifted a little too high and caught the edge of the spell protecting the locker on the other side. Energy ran through my particles, a touch of lightning that didn't actually hurt. But it was warning enough that the spell, while it might not be Aedh specific, would certainly react to my presence if I got too close.

I moved on. As I neared the junction of the inner and outer walls, I finally spotted what I was looking for—a slight crack between the concrete of the wall and the floor. I slithered in.

And found emptiness.

Well, almost.

There was magic here—it rippled through me like a mild summer storm—electric, yet not threatening. But that wasn't all there was.

Standing in the middle of the room were two upright stones. I'd seen their like once before—in the tunnels Jak and I had found underneath West Street. Those stones had turned out to be a gateway, though it wasn't one we'd been able to use, so we still had no idea where it went. Maybe these stones were the same.

I approached them cautiously. Warm yellow

light—similar in feel to the light that had danced across my fingertips when I'd touched the magic guarding the door—flared between the two pillars, shimmering and swirling softly in the darkness.

When I retreated, the light faded. I studied the stones for a moment longer, then dropped closer to the floor. The magic that protected the walls and ceiling wasn't evident here. After a moment's hesitation, I called to the Aedh and changed back to human form.

I was already low to the ground, so the drop onto all fours was a little more elegant than usual. I stayed there for several seconds, breathing deep, waiting for the quivering in my muscles and the fierce ache in my head to ease off. Both were the inevitable result of becoming Aedh—I wasn't a full blood, and therefore paid a price that few Aedh did. This time, though, the aftereffect was nowhere near as strong or fierce as it usually was. Maybe constant use was making me more adept.

I pushed carefully to my feet, and a cloud of fibers and dust swirled around me. Another casualty of the Aedh shift was my clothes. They disintegrated just fine, but re-forming them was trickier, as the magic didn't always delineate between bits of me and other particles. And—like the dirt that clung to my atoms when in Aedh form—I often ended up with a dustlike sheen covering my skin rather than fully formed pieces of clothing.

I do not think this course of action wise, Azriel said. His disapproval spun down the mental lines between us, sharp but holding a hint of frustration.

You're probably right, but we need answers, Az-riel, and we're not going to get them without taking chances.

You take too many chances as it is.

Maybe, but what other choice did I have? It wasn't like fate—or anyone else—was running around dropping clues at our feet. I drew my sword and stepped close to the gateway again. Fire flickered across Amaya's dark blade, spearing lilac light across the pillars and sparking the quartz within the stone to life. They stood about six feet tall and, like the ones we'd discovered underground, were covered in writing and symbols that resembled cuneiform. It was ancient, that writing—and *powerful*.

I swept Amaya in an arc around the floor, using her light to check if there was any sort of protection circle present. She was unusually quiet, which meant she detected no immediate threat. It should have been comforting, but it wasn't. Not when Azriel's tension flowed through me like a distant storm.

These pillars have no protection circle. The others did.

Maybe Nadler—or whoever else rents this storage locker—thinks the magic encompassing the perimeter was enough.

I frowned at the stones. *I wonder if these stones are a means of transport like the first ones we found were.*

That, he said, voice sharper, *is not something you should be discovering. Not when you have no idea of the type of magic involved or where it actually goes.*

Yeah, but as I've said, we're not likely to discover our answers by sitting here staring at the fucking things.

Risa—

I know. I know. I'm doing it anyway.

He didn't reply, but then, he didn't need to. His anger came through so thick and fast, it damn near suffocated me.

I gripped Amaya tighter. She began to hiss, the sound soft but fierce, filled with expectation. I continued to stare at the stones and hoped like hell I was making the right decision.

Then, before my courage gave way to common sense, I forced my feet forward and stepped in between the two stones.

Chapter 3

Nothing happened.

No light flare, no caress of magic, nothing. The stones were silent. Inert.

I raised a hand and tentatively brushed the stone's surface. Life pulsed under my fingertips. It was almost as if the rock had life and heart. The magic was there and ready to react. It just hadn't. Yet it had before . . .

I closed my eyes as the realization of what that meant sunk in. I'd been Aedh when they'd reacted, which meant these stones had been attuned to *that* form rather than human.

And there was only one being—one man—who had one, if not both, of those forms and who was also involved in the search for the keys.

Lucian.

Fuck! He really *had* taken me for a ride, and in more ways than one. The bastard had told me— constantly—that he couldn't take Aedh form, that the ability had been stripped from him by the Raziq when they'd tortured him for information. It seemed that might be yet another lie in a growing list of them.

He was not lying about being tortured, Azriel said. *Your father all but confirmed that.*

I raised my eyebrows. *You're actually defending him?*

In this, yes. And it grieves me greatly.

Amusement spun through me. *What about the whole "stripped of his powers" spiel? How much truth was there in that?*

I think it was skillfully mixed with untruths. I do not, however, believe he can attain full Aedh form.

So these stones might not be for his use? And did that mean we had another Aedh—someone we didn't know about—lurking in the background?

Azriel hesitated. *I am no expert in magic, but I suspect that if Lucian does use these stones, then they would be attuned to a full Aedh, in whatever form they might be in.*

Which might explain why they didn't react when I was in human form, but not why they did *when I was in Aedh.*

As I said, I am no expert in magic, but there would be little difference between you and a full Aedh when you take on Aedh form.

I grunted and sheathed Amaya. There was really only one thing I could do now—

Don't. Azriel's voice was as fierce as I'd ever heard it. *The risk is unnecessary. We can keep watch on this place and uncover whether Lucian—*

But even if we do confirm he's using these things, that won't tell us where these pillars take him. We need to know, Azriel. We need to start taking the advantage for ourselves.

But this—

Has to be done.

I cannot follow you when you are in Aedh form. The words practically stabbed into my brain. *No matter where those stones deposit you, until you take human shape again, I will not be able to help you.*

I know. But if I do get stuck, or I'm forced to change shape, I can use Amaya until you get there. She's more than capable of handling most things. I'd barely even finished the thought when Amaya's pleased hum began to run through the outer reaches of my mind. I shook my head in amusement. Trust me to get a sword that not only had a bloodthirsty bent, but also *liked* being complimented.

I am aware of that. I still think this is an unnecessary risk.

It undoubtedly was, but if we really wanted to get ahead of these bastards, we needed to do the unexpected.

I stepped out of the stones and called to the Aedh again. She came, changing me almost instantly, a storm of power whose force seemed even stronger than moments before. It shook me, and I couldn't help but wonder if it had anything to do with whatever Malin had done.

Then I thrust the thought away and drifted closer to the pillars. Once again they came to life, the light pulsing with the same beat I'd sensed when I touched the stone. Meaning I'd been right—they *were* primed to react to Aedh energy.

How they'd react to me actually entering them

was now the question to be answered—and I wasn't going to get that answer by hovering here staring at the damn things.

I forced myself forward, into the heart of the magic.

Just for a moment, there was no reaction.

Then power surged, tearing through my atoms, a sensation that was similar to and yet different from becoming an Aedh. It encompassed the particles of my being, then swept me into a bright orb of energy—where I hung, motionless, for several seconds.

Then the energy surged again, and I was suddenly back between two stones. But not the same two, I realized. These stones were smaller, darker, and stood in a square, windowless room rather than a storage locker.

Excitement and trepidation surged in equal amounts. I carefully moved from between the two stones, then slowly turned around. The room was small—maybe ten feet square—with white walls and coffee-colored carpet that had seen better days. There was nothing else besides the stones, although the carpet still bore the impressions of furniture that had once been present.

I turned fully around and found the door. It was closed and, on closer inspection, locked. Not that that was a problem in this form. I squeezed through the gap between the base of the door and the carpet, and found myself in a long, wide hall. Light flooded in from the ceiling-high, almost industrial-looking window to my right and, beyond it, there was a decent-sized courtyard. To my left were four more closed doors and, down at the far end, what looked to be a kitchen.

Other than the soft ticking of a distant clock, the house was silent. If someone was here, they were deathly quiet. I hesitated, then cautiously moved to the left. I wasn't about to take any chances, even though there was little chance of anyone seeing me in this form.

Anyone human, that was.

Which didn't mean I was safe. Whoever owned this place was, at the very least, involved with a magician. At worst, they were working with either Nadler or Lucian, or both. Either way, they were likely to be more knowledgeable about all things non-human than the average human.

The first door led into a small but neat bathroom, and the next two were bedrooms—both empty. I looked around for some clue as to who might be using them, but other than the fact they were male, I didn't find much.

The fourth door led to another bedroom, but this time, it wasn't empty.

I froze near the door and studied the man sprawled on the bed. The blankets were twisted around his legs, leaving part of his butt and his back uncovered. He was muscular and thickset—the body of a wrestler rather than a sprinter—and his skin lightly tanned. He had two tattoos on the upper part of his shoulders—one of a dragon with two swords crossed above it and the other a ring of barbed wire.

My stomach—or whatever the equivalent was in this form—sank.

We'd seen tats like these several times now, and not only on the man who'd unleashed the hell hounds on Jak and me when we were in the tunnel, but on the misshapen shifters who'd attacked me in a parking lot *and* on the man my father used to his deliver notes to a human courier.

Was this Razan the one from the tunnel? I really couldn't say because I hadn't taken all that much notice of what he'd looked like. But if he wasn't, why was he wearing the same branding as all the others? And why were there Razan involved with the machinations of a dark sorcerer in the first place?

I refused to believe my father was—in any way— involved with a sorcerer. Not when the magic he could command was stronger than anything a mere human—light or dark—could command. And given that he wanted the keys for his own quest of domination, it was hard to believe he'd be in cahoots with Nadler and his schemes. And yet his Razan appeared to have the same branding as this man and the others . . .

Then the reason clicked. Anger surged, so fierce and bright, and the man on the bed stirred.

God, I thought, I'm an *idiot*.

Lucian was the connection. He had to be. He'd been my father's *chrání*, so it was more than possible his Razan bore the same markings as my father's. And he was also involved with a woman who was a dark sorceress. She might not be the one we were after, but the odds were that she at least knew him. After all, how many damn dark sorcerers could there be in Melbourne?

The man on the bed rolled over onto his back and flung his arms wide. I waited for him to settle again, then drifted forward. It was a risk, because Razan were sensitive to the presence of Aedh. There was every chance my being in his room would tug at his awareness and subsequently wake him. But it was a risk I was willing to take, if only to confirm my suspicions about Lucian.

Not that they really *needed* confirming, but there was still some tiny, ever-hopeful part of me that wanted to believe I'd read the connections wrong, that I really *hadn't* been as big a fool as it was beginning to appear.

This room, unlike the previous one, was an utter mess. There were clothes strewn all over the carpet, shoes kicked into haphazard mounds, and piles of men's magazines opened to revealing images scattered everywhere. None of which told me much about the man's identity. But there was also a stack of change on the bedside table, and beside it were his wallet and watch. Unfortunately, the wallet was closed, and in this form I couldn't exactly change that situation.

Or could I?

If, as a half-breed Aedh in human form, I could reach inside a man's body, wrap my fingers around his heart, and squeeze the life from him, why couldn't I extract a driver's license from a wallet in *this* form? Or at least use the energy that was inherent in this form to open said wallet to get a better view of the contents?

It was certainly worth a shot.

I stared at the wallet and imagined the thing opening. Energy rippled along the length of my particles, then spun into a thin rope that glistened like lilac-tinted sunshine in the semidark confines of the room. I envisaged it wrapping around the wallet and, after a moment, the wormlike slither moved forward and did just that.

Pain ran through me, a sharp reminder that I wasn't anywhere near full strength and probably shouldn't be trying this if I wanted to function afterward. As ever, I ignored the warning and imagined the wallet flipping open. After a slight pause, the energy again reacted. The wallet flipped into the air, did a three-sixty, and dropped with a splat on the exact same side it had started on.

It certainly *didn't* open.

The man on the bed stirred, muttering something under his breath. I froze, ready to flee should he show the slightest hint of actually waking.

He reached down his body with one hand, roughly hauled the blankets over himself, then settled back to sleep. If I could have sighed in relief, I would have.

I glanced at the wallet again and tried opening just one side. All I achieved was flipping it completely over—but it was then I finally noticed the sturdy little press stud holding the wallet closed. Until that was undone, I didn't have much hope. As hot lances began to stab through my particles, I concentrated the energy on the press stud and somehow managed to undo it. I quickly flicked the wallet open—and none too soon, because the hot lances exploded into agony, and it was all I could do to maintain Aedh form.

I remained where I was, not moving, not doing anything, until the pain receded to a more comfortable ache, then carefully inched forward. The driver's license—visible through a somewhat grimy plastic window—said the Razan's name was Henry Mack. I might not remember what the Razan in the tunnel had looked like, but I remembered the name. It was a fake—one of two this man was using. His real name—which was part of the information Uncle Quinn had pulled from his mind—was Mark Jackson, and he lived in a Brunswick West warehouse rather than in Broadmeadows as his license stated.

I quickly checked out the rest of the place, but didn't find anything else. I hovered in the kitchen for a moment, staring out the window, wondering if I should risk using the stones to get back to the storage place or simply get there under my own steam. Or, given the lancelike flashes of pain that were beginning to stab through my particles, get as far as I could under my own steam.

Then I actually focused on what I'd been staring at rather blindly and realized it was two more stones. They were less than half the size of the ones in the small box room and formed part of the water feature that dominated one corner of the courtyard. But even from here I could see the cuneiform etched into the glistening stone, which in itself suggested they were at least created by the same hand as the others.

Curious, I headed out to investigate. The stones stood on a small rock island that had been built in the middle of the lily-filled pond. Water spurted from the top of each, then ran down their cuneiform-etched sides before trickling back into the pond.

As I approached the stones, they began to pulse with energy. This time, it was darker, more threatening. I hesitated, then mentally shrugged. I'd come this far—why stop now?

I entered the stones. Again the energy encaged my particles, then swept me not into brightness, but utter darkness. A darkness that was cold, devoid of sensation, and as frightening as hell. Then the energy surged, and I found myself in a very different garden. One that was lush and exotic, filled with plants and the happy calls of birds.

Where the hell was I? The air was hot and moist, and clung uncomfortably to my particles. Somewhere in the distance water bubbled, a soothing accompaniment to all the birdcalls. Yet no birds fluttered through all the greenery, and I soon realized why—the calls were being piped in from somewhere nearby. Then I saw the glass wall. I was in a greenhouse of some sort.

I moved in to the plant life. I had no sense that anything—living or otherwise—was close, but that didn't mean caution wasn't required.

After a few seconds I found a second glass wall, but this one looked out onto a backyard that ran down to sand and then sea. A sea that was blue and bright and vast and was nothing like Melbourne's own bay even on the best of days.

And I still had absolutely no idea where I was.

I followed the wall until I found a set of double doors that opened out into the yard and slipped underneath them. The outside air was cooler, but it was still far warmer here than in Melbourne. I slipped across the manicured lawn, then onto the sand. The sea rushed to greet me, its foamy fingers crashing upward, spraying my particles with salt water.

I studied the beach that stretched endlessly before me and suddenly recognized the long line of high-rise buildings that crowded the shore.

I was in Queensland—the Gold Coast, to be exact.

To have come this far meant those stones held some serious magic. Most transport spells—or at least the ones created by human witches and white sorcerers—were restricted when it came to distance. There were very few people with enough power capable of producing a spell that could take you from one state to another. Which meant that even if whoever the hell had made these stones wasn't involved with Lucian or the key quest, they were someone we needed to be very wary of.

I moved back through the greenhouse and into the house. As you'd expect of a property on such a prime piece of real estate, it was vast, bright, and expensive looking. The decor was minimal and modern, and this lower floor consisted mainly of a pool and barbecue area, as well as changing rooms and a bar. The entire first floor was devoted to a massive kitchen and living area, with panoramic folding glass doors opening onto a balcony that overlooked the beach. The second floor held all the bedrooms. There were no other standing stones that I could find, so maybe the ones in the greenhouse worked both as an entry and an exit point. The one we'd found underground certainly had.

The house was empty, and I could sense no other form of magic protecting it. Nor could I actually see any form of security system installed, which meant I could probably risk resuming my regular shape. I called to the Aedh once more, and the magic answered swiftly, sharply, sweeping me from energy to flesh in the blink of an eye before depositing me in an ungainly heap on the polished floorboards. Which was where I stayed, gulping down air, the pain in my head sharp enough to have tears rolling down my cheeks and my stomach jumping up my throat.

A heartbeat later, energy surged around me; then arms that were warm and familiar and oh so welcome wrapped around me and drew me close. As the side of my face pressed against Azriel's chest, I closed my eyes and listened to the steady beat of his heart, willing my own to match it. After a while, the rapid pace of my pulse began to slow, and the pain lessened.

He shifted his grip and held me at arm's length. "Are you all right?"

I took a deep breath and released it slowly. "Surprisingly, yes."

His gaze swept me, and his expression suggested he wasn't exactly believing that. No surprise, given he was connected to my chi and knew the truth. "Do you know where we are?"

I half smiled. "To paraphrase Dorothy: Toto, we're not in Kansas anymore."

"I'm bound to say that statement makes no sense."

"Do any of my statements ever make sense to you?" I brushed the solo tear tracking its way down my cheek with a somewhat shaky hand. I might have felt stronger changing to and from Aedh form, but the aftereffects still sucked. Big-time.

He rose and held out his hand. "On rare occasions, yes, they do."

I snorted softly and placed my fingers in his. He hauled me up gently, but the world did a brief three-sixty around me, and it was only his grip that kept me upright.

"Damn," I muttered, swallowing bile. "I really am going to have to eat something soon."

"I will refrain from saying I told you so."

"That's mighty big of you." I turned and studied the room. We were in what had to be the master bedroom, given it was twice the size of the other four. It was pin-neat, almost sterile, with little sign that anyone lived here. But someone surely had to—why else would the stones transport us here?

"I cannot say whether someone lives here or not," he said. "But there *is* magic in this place."

I raised my eyebrows. "Really? I didn't sense any when I was in Aedh form."

"That is because the magic has some form of sensory boundary around it. It is very subtle." He motioned toward the closet. "And comes from there."

I studied the double doorway somewhat dubiously, then pushed my feet into motion. The closet turned out to be another room—one as big as my bedroom and filled with enough designer shoes and clothes to make even Aunt Riley's heart sing. One side held feminine things, the other male, and in the middle stood several long, intricately carved Chinese sideboards. Now that we were close, the magic within them was easy enough to feel. It radiated from the drawers and cupboards in gentle waves, caressing my skin with an electricity that felt as dark and as dangerous as the stones in the greenhouse below.

I stopped and rubbed my arms. "Wonder what these things hold."

"The accoutrements of a dark sorcerer, from the feel of it. I would suggest you do not attempt to view them."

"There's not a chance in hell of me doing that." Even if part of me wanted to.

I swung away from the troubling source of magic, donned my gloves again, and went through the clothes, trying to find some clue as to the identity of their owners. Interestingly, all the male clothing—while exquisitely made—tended to be rather old-fashioned in design. If it weren't for the modern labels, it would have been easy to believe they belonged to a time when breeches and waistcoats were all the rage. In fact, they were the sort of clothes Jane Austen's men would have been perfectly at home in.

But again, there was nothing—not even a scrap of paper in pockets—to suggest that the clothes had ever been worn. It was as if we were dealing with a ghost.

But while a ghost could certainly haunt this place, one couldn't actually own it.

Frowning, I spun around and checked the other bedrooms. The result was, as I'd expected, more big fat zeros.

We headed downstairs. The kitchen was all shiny black and fitted out with silver appliances, and while the result was pretty spectacular, all I could envisage was the multitude of fingerprints and dust that would show unless you were vigilant about cleaning. Which whoever owned this place obviously was, because there wasn't a speck to be seen.

Thankful I hadn't ditched the gloves at the warehouse, I carefully opened the drawers and cupboards. All of them contained the usual kitchen paraphernalia, and all of them were as neat as the rest of the house.

"Whoever lives here doesn't seem to agree with your philosophy when it comes to storing things," Azriel commented.

I glanced at him as I moved over to the pantry. He stood in the middle of the oversized living area, arms crossed and expression wary. Like he expected something to jump out at us at any minute—and things certainly *had* during past investigations of places where we weren't supposed to be.

"And what philosophy would that be?" I said, opening the pantry door.

"To dump items wherever and worry about finding them again later."

I flashed him a grin over my shoulder. "Do my untidy tendencies bother you?"

"No. I just find them illogical."

"And now you sound like Spock. And I know that makes no sense because you have no idea who he is." I paused, my gaze falling on the small black organizer attached to the other side of the door. "Bingo."

He was beside me in an instant. "You've found something?"

"Bills." I plucked one out and opened it up.

My stomach dropped.

The person who owned this mansion was *no* stranger.

It was Lauren Macintyre—the dark sorceress who was Lucian's lover.

Chapter 4

"If you were looking for a connection between our dark sorcerer and Lucian," Azriel commented, "I think you just found it."

"But Lauren *isn't* the sorcerer we're looking for. Her magic felt different from the magic I sensed when that first key was stolen."

"And yet the cuneiform on all the stones—both the ones you discovered today and the one you and Jak discovered underground—bear the same markings and energy quality."

"Which suggests she's involved, not that she's the one we're looking for." I shoved the letter back, making sure it was in the exact same position. "Besides, it was a man I saw snatching the key, not a woman."

"You could have been mistaken. We were under extreme pressure at the time."

Extreme pressure was putting it mildly, given we'd been under attack from a horde of insane mutant shifters. "Yes, but I'm not mistaken. It *was* a man."

"There *are* male clothes upstairs. If Lauren is not the sorcerer we seek, then perhaps she lives with him."

That was certainly possible. "We need not only to find out more about her, but to keep an eye on her." I closed the pantry door. "Which means involving Stane again."

"This place has no security cameras that he can hack into."

"No, and that's an interesting point. Why would she own a massive place like this and have no obvious form of security?"

Did Lauren feel so secure about this location—or maybe even her own skills—that she felt no need for protection? Or was it, perhaps, that all her security was centered on the property's perimeter rather than within the actual house itself? It *would* make more sense to be aware of invaders long before they actually reached your door. And while I hadn't seen a security measure when I'd gone down to the beach, that didn't mean there wasn't one. Or that it wouldn't have reacted if I'd been in human form.

"Obviously, she has no desire for anyone to see what goes on in this house," Azriel said.

"Maybe it's not so much what goes on, but with whom."

That someone *wasn't* Lucian. The clothes upstairs hadn't been his size, nor, as far as I knew, his style.

For a change, Azriel made no comment on Lucian and simply said, "Did not Stane have a miniature camera device that proved useful once before?"

"He did." Said device had been made to resemble a bug, and we'd used it in an attempt to get information on a man we suspected of being not only a Razan, but perhaps involved with our sorcerer. Unfortunately, he, like many other of our leads, had turned out to be a dead end—in this case, literally. "I'm not sure if he managed to retrieve it, though."

"You can ask."

"True." I glanced at my watch and sighed. "But I'd better get back to work right now. I have to do Ilianna's shift, as she and Mirri are off celebrating their anniversary."

He raised an eyebrow as he took my hand and tugged me toward him. "An anniversary is something that should be celebrated?"

"Always." My gaze searched his. "I'm gathering reapers have no desire for such frivolity?"

"There is no need for it."

"Why not? I mean, it's not like you're incapable of emotion, and you do live in family units, so the concept of being with someone long term isn't an alien one."

"No." He hesitated. "Reapers do not view or feel emotions in the same manner as humans do. It is more about the harmony of energy than it is emotion."

"So a life mate—"

"Caomh," he corrected.

I made a face at him. "A *Caomh* is someone who is in perfect harmony with you energy-wise?"

"Yes. It is rare, which is why reapers tend to live in very large family units."

"Meaning parents, grandparents, etcetera?"

"Yes. Ready?"

I nodded. "So, what about your family? Do you have any brothers or sisters?"

The only answer I got was the surge of energy as he swept us from Lauren's mansion to the shadowed and minute-by-comparison confines of my office above the café. I blinked, caught my balance, then stepped back and said, "Well?"

"I have both. I do not see them."

Was that an edge to his voice? I frowned. "Why not?"

"I am a dark angel."

My confusion deepened. "So?"

He half shrugged and turned away, moving with easy grace to the sofa on the other side of the room. But red-tinged blue fire flickered down Valdis's sides—a sure sign Azriel was not as calm as he appeared. "Being a hunter is a punishment rather than a glory."

I moved around the desk and sat down. "But with the first gate down and the other two threatened, it's you guys who are holding everything together, not the supposedly more prestigious soul guides."

"They do not see it that way."

I stared at him for a moment, seeing the bitterness beneath the mask. "They don't, or you don't?"

A cool smile touched his lips. "Does it matter?"

"They're your family, Azriel—"

"And they're *not* important." This time there was no disguising the scathing edge, but I had an odd feeling that it was aimed just as much at himself as at me. "Nothing and no one else matters until the task that lies before us is completed."

I snorted softly and reached for the open bottle of Coke sitting on my desk. "And when this task is completed and you go back to hunting those who come through the dark portals, you still won't see them, will you?"

"Do you not have work you must do?"

Though his voice had lost the edge, there was a hard glint in his eyes and Valdis still flickered with angry fire. Frustration ran through me, but I resisted the urge to stoke the fire a little more and took a drink instead. He'd told me a whole lot more in those brief few seconds than he ever had about his reaper life, and while it was nowhere near enough to quench my desire to understand him more, I knew it was better to back away for the moment. Push too hard, and he'd make like a clamshell and not say anything else at all.

So I simply got back to work. It took me a couple of hours to get all the accounts done. Once I'd changed into clothes that weren't literally falling off me, I headed downstairs to help out with the waitressing. Tao was in the kitchen, but we were so damn busy that we barely had time to even smile at each other.

As it neared midnight—and the end of my shift—I counted the takings and secured the cash upstairs, then grabbed four glasses of ice and Coke and shouldered through the kitchen's double doors. The only person in the kitchen was our pot washer, Frank. Neither Tao nor Rachel, our other chef, was in sight, although the fridge door was open and the toe end of a brown work boot was visible. It had to be Rachel's—it was too small to be Tao's.

"Where's Tao?" I asked, handing Frank his drink.

The older man shrugged and wiped the sweat from his face with a brawny arm before accepting the glass with a smile of thanks. He was slightly simple, but he did a damn fine job and he seemed to enjoy it. At least he was reliable, unlike some of the kids we employed.

I swung around and headed for the fridge. "Hey, Rachel," I said, popping my head around the corner of the door. "There's a drink on the counter here for you. Where's Tao?"

"Outside I think, and thanks."

She didn't look up from her stocktaking, and I spun and headed out. The rear door was open, and the breeze was icy compared to the heat in the kitchen. I paused in the doorway, allowing my eyes to adjust to the darkness, but didn't immediately spot anyone.

I frowned. "Tao?"

There was a pause, then, "Here."

My gaze swung to the left, and even then it took me a minute to find him. He was hunkered down in the shadows of the Dumpster, his arms wrapped loosely around his knees.

"You okay?" I walked over and offered him one of the glasses. He smelled of sweat, grease, and ash. The latter had concern slithering through me.

"Thanks." He reached up and took it, but didn't lift his eyes. Didn't look at me.

"Tao, what's wrong?"

"Nothing." His voice was monotone. Clipped. "I'm fine."

"Then look at me." I squatted down in front of him and gently touched his chin. I might as well have touched a furnace, and I couldn't help the reflex to jerk my fingers back.

"Yeah," he said. "Nice, isn't it?"

"And the reason you're out here, I'm gathering." The fire elemental he'd consumed—the one he was locked in a constant battle with over control of his own body—didn't do too well in darkness and cold. Normally he'd just retreat to the freezer when the thing inside him started to threaten again, but with Rachel in there doing a stock take, the night air was the next best bet. I touched his chin again, ignoring the sting of heat as I forced him to look at me. His eyes—normally a rich, warm brown—were alien and fire filled. "Never turn away from me, Tao. You are not a monster, not now, not ever. Not to me, not to Ilianna, not to anyone that will ever matter."

He jerked out of my touch and snorted, the sound sharp with disbelief. "You say that now, but when the monster gains control, it'll be another damn story—"

"But it won't," I said sharply. "Because you're stronger than it is. So stop sitting there feeling so damn sorry for yourself and tell me about your date last night."

Just for a moment, I felt the flash of his anger—it rolled over me like the heated wind of a desert, drying my skin in an instant and sending little sparks dancing across my sweater. Then it dissipated, and he chuckled softly. "You really *do* like tempting the devil, don't you?"

"I have to deal with the devil in the form of Madeline Hunter on an almost daily basis, so maybe I've just become a little blasé about it." I sat down beside him, my shoulder touching his lightly. Although the heat was fierce, the tension within his body began to dissipate almost immediately. "And you avoid talking about your dates only when they go like crap. What happened?"

"Nothing. She was lovely, we had a good time, and we parted making plans for another date."

"So why all the doom and gloom?"

He sighed. "Because I'll have to break it off. She really *is* nice."

I frowned as I took a sip of drink. "I'm not understanding the logic of that statement."

"It's this." He waved a hand down the length of his body. "How can I commit to anyone for any amount of time when I have no idea just how long—if ever—it's going to take me to control this thing?"

I just about choked on my Coke. "Good grief, did you just admit to a connection? Is the lone wolf—the man who doesn't believe in long-term commitments—actually thinking he might have found the woman who could change that?"

He grimaced. "We went on *one* date—"

"And sometimes that's all it takes. You're a wolf, not a human or a monk."

He snorted. "I'm half wolf, and I'm certainly *not* a monk."

"Neat sidestep of the actual question, my friend."

He smiled. It was a somewhat pale reflection of his usual smile, but I was happy to see it nonetheless. "God, you're more tenacious than a dog with a bone. And yes, there was a connection."

"Then I can't see the harm in chasing it." I hesitated. "And it might just give you another reason to fight."

"Or another person I'm fearful of hurting."

"You won't." I nudged him gently. "I have faith in your strength, Tao."

He took a deep breath and released it slowly. "Yeah. And that scares the hell out of me, because you're seeing what I'm not feeling."

"Risa?"

I glanced up as Rachel appeared in the doorway. "What?"

"There's a gentleman here to see you."

"Business or personal?" I frowned as I glanced at my watch. It was after midnight, so it could hardly be business.

"He didn't say. Just said it was urgent." She shrugged, then added, "Tao, I may need help in a couple of minutes. A big group just came in from the Blue Moon wanting burgers."

"I'll just finish my drink and then I'll be in."

She nodded and disappeared. I climbed to my feet, then hesitated and looked down. "I can pull Danny off waiter duties to help Rachel if you'd like a few more minutes out here."

"It won't help much. I'll be fine." He squinted up

at me, expression half-mocking. "Isn't that what you're constantly telling me?"

It was a rebuke—a gentle one, but a rebuke nonetheless. I smiled, though it felt a little tight. "Yeah. And I'll keep saying it until you damn well believe it."

And with that, I left him. There was only so much I could say and do because, in the end, I couldn't help him win his war. He had to find the strength— and the desire—within himself to stop the elemental from taking over completely.

And, despite what I kept saying, part of me feared he wouldn't find either.

I walked back through the kitchen and into the café. The place was beginning to fill up again with wolves and a spattering of other non-humans, but we'd rolled into the next shift roster and there were plenty of people to deal with the rush. I couldn't see anyone obviously standing by themselves, so I poked my head back into the kitchen and said, "Where did you put him?"

"End booth, near the bathrooms," Rachel replied, without looking up.

"Thanks."

I headed down to the last booth, only to discover there was no one in it. But there was certainly someone standing in the shadows to the right of the booth. My gaze traveled up the long, lean length of him and clashed with his darkness.

This was no stranger. This was Markel Sanchez, one of the vampires who'd been ordered to not only follow me about astrally, but report my every move back to Hunter.

And as a Cazador, he was one of the most dangerous men I'd ever met.

I stopped abruptly. "Why are you here?"

"I am under orders, as you no doubt suspect." His voice held neither warmth nor inflection and yet somehow managed to be pleasant.

"So who's following me about on the gray fields right now?"

"Nick Krogan is currently on duty. Janice Myer shares the task at other times." He shrugged, the movement elegant. "It is my night off."

So they had female Cazadors? I guess there was no reason why they shouldn't, but it surprised me, for some reason. "And yet here you are."

"Because the wise in this world do not ignore the wishes of Madeline Hunter."

And yet I baited the bitch. What did that say about me? "Are you here to poke me into action or what?"

Amusement flickered through the darkness of his eyes and briefly warmed the coolness of his expression. "I am not here to poke. I merely deliver."

"Considering you're here under orders from Hunter, I'm rather hesitant to ask what, exactly, you're delivering."

The amusement was more pronounced, but he merely reached inside his rather classy-looking black trench coat and withdrew a small leather folder. With some trepidation, I took it and opened it up.

It was a badge. According to it, I was now an official investigator for the high vampire council. Talk about the shit-hole getting deeper.

I blew out a breath that did little to ease the tide of tension and shoved my shiny new credentials into the back pocket of my jeans. "Is that it?"

"For now, yes." He hesitated, his dark gaze flicking past me briefly. Then, more softly, he added, "Tread warily with Hunter on this one, Risa. She is ready to tear someone's throat out over this loss, and you are already close to pushing her past the limit."

I stared at him for a moment, then swallowed heavily. "Thanks for the warning."

"You are most welcome." A slight smile touched his lips, and just for a moment lent his austere features a surprising warmth. "I actually enjoy this duty. It makes a pleasant change from bloodshed, and you are certainly never boring."

I half smiled. "You obviously haven't been following me around for long enough, then."

"Perhaps not." He touched my shoulder lightly as he stepped past. "Be respectful. At least until this killer is caught."

"I will."

He nodded and walked away. I turned, watching him move through the crowd with ease, wondering how long he'd been a Cazador. He certainly wasn't the cold-blooded killing machine I'd grown up believing them to be—not on the surface, anyway. Of course, neither was Uncle Quinn, and he'd been a Cazador for centuries.

But that, I knew, was a rare feat. Most either died

on the job or were killed by the council after the endless killing sent them insane.

I headed back upstairs. Azriel still sat on the sofa, and I shook my head as I walked over to my desk to grab my coat, purse, and keys. "Don't you ever get bored, sitting there doing nothing?"

He raised an eyebrow. "Who said I was doing nothing?"

I glanced around. "Well, that's what it looks like from where I'm standing."

"Well, perhaps you should stand a little closer."

I grinned. "I keep trying. You keep pushing me away."

He rose and plucked the jacket from my grip, holding it out for me. "I did not mean in the physical sense."

I snorted softly as I shoved my arms into the sleeves. "Well, I can hardly get close to you mentally. The connection isn't two-way, remember?"

"I was not talking about either physical or mental connections."

I swung around, but he didn't move his hands, and his fingers trailed across my skin. His touch was warm, electric, and stirred to life the unsatisfied embers of desire once more. "What other connection is there?"

He hesitated. "For you and I, perhaps no other."

It was the "perhaps" portion of that statement that had me intrigued. "But reapers *do* have other choices?"

"Yes. It is the manner of our beings. This world of yours is filled with a vast array of energy harmonies, and it is a beautiful and wondrous thing to listen to."

"And rather noisy, I would have thought."

He smiled. "You learn to tune out the noisier melodies."

I arched an eyebrow. "You don't seem to have much luck tuning me out."

"No, but then, you're noisier than most. And more determined." His gaze lingered on mine for several heartbeats and, just for a moment, those bright depths showed a hunger as fierce as anything I was feeling. But it was gone just as quickly. He released his light grip and stepped away. "You're going to talk to the manager of Dark Soul now?"

I sighed in frustration, but there was little point in saying anything. He'd already stated that nothing would happen between us until I was stronger. "Yes. I'll drive, though. I feel like getting some air for a change."

He nodded. "I shall meet you there."

With that, he disappeared, making me wonder if he'd come closer to the edge than I'd presumed.

He didn't answer that particular thought, so I headed into the changing room, donned my leathers, then headed out to the secure underground parking lot where I kept my newly repaired Ducati.

Of course, she was no ordinary bike, but one of the first hydrogen-powered bikes to come onto the market. She was also the first thing I'd bought when RYT's finally began making a profit. And while she was nowhere near as efficient or as powerful as the current generation of hydrogen-fueled bikes, she was still sleek and sharp and comfortable, and that was enough for me.

I stashed my purse in the under-seat storage, then shoved on the helmet and sat down. The leather seat wrapped around my butt like a glove, and I couldn't help smiling as I fired her up. The vibration through the metal told me she'd come to life, although there was little other noise. Hydrogen bikes ran so silently that when they'd first become commercially viable, state laws had required manufacturers to add a fake engine noise device to warn people of their approach. I kicked up the stand and headed out. The night was cool and the streets relatively clear of traffic, enabling me to let loose. My grin just grew. Damn, I'd missed this.

Unfortunately, even though I'd taken the long way around, I reached Dark Soul far too soon. I reluctantly found parking up the road from it, then stored my helmet and walked back. Azriel appeared by my side as I neared the entrance.

"You should do that more often," he said softly.

"Do what?" It was said absently as I eyed the building in front of us. Dark Soul matched its name. It might not be a vampire-only hangout, but with blacked-out windows and smoke drifting out through the gothic metal gates guarding the doorway, it certainly gave off a dangerous vibe. Or maybe that was merely the haunting, ethereal melodies drifting from the shadowed interior.

"Ride your bike. It makes your soul glow."

I stopped abruptly and swung around to face

him. "Damn it, Azriel, you're going to have to stop doing that."

Confusion briefly crossed his features. "Stop what? *Complimenting* you?"

"Yes." I shoved my hands in my pockets and forced my feet onward again, feeling suddenly foolish.

He was beside me in an instant. "Why is this suddenly a problem?"

"Because," I muttered. "It just makes me want you more."

"Ah." Amusement laced his tones. "I see."

"No, I'm betting you don't."

"Then you would be wrong, Risa Jones."

I glanced up, saw that flare in his eyes again, and my breath caught briefly in my throat. Because it *wasn't* just need. Wasn't just desire. It was far deeper—far scarier—than that. Something that should not—could not—be, if only because we were two very different beings from two very different worlds. We might have made a decision to pursue this thing between us, but he was not of my world and never could be. What I'd just seen could *not* be anything more than an echo of my own emotions. It was an illusion—one that would turn to ash and totally destroy me once all this was over.

But maybe it was already far too late to start worrying about *that* happening.

I swallowed heavily. "Well, it wouldn't be the first time, would it?"

"No. And more than likely not the last."

Sadly, a truer statement had never been made.

The doorman opened the metal gates for us, and Azriel lightly cupped my elbow and guided me into the interior. It was, as the name suggested, a dark place, and it took a couple of seconds for my eyes to adjust. There was little noise in the room, even though it was full. Everyone's attention seemed to be trained on the stage at the far end of the room, their expressions one of rapture as they listened to the dark-skinned woman who played a pan flute. The music was haunting and beautiful and definitely not something you'd hear on the radio. I wasn't sure it was worthy of the rapture that seemed evident around us, but then, a pan flute, however nice the sound, wasn't really my cup of coffee.

The room itself was thin and narrow. A metal bar lined the left-hand side, and the scents emanating from it suggested it wasn't only booze being served, but synth blood. Maybe that was the reason behind the darkness—they didn't want to scare the human patrons with the knowledge of what they were serving vampires. It certainly wasn't illegal to serve synth blood, but it wasn't often done in places that catered to all races. Humans, vamps, and blood— even if only synthetic stuff—sometimes *weren't* a very good combination.

I made my way across to the bar. A small, thin vampire came up and gave me a pleasant smile. "What can I do for you?"

"I need to talk to the manager."

He raised a pale eyebrow, his gaze briefly skating down my length. Or what he could see of it, anyway, given the bar stood between us. Energy spun through the air, teasing the outer edges of my mind. He was trying to read me telepathically, but he didn't have a hope in hell, thanks to the superstrong nano microcells that had been inserted into my earlobe and heel. Nanowires—the predecessor of the microcells— were powered by body heat, but for the wires to be active, both ends had to be connected so that a circuit was formed. The microcells were also powered by body heat, but they were contradictory forces that didn't need a physical connection. Once fully activated, the push-pull of their interaction provided a shield that was ten times stronger than any wire yet created.

With them in place, no one was getting inside my head. Well, *almost* no one. Azriel certainly had no problems, and I suspected Lucian could read me more than he'd ever admitted.

And then there was Hunter, who always seemed to catch my thoughts at inopportune moments. Like when I was cursing her.

The energy died and he sniffed. It was a somewhat disdainful sound. "And who might I say is wanting her?"

"Risa Jones." I hesitated. "I'm here on orders of the vampire council."

"Really?" Amusement touched his mouth. "Just a moment, and I'll see if she's in."

"Tell her she'd better be, because she really *wouldn't* want a visit from Madeline Hunter right now."

The other eyebrow rose to meet the first, but he didn't say anything, just spun around and headed down the far end of the bar, disappearing through a rather solid-looking door.

I leaned back against the bar and studied the woman on the stage. "Do you think she might be our suspect?"

Azriel glanced at her, then shook his head. "She is a vampire. Whatever killed Hunter's friend was definitely something more."

"But the music she's playing seems almost hypnotic. I mean, look at them." I waved a hand around. "They can barely take their eyes off her."

"That is deliberate on her part. She feeds off them."

My gaze jumped sharply to his. "She's an *emo* vampire?"

"If that is a vampire that feeds off the life force of others, then yes."

"An emo feeds off emotion, not life force." I frowned at the woman. "Is anyone in danger?"

"I would suspect not. She appears to be taking only a small quantity from each—it amounts to little more than minutes from their lives."

"It shortens their *lives*?"

He raised an eyebrow, amusement lurking around the corners of his mouth. "Did I not just say that?"

"Apparently." I scrubbed a hand through my short hair. "Should we try to stop her?"

"That is not why we are here; nor is it your place to do so. If she takes it too far, the Directorate will deal with her."

"And will she? Take it too far, I mean?"

He studied her for a moment, his eyes narrowed.

"That possibility is there. It always is whenever a life depends on feeding from others."

"Huh." I glanced over my shoulder, saw the barman coming back, and turned around.

"You have a couple of minutes," he said. His tone held a mocking edge as he added, "Seems she'd prefer not to have Hunter after her."

"She's through that door?" I nodded toward the heavy wooden door.

"Yes." He picked up a tea towel and began polishing glasses, his expression one of disdain. Hunter's lackeys, it seemed, were not held in high regard in this place, even if the woman herself was feared.

I pushed open the heavy wooden door and stepped into a long, semidark corridor. Several doors led off it, all of them closed except the one down at the far end. Light flickered from within—some sort of computer screen, I thought, as I headed down. My footsteps echoed lightly, but no one came out to usher us into the room or greet us.

I paused at the doorway. The room was almost bare, with little more than a bank of security monitors and a large desk—complete with a light-screen monitor and keyboard—in the room. Behind the desk, in a chair that was larger than she was, sat a diminutive, dark-haired woman. She didn't bother looking up from whatever it was she was reading, merely waved a hand in a "come in" motion.

Given there were no seats on our side of the desk, I stopped in front of it and waited.

And waited.

She tests you, Azriel commented.

I gather that. My reply was grouchy. *Why is it that female vampires seem to be such bitches?*

Perhaps they feel the need to prove themselves more.

I snorted softly. *Or they just like being bitches.*

That is also possible. Perhaps you should flex a little muscle. Or would you prefer me to?

She's hardly likely to respect me more if I ask you to beat her up. By the same token, I doubted I'd actually have what it took to do that. I might be part were, but she was vampire. But then, I *did* have other talents I could call on—talents she *wouldn't* have seen before.

"You know," I said, keeping my voice conversational, "I came in here to ask a few polite questions about Wolfgang Schmidt, but if you'd rather do things the hard way, I'm more than happy to oblige."

She finally looked up, her expression mocking. "Am I supposed to cower in fear? Because, let's be honest here, a werewolf provides little threat to one such as I; nor does a man who wears the mask of death."

She sees you as a reaper?

Yes. To her, he added, "Then you are a fool."

"And certainly not a good judge of character." I raised a hand and called to the Aedh, then siphoned the surge of power into my raised fingertips. They went translucent in an instant, neither flesh nor Aedh, but somewhere in between. Her gaze went wide. I added, my voice still even, "Because, you see, I'm not *just* a werewolf. I'm someone who can reach into your chest, wrap my fingers around your heart, and rip it beating and bloody from your flesh."

She blinked, staring at my hand in awe and perhaps the tiniest touch of fear. And I have to admit, I *liked* seeing that, if only because I was getting a little sick of being on the wrong end of fear all the time.

Maybe it really *was* time for me to start flexing a little muscle.

"What are you?" she said after a moment.

"As I said, something more than a werewolf." I released the Aedh and let my hand return to full flesh. "Now, if you've finished with the games, tell me about Wolfgang Schmidt."

She shrugged. The fear—if indeed that was what I'd seen—was gone, but so, too, was her somewhat disdainful demeanor. "He's a regular, comes in two or three times a week."

"And he was in here last night?"

"Yes."

"With anyone?"

"No."

Obviously, she had every intention of answering what I asked and nothing more. "Then did he leave with anyone?"

"I can't say. I don't watch the movements of every single patron."

"Then why have the large bank of security monitors in the room?"

She smiled. "They are not trained on individuals. I simply like to be aware of what is going on in that room at all times."

A controlling bitch, in other words. Maybe I should have called Hunter instead of flexing a little Aedh muscle — the resulting fireworks might have been interesting.

"Then I want access to all the tapes from last night. Now."

"And you can prove you are actually from the council? Because I am not inclined to show those to any random stray off the street."

I ignored her jibe and tossed my badge onto her desk. She picked it up, briefly studied it, then handed it back. "Why do you wish to see the tapes?"

"Because Wolfgang Schmidt is dead. He was murdered last night after he left here."

"That is sad news indeed." It was hard to tell whether she actually meant it or not, because there was little emotion in either her voice or her expression. "You may view the tapes in the room opposite. I shall port them over to the screen there."

"Just the ones for the times he was here, not the entire night."

Another cool smile touched her lips. "Of course."

I spun and walked over to the other room. The lights came on as we entered, revealing another sparse room. At least there were two chairs here — one behind the desk and the other in front. I sat behind the desk, found the ported tapes on the screen, and hit PLAY. The quality wasn't top notch, but I guess it didn't have to be if the only reason she had the cameras was to source out trouble before it really started.

There was no sound, but the woman spotlighted on the stage seemed to hold the audience under the same sort of spell as tonight's woman. She had pale skin, black hair with an oddly jagged red streak in it, and coal-black eyes. She wasn't playing the pan flute, however, but some sort of short-necked lute. I hit FAST FORWARD and rolled through about an hour's worth of film before I spotted Wolfgang. He came in just after midnight, sat at one of the tables close to the stage, and watched the woman with the same sort of rapt attention as everyone else.

When the woman finished her set, she came down and sat with him. They chatted for another half hour or so; then the woman retreated—but not for long. She and Wolfgang left together.

We had a suspect.

I froze the screen on the woman's image, sent both Hunter and myself a copy of it, then switched off the computer and went back to see bitch-face.

"You were successful?" she said, without looking up.

"Who was the entertainer you had on last night? Wolfgang left with her."

"Her name was Di Shard. She wasn't one of our regulars, just someone brought in at the last minute."

"Have you got her contact details?"

"Yes." She reached into her desk and handed me a business card. *Classique Entertainers,* it said. *Specialist in art, chamber, and classical musicians.* She added, "Anything else?"

I hesitated. "If there is, we'll be back. Have a pleasant evening."

Her smile was as insincere as my words. "Oh, you, too."

I spun on my heel and got out of there. Once we were out in the cool air of the night, I drew in a deep breath and released it slowly. "I hate dealing with vampires. I know the world at large doesn't care about that, but I'm just putting it out there."

"You are right," a flat and all-too-familiar voice behind me said. "The world at large doesn't care. Nor do I."

I inwardly groaned, but somehow managed to fix a smile in place as I turned around. "And to what do I owe this pleasure? Or is it simply a matter of you not trusting me to do my job?"

Did Markel not warn you to be pleasant? Azriel commented. He was standing so close that Valdis's energy streamed over me, little flashes of fire that spoke of their readiness for action.

I am. It's not like I called her a bitch or anything.

Her dark eyes flashed. As usual, she'd caught the one thought I didn't want her to catch. One of these days I was going to learn.

Maybe.

"I was told you were here. I was close by, and thought I might get a report firsthand."

I grimaced. "There's not a lot to tell. Wolfgang left with Di Shard, last night's entertainment. I've already sent you her picture."

"Yes, and we're currently searching for all relevant details. Unfortunately, the entertainment agency that manages her maintains regular office hours, so we will be unable to talk to them until tomorrow."

How inconsiderate of them. "At least you can put an APB out on a woman matching her description or something."

"Hardly. She is mine to find and mine to kill."

There was death in her eyes. It might not be aimed specifically at me, but it would take only the slightest nudge and I'd be in her sights.

I had no intention of nudging.

"Then what do you want me to do? Until we talk to the agency or she kills again, the investigation has basically stalled."

"As I said, I have ordered a thorough search through both Directorate and council resources. We will uncover everything there is to uncover about this woman. In the meantime, you are to keep looking, as well."

"Of course." I said it politely, without inflection, yet still that darkness flashed. Sweat began to trickle down my spine, and my heart began to race. Never a good thing when standing in front of a vampire on the edge.

But all she said was, "Keep in touch."

I nodded. She shadowed, disappearing from my sight but not my senses. Only when the trail of her scent told me she had truly gone did I release my breath and turn around. "Will Hunter ever cross the line and become fodder for Valdis?"

"Hunter has crossed the line more than once, but Valdis will not taste her flesh unless she attempts to harm you."

"Damn. I was hoping you could bend *that* particular reaper ruling." It would be nice not to have to worry about the bitch, in any way, shape, or form.

A smile teased the corners of his mouth. "Trust me, I am most aggrieved by that particular ruling myself. Do you head home now?"

"Yeah. I'd better get some rest before I fall down dead or something." I rose on my toes and dropped a quick kiss on his lips. My own tingled in response, and it took a huge amount of willpower to step back. "I'll see you there."

He nodded and disappeared, though the heat lingering in the air told me he hadn't gone far. I walked back to my bike and rode through the almost empty streets, half wishing I could just keep following the road out into the darkness and the countryside, away from all the madness that had become part of my life of late. But that, unfortunately, wasn't an option.

Home was a square, two-story brick building situated in the heart of Richmond, and its somewhat bland gray exterior belied the beauty of its internal space. Ilianna, Tao, and I had purchased the old warehouse fresh from college and had renovated every inch of it—and were still regularly updating it with the latest and greatest technology.

After parking in the garage, I ran up the stairs to the thick alloy door that was both fire- and bulletproof and looked into the little security scanner beside it. Red light swept across my eyes, and a second later the locks tumbled and the door slid silently open.

The huge industrial fans that dominated the

vaulted ceiling whirled lazily, gently stirring the aromatic air. The place was silent, and though the electrochromic windows weren't on blackout, there was little light coming in from the street.

"Lights on low," I said as I strode toward the kitchen. Soft mellow light flared through the darkness, gleaming off the exposed metal struts and lending the brick walls additional warmth. Tao had left the remains of last night's roast in the fridge, so I made myself a sandwich and a coffee and worked my way through both as I sorted through the stack of mail sitting on the kitchen table.

With that done, I had a quick shower, then headed for bed. I woke hours later with the sensation that something was wrong. For several minutes, I did nothing more than lie there, listening to the silence and wondering what the hell it was that I'd sensed. The apartment was silent, and there was little in the air to suggest that I was anything other than alone.

And yet the wrongness remained, scratching along the outer edges of my consciousness.

Frowning, I groped for my phone. No messages. Not that I'd really expected any. Tao would have finished his shift several hours ago and was no doubt chasing tail at one of the clubs, and Ilianna was with Mirri. If I rang either—especially given it was barely eight in the morning—I would not be popular.

"Perhaps it is nothing more than a premonition," Azriel said.

I twisted around. He stood at the window, his

hands behind his back, his stance that of soldier on guard. Valdis was silent, but her hilt, touched by a glimmer of sunlight, gleamed like a star.

"I can do without premonitions like that, thank you very much." I rose and padded across to where he stood. Tension rolled briefly across his shoulders, but he didn't otherwise acknowledge me. "Especially when they're that fucking vague."

My gaze dropped from the broadness of his shoulders to the stylized tattoos decorating his well-defined back. While the biggest of these was the Dušan, there were others. Some were recognizable—like a rose, or an eye with a comet's tail—while others appeared to be little more than random swirls. He'd told me once they were his tribal signature, although I had no idea what that really meant.

I raised a hand and ran my fingertips along the length of one of the swirls. The tattoo pulsed with dark fire, and tension rippled down the muscular length of his back.

"Azriel—"

"What you want is not wise, Risa."

"I don't care."

"I know." There was a hint of resignation in his voice, but he still refused to turn around.

I let my fingers trail on, tracing the outline of a comet. The tension in him grew. "Tell me," I said softly. "If you and I were both reapers, would you be standing there with your back to me right now?"

"No, I would not."

"Then don't do it now."

He sighed. "You do not understand the risk—"

"If assimilation is our fate, Azriel, then it will happen whether or not we make love."

"I was not talking about assimilation."

"Then what were you talking about?"

He didn't answer. He never did when it came to questions like that. I tried a different tack. "You once said that reapers make love by combining energies. Can we at least attempt something like that, if you're so set against physical lovemaking right now?"

"We could." He hesitated. "But I doubt it would be any wiser, and for even more reasons."

"Damn it, Azriel, just this once, why don't you forget reason? What the hell do you *want*?"

For a moment I thought he wasn't going to answer. Then he sighed and said, almost inaudibly, "You."

And with that, he turned around, took me in his arms, and kissed me fiercely.

Chapter 5

There was nothing sweet about this kiss, nothing soft, because it was filled with all the hunger of a man in desperate need. I wrapped my arms around his neck and returned it in kind, and for what seemed like ages, there was nothing but the kiss and the desire that exploded between us.

When he finally pulled back, his eyes burned with a hunger deeper than anything I'd ever seen before. "Just so you know, reapers do not engage in kisses like that."

"Well, they sure as hell *should*."

He smiled, then caught my hand and led me toward the bed. "I agree that there is something rather satisfying about flesh-on-flesh contact, be it lips or something more intimate."

"Something more intimate?" Amusement bubbled through me. "That's a polite way of putting it, I guess."

"I am nothing if not polite." He released my hand and sat cross-legged on the bed, then motioned for me to do the same. "Press your knees against mine."

"If a reaper's idea of sex doesn't involve more

touching than this," I commented, "I don't think I'm going to like it very much. Especially given I'm naked and you're not."

"Trust me, our state of dress will not matter." His smile creased the corners of his eyes and made my heart do a happy little dance. "And I am not entirely sure this will even work—although there is enough Aedh in you that it should—so behave."

"I am yours to command."

"If only." Though his voice was bland, it held a hint of sadness that tugged at something deep inside. "Because you are still flesh based, we will have to take this slowly. Are you ready?"

I smiled. "You should know me well enough by now to guess that answer."

"True." A smile briefly lifted the corners of his mouth; then his expression became serious again. "Close your eyes and concentrate on nothing more than your breathing."

"That hardly sounds like fun."

"Stop talking and concentrate if you want to do this." It was softly said, yet held a note of iron.

I shut up.

"Now," he continued. "Let go of the awareness of all that is around you, until there is no sound, no scent, just you and every intake of breath."

Meditate, in other words. I closed my eyes and concentrated on nothing more than breathing in and out. My heartbeat began to even out, and a sense of peace settled around me. As the minutes slid by, my breathing slowed further, until I was on the edge of an almost trancelike state.

"Feel," he said, picking up my hand and placing it on his chest. His skin was warm under my fingertips, his heart a steady, strong drum. "The rhythm of my breath. Breathe in as I breathe out."

My fingers rose with every movement of his chest, so even though I couldn't hear his breathing, it was easy enough to set mine on a separate course to his.

"Now, feel my breath on your lips," he continued softly. "Let it run across your tongue and into your body. Let it fill you, become you."

Warm air teased my mouth. My lips parted and I drew it in, filling my throat with his taste and my lungs with the scent of him, until all I could feel and all I could sense was the energy of his presence. In me, around me.

"Open your eyes."

I obeyed, and stepped into an ocean of blue. It was beautiful, that ocean, beautiful, but turbulent, and oh so powerful. My body began to tremble, not just with expectation and desire, but also fear. I was reaching for something I didn't understand, and it was far more dangerous than even Azriel thought. My throat tightened, and the rhythm of my breathing momentarily faltered. His fingers came to rest on my chest, his touch warm, electric.

"There is nothing to fear, Risa." His voice swirled around me, soft and hypnotic. "There is no darkness here. There is just us, two beings connected by flesh, connected by air, and connected by the essence of all that we are."

The fear ebbed away, and once again there was

only him. His energy, his being. Against my skin and in my mind. Burning bright, within and without, making me tremble, ache. Want.

"Imagine there is no flesh to separate us," he continued. "That there is only energy and desire. Call to them, Risa. Become them."

It was as if his words were some sort of trigger. Power surged, became a rush of fire that invaded every muscle, every cell, breaking them down and tearing them apart, until my flesh no longer existed and I was one with the air.

As was he.

He was bright and fierce, a being that glowed like the sun and who was as beautiful as the moon. He drew me toward him, wrapped himself around me, until the music of his being began to play through mine and mine through his. It was a dance, a caress, a tease. It was movement, heat, and desire. It was crazy and electric, a firestorm that ripped through every particle of my being. It was pleasure unlike anything I'd ever experienced or felt before, and it took me ever higher. Our beings continued to entwine, tighter and tighter, until there was no separation—no him, no me, just the music of the two of us combined. And oh, the song we made was beautiful, and powerful, and *right*. Still the dance went on, burning ever brighter, until it felt as if the threads of our beings would surely explode.

Then everything *did* explode, and I fell into a storm of electric, unimaginable bliss.

I'm not entirely sure when, exactly, I came back to flesh, but when I did it was to an awareness of utter exhaustion. My body trembled, sweat trickled down my spine, and my breath was quick, shallow pants, as if my body couldn't get air quickly enough. And yet I felt alive in a way that was indescribable.

"God," I murmured, when I finally could. "Is it always like that for you reapers?"

He brushed a thumb lightly across my lips and smiled. "No, not always."

There was a note that almost sounded like amazement in his voice. I opened my eyes and looked at him. He glowed with health and vitality, his skin golden and his blue eyes shining. "You recharged?"

"Yes." He hesitated. "I hadn't meant to, but the intensity of the moment got the better of me. Unfortunately, it is the reason you are now so weak."

I raised an eyebrow. "Do you see me complaining?"

He smiled, then leaned forward and kissed me tenderly. "No. However, you should rest now."

"But I don't want—"

He briefly pressed a finger against my lips to halt my protest. "For once in your life, just do what I ask without argument."

"In honor of that amazing experience, I'll obey. Just don't expect it to happen too often. Me obeying, that is."

"Oh, I won't." His voice was dry as he rose gracefully from the bed. "Sleep, Risa."

I did. And for longer than I'd expected, because it was late afternoon by the time I woke. I stretched, and suddenly realized I felt better than I had in days, if not weeks. I was refreshed, revitalized. Normal, almost.

Or as normal as someone like me could ever get.

"The recharging appears to have gone both ways," Azriel commented. "Which is good, but extremely unusual."

I glanced around. He'd returned to his post by the window, but this time his stance was relaxed and his skin gleamed warmly in the afternoon sunshine. "Meaning recharging for reapers is usually only one-way?"

"No, but you are not reaper; nor are you full Aedh. It should not have affected you as strongly as it did."

"Well, I'm not complaining about it, that's for sure." I sat upright in bed, but as I did, that nagging, niggling sense of wrongness returned. I frowned and reached for my phone a half second before it rang.

I glanced at the number and saw that it was Rachel. No doubt she was simply ringing to let me know someone hadn't turned up again. But one glance at the clock told me they were midshift, not at the beginning. It couldn't be that.

Something was very wrong. Of that I had no doubt.

I hit the RECEIVE button and said, throat dry, "Rachel, what's up?"

"It's Tao," she said. "He's disappeared."

Disappeared? *Oh fuck, please don't let it be the fire elemental. Please let it be something—anything—else.*

"When?" I asked. My throat was so dry with fear, it came out harsher than I'd intended.

"About an hour ago. He said he was hot and was going outside to cool down. Didn't think much of it, as he's been doing that a lot lately."

Because he was losing the battle. I rubbed a hand across suddenly stinging eyes. Damn it, I didn't need this on top of everything else. But then, it wasn't like Tao needed it, either, and it was my fault he was in this mess in the first place. If I hadn't included him and Ilianna—

You cannot beat yourself up over decisions others are ultimately responsible for, Azriel commented. *Tao had the choice. He chose to help, just as he chose to save Ilianna by consuming the elemental.*

If he weren't there, he wouldn't have had to make the decision.

And Ilianna would now be dead. You cannot have all things, Risa. Fate is not a generous woman at the best of times.

Yeah, I'm learning that. To Rachel, I said, "Did you try his phone?"

"I can't, because all his belongings are still upstairs. He didn't even change."

Damn. I closed my eyes for a moment and fought for calm. "Do you need me to get someone in?"

She hesitated. "Jacques is due in next shift—perhaps if you could get him to arrive a little earlier? We're not usually rushed until after six most Tuesday evenings."

"I'll do that. Let me know if Tao does show up again."

"I will."

She hung up. I called Jacques and asked him to start early, then threw the phone onto the bed and glanced at Azriel. "I don't suppose it's possible for you to locate Tao via his life force, is it?"

"That would depend very much on which life force is in control. If it is the elemental, then no."

"Well, at least we'd know for sure if the elemental has taken over."

Azriel nodded. "It may take me a few minutes. Do not leave the security of this place while I am gone."

"I won't."

He disappeared. I picked up the phone again and dialed Ilianna. "Hey, gorgeous," she said, expression cheerful and green eyes glowing with happiness. "How are you?"

I couldn't help smiling. "The celebrations obviously went well last night."

"Very well. I'm one contented mare right now. Not even the fact that I have to meet Carwyn again can spoil it."

Carwyn was the stallion her parents were trying to set her up with. According to Mirri, he was rather hot—in bed and out—but given Ilianna's preferences, she was either going to have to be honest with her parents or get stuck with a mate she didn't want.

"When is that happening?"

She grimaced. "Tomorrow night. I think it was supposed to be just him and me, but Mirri is coming along. She thinks we should be honest with him."

"It can't hurt, can it?" She couldn't help her sexual preferences, and the sooner Carwyn was aware of them, the better it would be for them all.

"He's a horse-shifter," she said dryly. "A *male* horse-shifter. They don't think straight when it comes to mares."

"I'm still siding with Mirri on this one."

"Traitor." The fierceness of her tone was more than a little diluted by the glint of amusement in her eyes. "To what do I owe the honor of this call?"

I hesitated, then said, "Tao's walked out of the café and can't be found. I don't supposed you've had any particular vibes were he's concerned?"

Ilianna wasn't only a powerful witch, but also a very strong clairvoyant—and a far more reliable one than I'd ever been.

"No, I haven't." She frowned, expression suddenly concerned. "Is it the fire elemental?"

"I think it could be. I know he was having trouble controlling it earlier."

"I'll do a locating spell and see if I can find him."

"Great." I hesitated. "Though if the elemental has taken over, will a locating spell even work?"

"I don't know." She bit her lip for a moment. "A locator spell works on the energy of the person, so with Tao's body chemistry constantly changing—flowing from flesh to elemental depending on which being has more control—it's going to be difficult to pin him down. But I can try."

"Let me know the minute you find anything. In the meantime, I'll rope in Stane and Jak."

"Why the hell would you involve *Jak*?" Her

voice held a note of disbelief. "It's not like Tao needs someone like him—someone only after a good story—on his case."

"Jak has his nose to the ground and can hunt stories in places neither of us would get near," I said. To say Ilianna had a hate-on for Jak was like saying night followed day—blindingly obvious.

"You be careful with him, Risa. The last thing you need in your life is another heartbreak."

"Trust me, Jak is getting nowhere near my heart." I gave her a lopsided grin. "Or my body."

She harrumphed. "I'll be in contact."

"Thanks."

I hung up, then scrolled through the contacts list until I found Jak—though truth be told I knew the number by heart—and rang him.

All I got was a recording telling me to leave a message. I did so, asking him to let me know if he heard about anything unusual dealing with fire, then tossed the phone back onto the bed and decided to grab a shower while I waited for Azriel to return.

He'd done so by the time I'd dressed, and one look at his expression told me everything I needed to know. I swore and thrust a hand through my damp hair. "Now what are we going to do?"

"There is nothing we can do—not until he regains his flesh form."

"And if he doesn't?"

He studied me for a moment, expression giving little away. "If he doesn't, you have a choice to make."

I stared at him, my stomach suddenly twisting itself into knots. "No."

"There may be no choice," he said, voice even but somehow relentless. "If the elemental has won the war, then Tao is already lost to you."

"No!" I clenched my fists against the anger—the useless, sick anger that was fueled part by fear and part by the knowledge that he was right—and added, "I will not give up on him."

While there was life, there was always hope.

Besides, I'd promised Tao I would do all that I could to help him win. Giving up at the first major hurdle was not doing *that*.

"Risa—"

I made a chopping motion with my hand. "I don't want to hear it, Azriel. I don't care what you say. I don't care what fate plans. I don't care about being sensible. I will not give up on my friend. Okay?"

He studied me for several seconds, then crossed his arms and turned back to the window. Every inch of his muscular back seemed to radiate displeasure.

"Okay."

"Glad we agree," I muttered. I grabbed my phone, then stalked out to the kitchen.

I wasn't feeling particularly hungry, but I wasn't about to fall into the trap of not eating. Not when I actually felt reasonably healthy for the first time in ages.

I made myself a coffee, then sat down and consumed a large bowl of Coco Pops complete with lashings of whole milk. Not the healthiest of meals, but a slight step up from the chocolate cake that had initially tempted me.

As I rinsed the bowl out, my phone rang, and the funeral march tone told me it was Hunter. I closed my eyes and, for all of three seconds, resisted the urge to answer it. But Markel's warning loomed large in the back of my mind. I swore softly, then did the sensible thing.

"There's been another murder," she said before I could even open my mouth to say hello.

Of course there was. I mean, why *wouldn't* fate just chuck more fuel into the bonfire of insanity that was my life at the moment? "Same MO?"

"Apparently. The report came in via Directorate channels, and it is not someone I know."

Thank god for *that*. The last thing we needed was for someone to be targeting Hunter's friends or lovers. She was close enough to the edge as it was. "I'm guessing you want me to check it out?"

"Yes. The address has been sent, so get there." Something flashed in her eyes. Something that was almost unholy. "Find this thing, Risa."

She hung up. The phone beeped as her message came in. I glanced at it, noting that this time, the murder had occurred in the more middle-class suburb of Caulfield.

Azriel appeared in the kitchen. "How do you wish to travel there?"

I hesitated. "As much as I'd love to go on my bike, I'm thinking that when Hunter said 'get there,' she meant immediately." If not sooner. I grabbed some gloves out of the cupboard under the sink, then stepped toward him. "Ready when you are, chief."

His arms came around me, wrapping me in warmth. "Hardly an appropriate name when you never listen to a word I say, let alone do what I say."

Though his tone was light, there was an edge that suggested there was more emotion behind the comment than he'd intended me to hear. I glanced up quickly, but his power surged, sweeping us from flesh to energy in a heartbeat before zipping us through the gray fields.

"Azriel—" I said, as we re-formed, but the rest of the sentence was cut off by a sudden and angry, "What the *fuck* are you doing here?"

And the shit just hit the fan, I thought, but plastered a smile on my face as I turned around. Uncle Rhoan stood in the doorway of the ultramodern brick and concrete two-story house, his red hair glowing in the last remnants of daylight and gray eyes glinting with anger. Obviously, Hunter had *not* given me priority over the Directorate this particular time.

"I was asked here," I said. "Believe me, I'm no happier about it than you are."

He eyed me for a moment, expression disbelieving. "Are you saying Jack *ordered* you here?"

"Yes, I am." And heaven help me if Jack didn't back *that* statement up.

If Rhoan detected the lie, he gave no indication of it. He came down the steps and strode toward me. I held my ground in the face of his fierceness, even though all I wanted to do was run.

"Why the fuck would he do that? You're *not* Directorate."

No, I was something far worse—Hunter's go-to girl when it came to all things hell related. And while Jack might be the senior vice president of the Directorate and the man who ran the guardian division, it was Hunter who held the reins of overall control. She also happened to be Jack's sister, and he was undoubtedly wise enough not to go against her wishes—not even when it came to something that would ultimately cause him grief. Uncle Rhoan had *not* been a happy camper last time I'd been called in to help the Directorate, even though that had been totally accidental. The lunatic he'd been hunting just happened to be the same one I'd come across on the astral plane, and the creepy bastard had subsequently decided he only wanted to play his games with me.

It was a game that had almost killed me.

"Look, ring *him* if you want to chew out someone. I'm here in an advisory role only."

Rhoan snorted. "Don't get me wrong, Ris, because you know I love you to death, but what the hell can you give a murder investigation that I and everyone else at the Directorate cannot?"

"Hell is *precisely* what I can give you," I replied, voice grim. Damn it, while I understood his anger stemmed from fear for my safety, it was fucking annoying to get chewed out over something I could *not* control. Not if I wanted to keep on enjoying my life, anyway. "Or rather, a working knowledge of what is—and isn't—coming through the gates now that one has been opened. And then there's Azriel."

Rhoan's gaze cut briefly to the man standing quietly at my back. "And whatever happened to the option of saying no? You're not employed by the Directorate. They can't force you to do anything you don't want to do."

Yeah, but Hunter *could*—not that *that* was something I could admit to. I took a deep breath and released it slowly as I racked my brain for an answer that wasn't going to get me yelled at too much more. In the end, I went with the truth—or as close to it as I was likely to get in this sort of situation.

"I agreed because if whatever—whoever—is committing these crimes *is* a denizen from hell, then it's my damn fault that it's out there."

He continued to glare at me but, after a few minutes, muttered something under his breath and thrust a hand through his short hair. "I hate that you're involved with the Directorate, however peripherally. They have a way of sucking you in deeper and deeper and never letting go. Neither Riley nor I want that sort of life for you."

"I don't want that sort of life for me, either." I gave him the best fake smile I could manage. "Trust me, you're welcome to the investigation. I'm just here to see what you might be dealing with."

His expression remained uncertain. "You're hiding something, Ris. I can smell it a mile off."

"Honestly, I'm not."

He snorted softly. "Yeah, trusting *that* statement, too. But for now, I'll let it drop. Come on."

He spun and headed back up the steps. I let out a silent sigh of relief and followed, putting on the protective booties and gloves as he identified me to the hovering crime-scene recorder.

The inside of the two-story home was as modern as its outside. Crisp white walls, shiny wooden floors, bright abstract art, and leather and chrome furnishings. This time the murder had taken place in an upstairs bedroom rather than in a living space, but as with the first victim, this man was fully dressed and apparently hadn't noticed the web being spun up his body.

Rhoan stopped at the end of the bed. I halted beside him, Azriel still a warm presence at my back. The man on the bed was a thin, graying individual who looked to be in his midsixties, and he was as modern in the way he dressed as he furnished his house. But the expression frozen onto his face was one of pleasure, and his stomach bore the two fist-sized slashes that had been evident on Wolfgang. I flared my nostrils, trying to find some hint of the odd alien musk that I'd smelled at the first murder scene, but either it had dissipated, or it was lost under the scent of all the crime men and women coming and going in the room.

"Did you get here first?" I asked, glancing at Rhoan.

"Yes." He met my gaze. "Why?"

"Did you smell an unusual aroma? It's similar to the musk of a shifter, but odder, if that makes sense."

"It was faint, but yes."

"What about at the first victim's?"

"Also present." His expression remained noncommittal, but the anger in him suddenly ramped up again. "How did you know about the scent when it's not evident now?"

"Because, uh—" My voice faltered, and I cleared my throat, resisting the urge to step away from the anger that would undoubtedly follow if I finished that sentence. I knew he would never hurt me, but that didn't make him any less scary at times like this.

"It is a smell common to many of the darker spirits who inhabit this world," Azriel cut in smoothly. "Especially those who are also capable of shape-shifting."

Oh, good reason, I said to Azriel. *Thanks.*

It is also the truth, he replied. His mental tones were still frosty.

I sighed. *And just how long are you planning to remain annoyed at me over something so trivial, Azriel?*

I do not know. For as long as it takes for you to regain common sense, perhaps.

You could be in for a long wait.

I am a reaper. Patience is part of our nature.

I snorted mentally. *Oh yeah, you've so totally proven that.*

As you've said to me often enough, sarcasm does not become you.

"I do get the feeling," Rhoan said, "that there's a whole conversation happening that I know nothing about."

I glanced at him. "I was just asking Azriel if he could tell whether we were dealing with a spirit or a demon."

"And the answer?" His tone suggested he wasn't believing *that* for a second, either.

"It's not a demon, but he can't confirm or deny the possibility of a spirit because they're of this world rather than the other and therefore not his field of expertise."

"Huh." He crossed his arms. "Anything else you can tell us?"

I frowned, my gaze drifting up the body. The silken web that encased the victim had been leashed to the bed end rather than the floor this time, but otherwise it looked almost identical. I opened my mouth to ask if they'd found a Dark Soul business card in one of his pockets, then remembered I wasn't supposed to know about that. Subterfuge, I thought, sucked.

"Is that wound on his stomach the only one?" I asked instead.

"Yes. And whatever was injected through those slashes liquefied every inch of his innards," Rhoan said. "There's nothing left but a hardened outer shell of skin."

So it was definitely the same MO. "What about the victim? Is he human?"

"He's a hawk-shifter. He's also a perp with a long line of break-and-enter convictions behind him."

I glanced at him sharply. "So this *isn't* his house?"

"It's not even his *suit*." Amusement briefly touched the corners of his eyes. "The actual owner is one Shamus O'Callagan, and he's overseas on business. Apparently, old Sam here has been putting his psychic talents to good use and keeping himself off the street by not only sourcing out temporary high-end accommodations, but taking over the owner's identity."

"He might still be alive if he'd been on the streets."

Rhoan raised his eyebrows. "Meaning you think our killer has a taste for the high life?"

Maybe not so much the high life, but possibly a taste for those who are psychically endowed. It couldn't be a coincidence that the first two victims were both gifted in that area. "How strong a psychic was he?"

"Strong enough to easily convince doubters he really *was* O'Callagan."

"From what I've been told, the first victim was a strong telepath."

"Given he was an old vampire, that goes without saying."

Not all vamps were strong telepaths. There were a few—*a very rare few*—who missed out on that particular gift. "Then being a strong psychic of some kind *could* be the link." I half shrugged. "Of course, he was also rich. Maybe our killer is going after the wealthy. Maybe their innards taste better than us more ordinary folk."

He snorted softly. "You're about as ordinary as a blue diamond."

I grinned. "I think that's the nicest thing you've said to me for ages."

"That's because you keep doing dumb things." He nodded toward the body. "Is there anything else you can tell us?"

I sighed. "No. Bit of a waste of time, wasn't it?"

"Maybe, but at least we now know we could be looking for a spirit; it'll give the witches in the Directorate's employ something to do on this one." He gave me a stern look. "You're not going to attempt to track this thing down, are you?"

"Not unless I'm forced to." I gave him a lopsided smile, then rose on my tiptoes and kissed his cheek. "Tell Riley I'll see her on Thursday for lunch."

"I'd advise not missing this one, or she'll be royally pissed."

"And that's never very pleasant for anyone," I said. "Tell Jack I'm sorry I couldn't be of more use."

He nodded. I turned and headed out. At the front door, I stripped off the protective booties and gloves, dumping them in the hazmat bin before walking down the front steps.

"Now what do you wish to do?" Azriel said, as I stopped near the front gate.

"Run away to a desert island somewhere with a mountain of chocolate and a refrigerator full of Coke." But running away wasn't going to solve anything. Not when I had a world to save, keys to find, and beings willing to kill those I loved if I didn't get my ass into gear sooner rather than later. I sighed. "But I guess we'd better go home and see if we can do anything to pinpoint the location of the next key."

"Home it is," he said, and had us there in a heartbeat.

I rang Hunter, but this time, she didn't answer. I left a message that our killer appeared to be going after men who were psychically strong and asked if I could grab a copy of the crime-scene report when it came through.

My phone rang the minute I hung up. "Ilianna," I said. "Please tell me you've found him."

"Unfortunately, no." Frustration and concern filled her voice and expression. "If he's out there, then I can't see him. God, I hope he's okay."

So did I. "Would it be worth trying location spells every hour or so?"

"If he's in a state of flux, yes. If the elemental has full control, then no. But I'll keep trying."

"Just don't tire yourself out too much. That's not going to help anyone."

"I won't. Let me know the minute you hear anything, won't you?"

"Absolutely."

I hung up, then stripped off my jacket and said, "Com-screen on," as I headed into the kitchen. A light screen flared above the small, dome-shaped computer unit I'd left sitting in the middle of the dining table a few days ago. Several seconds later, a laser-light keyboard appeared on the table surface near the unit. I grabbed another Coke from the fridge, as well as a wedge of the cake I'd resisted earlier, then sat down and said, "Show last search result."

More than twenty-five names immediately scrolled onto the screen. All were museums located within the golden triangle, with the biggest of them being Sovereign Hill, the open-air museum that re-created life of the goldfields during the mid-1800s. It was probably the most logical place to hide a dagger—which was what the second key had apparently been disguised as—and yet, for some reason, I had a nagging suspicion it wouldn't be there. But maybe that was due to little more than the fact that nothing else had been easy of late, so why the hell would the search for the second key be so straightforward and logical?

Besides, the clue my father gave mentioned "soil being stained by rebellion," and that *had* to refer to the Eureka Stockade—one of the biggest and bloodiest rebellions in Australian goldfields history. Given the stockade had happened on Bakery Hill in Ballarat, that removed more than half of the search results. I ran an eye down the list, then grimaced and sat back in the chair. "This is going to take forever."

"Though your father has been surprisingly patient thus far, I cannot see him waiting out eternity for the keys," Azriel said.

"Especially since I'm not immortal and haven't got an eternity to search for them." I ate some cake, then added, "Hell, for all we know, the bloody dagger isn't even *in* a museum, but rather some private weapons collection."

"Possibly." Azriel studied the screen for a moment, then said, "Logically, a dagger would not likely be found in either a pottery museum or a fine arts gallery, so that would erase at least half of those names from the list."

"True." I leaned forward and looked at the list again. "If logic *did* play any part in the placement of this thing, then it's more likely to be at either

Sovereign Hill, the Eureka Centre, or the Aviation Museum. And maybe—if it was disguised as some sort of artifact—maybe the Aboriginal Culture Centre."

"Four locations is not an overly large search area."

"No, but it would be better to visit them when they're open." If only because I needed to be in flesh form to feel the presence of the key, and I could hardly just pop in at this hour of night and start wandering around. Security would be on me before I got three steps. And while Stane could hack into their systems, he needed more than a few minutes' notice. I munched on the remainder of the cake, then said, "The real problem is not going to be finding the key. It'll be keeping the damn thing long enough to figure out what we're going to do with it."

"With the Aedh out of the equation—"

"It wasn't Lucian who stole the first key," I cut in, more than a little annoyed at his continuing insistence on blaming all of our bad luck on Lucian. He was undoubtedly responsible for *some* of it, granted, but definitely not all of it. "It was a dark sorcerer. A *male* dark sorcerer."

"Who might well be connected to both Lucian and his dark sorceress lover."

"He also might not. The point, however, is not who is involved with whom, but how do we stop them from grabbing the second key."

"Simple. We tell no one—"

I snorted softly. "Yeah. Except that my father, the Raziq, and probably Lucian all have varying degrees of access to my thoughts. Hard to keep a secret when your mind leaks like a sieve."

"And there is nothing we can do about *that*. However, your father is more than capable of creating wards powerful enough to keep the Raziq and possibly the dark sorcerer at bay. Perhaps the time has come to lean on his capabilities a little more."

I frowned. "Do you really think he's going to agree to make wards strong enough to keep the Raziq out when it will also keep him out?"

"He can easily add a back door for himself in any magic he creates."

Given my father was responsible for the wards that currently protected this building, as well as creating the Dušans, that was undoubtedly true. And yet something within me didn't want to depend on him for *anything*. I didn't trust him.

"You don't have to trust him," Azriel commented. "You just have to exploit his abilities. Besides, if you wish to keep both the Raziq and the sorcerer from the key, then there isn't anyone else who has the power required to create such magic."

I took a deep breath and released it slowly. "Then let's go talk to the bastard."

I pushed away from the table and walked back into my bedroom. I'd stashed the communication cube my father had given me in a shoe box at the back of my wardrobe, hoping against hope that I wouldn't have to use the thing again. I should have known better.

I dug it out, then walked across to the bed and opened the box up. The cube sat within. It was little more than a white stone roughly the size of a tennis ball. Its surface was slick—almost oily—looking, and ran with all the colors of the rainbow.

I picked it up somewhat gingerly. It was warm against my fingertips, the energy within it muted and unthreatening. Yet it had been created using Aedh magic, and it was activated by blood—my blood—and that gave it a certain edge of darkness that made me wary.

Or maybe that wariness simply stemmed from the fact that I didn't trust the man who'd made it.

And yet he'd also made the Dušan on my arm, and she'd saved my life twice now.

I contemplated the cube for several more seconds, then tossed it on the bed and sat cross-legged in front of it. I glanced up as Azriel appeared. "I don't suppose you could get me—"

"Done." He offered me the knife hilt first, then sat opposite me and drew Valdis, placing her across his knees. Blue fire ran the length of her bright blade, a sure sign she was ready for action.

Hopefully, she wouldn't be needed.

I drew a deep breath, then released it slowly. It didn't do a lot to calm the nerves. I pressed the point of the knife against a fingertip until a drop of blood appeared, then turned my finger upside down and let the blood drip onto the cube. As it hit, the rainbow swirl of colors stopped, and everything went still.

Then light burst from the stone and quickly encased me in a cylinder of glaring white. Azriel disappeared from sight, and Valdis's fierce blue flames were little more than a shadowed flicker.

"Father, are you out there?" My voice echoed slightly in the odd silence of the white void.

For several seconds, there was no reply; then his voice—a harsher, more masculine version of mine—said, "I'm here. Why are you using this cube?"

"You gave it to me to communicate. I'm communicating."

"So you have found the next key?"

"Not yet."

"Then why are you using this cube?"

Impatience—and perhaps a touch of anger—swirled through the whiteness around me. My stomach tightened. I'd felt my father's anger once before. I did *not* want a repeat of the bruises that had ensued.

And yet I couldn't quite help snapping, "Because if you want the damn keys, then you're going to have to do a bit more than provide indecipherable clues."

"I cannot give you what I do not have. The Raziq who hid the keys are dead. I cannot call them back from whatever hell they may have gone to, so I am at a loss as to the point of this request."

"The request isn't more information." Which he'd know if he was reading my mind. The fact that he obviously wasn't meant either he was some distance away or something else was going on. Aedh could usually read the minds of anyone nearby, and my father had implied he could read mine anytime he desired. "I want to know if you can create a ward or something like that to keep both the Raziq and the black sorcerer who stole the first key out of whatever building I happen to be searching. It would need to be reusable."

He was silent for a moment, then said, voice cool, "When would you need such an item?"

"As soon as possible. I don't want to start looking for the key before we have some means of protecting ourselves from outside forces."

And that outside force included him.

If he heard that particular thought, he thankfully didn't react to it. "It could be done. It would not, however, keep anything flesh based out."

"Meaning it won't keep the sorcerer out?" If that was the case, then it was pointless.

"It will keep the sorcerer out if he uses magic to transport in. I doubt I can make something quickly enough that would also stop him from using magic to transport out if he happened to arrive in flesh form."

I frowned. "Aren't they the same thing?"

"No, they are not. It is easy enough to bounce magic to prevent entry. It is harder to contain once in."

Ah. You learned something every day. "What about the Raziq?"

"The wards will be designed to react to the energy of their beings, so will restrict entry regardless of the form they take."

"Does that mean they will also restrict Lucian?"

"My *chrání* has basically been reduced to flesh form, so no. But the restrictions that apply to the sorcerer would also apply to him."

Meaning he could not use any of his lover's magic to transport in and snatch the keys from under our noses, but he could certainly walk right in. If he managed to get past Azriel, that was.

"So how long would it take for you to get something like that to me?"

He paused. "Perhaps a day. I will have a Razan deliver it to you."

"Thanks." It stuck in my craw to actually say that, but being polite didn't cost me anything, and it was certainly a better option than pissing him off in some way.

"Just ensure no one else gets this key, or I will *not* be pleased."

"I'll do my best."

The energy in the cylinder became so electric, the hairs on my arms stood on end. "I am *not* interested in your best. I just want that key."

You and everyone else. I rubbed my arms and didn't say anything. A heartbeat later, the white light died and I found myself blinking at the abrupt darkness.

"You were successful?" Azriel said, then raised a hand and lightly brushed the hair from my eyes.

I nodded. "He said whatever he creates will not restrict anyone in flesh form from entering, though, so we still could be attacked."

"It wasn't so much the attack that was the problem last time, but the fact that the sorcerer used it to divert our attention from his arrival."

"Well, he can still arrive, just not via magical means." I paused. "It also means Lucian will not be blocked."

"Trust me, it will be my great pleasure to deal with him if he *does* attempt to take the key from us."

I eyed in him for a moment, then said, "You're hoping he does, aren't you?"

"Yes." His reply was short, sharp. Angry.

"Because you want a reason to kill him."

"Yes."

"Why? Because of me? Because he was using me?"

He didn't reply, but he really didn't need to. I could feel the answer echoing deep inside of me. I reached out and placed a hand on his leg. His muscles tensed under my touch. "You cannot kill Lucian because of me, Azriel. I don't want that guilt on top of everything else."

"The guilt would *not* be yours—"

"If you break reaper rules to gain revenge for the way he's treated me, then that *is* my problem. We've broken enough rules lately, Azriel. Let's not top it with murder."

"There are some rules worth breaking." He sheathed Valdis and crossed his arms.

Talk about closing himself off, I thought with amusement. But before I could actually say anything, my phone rang. I bounced off the bed and ran into the living room to answer it.

"Risa? It's Jak," he said, rather unnecessarily

given his rather handsome face was crystal clear on the phone's screen. "You wanted to know if I'd heard anything unusual concerning fires?"

My heart began beating a whole lot faster. "Yeah, I did."

"Well, I might just have something. But it'll cost you."

I snorted. "I'm not giving you a story, Jak. Not on this one."

He grinned. It touched his eyes, warming the dark-chocolate depths and creating the usual havoc with my pulse rate. He might have caused me untold heartache in the past, but there was still a tiny part of me that remembered—and maybe even hungered for—the good times.

"Oh, I don't want a story." He paused, and the spark in his eyes grew. "I want a date."

"No."

"Fine. I'll talk to you later—"

"That's fucking blackmail, Jak."

"Yep." His voice was cheery. "I believe there's still something between us, Ris. You keep saying there isn't, but you lie, and we both know it. A date should sort it out one way or the other."

"Jak, I'm not getting into a relationship with you." Annoyance filled my voice. "Accept that and move on."

"I had, but then you went and kissed me, and it just reminded me of how good we'd been together."

I rubbed my forehead wearily. I hadn't actually kissed Jak—I'd kissed Azriel. At the time, he'd been wearing Jak's image, as we'd thought Jak might have been the target of a sniper. Those suspicions had turned out to be wrong, but I couldn't entirely regret it, because that kiss was the reason Azriel and I had finally ended up lovers. What I *did* regret was telling Azriel to give Jak full memories of what had happened that night—kiss included.

"Jak, just tell me what you've uncovered. It's important."

"Answer the question on the table, and I just might."

I opened my mouth to say, "For fuck's sake, one date, no sex," but what came out instead was a flat, "No."

Jak didn't immediately say anything, but I could see his surprise. Hell, *I* was surprised. And yet, weirdly, I also felt free. I may not have wanted him back in my life, but at least confronting him had finally freed me from the pain of our past.

I could move on.

At least until Azriel got around to shattering my barely healed heart again.

"Look," I continued. "I'm not denying there's still chemistry between us, but I have to wonder how much of it is just the pull of our wolf natures."

"This is more than *just* that—"

"Jak," I cut in, exasperated. "I'm with someone *else*. I don't care how much lust might flare between you and me—or anyone else for that matter—it's *not* going to happen. If you can't accept that and move on, well, then, good-bye. But I won't be black-mailed into something I don't want." Not this fucking time, anyway.

He stared at me for several seconds, then took a deep breath and released it slowly. "Okay."

"Okay, you accept what I said, or okay, you're out the door?"

He smiled. "The former. You still owe me a major story, my dear, and you're not getting rid of me until I get it."

I couldn't help a chuckle. He really *hadn't* changed. "Then cut the crap and tell me what you've got."

"I just hope your reaper appreciates what you're giving up," he said, amusement teasing his lips.

"Who said it was the reaper?"

He snorted. "Anyone with two eyes and half a brain. Don't try to kid a kidder."

"Jak—" I warned.

"Okay," he said, the amusement on his lips becoming an all-out grin. "There have been several weird fire-related reports popping up on the scanner over the last half hour."

"This is the scanner you haven't got because they're illegal?"

"Do you want to hear the news, or not?"

I smiled. "I'm listening."

"There's been reports of fires breaking out on freeway verges near Strathmore, Keilor East, Calder Park Raceway, and another of a grass fire near Diggers Rest."

"And?" I said, hoping there was more to the reports than just that. Spot fires weren't unusual, especially along freeway verges. Cigarettes being thrown out of car windows started too many fires in the summer and autumn months.

"And," he said, "all reports mention a figure seen fleeing the scene."

I closed my eyes. Here it comes, I thought. "Was there any description?"

"Just one," he said. "They all said the man was made of fire."

Chapter 6

Damn, damn, *damn*!

Of course, there was always a chance it *wasn't* Tao, but deep in my heart I knew it was a very remote one. While he wasn't the only fire starter in Victoria, they all had one thing in common—even though they *could* make their entire body flame, they never appeared to be *made* of flames. Their features were always visible underneath them. If the figure seen fleeing the string of fires *did* appear that way, then there could be only two reasons why: Either a witch had conjured a fresh elemental, or Tao's elemental was now in control of his body.

I rubbed my suddenly stinging eyes. "How long ago was the last report?"

"The Diggers Rest report came in about ten minutes ago." Jak paused. "Ris, what's going on?"

"Nothing that I can tell you about." I swung around, walked over to the light screen, and quickly brought up Google Maps. I typed "Diggers Rest" in the search area and waited for the screen to respond. "When did the first report come in?"

"About twenty minutes earlier."

Meaning it had taken him roughly twenty minutes to travel the twenty or so kilometers from Strathmore to Diggers Rest. At that rate, he'd be in Gisborne in ten minutes. I kept following the freeway up with my finger, but stopped when I hit Macedon. Oh, *shit*. The elemental was going *home*. Going back to where the witch had created the flames that had given birth to it. It *had* to be. What other reason could there be for it to be heading up to Macedon? Obviously, the witch fire was still alive, though how that could be after all this time I had no idea. That was a question Ilianna would have a better chance of answering than me.

"Thanks, Jak —"

"Don't you dare hang up on me without —"

I hung up, then swung around to face Azriel. "I have to get out there and find Tao before he creates too much more damage."

"You wish me to take you?"

I hesitated, then said, "No. I'll go in Aedh form. It'll be easier to spot him that way."

"Remember, I cannot follow you or help you until you retain flesh form."

I nodded, then grabbed my keys and gave Azriel a quick kiss. "Wish me luck."

"I wish you safety," he said. "Luck is not something either of us should depend on at this point of time."

"True."

Ilianna's wards were still active, which meant I couldn't actually change inside the apartment. I headed out to the street, making sure the apartment was locked and the alarm on, then gripped my phone and keys tightly and reached down for the power of the Aedh. It swept through me instantly, a force stronger than ever before, switching me from flesh to energy form in the blink of an eye.

An unpleasant tingle ran across my particles, a telltale sign that the wards were definitely working. I spun around and headed skyward, arrowing northwest, straight toward Macedon. There was no point in following the roads—not in this form, anyway.

I was going so fast, the streetlights were little more than vivid streaks. The wind buffeted my body, occasionally throwing me sideways, but I still made good time. Soon the lights of the civilization started giving way to longer patches of darkness as I moved from the city to the country. After a while, I found the Calder Freeway and started following it, simply because the elemental seemed to be. For several miles, there was nothing more than the occasional car zooming past; then, gradually, a deeper, richer glow began to show up on the horizon. It was slightly off the highway, walking through paddocks, flicking flames through the undergrowth and sparking more spot fires.

I sped up. The closer I got, the more certain I became that it was Tao. Or rather, the elemental. Fear slithered through me, but it was fear for my friend, not fear for me.

Soon a fiery form became visible. It was trunk shaped, with thick arms and legs and no head. It dripped fire as it moved, the molten globules sizzling as they hit the ground. The dark energy that rolled off the creature crawled through my particles, making them quiver in discomfort.

This is Tao, I reminded myself fiercely. He wouldn't hurt me. I had to trust that, if nothing else.

I flew downward, shifting shape as I neared the ground. I landed on hands and knees and skidded forward, skinning my palms and ripping the knees out of my jeans. I cursed softly—more from the pain of those injuries than the incapacitating pain that usually followed such a shift—and forced myself upright. The abrupt movement had the world doing a brief three-sixty around me, but I ignored it and forced my feet forward. A heartbeat later, an all-too-familiar heat ran across my skin.

"I have no sense of Tao within that creature," Azriel said, voice soft and holding little in the way of emotion.

"You may not sense him, but he's still there somewhere."

"If he attacks, you must defend yourself."

"No." I glanced at him. "And you won't defend me, either."

Anger flickered through his eyes, even though his expression was as remote as it had ever been. "It is my duty to protect you from *all* danger. That includes threats from friends."

I stopped and swung around to fully face him. "If you even go *near* Tao, I'll fucking attack you myself."

"Tao is *not* in control of that being," he all but growled. The fury he was barely showing washed through my mind, a whirlwind of heat that left me singed. "And he *will* attack you."

"Maybe. But he won't kill me."

I had to believe that. *Had* to.

"I cannot stand here and watch—"

"You *will*," I cut in. "Promise me, Azriel."

"No."

"Damn it, I haven't asked *that* much of you. I'm asking this. Please, for me, stand back and let me deal with Tao."

He eyed me for a moment, then made a short, chopping motion with his hand. "Fine. I will not interfere unless I sense death is inevitable. I will *not* let you die. Anything more, I will not promise."

"Thank you."

I turned and walked toward the fiery form. Its steps were ponderous, as if its flaming trunklike legs were a weight it could barely lift. And yet, for all the appearance of slowness, it was covering a lot of distance fairly quickly.

The closer I got, the hotter it got. Heat rolled over me, furnacelike in its intensity. Sweat beaded across my brow and began to roll down my spine. But it wasn't all caused by heat. Some of it was definitely fear. No matter what I'd said to Azriel, no matter what I believed, I knew deep down that there was a very real possibility that this encounter would not end well for one of us.

Amaya's hissing began to fill the back of my thoughts. She wanted to kill, wanted to draw the life of the elemental into her steel and feed on its flesh.

I shuddered. *No way in hell, Amaya. This is a friend, not an enemy.*

Not, she replied. *Only way.*

I ignored her. I flexed my fingers, took a deep breath, and said, "Tao."

There was no response. The creature kept moving forward, its heavy steps making the ground quiver.

"Tao," I said, louder this time.

The creature paused, then slowly turned around. It didn't have a mouth or even a face, so, basically, it just stood there, dripping fire. I wondered what was going on within the creature, wondered if Tao had any awareness of what the elemental was doing and whether somewhere deep within the flames he still fought to regain control.

"You have to retake control, Tao. It's trying to return to the fire that created it. You can't let it." Because if it did, I'd never see my friend again. I was sure of that, if nothing else.

The creature twitched. Whether it was a response to my plea, I couldn't say. "Tao—"

The rest of the sentence was cut off as the creature raised a fist and punched. I swore and ducked, but not fast enough. The blow hit my shoulder rather than my face, melting my sweater and sending me sprawling backward.

Attack, Amaya screamed, her voice so strident, tears stung my eyes. *Touch you not.*

Damn it, no. I pushed to my feet, stripped off my still-smoldering sweater, and dumped it on the ground. The elemental had turned and was walking away.

I cursed and sprinted after it, looping around the left side of the creature until I was in front of it. "Damn it, Tao, listen to me—"

The creature swiped at me again. This time I was ready for it and ducked. The blow sailed over my head, but the heat of its flames was so fierce, it felt like my skin was burning. I backed away fast and kept out of fist range.

This *wasn't* working. Tao wasn't hearing me. Maybe he was gone. Maybe the creature was too strong ... I briefly closed my eyes. *No.* Tao was still within that fiery form. I was sure of it. I just had to find a way to draw him back out. But how?

Last time the elemental had tried to take over, I'd physically dragged Tao into the freezer and doused him with ice—something that was impossible to do out here in the middle of nowhere.

But what if it had been as much the physical contact between us as the ice that had helped Tao get the elemental under control?

No, Azriel said, the same time as Amaya screamed, *Will kill.*

Fuck it, both of you. Stop telling me what I can't do and start offering suggestions.

Azriel's frustration rolled through my mind, as sharp as Amaya's hissing. *You can use Amaya as a shield.*

How?

Flames, she said. *I eat.*

That will kill him, Amaya.

No. Weaken.

Azriel?

She's right. It'll weaken him. He paused. *But it will also kill him if she goes too far.*

His mental tones suggested this might not be

such a bad thing. Anger rolled through me, but I ignored it. I had bigger battles to fight right now.

I stopped moving, drew my sword, and held her—point first—in front of me. Lilac flames began to roll down her sides, and her hissing became filled with anticipation.

Okay, Amaya, I said. *Do what you have to do to drain his energy. But don't kill him.*

Kill not. It was somewhat begrudgingly said.

Her flames leapt from her shadowed blade, then raced across to the elemental and ran up one tree-trunk leg. Her lilac fire contrasted sharply against the red and gold flames of the elemental as she ringed the creature's rotund belly. For several seconds nothing happened; then, as Amaya began to hum softly—almost contentedly—her steel began to vibrate and the flames around the creature's stomach suddenly seemed less incandescent.

The creature never stopped moving, however, and the closer it got, the hotter it got, until I stood in the middle of a firestorm that tore at my hair and burned my skin. Until I felt as much a creature of fire as the one who was now only feet away from Amaya's tip. And yet, for all that it burned, the creature's heat *didn't* destroy me, and this close, it should have. Whatever my sword was doing, it was working.

"Tao," I screamed, more out of fear than any real need to raise my voice above the roar of the flames that swept around me. "You *must* get control of the elemental again."

The creature growled—an ungodly sound that

came from somewhere out of its flaming middle — and swiped at me. I didn't move — I didn't dare, lest I break the contact Amaya had with the elemental — but the blow never struck. It stopped inches from my ear, the heat of it singeing hair but not actually touching skin. The creature roared again, and this time, it was a sound of frustration. The vibration in Amaya's steel grew stronger, and fingers of dullness were quickly spreading from the creature's belly to the rest of its body.

If you're going to touch the elemental, do so now, Azriel said, his voice barely hinting at the anger and concern I could feel within him. *If Amaya drinks too much more of the creature's power, she will kill both the creature* and *Tao.*

Amaya, don't, I warned.

Fun, she grumbled. *You not.*

I snorted softly, then, as the creature roared and took another swipe at me, raised my hand and caught the flaming paw. This time, my skin *did* burn, and I screamed.

Risa! Do not expect me to stand here and see you harmed —

I can, I cut in fiercely. *And you will.*

Closing my eyes, I gritted my teeth against the agony and the screams that pressed up my throat and gripped the fiery paw harder. For several seconds, nothing happened, and I began to wonder if Azriel was right. Maybe Tao *was* lost and I was burning my hand for absolutely no reason. Then, suddenly, my fingers were touching flesh rather than heat. I opened my eyes. The flames were receding—grudgingly, but retreating nevertheless—from the point where my fingers clasped Tao's hand. His fingers twitched, then convulsed around mine, his grip fierce. It hurt like hell, but I didn't say anything, biting my lip and blinking back tears as the flames continued to retreat, first up his arm and then across his shoulders, revealing his head and upper body.

Amaya, release him.

No; want.

Do it, I said. *Now!*

She hissed her displeasure, but her flames unfurled from Tao's waist and dropped to the ground, slinking back to her blade with some reluctance.

As the remaining flames flickered and died, Tao opened his eyes and blinked. Then awareness surged, and horror spread across his pale, thin face.

"Oh god, Ris," he said, voice hoarse and raw. "What have I done?"

I quickly sheathed Amaya and tried not to think about the agony radiating from my left hand—a hard thing to do given it was so bad, all I wanted to do was throw up. "Nothing that can't be—"

I cut the rest of the sentence off as he collapsed, and I lunged forward to catch him. Azriel got there before me. He slung Tao like a sack over his shoulder, then swung around to face me.

"Your hand—"

"I can heal it when I change to Aedh form," I said, barely resisting the urge to cradle my hand and weep like hell. "Let's just get Tao home and worry about me later."

Azriel didn't look at all happy, but he merely nodded and disappeared from sight. I took a deep breath and glanced at my hand. *Bad* mistake. All I saw was a raw and swollen mess, and the pain—which had been bad enough up until that point—became overwhelming. A chill swept me, I began to shake, and my legs went from underneath me. But even as I hit the ground, my stomach rose, and I threw up.

Then Azriel was there, holding me, supporting me. The heat of his presence fanned through my body; a warmth and strength chased the weakness from my flesh and snatched the pain from my burned and blistered hand.

Eventually, I pulled away and glanced down. Though it was still red and tender, my hand was no longer blistered or weeping, and I could flex my fingers without pain. My gaze rose to Azriel's. "Thank you for healing me."

"I'm glad that I could." He brushed the sweaty strands of hair from my eyes, but despite the tenderness of his touch, there was anger in his expression. "You should not have endangered yourself that way, Risa. It could have ended very differently."

"But it didn't." I hesitated. "Where did you take him?"

"Home, as you wanted. I brought Ilianna in to tend to him." He placed a hand under my elbow and gently pulled me upright. "And we should go. The police are coming."

I glanced past him and saw the approaching red

and blue lights of the emergency vehicles. "At least no one got hurt."

"No one but you," he commented, as he wrapped his arm around my waist and swept us from flesh to energy form. He didn't immediately release me when we reappeared in the living room, simply continued to hold me close.

My gaze rose to his again, and there was an intensity, a ferocity, that had my heart doing an odd sort of dance. "What?" I said, almost breathlessly.

"Do not *ever* ask me to do something like that again," he said. "Because I will not."

Annoyance flared. I tried to step back, but his grip tightened around my waist, pressing me closer. "Damn it, Azriel. He's my friend—"

"And I mean nothing to you?" he cut in, his voice flat and even despite the fierceness that radiated from every inch of his being.

"You know that's—"

"What I *know*," he cut in again, "is that the link between us has evolved into something far stronger than a mere exchange of thoughts. I will not feel your agony like that again and *not* do anything about it."

My breath caught somewhere in my throat. "I'm sorry. I didn't know—"

"And wouldn't have cared if you had." His voice was grim. "I'm just giving you warning never to ask that of me again."

I took a deep breath and released it slowly. "Okay. But I also meant what I—"

"Oh, I am under no illusions where I stand when it come to your friends."

The edge of bitterness in his voice stung deep inside. "That's not fair, Azriel."

"And yet it is nevertheless true." He released me and stepped back. "Go tend to Tao."

"Azriel—"

He cut me off with a short, sharp motion. "You have what you wanted, Risa."

And with that, he disappeared, leaving me standing there feeling angry, confused, and oddly hurt.

"Risa?" Ilianna said.

I forced a smile and turned around. "How's Tao?"

"Unconscious." She hesitated. "Are you okay?"

"Couldn't be better. Is Tao going to be all right?"

"I don't know." Her expression was concerned. "What's going on between you and Azriel?"

"Nothing." And everything. "Is there anything I can do to help Tao?"

"The best thing you can do is get some sleep. You look like shit."

"Thanks."

"Seriously, I want you to get some rest. The last thing I need is to be looking after two of you. Especially given what a grouchy and unpleasant patient you can be."

I snorted softly. "I love you, too. Give me a yell if you need anything or he wakes, won't you?"

"I will."

I turned and headed for my bedroom.

"Ris?"

I paused and looked over my shoulder. "What?"

She hesitated. "Remember that Azriel isn't human. You can't expect him to react the way any human—or non-human, for that matter—would."

"I don't expect anything of him, Ilianna."

"Maybe that's the problem."

I snorted. "He's here for one reason only—the keys. He needs to secure them for his side, and he needs me to do it. No matter what I may or may not feel for him, that's the one truth that can never be ignored."

"But what if it's no longer the *only* truth?"

"It's the only truth that matters. In the end, he has his world, and I have mine, and as the saying goes, never the twain shall meet."

"Maybe you need to trust fate a little bit more. Or maybe you just need to enjoy what you currently have and not worry about the future."

How could I not worry about the future when the reality was I might not have one? "Fate is the one that got us into this mess, Ilianna. I'm not trusting her to get us out of it." I waved a hand. "I'll see you tomorrow."

With that, I went to bed and—surprisingly, given how much sleep I'd already had that day—slept.

A death march tone woke me. I groaned and rolled over onto my back, rubbing the sleep from my eyes and cursing the idiot on the phone for waking me. Then it twigged that the idiot was Hunter, and I lunged to answer it. But I hit the VOICE ONLY button—I had a feeling she wouldn't appreciate learning that I was still in bed.

"I haven't received the crime-scene report yet," I said, glancing at the clock. It was nine in the morning—no wonder my stomach was grumbling. What little I'd eaten yesterday, I'd thrown up last night. "So I really haven't got much more to report than what I've already said."

"I have no intention of discussing either your report or the Directorate's," she replied, voice snappish. Definitely not in a happy mood this morning.

But then, was she ever?

"So you're ringing me because . . . ?"

"Because another card was found in the pocket of the second victim—this one for the Blue Angels."

Which Rhoan would have no doubt already checked out. And I couldn't see the point in me doubling his work, especially given if he *had* found anything worthwhile, it would have been in his report. And *she*, subsequently, would now be hunting down the bitch behind the kills. All of which I wanted to say, but wisely refrained. "Is there any connection between the two clubs?"

"There is, actually. They both hired last-minute replacements from the same booking agency."

"I gather the Directorate has talked to the agency involved?"

"Yes." She hesitated. "And so have I."

Poor them. "And . . . ?"

"I told the agency owner to inform me of all last-minute requests for musicians," she snapped. "And he just did."

Hence the reason for the call. Wonderful. I

scrubbed a hand across my eyes and flicked the blankets off me. "I'm guessing you're not sending the Directorate to check her out."

"Rhoan hasn't your reaper, nor your ability to sense dark spirits."

The Directorate witches had the latter, if not the former. But again, I held the comment back. She didn't *want* the Directorate to find this killer—she wanted me to, so that she could then get her revenge. And what Hunter wanted, Hunter usually got.

Unfortunately.

I walked into the bathroom. Having a pee while talking on the phone wasn't something I usually did, but it was oddly appropriate when it came to Hunter—if only because I wished I could so easily flush her from my life.

"So where is the stand-in going to be playing tonight?"

"She'll be at the Hallowed Ground from midday today."

Which at least explained why Hunter wasn't going to interview the woman herself. She might be an extremely old vampire—and therefore able to stand far more sunshine than most—but the lunchtime hours were still as deadly to her as sunlight was to any of them. "Isn't it a little unusual for nightclubs to be open during the day?"

"Hallowed Ground has been around for a long time." She hesitated. "It is a haunt for those who might otherwise be alone during daylight restrictions."

Dread filled me. "Does that mean it's another blood whore club?" And if it was, why were they bothering to provide musical entertainment? It wasn't like the addicted vampires would care about anything other than getting their next fix.

"No," she said, voice cool but still holding an edge that sent chills down my spine. "Although it wouldn't matter if it was. You would still be going."

There was never any doubt about *that*. "I'll report back the minute I talk to her."

"If she *is* the one—report sooner."

Or else, her tone implied. I was suddenly grateful I'd had the foresight not to use the vid-phone. "Fine."

"Make sure you talk to the owner, not the manager. He is next to useless."

I frowned at the odd edge of amusement in her voice. There was something going on that I didn't understand. But I didn't bother questioning her because she had already hung up.

I tossed the phone onto the vanity, then had a quick shower. Once dressed, I headed into Tao's room. And noted, with some annoyance, that Azriel had yet to make his appearance. Apparently, when reapers were in a snit, they did it properly.

Ilianna was asleep on the chair next to Tao's bed, but started awake when I walked in. I grimaced. "Sorry. I didn't mean—"

She waved the apology away, then rubbed at her neck as she sat upright. "I've got to be up, anyway. I promised I'd ring Carwyn to confirm tonight's date."

I raised my eyebrows. "You're actually going?"

She frowned. "I told you I was."

"Yeah, but I figured last-minute nerves might step in and stop you."

She shook her head. "There's no avoiding it. Mirri's right." She hesitated. "Besides, he and I are destined to be, so I have to be honest with him."

"Destined?"

She wrinkled her nose. "It's just something I saw a long time ago."

I frowned. "Just because you foresaw this union happening doesn't mean you should let it override your own feelings for Mirri—"

She smiled. "It won't. You should know me better than that."

"Then why all this 'destined to be' shit? How much pressure is your dad putting on you?"

"Lots, but I can understand his reasons—a union with Carwyn has financial advantages for both families."

"So what? What you and Mirri have is more important than anything else."

"We may be in love, but we are also mares. It is a fact of life that mares end up in the herd of a stallion, whether we like it or not."

"Well, that sucks."

"Yeah, totally." She gave me a somewhat wan smile. "Trust me, I've done my best to avoid the whole situation, but the reality is, I have little choice. If I reject Carwyn, it'll be some other stallion—and maybe someone far less understanding and patient than he seems to be."

I sat on the arm of the chair and gave her a quick hug. "I'm sure you *will* work something out."

"And hopefully that something will be artificial insemination," she muttered. "I am *not* going to bed with the man if I can at all avoid it."

"So why not suggest that? What have you got to lose?"

She snorted. "Um, have I mentioned he's a stallion?"

"I'm sure even stallions are sometimes capable of thinking with their brain rather than their dicks."

"I wouldn't be betting on that," Tao muttered, his voice hoarse but nevertheless music to my ears. He opened bloodshot eyes and glared at us. "And don't you two know it's not polite to be talking about sex when a man is trying to get some sleep?"

I grinned. "A werewolf complaining about people talking about sex. I think the world just ended."

"I think it did for a while there." He closed his eyes and scrubbed a hand across his bristly jaw. "I'm sorry—"

Ilianna caught his free hand and squeezed it lightly. "Don't be sorry. Just be damn sure it doesn't happen again."

"And how the *fuck* am I supposed to do that?" His voice was a rich mix of anger, frustration, and fear. "This damn thing inside me is strong—"

"And so are you," she snapped back. "Or you would be, if you damn well stopped feeling so sorry for yourself and started taking the offense."

He glared at her. "It's not like I'm fucking sitting back, issuing the elemental an open invitation—"

"Isn't it?" she snapped. "Then why the hell aren't you looking after yourself? Why aren't you eating? You were told at the Brindle that you must keep strong both physically *and* mentally if you wanted to keep this thing contained."

"I'm trying—"

"But not fucking hard enough. You have to get serious about it, Tao, or this thing *will* win."

He snorted. "So you've seen that? Then what the hell is the point?"

"The point," she said, jumping to her feet and clenching her fists, "is that nothing is set in stone just yet, and I don't want you lost for eternity to flame. So, damn it, fight!"

My breath caught at the anger and desperation in her voice. Whatever she'd foreseen had been *bad*, and fear again stepped through me. I half reached out to her, but Tao beat me to it. He sat up abruptly, caught her hands, and tugged her into a hug that was as fierce as his expression was alarmed.

"I'm sorry," he whispered. "I promise, I'll try harder."

"You fucking better." She returned his hug for a moment, then pulled back and punched his shoulder. "Now I'm going to prepare you the world's biggest steak sandwich, and you will consume every fucking inch of it."

"Promise."

"Good." She turned, gave me a weak smile, then headed out.

I waited until she'd left, then met Tao's gaze. "How did the elemental get loose?"

He half shrugged. "One minute I was heading outside to cool down; the next I'm in some random field staring at you and realizing just how close I'd come to cindering my best friend."

"But you didn't." I dropped down into the seat, then raised my hand. "See, not even the smallest of blisters to show for my ordeal."

He eyed my fingers for a moment, then said, "I could hear you, you know, but I couldn't do anything. Not until you caught my hand and drew me out."

So I'd been right—touch *was* the key to breaking the elemental's control. "I knew you wouldn't hurt me, Tao."

"But I did, and we both know it." He took a deep, somewhat unsteady breath and released it slowly. "I think I'll remember your scream for the rest of my life. And it's because of that, more than anything, that I'll fight this thing." His gaze met mine. "It hates you, Ris. A witch created it to kill you, and the minute you spoke to it out there in the field, that's all it wanted to do."

"What it wanted was to return to the fire that created it."

"Primarily, yes. But if it regains control again, don't confront it. Because next time, I may not be able to stop it."

"Then, as Ilianna so politely put it, make sure there *isn't* a next time." I rose to my feet, then leaned over and dropped a kiss on his cheek. "Get better. I have to go hunt a dark spirit."

"Hunter's still on your case, huh?"

"Yeah. You rest up, and maybe I'll regale you with the whole sordid tale when I get back."

"I'll look forward to it."

I wouldn't—if only because in order to tell a story about hunting a dark spirit, I'd actually have to *do* it. I headed out to the kitchen. The smell of frying steak filled the air, and I took a deep breath, savoring the delicious aroma. My stomach rumbled happily. "Don't suppose you're cooking one of those for me?"

She glanced pointedly at the two waiting plates of buttered toast. "I'm vegetarian, remember?"

I grinned as I plopped my butt on the kitchen counter. "Hey, you're going on a date with a stallion tonight, so miracles can definitely happen."

She snorted. "Not twice in one day, they won't." She studied me for a minute. "Did you sort out your shit with Azriel?"

"No, because he isn't around."

"He's always around, and you know it."

"That's not the point."

"Then what is? The fact that you're scared of your own feelings?"

"Ilianna, stop, okay?"

She sighed. "Between you and Tao, I'm going to end up gray before my time."

I frowned. "Why? What have you seen?"

She hesitated. "Nothing."

"Yeah, like that sounded *so* convincing." I studied her for a minute. "So what, exactly, did you see in Tao's future?"

"Nothing. Nothing but flames." She stared at me,

and all I saw was her fear. "I think we're going to lose him, Ris."

No, we're fucking not. I forced a smile. "As I've said before, fate is a bitch who enjoys her games. She's just as likely to do the opposite of what you fear."

"God, I hope you're right." She poked the steak with a stiffened finger, then picked it up on a fork, slapped it onto a piece of toast, and handed it to me. "What are you up to today?"

"I've got to check out a few museums, and then I'm off hunting a dark spirit."

Ilianna's eyebrows rose. "Museums? You?"

I waved a hand. "Don't worry. I'm not on a culture kick or anything. We're looking for the next key."

"Do you want help?"

"No." Especially given what had happened last time I'd found one of the keys. I was already in danger of losing Tao. I wasn't about to risk losing Ilianna as well. I slapped the second piece of toast over the steak, then grabbed the sandwich one-handed and got off the counter. "If I don't see you before tonight, enjoy your date."

She snorted. "The only way that'll happen is if I get totally plastered first. And I've promised Mirri I wouldn't."

"Tell her she's a spoilsport."

"Oh, I have, trust me."

Grinning, I walked across to the dining table to transfer the search results from the computer to my phone, then walked into my bedroom to grab a coat and my purse.

Once I'd finished my sandwich, I stood in the middle of my room and said, "So, are you going to make an appearance, or is this snit going to continue?"

"As Ilianna has already noted," he said, voice even, "I am never very far away."

I swung around. He stood several feet away from me, his arms crossed and his expression back to its usual noncommittal self. "Then why couldn't I sense you?"

"Because I didn't allow it."

I frowned. "If you've always had the ability to stop me from sensing you, why haven't you?"

"Because I haven't always been able to."

I blinked. Definitely *not* the answer I'd been expecting. "Then why have you suddenly gained the ability?"

"For the same reason you are catching more of my thoughts and emotions than I might otherwise wish. The closer our link becomes, the more it opens some . . . abilities and closes down others."

"Meaning it's a two-way street?"

"Possibly."

Meaning yes. I briefly wondered just what it meant for me other than more insight into his thoughts and feelings, but I knew him well enough by now to know he was never going to tell me *that* sort of information. "And you can't stop it from happening?"

"No." He regarded me steadily for a moment. "We are going in search of the next key?"

"Yes. As scary as Hunter is, she has nothing on

the Raziq. If I don't start actively trying to find the keys, they just might stop threatening and start *doing*."

And Tao and Ilianna would be their first targets; of that I had no doubt.

A chill ran through me, although I wasn't entirely sure whether it was the thought of my friends coming under attack from the Raziq, or a premonition of trouble of another kind headed their way. Fast.

"How do you wish to travel to Ballarat?"

I hesitated, very tempted to ride the Ducati there and tell him where to shove it until he got over the moodiness, but I really didn't have the luxury of time. Not if that premonition was to be believed.

"You can take me, if you'd like."

Amusement briefly touched his lips, and there was something close to mischief shining in the blue of his eyes. "Oh, I *would* like."

I raised an eyebrow. "If I didn't know you better, reaper, I'd think not only was *that* a double entendre, but you were flirting."

"Reapers don't flirt." He stepped close and wrapped an arm around my waist. His body was warm against mine, his touch tender and yet oddly possessive. "It is merely a truth I cannot deny."

I rose up on my toes and said, my lips so close to his that I could almost taste him, "So you're saying that you want me?"

"From the very first moment that I saw you," he murmured; then his lips met mine and he kissed me fiercely and very thoroughly as his energy rose and swept us through the gray fields to the chill of Ballarat. Not that I actually felt, in any way, cold. Such a thing wasn't possible when Azriel's arms were still around me.

"God, get a room, will you?" a woman muttered as she walked past us.

I laughed softly and stepped back. His hand slipped from my waist, and my hormones mourned the loss. "Where are we?"

"At the Aboriginal Culture Centre."

I turned around. The building was modern in style, all concrete and glass, and painted in colors that reminded me of the outback—reds, gold, pinks, and browns. I frowned. "This really doesn't look like a museum."

"That is something we cannot be sure of until we go inside."

"True." I half shrugged and headed for the entrance, paying the fee for both of us but refusing the guided tour. It was interesting to look around, but there was nothing in this place for us.

"Well," I said, once we were back out. "*That* was a waste of time."

"At least there is one less option on the list." He pressed warm fingers against my spine, gently guiding me away from the cultural center. "What do you wish to do now?"

I pulled out my phone and glanced at my list. "Let's try the Aviation Museum. That's probably the next least likely."

"Done." He wrapped his arms around my waist again and took us there. The museum, it turned out, was a big tin shed.

"It is also not open," he commented

It certainly looked that way. The huge sliding doors that ran almost the entire length of the building were closed, and the tarmac forecourt was empty. I grabbed my phone, brought up the files I'd transferred, and checked the opening time. "What sort of museum is open only on weekends and public holidays?"

"This one, obviously."

There was amusement in his voice. I smiled and lightly nudged him with my elbow. "That was a rhetorical question, not one that wanted an answer."

I scanned the outside of the building. Though I couldn't see any physical guards, there were plenty of cameras on the outside and no doubt plenty of security measures on the inside. "I might just take Aedh form and have a quick look around."

"If the second key *is* in there, you will not sense it in Aedh form."

"I know, but at least we'll know if the place has any sort of military weapons on display."

"Presuming it *is* a military dagger."

"Yeah." Given the cryptic nature of the clues, who actually knew?

I called to the Aedh, and she swept through me in an instant. In energy form, I made my way through the fence, across the tarmac, and through the small gap underneath the massive doors. The shed was huge and filled to the brim with all sorts of old-looking airplanes—some single wing, some double wing, some with propellers and others without. I didn't know much about planes overall, but I had a feeling this collection was pretty impressive. There were also engines, various machine parts, and tools. But nothing that resembled an actual dagger. I turned around and headed out.

"Nothing?" Azriel said, as I became flesh again.

"Not as far as I can tell." I rubbed my arms against the chill in the air. "I guess we should try the Eureka Centre next. If the dagger isn't there, then we're left with Sovereign Hill being the most likely location."

"And yet you do not think it is there."

"No, but I've been known to be wrong before."

"I think it best I not say anything about *that* particular point."

I grinned and wrapped my arms loosely around his neck. "Wise man."

He smiled as his hand came around my waist again, but he didn't say anything, just swept us across to the Eureka Centre. Which was also closed—for renovations, this time.

"Well, shit," I said, staring at the sign on the door.

"Which leaves us with Sovereign Hill, I believe."

"And that's too big to check right now." I briefly glanced at my watch. "We've got only an hour and a half before we have to be at Hallowed Ground."

"Then what do you wish to do?"

I hesitated and stared up at the huge blue flag with its famous five eight-point stars that formed a cross in the middle of it. Though it was now a symbol of democracy and protest, it had originally been designed as a flag of war, and it was that symbol that spoke to me now. In very many ways I was in the middle of a war myself and, like the men who had fought under her on this very hill, my war was one I suspected could not be won. Not by me, anyway.

I pushed the rather gloomy thought away and swung around to look at Ballarat. "I don't know. Maybe we should wander down to the Visitors Center, on the off chance there's something the search missed."

"You wish to walk?"

I hesitated, then nodded and headed down the hill. He fell in step beside me, his arm brushing against mine and sending little slithers of desire skittering through me. It was, I thought with amusement, an almost normal moment in a life that had become insane.

With a little help from Google Maps, we found the Visitors Center and headed inside. It was, as was usual with these sorts of places, filled to the brim with information and souvenirs as well as local food and clothing. The thick jackets, I noted with amusement, seemed to be particularly popular today.

I walked across to the wall of information about local events, and almost immediately a brochure caught my eye. I picked it up and showed Azriel. "Well, looky here—an Arms and Militaria Exhibition."

"That is the one place we are certain to find military daggers. Whether it is the *right* place is another question."

"And one we won't answer until we go see it." I

flicked the brochure around. "It doesn't open until tomorrow and runs until Sunday. At least that gives us plenty of time to check it out."

He nodded. "And plenty of time for your father to come up with a way of keeping the sorcerer and the Raziq out."

"Yeah." I tucked the brochure into my pocket and glanced at the time. "I guess we can head to Hallowed Ground. Maybe we'll get lucky and she'll start her set early."

"Luck has not been particularly favorable to us as yet," Azriel commented, as he caught my hand and drew me closer. There was something in the way he looked at me that had my pulse racing. "And I can think of other, more pleasurable ways to fill in our time."

A smile teased my lips. "Can you, now? And what about the snit you were in not so long ago?"

"Would you rather talk yet again about the reasons for the snit?" he said, voice soft as he slid an arm around my waist. "Or perhaps explore the possibilities of a rather quaint human expression that goes something along the lines of makeup sex being the best kind?"

"Hard choice," I murmured, pressing myself against the warm, hard planes of his body. "But I've never really had the chance to test that expression out."

"Then perhaps we should."

"What, here?" I raised an eyebrow and glanced around the Visitors Center. "I might have werewolf blood in me, but I'm not that much of an exhibitionist."

He smiled and touched my cheek gently. "I meant in your bed."

"Perfect—"

His energy swept around me even before I could finish my sentence.

And I have to say, that old saying was right. Makeup sex *was* the best kind.

Needless to say, we did not arrive at Hallowed Ground on time. In fact, we were a good twenty minutes late. The club was situated on the corner of Wellington Parade and Simpson Street, not far away from what most Melbournians considered hallowed ground—the Melbourne Cricket Ground. The club was situated in a rather unusual two-story, redbrick building that had an old-fashioned concrete turret on one corner and small sash windows at regularly spaced intervals. The entrance was nondescript, and it would have been easy to pass by and think it was nothing more than an apartment entrance. Certainly, the small, discreet sign above the door did little to give it away.

Azriel opened the white-painted wood and glass door and ushered me inside. Darkness greeted me, and it took a moment for my eyes to adjust. The room was midsized, with a bar to the right and a stage at the back of the room. A thin woman with an oddly ragged red streak running through the middle of her dark hair was spotlighted on the stage. She was playing some sort of lute, and the music was strange and yet somehow evocative. There were more than a dozen people sitting at the various tables scattered throughout the room, and most of them had their eyes closed, listening with something close to rapture in their expressions.

I walked across to one of the tables sitting in the deeper shadows of the room and pulled out the chair. "Is she a dark spirit?"

Azriel hesitated, studying her as he sat down next to me. "It is difficult to tell. She has some sort of shield around her."

I frowned. "Meaning you can't break past it?"

"I could, but then she would sense that I am here. Spirits may not be the normal prey of dark angels, but they generally will not take a chance and remain in our presence if they sense us."

I studied her for a moment, noting her long, thin fingers and sharply pointed fingernails. Handy for plucking lute strings . . . or slicing stomach flesh, I thought, and shivered.

"Why would she have a shield up if she wasn't up to no good?"

"She is sitting in a room filled with vampires, many of whom are not above using their telepathic powers to seduce or influence the thoughts of others. It is natural she would have some means to protect herself from such events."

That *did* make sense. I continued to frown at the woman on the stage. There was something about her that made my nerves crawl, but maybe that was nothing more than my desire for this hunt to be easy.

"She'll have to take a break soon. We can interview her when she does." I leaned back in my chair and glanced at Azriel. He was little more than shadow in this darkness, but his eyes shone brightly—almost as brightly as his sword. "Why is Valdis reacting? Amaya's not."

Can, she said.

No. The last thing I wanted was her hissing like a banshee in my brain.

Banshee not. Her tone was a trifle huffy. Maybe she'd been taking lessons from Azriel.

"I had good reason for the huffiness," he replied evenly. "And I thought we'd moved past that."

My eyebrows rose. "You *heard* her?"

He nodded. "Through you. And a banshee is a spirit; she's a demon."

Better, Amaya grouched.

I snorted. "Tell me, do all demon swords have such attitude?"

He smiled. "The attitude of the sword very much depends on the attitude of the owner."

"So you're saying I'm a sweet-tempered, silver-tongued woman?"

He caught my hand in his, drew it to his lips, and kissed it. "Would I dare say anything else?"

"Usually, yes."

"Then maybe I am merely in an exceptionally good mood."

"Good sweaty sex will do that to you every time," I replied, voice wry.

His smile grew, touching the corners of his eyes and making my heart do several little happy skips. "Then perhaps I should get in a snit more often."

I laughed. The sound seemed to echo softly

through the darkness, and the woman on the stage turned to look at us. Though she didn't move, there was an almost imperceptible tightening in her shoulder and arm muscles.

"She knows what I am." Azriel squeezed my hand, then released me. "Get ready to move. I believe she's about to finish her set."

The woman on the stage finished the song she was playing, then rose and bowed to the audience. They didn't immediately respond, but as the spotlight died and she walked from the stage, it was as if a spell had been released and they all began to clap—some conservatively, some not.

I rose and wove my way through the tables, planning to cut the woman off before she could slip backstage. She was moving deceptively fast, however, and slipped through the curtains and disappeared from sight. I swore softly and ran forward, flipping the curtains aside and following the sound of her retreating steps down a dark corridor. Somewhere up ahead, a door opened and closed. I slowed.

Valdis's blue fire flickered across the walls, highlighting the peeling paint and dusty cobwebs. I shivered, not wanting to think about webs when I was chasing a woman whose alternate form could well be the world's biggest spider.

"I cannot sense her presence in the room ahead," Azriel said.

"Does that mean she's escaped us? Or is it simply a matter of the shield continuing to block you?"

"It could be either."

Meaning the only way we were going to find out

was to enter that damn room. I flexed my fingers and opened the door. Nothing immediately jumped out at me, but the room was pitch-black and my reluctance to enter grew.

I reached to the left and brushed my hand down the wall, looking for the light switch. Something skittered across my fingertips, and I yelped and jumped backward—straight into Azriel. He grabbed my arms and steadied me.

"It was only a small spider," he said.

I snorted. "I don't care if it's big or small; they're all spiders and they all deserve to die."

"Spiders are generally harmless creatures."

He reached past me. A second later, I heard the light switch being flicked up and down. No light came on, so the bulb was obviously blown.

"Can I remind you that this is Australia? We have some of the deadliest spiders known to man."

"That does not alter the fact that the one that touched you didn't actually harm you."

"That *isn't* the point." I stared at the darkness a moment longer, then drew Amaya and took a wary step. Lilac flame flared down her sides, providing enough light to view the immediate area. The room was small and furnished sparsely. There was a dressing table with an office chair in front of it, as well as a small sofa and a minibar fridge. I stepped farther inside and swung Amaya around. There was nothing and no one else in the room. Our musician *had* fled.

"Well, I guess that points to her—" Something dropped onto the back of my neck, and I swiped at it irritably. "What the hell?"

Something else dropped, but this time it raced under the collar of my shirt and down my spine. I yelped and flung myself backward at the wall, hoping to squash the hell out of whatever it was.

"Risa, I think we'd better get you out of here."

I gulped, my heart in my mouth and fear twisting my stomach. "Why?"

But I knew why even as I asked the question. There were more than just a couple of spiders in this room. I raised Amaya and looked up.

The entire ceiling was alive and moving.

Chapter 7

I opened my mouth to scream, but before I could, the whole damn lot dropped down, covering both the floor *and* me in a mass of tiny black bodies.

Horror filled me, and for a moment I couldn't move, frozen to the spot and praying like hell that this was nothing more than a nightmare. Then thousands of tiny fangs began to dig into my flesh, and I screamed and jumped and swung Amaya around wildly, swatting at the creatures I could barely even see.

Azriel pulled me into his arms, then swept us away. We reappeared in my bathroom, but it wasn't enough. I could still feel the fangs. I raced under the shower, throwing off my clothes and stomping on the black bodies that fell like rain around me. Despite the heat of the water, I was shivering like crazy, and my skin crawled with the sensation of movement.

"Are there any left?" I asked, spinning around almost wildly, trying to spot the creepy little bastards.

"No." Azriel caught my arm and made me stop. "They're gone. It's okay."

I shuddered. "It still feels like they're on me."

"No." He hesitated. "But we should go back—"

"There is no way in *hell* I'm going back into that room."

"If you'd let me finish a sentence occasionally," he said, voice a mix of amusement and annoyance, "I was going to suggest you talk to the manager while I investigate the room to see if the woman left anything behind in her haste to escape."

"Oh." I gulped down some air in an attempt to calm my still-racing pulse. "That I can do. Just wait until I get dressed."

He handed me a towel. "I was not intending otherwise."

I raised my eyebrows. "If I didn't know you better, reaper, I'd suggest there was an almost propitiatory note in your voice when you said that."

"Then you would be wrong."

"Really?"

"Yes."

"So if I started shagging Lucian again, you wouldn't care?"

He gave me a look. One that suggested I was being silly. I grinned.

"There is a *vast* difference between not caring about who sees your outer layer and whether you're with Lucian."

"So, Lucian aside, you wouldn't care if I found myself another lover?"

He crossed his arms, his expression giving little away. But tiny flickers of annoyance danced both along Valdis's sides and through the outer reaches of my mind, a sure sign that he was not as calm as he appeared. "That is not your intention, so why bring it up?"

"Because it's sometimes amusing to see your very human reactions." I rose on my toes and kissed him. "And now I'll get dressed."

"And I would like to point out that the workings of your mind are sometimes incomprehensible."

"Does that mean I sometimes make sense?" I brushed past him, dumped the wet towel down the laundry chute, then headed for my wardrobe.

His gaze followed me, a caress that sent a tingly warmth skittering all the way down to my toes. It was certainly a more welcome sensation than the tiny tickles of thousands of spidery feet.

"Occasionally. *Very* occasionally."

I grinned again. "Just think how boring your life would be without me."

"I do." He hesitated. "Possibly more than is wise."

I shot him a glance. "So you're actually going to miss me when this assignment is over and you leave?"

He hesitated again, and my amusement died. Hesitation was *not* what I'd expected. Not now. Not after all that had happened between us. And yet, as Ilianna had so rightly pointed out, the future was not something I should be worrying about right now. But, at the same time, how could I not when it came to him and me? Because I didn't *want* him to leave. Not now, not ever.

Yet that was the *one* thing that was never in doubt.

I ignored the ache that accompanied the thought and quickly waved a hand. "Sorry. Dumb question. Forget it."

I turned and grabbed the nearest clothing item. It turned out to be a short jean skirt that was more suited to summer than the chill of a day like today, but what the hell. I teamed it with a thick cashmere sweater that hugged me in all the right places, then wondered who I was trying to impress. Azriel certainly couldn't care one way or another what I was wearing.

Once I'd pulled on tall leather boots, brushed my hair, and grabbed my handbag, I turned around and gave him a bright smile. "Okay, let's go."

"Risa—"

I cut him off with a sharp motion. "Don't worry about it, Azriel."

"I can hardly *not* worry about it when you are." He caught my hand and drew me toward him. But he didn't kiss me, didn't do any of those things that a human—or non-human—male might have done. Instead, he said, "The future is in a vast state of disarray right now. No one, not even those of us whose duty it is to know the future of everyone who lives on this plane, can guess at where this quest might lead."

My gaze searched his. "Meaning death is becoming more and more likely?"

He shrugged and gently brushed a stray strand of damp hair from my eyes. "It has always been a possibility."

"And yet you got angry when I said my death might be a good thing."

"Because there is a huge difference between taking one's own life and a death that has been foretold. I would not like to see you end up as one of the lost ones."

"Trust me, it's not like I'd want that, either." Yet I couldn't shake the notion that *that* possibility was still on the table. I sighed. "As I said, let's forget it. We need to go talk to the people at Hallowed Ground before bitch-face rings and blasts me."

"Her time will come," he said. "Have no fear of that."

"Then I hope I'm still around to see it."

"I suspect that even if you are *not* instrumental in the event, you will at least be there," he said. "And no, I will not say more."

"Damn you—"

"I was and am," he said grimly; then his energy swept through us, zipping us across to the Hallowed Ground in no time at all.

He dropped me in front of the place, then disappeared again before I could question him. I cursed him softly and headed inside the club. Though there was no entertainer onstage, the club had lost none of its patrons. But I guess that wasn't surprising given it was barely one thirty and most of them were vampires. I walked across to the bar and showed the man idly polishing glasses my badge. "I need to talk to someone about the fill-in entertainer you hired today."

The bartender—a balding, pot-bellied vampire who smelled of an odd mix of garlic and alcohol— shrugged. "I'm afraid I can't help you, love. Not my line of work, that, and I don't talk to the entertainers much."

"Not even briefly?"

"No."

A non-chatty bartender was not what I needed right now. "What about the owner?"

"He's not here."

"Then who hired the replacement?"

"That would be Harry, the manager." Amusement lit his brown eyes. "But you didn't ask for the manager, now, did you?"

"I think it could have been taken as a given, seeing I asked to talk to whoever was in charge," I said, barely holding back the annoyance in my voice.

"Ah, but you see, if there's one thing I've learned over my many years of working in non-human establishments, it's that you should never take anything as a given or anyone at face value."

"Which isn't bad advice in general." I hesitated, remembering Hunter's warning, then gave a mental shrug. If she wanted answers, then I had to question the people who were here, whether she liked it or not. "Can I speak to Harry, then?"

"Sure. He's in the office down past the end of the bar."

"Thanks."

He nodded, and his gaze followed me, burning a hole in the middle of my spine as I headed down. I had a feeling that it would be a bad mistake to think he was as meek and as mild as he appeared.

The office door was open, and the vampire inside—a man with ebony skin and dark hair—

looked up before I could knock. His eyes were an almost incandescent green that glowed brightly against his skin.

"You wanted to see me?"

Obviously, the bartender had psychically warned his boss of my presence. "I did."

He waved a hand toward the somewhat scruffy leather chair on the other side of his desk. "About what?"

I sat down. "The fill-in entertainer you hired today."

He snorted. "I can tell you one thing: She won't be coming back. She did a runner well before her set was finished." He studied me for a second, something close to amusement in his eyes. "Seems someone scared her off."

And I had a feeling he knew it was me. "Unfortunate, given I need to speak to her."

I showed him my badge, and his eyebrows rose. "So we *are* hiring werewolves these days."

"Well, no, just me. You could say I'm special."

"Could I, now?" He leaned back in his chair and studied me for several seconds before adding, "And did they give you the nano microcells you're wearing?"

The amusement I'd glimpsed in his eyes was definitely evident in his voice, and I had to wonder what the hell was going on. "No, they are a means of self-preservation."

"Do they keep Hunter out?"

I hadn't felt him attempting to read my mind, but then, with the best telepaths, you didn't. "Mostly." I shrugged. "Probably as much as it has kept you out."

He smiled. "I can read only the occasional surface thought."

"As can she, and usually the worst possible ones."

His smile grew as he leaned forward and offered me his hand. "Harry Stanford, at your service."

His grip was firm, but not overpowering. A vampire who was confident in his own strength and who saw no need to display it—unlike Hunter.

I studied him for several seconds, mulling over our brief conversation, then said, a little hesitantly, "Are you, by chance, on the high council yourself?"

"And where would you get that idea, young lady?"

"It's a guess."

"Then it is a good one." He picked up a pen and began to tap the table lightly.

Unease slithered through me, and my pulse rate began to skip—never a good thing when cornered in a small room with a vampire.

"And, uh, were you on the side of those who thought I could be of use to the council, or one of the ones who thought it would be better for all concerned if I were killed?"

"Neither. I could not see the sense in killing you before we'd explored and discussed all possible outcomes." A half smile touched his lips. "And I would never, under any circumstance, side with Hunter."

"Oh." Great. He hated Hunter, and I was here under her orders.

"Never fear," he said, almost jovially. "There is no point in killing the messenger when it is the master I would rather see dead."

"If you *did* attempt to harm her," Azriel said, voice flat but nevertheless deadly. He rested a hand on my left shoulder as he reappeared beside me. "You would be dead before you even left your chair."

"Ah, the reaper himself. I was wondering when you'd turn up."

"I am never far away."

"Indeed." He studied the two of us for a moment, then said, "You do realize, don't you, that Hunter has no intention of ever letting you off her leash? Her plans for you are vast, and the keys play only a minor part of that."

The keys were hardly a minor part when the earth risked being overrun either by the denizens of hell or unhappy souls unable to move on. "I got that impression. But, for the moment, I need her. Or rather, I need her resources."

His snort was disparaging. "What, to find your mother's murderer? Do you honestly think she has any intention of allowing that? Or that she even cares, now that she has what she wants? You, in her pocket?"

My unease grew. Why the hell was he saying all this? I had no damn idea—but one thing was for sure. It couldn't be for any *good* reason. "There are Cazadors working—"

"There was one. He found no clues, just as the Directorate found no clues. Your mother's killer might as well be a ghost, for all the evidence he left behind."

I flexed my fingers, trying to relax, but it didn't help much. "I agreed to help her if she helped me. I cannot back out of that arrangement."

Yet, I added silently.

"Not unless you have the help of someone strong enough to rival her."

And there it was, I thought. The twist in the tale fate just loved applying to make my life even more interesting.

My smile was grim. "I may not know much about the inside workings of the high council, but I do know that if you thought yourself her match, you could challenge her anytime you wanted."

"I could, but that would be playing by the rules. She doesn't, so I see no reason for me to do so."

Wonderful. Another schemer. Just what I needed in my life right now. "If you're so powerful, how come you're the daytime manager of a club like this?" I hesitated, then added rather hastily, "No offense meant."

He waved a hand—an elegant gesture that nevertheless managed to highlight the muscular nature of his arms. "It amuses me to work here."

And it had the advantage of keeping him out of Hunter's eye, I suspected. Just as I suspected that *this* man was the reason for her warning about talking to anyone but the owner.

"Why are you saying all this to me?" I asked, a little hesitantly. "Aren't you afraid I'll tell Hunter?

Or that she'll pick the conversation out of my thoughts?"

"Do I fear the former? No." He leaned forward and crossed his arms on the desk. "As to the latter, she is welcome to whatever remnants she can retrieve past those nano cells. She knows I plot, just as I know she plots. It is a game we have played for a very long time."

"Well, it's not one *I* want to be in the middle of."

"And yet here you are, right in the middle."

"Uh, no. I'm working for Hunter on a case, nothing more, nothing less."

"Hunter intends to use you *and* the keys to become overlord of the council."

"And you don't?"

He smiled. It was quite a pleasant smile compared to Hunter's, but that didn't mean he wasn't as cold-blooded and calculating as she was.

"No, actually, I don't. I just believe that the council—and the world in general—would not only be better off if the gate situation remained as it is, but a hugely nicer place to live in without her polluting presence."

A sentiment I could totally agree with—and I had to wonder if he was choosing his words to match whatever thoughts he might be catching.

"I see no point in falsehoods," he commented, thereby confirming that he was, indeed, catching some of my thoughts. "Especially when Hunter herself is my greatest asset when it comes to convincing others she must go."

Something else I could agree with. "Look, I'm really *not* interested in either your plans or Hunter's. I just want to do what I have to do to get free."

"Which you will not do without assistance."

I couldn't help smiling. "Don't take this the wrong way, but I very much suspect asking for your help would simply mean jumping from the frying pan into the fire."

"Oh, I am far more honorable than Hunter. And I, at least, am sane."

"If she's insane, then she's doing a good job of hiding it." I didn't like her. I didn't trust her. But she would hardly be head of the Directorate *and* a high-ranking member of the high vamp council if she was off her rocker. The vamps, at the very least, would not have stood for it.

"Oh, trust me, she long ago mastered the art of hiding what she truly is."

"And you, of course, are a paragon of honesty."

He conceded that point with a regal incline of his head and a half smile. "Well, you know where to find me if you change your mind. And I very much suspect you will."

"Don't swear off drinking blood until that happens," I said, "because you might well starve."

Amusement crinkled the corners of his brown eyes. "I'm tempted to ask if you'd like to bet on that, but I suspect you are not the betting kind."

"Not on stuff like this." I crossed my legs, and his gaze briefly dropped. It was only then I remembered I was wearing a short skirt. I cleared my throat softly, drawing his gaze upward again. "Can we get back to the reason I'm here now?"

"Indeed we can." He leaned back in the chair again, his expression still amused. "What do you wish to know about our Ms. Jodie Summer?"

"For a start, have you used her before?"

"No. Whenever we need to cover a shift, we simply ring the agency."

"And that agency is Classique?"

"Yes." He reached to the left of his desk, picked up a business card, and handed it to me. It was the same card I'd gotten from the manager at the other venue. I flipped the card over, but there was nothing written on the back. "Have you got a contact there? I might have to talk to them."

"Either James Parred or Catherine Moore should be able to help you. I've dealt with both."

"Thanks." I tucked the card into my handbag. "Is there anything you can tell me about Ms. Summer? Did you notice anything unusual about her?"

"Aside from the fact she was neither human, shifter, nor vampire, you mean?"

I half smiled. "Yeah, besides that."

"No, because she had some sort of shield operating that I could not slip past." He hesitated. "It was neither a nano shield such as the one you wear, nor one of magic."

My eyebrows rose. "Meaning you have working knowledge of magic?"

"Those of us who have been around a very long

time do tend to become proficient in all manner of things."

Not just magic, then. And it did make me wonder what else Hunter had become proficient in. Beside killing and being a coldhearted bitch, that was.

He chuckled softly. "It *is* a wonder you're still alive if you're having those sorts of thoughts around Hunter. She can be somewhat highly strung when it comes to those who disrespect her."

"Yeah, noticed that," I muttered, then got back to the business at hand. "So there's nothing else you can tell me?"

"I'm afraid not."

Meaning I was at another dead end. Hunter was not going to be pleased. I hesitated, then said, "I don't suppose you could pull a picture of Ms. Summer from your security cameras?"

"If you give us a couple of minutes, Jonathan will have a printout waiting for you at the bar."

"Thanks." I rose. "You've been most helpful."

"But not as helpful as I could be," he said, expression back to being amused. He opened a drawer and drew out another business card. It was a simple card—black background and white writing—and said *Harold Stanford, manager, Hallowed Ground*, with a cell phone number underneath. "Just in case you change your mind."

I accepted it somewhat reluctantly. "I won't, you know."

He shrugged. "It never hurts to have an escape option, Ms. Jones. That is all I am offering."

"Thanks for your time." I tucked the card in the side pocket of my handbag and headed out. Once I'd collected the printout of our suspect, I walked back outside.

"Well, that was fun," I said, making a beeline for the 7-Eleven several doors down from the club. I needed a Coke and chocolate fix to calm my still-quivering nerves.

Azriel fell in step beside me. "*Interesting* is more the term I would use."

I glanced at him sharply. "You believed his bullshit?"

"I believe he intends to oust Hunter from the council. I also believe he desires your help to do it."

A chime rang cheerfully as I entered the 7-Eleven. "That doesn't mean I should trust him."

"I never said you should. But it is certainly worthwhile keeping his offer in the back of your mind. Especially since I will not be around once the keys are found."

Him not being around was something I did *not* want to think about. "I can hardly keep it in the *front* of my mind, given Hunter's predisposition for picking up all the wrong types of thoughts."

"She will be well aware that you have talked to Stanford."

"Yeah, but I'm not going to rub her nose in it." I plucked a can of Coke from the refrigerator, but there wasn't a whole lot of choice when it came to smaller chocolate bars. After a couple of seconds' deliberation, I grabbed a Mars bar, then paid for

them both at the self-service scanners. "And I'm
certainly not going to mention the fact that he
made me a counteroffer."

"If they are longtime foes, then she will guess
what he will or will not have done."

"You know, I really don't want to be talking
about Hunter right now."

"Then what do you wish to talk about?" He
opened the door and ushered me outside, one hand
pressed lightly against my spine.

"Nothing. How about we just walk down to the
gardens so I can eat my chocolate and enjoy the
quiet?"

"You? Requesting silence? A rare moment indeed."

I snorted and nudged him with an elbow. "No
smart remarks from the peanut gallery, thanks."

"And what, precisely, is a peanut gallery?"

I rolled my eyes. "Just escort me down to the
park before I die of caffeine withdrawal."

His nod was decidedly regal; then he offered me
his arm and said, "As you wish."

I slipped my arm through his and we walked
down to the park, where I found a bench seat near
the fountain and had my snack, listening to the
dance of water and the songs of the birds in the
trees. It was, I thought, another one of those rather
pleasant—almost ordinary—moments to treasure
in a life gone crazy.

Unfortunately, it didn't last. Just as I tossed the
empty Coke can into the nearby bin, my phone

rang. I dug it out of my handbag and hit the vid-phone's ANSWER button.

"Stane," I said. "How'd the date go?"

"Ah, the date," he said, a somewhat bemused expression on his face. "You could say it wasn't what I expected."

"Meaning it was worse, or better?"

"Better is something of an understatement."

I smiled. "So your mother wasn't so far off the mark when she arranged this blind date?"

"Nope. Holly Green is not only pretty, but she's a *gamer*." He sighed. "I think I'm in love."

"You haven't invited her around to your place yet. She might yet be a clean freak."

"No one who is a gamer can be a clean freak. The two are totally incompatible."

My grin grew. The lone wolf had been snagged, and *bad*. "I take it you'll be seeing her again—sans mothers this time?"

"Oh, hell *yeah*."

I laughed. "Is that the only reason you're ringing? To boast about your hot date?"

"Uh, no." He composed himself, his expression becoming a touch more serious. "Got a hit on that storage locker. Someone just came out of it."

"Who?"

"I don't know yet. I'm running a scan, but nothing has come up yet." He disappeared briefly as he scooted from one screen to another. "I just sent you a picture. It's a woman, so it might be Genevieve Sands."

"How long ago did she actually leave?"

He hesitated. "Just going out through a side door now."

"Let me know the minute anyone else enters or exits. And thanks, Stane."

"No probs."

As I hung up, my phone chimed, telling me a message had been received. I pulled up the pic, then glanced at Azriel. "You want to take us there?"

He nodded and did so, depositing us again in the side parking lot near all the shrubs. I swung around, but didn't immediately see anyone matching the image on the phone. Then I spotted the tail end of a white overcoat disappearing around the Hoddle Street corner and raced after her.

As I ran into Hoddle Street, I spotted her. Like the woman in the photo, she was tall and thin, with short dark hair and a long, almost manly walk. She also was twenty yards away and heading briskly for a taxi.

"Miss Sands?" I had to yell to be heard over the roar of passing traffic. "Can I talk to you?"

Thankfully, she paused and looked over her shoulder, a frown marring her pale, lightly lined features. I'd expected Genevieve Sands to be a much older woman, for some reason, but she looked to be in her midforties, if that. "Do I know you?"

I slowed to a walk, dug my badge out of my handbag, and showed it just long enough for her to see the badge but not read the finer print that said I was vamp council rather than anything more official.

"I need to ask you a couple of questions."

She frowned, her amber gaze skating my length briefly before rising to mine. I had the feeling that I'd been found wanting—and it oddly reminded me of Lauren Macintyre's initial response to my presence.

"In regard to what?" She looked down the length of her long, Roman nose at me, her voice cool and collected.

I hesitated. "John Nadler."

She turned fully around, her handbag clasped in front of her like a shield and her expression puzzled. "Who?"

"John Nadler, a businessman who recently died." I stopped in front of her and forced a smile. "I believe you're one of his three beneficiaries."

She blinked. "In what way?"

"As in, he's dead and you've been named in his will."

"Why on earth would I be named in the will of a man I don't know?"

"I don't know." I frowned. If she was putting on an act, then it was a good one. And yet there was something about her, an energy radiating off her that had the hackles rising at the back of my neck. "You haven't been contacted by his lawyers?"

"Not that I'm aware of." She hesitated. "But I've been out of town on business for a few weeks. It is possible that their communication is being held at the post office along with my other mail."

Which was a perfectly legitimate excuse, so why didn't I believe it?

"Is that why you're using one of the storage units here? Because you've been away?"

She frowned. "What on earth has my renting a storage unit here got to do with being the beneficiary of a man I don't know?"

"Please, Ms. Sands, just answer the question."

She huffed somewhat haughtily, then said, "I've been renting the unit for several months now. My house is quite small and I needed somewhere secure to stock several valuable items."

I pulled my phone out and pretended to look up some notes. "And is your unit G-18?"

"Yes." She frowned. "I'm really not seeing the connection here."

"It's in regard to the ongoing investigation into Nadler's death," I said. "We believe there might be some connection to your unit. Would it be possible for us to have a look at it?"

"No, it would not. Not without a warrant." She paused, looking me up and down. "Produce one, and I'll be more than happy to comply."

"That will take a few hours. It really would—"

"I do not care about what is easy or not," she cut in coldly. "The law is the law, young lady, and I will not be railroaded into doing anything that might not be advantageous to myself."

"I'm not implying that you're in any way involved—"

"Then what are you implying?"

"As I said, I'm merely trying to tie up some loose ends."

"Well, this is one end that will remain loose until you get the proper paperwork, and not before."

Okay, then. I forced another smile. "If you happen to remember just where you know John Nadler from, could you perhaps give me a call?"

"That I can do." She took out an old-fashioned notebook and pen, then looked at me pointedly. "Number?"

I gave her my cell phone number, then added, "I'm sorry to have delayed you so long, Ms. Sands."

She nodded, tucked her notebook back into her bag, then turned and strode to the still-waiting taxi.

"What do you think?" I asked, as she climbed into the cab and slammed the door.

"I could not read her."

I glanced at him, surprised. "That seems to be happening an awful lot these days."

He shrugged. "There *are* humans we cannot read."

"You said it was rare."

"It is. We just seem to be coming across more of them than usual."

"So she *is* human?"

"Yes." He glanced at me. "Why?"

"Because there was something about her that didn't feel right."

"Well, given she was exiting a storage locker containing a sorceress's transport gate, it is very possible she is either in league with said sorceress, or the sorceress herself."

"It can't be the latter." I watched the taxi's

blinker come on as it readied to pull away from the curb.

"Why not?"

"Because she didn't have the same build as Lauren Macintyre."

"I cannot see—"

"Face-shifters can change only their *facial* shape, not their bodies."

"That does not mean there cannot be those who *are* able to do a full-body shift."

"If there is, I've never heard of them." As the taxi pulled into the traffic, I added, "I'm going to follow her."

"Be careful."

"That goes without saying."

"But given your somewhat reckless nature, it bears repeating."

"If I had the time, I'd be offended by that statement."

"It can hardly offend when it is the truth."

"Only as you see it. Meet you back home." I dropped a quick kiss on his lips, then slung my handbag over my shoulder and called to the Aedh. She came in a rush, and within a heartbeat I was trailing after the taxi.

We followed Hoddle Street, went under the Swan Street rail overpass, then followed Punt Road for several miles until the taxi turned left into Greville Road and stopped at a redbrick and concrete house that looked totally alien among all the more traditional terraces.

I waited until Genevieve had stepped inside and

slipped in after her. A quick look around her house didn't reveal anything out of the ordinary. It was neat and obviously well lived in, with plenty of clothes in the wardrobe and little dust on the furniture. I briefly wondered how long she'd been away, because surely if it had been any length of time, there would have been dust. And if she'd had the time to dust, why wouldn't she have collected her mail?

She dumped her coat and bag on her bed, checked her answering machine, then headed into the bathroom. I waited until she'd filled her bath and climbed in before I gave up and retreated.

"Anything?" Azriel grabbed my arm as I reappeared in my bedroom, steadying me.

I shook my head, gulping down air as dizziness swept me and my stomach briefly rose. But this time, there was no my-head-is-going-to-explode pain accompanying the shift back to flesh form, and though my legs felt weak, they didn't collapse underneath me. Although no doubt Azriel's grip had something to do with that.

He guided me across to the bed and sat me down. He plucked the phone from my fingers, dropped it lightly on the bed, then squatted in front of me and clasped my hands between his. Warmth began to flow through me, gently chasing away the remaining weakness.

"What did she do?"

"Nothing. She just went home and had a bath." I grimaced. "I don't know. Maybe I'm just jumping at shadows, but she still feels wrong to me."

"Perhaps our next step should be uncovering whether there are shifters capable of full transformation."

"Yeah." I took a deep, somewhat shuddery breath, then pulled my hands from his and picked up my phone. "Uncle Rhoan," I said, and watched the psychedelic swirls run across the screen as the call was connected.

"Ris," he said, after a couple of moments. "What can I do for you?"

"Got a weird question for you—are there such things as face-shifters who are capable of transforming their whole bodies?"

He frowned. "Well, I've never come across one, but I can't see why there wouldn't be. They're probably rarer than hens' teeth, though."

"Would something like that be registered on a birth certificate?"

"I doubt it. Even face-shifters are registered only as shifters—and only if they come from a known line of shifters. If it's an out-of-the-blue occurrence, or they're the product of a human-shifter mating, then probably not." He hesitated. "Why?"

"I was just following a woman who reminded me of someone else, but she looked nothing like her."

"Could she be a sister or a relation?"

"We can't uncover much about her, let alone anything about her family. She may exist, but there's not a whole lot of paperwork to prove it."

"So you're thinking a fake ID?"

"Maybe." I scratched my nose. "I don't know."

He studied me for a moment, gray eyes narrowed. "I hope this woman has nothing to do with our two spiderwebbed victims."

"Not a thing. It's key related."

"Huh. Well, the best I can do is run a search for you, but I doubt anything will come up."

And I doubted whether a search done by Directorate resources would bring up anything more than one done by Stane, but I guessed it couldn't hurt. "The woman's name is Genevieve Sands. She lives at sixty-five Greville Road, Prahran."

"Posh address."

"Posh woman." I hesitated. "Speaking of the other deaths—"

"No, Risa."

"Damn it, I'm just curious—"

"And you know what *that* did to the cat," he said with a smile. "You've got enough on your plate. Don't go stealing my work as well."

I half laughed. "You're welcome to your work. I'm just curious as to whether you'd uncovered anything interesting—"

"If I did, I wouldn't be telling you. Talk to you later, Ris."

"With some interesting information on Sands, hopefully," I said, and hung up. I tossed the phone back on the bed and sighed. "Another dead end."

"Possibly not. Despite her assertions to the contrary, she must know who Nadler is, because she would not be named heir otherwise, true?"

"Well, maybe. You occasionally see reports of strangers or even animals being gifted money in wills."

"But it is unlikely to be the case here."

"Very unlikely."

"And we also know she must have some acquaintance with Lauren Macintyre, as that transport portal ultimately leads to her place."

"Actually, it leads to the house Lucian's Razan are staying in. There's another portal that goes to Lauren's from there."

"Lucian's Razan?"

The edge in his voice had me frowning. "What, you didn't pick that information up from my thoughts?"

"No, I did not."

"Oh." I hesitated. "Why the hell not?"

He waved the question away. "The Razan?"

"There was only one there, but his name is Mark Jackson, and he was the one we knocked unconscious in the tunnel."

"Why are you so sure he is Lucian's Razan?"

"Because there's no one else he could belong to."

"Your father—"

"Would not be dealing with a dark sorcerer. I might not be sure of much, but I'm pretty sure of that." I shrugged. "Lucian was his *chrání*, and you said yourself that they often shared the same markings as their masters."

"It would be interesting to uncover whether—if Jackson *is* the Aedh's *chrání*—he was a recent creation or one that was created before his power was ripped from him by the Razan."

I frowned. "What difference would it make?"

"If before, then not much. If the latter"—he

paused, something close to hatred glimmering briefly in his eyes—"then he has thoroughly concealed his true self and is far more powerful—and dangerous—than I suspected."

"Meaning he *could* take on his energy form?"

He hesitated. "No. There is no doubt he has been trapped in flesh form for eons. But it *is* possible he could not only take on partial form, but have all his other powers available as well."

I frowned. "What sort of powers would we be talking about?"

"The ability to use magic, for a start. The Raziq are proficient in its use—they have to be, as masters of the gates."

"I thought the priests were the masters?"

"And the Razan were once priests. Lucian, as your father's *chrání*, is very likely to be magically strong. Your father would not have taken him otherwise."

Meaning Lucian had never had to enlist Lauren's help to spell me—he could have done it all himself. I frowned. "So why did he get Lauren to make that cube? Why wouldn't he have made it himself?"

"Because he would have wanted to belay any suspicions. *His* magic would feel very different from that of his mistress."

"But I've never felt any of his magic."

"And perhaps never would. As I said, he would be extremely strong and—I suspect—very adept at hiding it after all those years on this plane."

I blew out a breath. "I really was fooled by him, wasn't I?"

"But not for as long as he might have desired."

"Thankfully," I muttered, then jumped as my phone rang. The tone told me it was Hunter, and I groaned. "Like I need to speak to her right now."

"Talking on the phone is preferable to talking in person, is it not?"

"There is that." I hit the ANSWER button and said, "I had nothing to report, which is why I didn't report."

Her voice was cool and disbelieving. "So the woman wasn't there?"

"No, she was there, but she did a runner on us. We chased her to her dressing room, but she escaped and left lots of little friends behind to play with us."

And the memory of it had my skin crawling all over again.

Amusement briefly touched Hunter's lips. "Spiders, I'm guessing?"

"Lots of them, as I said."

"How quaint that you're afraid of something so small."

"We all have an Achilles' heel. Spiders just happen to be mine."

Something glimmered in her eyes. Something that could have been humor but felt like something far darker. "Oh, you have more than just spiders, my dear."

I found myself clenching the phone so tight, I was in danger of cracking the case. "What weakens can also give you strength. You might want to remember that sometime."

"My, my," she murmured. "Aren't we all aggressive this afternoon? I wonder why."

I took a deep breath and released it slowly. "Talking to uncooperative vampires tends to do that to me."

"I gather you mean those who run Hallowed Ground rather than myself?"

"Of course." I kept my voice flat, without inflection. To have done anything else would have been dangerous. "I didn't learn much, but I did get a picture of our suspect."

"So she *is* the one we're after?"

"Hard to tell, because she was using some sort of shield that stopped Azriel sensing what she was. But given she had a boatload of spiders sitting in her dressing room, I think it likely."

"So she left nothing behind other than the spiders?"

"No." I hesitated. "But she's killed two nights in a row, so I'd bet she'll attempt to do so again tonight."

"More than likely." Hunter studied me, a deeper darkness creeping into her eyes. "I believe you talked to Stanford, despite my warning not to."

I shivered, wondering how she'd known. The bartender, perhaps? Then I remembered—I had a damn Cazador following me around, reporting every little move back to her. "I had no choice. The owner wasn't there and the bartender didn't know anything."

Hunter snorted. "Bartenders know *everything*."

"Well, this one wasn't talking." At least not to

me. "The only way to get any information was to talk to Stanford."

"And did he have anything interesting to say beyond his lack of knowledge about his fill-in entertainer?"

I hesitated. Stanford might be planning to oust Hunter, but he could also be doing nothing more than stirring the pot. Hell, for all I knew, he'd picked up the phone and talked to Hunter the minute I was out the door. Which meant that no matter what I said, it wasn't going to make her happy.

Although I could hardly lie, given the Cazador.

"Nothing worth listening to," I said eventually.

Amusement touched her lips. "I'm glad to hear it."

I bet she was. Couldn't have her pet joining the opposition, after all—not before she'd done what was expected of her, anyway.

"He did give me his contacts at the entertainment agency. I thought I might go talk to them, unless you'd prefer—"

"If I wanted to get deeply involved in this case, I would have," she said. "Report back to me if you uncover anything else."

And with that, she hung up.

"Hunter was her charming self, I see," Azriel murmured.

I laughed, as he'd no doubt intended. "Yeah, she was."

He caught my hand and rose, dragging me upright with him. "Tao is about to call for you."

"Why?"

"I believe he is hungry." He gave me a somewhat

stern look. "And you should be eating something, too."

"Yes, Mom," I murmured, as I brushed past him.

"Hey, Ris?" Tao called, just as I neared his bedroom door. "You out there?"

I poked my head around the door. "I am. What can I do for you?"

"Ilianna threatened to make the old boy go limp for the next three months if I got out of bed for anything more than a pee," he said, expression amused. "But she hasn't come back from her shopping expedition, and I'm absolutely starving."

"So get up and get something. She's not going to know."

He snorted. "Maybe, but I enjoy sex too much to risk it."

I grinned. "What would you like?"

"Anything that involves lots of meat."

"Steak, eggs, and chips?"

"Perfect." He grinned. "And I'll have a beer while I'm waiting."

I raised an eyebrow. "Did Ilianna really make that threat? Because you seem to be milking it a little here."

"Hell yeah." He grinned. "Having you run around waiting on me hand and foot isn't something that happens every day. Gotta make the most of it."

I snorted softly and headed into the kitchen. Half an hour later, I dished up two plates and walked back into his room.

"That," he said, practically drooling as he accepted the plate, "smells divine."

"Then eat up." I sat down on the chair beside his bed and followed my own advice. I was about half-way through my meal when my phone rang again. This time the tone said it was Stane.

I cursed softly. "I swear, people are intent on not letting me eat today."

"So ignore it," Tao said sagely. "It's not like you can't ring him back."

Azriel appeared by the chair and offered me the phone. "It could relate to the storage unit."

"Yeah." I accepted the phone and hit the ANSWER button. "Stane, what's up?"

"Genevieve Sands just got out of a taxi in front of that storage place again."

I glanced at Azriel. "Maybe we spooked her."

"Could be."

"I think we should go see what she's doing." To Stane, I added, "I discovered her address today. Do you think it'll help you dig up any other information about her?"

"Worth a try."

I gave him the address, then added, "And while I'm thinking about it, have you still got that bug we used at the nightclub?"

"Certainly do. I wasn't about to let that baby go—do you know how hard those things are to get?"

Given they were black market, I'd imagine very hard, and very expensive. "What's the range of the thing?"

"Fairly extensive. Why?"

"So if I were to place it in an apartment up on the Gold Coast, you'd be able to pick up its signal?"

"No, but if you were willing to fork out the cost of hiring a buddy of mine, I could get him to pick up the signal and bounce it down to me."

"Done. Can we pick it up later, after we've checked out the storage unit?"

"You can, but I won't have everything in place by then. And I'm not sure if Fitz will have the necessary relay stuff on hand."

"Do what you can."

"I will."

"Thanks." I hung up and shoved my plate toward Tao. "You want to finish any of that?"

He snagged the rest of the steak and gave me a thumbs-up. I took the rest out to the kitchen and dumped it in the trash, then grabbed my bag and coat and turned to Azriel. "Let's go."

We reappeared in the side parking lot again. The evening air was cold enough for my breath to fog, so I pulled my coat on as I walked toward the entrance.

But I'd barely taken half a dozen steps when the building exploded in a gigantic ball of flame.

Chapter 8

The force of the blast knocked me off my feet and sent me tumbling. I landed in an ungainly heap near the shrubs that lined the parking lot, with bricks, metal, and wood thudding all around me. I didn't move, just squeezed my eyes shut, threw my hands over my head, and prayed like hell that I wasn't hit. Then Azriel landed on top of me, knocking out whatever breath I'd had left.

But the minute his body covered mine, the debris stopped falling—not just on us, but around us. And it became quiet. Whisper quiet. I frowned and opened my eyes. We were surrounded by a halo of blue fire.

"What the *hell*?"

"Valdis shields us." His warm breath tickled my ear. "She formed it the minute the building exploded."

"Is that why you're lying on top of me?"

"Yes. It was easier than transporting us both out of here—especially given you would only want to come back." He hesitated, then added, with a hint of a smile in his voice, "Of course, this way I also get to touch you more fully, and that is not entirely unpleasant."

I snorted. "You're beginning to sound like a regular male, and that's scary."

"Right now, I feel like a regular male."

Laughter bubbled through me. "Well, I *was* going to be polite and not mention that bar you have—"

"I meant," he cut in, the amusement in his voice deeper this time, "that I was feeling protective. You, Risa Jones, have what I believe is called a dirty mind."

"Hey, I'm *not* the one manning up."

"*That* is a function of *this* body I have no real control over." Valdis's shield flickered and died, but he didn't immediately move. "Are you all right?"

I opened my mouth to say yes, but the word never came out. With the shield gone, the noise hit, and it was *horrendous*. But the creak and groan of a dying building wasn't the worst of it. It was the screams of those trapped and injured that were the hardest to take.

"Oh god, Azriel, we have to help—"

"We cannot," he said, voice firm. "It is too dangerous to go in there just yet."

I bucked my body, trying to get him off me, but I might as well have tried to shift a brick wall. "Damn it. I can't just lie here—"

"You can, and you will," he said. "It is not within your ability to save those people."

"But it *is* within your ability."

"No."

"Azriel—"

"*No.*" This time there was an edge of anger in his voice. "I am not here to alter the hand fate has dealt to any of those people inside."

"Not unless it had something to do with the keys, which this *does*."

"Only peripherally. I have no justification for interfering in either the life or the death of those within that building."

"What about Genevieve Sands? She might be connected to both the dark sorcerer *and* the keys, so why can't you at least go in there to see if she survived?"

"Look at the building, Risa. Do you really think it possible she could be alive?"

I twisted around and my gaze widened. Flames leapt high from either end, but it was the middle of the building—in the area that had held Lauren Macintyre's storage unit—that had taken the brunt of the explosion. It was *completely* destroyed. There was nothing left but the charred remnants of brick walls and the twisted remains of metal. There is no way in hell anyone in that area could have survived.

"There's no guarantee she was actually *in* there at the time of the explosion. She might have set it all up and then used the stones to escape." That was what I would have done if I'd been in her somewhat ugly shoes. "We need to go check the Razans' place and see if she's there."

Azriel's expression went back to being noncommittal. "You cannot go in Aedh form, as they will sense you."

I met his gaze. "You could go."

He hesitated. "I prefer not to leave you—"

"Who's going to attack me here? The Raziq are

waiting for my father's appearance, Hunter still has use for me, and anyone else I can cope with."

"Given you do have the unfortunate habit of attracting danger, that is no comfort."

I smiled. "It's going to take you a couple of minutes, if that, to check. What trouble could I get into in that amount of time?"

"Plenty, I suspect." He rose, his movements fluid and graceful, and offered me a hand. "Do not go into that building."

"I won't." Not in human form, anyway.

"Risa—"

"Stop being such a worrywart and go before she escapes us again."

He did. I brushed the dirt and grit from my hands and clothes as I studied the blackened, broken building. There was little sound coming from the building now—little in the way of human sound, anyway—but the flames were intense, a caress of heat that would burn my skin if I got any closer. But I had to get closer, no matter what Azriel said. Though the approaching wail of the emergency vehicles was barely audible over the fierce burn of the fire, they were little more than a couple of minutes away. If I wanted to check if anything in that locker had survived the blast, I'd better do it now, before officialdom descended and perhaps destroyed whatever evidence still survived.

My gaze went to the front of the building. Fire licked along the roof, but much of the front office still seemed to be standing. Which meant that Maggie, the cheerful receptionist who'd been working there yesterday, might still be alive.

And I couldn't escape the sudden notion that I needed to check—not only to save her life if that were possible, but for the sake of our mission.

My clairvoyance sure picked the oddest times to kick in.

A good-sized crowd had gathered across the other side of the road, but few of them were looking in my direction. I called to the Aedh and she rushed through me, changing my form in an instant.

Heat and dust whispered through my particles as I moved closer to the building, an unpleasant combination that made me want to scratch even though I had no flesh. I slipped through the ugly hole blown in the side of the building and made my way above the debris that had once been a corridor. The storage units on either side were little more than skeletal remnants, with boxes and god knows what else hanging out of them like the innards of a gutted body.

But the wall between the storage section and the office area was still basically intact, and though it was barely visible through the smoke and flames, hope rose.

The door into the office area hung limply from one hinge, tilted inward by the force of the explosion. Flames licked the doorframe and slipped fiery tentacles along the inside ceiling. I went through, mentally wincing as the flames danced through my energy form. It felt like red-hot fingers were being shoved inside me.

The office itself hadn't escaped damage, despite the buffer of the standing wall. Furniture was strewn everywhere, paper and glass littered the floor, and the front windows were smashed and were held in place only by the thick mesh grills covering them. The air was a morass of dust, smoke, and heat.

I spun around, searching for any sign of life, but couldn't immediately see anything. The desk where the receptionist had been sitting had tipped over sideways and was now covered by part of the ceiling. There was no sign of life. But, by the same token, there was no evidence of blood or broken body parts.

Then what sounded like a groan came from under the debris of the desk. I swore mentally and shifted back to flesh. The air was so damn hot that it felt like I'd fallen into an oven set on high, and the thick, heavy smoke swirled around me, stinging my eyes and catching in my throat, making me cough.

"Maggie?" I had to shout to be heard above all the noise. "Where are you?"

No answer came, but after a moment, I heard another groan. It was definitely coming from underneath the desk area.

I began grabbing bits of plaster and rubbish from the pile covering the desk and tossed them to one side. Another explosion ripped through the building, and the walls around me shuddered. I ducked instinctively, scraping my thigh along a jagged piece of wood as dust and bricks fell around me. The remnants of plaster still clinging to the ceiling began to crack alarmingly; it wouldn't take much to bring the rest of it down.

I swore and drew Amaya. *Don't cut or burn the woman's flesh.*

Will not, she replied.

Fire ignited along her blade, the lilac flames bright in the smoky darkness. I used her steel to hack apart the larger chunks of wood, plaster, and metal that lay between me and the receptionist, kicking the smaller bits aside as Amaya's flames consumed everything else.

From somewhere under the mess came another groan.

"Maggie? Can you hear me?" I shoved Amaya's tip under a long piece of wood, then thrust it up and back.

There was a pause, then a weak, "Here. Help."

Something shimmered in the smoky shadows near the door. I tensed, my fingers tightening around Amaya, then realized it was a reaper. She wore the image of an elderly woman and had a kind face and sorrowful blue eyes.

"You can't have her," I said fiercely. "She's not going to die."

"That is neither your decision nor mine," the reaper replied softly.

I blinked. None of them had ever talked to me before. None of them except Azriel, anyway.

"That is because you have never spoken directly to any of us before now," she said, her expression somewhat amused.

"I had no real reason to before now," I muttered.

I grabbed another chunk of wood and threw it away.

A flash of familiar heat across my skin told me Azriel had also appeared. "I thought you weren't coming in here in flesh form," he said.

"Yeah, well, you knew it was a lie, so why sound so aggrieved now?" I shoved another piece of wood out of the way. "You could help, you know."

"I cannot interfere in this one's life or death, Risa, and you know that."

"Damn it. I'm *not* asking you to interfere. I'm just asking you to help me remove some of the rubbish on top of her."

"I cannot."

"Well, fuck you *both*, then!" I raised Amaya and brought her down hard. Her blade hit the desk and, with a resounding crack, split it in two. As her lilac flames began eating into the wood, I raised a foot and kicked half of the desk with all the force I could muster. It tumbled up and back, revealing the bloody and bruised torso of the young receptionist.

I squatted beside her and gently brushed the hair from her eyes. "Maggie? Can you hear me?"

She nodded, though she didn't open her eyes, and the movement was so weak it might have been imagination on my part.

My gaze slid down her length. Her hips and legs were trapped under the remains of the desk, and the blood I hadn't seen earlier was there. Everywhere. I bit my lip, then added, "I'm going to get you out of here, okay?"

Her eyes fluttered open. She blinked, and just for

a moment, confusion briefly outshone the pain in her eyes. "You. Changed again."

I frowned, not sure what she meant. Not even sure if she was seeing me. "Your legs are trapped under the desk, Maggie. I'm going to free you, but it could hurt. Okay?"

She swallowed, then nodded and closed her eyes again. I rose, stepped over her, then, as quickly but as gently as I could, grabbed the edge of the desk and flung it up and over her. She screamed. The sound cut through me, as sharp as a knife, then abruptly stopped.

The reaper stepped forward.

"No," I said. "Please, don't."

"Her decision is made. Her soul moves on." The elderly reaper's voice was filled with gentle understanding. "There is nothing you can do for her now."

"Damn it, no," I said, and looked down. A soft shimmer rolled over the receptionist's body; then her soul pulled free. She looked at peace, happy almost. I closed my eyes, not wanting to see her spirit take the reaper's hand and move on.

Not wanting to acknowledge my failure to yet again save someone.

Another explosion ripped through the building. Above, the ceiling cracked and plaster began to fall, the pieces small at first, then getting gradually larger as the cracks grew and joined.

I swore and called to the Aedh, changing form just as the remainder of the ceiling crashed down. It would have crushed me if I'd still been standing there. As it was, dust and debris plumed through my particles, making me feel as if every inch was coated in grime.

I headed back into the hellhole that the main storage area had become, quickly winding my way through the remnants of the corridor until I found Genevieve's storage locker. Or rather, where it once had been, because this area was definitely ground zero. There was very little left here, nothing but a few blackened, twisted metal remains. I turned around, trying to find the middle of the unit where the stones had stood. What I found instead was the remnant of a leg—though it was little more than crisped strips of skin and meat hanging from a cracked and blackened femur. I looked around for the rest of the body, but couldn't see anything. Why just that section of whoever's body it was had survived was anyone's guess.

There was little evidence left of the stones, which no doubt had been the intention of the blast. Genevieve Sands obviously didn't want to risk me investigating this locker. It's just too bad for her that I already *had*—something she would have known if she'd accessed the site's security system. For once it seemed that fate had played us a better hand than the bad guys.

I checked the rest of the storage units in the hope that someone else might have survived, but the effort was futile. All I found were bodies. There was nothing else I could do, so I turned around and headed home. Once there, I stripped off and show-ered, although the dust was so ingrained, I had a sneaking suspicion I'd be rubbing it out of my skin for the next week.

Once I'd finger combed my hair, I headed out to find Azriel. He was back in his usual spot.

"What is it about you and windows?" I grabbed some socks out of the nearby dresser and plopped down on the bed to pull them on.

He shrugged. "It is, quite literally, a window to a small section of your world. It is endlessly interesting watching what goes on."

"Meaning your world is boring?"

"My world is one of rules and duty. It is not so much boring as that nothing ever changes."

"I can't imagine the life of a Mijai would be too boring."

"The life of a hunter-killer is exciting for only the first couple of millennia."

I stared at him for a moment, not quite sure I'd heard him right. "Millennia?"

He glanced at me, amusement briefly touching his eyes. "I am young in Mijai terms."

"But ancient in mine."

His eyebrows rose. "And this is a problem?"

"No, just surprising, that's all." I pulled the last sock on, then reached for my boots. "Did you find Genevieve at the Razans' place?"

"No, she had already moved on."

"To the place on the Gold Coast?"

"I checked both there and her house in Prahran. She was at neither."

"Damn." I thrust a hand through my hair and

wondered if that meant she were dead, or if she were merely being cautious.

"That is a question that cannot be answered until she turns up either alive or dead."

Very true. We had no idea how involved Genevieve Sands might be with either the magic or the key quest, and it was certainly more than possible that she *was* dead—but I was betting on the former rather than the latter. Something about the grim remains I'd seen just seemed a little too convenient. "So what do we do now?"

"Given we can do nothing on our own quest until tomorrow, perhaps we should concentrate on Hunter's."

"I guess." I glanced at the clock. It was just after four, so there was still plenty of time to head on over to the entertainment agency and talk to either James Parred or Catherine Moore, the two contacts Stanford had given us for the agency. "I might go over to the agency on my bike. My head still feels achy after all the shifting to and from Aedh form."

"That you have shifted so much and have not suffered the consequences suggests you are becoming more adept at the process."

"Or it's a result of whatever Malin did to me."

He hesitated. "Yes."

I snorted softly. "You're determined not to give me any information about that, are you?"

"You know I cannot. Your dealings with your father are dangerous enough as they are."

"Just because I understand your reasons doesn't mean I'm not frustrated by them." I gathered my phone and ID, then walked to the wardrobe to get my leather bike gear. "I'll meet you at the front of Classique Entertainers."

He nodded and disappeared. I headed down to the garage, gearing up in my leathers before I hopped on the Ducati and drove out.

Of course, going anywhere near the city approaching peak hour always added far too much time to the journey, so it was close to 4:45 by the time I got to Port Melbourne.

The agency was located in an area that was all concrete warehouses and office buildings. I found parking under one of the trees lining the center strip, then pulled off my gloves and helmet, shoved them into the under-seat storage, and headed across the road to Classique. It was situated in a building that was basically a glass-fronted concrete box, though the colorfully painted wooden strips lining the upper half of the building on either side of the windows at least gave it a bit of personality that was sadly lacking in its neighbors.

Azriel joined me as I walked toward the steps. "Would not a disguise be useful at this point, given that your uncle would not be pleased to discover you're investigating these crimes?"

I stopped cold. "Shit, yes. Thanks for reminding me." I did a quick look around, scanning the nearby building to see if there was anyone staring out the window. There didn't appear to be, so I imaged myself with a long, thin face, with freckles over a somewhat large hooked nose, and spiky red hair. Once the shifting magic had done its work, I glanced at Azriel. "Well?"

"Definitely *not* an improvement," he said, barely managing to restrain his smile.

I laughed. "What about you? There may be cameras inside, and we can't risk Uncle Rhoan recognizing you any more than we can me."

"Both human and electronic eyes will see a leather-clad, hairy-faced individual of impressive proportions."

"Hopefully not too impressive—we don't want to scare them."

"Impressive proportions toned down, then."

I grinned, loving his growing sense of humor more and more, and all but bounced up the steps. I pushed open the bright red metal doors, then stepped inside. The reception area was as modern as the outside of the building, with glass and bright colors being a central theme. The seated woman did something of a double take as we walked in. Her eyebrows rose slightly, but all she said was, "Can I help you?"

I dug my ID out of my pocket and showed it to her. "I need to talk to either James Parred or Catherine Moore about an entertainer they booked for Hallowed Ground this afternoon."

She studied the badge for a moment, then frowned. "An investigator for the high council? What the hell is that?"

She had good eyes, because I'd deliberately kept the badge some distance from her.

"It means I work for the vampire high council."

I kept my voice in the lower tonal ranges. There was a security camera in the corner, and while it was focused on the door, I had no idea if it was sound capable or not. The last thing I needed was Uncle Rhoan raiding their system and hearing me.

"So, not Directorate?"

"No." I hesitated. "I take it they have been here, though?"

"Yes. Yesterday." She frowned. "So are you a cop or what?"

I gave her what I hoped was a reassuring smile. "I lean more toward being a private investigator than something as official as a cop."

"Meaning you don't have the same sort of powers?"

"No." And I could see where this was leading—me being shown the door. I glanced at Azriel. *Don't suppose you can apply a little reaper charm, could you? I know you're not supposed to, but we need to get this case moving so we can concentrate on our own.*

He raised an eyebrow, but he gave the woman a full-wattage smile and said, "We tend to be the intermediaries between the council and the Directorate. We're used when the council does not wish a more official investigation."

"But they *are* involved with whatever you are here to ask about, aren't they?"

A woman immune to your wily ways, I said, amused. *How amazing is that?*

I suspect the reason is all the hair. She does not find it attractive, apparently.

Amusement bubbled through me, although I

could certainly sympathize. Lots of hair wasn't on my must-have list when it came to men, either. *Can you give her a little push into accepting us?*

Only if it was key related, which this is not.

I mentally sighed, then said, "Look, we just have a couple of quick questions, but if you think either James Parred or Catherine Moore would prefer to speak directly to the guardians, that can be arranged."

She bit the bottom of her lip, her expression uncertain, then made her decision and picked up the phone. "James, there are some investigators from the vampire council here who wish to speak to you about Ms. Summer."

"Another bloody complaint, no doubt," he replied, voice clearly audible even from where I stood. As was his annoyance. "Send them in."

The woman hung up and motioned to the vibrant yellow door at the far end of the desk. "Through there, green door on your left."

"Thanks."

We followed her directions, and a balding, middle-aged man rose from his chair and gave a welcoming—if somewhat tense—smile. "James Parred, at your service."

I shook his offered hand. "Annie Logan and Bear Brown," I said, grabbing at the first names that came to mind.

He glanced at Azriel, amusement briefly touching his lips. "Bear?"

"It is more a nickname," Azriel replied, giving me a "must-you?" sort of look.

"Well, it's certainly appropriate, if you don't

mind me saying." He waved a hand toward the seats, then sat back down himself. "What do you wish to know about Ms. Summer?"

"We went to Hallowed Ground to talk to her this afternoon, but she disappeared—"

"Yeah, damn annoying, that was," he cut in. "She did me out of a booking fee and annoyed a good customer."

"Have you been in contact with her? Do you know why she ran?"

He shook his head. "I tried calling her, but she's not answering her phone."

"And have you had any problems like this with her before?"

"Like this? No."

"But you have had problems?"

He hesitated. "Earlier this week we were having problems contacting her, but she called yesterday and said her phone had been on the blink." He grimaced. "Obviously, it still is."

Either that, or the shape-shifting spirit behind these kills had decided to abandon the Summer identity. And that, in turn, meant we were dealing with a spirit with more intelligence than I'd thought them capable of. Although why I'd thought them incapable of logical thought, I couldn't say. Maybe I'd just figured dark spirits were all about the need to kill and little else.

"What about Di Shard?"

He blinked. "What about her?"

"Well, have you had a similar problem with her recently?"

DARKNESS UNMASKED   215

"She was out of contact for a couple of days, but it wasn't a problem because we didn't actually have her booked for anything." He shrugged.

"Have you been in contact with her recently?"

"She called this morning to ask if there were any bookings."

"And were there?"

"Nothing last moment. But I did have to remind her about her regular midnight booking at the Falcon Club, which was a little odd."

Meaning if our dark spirit *had* taken over the identities of both Summer and Shard, the Falcon Club was most likely her next hunting ground. "Have you got a picture of the two women?"

"Sure."

He rifled through the paperwork on his desk and handed me two photos. Both women were tall, with thin features and dark hair. Other than the fact one had pale skin, the other dark, they could have been mistaken for sisters.

I glanced up at Parred. "Until recently, how reliable were they?"

"Very." He grimaced. "Reliability and quality performances are necessary assets in this business. Without it, you don't survive that long."

"I don't suppose you could give me their addresses?"

He frowned. "No, I'm sorry, but information like that is private. I couldn't hand it over without a warrant."

"What about a cell phone number? It's urgent that I speak with both women."

His frown deepened. "I'm not sure—"

"It's only a cell phone number," I said, using my most persuasive voice. "It's not like I can use it to track down their addresses or anything."

He snorted. "The Directorate could."

"The Directorate could have just pulled their driver's license details and gotten the information from there."

I could have, too—or rather, Stane could have. But I needed to take all the right steps to satisfy Hunter, and that had to include talking to the people who employed the two women.

He studied me for several seconds, then half shrugged. "I guess it won't hurt."

He leaned forward, pulled an old wireless keyboard out from under his desk, and began typing. I glanced at Azriel. *Don't suppose you could take a sneaky look over his shoulder without him noticing?*

I could. His tone was amused.

I smiled. *Then would you?*

Of course.

He appeared behind Parred. *Shard lives in flat one, ten Martin Street, St. Kilda, and*—he hesitated, waiting as Parred did some more typing—*Sands lives in flat eleven, one twenty Newman Street, Kensington.*

He reappeared on the seat beside me just as Parred grabbed a piece of paper and scrawled two phone numbers onto it. "Here," he said, sliding the paper across to me. "The first is for Shard, the second for Sands. Hope you have better luck contacting them than I have of late."

"Thanks for your help."

"Anytime."

We headed out. Once safely across the street and well out of earshot, I pulled out my phone and gave both women a call. Neither one answered. No surprise there, I guess. Especially when it was more than likely that both women were either incapacitated or dead.

I shoved my phone away and glanced at Azriel. "We'll try Di Shard first. She's slightly closer."

"I will meet you there."

He disappeared. I called to the shifting magic and made my face my own again, then pulled on the helmet and climbed onto the Ducati.

The trip across to St. Kilda was hell, thanks to the traffic, and by the time I got to Martin Street, I was more than a little pissed off and totally wishing I'd simply come here via Aedh form.

I cruised slowly past the apartment building, then parked around the corner, stored my helmet, and walked back. Ten Martin Street was a modern glass and concrete building that looked like a series of receding boxes, each layer sitting farther back, giving that "box" more of a courtyard than the one below it. The top layer apparently had enough room for a large outdoor umbrella to be set up.

I glanced at Azriel as he appeared beside me. "Can you sense anything inside?"

"There is life in the first two apartments; nothing in the other two."

"Are there any bodies?"

"If death occurred some time ago, as you suspect, I would not sense it. A soul's resonance does not last beyond a few days in this world, unless they become one of the lost ones."

"So if Shard is dead in there, this death was meant to be?"

"Yes."

I studied the building a minute longer, but I was only delaying the inevitable. "Right. Let's go."

I wrapped my fingers around my keys and phone and called to the Aedh. Once I'd changed form, I moved across the road, hesitating briefly to study the names on the intercom before slipping through the small gap between the door and the floor. Flat one, according to the directory, was up on the first floor. Shard's flat was the only one on that floor. I went in.

At first glance, there didn't seem to be anything wrong. The place was tidy, but not overly so. There was a small stack of mail sitting—unopened—on a glass side table near the door, dishes draining on the sink in the kitchen, and laundry sitting in the basket in the small laundry room. There was nothing that immediately jumped up and screamed "problem." Not until I went into the bedroom, anyway.

Because the entire room had become one gigantic web. Even though I was little more than particles, it seemed to cling to me, making me feel itchy and sending horror coursing through me. I backed away faster than I'd ever done before—in either form—and returned to the relative safety of the doorway.

I hadn't noticed any motion sensors in the flat, so

I shifted back to flesh form. Dizziness swept me, and I had to grab the doorframe to steady myself—but the pain that slithered through me was next to nothing when compared to the state I was usually in after a shift. I might not know what Malin had done to me, but if this lack of pain was one of the side effects, then I couldn't entirely be sorry about it.

The cobweb hung from one side of the room to the other, the gossamer strands shining like gilded silver in the evening light filtering in through the bedroom window. Little white pods hung in various corners, but all of them were split open and empty of contents. I couldn't be sorry about that, considering what they'd probably held was spiders. Lots and lots of baby black spiders. Goose bumps fled across my skin, and I rubbed my arms, trying without succeeding to warm the chill from them. Even Azriel reforming behind me couldn't do anything about that.

Di Shard lay on the bed. Or what remained of her did, anyway. Like the two male victims we'd seen, she was wrapped in spiderweb and her skin was like parchment—brittle and almost translucent. The only difference was, she didn't have just two slashes in her abdomen. Instead, her body was littered with little cuts. Tiny cuts. As if they'd been made by the fangs of thousands of little black spiders.

Another shiver ran through me. I could only hope she'd been dead when they'd begun consuming her.

"Well," I said eventually, "this really doesn't tell us much."

"Other than the fact that she has been dead for

at least a week." His hand rested lightly on my hip, the touch comforting rather than sexual.

My gaze swept the room again, but there wasn't much to find in the way of clues. "Why would she be consuming the men herself, but leave the women for her young?"

"She would probably need to keep her own strength up if she is in a breeding phase."

"Any idea how long that phase is likely to be?"

"No. As I have said before, I normally do not hunt spirits." He half shrugged, a movement I felt rather than saw. "But her actions so far suggest she is not working purely from instinct, but rather from intelligence."

I glanced up at him. "Meaning not all dark spirits are capable of logic?"

"There are levels of spirits, just as there are levels of demons. This one is obviously one of the higher ones."

"So the Rakshasa we hunted would be have been considered a higher-level spirit?"

"Yes. Although perhaps not as high as the spirit we seek here, because she could not ignore the call of the ghosts."

"Does that mean she won't be hunting tonight? I mean, she knows we're looking for her after this afternoon's events."

"Yes, but remember, she is also in breeding mode. That is an imperative not even intelligence can ignore." His grip tightened on my hip, and the tension suddenly evident in his touch echoed through my being. "We should go. Someone comes."

"Who?"

He hesitated, then said, "Directorate. Your uncle."

I swore softly, called to the Aedh, and hoped like hell that I hadn't been in human form long enough for my scent to linger in the air. And thanked whatever gods that happened to be listening that I'd parked my bike around the corner rather than directly opposite the apartment as I'd first planned.

I swept out as Uncle Rhoan walked in. He hesitated, as if he'd sensed me, but I just kept going. Hanging around to see if he actually *had* would not have been a bright idea.

"What do you wish to do now?" Azriel said, the minute I re-formed beside the Ducati.

I grabbed my helmet and shoved it on. "Go home and make mad, passionate love to you."

Amusement touched his lips, and desire flared briefly around me, bathing my skin with its warmth.

"That is something I would not find unpleasant." His voice was even despite the desire that pulsed between us. "I suspect, however, you merely tease."

"You suspect right. We need to check out Summer's place before my uncle beats us to it." Hell, for all I knew, he already *had*. Maybe there was a cleanup team there right now, photographing, cataloging, and pulling apart any clues that might be left. I had no doubt that Summer had suffered the same fate as Shard.

I flipped the helmet's visor down. "I'll see you there."

He nodded and disappeared. I booted up the

bike and headed across town. Thankfully, peak hour had eased now that night was setting in, and it was definitely more pleasant to be on the Ducati. At least I could weave my way through the traffic without having to worry about some impatient motorist suddenly swinging into my lane.

One twenty Newman Street turned out to be one of those modern, split-level town houses that had been popular with the upwardly mobile about fifty years ago. This one was showing its age more than most, the redbrick darkening with grime and the concrete portions showing remnants of past graffiti attacks. Still, it was in better shape than some of its neighbors, which looked to have been abandoned for many years—decidedly odd given how close to the city Kensington was. At the very least, a developer should have stepped in and purchased the land because it would have been worth a fortune if developed properly.

And maybe I was thinking about *that* sort of nonsense rather than contemplating what might be waiting inside.

I glanced around. There weren't any Directorate cars about, and nobody seemed to be watching, so I shifted shape and silently made my way into the town house. Summer's place, like Shard's, looked lived in—there was an empty dinner plate sitting on the coffee table, a mug with a tea bag sitting ready near the kettle in the kitchen, and clothes in the dryer, ready to be pulled out. For all intents and purposes, it looked as if someone were living here. And maybe they were. Maybe this was where our dark spirit had made her lair. Which meant that maybe this was where all those tiny spiders were living ... My gaze jumped to the ceiling, but it was free of movement or threat. There wasn't even a spiderweb decorating any of the corners.

Which didn't mean there weren't any in the bedroom.

The bedroom door was closed, and there was no way in hell I was going to slip underneath it until I knew for sure what waited on the other side. I shifted back to flesh form, then flexed my fingers and made my feet move forward. As I gripped the door handle, I closed my eyes and sent a brief prayer to whatever gods might be listening that there wouldn't be anything untoward waiting beyond this door.

But, as usual, they had the IGNORE button pressed when it came to me.

What lay inside wasn't only the biggest damn spiderweb I'd ever seen, but a goddamn army of little black crawly things.

I jumped back, a squeak of fear escaping my lips, and hit Azriel so hard that I actually forced him back a step before his hands gripped my arms and he steadied us both.

"Her nest," he said, rather unnecessarily. "But I suspect it is not her only one."

I swallowed heavily, my gaze on the ceiling and all the critters up there. There was no way in *hell* I was getting any closer to that room. They didn't appear to have noticed me, and I had no inclination to change that situation. "What makes you say that?"

"These spiders are larger than the ones who attacked us and therefore more likely to be older."

That a dark spirit was capable of having more than one cache of babies was something I did *not* want to think about. I forced my gaze from the creepy-crawlies and studied the body on the bed—although to call it a body was something of a misnomer. The other victims we'd seen might have been little more than preserved skin, but there wasn't even *that* much left of Summer. Just some dark hair on the pillow and a few bits of what looked like nails and bone remnants.

A shudder ran through me. Azriel rubbed my arms, but the heat of his touch did little to combat the chill.

"Why would she have more than one lot of babies?" I asked. "And if she does, why the hell aren't we overrun with spiderlike dark spirits here on earth?"

"I would suggest the reason is because they're cannibalistic."

"What?"

"Look at the carpet. It is littered with carcasses."

He was right. It was. In fact, the remnants of little black bodies were so thick that the gray carpet looked like patchwork. "So she kills the victims to feed her young, but when the young get old enough, they feed on one another? How does that make sense?"

"It would ensure only the strongest of them survive. It is not unusual behavior."

"Maybe in your world, but not in mine," I muttered. I knew that there were some animal species where the young *did* eat one another, but only if there wasn't another food source, and it was generally rare.

"Children are not as common in my world as yours and therefore somewhat revered." His voice held a hint of censure. "We certainly would *not* allow them to harm one another in *any* way."

Which wasn't what I meant and he knew it. But I let it slide and glanced up at him. "I thought reapers lived in big family groups?"

"We do."

"Then why would children be rare? Do you suffer the same sort of problem that has killed off most of the Aedh?"

"No. Aedh breed only when their death is imminent, which kept their numbers stable for millennia. No one can say what changed, but we think the Raziq had a lot to do with it."

That raised my eyebrows. "They killed off their own kind?"

"They believe in their cause and would certainly be capable of wiping out all opposition. In this case, that would mean those who tended and believed in the current viability of the gates."

"All of which doesn't explain why reapers don't breed willy-nilly."

He hesitated. "It is a combination of our long life spans and the fact that our recharge partners aren't always our Caomhs."

"Can you have both?"

"Rarely. And if a reaper only ever finds his recharge companion, he will not be blessed with children."

"And have you any children?" I asked, curious and perhaps a little . . . afraid. Because if he had children, that would mean he'd met his Caomh, which in turn meant there was never any hope for us.

Not that there ever really was.

His expression closed over. "I am not the Aedh, Risa. I do not want or need multiple partners. If I had a Caomh waiting in the fields for me, I would not be with you."

Summarily—though gently—chastised, I pulled my gaze from his and stepped back onto safer ground. "So what do you suggest we do about these spiders? Do we leave them, keep watch on the apartment, or what?"

"You do not wish to call your uncle?"

I hesitated. "How likely are the spiders to attack anyone who enters that room?"

"Very. Their hunger stings the air."

"So why aren't they attacking us?"

"Because we have not entered their lair."

And I had no fucking intention of doing so. "Can they be destroyed by something like pest spray, guns, or even fire?"

"Not ordinary fire. Though they wear flesh, they are spirit in design. Witches would more than likely be capable of destroying them, but not someone like your uncle."

Which meant I either had to ring Rhoan and warn him—and get the shit blasted out of me for interfering in his case again—or get rid of the damn things myself. Great. Just fucking great.

Can kill, Amaya said with an eagerness that had me shaking my head. *Will enjoy.*

No doubt. I glanced up at Azriel again, and he nodded a confirmation. "It will not draw our dark spirit to us, though. She obviously does not look after her young any more than the initial feeding."

"So how come we were attacked at the club? She wouldn't have had time to lay her eggs, let alone for the things to hatch. She was only the fill-in entertainer."

"She may have been carrying some young on her. Do not some spiders do that?"

"None that I want to meet," I replied, with another shudder. I drew Amaya and held her in front of me. Lilac fire raced down her sides, and her eagerness ran through the back of my mind. "Go for it."

She did. Fire exploded from her tip and spread out in a deadly wash that consumed all that stood in front of it without actually burning the walls or ceiling. The fire alarms went off regardless, but their strident ringing was almost lost to the roar of Amaya's flames. The thick web shriveled against the onslaught of heat, dripping in silver globules onto the carpet. The spiders tried to flee, attacking one another as they scrambled to seek refuge from the flames. Only there was no refuge—Amaya devoured everything. Web, spiders, furniture. Even Summer's few remains fell victim to her hunger.

Soon there was nothing left. Nothing but scorched

plaster and melted carpet. Amaya's flames retreated back to the steel, and her roar became little
more than a contented hum. If she'd been a cat, I
suspected she would have been purring. Loudly.

I sheathed her, then rubbed my arms. It didn't do
a lot against the chill still invading my limbs. "Would
she have felt the death of her young?"

"I do not know enough about her kind to say for
sure, but it is a possibility."

"Meaning she might not turn up for her perfor-
mance tonight."

"If she has more young to feed, she might have
no choice."

"Meaning it would be helpful if we knew more
about the breeding habits of the Jorōgumo—if
that's what this thing is." I bit my bottom lip for a
moment. "I wonder if the Brindle witches can tell
us anything about them."

"Given they are the keepers of all witch knowledge, it is more than likely they could."

"Then that's where we'll go next." My phone
rang, the abrupt noise making me jump. I took a
calming breath, then hit the ANSWER button and
said, "Mirri, what can I do for you?"

"You haven't heard from Ilianna, have you?"

I frowned. "No. I thought she was supposed to be
meeting you. Didn't you have that date with Carwyn tonight?"

"That's the thing—she hasn't turned up."

My heart began to beat a whole lot faster. "What
do you mean? Has she backed out again?"

"No. At least, I don't think so. She was pretty determined to hash everything out with Carwyn tonight." She paused, and even through the phone's tiny screen, her worry was evident. "Risa, I think something has happened to her."

Chapter 9

For a second I swear my heart stopped. Just thinking that something had happened to Ilianna made my stomach churn so badly, it felt like I was about to vomit. Damn it. I *couldn't* lose Ilianna. Not when there was a very real possibility we would lose Tao.

Panic surged, thick with fear, but I somehow reined it in and said, "Have you tried calling her?"

"Of course—"

"What about Tao? Or her parents?"

"Yes and yes. No one's heard from her, Risa. She's just gone. Completely and utterly disappeared."

No, I thought, swallowing heavily against the bile rising up my throat. She hadn't disappeared. She *was* somewhere. It was just somewhere Mirri couldn't find.

"What about the hospitals?" As much as I hoped she hadn't been hurt, it was always a possibility, and certainly one we had to consider before we pressed the panic button too far.

"Also checked. Nothing."

At least that was *something*. I took a quivering

breath and released it slowly. "I'll find her, Mirri." I hesitated. "What about Carwyn?"

"He's here with me at the restaurant. He's got a friend in the police force he's going to hit up for any information that might come through official lines."

If it came through police sources, then it wouldn't be good. But Mirri knew that just as well as I did. "I've got to go across to the Brindle, so I'll talk to Ilianna's mom. Maybe she can scry for her or something."

"It's worth a shot." There were tears in Mirri's dark eyes. "You don't think something bad has happened to her, do you?"

"No." I gave her a reassuring smile and hoped it didn't look as forced as it felt. "I'm sure it's just something dumb—like her phone running out of charge and her car breaking down."

A tremulous half smile touched her lips. "She does have a habit of letting her phone run out of charge."

"Yeah, she does." But rarely to complete emptiness. "We'll find her, Mirri. I promise you."

"Let me know the minute you hear or find anything."

"I will."

She hung up. I pocketed my phone, then glanced at Azriel. "I don't suppose you could do a sweep and see if you could find her."

"I'll try." He studied me for a moment. "What do you plan to do?"

"Go to the Brindle, as I said. I vaguely remember

Ilianna saying her mom was on night shift this
week, so I can kill two birds with one stone." My
stomach tightened as the words left my mouth.
Damn it, she *wasn't* dead. I'd know. Surely to *god*
I'd know. I hesitated, then added, voice a little
hoarse, "If she *were* dead, would you know?"

"No." He hesitated. "But I could find out if you
wish."

"That would be good. Thanks."

He nodded and disappeared. I took another of
those calming breaths that did jack all to calm, then
called to the Aedh and got the hell out of there. I
left the Ducati where she was—right then, I didn't
particularly care if Rhoan saw it or not. All that
mattered was getting to the Brindle and talking to
Ilianna's mom. If anything *had* happened to her,
surely she'd be the one person who *would* know.

I zoomed through the night with all the speed I
could muster, reaching the Brindle in record time. I
shifted shape, splatted with my usual inelegance
onto the carefully manicured lawn in front of the
building, then thrust to my feet and pulled the remnants of my clothes into some semblance of order
as I ran for the front steps.

The Brindle was a white, four-story building that
had once been a part of the Old Treasury complex.
It had been built in the Victorian era and was both
beautiful and grand in design. It wasn't until you
neared the steps and felt a tingling caress of energy
against your skin that you realized this place was
very different from its brethren. It was the home of
all witch knowledge, and it was protected by a veil

of power so strong that it snatched away the breath of those who were sensitive to these things. I'd never considered myself overly sensitive to magic, but I'd always been aware of it. This time, though, the feeling was weirdly different. It wasn't just awareness—it felt like the power of this place was alive. Fingers of energy crawled across my skin, its touch sharp, electric. It made my flesh itch—crawl—and almost felt as if it were testing me. The Brindle didn't suffer evil to enter, but it had never troubled me in any way before.

So why the change? Did it have anything to do with the key quest or what the Raziq had done to me?

Possibly. And yet Kiandra—who was the head witch at the Brindle—had told me that as powerful as the magic around the Brindle was, it could not stop the Aedh from entering. Logically, therefore, it shouldn't be able to stop me. But then, I wasn't full Aedh. I was both flesh *and* energy.

That will change, an inner voice whispered darkly.

I shivered, but thrust the odd premonition out of my mind and took the steps two at a time. The huge—almost medieval-looking—wood and wrought-iron doors had been closed for the night, so I walked to the left side of the massive entrance and pulled the discreet cord. Deep inside the building, a bell chimed. I waited, and after a few minutes, footsteps approached. One door opened, revealing a brown-haired, slender, tunic-clad figure. It wasn't someone I'd met before.

"I'm sorry, but we're closed for the night." Her voice was soft, gentle. Raised voices were rarely used in this place of power.

"I know, but I need to speak to Custodian Zaira, please." I hesitated. "It's urgent."

"I'm not sure that she's here—"

"Then check," I cut in. Then, at the flash of annoyance that crossed her face, added, "Please. Tell her it's Risa Jones, and it really *is* important."

Her gaze swept me assessingly; then she nodded and closed the door. I listened to the retreat of her footsteps and wondered whether she was simply walking away or doing what I asked. After a few minutes, I heard her talking. Misplaced mistrust, I thought, and gave myself a mental slap. After a few minutes, she returned and opened the door, wider this time.

"Zaira has agreed to see you. Please, come in."

"Thank you."

I stepped through the doorway. The foyer wasn't exactly inviting, even in the daylight, but at night, its sheer size seemed to weigh on the shadows, so that they almost appeared to loom over me. It was a weird sensation—almost as if the walls themselves were standing in judgment of not only me, but all those who walked past.

I very much suspected I would be found severely wanting. At least at the moment.

"This way," the woman said softly.

She led the way down the long hall. The energy of this place was so strong that every step was accompanied by a spray of golden sparks. The old-fashioned electric sconces threw just enough light to ensure we didn't run into the walls, but they did little to otherwise lift the shadows.

The young witch led me into the visitors' waiting room, told me to wait, then went through the door behind the small desk and closed it firmly behind her. I knew from previous visits that you didn't get past this area without either a witch escort or special dispensation from Kiandra, but I was a little surprised at being held here this time. I'd have thought Ilianna's mom would have been here given I'd mentioned it was urgent.

That she wasn't probably meant we were all panicking over nothing.

No, that dratted inner voice whispered, *you're not.*

I crossed my arms and began to pace. Several minutes crawled by, ratcheting up my tension and frustration. When footsteps echoed in the hall outside, I swung around and all but ran out—and almost collided with Ilianna's mom in the process. Only quick reactions on *her* part kept us both upright.

"Risa," she said, her soft tones holding a hint of surprise and perhaps amusement. "This is not a place where speed is required."

I took a deep breath and tried to calm down. "I know, and I'm sorry."

She nodded. Ilianna had inherited her palomino coloring and her shifting abilities from her dad, as Zaira was human. But Ilianna had the same powerful green eyes as her mom and right now they'd narrowed considerably. "What can I help you with?"

"Two things." I hesitated, but there was no easy

way to say it, so I just came straight out with it. "First off, we think something has happened to Ilianna."

Zaira frowned. "Mirri called earlier looking for her, but I didn't get the impression that she was in any way worried."

Then Mirri was better at containing her concern than I was. "I know. But Ilianna hasn't turned up for her date with Carwyn, and we can't get her on the phone."

The older woman smiled, although there was a slight edge of tension emanating from her now. "Well, given she isn't too pleased about our matchmaking efforts, her standing him up again is *not* entirely surprising."

I was shaking my head before she'd even finished. "Not this time. Mirri said she was determined to talk to him about the match."

"Talk him out of it, you mean," she said. But the tension in her ratcheted up several more notches. She studied me for a moment, then abruptly turned and walked away.

"Come along, child," she said over her shoulder, when I didn't immediately follow.

I hurriedly caught up. "I was hoping you could do a scrying or location spell for her."

"A location spell won't work." She opened a door and walked into another dark hall. "She learned to divert such spells at a very early age."

There was an odd mix of annoyance and pride in her voice. I half smiled. "How young?"

She hesitated. "She was twelve. Even at that age it was evident she was very gifted."

"So why wasn't she ever asked to become a custodian?"

Our footsteps beat a sharp tattoo against the marble floor, and the sound echoed in the hushed shadows that surrounded us. I half wondered if we'd wake anyone up. I knew from past experience that there were at least two dozen witches staying here at any one time, some of them permanent residents like Kiandra, and some, like Ilianna's mother, here only when rostered on for duty.

Zaira turned left at the end of the hall and started up some stairs. Lights flickered on as we approached, then went dark once we'd passed, and there wasn't a sensor to be seen.

Zaira gave me a quick but nevertheless shrewd glance over her shoulder. "She did begin training as a custodian, but her tenure was brief."

I knew that. I also knew she'd seen something that scared the hell out of her. "She has mentioned that, but she's never said why she left."

"No, she would not." We entered another hall. For a moment I thought that was the end of the conversation, but she surprised me by adding, "This place, and all the wisdom it holds, is not only protected by magic, but sometimes by steel and bloodshed. Ilianna witnessed a latter event and was too young to understand the necessity."

"She's not too young now."

"No." There was a smile in her voice. "But she *is*

incredibly stubborn. I fear she will not come back to us until Kiandra leaves."

Meaning Kiandra was the one who had done the bloodshed, obviously. Still, it was odd. Ilianna wasn't the squeamish type; nor was she illogical. And she was certainly more than capable of understanding the necessity to sometimes use force to protect what was, basically, the spiritual home of witches here in Australia. There *had* to be more to the story.

"So what did she see?"

"That, I'm afraid, I cannot tell you."

I guess I had to be thankful she'd told me as much as she had, although it was certainly frustrating to pick up a little more knowledge and yet know there was a whole lot more to uncover.

We continued on down the darkened hall. This was an area I'd never been through before and, if it had been day rather than night, I might have slowed and had a good look around. As it was, I could barely see anything more than the darkly stained wood panels that lined the hall.

"What was your other reason for coming here?" Zaira asked.

It took me a moment to remember. "Oh. Yeah. Do you know anything about Jorõgumos?"

She frowned. "I am by no means an expert, but I *can* tell you they are particularly nasty spirits."

"*That,*" I said grimly, "they are."

She shot me a glance. "Meaning there's one active here in Melbourne?"

"Maybe. Anything you can tell us about them would be helpful."

She grimaced. "They're often called whore spiders, and for good reason. When they come into season, they take on the form of beautiful women and lure their chosen victims by playing magical Biwas, which is a type of Japanese lute. Once their prey is ensnared, the Jorōgumos bind them in order to either devour them or feed them to their young, depending on where the particular Jorōgumo is in her breeding cycle."

Which was an exact description of what was happening. This thing *was* a Jorōgumo. "Do you know how many kills they need per breeding cycle?"

"Up to half a dozen." She shrugged. "Depends on the size and age of the Jorōgumo."

Meaning this spider spirit wasn't finished hunting yet. "I don't suppose you know an easy way to find this one."

"No. But they rarely stray from established hunting patterns. Work that out, and you should be able to ascertain where she will attack next."

In other words we were already on the right track. Zaira opened a door about midway down and flicked on a light. As had been the case in the hall, warm light spread across the room but barely lifted the shadows.

We were in a small, sweet-smelling office that was basically furnished. An old wooden desk dominated the center of the room, and with it was a leather chair that had seen better days. Shelves lined all the walls and were overflowing with books of every size and color. The weight of them had many of the shelves bowing, and the smell . . . I drew in a deep breath and sighed in appreciation. There was nothing quite like the scent of old books, even when it was almost overwhelmed by the richer scents of lavender and rose.

Zaira sat down at her desk, pulled open a drawer, then carefully lifted a silk-covered ball onto her desk. This wasn't any old ball, but one of power. I could feel the energy radiating off it even from where I stood in the doorway.

"I'll attempt a scrying," she said. "But there's no guarantee it'll work. As I've said, she learned long ago to block my efforts of tracking her."

I crossed my arms and leaned a shoulder against the doorframe. "I just want to know if she's okay. I know I may be panicking over nothing, but—"

"But you are your mother's daughter and, in many respects, even more powerful. I would never ignore your premonitions, however slight, and neither should you."

Surprise rippled through me. More powerful than my mother? That was unlikely, because her talents had been sharpened and honed in a madman's laboratory. While I was more than adept at using my psychic skills, I'd certainly never honed them—something that *had* frustrated the hell out of Mom.

But all I'd ever wanted was a normal life—or as normal as it could ever be given who my mother was and how wealthy we were—and in many respects, my psychic abilities had stood in the way of that desire. I *had* learned to control and use the skills that being half Aedh endowed, simply because Uncle Quinn had always stressed the danger of doing otherwise. I might be stubborn, but I wasn't a fool.

But it was moments like this, when I was standing here in Zaira's office, having to rely on her for information, that I wished I'd listened to Mom.

Zaira unwrapped the crystal and placed her hands on either side of the ball. Light flickered deep in its heart and sent sprays of silver cascading around the walls. Zaira took a deep breath, released it slowly, then closed her eyes and placed her palms on either side of the crystal. Her breathing grew deeper and, after several minutes, the crystal became cloudy and the silver cascade muted.

I watched, wondering what she was seeing and whether it involved Ilianna. Mom had sometimes used a crystal ball when trying to contact the dead for her clients, but it was never her favorite method. She preferred séances, simply because a physical connection with the living relative made communication with the dead easier. For her, it was also less taxing and more accurate.

But Zaira was witch trained. She would be able to do far more with a crystal ball than Mom could ever have imagined.

Time seemed to slow to a crawl, and tension curled through me. I hating waiting, hated not knowing what, if anything, was happening. The only reason I didn't start pacing was the knowledge that it would more than likely disrupt Zaira's scrying.

But eventually she sighed and removed her hands from the crystal. The cloudiness eased immediately and the swirling silver light returned.

Zaira leaned back in her chair and rubbed her forehead wearily. "Well, the good news is that she's not dead."

That was at least something, though it didn't exactly ease the tension still curling through me.

"But?" I said, because there very obviously was one.

"But I can get no feel for her. Something is blocking my ability to pin down her essence, and I cannot tell whether that something is her own magic or something else."

I frowned. "What else could there be?"

She shrugged. "All magic can be blocked, whether by magical means or physical."

"Physical? How do you block magic physically?"

"Certain elements—white ash and iron, for instance—are immune to magic and therefore can be either used as a weapon or shield against it." She wrapped the silk covering around the ball and placed it carefully back in her drawer. "Whatever is being used, I'm afraid I can't get past it."

"Damn."

"Indeed." She rose. "And it might just mean, despite her assertions to the contrary, she had last-minute qualms about meeting Carwyn. Which would be unfortunate, because she would not find a better match herself."

It was a point Ilianna had finally acknowledged—if only to me—but it didn't change the fact that she'd rather remain in a relationship with just Mirri than join Carwyn's herd and risk the dynamic between them changing. I couldn't actually say that to Zaira, though, given she didn't even know her daughter was gay.

"I know she doesn't want to be forced into a herd, but I doubt she'd back away at the last minute. Not without informing Carwyn, at the very least. She has better manners than that."

Zaira smiled as she walked around the desk. "That she has."

She motioned me into the hall, then walked beside me as we made our way back down to the foyer.

"You'll call me the minute you find her?" she said as she unlocked the front door.

"Yes, of course." I touched her arm in reassurance. "And I'm sorry to have worried you over what will probably turn out to be nothing."

"When it comes to the safety of my daughters, I would rather be worried over nothing than something." She placed her hand briefly over mine and lightly squeezed. "Be careful. I might not have found Ilianna, but I did sense the shadows that surround you. There are people in your life who are more dangerous than you know."

Which wasn't something she needed to tell me. I forced a smile. "Thanks. I will be."

I headed out. The night air was cool after the warmth of the Brindle's halls, the gentle breeze like ice. I zipped up my jacket as I ran down the stairs. Azriel reappeared in front of me, forcing me to stop on the bottom step.

"I could not find her," he said. "But she is alive. Her death is not slated for this time."

"Just because she's not meant to die now doesn't mean she won't. Accidents happen." Nevertheless, relief slithered through me. If both Zaira and Azriel were saying she was alive, then surely to god she was. But that didn't mean she couldn't die. That she wasn't in trouble. "Damn it, something *is* wrong, I can feel it."

"Then what do you wish to do next?"

"There's nothing we really *can* do." I bit my lip for a moment, then said, "Maybe Stane can locate her through the GPS in her car."

"And if she is not in her car?"

"Then maybe via her phone." I half shrugged. "It's the only option I have left."

"Then we will try it."

He held out a hand. I placed my fingers in his and allowed him to tug me into his embrace. For a second, he did nothing more than hold me, surrounding me in his warmth and silently offering me the comfort I so desperately needed. Then his energy surged and we swept through the gray fields to Stane's.

He jumped and swore a blue streak when we reformed in the middle of his living room.

"Don't *ever* do that to me again," he said, leaning back in his chair and holding his hand rather dramatically over his heart. "I don't think I could survive the shock a second time."

"You are not slated for death until you are old

and gray," Azriel commented. "So do not fear the strength of your heart."

Stane gave him a somewhat dubious glance. "I'm not entirely sure whether to be comforted by that statement or not." He glanced at me. "I'm gathering something dramatic has happened?"

"Yeah. Ilianna's gone missing." I sat in one of the spare chairs and scooted it across to his "bridge" of computer screens. "I need you to hack into either her car's GPS signal or locate her via her phone."

He gave me the sort of look a father might give a child that was being exceptionally dumb. "And have you tried using Latitude?"

"Um, no?" Mainly because I was of the opinion that if my friends wanted to find me, they could damn well ring and ask me.

He sighed. "Did I not tell you all to sign up for it some time ago?"

"Yes, but—"

"No buts. I told you, it's the easiest way ever invented to uncover where your buddies might be hiding, and it doesn't even require GPS." He swung around, swiped one of the screens across to Google, and logged in. A map of Melbourne appeared, dotted with arrowed face pics. He leaned forward a little, studying all the names, then grinned.

"Here you go," he said, enlarging the screen. "She's at South Bank."

Which wasn't that enlightening given how big the place was. Although, if I remembered right, Carwyn had booked a table at Harvest Time—did this mean she *was* headed there? That she was okay, despite being incommunicado? "Where in South Bank?"

He frowned, zoomed the screen in a little more, then said, "According to this, she's at Wilson's Parking, just off Freshwater Place." He glanced up at me. "It's the riverside quay area, if you don't know it."

"I don't, but we'll find it." I jumped up and dropped a kiss on his unshaven and definitely scratchy cheek. "Thank you."

"No probs. Just give me some warning next time you decide to drop by." He gave Azriel another dubious look. "Despite what your friend here says, my heart really *can't* take surprises like that."

I grinned. "I'll send some more champers to make up for it."

He snorted. "I haven't got the last lot yet."

"You will."

"And I'll need it if you keep popping into existence willy-nilly. Now, go find Ilianna so I can get back to my gaming."

"Done."

I stepped into Azriel's arms and he whisked us out of there. We reappeared on the center strip that divided the two lanes of Freshwater Place, the eight-story parking garage in front of us and the remaining wall of an old brick warehouse behind us. Several cars zoomed past, briefly spotlighting us before sweeping on.

I grabbed Azriel's hand and ran across the road. "Can you sense her?" I asked, as we headed into the garage via the exit lane.

"No." His fingers squeezed mine lightly. "But that does not mean she is not here."

Didn't mean she was, either. I ignored the fear that rose with the thought and hurried on. The garage had eight levels, and we found Ilianna's car on the seventh.

She wasn't in it.

I swore vehemently and punched the roof of her Jeep hard enough to actually dent it.

"There are security cameras dotted around this place," Azriel commented. "I would suggest you avoid such outbursts unless you wish company."

I flexed my fingers, somehow managed to control the somewhat insane desire to continue to take my frustration out on Ilianna's car, and peered in through the windows instead. And there, sitting on the front seat, were not only her phone, but her purse and coat as well.

Ilianna might have left her phone behind if it had gone dead, but she sure as hell wouldn't have left her purse.

Something *had* happened to her.

"Damn it!" I all but exploded. "What the *hell* is going on?"

"I don't know—"

"Neither do I," I cut in, voice bitter. I leaned back against the car and closed my eyes. "This day has just gone from bad to fucking worse. Maybe we should just quit while we're ahead."

"A sentiment I would agree with, except for the fact that Hunter, at the very least, would not be pleased by such an event."

As if on cue, my phone rang. And the tone told me it was Hunter.

"The bitch obviously has her phone linked to my thoughts," I muttered, but nevertheless dug it out of my pocket and hit the ANSWER button. "No, I haven't found her yet. I haven't found anyone fucking yet."

Amusement touched her lips, though it did little to lift the shadows from her bright eyes. "I take it the day has not been a good one for you."

"No. Ilianna has gone missing." I paused. "I don't suppose you'd know anything about that, would you?"

She arched an eyebrow. "And why would I bother with such an endeavor?"

"Well, you did make less-than-veiled threats against my friends if I didn't do what you want."

"Ah yes, I remember." Her amusement grew. "But given you are doing as I desire, there is no need for such action as yet, is there, now?"

Her reply was almost purred. If I could have reached down the phone and strangled the bitch, I would have.

"I guess not." It was said through somewhat clenched teeth. "But the fact of the matter is that I'm not having much luck tracking down the Jorōgumo."

"But you found two of her nests. Or was the burned-out bedroom not your handiwork?"

I mentally swore and rubbed my forehead wearily. I was starting to get one hell of a headache, and I suspected it wouldn't go away in a hurry. Not unless I drowned it under several gallons of alcohol, and that wasn't particularly practical right now—even if it sounded like the best idea I'd had for ages.

"What did Rhoan say in his report?"

"That something or someone destroyed what appeared to be a nest of spiders in one Ms. Summers's bedroom."

And how had he come to that conclusion given that Amaya's flames had consumed just about everything? And why hadn't I received a phone call demanding to know why the hell I was even anywhere *near* the place given my promise not to investigate? He surely wouldn't have missed the fact that the Ducati was parked right outside. *If* she was still parked outside, that was. Knowing my uncle, he'd probably ordered her confiscated, just to teach me a lesson.

"I burned the bastards because I didn't think anyone would want a friggin' nest of Jorõgumos remaining in existence," I said, with a touch more annoyance than was probably wise. Just because she seemed to be amused didn't mean she actually was. "They were too young to be in any form other than spider, so it was unlikely the Directorate witches would have gotten any information out of them."

"And what about the mama spider?"

"Well, she's supposed to be performing at someplace called the Falcon Club at midnight, but I don't like our chances of catching her there."

The amusement faded. Rapidly. "And why would that be?"

Because I burned her babies and it's more than likely she sensed it. But I wasn't about to actually say that. My life might not be fun at the moment, but I sure as hell wasn't ready to see it end just yet.

"Because we're not dealing with a dumb spirit here. She spotted me at Hallowed Ground and did a runner. She knows we're after her."

"Not even a spirit can deny the urge of a mother to feed her young," Hunter commented. "She didn't kill this afternoon, so if she still has young to feed, she will be forced to do so either tonight or tomorrow."

Undoubtedly. "So do you want me to go to the Falcon Club, or would you rather?" I kept my fingers crossed for the latter, because the last thing I really felt like right now was traipsing off to another bloody club.

As usual, it was a forlorn hope.

"I have no desire to be involved in the grunt work of investigating. That is what underlings are for."

A smile touched her lips, but it was in no way a nice smile. Just for a moment, I thought about Harry Stanford's offer and was tempted. *Seriously* tempted.

But only briefly. However desperate I might be feeling, I wasn't insane, and there was no way in hell I was going to cross the line and go up against Hunter.

"Just remember to contact me once you have found her," she continued, in that same sweet, do-it-or-I'll-kill-you voice. "Because I very much intend to do to her what she did to Wolfgang."

Consume her? Not just her blood, but her intestines, guts, and brain? Surely to god that wasn't possible for a vampire to do—blood yes, but not the innards as well? And yet if any vampire *could* be capable of it, then it would be Hunter.

Somehow, I managed to keep the horror out of my voice as I said, "You'll be the first person I call."

"I had best be the only call you make where this case is concerned."

I'd meant the comment sarcastically—it wasn't like I could call anyone else, anyway. But I didn't bother replying. I just hung up, shoved the phone away, and glanced at my watch. "Well, it's nine o'clock. Given I can't do anything else to find Ilianna, and I have no intention of going to that damn club earlier than I have to, we've got only one option left."

"And that is?" Azriel said, the slightest hint of a smile breaking his otherwise bland expression.

"We go home and make mad, crazy love to each other. Let's grab a moment of utter normality before the shit hits the fan completely."

Because a storm *was* coming. I could feel it. And I had a bad, bad suspicion I might not survive it.

Azriel caught my hand and tugged me into his arms. "While I am alive, you will remain so. I promise you that, if nothing else."

I melted into his embrace and listened to the strong, steady beat of his heart. "If death is my fate, even you cannot change that."

He didn't answer, and my stomach dropped. I looked up quickly and caught the flash of ... something dark—perhaps even a little guilt—in his eyes. Then it was gone, and all that remained was tenderness.

"Can you?" I asked, frowning.

"That is a question I hope I will never be forced to answer," he said. Which wasn't exactly an answer, but I knew him well enough now to understand it was all I was about to get. "Now, about this business of mad, crazy lovemaking. I'm not sure I understand the concept."

I smiled. "Then take me home and I'll show you."

He did, and I did.

And it was glorious.

Chapter 10

The Falcon Club was decidedly seedy. The air was thick with the scents of cigars, alcohol, and unwashed flesh, and it was packed with people—mainly men, but there was a good smattering of women here as well, most of whom were scantily dressed and very obviously working the room. Sex, I suspected, could be found here for a price.

My nose twitched at the unpleasant aromas surrounding me, but I ignored them the best I could, grabbed a drink from the bar, then wound my way through the shabby tables, choosing one in the thicker shadows near the bathrooms. It was far enough away from the bar—and most of the patrons—that the air was almost breathable and had the added bonus of affording a good view of the small stage situated to the left of the bar.

I sat down and nursed the icy glass of beer between my palms. This club obviously wasn't one of your more upmarket ones, so it was a little surprising that they'd employed someone like Di Shard to provide their entertainment. Given the state of this place—and the less-than-dapper look of its customers—a stripper would probably have been more appropriate. Or, at the very least, a rock band—although given the club's close proximity to homes, noise regulations would probably have stopped that.

I took a drink of beer and briefly caught the eye of a tall, somewhat hairy individual several tables over. He reminded me somewhat of the visage Azriel had said he'd adopted when we'd visited Classique, and I couldn't help smiling. The bear-shifter—he couldn't really be anything else looking like that—obviously took my smile as a go-ahead signal, because he rose, hitched up his trousers, and began wandering over. He was little more than four feet away when he abruptly turned and headed off toward the bar.

I just about choked on my drink. *And here I was thinking you couldn't interfere with the thoughts or actions of others unless it involved the key search in some way.*

Given the direction of that man's thoughts, you should be thankful I did turn him away.

I grinned at the annoyance in his mental tones. *And what if I'd wanted to be mauled by a hairy bear type?*

You have far better taste than that.

The amusement bubbling through me got stronger. *That wasn't what you were saying when I was with Lucian.*

The Aedh's attraction was magic enhanced.

And the fact that he was also a fantastic lover had absolutely nothing *to do with it.* That comment was greeted by stony silence. I somehow controlled my amusement and switched to safer subjects. *No sign of our spider-spirit yet?*

We'd decided that—given the Jorōgumo's sudden retreat last time we'd tried to confront her—it might be wiser if Azriel remained outside, in the vague hope that out of sight would mean out of sensory range. I could hide my features easily enough—and was, in fact, now green-eyed, brown-haired, and definitely not anything you'd label pretty—so it was unlikely she'd even recognize me, let alone sense I was anything more than just another non-human. Spirits, Azriel had assured me, weren't often attuned to the Aedh. Amaya's presence on my back was another matter entirely, but given I wasn't about to go anywhere without having her close at hand, it was a risk we had to take.

No sign of her, he said. *But she is unlikely to arrive early given she is aware that we hunt her.*

Which makes me wonder if she'll even turn up. I mean, if she's as smart as you said, she'd be stupid to come here.

But, as Hunter noted, sometimes maternal demands overrun common sense.

I took another sip of beer. It was, despite the grimy air of the place, surprisingly good. A couple walked past me, the man radiating lust and grinning with expectation. The woman's expression was rather world-weary. Just another mark for her, I thought, as they made their way into the bathroom. I grimaced at the thought. If the bathrooms were as grimy as the rest of this place, it sure as hell wouldn't have been *my* first choice for a rendezvous. Even the lane behind this joint would have been cleaner.

Trying to tune their noise out, I said, *If she merely wishes to feed her young, why wouldn't she just snatch someone off the street?*

Perhaps she requires more in a victim than just mere flesh and blood. Her male victims were strong psychically, remember. And she *consumed them, not her young.*

Meaning maybe I should do a quick reconnoiter and see if I can sense any psychically strong targets in the room.

You do not need to subject yourself to the less-than-savory nature of those in the club. His mental tones held a note that I would have sworn was proprietary had it been anyone else. *There are four such people in the room.*

Who?

As I am not in the room, I cannot say precisely. I merely sense the vibrations of their souls.

Which isn't much good given the room is packed. Our task would be easier if we knew who to keep an eye on. I downed my drink in several gulps and rose. *I'll take the long way to the bar and see what I can uncover.*

If you wish. His tone suggested he didn't think it was necessary, and I couldn't help grinning all over again. My reaper might have accused me of being jealous over his flirting with other women on more than one occasion, but it really was beginning to sound like he was suffering from the same affliction. And I couldn't help but be happy about that, if only because it suggested that I wasn't imagining the caring I sometimes sensed in him.

Of course, taking the long way to the bar did mean walking past a lot of very merry men, many of whom seemed to think a female rump in close proximity really *did* need a pinch, if not a good fondle. It irked the hell out of me, but I kept my temper in check and a smile on my face and was rewarded by finding all four psychics. Two had parked themselves at the bar, one was sitting with a dark-haired woman near the front door, and the last one leaned casually against the wall opposite the bar, sipping his beer and idly surveying the crowd.

His gaze met mine briefly, and a frisson of recognition raced through me. Not because I knew him, but because I knew the *type*.

If he wasn't Directorate, I'd eat my damn hat. If I'd been wearing a hat, that was.

At least his gaze slid past me and continued on. My inner devil was tempted to go over and chat him up, not only because he was one of the few half-decent-looking guys in the room, but because it would have been interesting to see if I could tease any information out of him.

But we were both here to catch a killer, and *that* sort of behavior wasn't something either of us needed. Besides, it wasn't like I needed another man in my life, however briefly I might flirt with the idea.

I made my way back to my table, but had barely sat down when Azriel said, *She's here.*

Where?

Just entering the club via a rear door. He paused. *She can sense me.*

I swore softly and pushed up from the table so quickly that I half spilled my beer. *Meaning she's running again?*

No. I retreated fast, and she remains.

I sighed in relief. *Keep your distance, then. With the Directorate here, we can't do anything until she picks out a victim and leaves with him.*

The guardian will follow her, just as we plan to.

Yeah, but we can knock out his car or even him. Though it would undoubtedly be easier to do the former rather than the latter. He might be a shifter rather than a vampire, but he was still a guardian and therefore dangerous.

I sat back down and took a sip of beer. I had only half of it left, but I wasn't going to walk over to the bar to get another one. Given our target had entered the building, it was better if I remained where I was.

After a few more minutes, a tall, thin man walked onto the stage and lightly tapped the microphone to get everyone's attention. Unfortunately for him, just about everyone but me ignored him.

"I'm afraid tonight's entertainment has been canceled. The lively Di Shard called in sick at the last moment, and we weren't able to get a replacement."

The news was greeted by general indifference, but it had me frowning. *Azriel, has she left again or is she still here?*

She's there. I cannot pinpoint her location precisely because doing so means moving closer and increases the chances of her sensing me again.

So why the hell would the manager announce she was unavailable?

I cannot say.

Neither could I, and it was damn worrying. And it wasn't like I needed anything else to worry about given the whole key situation and now Ilianna's disappearance.

I searched for the four psychics again and spotted all but the guardian. I saw him a couple of seconds later as he jumped onto the stage and followed the manager into the back room. He was obviously intending to question the man—something I really would have liked to have done but now couldn't. The guardian might not have recognized me, but he'd know I was wolf. The last thing I needed was him reporting a werewolf working for the vamp council questioning the manager. Rhoan could put two and two together as easily as the next man.

My gaze swept the room again, but I didn't see anything that spiked the internal radar. Then a tall, somewhat slender woman pulled away from the deeper shadows to the left of the stage—in fact, it looked almost as if she was *re-forming* from them. And maybe she was.

She was tall, brown-haired, and had a faint red stripe running along her center part. She didn't physically resemble either Shard or Summer—except for that stripe—but then, that was no surprise given she was able to take on different forms. And she would, because she knew she was being chased.

I wrapped my hands around my almost empty glass and tried not to be overly obvious about watching her. She looked around the room for several minutes; then her gaze centered on one of the shifters standing near the bar. She strolled toward him and trailed her fingers along the nape of his neck as she sat on the vacant barstool beside him. He jumped as if he'd just been stung, and maybe he *had*. She was a spider after all.

They began to chat and were soon as animated as old friends. She wasn't overly obvious with her flirting, just went with encouraging smiles and the occasional casual touch. But the psychic energy radiating off her was strong enough that I could feel it from here—and it felt *hungry*.

I shivered. In the back of my mind, Amaya began humming, the soft sound filled with expectation. *This one is not for you, I'm afraid.*

It hunts, she replied, somewhat testily. *Should kill.*

Oh, she will be killed, just not by us.

Task mine.

Not this time.

I swear she swore—although if she *had*, it was in a language I couldn't understand. Did demons even have their own language?

Of course, Azriel commented, his tone amused. *All sentient beings do.*

I guess I just didn't expect it from a demon in a sword.

Remember, before she was in the sword, she was

a very powerful demon causing a great deal of havoc.

Havoc good, she commented. *Should cause more.*

I snorted. *Bloodthirsty little beast, aren't you?*

She preened. I shook my head, then tensed as the shifter and the Jorōgumo rose in unison. My gaze swept the club, but I didn't see any sign of the guardian. Maybe he'd left after talking to the manager.

Not entirely, Azriel said. *He's outside, watching the entrance.*

Damn. I should have guessed a guardian wouldn't abandon his post so easily. Or that we'd be *that* lucky. *We need to take him out.*

The shifter and the spider-spirit didn't head for the front door, however, but rather turned and walked, arm in arm, in my direction. I swore softly, but kept my head down and sipped the remains of my beer.

Awareness crawled across my skin. The closer she got, the worse it got, until it felt like thousands of tiny black feet were skittering all over me. My grip on the glass became so fierce, my knuckles went white—how it didn't shatter, I had no idea.

They walked past, whispering like lovers. I resisted the urge to jump up and follow them, forcing myself to remain still and listen to their retreating footsteps. They didn't go into the bathroom as I'd half expected, but rather through the rear fire exit.

I thrust to my feet and followed them, catching the door with my fingertips before it closed again.

The alarm, I noted, had been disconnected—and had been for a while, if the state of the wires was anything to go by. Obviously, the Jorõgumo and her lover were not the first to make a retreat out the rear door.

I cautiously peered out. The two of them were halfway down the small lane that ran the length of the row of buildings in this block. I waited until they'd neared the main street, then slipped out, stopping the door from slamming closed before moving— as stealthily as I could—down the lane. The minute the two of them turned left and were out of my sight, I quickened my pace but didn't run. Even a drunk shifter had damn good hearing. While he might not connect my footsteps with them being followed, he might just mention it. I couldn't risk the Jorõgumo fleeing again.

Where are they going? I asked.

They have stopped near a car. Azriel paused. *The guardian is on the move as well.*

Shit. He must have put either movement sensors or temporary cameras in the lane. My gaze swept the shadows around me, but I couldn't spot either of them. Of course, he very obviously wouldn't have put them anywhere that they *could* be easily seen.

If there were damn cameras, though, it might lead to trouble for me. A brown-haired woman following the Jorõgumo and her next victim might not make *this* guardian suspicious, but it certainly would prick Uncle Rhoan's internal radar.

Where is he?

He's just turned left into the street you move toward.

Great. Unless I wanted him following the Jorō-gumo and perhaps interfering with Hunter's desire for revenge, I had to take him out. I looked around for some sort of weapon, but there wasn't anything particularly handy lying about. But there was some sort of industrial Dumpster near the far end of the lane. I spun, ran back, and climbed in. After a few seconds of fishing around the stinking refuse and building rubbish, I found something usable — an old chair leg about one foot long.

I jumped out of the Dumpster, brushed off the worst of the gunk clinging to my jeans, then shoved a hand in my purse and wrapped my fingers around my phone and keys as I called to the Aedh. The magic transformed me in an instant, and I scooted down the lane. Now I just had to hope that the guardian wasn't sensitive to energy forces.

I paused at the junction of the lane and the street and glanced left. The shifter and the Jorōgumo were about one street down, getting into a pale blue Toyota. I swore mentally and spun left, searching the shadows flowing across the footpath for the guardian.

He was moving with surprising speed for some-one who wasn't a vampire, and something silver glinted in his fist. Tracker, I thought. That was the last thing I needed.

I flowed past him, then spun around and moved up behind him. How the hell was I going to knock him out? Total re-formation was out of the question, especially given my less-than-stellar re-formation technique. Which left me with the option of doing a partial one—something I *had* done when in flesh form, but never from Aedh. Or on the move.

I snuck closer, then called to the Aedh. This time, I controlled the surge of power, channeling its fury, containing its strength, focusing it on just the arm that held the old chair leg. Making both real and solid.

The guardian must have sensed something was happening because he suddenly spun, but I'd already let loose with the chair leg. It smashed against the side of his head with a heavy crack, and he dropped like a ton of bricks. Guilt flickered through me. I hoped like hell he wasn't hurt too badly, but it wasn't like I could stop and check.

I drew my arm back to Aedh form and raced down the street just as the shifter's car pulled away from his parking spot.

He drove fast, obviously eager to get home, and I had to wonder what the hell I'd do if he got pulled over by the cops. I couldn't keep attacking law enforcement officers—especially given few cops traveled alone these days, and all of them had onboard cameras in their cars.

But he wasn't pulled over, and eventually he stopped in front of a small weatherboard home that looked as unkempt as the shifter. Obviously, it was just the psychic power our dark spirit was attracted to rather than the sort that came with success and wealth.

He climbed out of the car, ran around the rear of it, and opened the Jorõgumo's door, ushering her out and taking her arm as he escorted her through the front gate and up the steps. I waited until they'd gone inside, then re-formed. Once I'd picked myself up off the pavement and sorted out my clothing, I grabbed the phone and rang Hunter.

She answered almost immediately. "I do hope it's good news, Risa dear," she drawled. "I am not in the mood for the other sort."

"I'm standing outside of an old weatherboard house. The Jorõgumo is inside, about to feast on an-other victim."

Something dark, dangerous, and very, very hungry flashed in her eyes. "Give me the address immediately."

I did. "What do you want us to do? Wait here or leave?"

"What I want you to do is go in and pen the bitch. As much as I do not care about the shifter himself, Jack has insisted I not risk more lives than necessary in my quest for revenge."

Meaning Jack actually held some sway over her actions? Somehow, I suspected *that* would be the case only if his requests meshed with her own desires.

"I have no idea how the hell I'd pen—"

"I don't care how you do it; just do it," she cut in. "I will not be pleased to arrive and find her gone."

A displeased Hunter was *not* someone I wanted to face. "Fine," I muttered, and hung up.

Heat swirled through me, warm and familiar as Azriel appeared beside me.

"Is it safe for you to re-form?" I leaned my shoulder against his to steal more of his warmth. The night air hadn't gotten any warmer, that was for sure.

"I am as far away now as I was back at the club, so I would presume so."

"How the hell are we going to cage her?"

"Not we," he said grimly. "You. The minute I get nearer, she will run."

"Oh, fabulous." I rubbed my arms, but it didn't do a whole lot against the sudden sense of dread. "What do you suggest?"

"Amaya should be capable of containing her long enough for me to get in there and help complete the task."

"She's capable of consuming her, too," I muttered. My sword's response to this was what sounded like a wicked chuckle.

"Yes. You will have to be firm with her."

Easier said than done. "When the Jorōgumo appeared in the club, she seemed to merge from the shadows—can she actually do that?"

"Most spirits who can take on flesh can just as easily dissolve. You will have to be quick to capture her."

"And hope like hell she doesn't decide to attack rather than run."

"If she attacks, I *will* be there."

If she flung little black babies at me, him arriving quickly was *not* going to help. "So, wish me luck."

"I wish you speed and strength," he said. "As I

have noted before, it is not wise to rely on luck in this sort of situation."

I guess not. I drew Amaya and gripped her fiercely. *Okay, we are going to cage her, not consume her; you got that, Amaya?*

Fun not.

I don't care.

She muttered for several seconds, the words indecipherable but their meaning clear. Happy not, as she would say. Then she said, *Can nibble?*

Not even a little taste. She is Hunter's meal, not yours.

Eat Hunter, she muttered.

That, I replied grimly, *might yet be an option in the future.*

She perked up no end at this and began humming happily. I took a deep breath, released it slowly, and wished the nerves and the tension would just fuck off. They didn't, however, so I just called to the Aedh once again and carefully made my way inside the house.

To hear music rather than the sound of lovemaking.

I inched forward, following the haunting, melodious sound, and found the shifter and the Jorōgumo in the living room. He was sitting on a chair, his jacket dumped on the floor and his shirt undone to the waist. His eyes were closed, and his expression was one of bliss. I couldn't actually see why—the music, while different, wasn't exactly a sound that would put me into raptures. But then, my tastes tended to run to pop and rock rather than more classical stuff.

Besides, his state didn't really have a whole lot to do with the actual music, but rather the lute it came from. Zaira had said the instrument was magic, and the room was thick with it.

The Jorōgumo knelt at his feet, her head bent and her dark hair cascading over what looked to be a small, odd-shaped lute. She plucked the strings with nails that were long and glistened with silver—silver that fell onto the wood floor and spun up and around the shifter's sneakered feet.

Her web.

The music spelled him, distracted him, while she spun her cocoon around him.

Remember, I said to Amaya, although I wasn't entirely sure she could hear me when we were both little more than energy particles. *No consuming. Just containment.*

With that, I called forth the Aedh and re-formed—but only enough to give Amaya room to do her stuff. There was no way in *hell* I was about to risk baby spiders being thrown at me.

The minute Amaya formed, she flung fire at the Jorōgumo, but the spider woman reacted with lightning speed, throwing herself sideways and out from under the range of the flames. They chased her, eagerly crawling across the floor toward her, but already she was dissolving, her face and torso becoming little more than wisps that trailed behind the rest of her body as she continued to run from Amaya's flames.

"Fuck," I said, and regained full form. "Amaya, grab her legs!"

A rope of fire lashed out instantly, whipping around what remained of the Jorōgumo's limbs. She screamed and stumbled, crashing to the floor and finding form again.

Only her form was spider rather than human this time, and she was big and black, with skin that writhed and pulsated. I did *not* want to know what was causing that movement. I really didn't.

The Jorōgumo lunged at me, her fangs bared and as thick as my arm. I yelped and jumped backward, but my calves clipped the edge of the coffee table and I tipped ass over the top of it. I landed awkwardly, but had barely rolled onto my back when Amaya screamed a warning. I looked up to see a hairy black leg coming straight at me. I swore, swung my sword, and steel met flesh with a clang that sounded oddly like a death knell. Not mine, I hoped. Amaya's screaming was fierce as her steel bit deep into one of the fleshier parts of the Jorōgumo's leg, and blood flew. As did little black objects.

It was my worst fear come to life. There were baby spiders *under* her skin.

Somehow I kept a lid on the utter horror that crawled through me and rolled out from under her leg.

"Azriel!" I screamed, wrenching Amaya free as I jumped upright. "I need some damn help here!"

Already here.

His mind voice was sharp, distracted, and I risked a glance across the other side of the room as I con-

tinued to back away from the Jorōgumo. A second
creature had appeared, only this one was made up
of thousands of little tiny bodies that writhed and
moved and hissed and yet acted as one deadly enemy. Azriel attacked the mass with Valdis's steel
and flame, moving so fast, he was little more than a
blur. But for every part of the mass they destroyed,
others just crawled in and resumed the attack.

Fuck, fuck, *fuck*!

Mom Jorōgumo lunged at me again, liquid dripping from her fangs. I ducked away from her attack
and smashed Amaya across her fangs. One went flying but the other remained. Liquid splashed across
my clothes, stinking to high heaven and stinging
where it hit flesh. Hoping like crazy the stuff had to
be injected to actually work, I batted away another
attack, then leapt high, twisted in midair, and came
down on the middle part of her body, right behind
her eyes. Amaya screamed again, the sound echoing across the room as well as in my head.

Don't kill, I ordered her fiercely. *Just blind and bind.*

Then I swung her with all the strength I had. Her
steel bit into the bitch's eyes just as the Jorōgumo
flung herself at the wall. We hit hard, and breath
whooshed from my body. Not satisfied with merely
winding me, the Jorōgumo hissed and writhed, and
I fell, ending up on the floor underneath her. One
foot scraped my leg, cutting deep, and a scream
rolled up my throat. I bit down on it and crawled
out from underneath her, barely avoiding several
strikes of fang and leg. A hand grabbed me and
dragged me upright.

"Amaya!" Azriel said. "Flame and ensnare. *Now!*"

My sword responded instantly, and twin lances of flames rolled out from the swords, shooting across the writhing creature's body, spreading out in vibrant fingers, weaving in and out of each other, joining the rope of flames that still encased two of the Jorõgumo's legs, until it had formed a net that encased the spider-spirit's entire body.

She didn't stop writhing and screaming, but she was trapped and not going anywhere.

I collapsed back against the wall and closed my eyes in relief. My head was pounding, and my leg was bleeding, I was aching all over from my encounter with the wall, but hey, I was alive and the spider *wasn't* dead. As outcomes went, it wasn't all that bad.

"I guess the fact you have only one injury *is* something to be grateful for," Azriel agreed, voice wry. "However, it would have been nice if you could have remained wound free for a change."

"Tell *that* to the bad guys who keep attacking me." I opened my eyes. Azriel stood several feet away, his body covered with tiny wounds that gave his skin a bloody glint. Concern rolled through me. "Are you all right?"

He nodded. "I am energy, remember."

"But you're wearing flesh." I pushed away from the wall, took two steps, and gently ran my fingertips across the worst of the wounds on his arm. "If the babies were as venomous as their mom—"

"I will burn off their venom the minute I return to energy form." He gave me a sweet, somewhat lopsided smile. "But I appreciate the concern."

"Hey, I don't want to lose you over something dumb like getting bitten by a damn spider."

"That is not something I would be overly pleased with, either."

Amaya's steel began to vibrate in my hand, and I glanced down with a frown. Both swords were still blazing, but Amaya's flames were beginning to pulse. It was almost as if her strength was faltering.

"It is," Azriel commented. "Which means she's now drawing on your strength to help hold her share of the net."

"Why can't she hold it herself?"

Strength not right, she muttered, the surliness in her mental tones suggesting she was very put out by the fact.

"She's young in demon terms," Azriel commented. "She will get stronger with both age and your continuing merger."

Merger. Not something I really wanted to be doing with a demon spirit with a hankering for bloodshed, but I guess that option had gone out the window the minute I'd taken her steel and stabbed her into my flesh.

And, if I was being at all honest, for all my wariness about owning a demon sword, I really wouldn't want to be without her now. Having her so readily at hand had saved my ass more than once.

"I hope Hunter gets here quickly, then." I paused. "Or can you and Valdis hold the Jorõgumo yourselves?"

"We can kill her, but containing her as we are takes more strength and generally requires two swords." He grimaced. "They were never designed for this."

I guess they weren't—and they were doing it now only because Hunter wanted bloody revenge.

"Speaking of Hunter, she approaches the front door."

"Meaning we now have the problem of getting her *into* the house." As a vampire, she had to abide by the old "invite only" rule.

"Can she not telepathically order such an invite?" Azriel said.

"No. It has to be freely given."

The doorbell rang. I shot a look down the hall and saw her silhouette through the glass panes. "Now what do we do?"

"I would suggest you get the door open, Risa dearest," Hunter replied, proving the keenness of her hearing yet again. "Otherwise I will not be pleased."

"Kinda hard to do when the owner is unconscious." But I walked over and booted the cobwebbed heel of his shoes. "Hey, wake up."

He didn't flinch. I tried again, harder this time. Still nothing. "Can you wake him?" I said, glancing at Azriel.

"I shouldn't, but given the growing precariousness of the situation—" He paused, his expression one of concentration. After a moment, the shifter groaned and rubbed his eyes. Then he saw us.

"What the fuck?" He jerked upright abruptly. "Who the hell are you two? And what the *fuck* is *that*?"

"That," I said grimly, "is the woman you brought home."

"No fucking way."

"Look, I don't particularly care if you believe me or not," I said, voice tart. "The fact is you have the mother of all spiders in your living room and you were almost her dinner. Now, be a good chap and go invite Director Hunter into your house so she can deal with the beast."

He blinked. "The director? As in, the Directorate?"

"Yes," I said, and mentally ordered the man to just go. It wouldn't have done any good, of course, even if I *had* been telepathic, because of the whole "freely given" restriction.

But if he *didn't* hurry, things were going to get bad pretty quickly. The throbbing in Amaya's steel was stronger, as was my damn headache. And I didn't even want to think about the amount of blood I was losing, but my socks were beginning to feel rather wet.

"If this spider escapes the power net," I continued, "we'll all be damn dinner. So please, just go open the door."

He looked from me to the spider, then to Azriel, and rose—and just about fell flat on his face again. I'd forgotten about the web wrapping his feet and lower legs.

"Fucking hell, it *was* trying to eat me!" His voice held edges of both anger and hysteria.

"But it didn't!" I cut in harshly. "Just hop down

the damn hall and open the door. We can't hold this bitch much longer." I paused. "We'll explain everything later."

He gave me a "you'd better" look, then hopped in a rather ungainly fashion down the hall and opened the front door. Two seconds later, Hunter was striding toward us. There was little emotion on her face, but her pupils had expanded to the point where there was little green left and the sheer depth of hunger that radiated off her stole my breath and had my gut churning. This was Hunter as I'd hoped I'd never see her—eager for her revenge, ravenous for the blood of her enemy.

Thank god I had Azriel with me.

I glanced back down the hall. The shifter was still standing by the open door, but his expression was slack.

"His expression is as empty as his mind," she said, her low voice vibrating with anticipation. "Do you think I desire a witness to what I am about to do?"

I swallowed heavily. "We're witnesses."

She turned her black gaze on me, and I took an involuntary step back.

"Yes," she murmured, voice silky. "But I have nothing to fear from you; do I, Risa dear?"

I felt like a rabbit caught in the spotlight, only this particular one shone with a dark, dark light and promised a bloody, brutal death.

"Your threats grow tedious, Hunter." Azriel's voice held little inflection and no doubt for good reason. It wouldn't take much to set her off. "And you are here for the Jorõgumo, remember."

"Yes."

Hunter's gaze returned to the caged spider, and the energy radiating off her suddenly spiked. Only it wasn't aimed at any of us, but rather the Jorõgumo herself. Her form began to flicker, change, shrink, until what stood before us was once again a woman.

A woman who looked suddenly scared.

Just for a fraction of a second, I almost felt sorry for her. Then I remembered what she was and what she'd done. The death Hunter was about to give her was surely quicker than the one she'd given any of her victims.

"Lower the force of your flames and allow me access," Hunter said.

Chills raced across my skin. There was nothing human behind those words.

Lower Amaya's flames so they leash just her legs, Azriel said.

I echoed his words to my sword, and she obeyed. *Hurry must,* she said. *Weak growing for both.*

Yes, it was. I bit my lip and tried to ignore the fact that my head felt like it was about to explode.

Amaya's flames followed Valdis's down the Jorõgumo's body until they encased just the lower half of her legs. The spider-spirit didn't move. I suspected the energy radiating off Hunter had a whole lot to do with that.

"For the crime of killing four, you are sentenced to death," Hunter said, stepping so close to the Jorõgumo that she was practically in her face. "But for the crime of killing one of those four, you are sentenced to death by *me*."

And with that, she attacked.

But she didn't just sink her teeth into the Jorõgu-mo's neck and drink her blood. She rendered her apart and consumed everything.

Absolutely everything.

Even her soul.

Chapter 11

It was sheer survival mode that kept me rooted to the spot and watching, even though every instinct in my body was screaming to get the hell out of there—to get away from the monster that was consuming one of its own kind.

Hunter might not be a Jorōgumo, but given what I was witnessing, it was impossible to think of her as just another vampire—however powerful and old she was.

Normal vampires didn't consume flesh and bone and brain matter. Normal vampires didn't drink souls.

How I didn't lose the entire contents of my stomach, I'll never know.

Unbidden, Harry Stanford's words came back into my mind. *Oh, trust me, she long ago mastered the art of hiding what she truly is.*

I guess the question that needed answering now was, what sort of monster had she become?

Unfortunately, it wasn't a question I could exactly ask anyone in the know. I had a more than vague suspicion questioning Hunter herself would not be a good idea, and the only other people I could approach who might have some clue were

Uncle Quinn and Harry Stanford himself. Both were out of the question, for very different reasons.

So I swallowed the bile backing up in my throat, kept my knees locked, and ignored the ever-increasing shuddering in both Amaya's steel and my body. And found myself looking anywhere but at the scene in front of me.

But it seemed to take far too long for the Jorōgumo to meet her end.

My knees and Amaya's flames gave out at the exact same time. I hit the floor with a grunt and drew in shuddery breaths, my head swimming and my body on fire.

A heartbeat later, Azriel knelt in front of me, his concern radiating through me like the wash of a warm summer breeze. He pressed his hand against the wound, my blood oozing up through his fingers as energy radiated from the epicenter of his touch. It flushed strength through my shaking muscles as it began to heal my leg, and, after a few seconds, I felt decidedly better.

My gaze met his. In the depths of his differently colored eyes, barely leashed fury burned.

If she but gives me the tiniest of excuses, he said, mind voice flat and in many ways scarier than even Hunter herself, *she will be dead.*

She won't. I lightly brushed some spider goo from his cheek. His skin was far cooler than usual, and concern sharpened anew. *Will you please shift into energy form and burn away the venom?*

Your wound is not fully healed, and I am in no danger as yet—

I don't care about my wound—

A continuing problem with you, he cut in. There was both amusement and frustration in his mental tones.

I smiled. *I'm okay, so just humor me and heal yourself, will you?*

If you insist.

He disappeared, leaving me once again staring at the scene in front of me. There actually wasn't that much to see anymore. All that remained of the spider woman were the bits I'd sliced off—some leg pieces, her fang, and one of the spinnerets. Everything else—all the gore and other body parts—had been consumed.

Hunter turned and our gazes met. I froze again, pinned by the awful darkness of her eyes, and for a moment feared that I was about to become her second victim. Then she blinked, and the darkness retreated.

But the air still burned with the wrongness of her being. Worse still, blood and flesh covered the lower part of her face and dripped from her chin, and her shirt was soaked with gore.

My stomach once again threatened to rebel, but I had a feeling vomiting all over her no-longer-shiny shoes would be a sign of weakness I could *not* afford. I just wished I could control my pulse rate as easily, because right now it was through the roof.

"So," she said, "have you got anything to say?"

Her voice was cool, unthreatening, but my skin crawled. "Absolutely nothing."

She smiled, revealing razor-sharp, blood-stained canines. "Wise choice."

I swallowed heavily and wished like hell I could take back the words that now bound me to this woman. But breaking our deal was an option I'd never really had, no matter how much I might have flirted with the idea. Yet I had no doubt *those* flirtations were the reason behind her revealing her true nature here today. She'd wanted to show me just what would happen to Ilianna and Tao if I ever stepped out of line.

It was my desperate need for revenge that had led them into this woman's sights, and I hated myself for that.

But what was done was done, and regretting the path I'd chosen in a desperate moment of pain and anger didn't help anyone, particularly them.

I licked dry lips and said, "Are you going to call in the Directorate, or do you want me to?"

"Oh, there's no need for them to be advised of events here." There was cold amusement in her voice. "The Jorōgumo is dead and I will erase the shifter's memory. I'm afraid this is destined to become just another of the Directorate's cold case files."

And how many of those files, I wondered, were cold because of Hunter's intervention?

"Then I can go?" I tried not to sound overly eager, but failed dismally, if the gleam in her eyes was anything to go by.

"You may. Just remember, I want to be advised if

you do find the next gate key at that gun exhibition later today."

"Given you have Cazadors following me about like trained puppies, that goes without saying," I snapped, and regretted it almost instantly.

That darkness flared in her eyes again. My breath froze in my throat, and I took an involuntary step back. Even that one small movement had her half baring her teeth, and it wasn't only Amaya who began screaming inside my head. I was at full voice, too.

Then Azriel appeared in front of me, providing a physical barrier against the wash of hunger and darkness coming from Hunter and allowing me to breathe normally again—although the fury and tension rolling off both him and his sword wasn't any less breathtaking.

"Do it," he said softly. "I will enjoy watching your soul be escorted through the gates of hell."

For a moment, she didn't move. Didn't even blink. Then she smiled—still all teeth—and said, "Oh, I will give you your chance, reaper, but not now. Not yet. There is still much to be achieved."

Yeah, first high council domination, next the world. Azriel reached back and caught my hand, squeezing it in either reassurance or in warning. Then his energy surged around us, tearing us apart swiftly, but he didn't take his gaze off Hunter until the gray fields were around us.

"What the *fuck*," I said, as we reappeared in the secure surrounds of my bedroom, "has she become?"

"I cannot say." He turned around, but didn't immediately release my hand. "I suspect the only people who would know are the two people you've already noted."

Stanford and Uncle Quinn. I rubbed my free hand across my eyes wearily. "What the hell are we going to do, Azriel? Stanford is right about one thing— whatever she is, she's *not* sane."

"Actually, I would suggest the opposite. However, she is a being without emotion, someone whose soul lost contact with all that is humanity a very long time ago. She is incapable now of seeing beyond her own needs, desires, and plans."

I frowned. "You can't say she's without feeling given she had us chasing the Jorõgumo for revenge."

"That did not come from either the heart or the soul, but rather a far darker place. Someone took something of hers, and she could not let the matter slip unchallenged."

"So if I ever *did*?"

His smile was somewhat wry. "You challenge her every time you speak to her."

I grimaced. "I meant seriously challenged. As in, agree to work with Stanford."

"Then you'd better hope I am still around to defend you."

Fear swirled through me. I knew I wasn't any sort of match for Hunter, even with Amaya at my back, but still, hearing Azriel basically confirm it was as scary as hell.

"Well, it's not actually something I'm planning, however much I'd like to see the bitch dead."

"Which is the first sensible statement you've made for quite a while."

"I am capable of sensible on occasion." I rose up on my toes and quickly kissed him. "I'm going for a shower. If you want to be useful, you could make me something to eat."

His eyebrows rose. "I am not adept at human domestic duties."

"Now, *that*," I said, voice wry, "is a comment echoed by men the world over. All you need to do is slap some of the lamb that's in the fridge between a couple slices of bread, squeeze on some tomato sauce, and I'll be one happy lady."

"That I can manage." He raised my hand, kissed my fingertips, then disappeared.

I checked my phone to see if Ilianna—or anyone else for that matter—had called, then headed into the shower. By the time I'd dried my hair, dressed in comfortable jeans and an old sweater, Azriel had set the dining room table with not only a sandwich, but a glass of Coke and a steaming mug of coffee.

"You know," I said, as he pulled out a chair and seated me. "You might just become a keeper if you carry on like this."

He didn't immediately answer, but when he did, his voice was oddly formal. "And would you wish that, if the situation were different?"

I paused, the sandwich halfway to my mouth, and met his gaze. "If the situation were different, if we weren't who we were, and the option was there, yes, I would like that very much."

He nodded, and it oddly felt as if an agreement

had been reached. I frowned, wondering what exactly that might have been, but his expression—or lack thereof—very much suggested he wasn't about to elaborate.

"Because there is nothing to elaborate," he said softly. "What happens next lies in the hand of the fates."

I swallowed against a suddenly dry throat and tried to ignore the tiny slivers of both hope and fear that began coursing through me. "Meaning there *could* be some way we could explore this thing further?"

While that possibility scared the hell out of me, I couldn't help the leap of excitement at the thought of being able to explore whether what was between us had the strength to blossom into something real *and* permanent.

But all he said was, "That is for the fates to decide."

"Then the answer is probably no, because fate and I have not been on friendly terms of late."

He didn't reply, and there was little to be read in his expression. I bit into my sandwich and had to bite back a groan of sheer pleasure. Besides sex and a cold glass of Coke, the best thing in life had to be a fabulous lamb sandwich.

My phone rang just as I finished my meal. The tone told me it was Jak, and my heart began to beat a whole lot faster. Something was wrong. I was certain of it even before I answered the damn thing. I pushed up from the table and ran across to my handbag, fishing around for several seconds before I found my phone.

"Jak," I said, my heart seeming to beat somewhere high in my throat. "What's up?"

"I need to talk to you. Urgently."

Despite his words, he neither looked nor sounded worried. In fact, he looked rather distracted.

I frowned. "What about?"

"Can't say on the phone, but you'll want to hear it, believe me."

I bit my lip, frustrated with both his reticence to answer the damn question—although *that* was something I should have gotten used to, seeing as everyone was doing it of late—and that inner voice that kept insisting something was wrong. But was it clairvoyance, or the simple knowledge that every time the phone rang, the shit got deeper? "Where?"

"At Larry's, in Brunswick."

It wasn't a place I knew, but then, that was what Google was for. "When?"

He paused. "Ten minutes."

"Shit, Jak, you're not giving me much time to get—"

I cut the rest of my sentence off as my damn phone beeped, then shut down. The stupid battery was dead.

I swore softly, threw it down, then stalked across to the computer and Googled Larry's in Brunswick. It was situated on Hope Street, not far down from Sydney Road.

I grabbed my keys, then glanced at Azriel. "I'll meet you there."

"You do not wish me to take you?"

I hesitated. That niggly sense of wrongness was

still present, but I wasn't really sure whether it was related to Jak, or the still-missing Ilianna. I bit my bottom lip, weighing options, then said, "Can you go to Stane's first and ask him to keep an eye on police reports, just in case something comes through about Ilianna?"

He frowned. "Why not ring him? He does not appreciate me suddenly appearing on his premises."

No, he didn't, but he wasn't about to keel over in shock from it, either, according to Azriel, and he should know. Besides, I needed information on Ilianna, and Stane was probably our best method of getting it—and it was stupid of me not to have asked him when I was there earlier. "My phone is dead, and I don't want to waste time going there myself. And I'm only meeting Jak. He's not a threat."

"Perhaps not, but given your own sense of unease—"

"Look," I said, impatience edging my voice— which wasn't really fair given he was only trying to keep me safe. But there was safe and there was mollycoddling, and this had the feeling of the latter. "It'll take you all of three seconds to get to Stane's and less than that to ask him to scan the police frequencies. I can hardly get myself into too much trouble in that short time."

Surely even *I* wasn't that clever.

He studied me, clearly unhappy, then nodded abruptly and disappeared. I headed out the front door, locked up, then called to the Aedh. A sliver of pain ran through my head, but I wasn't entirely sure whether it was a warning that I was pushing my limits again—despite the energy Azriel had given me—or the mere fact that I was too close to the wards that prevented the Raziq from entering our home. But if pain and pushing my limits found Ilianna, then I really didn't care—though I had no idea why I thought Ilianna might be the reason behind Jak's sudden demand for a meet. Maybe it was nothing more than stupid hope.

I zoomed through the streets, the bright lights little more than a blur underneath me. Larry's, it turned out, was an old, somewhat rambling warehouse structure that had obviously been no more successful as a bar than it had as a warehouse. I reformed and pulled the somewhat holey remains of my sweater together, my gaze sweeping the grimy, blue-painted building dubiously. I couldn't imagine any good reasons for Ilianna being in a place like this, and I sure as hell did not want to think about bad reasons. But maybe this *wasn't* about her—after all, it was Jak who'd collected the information that had led us to the standing stone gateway under the run-down warehouse near Stane's. Maybe he'd found another one.

I walked across the road, every sense I had attuned to the old building. Nothing stirred, and I couldn't see or hear anyone near. The night air was cool and whispered through the holes in my clothes, chilling my skin and causing goose bumps. Or maybe they were simply the result of growing unease.

"Jak?" I kept my voice soft. If he was here, he'd hear.

"Inside." His voice was as hushed as mine, but oddly lacking warmth.

Unease growing, I grasped the door handle and wrenched it open. Unfortunately, I used more force than necessary and it crashed back, trapping my hand between the door handle and the wall. I bit back my yelp and shook my fingers, my gaze searching the dark room as I eased inside. I couldn't see anything, couldn't hear anything.

"Where are you?"

"Here."

He sounded closer, but no warmer. Trepidation prickled across my skin, and my footsteps slowed even further. "Where the hell are the lights?"

"Can't risk them."

"Why?"

"Get in here, and you'll see."

Impatience threaded his distant tones, and just for an instant, he sounded like his old self. Maybe I was just being paranoid.

Maybe I should just wait for Azriel . . .

Damn it, *no*. I couldn't keep relying on him to keep me safe. Sooner or later, he would leave, but I was stuck with Hunter long term. If I wanted to survive *her* post-Azriel, then I had better *not* start jumping at shadows the minute he wasn't at my back.

Still, it was with a whole lot of trepidation that I continued to move into the darkness. "Jak, I can't see a goddamn thing in here. Can't you at least use the flashlight app on your phone?"

I'd certainly be using mine if the damn thing hadn't decided to die on me.

"No." He paused. "Take three steps to your right, then five to the left. Watch the table—"

I crashed into said table and bit back another curse. "Warning me a little earlier might have been handy."

"Sorry."

There was little amusement in his voice, and again I frowned. This whole thing felt decidedly off . . .

"Almost there," he added. "Just one more step."

I hesitated, then cursed myself for doing so. Jak wouldn't harm me. Bed me—given half a chance—yes, but not harm. Not only did he need me to get his story, but he was well aware just how thick and fast trouble in the form of Uncle Rhoan would hit him if he in any way caused me damage—physical or emotional.

I took that step.

Realized almost instantly it was the wrong thing to do when something grabbed me and held me.

But that something wasn't flesh and blood but rather magic. I had one moment to wonder what the hell—who the hell—had me this time and even less time to fear; then thought was torn away and I knew no more.

Waking was a slow process and felt rather like the tedious climb to awareness that often accompanied a heavy alcohol binge. Thanks to our faster metabolic rate, it was harder for werewolves to get drunk than humans, but it *was* certainly possible if you applied yourself well enough. I had on several occasions, generally when I'd stupidly embarked on a drinking contest with Liana and Ronan, Riley's two eldest. But at least I'd had the pleasurable buzz of consuming all that alcohol first. There was none of that joy here, just the sick queasiness and thick head that generally hit after consumption had well and truly finished.

For several minutes, I did nothing more than simply lie there, willing my head to stop pounding even as I wondered where the hell I was.

But as awareness of my surroundings grew stronger, I discovered that not only was I in a bed *and* naked, but I was spread-eagle, with my hands and feet tied.

What the *hell* was going on?

My first thought—naturally enough—was that I'd been raped, but I had no sense of violation. It didn't feel like anyone had abused me in any way other than tying me. My body *did* ache, but I suspected it was more a residue of whatever magic had knocked me out rather than someone having forced themself on me.

Of course, no one ever *had*, so how could I be so certain that it *hadn't* happened? God, the way I was tied certainly suggested that even if it *hadn't* happened, it was very much in the cards. It was a thought that should have frightened me, but all it actually did was make me mad. Werewolves had a free and easy attitude when it came to sex, but force was an entirely different matter—and one that was *not* dealt with lightly. Fortunately, it was something that rarely happened among werewolves. But then, rape was rarely about sex and all about either gaining power over—or causing degradation to—another person.

Who the hell would wish either of those on me?

Even as the thought hit, the answer came. Lucian.

Touch not, Amaya said, her sharp voice cutting like razor blades through my brain. *Tried.*

Lucian?

Him, she spat. *Tried to slice it off. Missed.*

I blinked. As statements went, *that* was pretty dramatic, and it was one that had just a touch of amusement vibrating through me. At least I'd had a defender when I was unconscious.

It was just a damn shame that she'd missed.

I very much wanted to open my eyes and see where the hell I was, but caution prevailed. Until I had some sense of what was going on around me, it was better that Lucian thought I was still unconscious.

There was little in the way of movement or sound—other than the nearby rumble of traffic—to indicate there was anyone close, but the air was thick with the scent of dust and mold and age. Wherever we were, it wasn't Lucian's apartment. But he was here. His scent—lemongrass, suede, and musky, powerful male—was a strong undercurrent to the other scents.

So why wasn't Azriel here, ripping Lucian's head off his fucking shoulders?

Can't, Amaya muttered. *Blocked.*

She had to mean magically, because there were few physical forces that could actually stop him.

So did those same restrictions apply to me becoming Aedh? I quickly reached for the magic. The pounding in my head sharpened dramatically—suggesting that part of me *was* trying to respond—but I remained as I was. In flesh and bound.

And *that* was a little frightening. We'd guessed Lucian had been capable of magic, but I hadn't thought it possible that he could create a spell powerful enough to either bind an Aedh to human form or stop the movement of a reaper. And if he could do *that*, then he probably knew how to kill them, too. It made me suddenly glad that Azriel wasn't here.

Besides, I wanted the pleasure of killing the bastard myself.

Not self, Amaya said, her background noise ramping up a notch. *Me include.*

Trust me, you'll be included.

The hissing changed to a happy humming. I still wasn't entirely sure whether that was an improvement.

I pulled on the ropes binding me to test their strength. There was no give and no sign that they'd break easily. No surprise there, I guess. Lucian was well aware of what I could and couldn't do.

Just as, I suddenly realized, he was well aware that my friends were very much my Achilles' heel.

God, was *he* the reason for Ilianna's disappearance?

I hoped like hell he wasn't, but the dread that filled me suggested otherwise.

I opened my eyes. The ceiling was wood and heavily stained and draped with cobwebs that hung in long, dusty strings. The walls to the left and the right had been semidemolished, but there was little to see in the rooms beyond except rubble.

The bed itself was wide and would have been comfortable if not for the ropes holding me so tightly. They snaked from my wrists and my ankles over each corner of the bed and were, I presumed, anchored somehow to the floor.

I lifted my head to see if I could spot anything else. There were industrial-looking windows running the length of the wall in front of me, but they were all covered with black plastic. Wouldn't want the neighbors seeing what he was up to, after all.

Why the hell was I even here? Why hadn't I been rescued? Azriel might not be able to get into this place, but he'd have to know I was here. Why hadn't he called for help from Riley, Quinn, or even Tao?

I had absolutely no idea, and given it was a question that couldn't immediately be answered, I turned my attention back to the ropes. They were thick, coarse, and tight, and my wrists were red but not yet bleeding. I yanked on the left one as hard as I could, but the only thing I managed to do was rub my wrist raw. The fucking rope didn't give.

Amaya, any chance that you can cut the damn things?

She didn't answer, but half a second later, her energy began to burn through my flesh. Slowly but surely, she moved from her position near my spine to the right side of my body, then into my shoulder. It was a weird sensation, and even weirder to see the broader end of her blade and her hilt find substance and stick out of my shoulder. Her sharp tip appeared near my wrist, and a second later, that arm was free.

She repeated the process with my left arm. This time, the Dušan twisted around to watch, though it kept its tail firmly wrapped around the bracelet of leaves inked into my skin. Of course, it was no more a tat than the Dušan was—it was one of Ilianna's charms that the Dušan had made a permanent part of me. Just how she'd done it, nobody knew. The Dušans weren't supposed to be active on this plane, but for some reason no one could explain, mine was.

The minute both wrists were free, I sat upright and reached for Amaya.

But in that moment, I realized I was no longer alone.

"Make no further move to free yourself, my dear," Lucian said, "because I really *would* hate to shoot you."

His familiar tones flowed over my skin like a warm summer breeze and made me hunger for the touch of his clever fingers. It was a reaction that annoyed the fuck out of me, if only because I knew my response couldn't entirely be blamed on the spell he'd placed on me. Some of it was simple, old-fashioned lust.

He stood in the wide, unfinished doorway, an image of golden perfection, holding a gun. He was tall, muscular, and, if I was being at all honest, a perfectly formed piece of manhood. Lucian's faults were internal rather than external, emotional rather than physical. *His* wishes, *his* desires were all that mattered to him. The wants and needs of others were of little relevance, even if he sometimes offered others utter bliss. He'd certainly offered it to me often enough, but he'd also magically bound me to ensure I kept coming back to him. He might have wanted my body, but he'd also wanted the knowledge of not just what was happening with the key search, but also my father and the Raziq. Lucian hated them with a passion and depth that was as fierce as it was frightening.

And the only way he could completely keep track of both their movements and mine was to read my mind when we fucked.

"What the hell are you doing, Lucian?" My voice was amazingly calm given the anger that surged through me. "Have you got a death wish or something?"

"The reaper may want to kill me," he said with a half shrug. "But he will not overstep the rules to justify his own petty desires."

"That's where you're wrong." My fingers twitched against Amaya's hilt, and it took every ounce of willpower not to aim her steel at his black heart and release her. But he wasn't a fool, and that meant I couldn't be. Not until I knew the full length and breadth of whatever he had planned. "By kidnapping me, you've given him carte blanche to break the rules where *you're* concerned."

"Then he is most welcome to try to kill me. But I doubt that he will."

His confidence was as irritating as it was unnerving. "What do you want, Lucian?"

"What I have always wanted." His low tones were laced with amusement and slid across my skin like silk. "I want to fuck you senseless."

I shivered—a reaction that was a weird mix of loathing and desire. "And suck me dry information-wise."

"Well, yes, that *is* a luscious side benefit." He grinned. "You cannot deny that our time together was mutually satisfactory."

I snorted. Side benefit, my ass. If anything *had* been a side benefit, then it was the sex. And yeah, it had been great, but the truth of the matter was, I was just another cog in the many wheels he had spinning.

"And you were so damn sure of your prowess in bed that you had to place a spell on me to ensure I came back."

Something flickered in his eyes. Something that was dark and ultimately dangerous. It was a quick reminder that for all the time I'd spent fucking this man, I didn't really know him.

"Let's not kid ourselves, Risa." His voice was as soft as his expression was dark. "It was not just the spell that kept you coming back, but your own insatiable desire. And we both know if I were to touch you now, you would beg me for more."

"If you tried touching me, the only thing you'd feel is Amaya's steel." I paused, then added somewhat cattily, "Oh, that's right, you've already *had* a close encounter of the ugly kind with her."

He laughed. It was a short and sharp sound, but held little of the anger and frustration I could sense within him. "Yes. I wasn't aware that demon swords were capable of thought or action when the bearer was out of it. To discover the sharp end of a sword literally sticking out of your cunt was something of a surprise."

Thank you, thank you, thank you, I said silently to my sword.

Kill him to thank.

I have to admit, it was a very tempting thought. But until I knew whether he was at all involved with Ilianna's disappearance, my hands were still as tied as my feet.

"So you kidnapped me just to fuck me?"

"Oh, I didn't intend to just fuck you, my dear." Amusement played about his mouth, but there was something decidedly dark in the green depths.

"Then what the hell *did* you intend?"

"What I intended," he drawled, "was to seed you with my child."

Chapter 12

For a moment I simply stared at him, wondering if he'd gone absolutely bonkers in the brief time we'd been apart. He'd been in this world long enough to know it was law that all werewolves—even those of us who were half-breeds—had to be chipped at puberty to prevent conception. The government still seemed to think—despite centuries of evidence to the contrary—that just because we fucked like rabbits, we'd breed like them, too.

"Well, you wouldn't have had much luck with that," I bit back. "Even without Amaya's well-placed intervention, I'm chipped. If you took it out, it would still take several cycles for me to conceive."

He smiled. It held a very nasty edge. "Yes, but you are no longer what you were. You have been remade by the Raziq."

My stomach flip-flopped, but I didn't let the sudden surge of fear show. "Meaning what?"

"That you are fully fertile, for one thing." His gaze slid down my body, and despite the distaste that rolled through me, I nevertheless reacted as strongly as I ever had. My hormones, I thought in frustration, needed to be bitch slapped. "It is such a shame your sword intervened, but in truth, I am not so annoyed. I do prefer my partners awake and willing."

A statement that had trepidation crawling through me all over again. But what was more interesting was the fact that he'd intended to breed. Aedh felt that imperative only when their life was coming to an end. Of course, thanks to an Aedh's long life span, that end could be many years away. Hell, my father was still going strong, more's the pity.

"I'd love to say I'm sorry to have disappointed you, but I'm not. Now, why don't you just put that fucking gun down and release me. You're not going to get what you want from me—no baby, no fucking keys, no revenge—"

"Oh," he cut in, his expression altogether too confident for my liking. "That's where you are very, *very* wrong."

Again that sick, fearful feeling began to rise up my throat. My fingers tightened against Amaya's hilt, but I didn't draw her free from my flesh and throw her at the bastard's heart. But I wanted to. Oh, how I wanted to.

"What do you mean?" The edge in my voice was fear and anger combined.

"Simply that I have combined my need for offspring with my desire for revenge on all those who have made me less than I am."

That feeling of dread ramped up several notches. My throat was so restricted, I could barely even say, "How?"

But I knew.

And he knew I knew. That was very evident by the amused glitter in his bright eyes. "Ilianna."

My reaction was instant. Without thought. In one smooth movement, I drew Amaya free, swept her across the ropes binding my ankles, then lunged at him. But he was even faster than me. He jumped back and fired the gun. The shot tore through my hand, blowing apart two fingers before it hit Amaya's hilt and ricocheted into the nearby wall. Pain and blood surged, but all I felt was anger. My anger, Amaya's anger, and the utter need to just rid the world of the man who might well have destroyed my best friend. I attacked him, Amaya raised high above my head and screaming for blood.

Just for a moment, surprise flitted across his features; then he retreated from my onslaught and held up the gun.

"Know that I will shoot you again if I need to," he said. "And know, too, that if I die, so will Ilianna."

That stopped me. Even Amaya muted her screams. "What do you mean?"

"Just that." He paused, but the tension in his body suggested he was very much ready to react the minute I so much as twitched. "If I do not contact the people holding your friend every hour, they will kill her."

"You *bastard*."

Amusement flitted across his features. "All Aedh are bastards, dear Risa, because we seed and leave. We are not prey to the emotions and needs that wreck so many human lives."

And were poorer for it. "But to rape Ilianna—"

"There was *no* rape," he cut in, sounding oddly annoyed. "An Aedh's kiss always ensures that their chosen breeder is more than willing."

"Ilianna is *gay*. You would have had to force a kiss, if nothing else."

Though anger kept the worst of the pain at bay, I was bleeding all over the place and would be in very serious trouble if I didn't do something about it soon. Yet I remained still. To do anything else would not have been wise right now.

"Well, yes, but we both know I was not her first male lover."

No, because Ilianna *had* experimented when she was young. After the attack on her sister had left her incapable of conceiving, her parents' desire for grandchildren had fallen solely onto Ilianna's shoulders. The weight of their expectations had all but forced her to least *try* to have a relationship with a male. But she could no more change her orientation than the moon could rise during the day.

"That doesn't alter the reality that you forced yourself on her. Whether the magic made her willing or not doesn't matter in the end." And I would kill him for it. If not now, then later.

I shifted Amaya to my left hand and tried to ignore the warm slickness covering her hilt. The pain was getting stronger, a monster ready to consume. I clenched what remained of my fingers on my shattered hand, but it did little to stem the tide of blood.

He made a "who cares" motion with his free hand. "It has been done. She will bear my child, no matter what happens to me. The decision *you* have to make is whether *she* actually gets to live or die."

"And why the hell would you impregnate her if all you intended to do is kill her?"

"Come now, let's not play dumb, Risa. She is captive to your good behavior. And, of course, she is not the only one I have seeded." His smile was all arrogance. "The Raziq may have stolen many things from me, but they did not take my potency."

I wished they fucking *had*. "So does your dark sorceress know she's about to become a mom?"

"You always did catch on to the inconsequential things faster than most," he murmured, looking amused. "But no, she does not. It is not necessary. Besides, she has not entirely upheld her part of our agreement, so I see no problem in not entirely upholding mine."

"That's a decidedly risky game to play when dealing with a sorceress as powerful as Lauren Macintyre." But maybe she'd kill him and save the rest of us the trouble.

"Yes, but there is also great pleasure to be found in playing such games."

I resisted the urge to glance at his body and see for myself just how much delight he was taking in this game. "So what's next?"

"Why, you find the keys; then we both go to retrieve them, of course."

"Of course." Dizziness swept me. I licked my lips and tried to ignore the trembling that was beginning to hit my muscles. "But what the hell are you going to do with them once you get them, Lucian?

It's not like you can get onto the gray fields anymore."

Again that dark and dangerous energy flashed through him. "Perhaps, but I can use them as a bargaining chip with the Raziq."

"If you think they'll agree to restore you to full Aedh in exchange for the keys, you're not playing with a full deck."

"They will have no choice."

I snorted. "They tortured you once for information on the keys. What makes you think they won't do it again?"

"Because I will have them placed where even the Raziq can't get them—hell itself."

I stared at him. He was insane. He had to be to even think *that* was a logical solution. "I'm sure the inhabitants of hell are going to be as happy as all get-out when they discover what they've been handed."

"I am not so foolish as to simply hide them," he growled. "They will be guarded by the most powerful demons in hell."

"And suddenly Lauren's presence in your life makes sense."

"Everything I do, I do for a reason, Risa." He nodded down at my hand. "You'd better do something about that. I need you fit and able to find the keys later today."

"So much for being able to read my mind only during sex," I spat. "Is everything that comes out of your mouth a fabrication?"

"Only when it suits me." His smile was lazy and

arrogant. "That, however, was not a total lie. The only time I *can* generally read you is during sex—it just doesn't have to be between you and me."

My stomach clenched, and I came so close to throwing up that the bitter taste of bile filled the back of my throat. *Every* time I'd had sex with Azriel, *he'd* been reading me. God, was there no end to this man's depravity?

"I'm going to fucking kill you. You know that, don't you?"

He laughed softly. "Keep believing that if it makes you feel better, Risa. However, you are no more capable of doing that than I am of sprouting wings—and not even the banshee you hold in your hand will alter that one fact."

Banshee not, Amaya growled. *Throw. Will gladly eat.*

Not until we find Ilianna. To Lucian, I said, "You always were an arrogant sod. I just didn't think you were stupid."

"I guess only time will prove which of us is right." He shrugged, the movement casual and elegant. "Now, as I suggested before, you'd best heal that hand."

I glanced down. Blood streamed from what remained of my fingers, and the ever-enlarging pool underneath them shimmered softly in the semilit darkness. And just like that, the anger gave way and the pain hit. My legs started trembling, and my head began spinning so badly, it was all I could do to remain standing.

I wasn't even sure I could heal a wound this bad,

but if I didn't try soon, then I'd be unconscious and in his power again. *If he moves near me,* I ordered Amaya, *slice him up. Just don't kill him.*

Pleasure.

I closed my eyes and called to the Aedh. It came in a trickle rather than a rush, a sure sign the magic that had prevented me from changing in the bedroom still held some sway out here. Either that or I was simply reaching the limits of my strength. And in the end, the result was pretty much the same.

I grabbed at that trickle fiercely, forced it down into my arm, imagined my fingers and hand fading into energy. I felt the burn of power roll down the muscles, and an instant later, the ever-growing throb of pain was gone as my lower arm and hand became particles rather than flesh.

The trembling in my body grew stronger, and my control began to slip. I bit my lip, called up the Aedh again, and imagined fingers that were healed and whole. But this time, the energy was little more than a weak wash.

Then my knees went out from under me and I hit the concrete. Hard. I bit back a yelp and, with some trepidation, opened my eyes. I had four whole fingers back on my hand, but they were still a bloody— and very painful—mess. But the bleeding had at least slowed to little more than a trickle.

I met Lucian's gaze again. "Now what?"

His gaze slid insolently down my body and my stomach clenched. *He not touch,* Amaya warned. *Will slice.*

Her fierce readiness to defend my honor was infinitely gratifying, but I had no doubt that having sex with him would be the ultimate price for setting Ilianna free. He didn't want just *any* offspring, no matter how much he'd loaded the bases with Ilianna and Lauren. He wanted *our* offspring. Wanted a child that was as close to full Aedh as someone like him was ever likely to get.

And if that was the price of freeing Ilianna, then it was one I would pay, however much I—and my sword—might hate it.

"What do you think is next?"

The desire radiating off him was so fierce and strong, it hit like a summer storm. My body trembled under its force, and my nipples puckered, reactions that only increased the strength of the storm.

"If I knew, I wouldn't have asked." I continued to meet his gaze steadily, even though my heart was beating a million miles an hour and my throat was dry.

A smile played about his lips. "You lie, Risa Jones."

I didn't reply, because there was very little I could say or do at this point. If sex was what he now intended, then it would happen, no matter what. And if I killed him, as I ached to, it would be Ilianna who paid. I was the reason she'd been kidnapped, raped, and impregnated, and that was guilt enough. I couldn't bear the weight of her death as well.

He took several steps toward me, then stopped. "Get up."

I rose slowly and somewhat unsteadily. Lust continued to roll off him in waves, and tiny beads of perspiration began to dot my skin. My damn nipples were so hard, they ached and, as much as I hated it, I couldn't entirely ignore the desire that slithered through me. And while most of it was undoubtedly the spell he'd placed on me, some of it was not.

I might hate him, but I also wanted him.

But I'd be damned if I admitted it.

Our gazes clashed for several more nerve-racking minutes; then he raised a hand, pressed a fingertip between my breasts, and pushed me backward. Amaya's screams echoed in my head, and I ordered her to shut up and *not* cut.

My back hit the wall, the wood rough and grimy against my skin. He kept me pinned, not moving, not saying anything, just watching me with that smug, insolent expression I was beginning to hate.

Then he stepped back.

For a moment, hope leapt, but the amusement touching his lips soon killed that.

"Undress me," he ordered. "Slowly."

I flexed my fingers, battling anger and the urge to do as Amaya desired, then raised my hands and unbuttoned his shirt. When the last button came undone, I placed my hands on his skin and slid them upward, over the taut muscles of his stomach and chest and then under the shirt. As it slipped to floor, I ran my hands back down his body and played with the waist of his pants.

His warm breath fanned across my skin, its tempo one of expectation. Mine was no better, despite my loathing of the situation. My gaze rose to his. Desire burned in those green depths, but so, too, did warning.

I unfastened his pants. His cock strained against the restriction of his silk boxers, thick and hard and ready for action. I hooked my fingers into the waist of both and slid them down his legs. He stepped out, then pressed a hand against my head, keeping me down.

"Suck me."

I did as he bid, sucking and licking and teasing until the salty taste of come began to fill my mouth.

Abruptly, he tangled his fingers in my hair and yanked me upright. He spun me around so that I faced the wall, then pulled my head backward, kissing me fiercely as he entered me from behind. What followed was animalistic and hard, and, despite my loathing of both him and the situation, felt good. But I did *not* give voice to my pleasure. There wasn't much I could keep to myself given the situation, but I refused to give him *that*.

He came with a shout that was as fierce as it was triumphant, pumping hard as he emptied himself inside me. I closed my eyes, my body still trembling with unfulfilled desire, his fluids dribbling down my thighs and hate in my heart.

He withdrew, turned me around, and kissed me fiercely again. But just as quickly, he pulled away.

"Respond like you mean it, dear Risa, or I will not make the call that is keeping your friend alive."

"You can't keep either of us forever, Lucian," I said, my voice edged with the anger I was barely keeping leashed. I could almost taste his death, and god, it tasted *sweet*. "Sooner or later, this will have to end."

"Oh, it will." He bent, picked me up in his arms, then spun and walked back to the bedroom. "But the military exhibition does not open until ten, and that gives me five hours to fuck you senseless."

He threw me onto the bed, but didn't immediately join me. "By the time you leave here, you will be carrying my child. And *that* will be the greatest revenge I could ever have on your reaper."

My *flesh-and-blood* reaper. If he could bleed, if he could gain human emotions when in flesh too long, why then would he not also be fertile? If the Raziq *had* taken the chip out, then it was more than possible that I was *already* pregnant.

God, wouldn't that be the perfect twist? If I had to be pregnant, then I would much rather the father be someone I actually cared about than someone I intended to kill.

Of course, given fate's apparent desire to crap all over my life, it was *not* a likely outcome, but my heart still sang at the thought.

And it was a hope that got me through the hours that ensued.

I woke to the scent of mold, dust, and age. Similar scents, yet different from what I'd woken to before. Disoriented, I rolled onto my back, feeling the rough edges of wood rather than the silk of sheets. My eyes were heavy and my head was booming, and that "drank too much" sensation was well and truly back.

He'd obviously transported me magically rather than just letting me go. I couldn't remember his doing it, but then, I hadn't *actually* been around for the last few hours of our encounter. I might not have done much astral travel, but I'd learned enough to get the hell out of my body. Lucian either hadn't noticed or hadn't cared. He might have paid lip service to wanting me to be an eager, vocal participant, but in the end all he'd wanted was a body to impregnate.

And I wasn't entirely sure what I'd do if I *was* pregnant, especially since there was just as much chance of it being Azriel's as Lucian's.

God, please, let it be Azriel's.

A desperate plea that in itself suggested the psychic part of me already knew my fate in *that* regard.

I opened my eyes. Daylight drifted in from the grimy windows to my right, highlighting a mess of upturned tables, broken chairs, and graffiti-littered walls. It had to be Larry's, and I wondered if Jak had ever been here. Lucian was much more than we'd *ever* suspected, and maybe magic wasn't the only thing he'd become adept at. Maybe he could imitate voices, as well. Right now, I wouldn't put anything past him.

I pushed into a sitting position. The first thing I saw was the ring of black stones that surrounded me. But they weren't just any old stones; they were wards. I raised a hand and carefully touched one. Color swirled through its dark heart, but it didn't react in any other way. Their presence, however, might explain why Azriel—or anyone else, for that matter—hadn't come to my rescue. Warding stones were generally used to keep things either out or in, but I knew they could also be used to confuse. Maybe no one had rescued me simply because they'd been unable to pin down my location.

I carefully flicked the nearest stone out of sequence. It rattled noisily across the old floorboards, the sound almost thunderous in the hush holding the building captive. A heartbeat later, energy burned across my skin and Azriel was in front of me, pulling me into a hug as fierce and as desperate as any I'd ever experienced.

I melted into him, enjoying the security and warmth of his embrace. "I'm okay," I said eventually. My words were muffled against his chest, but I wasn't about to move. Not yet. Not until the trembling that was as much utter relief as it was weakness stopped. "I wasn't there for most of it."

"The Aedh's death will be slow and very painful." Azriel's voice was flat but filled with such fury, it momentarily stole my breath. "And I will savor every single moment of it."

"But not until we find Ilianna."

"He cannot get away—"

"You will *not* kill him." I pulled away from him, my gaze searching his. Saw the anger, the pain, and knew it was all for me. It warmed me just as much as it worried me. "Far worse can and has been done to me, Azriel. Ilianna is a hostage against my good behavior, and until we can find her, then Lucian has to live."

He said something in his own language, the

words soft but vehement. It didn't take much imagination to know he was swearing. "You can*not* seriously think we should allow him in on the search for the keys. That is taking things too far."

Things had already gone too far, and it was too late to stop it all now. "I am, and he will." I gave him a lopsided smile. "At the very least, it means we can keep an eye on him."

"I would much rather keep a sword on him, if it's all the same to you." He tugged me close again and wrapped his arms around me. It felt like heaven. "Let's get you home."

If I was in his arms, then I *was* home, but I didn't give that particular thought voice. His energy swept around me, and in no time we'd zipped through the fields and were re-forming in the middle of my bedroom. I stepped back and glanced at the clock on my side table. It was just after ten.

"I'll have a shower and clean up; then we can go see if the key is at the exhibition."

"And if we find it?"

I shrugged. "I guess what happens next depends on what sort of security they have in place."

He studied me for a moment, then said, "What of the Aedh?"

"He's going to meet us there at eleven thirty."

"So we should try to get there sooner—"

"No," I cut in. "Remember Ilianna."

He swore again. I smiled, dropped a quick kiss on his lips, and said, "I know. Trust me, I know."

"I bet you do *not*."

He caught my broken hand and gently ran his

fingers over the mangled remnants of mine. Energy
flowed from his touch, renewing my reserves even
as my fingers began to heal. Or rather, heal as much
as they were ever going to. But I could bend them,
use them, and the scars—which were red and fierce-
looking right now—would eventually fade. I'd been
lucky, and I knew it. If not for the fact I was half
Aedh, I would have lost them.

He raised my fingers to his lips, brushing a sweet
kiss across them, then said, "Go. I will prepare you
something to eat."

He disappeared, and I headed for the shower.
For the longest time, I did nothing more than stand
under the water, letting the heat wash the ache
from my bruised body and the scents of lust and
Lucian from my skin. I wished it could similarly
wash the niggling sense of violation from my mind,
but there was nothing in this world that could do
that except time.

I ran my fingers across my belly and wondered if
I did indeed carry the beginnings of life deep inside.
Wondered how I would feel if it turned out to be
Lucian's rather than Azriel's.

Another two questions only time could answer.

I took a somewhat shuddery breath, then got the
hell out of the shower and dressed. Worrying over
events far in the future was not particularly the best
way to spend my time at the moment. Not when I
had keys to not only find but, hopefully, this time,
keep. How we were going to do that given the
whole Lucian situation, I had no idea, but one thing
was certain. The bastard might think he held all the

cards, but there was always, *always*, a way out. You just had to look hard enough.

And perhaps be willing to pay the ultimate price.

But that price would *not* be Ilianna's death. That was the one place I would *not* go.

Azriel, it seemed, had been picking up cooking tips from somewhere, because this time he'd produced the world's biggest steak and some steamed veggies.

I sat down and tucked in with gusto. Once I'd demolished everything on my plate, I grabbed my Coke, sat back, and asked the one question that had been quietly bugging me. "Why weren't you able to rescue me?"

"Because, as you have already guessed, he used magic to not only snatch you, but to disguise your whereabouts."

"And Jak?"

"Unharmed." His voice was as neutral as his expression. "I will admit to a somewhat angry response to his part in your abduction, but I controlled it the minute I realized he was an unwilling participant."

"Meaning you beat him up, then healed him?"

"Something like that." He returned my gaze evenly. "He does not now remember the event."

Meaning the event, as he put it, had been pretty bad. "I told you Jak wouldn't willingly betray me, Azriel."

"He has before, so that is an illogical statement."

Perhaps it was, but I nevertheless believed it. "What, exactly, did Lucian do to him?"

"Nothing more than luring him to the warehouse with the promise of a story, then capturing his mind."

Which was why Jak hadn't really sounded himself. They had been Lucian's words, not Jak's. I drank some Coke, enjoying the fuzzy goodness for several seconds before saying, "We need to find Ilianna. Until she's free, we're stuck doing whatever Lucian wants us to do."

"I would suspect that he has her position well hidden by his magic."

I frowned. "Does it take much magic to do that sort of thing?"

He shrugged, the movement brief but somehow elegant. "I am not knowledgeable when it comes to magic, but I would suspect so."

"So perhaps what we need is someone who is not only knowledgeable in all matters magic, but who is able to detect such things."

"Ilianna's mother."

I nodded and thrust upward. "We need to go see—"

I cut the rest of the sentence off as a phone rang. It wasn't my phone—I hadn't yet gotten around to charging the damn thing—but rather a phone coming from Tao's room. It was answered after a few seconds, but that didn't do much to ease the tension suddenly running through me.

I knew who was making that call. Knew why.

After a few minutes, Tao stumbled out, looking somewhat disheveled and far from awake. "It's Mirri," he said, thrusting the phone at me. "She's not making sense. Is Ilianna missing or something?"

"Yes." I grabbed the phone and said, "It's okay, Mirri. I know what's happened to her, and she's okay."

"Oh, thank god." Tears filled her bright eyes. "I was so afraid something bad had happened to her. Where is she? Why hasn't she contacted me?"

Something bad *had* happened, but I wasn't about to tell her that. At the same time, I couldn't *not* tell her what was going on. I hesitated, then said, "I'm afraid she's being held hostage against my good behavior. She hasn't been hurt, and won't be, as long as I do everything her kidnapper says."

"Oh, *fuck*."

That, ten times over, I thought grimly. "I think we've worked out a way to free her, Mirri—"

The phone was snatched from her hand, and suddenly I was staring at a man with piercing, light blue eyes, pale skin, and silver-white hair. Albino, I thought, and then realized this was probably Carwyn.

"I want in on any rescue attempt," he said, voice deep and fierce.

"I doubt that Ilianna would—"

"I may not yet be her mate," he cut in. "But I will be. Whoever did this to her must pay."

And *that* was both the stallion *and* the man speaking, I thought grimly. And yet I couldn't do everything. If I were to have any hope of prizing Ilianna away from Lucian's clutches, then it would have to be when Lucian was otherwise distracted.

"We've got to find her first," I said; then, when he opened his mouth to obviously argue, I quickly added, "The minute we do, we'll ring you."

"I'll be standing by."

"Great." I hung up and handed the phone back to Tao, who was looking decidedly more awake.

"Ilianna's really missing?"

"Lucian's snatched her and hidden her location through magic. I'm about to go over to the Brindle to see if her mom can find her."

"What can I—"

"No," I cut in. "Time is of the essence. We'll come back here the minute we uncover anything."

"To echo Carwyn's words, I'll be standing by." He half turned, then clicked his fingers and added, "Oh, a parcel was delivered for you an hour ago. I dropped it on the coffee table so you'd see it coming in, which you obviously haven't."

No, because I hadn't come in the regular way, but rather via the Azriel express. I walked across to pick up the small white box. It wasn't particularly heavy, and the writing was my father's. This *had* to be the wards he promised. Heart beating a whole lot faster, I glanced up at Tao and said, "Thanks."

He frowned. "It's not one of *those* parcels, is it? Because you're suddenly looking a whole lot paler."

"It is, but it's something I've asked for this time." I forced a smile. "Hopefully, it's something that'll keep the hordes at bay while we grab the next key."

"Shame it couldn't also keep Lucian at bay," he muttered.

"A sword would," Azriel commented, voice as

flat as his expression. "And I know two that would
gladly cooperate."

"He does make an excellent point," Tao said,
then held up his hands as I opened my mouth.
"Yes, I know. We can't do anything until Ilianna is
safe. But that doesn't stop either of us from wishing
the worst on the bastard, does it?"

"You can't wish anything worse on him than *I*
am, trust me."

I couldn't stop the bitterness in my voice, and
Tao's gaze narrowed. "Is there something else going
on you're not telling me about?"

"No." He didn't look convinced, but then, I guess
he *had* known me a long time. "I'll call you when
we find anything."

"You'd better."

I turned to Azriel. He caught my hand unasked,
drew me to him, and whisked us through the fields
to the Brindle. I handed him the box, suspecting the
Brindle would *not* react kindly to Aedh magic being taken into its midst, then ran up the steps and
into the foyer. A geyser of golden sparks followed
me as I ran through the shadows.

A gray-clad woman appeared. "Please, there is
no need for haste—"

"There's *every* need," I bit back, but I nevertheless slowed. "I urgently need to see Custodian
Zaira."

"I do not think—"

"Risa, what draws you here in such a state?" The
familiar voice was as soft as the shadows around us
and just as powerful.

I glanced past the gray-clad young woman and watched the willowy figure approach. Kiandra wasn't only the woman charge of the Brindle, but one of the most powerful witches I'd ever met. "I need to speak to Zaira urgently."

"As Indara was no doubt about to tell you, Zaira is not on duty today." She stopped several feet away and studied me. The power so evident in her gray eyes, was breathtaking. "Is this about Ilianna?"

"Yes. She's been kidnapped, and we suspect magic is being used to stop anyone from finding her."

"And you wish us to find her by tracking the magic itself?"

"Yes. I have no idea if it's possible—"

"It is." She tilted her head, and just for an instant it felt like she was seeing into my mind, reading all my hopes and fears. Judging me. My breath caught somewhere in my throat, and I found myself hoping I came up to scratch. After a moment, she added, "This way."

Once again I was led through the Brindle's quiet, shadowed halls and into yet another area I'd never been before. This one felt and looked far older than the other areas I'd visited, and power seemed to ooze off the walls. It was almost as if the centuries of spell making had infused the old stones with a magic all of their own.

We made our way through the dimly lit corridors, each one getting progressively smaller and darker, and eventually stepped into a room that appeared little more than an antechamber. The air was rich with such a riot of scents that my nose twitched and

I didn't even bother trying to sort them all out. There was power here, too, and the force of it made my skin itch and tingle.

"Wait here," Kiandra murmured, waving an elegant hand toward the two small chairs that were positioned on either side of the doorway. "You are not an initiate and therefore cannot follow me into the next room. I will see what magic there is to be found."

"It won't feel like human magic," I said. "Because it isn't."

She didn't ask what type of magic it could be, but then, given she appeared to know all about my key quest and the forces that fought for control of both me *and* them, maybe she didn't need to.

Without further comment, she turned and walked into the next room. The door closed behind her with a heavy *click*, leaving me alone in the silent shadows. I sat for all of three seconds, then got up and began to pace. I couldn't help it. So much of what we could do next depended on the information Kiandra did—or didn't—find for us.

It seemed to take forever. I didn't have my watch or phone, but I guess the reality was closer to ten minutes. I spun around as the door opened and she reappeared, a slight haze of smoke and magic accompanying her as she walked toward me. Her expression gave little away, so it was with some trepidation that I asked, "Did you find her?"

She stopped and clasped her hands in front of her. Her expression held an odd sort of excitement. "Ilianna is with child?"

I closed my eyes for a moment and swore internally. If Kiandra knew, then Ilianna's mother would more than likely find out sooner rather than later. Given her desire to see Ilianna join Carwyn's herd, I wasn't entirely sure how'd she react. Or, indeed, how Carwyn would.

"It's more than possible. The man who holds her is an Aedh—"

"And her child will be as you are: born of two worlds, powerful in magic, and gifted with foresight."

I frowned. "I'm not—"

"Just because you do not acknowledge such things does not mean they do not exist or that you are not capable." She paused, her gray eyes glowing molten silver with the shadows that held the room hostage. There was more than just power in her gaze now. There was excitement. "The old ritual site on Mount Macedon would not have acknowledged you in the manner that it did if it were not so."

The site had acknowledged me? When? Then I remembered the odd sense of watchfulness and the feeling that the trees themselves were sentient. Remembered that I'd been able to become Aedh when the magic of that place barred all such beings entry.

"Ilianna may not choose to keep—"

"She will," Kiandra said, with a certainty I couldn't help but believe. "Because she knows, as I know, that this child has been a long time coming, and a long time needed."

I frowned. "I don't understand—"

"No," Kiandra agreed. "But Ilianna does. There are many reasons she ran from us. What she witnessed when young was the excuse but not the truth."

I rubbed my forehead wearily. Fate, it seemed, had been brewing her plans for us all for a very long time. "Look, right now, all I want to do is rescue her. Did you find her?"

"Yes. And you were right—great magic holds her."

"Meaning we won't get past it?"

"Meaning that neither you nor your dark defender will. It is aimed at energy beings rather than mere flesh and blood."

"So Tao and Carwyn would get past it?"

"I suspect so." She hesitated. "There are beings within who guard her, but I could gain no true sense of them. They may or may not be human."

"Well, neither are Tao and Carwyn, and both are pretty pissed off right now."

She nodded. "It may be enough. Just tell them not to go in all guns blazing, because that will have dire consequences."

For Ilianna, I thought, not for them. I swallowed and nodded. "I'll pass on the message."

She nodded. "She is being held in an abandoned warehouse in Link Court, Brooklyn. The magic lies within the building, not along the perimeter."

"Meaning they'd need to be wary of other security measures?"

"Yes." She moved past me and led the way back through the warren of shadowed, powerful corridors. When we neared the front door, she stopped and lightly touched my shoulder. "Be careful, Risa Jones. There are more games being played than you realize."

My smile was almost a grimace. "Tell me something I don't know."

"There are two people in your life who are in reality one, and their deception goes deeper than you think."

I blinked. "What do you mean?"

She half shrugged. "What I see is not always clear. But I would suspect that a shape-shifter of some kind has entered your life."

"There is—he stole the first key. It's tracking the bastard that is proving the problem."

"Then perhaps you should start looking closer to home."

I frowned. "Are you saying it's a friend?"

She hesitated. "Acquaintance, perhaps. As I said, these things are not always clear."

Then I wished she hadn't mentioned it, because now I'd be looking at everyone suspiciously and suspecting the worse. But I forced a smile and said, "Thanks. I'll keep an eye out."

She nodded and, with one eloquent gesture, ushered me out of the building. But I was aware of her gaze as I ran down the steps, and it made my back itch. She knew more than what she'd said; of that much I was sure.

Azriel appeared near the bottom step. "You were successful?"

"Yes. Now we just need to plot our next move."

"Back to your apartment, then."

"No. I need to go see Aunt Riley. She's the expert in this sort of stuff. As much as I hate to do it, I think I need to bring her in rather than risk using only Tao and Carwyn."

"And once again, you do something thoroughly sensible. There is hope for you yet, I think."

I grinned. "Don't say that too loud. Wouldn't want the word getting around and spoiling my reputation."

"Your secret is safe with me." He wrapped his arms around my waist, dropped a kiss on my nose, then zapped us across to my aunt's.

To say our sudden appearance in the middle of her living room was something of a surprise would be the understatement of the year. I waited until she stopped swearing, then dropped a kiss on her cheek. "And good morning to you, too."

"Well, it was a good morning until you scared the life out of me *and* made me spill my coffee." Amusement teased her mouth and lit her gray eyes as she walked into the open kitchen area and grabbed a cloth. She tossed it to me, then added, "Seeing as I have to make a fresh cup, do you want one?"

"No, I haven't the time." I bent and wiped up the spillage. "I'm actually here for help."

"I'm gathering it's not key related, given your determination *not* to involve any of us in that search." Her voice was wry. "Which, by the way, is neither warranted nor necessary. We have faced far worse in our lifetimes than rogue Aedh."

"Which is precisely *why* I don't want you involved." And she *knew* that. "But this is related. Sort of."

"Go on."

She crossed her arms and regarded me steadily. A rock I could always depend on, no matter what, I thought with a half smile.

"Lucian has kidnapped Ilianna and is holding her hostage against my good behavior at a warehouse in Link Court, Brooklyn. According to the Brindle witches, she's protected by magic that will allow neither Aedh nor reaper entry."

"Then I'm surprised Lucian is still alive. In a similar situation, I would have killed the bastard."

"A sentiment I totally agree with," Azriel said.

I gave him a look over my shoulder, but he merely raised an eyebrow at me.

"Then why isn't he dead?" Riley said. "It would solve the problem of being forced to do what you do not wish to."

"If he doesn't report in every hour, the men holding her have orders to kill her."

"Ah."

"Also, I do not think those men are human."

She shrugged. "Non-human I can deal with."

"Yeah, but these are non-human *and* Razan."

"Meaning the fight will be infinitely more exciting." She grinned and cracked her knuckles. "I haven't had a good fight in quite a while."

"That is because you're *supposed* to be settling down to a quiet life." Uncle Quinn's gently lilting tones seemed to come out of the air itself. "And you *were* intending to call me in on this, weren't you?"

He re-formed next to Riley, his expression a mix of love and amusement. Like me, he was half Aedh, and was, in fact, the man who had taught me all of my skills.

"Of course," she replied, a smile on her lips and her eyes sparkling. "I wouldn't want you to miss out on the excitement."

Quinn rolled his eyes and glanced at me. "What do we face?"

"Magic, electronic security, and more than likely Raziq." I hesitated. "Tao and Carwyn—Ilianna's potential mate—want in on the action."

Quinn frowned. "Given we face an unknown number of combatants, I don't think it wise to involve anyone who isn't fight trained."

"Maybe, but the magic is aimed at those who are energy or half-energy beings, so it'll prevent you from getting in." I switched my gaze to Riley. "I know you're one of the best, but I don't want you going in there alone. I couldn't stand to see you hurt." Or worse. I didn't say it, but it hovered in the air, regardless.

"I won't be alone. I have a twin, remember, and he loves a fight even more than I do." She smiled, walked over to gather me in her arms, and hugged me fiercely. "It'll be all right, Risa," she added softly. "It always is."

Tears stung my eyes, and I blinked them away rapidly. And wished, with all my heart, that I could believe her. But deep down I knew it *wasn't* going to be all right, that it was never going to be all right. All right had long ago passed me by, and I was sliding faster and faster into the darkness that my mother had foreseen wrapped around me all those years ago.

"What we need," Quinn said, "is eyes on the situation. Once we know what we face, we can plan our attack."

"Stane can hook into all the security cams in the area—"

"So can the Directorate," Riley said. "And it'll be easier and faster. I'll get Rhoan on it immediately."

I frowned. "I'm not sure it's a good idea—"

She waved my objection away as she picked up her phone. "Jack owes me more than one favor. Besides, if this goes sideways, it's better that the Directorate be involved."

Please, God, don't let it go sideways. I licked my lips, then nodded. As Riley made the call, I glanced at Quinn. "I'm meeting Lucian at eleven thirty. I know that doesn't leave much time to plan anything, but I can delay him for at least an hour."

He said, "The longer you can delay, the better it will be. We'll ring—"

"You can't. My phone is dead and I left it home."

"Then I will shoot you a telepathic message when we've freed her."

"But I'm wearing nano microcells—"

"Which have not the capacity to stop me, no more than they could Riley." Quinn glanced at her as she got off the phone. "All set?"

"Rhoan is gearing up surveillance as we speak, and Jack has approved full Directorate participation." Her gaze met mine. "He said he owed you a favor. Care to explain that?"

I kept my expression—and thoughts—carefully neutral. "I was asked for advice on some demon-related killings Rhoan's investigating. Couldn't do a whole lot to help, though."

"Hmm." Her expression suggested she very much *didn't* believe my reply, even though it was the truth as far as it went. "We're not going to need your friends, so tell Tao and Carwyn to cool their jets. We'll contact them the minute we can."

If they are not going to help free Ilianna, perhaps we should bring them in on the key—

No, I said, before he could finish. *Definitely not.*

Risa, I do not trust the Aedh, and it might be wiser—

I won't risk my friends again, Azriel. I've already done enough damage to them. Out loud, I said, "You'll let me know the minute you have her? And you'll both be careful?"

"We will, on both counts." Quinn glanced at his watch. "If you were planning to scout the area before you met Lucian, you had better hurry. It's almost eleven now."

We left.

But not without a prayer to the fates and whatever gods were listening that everything went as planned and everyone got out alive.

And that included me and Azriel.

Because the shit, I suspected, was about to hit the fan big-time.

Chapter 13

The Arms and Militaria Exhibition was being held in a beautiful redbrick building that had once been a post office. It sat on one corner of a street that was a mix of old architecture and more modern—but infinitely uglier—concrete buildings, a grand old lady that time had not diminished.

The street itself wasn't crowded, although the parking lot across from the old post office was full, and I doubted they were all here for the nearby florist or the computer shop.

A roundabout was situated at the right end of the old building, but to the left there was a small metal gate and a green covered pathway that led—presumably—around to the back. Handy, given I had to set up the ward somewhere it wouldn't be noticed—presuming it *was* a ward in the box my father had sent, and not something else.

"Whatever lies in the box," Azriel said, "it certainly involves some form of magic. It crawls over my skin."

I frowned. "Why would it have that reaction? It's supposed to keep the Aedh out, not you."

Azriel's smile was tight, without humor. "Your

father does not want me in possession of the keys any more than he does anyone else."

I rubbed my head wearily. "You know, I hadn't even *thought* of that possibility."

He shrugged. "It is better to have us all locked out than none of us."

"You can bet my father won't be locked out. Or the Razan." Not to mention the dark sorcerer. I doubted *he* was going to miss out on the action, given his success stealing the first key.

And then there was Lucian, the joker in the mix.

My gaze dropped to the box Azriel still held. "Should we use it, then?"

"Yes." He handed it to me. "I can patrol the perimeter and cut any off who attempt to breach the wards."

"What about my father?"

"Your father can't gain flesh form, so even if he has created a back door in the ward's magic, he still needs you to actually find and retrieve the key."

"He needs me to find it," I said darkly. "But he has Razan to retrieve it."

"And if any *do* get past me, the Aedh will be beside you to stop them."

I gave him a surprised look. "I can't believe you just said that."

"I would rather Tao be in there beside you, but it is an inescapable truth that the Aedh wants the keys for himself. He *will* fight anyone who gets in his way." He regarded me steadily. "Do not turn your back on him."

Definitely not. The bastard was just as likely to

fuck me as kill me. I glanced down at the box in my hand, then took a deep breath and, with slightly shaking fingers, opened it. Inside were four small stones in varying shades of gray and a note. I tucked the box under my arm and opened the note.

Place these wards on each corner of the building, it said. *Activate them in sequence, light to dark, with a drop of your blood.*

Losing more blood, even if it was only a couple of drops, wasn't exactly what I needed right now. Especially to activate damn wards. Still, if it kept the hordes out, then I guessed it was worth it.

I rolled the stones out onto my hand. They felt extraordinarily light and yet oddly warm. I couldn't sense any magic in them, but my skin still crawled at their touch. I forced my fingers closed around them, then glanced up at the building again. Placing stones on three sides of the building would be easy enough, but the last side was right on the intersection corner, with only a small strip of pavement between it and the roundabout. Placing a stone there, however close to the building, was risking it either being kicked away or picked up by some curious kid. Not that there were actually kids in the street at the moment, but knowing my luck, they'd flood the place the minute I started activating the wards.

"What about the roof?" Azriel said. "He did not define that the corners had to be the base of the building."

I glanced up. The roof was tiled and not particularly steep, but it was very visible from all parts of the street. If I got up there, I'd attract all sorts of unwanted attention.

"Then you must risk the last stone at the corner."

I guess I did. I took another deep breath that did next to nothing to release the tension in me, then said, "Let's get this done before Lucian turns up."

I walked across the road, glanced up and down the footpath to see if anyone was paying undue attention to us, then pushed through the old wrought-iron gate and quickly headed around the corner. Ivy and shrubs crawled all over the fence lining one side of the path, which would have been the perfect place to hide a stone except for the fact they had to be on the corner of the building. I found a crack in the concrete that was as close as I was ever going to get and wedged the lightest-colored stone into it. "Blood," I said suddenly. "Amaya won't cut me, will she?"

"She is incapable of doing so, even if requested." He drew Valdis and held her point down, near my leg. Her steel flickered with an odd purple fire. It was almost as if she were displeased. "She is."

I raised an eyebrow. "Why is that?"

His hesitation was brief, but nevertheless there. "Because of the connection we have formed."

I studied him for a moment, sensing that was the truth as far as it went, but knowing there was a whole lot more to it than that—and that he wasn't about to explain it. I lightly pressed a fingertip against Valdis's point. Blood welled. I let it drop onto the ward. In an instant it was gone, sucked into the stone itself. Dark, bloody light flickered deeply in its heart, then stilled. But it was not inert. It was waiting.

I shivered, then stood and walked to the next corner. This time I wedged the ward into the strip of garden bed that ran the length of the rear of the building. When I dropped blood onto it, that dark, bloody light began to beat very slowly.

They were coming to life.

I repeated the process with the third stone, and this time the magic was tangible. It crawled across my skin, a force waiting for completion.

I jumped over the rear fence and walked up to the final corner. There was absolutely nowhere to safely put the ward. It was pavement right up to the edge of the building, and there were no cracks in either the concrete or the bricks.

"Then let me make one." Azriel pressed Valdis's sharp tip against the lowest visible brick near the corner of the building. Her flames flared briefly and, in seconds, there was a small, thumb-sized hole large enough to securely hold the last ward.

"Perfect." I squeezed my finger to get a final drop of blood, put it on the stone, then hurriedly dropped it in place.

The energy that crawled across my skin expanded in a rush, sweeping out and up, creating a wall of power that was invisible, but not entirely silent. It reminded me of the crackle and hum often heard when standing under high-voltage power lines. It would certainly be a warning to those who were sensitive to such things that something major now protected this building.

I rose and met Azriel's gaze. "Are you sure the wards will keep you out?"

In answer, he raised his hand and held it close to the wall. Little bolts of lightning shot toward his fingertips, a warning of what was to come if he pressed closer.

He lowered his hand. "The Aedh is here."

"The bastard is early." I flexed my fingers against the sudden urge to grab Amaya and thrust her sharp point into Lucian's dark heart, then forced a smile and walked around the corner.

He waited in the middle of the three arches that made up the main entrance into the building. "Lucian," I said, voice somehow very neutral. "How pleasant to see you."

Amusement touched his lips. "And said with such sincerity, too. Just as well you're a restaurateur rather than an actress, my girl."

"I'm not *your* anything." I stopped several feet away and crossed my arms. "It's seven bucks an adult to get into the exhibition. You can pay."

"My pleasure." But his gaze wasn't on me; it was on Azriel. "And it was, many times."

The anger that exploded from Azriel was so strong, it actually forced me forward a step. How he managed to rein it in, to *not* attack Lucian, I had no idea. But he did.

He didn't say anything, either. Maybe he simply couldn't, lest it break the wall of control.

"Lucian, cut the shit and just get inside," I growled. "We're here to find the key, remember?"

"So we are," he murmured. "But it is infinitely

satisfying to know that I have succeeded where *he* has failed."

"I wouldn't be so certain of that," I bit back, then pushed him up the stairs. Just for a moment, darkness flared in his eyes, yet another reminder that the man I'd spent so much time with was *not* the person he truly was.

I followed him up the steps and into the shadowed confines of the building's foyer. Old bank-teller-type windows lined one wall, and it was behind several of these that tickets could be purchased.

"I see your father has done his bit to make this place safe," Lucian said, smiling at the woman as he paid the entrance fees.

"It's just unfortunate he was unable to keep the likes of *you* out."

Lucian chuckled softly, handed me a ticket, then grandly ushered me forward. "After you, my sweet."

"You can stick the politeness where the sun don't shine," I muttered, then handed the ticket to the collector at the main door and went in.

The next room was vast and had obviously once been the main mail sorting area. There were three rows of exhibits here and, at the rear, a sign stating there were more up the stairs. There were also about a dozen people wandering around and a guard for each of the aisles.

I scanned the room for security cameras and saw four—one on each corner. Between them and the glass covering the majority of the display tables, there was little chance of snatching the key inconspicuously—if it was here, that was.

I made my way to the first aisle and slowly walked through, lingering near each table for several seconds to see if I got any reaction to the items within. This aisle seemed to be a mix of pistols and swords, but none of them set off the internal radar. I walked on.

It was a slow process and one that was utterly nerve-racking. Not just because I needed the key, but because of the rising expectations of the man who followed so closely behind me. Of course, the growing sense that the shit was about to hit the fan didn't help all that much, either. By the time I reached the end of the last aisle, I was so wound up, I was shaking.

I flexed my fingers again, trying to relax. A hard thing to do, given the tension radiating through me and around me. Tension that was mine, Lucian's, *and* Azriel's, all combining to make a stomach-churning mix. How I was managing to *not* throw up was a miracle.

"There are more exhibits upstairs." Lucian wrapped his fingers around my upper arm and propelled me forward.

I wrenched my arm free, but bit back the anger and somehow managed to say, almost civilly, "I'm well aware of that. There's no need to manhandle."

He glanced at me, the amusement playing about his lips at odds with the cool distance in his eyes. "You and I both know that you are not averse to a little force now and again, no matter how much you might say otherwise. This morning's efforts are a case in point."

Which explained the bruises I couldn't remember getting. God, how had I ever been fooled by this man?

Because he hid behind magic and years of pretending to be what he never was, Azriel said.

You weren't fooled.

No, but then, there were other reasons for that. He paused. *Be wary. The Raziq approach.*

Concern shot through me. *How many? God, don't fight them—*

I will do what I must, he said, in a tone that suggested he wasn't about to listen to reason no matter what I said. *You worry about finding the key. Let me do what I am here to do.*

I grabbed the banister and began climbing the stairs. *You're here to keep me safe and find the keys. Getting dead isn't a part of that.*

I have no plans in that direction.

It isn't your *plans I worry about.*

Ah, but you should, Risa, he said, his mental tones soft and almost wistful.

I frowned. *Azriel, I really don't need to be worried about your motives on top of everything else, so quit it.*

I wasn't talking about motives, he said, then, in more normal tones, added, *But as you say, this is not the time. Razan have arrived.*

Fear shot through me. *What about the Raziq? And how many Razan?*

I reached the top of the stairs and hesitated. The floor plan was a mirror image of the one below, but there were more people up here. My gaze swept the walls. Another four cameras. I wondered if anyone was watching them, or if they merely recorded events for viewing later if something went wrong.

Because something was most *certainly* about to go wrong. Just not in the way they suspected.

The Raziq keep their distance and wait. There are six Razan. Azriel hesitated. *They do not feel right.*

Oh, great. *Meaning?*

They have been infected with magic.

My stomach twisted a few more knots. *You mean like the ones who attacked us when we lost the first key?*

The same. His mind voice was grim. *I will stop them, but it will attract attention. It is also possible they are little more than a diversion. Stay wary.*

"I suspect your mind is not on what you are supposed to be finding," Lucian murmured, cupping my elbow and propelling me toward the row of long rifles. "Wouldn't be bitching to the reaper, would you?"

"What would it matter to you if I was?" I snapped, and yanked my arm free again. "But as it happens, he was informing me that Razan have arrived. Wouldn't be yours, would they?"

His expression darkened. Meaning he *wasn't* overly excited by this news and, warped or not, it cheered me up no end. I mean, anything that pissed *him* off had to be a good thing, if only marginally, right?

"I do not have enough magic left to create Razan," he said. "So if they come, they are not mine."

"But has your dark sorceress got enough magic to create them? Or something similar to them?"

He shot me a glance, his expression unreadable. "What makes you think that?"

"Call it an educated guess. You're the one who said you don't do anything without reason. Perhaps your apparent lack of magic strength—by Aedh standards, I'm guessing, not human—is the real reason you're making out with a very powerful sorceress. I bet she could create all manner of magic with a little help from you."

"Perhaps," he said. "But those Razan are not here under my orders."

"Yeah, but maybe they're here under *hers*."

He didn't answer that particular accusation, meaning I'd hit the nail on the head. And if she was behind the creation of the twisted Razan who'd run interference when the first key was stolen—and who were here now—then maybe she was more involved than we'd thought. After all, there *had* been male clothes in her Gold Coast apartment. Maybe Lucian was being played just as much as he was playing us.

"Just find that key," he growled.

"It may not even be here," I reminded him. "And don't stand so fucking close."

"Or you'll do what?" he mocked. "Let's not forget who holds all the cards here."

"Not *all* the cards," I retorted. "You still need me to find the damn keys, and standing so close, radiating tension all over me, is interfering with that."

He stepped back, but only a pace or two. Still, it gave me not only breathing room, but room enough to draw Amaya if I needed to.

From downstairs came a shout, then the sound of fighting. I knew Azriel was involved, but I resisted the urge to reach out to him. Distractions were the last thing he needed.

I walked on, scanning the displayed weapons, finding nothing, sensing nothing. Then, as I reached the end of the aisle, energy slithered across my skin—a caress so light, it barely brushed the hairs on my arm. But the Dušan stirred in my flesh and my gaze swept the remaining aisle. It was in one of them, somewhere.

"You've found something?" Lucian said, excitement in his voice.

"Not exactly." I hesitated as another wash of energy ran over my skin, but this one was stronger and darker. "There's something wrong."

"Aside from the hullabaloo your reaper is causing downstairs, you mean?"

"Yes." My gaze swept the room. There were still a dozen men up here, and none of them seemed overly interested in what was going on downstairs. In fact, they appeared to be deliberately *ignoring* it. Even the guards. Unease stirred. "It just doesn't feel right."

"The wards your father so kindly created have stopped the Raziq. Your reaper is taking care of the Razan. There is nothing and no one else here to worry about, Risa."

He was wrong. Totally wrong. But I guessed he knew that. Guessed whatever or whoever I was sensing were either his people or his magic, or those belonging to his dark sorceress.

I forced myself to keep moving and tried to catch the elusive sensation that would lead me to the next key. The awareness of danger grew until it was a pulse beating in tune with my heart. My skin itched and sweat began to trickle down my spine, and all I could smell was fear. It was thick and rich and it was all mine.

I walked down the next aisle, drawn by the growing pull of power. The Dušan's movements grew stronger, and she appeared to be moving from the left to the right. Knowing that the last time she'd done this, she'd actually been hinting at the key's location, I walked to the end of this aisle and into the next one.

And stopped abruptly. The key was here.

But every sense I had screamed that pinning down its exact location was *not* a good thing to do right now.

"You've found it." It was a statement, not a question, and again suggested that Lucian had not been altogether truthful when he'd said he couldn't read my thoughts. Like *that* was a surprise.

"It's there somewhere." I pointed to the largest of the three remaining display cases.

But the words were barely out of my mouth when the shit hit. The dozen strangers in the room turned as one, and for the first time I saw their faces. They *weren't* just men. They were the half-human, half-animal beings that had attacked us the first time.

Fuck.

Lucian yanked me backward and drew a long

knife from god knows where. Its sides gleamed with an unearthly fire that matched the glow in his eyes. "You will *not* take it from me this time," he growled.

And with that, he attacked. Three of the shifters met his charge head-on. The remainder flowed around him and came straight at me.

I swore, drew Amaya, and fell back. Her anger filled me, but it did little to shore up my courage. I knew what these fucking things could do, and I knew that against so many I stood little chance.

I swung my sword, slashing right and left, Amaya's blade little more than a blur as she cut through the air and flesh with equal efficiency. Blood and body parts flew, and my arms shuddered with every strike, but nothing seemed to halt the creatures' onslaught. They didn't feel pain, didn't even acknowledge limb loss, never hesitated for one moment in their mad charge. Their eyes were filled with the desire to kill, to rent and tear and taste blood, and yet, oddly, they didn't. They attacked, but it was nine against one, and even with Amaya in my hands, the odds *should* have been overwhelming. But while they kept forcing me back, they hadn't yet done any serious damage.

And maybe that was the whole point. Distraction, *not* destruction.

The key, I thought, and desperately jumped sideways, trying to see past the wall of twisted flesh. A dark figure stood near the display cabinet, sweeping everything within it into a large rucksack.

"No," I screamed, but was hit by one of the shifters and sent tumbling backward, over the guardrail.

I hit one of the display cases below with a resounding crash and for a moment saw stars. Every breath hurt, and pain slithered down my back and right leg. Then twisted flesh replaced the spinning stars, and I threw myself sideways, off the broken display case and onto the floor.

"Hey, what the hell do you think—" someone shouted, but the sound was cut off abruptly as one of the shifters leapt at him.

There was a gargled cry and somewhere a woman started screaming, but I barely had time to scramble to my feet before the rest of the shifters were on me. I slashed Amaya across the face of one, sending bits of flesh and blood flying, then spun and stabbed upward, hitting another square in the chest. Amaya screamed as her flames leapt from steel to flesh, eating into him even as she sucked his life into her steel.

I shuddered at her voraciousness, then pulled her free and ran as hard as I could for the stairs. The remaining shifters came after me, snapping and snarling at my heels. Fingers snagged my foot on the third step and brought me down. I twisted and booted the shifter in the face with my free foot. His head snapped back under the force of the blow, and he snarled, revealing a bloody mouth and broken canines. But he didn't let go. I swore and swept Amaya from left to right. Her steel bit into the shifter's neck and she screamed in pleasure as she severed arteries and sprayed blood all over us both. I bit back bile and scrambled to my feet, only to be brought down again by another shifter. Teeth tore into my arm, and I screamed as he worried at my flesh like a dog with a bone. I hit him with my free hand, clawing at his eyes, trying to force him to release me. His teeth were biting deeper and deeper, and my fingers were beginning to lose strength. Amaya was stuck like glue, but it was her doing, not mine. I gouged my fingers deeper, until one of his eyeballs popped. He snarled and his grip on my arm momentarily lessened. I pulled free, clenched my bloody fist around Amaya's hilt, and hit him, as hard as I could. His head snapped backward and he went tumbling back down the stairs, knocking down several others in the process. But they were only down, not out, and already others were leaping over them and coming at me. I spun and raced up the rest of the stairs.

And saw Lucian thrust his arm into the middle of a shifter's chest and literally blow him apart.

I stopped cold.

Watched the bloody body parts fall as if in slow motion. Saw in the way they fell an echo of my mother's death.

And knew, with absolute cold certainty, that it had been Lucian who'd killed my mother.

Chapter 14

My mind went dead.

For several seconds I couldn't move, couldn't think, couldn't do anything. I just stood there, horror filling every part of me, as the man who had fooled me in more ways than I'd ever imagined stepped over the broken remnants of the body and turned around. He didn't see me, didn't even look in my direction. He just raised the knife and ran at the darkly shadowed person still stuffing weapons into the rucksack.

The thief swore; the voice was male, not female. Not Lauren, then, some distant, still-aware part of me registered. Then magic surged and the cloaked stranger disappeared. Lucian screamed his fury, and it was that sound, more than anything, that unfroze my lips and got my mind working again. Suddenly, I became aware of the footsteps behind me and Amaya's screams. I swung, lashing out as hard and as fast as I could, slicing across the chest of the nearest shifter. As blood flew, I twisted and lashed out with a booted foot, knocking the second into the first and sending them both back down the stairs. Then I turned and ran straight at Lucian.

He saw me. He was always going to see me, given the noise Amaya was making. He made a mocking half bow, then threw something to the floor. Power surged, and he began to disappear. No fucking way, I thought, and threw myself at him. I hit him at the precise moment the energy reached its peak, and the power tore through us both, disintegrating flesh and body and bone in a manner very similar to the Aedh shift. It swept us into a void that lasted for several seconds; then the power surged again, and suddenly we were skin, rather than energy, and tumbling to the ground in a tangled mess.

Ground, not floor, not concrete. Wherever the hell we were, it *wasn't* back at his apartment, as I'd half expected.

He threw me off, then scrambled to his feet. "What the fuck are you playing—"

I didn't give him a chance to finish. I just attacked. Amaya was little more than a blur of my hands, and her steel spat flames that sprayed all around us. Lucian swore and parried every blow with his long knife, retreating slowly but surely, his expression intent but not unduly worried.

When energy surged around me, I realized why. By reacting without thinking, I'd very neatly stepped into his trap.

He lowered his weapon and shook his head, his expression somewhat bemused. "This cage was not meant for you, but I'm damn glad I set it up, all the same."

I slammed Amaya against the wall of power that surrounded me. Spidery veins of red spread for several inches from the impact point, then faded away, and Amaya hissed in fury.

Break can, she said. *Time needed.*

"That cage was designed to hold a sorcerer," Lucian said, amusement in his voice. "Neither you nor your sword have the power to break it."

"Why did you do it, Lucian?" I growled, hitting the wall again. This time, I left Amaya against it. She hissed and spat, her steel throbbing as she sucked at the power of the cage. "Just tell me that."

He frowned and held his hands wide, as if pleading his innocence. For the first time it actually registered that we were underground. Both the walls and ceiling that soared high above us were stone, and the air was thick with the scents of moisture and damp earth.

"I didn't steal the key, Risa. Indeed, I was hoping to trap the thief in the cage that now surrounds you."

"I'm not talking about the fucking key, Lucian, and you *know* it."

His frown deepened. For half a second I honestly believed he had no idea what I was talking about; then I remembered what a consummate actor he was. What a liar he was.

"Trust me—"

Never again. "I'm talking about my mother. You *killed* her."

"Ah." His voice was soft. "That."

Rage exploded, and I leapt at him without thinking. The cage bowed under the force of my impact but it didn't break, and I was flung backward, landing in an inelegant heap on the floor.

"*That,*" I hissed. "That's all you've got to say about my mother's *murder.*"

He shrugged. "She died well, with great grace, if that is of any consequence."

"But you killed her."

Amusement touched his lips. "Yes, I believe we've already established that fact."

"But *why*?" The word was torn from me. "What the hell did my mother ever do to you?"

"Nothing, of course. But without her presence, without her advice, you were infinitely more alone and vulnerable."

So he'd killed her merely to make me more accepting of his advances?

"You *bastard.*" Bastard, bastard, *soon-to-be-dead fucking bastard.*

"Another fact we have already established." His amusement was stronger this time. "It's not as if I have taken her from you for all eternity, Risa, so please cut the dramatics. You and she will meet again on another plane."

"*That* is beside the point!"

"No, it is not, because I could have done otherwise."

A chill went through me. "What do you mean?"

He smiled, but this time, there was nothing pleasant or amused about it. "I may be one of the fallen, but I still retain my power over souls. I could have stopped her from moving on, if I'd so desired. You should be grateful that I left you the chance to meet her again in another lifetime."

"Grateful? *Grateful?*"

He tsked. "Enough with the dramatics, Risa. It is time to concentrate on things we *can* still do something about. Like retrieving the key."

Amaya, I hope you're going to get that fucking wall down soon.

Trying, she growled. *Patience must.*

Coming from my sword, *that* was almost amusing. I rolled my shoulders, trying to ease the tension. It didn't do much, but I suspected little would. Not until the Aedh in front of me was in bits all over the floor.

"So are you intending to enlighten me on who stole the damn thing? Because it's very obvious you know them and are maybe even working with them."

"*Working* is not quite the right term to use," he replied. "Let's just say we have a somewhat fluid agreement."

I snorted. "Meaning you're both doing your utmost to stab the other in the back."

"It does add a degree of excitement to the proceedings," he said, voice droll. "Much like fucking you, really."

I snorted. "Only in that you're betraying us both."

"And fucking you both."

I blinked. "The person who took the key was a man—"

"So? As I have said before, it is pleasure that matters, not source."

"So you're fooling around with *two* dark sorcerers?" I asked incredulously.

"Perhaps," he replied. "Perhaps not. I am hardly likely to give you such information, my dear, when I still need cards to play if I am to survive this encounter."

"And we both know you're *not* going to survive; otherwise you wouldn't have been such a busy little beaver trying to impregnate any woman you could get your grubby little paws on."

"*That* was merely a precaution." He glanced at his watch, and I suddenly remembered Ilianna.

Fuck, fuck, *fuck*! Had she been rescued, or had the whole thing gone ass up?

"A precaution?" I bit back, relief filling me when he didn't immediately dig out his phone. We obviously still had some time left before he needed to make his next call. "Another lie. Aedh breed only when their death is imminent."

"As your father only bred?" He shook his head. "Like him, I have a few years left before I am forced to leave this world permanently."

Amaya's steel was getting heavier in my hand, her hissing more strident in my mind. I hoped that meant the wall was weakening rather than her.

"Is the person who stole all the weapons out of that display case," I growled, "the same person who stole the first key?"

He considered me for a moment, expression a mix of amusement and condescension. "It was."

"And is that person a dark sorcerer who is also a shape-shifter?"

God, it felt like we were playing twenty questions. But this wasn't a game, and I had to get as much information out of him as I could while I was still trapped, because there *wasn't* going to be any talking once I was free. Not by me, anyway.

Amaya, on the other hand, was a whole different story.

"I believe that might also be correct." The amusement got stronger. "You will never guess their identity, Risa, but you are most welcome to try for as long as you like. However, it will not get us that key back."

"Is it even possible to get the key back, given what happened to the first one?"

"The difference that time and this," he said, "is that it wasn't only the key stolen, but rather a whole bunch of weapons in which the key is just one. Our thief has not the capability to find it himself and will need our help."

Relief slipped through me. We may have momentarily lost the key, but it still was within the realms of possibility that it could be retrieved. That was something, at least.

"Our help, or yours? You can sense the key when you're close, can't you?"

"Yes, but I need you to pin down its location. Which is why I suggest an agreement would be in order—"

I snorted. "The only agreement you're going to get from me is one at the end of a sword."

He tsked again. "Now, let's not forget Ilianna here. I would hate to have to kill her after all the effort I've put into snatching and seeding her."

Amaya—

Close, she growled. *Close.*

"What sort of agreement?" I spat. "And why the hell would you even expect me to believe you'd actually uphold your end of it?"

"I don't expect trust," he said. "But I do expect that you'll remember I hold your friend's life in my hands and that you'll control not only your own need to kill me, but that of your reaper's."

"In exchange for what?" I spat.

"In exchange for the key, of course. What else matters?"

Indeed, what else did? For him, my father, the Raziq, and even Azriel, there *was* nothing else. And if Lucian thought I could control the actions of *any* of them, then he was seriously insane.

"I can speak only for myself and Azriel, but we both know there are other players in the mix who want the key just as much as you."

Ready soon, Amaya said.

Anger—and the need to kill, to rent and tear— surged, and I could almost taste his death on my tongue. And I knew that *this* time, it wasn't Amaya's need, but my own. I wanted his blood on my hands, wanted to feel his life slipping away, wanted to watch the realization of defeat dawn in his eyes.

"With the keys in my possession, neither your father nor the Raziq will be a problem," he said. "Because they will not move against me until they are sure of the keys' location."

I pushed to my feet but made no other move to give away my readiness to react the minute I got the all clear from both Amaya and Uncle Quinn. *God, please, let him contact me soon.*

"You're overconfident, Lucian, and that's never a good thing."

"I have lived many lives in this world in that state, and I have always surpassed my own expectations." He glanced at his watch again. "And now, I believe, a phone call is required."

Amaya!

Through, she screamed back. *Attack!*

At the same time, Uncle Quinn's lilting tones said, *We have her. She's safe and well.*

As Lucian dug his phone out of his pocket, I launched myself. There was a brief flare of magic, a moment of resistance, and then I was free and running. He looked up and swore, the phone smashing to the stone floor as he brought his sword up. Steel clashed with steel, and Amaya screamed, the sound one of fury.

Magic, she screamed. *Burns.*

I guess it was no surprise that Lucian had a weapon prepared against Amaya, given he was well aware I never went anywhere without her.

I pivoted and lashed out with a booted foot, hitting him square in the chest and forcing him backward. He laughed—laughed!—then brought the long knife down. I jumped back but not fast enough, and the knife slashed through my boot and into flesh. The warmth of blood began to flood my boot, but I ignored it, ducked under another blow, then thrust upward with Amaya. He twisted out of her way, but not fast enough, and her sharp steel skated along his ribs, instantly drawing blood.

More, she screamed, her noise within my head and without.

Lucian's eyebrows rose. "It talks?"

"Yeah," I bit back, "and *she's* eager to drink in your death."

He avoided another blow, then lashed out with a clenched fist. I ducked but not fast enough. It skimmed my chin and rattled teeth, and I almost missed his follow-up. I jumped over the sweep of his legs, then raised my sword and brought her down hard. He twisted, so rather than splitting his head open as I'd intended, it hit his shoulder. A shudder ran through her steel; then blood sprayed and his arm was swinging uselessly from the few remaining bits of flesh and tendons that Amaya hadn't severed.

And just like that, all his amusement was gone.

What remained was anger. Anger that was deep and dark and utterly, *utterly* inhuman.

"For that, you will wish you were dead."

"You can't kill me," I retorted. "You can't find the fucking keys without me, remember."

"I never said I would kill you," he replied softly. "I merely said you will *wish* for it."

And with that, he attacked, a whirlwind of power and speed and sheer, bloody force. I weaved and dodged and blocked, using every skill, every instinct. Amaya was a blur in my hands, her flames sparking off every stone and her fury stinging the air itself.

But as fast as I was, as fast as *she* was, he was faster. He was also bigger and heavier, and his reach was twice that of mine.

It was inevitable that some of his blows would get through my defenses; one slashed my hip, another my thigh, but I was still upright, still mobile, after several minutes of heavy fighting. And he was hampered by his useless left arm and was now bleeding from wounds on his chest and legs. It enraged him further, as I'd hoped it would. I needed him reacting, *not* thinking. It was only through blind rage—his, not mine—that I truly had any hope of winning.

He came at me again, a blurring mass of muscle and sheer bloody anger. I spun and kicked. Lucian sucked in his gut, and my blow missed. Not so his knife. It sliced across my foot and sheared the end off my boot. Only quick reactions on my part stopped my toes from joining it on the stone. But it was the same foot that had previously encountered his blade, and without the boot to restrict it, blood began to flow more readily and pain surged.

I jumped back, limping now.

He laughed, the sound a weird mix of anger and amusement. "The first of many, dear Risa."

"I'm glad you're enjoying yourself, Lucian," I said, catching the edge of his blade with Amaya, holding it still as her flames leapt from her steel to his and she screamed blue murder. Nothing happened. The knife didn't melt. Amaya's flames died even as I added, "Because as an aunt of mine has been known to say, a condemned man should always enjoy his last meal."

He merely laughed and attacked. Again and again. I dodged, attacking him when opportunities arose, taking more and more hits but unable to find a way through his defenses. In the end, I knew there was only one way I was going to get the upper hand.

Do what must, Amaya said.

Do what must, I repeated grimly, then lowered her steel and stepped into his next blow. His blade punched into the middle of my stomach and right out the other side. As his fist came to a rest against my skin, I swung Amaya low and hard. Her blade reverberated as she hit flesh, but then she was cutting, sawing, burning her way through his legs. He barely had time to open his mouth when he dropped, dragging his long knife from my stomach as his body went one way and his legs the other.

I swung Amaya again, removed his good arm, then dropped to my knees and pressed one hand over my stomach, vainly trying to stop the flow of blood and gore as I stared at the man I had all but beaten.

His expression was one of utter amazement. There was no pain, no sense of loss, just sheer disbelief I'd done what I'd done.

Kill! Amaya screamed. *Finish!*

Not you. Me.

And with that, I released her, and with my now free hand, I dragged myself forward.

"You killed my mother," I said softly. "You raped

my friend; you worked with a dark sorceress to steal the keys and threatened the safety of this world. You betrayed me in more ways imaginable, and for all those crimes, you must die."

And with that, I dredged up the last of my reserves, called to the Aedh, and forced it into my arm. Then I shoved my fist into his chest and blew him apart.

Just has he'd blown my mother apart.

Chapter 15

It was over. I'd done what I'd sworn to do—found my mother's killer and dealt with him. Without help, on my own.

There should have been a sense of victory. Should have been a sense of relief. There wasn't.

There was only an odd numbness.

It was almost as if I'd given all there was to give and there was nothing—absolutely nothing—left inside of me. I raised my re-formed, bloody hand and, as if from a great distance, watched the bits of flesh and blood dribble toward my elbow.

Then, without warning, my stomach heaved and I threw up. The pain hit seconds later, and I was shaking and crying and wanting nothing more than to just let it all go. The pain, the horror, the guilt, and the expectations of others, just let it all wash away and become someone else's problem.

Can't, Amaya said sharply. *Finished not.*

Isn't it? I wondered. I closed my eyes and fought the wash of weakness in my body, and yet I could not deny the allure of ending it all here and now. Why not let fate take whatever course she'd decided to take and no longer fight it?

Everyone would be better off without me. *Everyone*. No one could hold them hostage against my behavior; no one could kidnap and rape them, and—perhaps best of all—there would be no one to find the remaining keys and threaten the very safety of the world.

That alone was worth one life.

That alone was certainly worth *my* life.

Everyone not safe, Amaya said. *I not. The life within not.*

A life that might well be Lucian's. God, he'd murdered my mother—how on *earth* was I to survive looking at his child every day and being reminded of his deed? How was that fair to the child? Or to me?

I couldn't. I wouldn't.

The death I'd seen so long ago wasn't the truth. I wasn't going to die in an automotive accident. I was going to die here, underground, all alone except for a nagging sword.

My arms collapsed underneath me, and I fell face-first onto the stone. For several minutes I simply lay there, my breathing becoming more and more labored and my life leaking out through various wounds in not-so-slow rivers.

And wondered, just for an instant, where Azriel was.

Magic, Amaya spat. *Stops.*

It was a shame. I wouldn't have minded seeing him just one more time . . .

No, Amaya screamed. *Go not!*

Must, I replied, the roar in my mind going stronger. *It's too late.*

Not! she bit back; then she was in my hand. Power exploded around us, through us, merging steel and flesh with equal ferocity. It was a storm that tore my core apart, fiber by fiber, then pieced me back together, all within a matter of heartbeats.

Then it was no longer me, but *we.*

Die not, she said with fierce determination. *Live must.*

And with that, she forced my limbs into action, and I found myself crawling, slowly, painfully, past all the bloody, broken remnants of flesh toward two standing stones I hadn't even realized existed. Only they weren't just standing stones, but ancient, cuneiform-marked ones. Another gateway.

She kept me crawling, even though every movement had more blood pouring out and the pain was so intense I could barely even breathe. Energy washed across my skin, fierce and dark, but something was wrong with my eyesight because I could no longer see the stones, let alone tell whether they were active.

Not go! Stay!

I can't—

She wasn't listening. She never did, I guess. That surge of energy grew closer and closer even as my mind seemed to drift farther and farther away. It tore through me like a summer storm, sharp and electric, breaking me apart, then sweeping me away. I have no idea where it deposited me. I was no longer capable of caring.

My world was one of darkness and peace, and I smiled. *Yes,* I thought, *I'm ready.*

And not even Amaya's howls of protest could stop me from stepping free of my soul.

Light flared all around me, light that was warm and golden and peaceful. The figure of a woman appeared, her face glowing and serene. I smiled, unsurprised that the image the reaper who'd come to escort me onward had chosen to wear was the countenance of my mother. Of everyone I knew, she was the one person I trusted utterly.

Though Azriel had come pretty close.

As my thoughts turned to him, the light around me seemed to dim. No, I thought with determination. I *was* ready to move on.

The reaper wearing my mother's face smiled and offered me her hand. I hesitated and, just for a moment, thought of Tao and Ilianna, Riley and Quinn, Rhoan and his partner, Liander, and everyone else I was leaving behind. They would undoubtedly mourn my loss, but by my leaving, they could no longer be hurt by the madness that surrounded me.

And this was my chance, perhaps my only chance, to be with my mother again. I wanted that. More than anything, I wanted to see her, be with her, one more time.

I closed my eyes briefly, took a deep breath, then stepped forward.

It was then that Azriel appeared and blocked my path to the reaper.

What on earth are you doing? The words seemed to echo across the golden light, and an odd hush fell around us.

I'm sorry, Risa, but this cannot happen.

It is my time—

Yes, it is, but that does not mean I can let you go.

It is better for everyone—

Not everyone, he said and with such ferocity the very world around us quivered under its force. *Definitely not everyone.*

Then he reached out, grabbed my arm, and yanked me forward.

Not into death.

Into life.

I have no idea how long it took me to wake. I know I fought it for a very long time, desperate to snatch back what had been taken. Desperate to find that reaper again and move on, to be with my mother and far away from the pain and the hurt and the guilt and the never-ending expectations of others.

But that was an option that was not mine to take. Not now.

When I finally did open my eyes, it was to discover I wasn't alone. I guess that was no surprise. I did have people who cared for me, even if a tiny part of me actually resented that fact right now. If I'd moved on, as fate had destined me to, then I would not once again be responsible for their safety.

You are not responsible for our safety, Risa. We are more than capable of taking care of ourselves.

The voice wasn't Azriel's. It was Aunt Riley's.

I turned my head and looked at her. She was standing at the end of my hospital bed, her arms crossed and her expression severe. "You, my girl, will stop wishing yourself dead and start celebrating the fact you were given a second chance."

"I wasn't given anything," I retorted. "It was *forced* onto me."

"Running away, however you intended to do it, is never the answer—trust me on that."

"It would have been a hell of a lot easier than remaining here and being forced—"

I cut the words off before I could reveal a little too much, and she narrowed her eyes. "Being forced to do what?"

"The bidding of the fucking Raziq and my father and god knows who else. Ilianna was kidnapped because of me. Tao fights for control of his own body because of me. My mother is dead because of me—"

She sucked in her breath. "How did Dia get into this?"

Tears stung my eyes, and all that anger suddenly just washed away. "It was Lucian who killed her."

"And he's dead?"

"Well and truly."

"Good." She moved up the side of the bed, then sat and gathered my hand in hers. "I know it feels right now that death would be the easier option, but trust me, it isn't."

"But the keys—"

"We can sort out the key problem together," she said. "But you cannot allow yourself to fall into the trap of death. There are those in this world who can recall spirits and force them to do their bidding. What makes you think they will not do that to you?"

"Because they need me in flesh form to find—"

"So they've told you," she cut in, "but are you certain it's the truth?"

No, I wasn't. I took a deep, shuddering breath and released it slowly. "Life," I said softly, "sucks."

She laughed and bent over to drop a kiss on my forehead. "Yeah, it often does. But I'm so glad you decided to stay with us. I couldn't bear to lose you so soon after losing your mother."

If she'd wanted me in tears, then she'd damn well succeeded. She smiled and brushed them away with a gentle finger. "I couldn't be more proud of you if you were one of my own. You know that, don't you?"

I knew. In her eyes, she'd always had six children, not five. Dia might have given birth to me, but Riley had nevertheless adopted me. And I loved her almost as much as I loved my own mother. Which was why I couldn't let—

She pressed her fingers against my lips. "Enough with the self-sacrificing behavior. You can and will have our help, whether you like it or not. Now," she added, brisk and businesslike, "Ilianna is waiting out in the hall, desperate to see you, but she's under strict orders from the nurses and from me *not* to be more than a few minutes. Okay?"

"Okay."

She went out. Two seconds later, Ilianna appeared. I smiled, utterly relieved to see her safe and sound, but there was tension in me, too. I was ultimately responsible for what had happened to her, after all.

But when my gaze rose to hers, all I saw was complete and utter acceptance of all that had happened. There was no hate, no bitterness, not even regret or reproach. Just acceptance.

And I found myself wishing I could find even *half* of her serenity. Those damn tears welled again. "God, Ilianna—"

"Ris, it's okay," she said. "This event was foretold a long time ago, and even though I *had* thought it would be Carwyn's child I'd bear, I can't regret what happened. Not knowing what I do of her fate."

"But he forced you—"

"He used magic, yes, and it wasn't pleasant, but neither was it life-ending. I hate him, but I can't hate the result."

Which made me all the more ashamed, because I *could*. I didn't want to bear Lucian's child. No ifs, buts, or maybes.

But could I abort the child? Could I do that, when there was also a slim chance that the child was Azriel's?

That was a question I just couldn't answer.

I caught Ilianna's hand and squeezed it lightly. "Where's Tao? And Carwyn? Last time I saw them, they were both all fired up to ride to your rescue."

She smiled. "Well, right now they're both more than a little pissed at missing all the action. I believe Carwyn had pictured himself coming to my rescue and sweeping me off my feet in the process."

"Oh, I have no doubt about that." I hesitated. "Does he know what happened?"

"Not yet. But I'll tell him soon."

"How will that affect things?"

"It won't. He's after the merger with my family more than just me." She shrugged, expression unconcerned. But then, it wasn't like it was a love match. She had that in Mirri. "Stallions never take kindly to the offspring of others, but he won't hurt the child, and she'll be allowed to remain in his herd until grown."

"I guess that's something."

"That's everything. At least everything that matters." She smiled. "Tao said he'd visit tonight, seeing your aunt is adamant you get no more than one visitor at a time, lest it weaken you."

"She can be rather fierce about these things," I said with a smile.

"Too right she can," the woman in question said. "Ilianna, time's up. You can visit her tomorrow. Right now, she needs to rest."

Ilianna dropped a kiss on my cheek, then, with a promise to be back, left.

And that, basically, was the pattern of the next four days. Visitors in between bouts of resting, but no sign of the one person I really wanted to see.

Azriel.

It was deliberate on his part; of that I had no doubt. He'd crossed a line, with me and with death, and there would be a price to pay. Whether by me, or by him, or by us both, I had no idea.

On the fifth day, the doctors declared my werewolf heritage had worked another goddamn miracle and that I was fit enough to go home. *That* was music to my ears.

I rang Ilianna and arranged for her to pick me up, then climbed out of bed and took a shower. I was clean, dressed, and ready to get the hell away from the hospital and the awareness of death that continuously washed over me, thanks to the presence of the sick and the dying, when a different kind of awareness hit.

Azriel had finally decided to show up.

He appeared on the other side of the room, his arms crossed and his stance easy. And, as usual, his expression gave nothing away. He was holding his emotions—and his thoughts—very much in check.

I studied him for a moment, then said, "What did you do?"

"You know what I did," he replied, voice even. "I made you live."

I snorted softly. "Okay, let me rephrase that. *How* did you do that?"

He hesitated. "By leashing our energy beings together."

Fear curled through me. A fear unlike anything I'd ever experienced before. "You leashed our beings? As in, forever bound together?"

"Yes."

"So if you die, I die?"

"If I die, you take my place."

I stared at him. Did that mean . . . ? "No, that's not possible. I'm a flesh-and-blood being. I can never be what you are."

"You were never *just* flesh and blood, Risa. You were born half Aedh and became more so after what Marin did. When I snatched you from fate's pathway, I altered not only your destiny, but your very being."

No, no, *no*! How was something like that possible? How could I be born one thing and be made, on death, into another?

"What if *I* die? What if I decide to kill myself rather than become something I never wanted to be?"

Something flickered through his eyes. Anger, fear, hurt. I wasn't entirely sure. "You would not kill yourself."

"But what if I *did*?" I all but shouted.

"Then you would still become what I am—a dark angel."

I just stared at him. I couldn't do anything else. I was stunned. Broken. Betrayed. Again.

"Damn it, Azriel, *why*?"

"You know why."

"The mission. The key." I swung away, not wanting to look at him, not wanting him to see the hurt. It was always the *damn* key. Always about the damn mission.

"It *wasn't* about the damn mission or the key!" The sharp denial was accompanied by an explosion of anger that rolled my senses and just about fried my mind. "And if you'd listen to your heart *and* your body, you'd know it!"

I closed my eyes. Listen to my body, he said. Which implied he knew not only that I was pregnant but that the child was his.

So he'd saved what was rare and precious in his world. Not me. Never me.

"Damn it, Risa, that's not—"

"Isn't it?" I cut in and scrubbed a hand across suddenly aching eyes. I wouldn't cry. I *wouldn't*. "I listened to my heart, Azriel. I let you in. And you repaid that trust by taking away everything from me—"

"I haven't—"

"You took my *future*, Azriel! When I die, I won't move on. I won't be reborn." Wouldn't ever meet Mom again. "How can you stand there and say you *haven't* taken everything away?"

He didn't say anything. Didn't deny anything.

I closed my eyes and leaned my forehead against the windowpane. "I can't do this anymore, Azriel."

"Do what?"

Just for a moment, I swear there was fear in his voice. But that had to be imagination. Reapers didn't do fear. Didn't do emotions. Not the way I wanted emotions, anyway.

"You. Me. I can't do it. I don't want you near me. I don't want you in my life. I don't want you following me around anymore."

"Risa, that's not possible without—"

I swung around, my fists clenched against the sudden explosion of anger. "I don't *care* what is or isn't possible. I just want you out of my life!"

He stared at me for several minutes, his expression stony. Not even Valdis was emoting. "If you take this step, if you force me to go, I may not be allowed to come back."

"And I should be sad about that?" I spit out.

"Besides, it's not like you *won't* know what's going on. Not with the chi link—"

"That link was cut when you stepped onto death's plane."

"So why are you still able to read all my thoughts and emotions?"

"Why do you *think* I can, Risa?"

"Goddamn it," I said, my voice rising again. "If I knew, I wouldn't be asking!"

"Wouldn't you?" he said, bitterness edging his tones.

Leaving me none the wiser. But then, nothing was ever easy, nothing was ever straight, when it came to my reaper.

"No more, Azriel. I just—" I shrugged. "I can't. I won't."

He made a short, sharp motion with his hand. "So be it, then."

He winked out of sight, and I closed my eyes against the instinctive need to call him back and tell him I didn't mean it, that it was just anger and fear talking.

But I didn't.

Because it wasn't. Not entirely.

One thing, he said, his mind voice cool and distant as it flowed through my thoughts. *Rephael.*

What?

It is my name. If you ever need me, for whatever reason, say it. Wherever I am, whatever I am doing, I will hear.

And with that, he was gone, leaving me wondering if I'd just made the biggest goddamn mistake of my entire life.

Fuck it, no!

I *would* stand on my own feet and get on with whatever life I had left. I *would* sort out the mess that was the keys and Hunter and the Raziq the best I could, and I *would* goddamn survive in the process.

But the very first thing I needed to do was get drunk. Absolutely, mind-numbingly drunk.

Because before I could do anything else, the first thing I needed to do was *forget*.

If only for a day or so.

Don't miss the next exciting novel in the
Dark Angels series,

Darkness Splintered

Coming from Signet in November 2013

I woke up naked and in a strange bed.

For several minutes I did nothing more than breathe in the gently feminine—but totally unfamiliar—scents in the room, trying to figure out how, exactly, I'd gotten here.

And where the hell "here" was.

My brain was decidedly fuzzy on any sort of detail, however, and that could mean only that my mission to consume enough alcohol to erase all thought and blot out emotion had actually succeeded. And *that* surprised the hell out of me.

Thanks to our fast metabolic rate, werewolves generally find it difficult to go on a bender. I might be only half were, but I usually hold my alcohol fairly well and really *hadn't* expected to get anywhere near drunk. I certainly hadn't expected to be able to forget—if for only a few hours—the anger and the pain.

Pain that came from both the worst kind of betrayal and my own subsequent actions.

My eyes stung, but this time no tears fell. Maybe because I had very little in the way of tears left. Or maybe it was simply the fact that, somewhere in the alcohol-induced haze of the last few days, I'd finally come to accept what had happened to me.

Although it wasn't like I had any other choice.

If I *had*, then I would have died. *Should* have died. But Azriel, the reaper who'd been my follower, my guard, and my lover, had forced me to live and, in doing so, had taken away the very essence of what I was.

Because in forcing me to live, he not only ensured that my soul could never be reborn, but he'd made me what he was.

A dark angel.

The next time I died, I would not move on and be reborn into another life here on earth. I would join him on the gray fields—the unseen lands that divided this world from the next—and become a guard on the gates to heaven and hell. And that meant I would never see my late mother again. Not in any future lifetime that might have been mine, because he'd stolen all that away from me.

What made it all that much worse was the knowledge that he'd saved me not because he loved me, but because he needed me to find the lost keys to the gates.

And because I might be carrying his child.

The stinging in my eyes was *nothing* compared to the pain in my heart. I curled up in the bed and hugged my knees tightly to my chest, but it did little to stop the tidal wave of grief washing over me.

If he'd said, just the once, that I mattered more than any quest or key—or even the child we might have created—then perhaps the bitterness and anger would not have been so deep, and I wouldn't have banished him from my side. But he hadn't, and I had.

And now all I could do was try to figure out what had actually happened in the days that had followed his departure, and move on.

Because despite what he'd done, my task in *this* world had not changed. I still had keys to find, and I very much doubted whether the patience of either my father or the Raziq—the Aedh who'd jointly created the damn keys with my father before he'd stolen and then lost them—would hold for much longer.

Hell, it was surprising that one or both of them hadn't already appeared to slap me around in an effort to uncover what the hell had gone wrong *this* time.

But maybe they had no idea that I'd actually found the second key. After all, this time it had been stolen not only from under my nose, but *before* I'd managed to pinpoint its exact location. Which meant the thief—the same dark sorcerer who'd stolen the first key, and who'd permanently opened the first gateway to hell—wouldn't know which of the many military weapons he'd stolen was the second gate key in disguise. Thanks to the fact that my father's blood had been used in the creation of the three keys, only one of his blood could find them.

And I *would* find them. Without my reaper. Without my protector.

A sob rose up my throat, but I forced it back down. *Enough with the self-pity,* I told myself fiercely. *Enough with the wallowing. Get over it and move on.*

But that was easier said than done when my entire world had been turned upside down.

I scrubbed a hand across gritty eyes, then flipped the sheets off my face and finally looked around the room. It definitely wasn't a place I knew, and I very much doubted it was a hotel room. There were too many florals—the wallpaper, the bedding, and the cushions that had been thrown haphazardly on the floor all bore variations of a rose theme—and the furniture, though obviously expensive, had a well-used look about it. There was a window to my left, and the sunshine that peeked around the edges of the heavy pink curtains suggested it was close to midday.

Curious to see where I was, I got out of bed and walked over to the window. My movements were a little unsteady, but I suspected the cause was more a lack of food than any residual effect of my drinking binge. Alcohol cleared from a werewolf's system extremely fast, which was why it was so damn hard for us to get drunk. And *that* was definitely a good thing if I *was* pregnant, because it meant my desperate attempt to forget wouldn't have done any harm to my child.

I drew one curtain aside and looked out. In the yard below, a dozen or so chickens scratched around a pretty cottage garden. To the left of the garden were several outbuildings—one obviously an old stable, the other a large machinery shed—but to the right there was nothing but rolling hills that led up to a thick forest of gum trees.

It definitely *wasn't* somewhere familiar.

Frowning, I let the curtain fall back into place

and turned, my gaze sweeping the small room again. My clothes were stacked in a neat pile on the Georgian-style armchair, and flung over the back of it was a fluffy white dressing gown. Set on the nearby mahogany dressing table was a white towel, as well as bathroom necessities. Whoever owned this place at least didn't intend to keep me naked or unwashed. Whether they intended me other sorts of harm was another matter entirely.

Not.

The familiar, somewhat harsh tone ran through my mind and relief slithered through me. I might be without my reaper, but I still had my sword, so I wasn't entirely without protection. Amaya—the name of the demon trapped within the sword—was as alert and as ready for action as ever. The sword itself was shadow wreathed and invisible, so the only time anyone was truly aware of her presence was when I slid her dark blade into their flesh. Although she *did* have a tendency to be vocal about her need to kill, so she certainly could be heard on occasion— generally when she was about to kill someone.

What do you mean, not? I walked over to the Georgian chair and started dressing. Like the room itself, my clothes had a very slight floral scent, although this time it was lavender rather than rose, which was definitely easier on my nose.

Harm not, she replied. *Foe not.*

Which didn't mean whoever owned this place was a friend, but my sword had saved my butt more than once recently and I was beginning to trust her judgment.

Should, she muttered. *Stupid not.*

I grinned, not entirely sure whether she meant she wasn't stupid or that I'd be stupid not to trust her. I sat down on the chair to pull on my socks and boots, then headed for the door. It wasn't locked—another indicator that whoever had me didn't mean any harm—but I nevertheless peered out cautiously.

The hall beyond was thankfully free of the rose scent that had pervaded my room, and it was long, with at least a dozen doors leading off it. To the left, at the far end, was a wide window that poured sunshine into the space, lending the pale green walls warmth and richness. To the right lay a staircase. There were voices coming from the floor below, feminine voices, though I didn't immediately recognize them.

I hesitated, then mentally slapped myself for doing so and headed toward the stairs. My footsteps echoed on the wooden boards, and the rhythmic rise and fall of voices briefly stopped.

I'd barely reached the landing when quick steps approached the staircase from below. I paused on the top step and watched through the balusters. After a moment, a familiar figure strode into view and relief shot through me.

"Ilianna," I said. "Where the hell am I?"

She paused and looked up, a smile touching the corners of her green eyes. Ilianna was a shifter, and her human form echoed the palomino coloring of her horse form, meaning she had a thick mane of pale hair and dark golden skin. She was also a powerful witch, and one of the few people outside my adopted family I trusted implicitly. Tao, our flat-mate; Mirri, Ilianna's partner; and Stane, Tao's cousin, were the others.

"We're at Sable's winter retreat," she said. "And it's about time you woke up. I was beginning to think you intended to sleep the rest of your life away."

Sable was Mirri's mom. I'd met her only once, but I'd seen her often enough on TV. The woman was a cooking phenomenon, with two top-rated cooking shows behind her and a slew of books on herbs and healing still among the country's best-sellers. Mirri's dad, Kade, had worked with my aunt Riley years ago, but had unfortunately been killed in action when Mirri was little more than a baby. It had been Sable who had looked after his herd and kept them all together when he'd died.

"After the events of the last week or so, sleeping the rest of my life away certainly has its appeal." I couldn't help the grim edge in my voice. "Why the hell are we at Mirri's mom's rather than at home?"

"Because we figured a change of scenery might get you out of your funk. You coming down for lunch?"

"Funk" was definitely the *polite* description of what I'd been through the last few days. "Lunch would be good," I said, even as my stomach rumbled rather loudly.

Ilianna's eyebrows rose at the noise. I grinned and walked down the rest of the stairs, only to be enveloped in a hug so fierce I swear she was trying to squeeze the last drop of air from my lungs.

"God," she whispered. "It's good to have you back."

I blinked back the sting of tears and returned her hug. "I'm sorry, Ilianna. I didn't mean to worry you. I just—"

"Needed to cut loose a little," she finished for me. "I understand. More than anyone else ever could."

It was gently said, but nevertheless a reminder that I wasn't the only one who'd been played and abused. Guilt swirled through me and I pulled back, my gaze searching hers.

"Are you—"

"Yes," she said, interrupting before I could finish. "As I said in the hospital, my pregnancy was meant to be, even if the method of conception was both unforeseen *and* unwelcome. But we are *not* discussing me and my pregnancy right now."

I half smiled. No, we were discussing me and mine. "I've a feeling I'm about to be told off."

"Not told off. Just . . . warned."

Tension rolled through me. "About what?"

She hesitated. "While I understand your need to cut loose after everything that has happened recently, others do not, and they are looking for you. Specifically one person. And she's not someone any of us should piss off."

"Hunter." I practically spat the word.

Madeline Hunter was the head of the Directorate, a top-ranking member of the high vampire council, and a monster clothed in vampire skin. She was also, unfortunately, my boss, thanks to an agreement I'd made the day I'd scattered my mother's ashes.

Of course, that agreement technically no longer

stood, because I, not Hunter, had been the one to find and kill the man who'd murdered my mother. That man had been my Aedh lover, Lucian, who had managed to fool me in more ways than I was willing to think about. He'd not only been responsible for my mother's murder, but he'd also been involved in the theft of the keys.

And, as a parting gift, he'd kidnapped and impregnated Ilianna, and had tried to do the same to me.

I still wasn't sure that he hadn't succeeded, despite Azriel's statement that the child I apparently carried was his.

Ilianna grimaced. "Yeah. Tao's fobbed her off a couple of times now, but she's getting pretty scary."

Scary was a normal state for Hunter, but I certainly didn't want to piss her off any more than necessary. Not after what I'd seen her do to the dark spirit who'd murdered her lover.

Still, it was decidedly odd that she didn't know where I was. "Why would she be hassling Tao, or anyone else for that matter? She knows *exactly* what I'm doing every single minute of the day, thanks to the fucking Cazadors."

Cazadors were the high vampire council's kill squad, and they'd been following me about astrally for weeks, reporting my every move back to Hunter.

"In this case, she doesn't, because they *can't* follow you here." Ilianna tucked her arm through mine and escorted me down the hall.

I raised an eyebrow. "You've *spelled* the place?"

She nodded. "Mom found a spell that automatically redirects astral travelers every time they approach the spell's defined area."

Just astral travelers, not Aedh, I guessed. Which was logical given that the only spell we had to keep the Aedh out was the one we were using around our home, and that had originated from my father. Which meant my father and the Raziq could get to me here. I shivered and tried to ignore the premonition that I'd be confronting both far sooner than I wanted.

Still, some protection was better than nothing, and at least we could plan our next move without the Cazadors passing every little detail onto Hunter. "There wouldn't happen to be a mobile version of that spell, would there?"

"Unfortunately, no."

Of course not. Why on earth would fate throw me a lifeline like that? "Then I guess I'd better give the bitch a call ASAP."

And pray like hell she didn't have another job for me. I really didn't need to be chasing after escapees from hell right now—especially, I thought bleakly, when chasing hell-kind was all I had to look forward to in the long centuries after my death.

Besides, I needed to find the sorcerer and snatch the second key back. While he might not know which one of the items he'd stolen it was, there was nothing stopping him from taking them all to hell's gate and testing them out one by one.

And while my father and the Raziq had been relatively patient so far when it came to my lack of progress on the key front, I doubted that would last.

They'd already threatened to destroy those I loved if I didn't find the keys. I wouldn't put it past any of them to actually kill someone close to me just to prove how serious they were.

As if tearing *me* apart to place the tracker in my heart hadn't already proved that.

"Calling her should definitely be a high priority," Ilianna agreed. "But come and eat first. You look like death warmed up."

No surprise there, given I nearly had been. "So what's stopping Hunter or the Cazadors from *physically* finding us?"

"She probably could, given enough time. While the spell is designed to confuse astral senses, they'd still have a general idea of location."

"But all she has to do is hack into my phone—"

"Which was left at home," Ilianna interrupted. "Along with anything else that could be used to track you. We're not that dumb."

No, they weren't. And Hunter was undoubtedly hassling Tao simply because she couldn't get to anyone else. Even *she* had more sense than to contact Aunt Riley. I might not be related to Riley by blood, but she and her pack were the only family I had left. They would not have reacted nicely to the news that Hunter was after me.

"Knowing Hunter as well as I now do, I'm surprised she hasn't done more than merely threaten him."

Hell, she probably considered a spot of bloody torture a good way to start the day. Although, given that Tao was rapidly losing the battle with the fire elemental he'd consumed, maybe I should've been hoping the bitch *did* attempt to torture him. Crispy-fried Hunter was a sight I wouldn't have minded seeing.

"She's given him until tonight to find you, so there's time. You need to regain some strength before you run off to confront that psycho bitch."

"Ain't that the truth," I muttered. "Especially now that I have to do it alone."

Ilianna hesitated, then said quietly, "Look, I don't know what actually went on between you and Azriel, but—"

Something twisted deep inside me. Pain rose, a knife-sharp wave that threatened to engulf me. *No,* I reminded myself fiercely, *you can't go there.* Not just yet. Not so soon after waking. I needed at least *some* time by myself to mull over the implications of my actions.

"Ilianna," I said, when I could, "leave it alone."

"But he wouldn't have left you—"

"He did, because he had no choice. I banished him." *How* I'd actually managed that, I had no idea. I mean, he was a reaper, a Mijai, and my telling him to leave me alone had never worked before. So why the change?

"Why the hell would you do that? Damn it, Ris, you need—"

"Ilianna," I warned, the edge deeper in my voice this time.

She drew in a breath, then released it slowly. "When you want to talk about it, I'll be here. But just remember one thing—he's not human. He's energy, not flesh, and he doesn't operate on the same

emotional or intellectual levels as we do. But whatever he did, he did for a reason. A *good* reason. And no matter how absolute or final his actions may seem to you, it may not be a truth in his world."

"The truth," I replied, bitterness in my voice, "is that the keys were always first and foremost to him."

And I wanted more than that. Wanted him to feel about me the way I felt about him. But was love an emotion reapers were even capable of?

I blinked at the thought. I *loved* him. Not just cared for him, but *loved* him. How or when it had happened, I had no idea. It wasn't like love and I were on familiar terms. Quite the opposite really, given the only other man I'd loved had been Jak — the werewolf reporter who was one of the people we'd pulled in to help with our key search — and that had turned out to be a complete and utter disaster.

Maybe love and I just weren't meant to be.

Ilianna said, "I would not be so —"

"Ilianna," I warned yet again.

She sighed, then pushed open the door and ushered me through. The twin scents of curry and baking bread hit, making my mouth water and my stomach rumble even louder than before.

The room itself was a kitchen bigger than our entire apartment. The country-style cabinets wrapped around three of the four walls, providing massive amounts of storage and preparation space, and there were six ovens and four stovetops. A huge wooden table that could seat at least thirty people domi-

nated the middle of the room, and it was at this that Sable, Mirri, and two other women sat.

They glanced around as we entered. Sable smiled and rose. In both human and horse form she was a stunningly beautiful woman, with black skin and brown eyes that missed very little. Mirri, a mahogany bay when in horse form, had taken after her dad.

"Risa, I'm so glad you've recovered." Sable kissed both my cheeks, then stood back and examined me somewhat critically. "Although you do need some condition on you. You, my girl, are entirely too thin."

I smiled. "Werewolves tend to be on the lean side."

"Not this lean, I'll wager. The ladies and I are just about to go out, but there's a curry in the oven and the bread should be done in about five minutes."

"Thank you—"

She cut me off with a wave of her hand. "Ilianna is family, and her family is my family. So please, don't be thanking me for something we'd do for anyone in the herd."

I smiled. At least Mirri's mom had accepted her relationship with Ilianna. The same couldn't be said of Ilianna's parents—although I personally thought they *would* come round if they actually knew about it. But Ilianna refused to even tell them she was gay.

Sable collected her coat and bag from the back of one of the chairs, and then she and the two women retreated out the sliding glass door.

I raised an eyebrow and glanced at Mirri. "That felt like a deliberate retreat."

Mirri grabbed a couple of tea towels and rose. "I told them you and Ilianna needed some alone time for a war council when you woke up."

"War council? Sorry, but whatever I do next—"

"You're *not* doing alone." Ilianna grabbed some plates from a nearby cupboard and began setting the table for the three of us. "Azriel may be gone, but Tao and I are still here. And we're a part of this now, Risa, whether you like it or not."

I didn't like it. Not at all. She and Tao had been through enough because of me and this damn quest. I wasn't about to put them through anything else. But I also knew that tone of voice. It was no use arguing—not that that ever stopped me from trying.

"The first thing I have to do is find the damn sorcerer who stole the key, and that's not something I want you involved with. It's too dangerous, Ilianna."

"Maybe," Ilianna said, giving me a somewhat severe look. "But the Brindle is more than capable of taking care of a dark sorcerer. There aren't that many in Melbourne, you know, and they'd be aware of all of them."

The Brindle was the home of all witch knowledge, both ancient and new. Ilianna's mom was one of the custodians there, and Ilianna was powerful enough to have become one—and in fact had started the training when she was younger. She'd walked away for reasons she refused to discuss, but if the predictions of the head witch, Kiandra, were to be believed, not only would Ilianna one day finish that training, but her daughter would save the Brindle.

"Yeah," I said, "but given Lucian was probably working with him, he'll know about my connection to both you and the Brindle." I grimaced, then added, "I'd bet my ass he's taken steps to ensure you—and they—can't find him."

"But it would take *major* magic to achieve something like that, and that in itself can also be traced."

Undoubtedly. But it still meant dragging more people into the search, and I really didn't want to do that unless absolutely necessary. It was just too damn dangerous.

"It's an option." I sat down. "But it wouldn't be my first."

Ilianna placed the hot bread on the table. "Why not? There's no easier way to find a sorcerer than to trace his magic."

"A normal sorcerer, perhaps. But this one has been working with an Aedh, and has probably acquired much of his knowledge." Which was another reason to be glad Lucian was dead. At least the bastard couldn't pass anything else on to our ever-elusive sorcerer. "Besides, our best option right now is to go through Lucian's things and see if he left any clues behind."

Mirri snorted as she began dishing out the huge chunks of curried vegetables—which wasn't normally a favorite of mine, but it smelled incredible. "Forgive me for stating the obvious, but you've been on a bender for three days. That would have given our sorcerer plenty of time to go through Lucian's things and ditch whatever evidence there might have been."

"Lucian was clever enough *not* to leave such information in easy reach. If there *is* incriminating evidence to be found, then it would be somewhere ultimately safe from everyone but him."

And that, I realized suddenly, could mean the gray fields. They might be the unseen division between worlds, but they were as filled with life as anyplace in *this* world. And given Lucian had once been an Aedh priest under my father's tutelage, then maybe the first place I should look was in temples near the gates of heaven and hell. I had no idea whether the temples still stood now that the priests had all but disappeared—or if someone like me would even be able to see them—but what better place would there be to secure information? It was doubtful whether the reapers or the Raziq would bother to look through ruins in an effort to find information on a dark sorcerer.

Of course, that was presuming Lucian had been able to get onto the fields. The ability to attain full Aedh form had apparently been ripped from him by the Raziq, but that hadn't stopped him from shoving his fist into my mother's chest and blowing her apart.

Which was exactly how I'd killed him.

I'd had my revenge, but its taste wasn't as sweet as I'd expected.

I swallowed heavily and added, "The bastard was more cunning that a basketful of foxes."

Ilianna's smile was grim. "But not cunning enough in the end."

"No." I tore off a chunk of bread as Mirri slid a

plate of curry my way. "I'll search his place first; then I'll do the same to his lover's place."

"And if you find nothing either there or on the fields?"

If I found nothing, we were up shit creek without a paddle, because I honestly didn't think the Brindle would be able to help us. Not in this. Not when Aedh magic was involved. And there had to be; the ancient cuneiform that gave the magic to the transport pillars we'd found—pillars both the dark sorcerers and Lucian had been using to move around undetected—could have come only from Lucian.

"If I find nothing," I replied as I dipped a chunk of bread into the curry, "then I guess I have no choice but to involve the Brindle."

"Good," she muttered. "Because I was going to involve them if you didn't. You can't do this on your own anymore, Ris."

I snorted softly. "I was never doing it on my own, and look where it's gotten—"

I cut the words off as awareness ran through me. Something approached the house.

Something that wasn't human, or in human form. An invader that was as silent as a ghost, and yet accompanied by such a wash of heat and power that the hairs on my arms stood on end.

It was a sensation with which I was more than a little familiar.

An Aedh approached the house, and he was in energy form rather than physical.

Only it wasn't any old Aedh.

It was my father. And he was *not* happy.